SCARLET TEARS

A Novel

By

D. Allen Miller

Infinite World Communications, LLC
P.O. Box 470006
St. Louis, MO 63147
Phone: 314-456-3003
www.infiniteworldcomm.org

Copyright © 2007 by D. Allen Miller.
All rights reserved, including the right of reproduction
in whole or in part in any form.

Cover Graphic Design by Watchmaker Publishing

Library of Congress Catalog Number: 2007929452

ISBN: 1-60386-007-X
ISBN: 978-1-60386-007-9

All characters, places, and events in this work are
purely fictional.
Any resemblance to actual persons, living or dead, is
coincidental, except for by agreement.

Visit Infinite World Communications at
www.infiniteworldcomm.org

Printed and bound in the United States of America.

ACKNOWLEDGMENTS

I owe a very special thanks to my mother and father, Tecora Miller, Bishop Kenneth Ulmer, Traneen Young, Felicia Gayden, Ticarol Smith, Derricka, Lauren, Cresleonyta Thompson, Yvette Tanner, Yasha Henderson, Jeri Betts, my family and friends, and to the many individuals in the federal prison system who helped breathe life into this novel. You know who you are, and I couldn't have completed this novel without you.

This is for the women, those who have stood the test of time . . . those who have been forgotten.

NEVER GIVE UP! SUCCESS'S LIGHT FOREVER BURNS.

A NEWS UPDATE

January 13, 2000, the St. Louis Post-Dispatch:
**THIRTEEN DAYS INTO NEW YEAR:
NINE ARE SLAUGHTERED**
New program on fighting crime is implemented

January 31, 2000, the St. Louis American:
**MASS TURMOIL THREATENS
ST. LOUIS METRO**
Citizens cry for resolution

February 8, 2000, the St. Louis Metro Evening Whirl:
**GANG MEMBER FACES LIFE
IF FOUND GUILTY FOR
"CRACK COCAINE"**
City tired of drug pushers

February 15, 2000, the Alton Telegraph:
LAW AND DISORDER
Rape, murder, robbery, assault, car theft at an all-time high

February 22, 2000, the Belleville News-Democrat
**SOUTHERN DISTRICT OF ILLINOIS
SPARES NO LENIENCY**
Says all drug cases are serious

March 10, 2000, the East St. Louis Monitor
**FOUR DIE IN HOME FIRE:
THREE ARE CHILDREN**
Foul play is suspected

March 19, 2000, the St. Louis Argus:
**CHAOS REIGNS SUPREME IN
URBAN AMERICA**
Study on "Black-on-Black" crime is being conducted

April 1, 2000, Midnight X-tra:
**49-MAN INDICTMENT ISSUED
FOR DRUG THUGS**
The "Great Sweep" of 2000

April 11, 2000, the St. Louis Metro Sentinel:
**DAUGHTER OF POPULAR POLITICIAN
SLAIN**
He says, "Inner-city St. Louis is at war with self."

May 2, 2000, the Granite City Press Record:
**ARMED 12 YEAR OLD THREATENS
SUICIDE**
Upset over parents neglect and domestic abuse

May 13, 2000, the North County Suburban Journal:
**RESIDENTS STILL SEEKING 'THE TRUTH'
OF FEDERAL AGENT'S BEHAVIOR**
Injustice storms the Black suburb

ONE

"Jessica! Jamie!" Mahogany called, standing with her family.

Jamie and Jessica stopped. They turned towards Mahogany. Smiling, Jamie held up her camera to her left eye. She focused and took a picture of Mahogany.

"Girl, we've been looking all over for you," Jessica said, her Bachelor's in hand.

"Well," Mahogany paused, stretching out her arms, "here I am."

Excited like small children at the local park, Mahogany, Jessica, and Jamie embraced and congratulated one another. It was Commencement Day, May 26, 2000, at the University of Houston.

"Hey, let's take a few pictures together before I begin to look like a complete mess," Jamie suggested, her eyes watery.

"Are you getting ready to cry, again?" Jessica asked. "Girl, you're too sensitive."

"Don't say that, Jessie," Mahogany said, reaching for some facial tissue from her mother.

"So I finally get to meet your parents," Jessica uttered. She smiled at Mahogany.

Mahogany stared at Jessica. *Please not now, Jessica. Are you ever going to grow up?* she thought. Mahogany then handed Jamie the facial tissue. She turned and looked at her family. "By the way, you all, this is the fabulous Miss Jessica Francis, Conference USA track and field extraordinaire." She paused. "And this is my dear friend, plus two-year roommate,

Jamie." Mahogany and Jamie smiled at one another. "Jessie, Jamie, this is my mother, the lovely Sophia Brown. My beautiful aunt, Karen. My favorite cousin, Stefaughn. And my wonderful father, Daddy Brown."

"I'm very pleased to meet you young ladies," Mr. Brown said with a deep voice. He was well dressed in tan slacks, a cream-colored dress shirt, a russet-and-cream plaid sports jacket, and a pair of tan-and-beige crocodile dress shoes.

"The same," Jessica replied.

"My pleasure, sir," Jamie said.

Everyone exchanged handshakes, smiling at one another. All graduations were common grounds for kind gestures and encouraging words. Is it all sincere? Who knows. Taking an educated guess, the Academy Awards was an affiliate association with all college graduations. Awful . . . but welcome to America.

"A gorgeous spring day I'd say for such a terrific occasion," Sophia said.

"Yeah, we kind of got lucky this year. The weather for last year's graduation prohibited an outdoor ceremony," Jessica added.

The Texas sun was friendly. The sky was clear, and there was a soft breeze more humble than the perfect gentleman. Cameras flashed. People were everywhere, laughing, talking, and smiling.

Mahogany noticed Stefaughn gazing at Jessica. He licked his lips. Jessica gazed back with an endearing smile.

"Uh, let's take a picture, everybody," Mahogany said.

"Hold on. I have something to say," Karen interrupted.

"All praises to God but through Jesus. And I'm so proud of you, ladies."

Oh no! Please no sermons. This isn't the time, Aunt Karen, Mahogany thought.

Karen continued, "I commend you on your accomplishment. And if either of you ever find yourself lacking spiritually, please don't hesitate to contact me." Karen gave Mahogany, Jamie, and Jessica, each, one of her spiritual cards. "I'd love to be of any assistance."

Mahogany read the front of the card:
GodsKaren@hotmail.com
Mahogany flipped the card over and read:
Fulfilling God's mission
(In the Perils of Storm)
Available for all types of
speaking engagements.
Price negotiable

Mahogany thought aloud, *This is a business card, Aunt Karen. Not a spiritual card.* She then asked, "Can we take pictures, now?"

"Sure, Mahogany. We definitely don't have all day," Mr. Brown answered. "And I'm certain your friends have to get back to their respective families. So just let me know when you, angels, are ready."

Jessica scrambled for the middle, a junky for attention. Mr. Brown and Stefaughn snapped away as the graduating trio exchanged positions and poses.

"Hey, Jessica, can I have one of you alone?"

"Sure thing, Stefaughn." Jessica removed her mortarboard; her pose was inviting. Stefaughn snapped three pictures instead of one.

Jamie, an emotional wreck, snapped a few pictures of her own. Her and Jessica expressed their farewells and walked away. Jamie didn't live very far from the U of H. She was from a small town there in Texas, named New Bethel.

Mahogany and Jessica were from St. Louis, Missouri, but from two very different sides of town. Their journey home would be extensive, eight hundred, sixty-two miles.

Time passed fast. Mahogany and her family appeared to be getting restless. Robertson Stadium thinned out, quieting as if it was time for evening prayer.

Sophia looked up from her watch. "Well, it's seven minutes after six. Let's not forget we have dinner reservations for a quarter after seven. So let's put a rush on it."

Exiting the stadium, Mahogany took one final look at what she was about to unwed. Tears streamed from her eyes, although athletics at the U of H was wounded like an ailing veteran. The U of H was home to the NCAA's "Phi-Slamma-Jamma" in 1983, a fabulous memory in the distant winds. However, Mahogany didn't attend "The Big Red and White" for athletics. She majored in Business Management and minored in Business Law.

Being closely involved with the university's student body, recollections of fun moments and special occasions flashed through Mahogany's mind. Memories of dear acquaintances wrapped themselves around her caring heart. Letting go of it all was painful.

"It's okay, sweetheart. Mom and I have been there before,"

Mr. Brown consoled, hugging his daughter. "I promise you that everything will be all right. And we're here for you, my love."

TWO

"May we now have dessert, please?" Mr. Brown asked.

"Sure. I'll have it coming right up, sir. Is there anything else I can get for you, lovely people, besides removing some of this dishware?"

"No. Just the dessert will be fine, dear," Sophia replied. "So how did you like your dinner, Mahogany?"

"It was delicious, Mom. And I thank the all of you for loving me," Mahogany said. "Also, I've heard a lot about this place around campus."

"Yeah, La Gri . . . La Griglia's is a popular restaurant, here, in H-Town. It's known for its class, great choice of wines, excellent service, and delicious steaks. Especially their sixteen-ounce ribeye served with Capellini marinara. Oh, and their rotisserie roasted duck with wild rice is mouthwatering. My colleagues and I come here every year when we have our national convention at the Wyndham Hotel during October. Everyone mostly order lamb T-bones grilled in butter sauce," Mr. Brown elaborated.

Mahogany was puzzled why her father would inform them about the restaurant's most popular dishes after they'd finished eating. Men of course.

"Having mentioned a hotel. . . . Mahogany, I hear that Adam's Mark back home has offered you a position in their executive offices with an annual starting salary of thirty-nine thousand dollars." Karen paused. "I guess it pays to graduate in the top ten percent of your graduating class. You know, that's a lot of dough for a twenty-two-year-old, single Black female without children. You go, girl!" Karen reached over the dinner table for Mahogany's hand smack. "See there, Stefaughn. Do you see what finishing college can do for you?"

Scarlet Tears

"Come on, Momma. This isn't the place or the time," Stefaughn said.

"Auntie, I appreciate Adam's Mark giving me the job. I'm very excited about it. But I wonder if they only hired me because of the discrimination allegations they're facing."

"Child, don't even worry about that. You gotta live for you, today. As soon as those people get an offer to settle out of court, they'll be the first ones right back spending money with Adam's Mark. Trust me . . . I've seen it a million times before."

Stefaughn sat holding his head down. His mother, Karen, was revved up, seemingly in the mood for the sister-to-sister thing. Mr. Brown rubbed his forehead, looking from side to side. Sophia sat smiling, squeezing her cloth napkin.

"Karen, how are the final touches coming along at The Rhema Church?"

"Everything is going well, Sophia. This is supposed to be the last weekend for the contractors. Why? Are you and your family thinking about attending services soon?"

"Um, that's a possibility." Sophia looked at her husband. "You agree, darling?"

"Uh . . . yeah . . . yeah, I don't see it as a problem."

"Excuse me, everybody. Here's dessert as requested," the young waitress announced.

Stefaughn gazed at the young Caucasian waitress in fitting black slacks. She had a body like a curvaceous "sister," one of those young, vibrant African-American honeys who inspire grown men to act like a damn fool. WHOA! SO FINE!

"May I take this out of your way, please?"

"Why sure," Mahogany said to the waitress.

Having cleared the table directly in front of Mahogany, the waitress continued, "And here. I'm certain this is for you."

"Congratulations, Mahogany!" everyone said.

Her mouth agape, Mahogany peered at the adorned little box with a white bow on top. She wondered what was

12

inside of the box, what was about to add or subtract value from her life.

Observing the expressions on everyone's face, Mahogany experienced a sudden rush of delight. Just watching Karen with all of her antics, the surprise was basically hurled out the window. So much for the adjectives calm, cool, and collect.

The restaurant's other dining customers watched closely. Smiling away, Mahogany felt like Tupac Shakur: "All Eyez on Me."

"Go ahead and open it, dear," Mr. Brown suggested. He took a scoop from his fudge a' la mode dotted with pecans.

"Okay, okay. I'm a bit nervous."

"That was a great choice of wrapping," someone said in the near background.

"I bet she feels special," background voices continued to speak.

"Oh my God!" Mahogany said. "I can't believe it. Is all of this for me?"

Inside the silver-dressed box, there were a cashier's check for one thousand dollars, which was from Mahogany's maternal grandparents in Topeka, Kansas; seven freshly-printed Benjamins from Karen and Stefaughn; a trendy pair of Gucci shades; a six-month prepaid Allstate insurance card; a key to a brand new convertible Ford Mustang GT; and a personal check for five hundred dollars from her paternal grandparents with a short letter and poem attached. It read:

Dear Mahogany,
We know that today is a very special day for you. We sincerely apologize for our absence. Today is a commemorative occasion. However, you'll always have our affection and support as the good Lord allow. We're positive you'll understand our predicament. In poem, we sing to you:

New Butterfly

Along born a grandchild,
When to the whispers blew softly,
Having known in our hearts,
She was the precious of arts,
It sparked the pearl in her eyes,
That inspired us to smile,
We knew at such while,
She would soar to the skies,
So we pen to express,
And the truth we've confessed,
That you're the greatest of best!
   Love always,
   Grandma and Grandpa

P.S. We'll speak with you soon, and we promise to send more in nearing time.

  Weakened by the moment at hand, Mahogany began to cry. She rested her head against her mother's bosom, welcomed by a gentle drum of affection.
  "Karen, look in my purse and please hand me that package of Kleenex," Sophia said, caressing Mahogany's back. "Thanks, sis." Looking down at her daughter, Sophia continued, "Here, Mahogany. Dry those tears."
  "Didn't I tell you, honey, that everything was going to be all right?" Mr. Brown uttered to his daughter.
  Mahogany flashed her father a smile. "I know, Dad. But I'm so . . . so. . . ."
  "We know, baby. No need of explaining yourself. And we're so proud of you," Sophia said.
  Mahogany and family finished what was left of their desserts, excluding the ice cream that had melted. Adrift in tomorrow, Mahogany envisioned herself cruising through the streets of West County, an affluent St. Louis suburb, with her childhood friends.

"I'm sorry, miss. Will you please take a couple pictures of us together?" Sophia asked the waitress as she refilled Stefaughn's glass with water.

The waitress agreed. Mahogany and family took several pictures. Mr. Brown then asked for the evening's check. He glanced at his timepiece and reminded the group that a good night's rest was pertinent.

"Here's the check. And please feel free to pay at your convenience."

Mr. Brown looked down at the yellow check. "We'll gladly pay now." He handed the waitress his Platinum American Express credit card.

"Dad, how far is the hotel we're staying at from here?"

"It's about ten to fifteen minutes from here."

"Whew! . . . Pardon me. It's twenty-five minutes after nine, and I can use, both, a hot shower and some sleep. It's been some day. Don't y'all think so?" Karen implied after looking at the time on her cellular telephone. She belched. Karen apologized and leaned her head on her son's shoulder. She closed her eyes.

Stefaughn sniffed the air. He turned his head.

"Yeah, it's about time, sis," Sophia said.

Mr. Brown snarled at Karen. She rolled her eyes.

"Mahogany, what's up with the night life around this part of town?"

"Personally, I'm unsure, Stef. I hardly left the Third Ward. But I've heard a lot about this joint named Jamaica-Jamaica over on Kirby and Richmond. Then there's Dave and Busters, Slick Willy's, Cornbread . . . uhh, and Maxis Two-Thousand. Oh yeah, I have been to Carrington's a couple of times over on South Main. Now that's a pretty cool sports bar."

Mr. Brown stared at Stefaughn. It was quiet.

"Excuse me again, everyone. Here's your credit card, sir. And could you please sign the receipt." The waitress paused. She picked up her gratuity, $40.00, and one of Karen's spiritual cards from the table. Wearing a big smile, the waitress thanked Mahogany and family and walked away.

"Mom, why did you waste that card? You know good'n well that girl don't wanna hear about God from a Black woman, especially one from Saint Louis."

"How would you know, Stefaughn? Jesus just might incite her to leave me an E-mail," Karen said.

"Well, I think it's time we leave," Mr. Brown said. "Sophia, would you happen to have the valet ticket?"

"I sure do, love."

Mahogany and family rose from the dinner table. They walked through the dining room into the plant-adorned lobby and waited for the valet attendant to fetch their vehicle. Karen stood rubbing her stomach. Sophia stood taking a deep breath. Stefaughn leaned against the wall. Mr. Brown stood with his hands in his pants pocket staring out the large glass window.

Mahogany smiled at them all, yearning for the nearest bed.

THREE

Driving westbound on San Felipe, silence reigned inside of the black Ford Expedition, except for Stefaughn's snoring.

"Sophia, can you put this in the CD player for me?" Karen asked, handing her sister a CD from the backseat. "And let it play from the beginning, please?"

"Sure. Hand it here, sis," Sophia replied, reaching over her left shoulder. She inserted the CD inside of the CD changer, turned on the stereo, and pushed the CD button on the stereo panel.

The remix version of Kirk Franklin's "Stomp" came blasting through the vehicle speakers. Having the shit scared out of them, everyone jerked in perfect key.

"Goddamn it!" Mr. Brown yelled, smashing the accelerator as if a gang of wild gunmen had fired a few rounds or more. "Y'all gone make me lose my religion up in here!"

Everyone busted into laughter.

Karen was "live" on VH1, singing along with Kirk Franklin and God's Property. Her voice was on a rampage, ruining lyric after lyric. It's as if Karen was singing karaoke down at the local bar—maybe tipsy from rum.

Stefaughn couldn't listen to his mother continue butchering the gospel masterpiece. He covered his ears. Seemingly not caring, Karen stared at him, rolled her eyes, and continued to sing.

"Hallelujah! Praise the Lord fo' that song," Karen glorified. "*Girrrl*, Kirky Boy is my main man! And that's my jam right therr!" Karen stomped the floor of the SUV and blurted, "STOMP!" Oh yes, she grooved; she stomped; she snapped her fingers. Karen slipped into a spiritual trance.

17

Scarlet Tears

Mahogany sat laughing. She then cued her mother to give Karen a boost in amperage.

"Go, Karen! You can do it! It's yo' birthday!" Mahogany and Sophia sang, clapping their hands to the beat.

Karen was now super-charged. She was all in, dancing and stomping as if a pair of jumper cables was clung to her DNA's positive and negative from a brand new Die Hard automobile battery. My God, she stomped. Karen spoke in a foreign vernacular . . . in tongue as some would say. This girl had rocketed off into some unknown constellation.

Mahogany and Sophia continued to hype up Karen. It was a late evening fiesta, the motherf---- grand finale. Mahogany laughed her heart out until her cheek muscles had begun to hurt. Now how about that for dessert?

"Will you look at this crazed woman," Mr. Brown said. "Somebody stop her before I have a wreck."

Karen didn't stop; she was the star of the holy powwow.

Approaching a large, illuminated street-side advertisement that said Drury Inn Suites in bright white letters, Mr. Brown drove onto the hotel parking lot. Cars were parked everywhere.

"I've made it. Oh yes, I've made it. Thank God! Thank God Almighty, I'm free at last!"

"Well, okay then, Mister Civil Rights," Mahogany said to her father.

Mr. Brown found a parking space and parked the SUV. He turned off the radio then the engine. Suddenly, there was no more Karen; the *black diva's* gospel career had been brought to the cross. Karen looked at everyone in the SUV. She smiled at Stefaughn slowly shaking his head in disbelief.

"Dad, will you open the rear door so I can grab my travel bag?"

"Sure, Mah----"

"Don't bother, cuz," Stefaughn butted in. "I'll carry it for you."

"Oh really?" Mahogany smiled. "Is there a fee?"

"Fo' sho, cuz." Stefaughn paused. "Just continue being you."

Everyone exited the Expedition, his or her belongings in hand. Beneath the starry night sky, Mahogany and family walked across the well-lit parking lot. A cool breeze streamed through the night air. Now watching her father's hand slide down her mother's back to her butt cheeks, Mahogany chuckled as Mr. Brown squeezed the Charmin.

Entering the hotel lobby, there was no movement. Sophia approached the front desk, handed the night attendant her driver's license, and asked for the programmable card to their additional, reserved suite.

The night attendant, chewing gum, keyed information into the computer. "Okay, here you are." She paused, reaching away from the computer. "Here's your card, ma'am. The suite is next to yours, and could you please sign next to the X."

Sophia wrote her signature on the paper.

"Thank you, ma'am. And would you like a wake-up call?"

"Yes. Eight a.m., please," Sophia replied.

From the front desk to inside the elevator, there wasn't much speech between Mahogany and her family. Mr. Brown went over his duties for the following day. Stefaughn stood gazing at the advertisement on the elevator wall regarding a free continental breakfast. Karen was . . . apparently sleep standing for lack of a better description. A bell rang, and the number three became aglow above the elevator doors. Slowly, the elevator doors opened. Through the elevator doors, down the quiet corridor, Mahogany and family walked to their suites.

Inside suite 333, Mahogany bathed, brushed her teeth, moisturized her body, pinned up her hair, and slid on a short, pink satin gown. She stood in front of the body-length mirror and thought: *I'm a prize-winning catch; sexy at five-feet, nine inches; thick in the thighs; conserved; have a caramel skin complexion with shoulder-length, naturally curly black hair; my eyes are hazel, shaped like those of an Egyptian; I have a*

Scarlet Tears

bad-ass walk; I'm classy and intelligent; then I'm blessed with a good job. As Jessica would say, "I'm all that! Da baddest bi. . . ." Even better, I got a cherry on top.

Away from the mirror, Mahogany sat at the glossy wooden desk in her suite. A dim gleam of light shined on the desktop from a wall-mounted lamp. Mahogany archived the day's events in her scarlet-colored journal, titled "A Life to Remember" in gold Boulevard letters with a scarlet silk ribbon for a tie.

Finished with her day's memoirs and resting comfortably between the sheets—just like a well-seasoned, grade A steak lying tenderly between slices of fresh white honey bread—Mahogany watched CNN News.

Abruptly, a rhythmic pounding that sounded like a jackhammer busting through the suite's wall distracted Mahogany. She stiffened. She listened closely. Mahogany eased into a smile.

Mom and Dad are at it again. And, Dad, slow down, Mahogany thought. She snuggled into a fetal position and drifted away into dreamland.

FOUR

Ring . . . ring . . . ring. . . .

Mahogany rolled over in bed. She answered the telephone.

"Good morning, honey. It's after eight a.m. Time to get up."

"Mom, I'll be ready shortly. And tell Dad I said good morning," Mahogany said with a raspy voice. "Is Karen and Stef up?"

"I don't know. I'm going to call them, next."

Mahogany ended the telephone call, got out of bed, and stretched. She paused then fell backwards on the bed. Mahogany thought about home and her life as an adult. No more depending on Mom and Dad. Each decision would need to be carefully measured. Moreover, responsibilities sang her a love song.

Moments later, everyone was ready. They bypassed the free continental breakfast and checked out of the hotel.

"Hey, it's five minutes after nine, so let's quit dragging our feet," Mr. Brown said, his voice rather stern. Everyone stared at him. "Ease up. I didn't mean it like that. Anyway, Sophia, look in the glove box and hand me that tire gauge. Stefaughn, load in the luggage. And, Mahogany, please throw this bag of trash away for me."

"Yes sir, Captain Jackhammer!" Mahogany saluted her father.

Looking at Mahogany, Mr. Brown laughed. "Where did that come from?"

"I'm not telling."

Scarlet Tears

"How about IHOP for breakfast, everyone?" Sophia asked.

Everyone agreed.

The morning was sunny. The SUV was ready for travel. Mr. Brown fired up the engine and said, "All aboard!"

Passing Westheimer Road and driving south on the West Loop, Mr. Brown bumped the oldies on Majic 102 FM. Everybody bobbed their heads, grooving to "Summer Breeze" by the Isley Brothers. In the mood, Mahogany pictured herself cruising in her convertible Mustang, again. Yet, she didn't have an appetite for the jams of yesterday. Mahogany was a modern-day music enthusiast; her favorite music artists were Jay-Z and R. Kelly, and Nelly's "Country Grammar" was quickly becoming her song of choice. June 27, 2000, the date of Nelly's world debut, couldn't come fast enough.

Mahogany and family arrived at the International House of Pancakes, welcomed by the smell of grilled sausage, hotcakes, and other breakfast favorites. They were led to a table by a short, overweight waitress who favored talk show host and actress, Rosie O'Donnell.

"Hey, Mahogany, would you like to attend church with Stefaughn and me tomorrow morning?" Karen asked, replacing her menu on the table. "There are a lot of productive people I would like for you to meet, and you can ride with me."

"No problem, Aunt Karen. Does Pastor Taylor still minister there?"

"Yes he does. And, girl, he just keeps getting better with age." Karen paused. She swallowed her food. "He's so wise, so real, so inspirational, and definitely blessed with God's anointing."

"Well, I look forward to going with you, tomorrow, Aunt Karen."

Everyone ate breakfast, talking about a little bit of this and that. Karen kept it spiritual of course. Mr. Brown paid for breakfast. Karen and Sophia left the tip. Mahogany and family then returned to the SUV.

Ready to say farewell to Texas, Mr. Brown drove to the nearest gas station, Chevron. Gas was purchased; snacks were purchased; ice was purchased; and soft drinks were purchased. Mahogany rejoiced in the moment, adoring the beautiful day.

Traveling north on the West Loop, Mahogany waved goodbye to Galleria Mall, her ideal mall for shopping. Everybody relaxed and chilled to the oldies again. Stefaughn couldn't stay awake to save his life; he and traveling apparently didn't get along.

"Hey, Karen, I just know this ain't "I Love You" by Lenny Williams. Girl, they can't be getting' ready to play this song. Now this is whutcha call music. I mean this is when R and B had soul." Sophia peered over her shoulder. "Mahogany, you betta listen to this jam, girl. 'Cause it'll nevva be anutha Lenny Williams."

Mahogany thought aloud, *Yeah, and it'll never be another R. Kelly.* Nonetheless, Mahogany enjoyed listening to "I Love You." Goose pimples grew on her arms.

"*Girrrl,* you know you right 'bout that song. Whew! I can see me now back in those days. Huh . . . I was hard to handle," Karen reflected. "You could've called me Miss Hot Thang, 'cause I was like that and some, honey! Hmmph! Just hearing that song does sumptin to me. Mmm-mm! Lord, you know I need a cold shower."

Mr. Brown stared over at his wife. He didn't smile. He looked away and quickly stared at Sophia again. Sophia slowly grooved the moment away.

"Baby, remember this song when we were younger?" Sophia asked her husband.

"Um . . . talking to me?"

"Who else could I be talking to?" Sophia paused. "Is everything okay?" She smiled, stroking the rear of Mr. Brown's neck.

"Yeah . . . I'm okay. Just glad you don't know Brother Lenny personally."

"Why worry, big boy." Sophia smiled again. "Especially when you have all of me and more."

Scarlet Tears

Driving along on I-10, Mr. Brown leaned over and kissed Sophia. Everyone soon fell asleep, except Mahogany and her father. Mahogany sat back in her seat with her eyes closed, entertaining thoughts more pleasant than a rose garden. Mr. Brown changed the radio station to a weather channel:

Good afternoon, all listeners. Here's your local broadcasting weather update. We currently have clear skies from as far as Houston, Texas, to Lafayette, Louisiana, with light winds at seven miles per hour. The temperature is presently eighty-five degrees, but that's to change within the next three to four hours. For there's a severe thunderstorm with heavy rains, lightning and winds up to seventy-six miles per hour traveling west from the southern region of Alabama and Pensacola, Florida. Responsible for two deaths already and massive traffic problems—today's storm is on a roll. So, if you can avoid traveling until the storm has passed, I ask that you please do. This is Jane Siegel from WTPI, your local weather broadcast.

Mahogany's heartbeat increased; she quickly opened her eyes. Well aware of the dangers characteristic of storms developing in the Gulf of Mexico, Mahogany glanced from left to right. The sky was but a clear heaven, and the Sabine River beneath the bridge they were crossing into Louisiana appeared unruffled.

Five minutes into the State of Louisiana, Mahogany noticed a Louisiana State Patrol car following the SUV with its sirens flashing. "Dad, I think we're being flagged."

Looking through his rearview mirror, Mr. Brown said, "Now what in the hell does he want?" He slowed down and pulled over on the gravel-sided interstate.

"Baby, what's the matter?" Sophia asked, jumping out of her sleep.

"Shoot, I don't know. Some damn cop decided to pull me over."

"Were you speeding?"

"No. I had the damn thing set on cruise control," Mr. Brown replied to his wife. "Racial profiling is all this is."

Glaring through the driver's side rearview mirror, Mr. Brown lowered his window.

"How y'all, folks, be doin', sir?"

"I'm just fine." Mr. Brown seemingly forced himself to smile. "And how about yourself, officer?"

Mahogany stared at the red-faced police officer wearing dark tinted shades and shiny black boots. She listened closely, hoping for the best.

"I be doin' alright for a good ole boy from bayou country. You be knowin' the reason I'm pullin' you over, sir?"

"No, I really don't, officer." Mr. Brown sniffed.

The police officer grinned. "You be doin' an awful lot of lane switchin' without usin' yo' turn signals, there, son."

"Are you sure, officer? I've been driving in the slow lane for a while, now."

The police officer straightened his face. He took a step back and tapped the butt of his firearm with his right hand. "This be yo' truck? I'm an ole Ford boy myself, yeah."

A redneck. Probably a stick-in-the-mud confederate, Mahogany thought.

"No. It's a rental, officer."

"It is a mighty nice truck, then, sir." The police officer paused. "Well, I'm gonna need be seein' yo' license and rental agreement, yeah."

"Baby, hand me that agreement from out of the glove compartment." Mr. Brown leaned forward, reaching into his rear pants pocket.

"Take it slow there, son." The police officer rested his right hand on the butt of his automatic firearm.

Watching her father stiffen in his movement, Mahogany felt raped, maimed by the unbelievable. Her eyes became watery with pain, her heart disgust with an ache more severe than heartbreak.

Slowly removing his wallet from his rear pants pocket, Mr. Brown sat straight in his seat. He carefully removed his driver's license from his leather wallet. Not looking to his left, Mr. Brown extended his right arm over his body. "Here you are, officer."

Scarlet Tears

Accepting the driver's license, the police officer asked, "Where is it y'all be comin' from?"

"My daughter's college graduation at the University of Houston."

"Cougarsville, yeah. A good school, I'd reckon." The police officer lips twitched. "She's in here?"

"Yes she is."

The police officer peered behind Mr. Brown's head. "That be you right there, hon?"

"Yes, sir," Mahogany answered. She didn't smile and then met eyes with her mother. Sophia appeared helpless . . . maybe even hopeless.

"I be offerin' my con . . . congr . . . congratulations to you, ma'am."

Mahogany said nothing to the police officer. A still quietness shifted through the SUV.

The police officer looked at Mr. Brown then at his driver's license. "It be good y'all, folks, wearin' yo' seat belts. Ya know . . . seat belts done saved a many lives down here in da bayous," he said. "I take it you, folks, headin' back to Creve Coeur, yeah? Hopefully, I pronounced that right."

"Yes, Creve Coeur is home," Mr. Brown uttered.

"Exactly where is Creve Coeur, my friend?"

"It's a suburb community in Saint Louis County, officer."

"Is that where you, folks, originally from?"

"I'm originally from Kansas, officer."

"I be gotten family up there, myself. Lawrence, Kansas, that is. Yeah, I like the ole Sunflower State, I'd say." The police officer lips twitched again. "Well, I'm gonna be doin' you a favor, sir. If everything comes up fine on the computer . . ." he smiled, "I'ma be lettin' you go with a warnin' this time, yeah."

"I thank you ahead, officer."

Looking out the tinted rear hatch window of the SUV, Mahogany and family noticed several patrol cars had arrived. Without smiles, the police officers exited their cars one after another.

"Will you look at this?!" Karen cried in apparent fear or antipathy. "Now this doesn't make any sense. All the crime going on in this country and these no-good racists wish to waste time chastising us. It ain't nothing but the devil in them." Karen paused. She licked her lips. "I forsake, you demons!"

"I feel you, Karen," Mr. Brown said. "And I hate to speak like this. But a black man has it rough in this country."

The police officer approached the vehicle again. "Excuse me, sir. Here yo' papers and license be." He spit out a wad of chewing tobacco. "Sorry for that." He grinned. "Anyway, you know there's a lot of drug traffickin' in this part of da nation. Just da other day a friend trooper of mine and me stopped a ni---- I mean fellow." The police officer grinned, his face flushed with red. "He was headin' y'all's direction and speedin' with forty-five pounds of coke. And I ain't talkin' 'bout soda water, either. He was in this here same type truck, yeah." He smiled again, chewing tobacco having stained his teeth to the point of coffee brown. "Anyhow, they say awful big storm be headin' this way. Y'all, folks, be careful in this big, fine truck. And stay away from these here marshlands. They say it's gators 'round this neck of da woods. Be havin' a safe trip home, yeah." Stepping away from the SUV, the police officer waved with a smile, his right hand returning to the butt of his firearm.

Mr. Brown drove onto the interstate. Sophia massaged his shoulder.

Disheartened, Mahogany wondered if she should have majored in civil and criminal law. She liked being an African American. Considering herself as being a second-class citizen was the unthinkable. Nevertheless, Mahogany wasn't exempt from experiencing the eternal sting of racism and discrimination.

Stefaughn seemingly had no desire to discuss what had just happened; he immediately returned to sleep. Karen talked about the situation a little bit more, whipped out her mini-sized Bible and read some Scriptures.

Two-and-a-half hours quickly passed while traveling the interstate. Swamps and miles of woods flanked both sides of the interstate. Traffic was mild, a typical Sunday.

"I'll never rent another Expedition. These things guzzle gas like winos gulp booze. And the ride sure isn't anything to brag about. Ford I guess," Mr. Brown suddenly said.

Their faces glued to the windows, nobody responded.

"Boy, it sure looks creepy out there," Sophia announced. "Didn't I hear that officer say it was a storm heading this way?"

"Yeah. They'd also mentioned it on the weather station a while ago," Mr. Brown replied. "I just figured I'd drive as far as I could until driving conditions possibly get too bad."

"Man, the sky looks dreadful," Mahogany alarmed. "It's kind of unique, though. Maybe we should take a picture of it. There's dark purple. An orange red. The clouds are dark and gray. The sun is masked." She paused. "Everything just looks artificial. And I don't see a single bird."

"Birds have plenty of sense," Karen said. "It'll take a fool to keep flying or driving around beneath a sky like that."

"Yeah, it is kind of gloomy-looking ahead," Stefaughn added, somehow awakened from the dead.

"As long as it's not raining too. . . . Well, it's here." Rain bombed the windshield. The sky darkened. "I hope it'll all pass right over. That way we can keep right on trucking."

"Watch out, honey!" Sophia screamed.

"Oh shit!" Mr. Brown exclaimed, quickly turning the steering wheel to his right.

"Good God! What kind of creature was that?" Sophia asked.

"I don't know. That thing sure looked weird. Hey, did you, guys, feel the truck slide?"

"Yes, I felt it, Dad," Mahogany answered. "We probably need to go ahead and pull over. It has gotten too bad out here. And that possibly could have been an omen."

"It sure is getting real dar----"

There was a loud clap of thunder. Lightning streaked across the firmament. Mahogany and family screamed for dear life, ducking in the name of safety. A downpour succeeded as if it was the Great Flood all over again.

"Oh, Jesus, Jesus, Jesus—Jesus!" Karen bawled. "Please don't let this mad man kill us!"

"Karen!" Mr. Brown yelled. "That's the la----"

Heavy rain stormed the windshield, seriously impairing visibility.

"There's a rest area just miles ahead not far from Baton Rouge. I'll pull over off the road, then. Because I'm not pulling over on the side of this highway with all these woods and Lord knows wh----"

Bomp-bommmmp blared the air horn of a passing eighteen-wheeler. The truck pulled a trailer with a McDonald's advertisement.

"Hmmph! That was close," Mahogany said after taking a train of deep breaths and praying that her father would pull over. "I hope you're not riding in both lanes, Dad."

"Will you look at that fool!" Sophia fussed. "Speeding like a bat out of hell. I know McDonald's isn't that hard up for some hamburger buns and French-fries."

Mahogany and family were clearly afraid. The driving conditions had gotten terrible. There wasn't an exit in sight. Darkened woods haunted the journey. The weather wasn't letting up, and lightning continued to ignite the eerie heavens.

"Everybody, let's just be quiet for a moment, so I can pray for us," Karen instructed, obviously staying true to the message on the rear of her spiritual cards. Stefaughn, Karen, and Mahogany joined hands on the second row of seats. "Dear Heavenly Father, my Great Lord, I pray unto You in this time of danger for Your protection and guidance. Lord . . . watch over us and please keep us safe. We are encountering a complication at this time. And shall it ever b----"

"Holy shit!" Mr. Brown blurted.

Scarlet Tears

A loud, crushing noise sounded from beneath the SUV. Silence loomed. Everyone stared at one another. The numbness of death was in the air.

"I don't like the tires on this truck. I've felt this thing hydroplane twice. And I'm not driving anywhere near the speed limit. It slides too much, and it takes too long to slow down," Mr. Brown complained. "You don't have to *ever* worry about me buying some Firestone tires. Anyway, maybe if I put it on four-wheel drive it'll handle the road a little better."

"Uhh, Dad? What was that?" Mahogany asked.

"Probably an armadillo from the way it sounded."

The rain began to dwindle; thunder began to silence; yet lightning continued to streak the heavens.

Now at the rest area, Mahogany could feel her heartbeat slowing. There was life again.

"Well . . . is everybody, okay?" Mr. Brown asked.

Nobody answered. Mahogany, Karen, Sophia, and Stefaughn had their faces glued to the windows, again.

"It feels like I have to throw up," Mahogany said, rubbing her abdomen.

"Are you okay, darling? It should be some Sprites left inside of the cooler," Sophia said. "I'll walk with you over to the restroom if you want me to."

"That's okay. It's still raining quite a bit. I think I'll be fine."

"Are you sure, Mahogany?" Karen asked.

"Yeah, I'm all right, Aunt Karen. It's just that nasty crushing sound I can't get over. I think that is what's upsetting my stomach."

"Oh, you'll get over it, especially riding out here in this crazy weather," Stefaughn said.

"As a matter of fact, let's see what the radio is saying about the storm." Mr. Brown turned up the stereo volume. He searched for local weather broadcasting. "Ah, here it is."

'll in effect is a rigorous thunderstorm that continue to dominate the southern parts of Western Mississippi, Louisiana, and Southeastern Texas. In its wrath, the storm

carries some very harsh winds and heavy downpours. There are frequent flashes of lightning and a lot of debris spread across roads and highways. The temperature is currently seventy-five degrees in and around the Baton Rouge vicinity. And six deaths have been reported from today's storm. If you're driving, we ask that you please be careful and buckle up. This is your emergency weather broadcast station, WERP.

"Well, the storm seems to be just about finishing up, here. We're catching the tail end now. I think we'll be okay with this thing now on four-wheel drive. Believe me, I have no intentions being stuck on this highway all night. Another nine hours or so and we'll be at home," Mr. Brown explained.

"I guess it is okay," Sophia said, observing her surroundings. "Everybody else is getting back on the interstate."

"So, does anyone need to use the restroom before I pull off?"

Everyone said no.

Mr. Brown returned to the interstate, soon connecting with I-55 North. Mahogany loved her father, possessing many of his characteristics. She didn't believe in *I can't*, yet was discerning. Life was Mahogany's playground, and she wanted to both explore it and enjoy it.

FIVE

It was early Sunday morning, and the sun shined bright. The winds were tickling the trees at 1919 Villa Hill. Mr. and Mrs. Brown were in their bedroom. Mahogany had just finished drinking a cold glass of OJ and speaking with Karen on the telephone.

Through the home intercom system, Mahogany informed her parents that she was preparing to depart for Karen's. She exited through the kitchen door that leads into the three-car garage, her purse in hand. Mahogany pressed the white button on the wall-mounted electrical garage door opener. Rays from the sun burst into the garage. Mahogany walked over to the driver's side door of her new car, opened it, and was delighted by the scent of fresh leather. Leaping from a 1994 Honda Accord, coupe, to a 2000 convertible Mustang GT 5.0 was thrilling.

"Well my, my, my, look at Miss Pocahontas," Sophia said. "Here, take my cell phone and call me when you get to Karen's."

"Okay."

"Make sure you have your house key, dear. We'll probably be gone by the time you return," Mr. Brown said. "And drive safe, sweetheart."

Mahogany fastened her seat belt and assured her parents that everything would be fine.

"Honey, do you have your driver's license and insurance card? Oh yeah, the vehicle registration is in your glove box."

"I got everything, Mom." Mahogany turned the ignition switch.

Scarlet Tears

Vroom roared the high-performance engine beneath the hood of Mahogany's car. Mahogany smiled and gripped the steering wheel. She could sense the increase in horsepower and decided not to lower the convertible top. Mahogany wanted to save her hairdo for church.

Desperate to have the time of her life, Mahogany fantasized dazzling St. Louis. On the down low, she believed herself to be the African-American bombshell of the Midwest. From the latest fashions, wearing the hottest hairdos, Mahogany had become of age.

Easing out of the garage, Mahogany waved goodbye to her parents. She opened her purse, removed R. Kelly's R. double CD, and inserted disc one into her Mach stereo. Mahogany turned the volume midway. The music instantly galvanized Mahogany into an exalted mood. She felt wanted, sexy, touched in a special way. The sound system was clear and well balanced, very satisfying.

Maneuvering through her neighborhood, Mahogany drove onto Highway 40 and steamed east—but with R. Kelly stroking her fantasy.

Approaching North Kingshighway, Mahogany exited the interstate. She cruised towards her aunt's home, however, stunned by the many African Americans aimlessly wandering the trash-laden inner-city streets in tattered clothes.

Damn, she looks tired and hopeless, Mahogany thought, having just passed a young woman in tight, multi-colored clothes who shuffled down the sidewalk as if her feet were tender from walking on hot coals. Mahogany thought she was at the movies, unaware that true hell was only minutes away from her home.

Mahogany arrived at Maffit, a seemingly quiet, clean street on the city's West Side. Karen lived on Maffit, and all the lawns were well manicured. The houses were well kept. Grass was green, and the trees were trimmed. Noticeably, the spirit of community hadn't been strangled on Maffit.

Twenty-seven, twenty-one, Mahogany said to herself, reading the shiny brass numbers on Karen's house. She parked her car and called her mother on the cellular telephone. They talked briefly. Mahogany then exited her car, chirped the alarm, and walked up the five concrete stairs that lead to the front door of Karen's home. She peered at the elongated doorbell, pushed it, and waited.

The door opened.

"Damn, you look good, cuz!" Stefaughn said. "Don't tell me you're looking to snag you a religious man." He smiled. "For a minute I thought you were the black Cinderella. Or maybe Halle Berry paying me a surprise visit." He paused, staring outside. "And nice wheels, cuz."

Mahogany blushed. She shoved Stefaughn to the side. "Boy, you're so silly. Thanks, anyhow. And what happened to good morning?"

"Oh, I forgot . . . Miss Suburbia is here." Stefaughn chuckled. "Why good morning, Mademoiselle Mahogany Brown."

"Yeah, whatever. You don't know any French. Quit fronting." Mahogany placed the palm of her hand in front of Stefaughn's face.

Karen pranced into the living room. "Well good morning, Miss Angel. And look at you." Karen paused, looking at Mahogany from head to toe. "You look *goood*. Now don't make me have to go and change." She placed her hands on her hips.

The compliments flattered Mahogany; her spirits danced in joy.

"Good morning, Aunt Karen. And you're already dressed to impress."

"Oh well, that's all I needed to know." Karen smiled. She walked out of the living room.

"Hey, Momma, have you seen my Bible?" Stefaughn shouted, searching under the sofa pillows.

There was no reply. Mahogany took a seat in the armchair, shaking her head at Stefaughn.

"Oh, I know where it is." Stefaughn walked into his bedroom.

Mahogany overlooked the living room. *Nice, but gaudy*, she thought.

Scarlet Tears

"I found my Bible, cuz," Stefaughn said, returning to the living room.

"Good for you. Have you been reading it?"

"Hey, hey, hey, are you trying to tell me something, cuz?"

"No. I just asked a simple question."

"Then I'll just give you a simple answer a little later."

Mahogany and Stefaughn laughed.

Soon, Mahogany, Karen, and Stefaughn marched out of the front door, armed with Bibles, note pads, ink pens, and belief in God. The Rhema Church was their destination. And NO . . . Karen didn't forget to set the house alarm. Paradise wasn't exempt from burglary.

Driving down Dr. Martin Luther King Drive, Karen complimented Mahogany's car. Mississippi Mass Choir was playing on the stereo. It was little talking. No smiling. Just intense listening. Clearly, it was God's time.

Mahogany and family arrived at church. They hurried from the car; service was beginning.

Now inside of The Rhema Church, Karen wore a smile, one that was picture perfect. Her gold tooth twinkled, and she waved hello to practically every brother and sister in the congregation. Karen's diamond rings were glinting, but her broad-brimmed straw hat, along with its red silk band, stole the show.

Walking alongside Karen, Mahogany was nervous. She felt like the new kid on the block, under scrutiny by a thousand eyes. Karen had told Mahogany that Sunday services were videotaped, edited, and available for purchase. Therefore, Mahogany wanted to look and feel relaxed, to be fully in tune with God.

TRC was Karen's house; the evidence was revealing. To Karen, Hollywood had packed up and relocated to the STL. Her swagger didn't lie. Yes, Ms. Angela Bassett was on the scene.

Mahogany and family were ushered to reserve seating. Karen allowed Mahogany and Stefaughn to sit first. She wanted the aisle seat. Mahogany chortled and thought, *My aunt is off the chain.* Truthfully, Karen was adorable. She kept it real, always caring, sharing, and loving.

The whole while, TRC's choir rocked the house. "My Precious Lord," the remix, was the selection. Women shouted. A sea of hands slowly drifted through the perfumed air. Men and women rocked from side to side. Brothers sat slowly shaking their heads as if guilt was the emotion lashing at their hearts. Others appeared to be mourning, trapped in a matrix of grief. Many cried "Praise Jesus!" over and over again. Undoubtedly, the Holy Ghost had been stirred up, elevated to the forefront.

All of this was fairly new to Mahogany. Until age fifteen, she was reared under the strict principles characteristic of the Jehovah's Witnesses. Mahogany parents withdrew from the religion, unable to flourish through life poisoned by fear and hope for an earthly paradise where everyone would coexist as one big happy family.

Mahogany sat attentively, rattled by the unknown, her skin covered with goosebumps. Beads of sweat dribbled down her backside. She repeatedly tried wiping her forehead free of perspiration. Quietly, Mahogany wanted to escape the religious bonanza.

Unlike Karen, Stefaughn noticed Mahogany's uncomfortableness. He was tickled purple. Mahogany shot him a bow, warning him to stop giggling. Well, Stefaughn seemingly couldn't help himself. Mahogany became more nervous, praying she wouldn't fall victim to a panic attack. She damn near wanted to scream, to remove the unusual feeling she was experiencing. Anxiety was relentless. Then maybe it was true joy, God's way of letting Mahogany know that she'd found home. There's one thing for sure, Mahogany was vulnerable to catching that sudden urge to just let go, to unleash whatever spirits that dwelled within.

Mahogany felt pressured to speak in tongue; strange images raced through her mind. She fought hard to contain the abnormal feelings that sought liberation. *What happened to Karen's niece? Is my child all right? Girl, that bitch is crazy! Did you see that new sister shouting and speaking like some*

Scarlet Tears

damn heathen? Girl, Mahogany was attacked by demons. These would have been the inquiries and statements typical of many, Sunday's after church gossip.

Regardless of the encounter, Mahogany tried enjoying and learning from the pastor's sermon. She endured; she overcame another struggle. But would victory last?

Service had ended. The congregants smiled; they shook hands and hugged one another. Seemingly, the congregants were filled with new hope, ready to fight through another week of trials and tribulations.

Mahogany observed those around her. The brothers couldn't keep their eyes off her. Mahogany felt like prey, the last steak in the lion's den.

Karen introduced Mahogany, well, showcased her, to the entire church clergy and almost half of the Christian congregation. Mahogany found herself answering question after question, several brothers inquiring to see if she was single and interested in further attendance at TRC. Mahogany wished they would have just asked for her seven digits. Men's beating around the bush was annoying. She knew what they wanted, someone fresh, somebody delectable like milk chocolate, a virgin princess.

Figuring what the hell, Mahogany joined Karen in theatrical school. She chose to be Nia Long. Mahogany did just fine, actually loving the good ending.

SIX

Away, adrift in the privacy of her bedroom bathroom, Mahogany was home alone. She sat in the bathtub, submerged in bubbles. The scent of fresh pears hovered in the air, reminiscent of the perfect orchard. Victoria's Secret was being revealed, while the mellowness of candlelight softened the moment like Granny's age-old feather bed.

With her back lying against the rear of the bathtub, Mahogany slowly slid more of her body into the warm water. She enjoyed some me-time, making the best of her Sunday evening. With the sun declining from its prime, Mahogany looked forward to an even better time—wherever, however.

Hadn't long ago spoke with Jessica and her high school comrades, Astarte May and Sarah Warrenberg, Mahogany reflected upon the plans they'd set up for the evening. She believed true fun mostly came about on a whim, something that was entirely unpredictable.

Astarte May, an engaging African-American young woman, wasn't popular in high school. She was perceived as an intelligent klutz, but well respected. Astarte bypassed traveling off to a four-year university; she remained home after high school to help her parents manage their real estate enterprise. Soon after, Astarte enrolled as a part-time student at Maryville University at Town and Country, studying towards the acquisition of a baccalaureate in Accounting.

Sarah was a glamorous European American who lived with her parents seven minutes from Mahogany in a gated community of breathtaking homes. In high school, she was known for her splendid memory and fitness fetish. Parkway North High School in the West Suburbs was where Sarah developed to be a spectacular cheerleader her junior and senior year. She scored exceptionally high on the SAT but didn't attend college.

Being the youngest sibling of the Warrenbergs, an affluent family of politicians and lawyers who'd accumulated a fortune through the stock market and private investments, Sarah was now a cheerleader for the 2000 Super Bowl champs, St. Louis Rams. Away from the public's eye, she'd acquired an unrelenting appetite for chocolate-covered men, those fulfilling exuberant, wealth-aggregating contracts.

Well-educated products of St. Louis County's highly esteemed Parkway School District, well endowed with family support and a host of other productive resources, Mahogany, Sarah, and Astarte were the dream little orphanage girls often dreamt.

Jessica and her family had made it home without harm from Houston, Texas, early that morning. Jessica lived with her mother and younger sister on the top floor of a two-family flat on Walton Avenue. She hadn't long awakened from a nap when Mahogany called and was excited about their planned evening. Jessica was Mahogany, Astarte, and Sarah's key to all the happenings around town that was associated with young African-American adults. Claiming that she had inner-city connections, Jessica was imbued with passion to establish it in her hometown that she was the big kahuna.

The winds were mild, and the evening sun was cordial. Puffy white clouds graced the sky here and there. Mahogany dressed in DKNY summer apparel, a close-fitting outfit that had no intentions of confining her curvaceous body. Revealing, the awe of a beautiful day, Mahogany was male stimulation to the first degree.

Astarte dressed down; she was more of a conservative. Her natural appeal made a clear statement: RESPECT ME OR GIVE ME FIFTY FEET.

Judging Sarah, she was overly disclosing, a grandparent's nightmare. She was practically naked, yet damn proud of her model-perfect body. Sarah's long brunette hair danced in the running winds; her cleavage sparked thirst; and her tanned legs appeared as if they were carved with the master's touch.

Cruising down the interstate, Mahogany, Sarah, and Astarte were a sensual road hazard, a gorgeous trio of God-blessed jewels. Brake lights flashed. Strangers tried keeping up. Hands waved. Boys and men had it bad.

Mahogany and company loved the attention. They had fun, whipping in and out of traffic as if they were making a last-minute dash for the finish line.

Laughing, sporting expensive shades, and reminiscing their high school days, the suburban "Supremes" arrived at Jessica's apartment. Mahogany dialed inside from her cellular telephone and informed Jessica that she and the crew were waiting outside in her car.

As they waited, boys and men, young and old, crowded to the street. The onlookers stood gazing, some flirting and others sharing obscenities. High fives became constant throughout the crowd of men. Booze, cigarettes, and "joints" were passed from hand to hand, the chemical controllers of the underworld. Then there were the promiscuous managers of hell; those with gold teeth; those who thought gripping the crotch of their pants was cool. The sight of such beautiful women on Walton Avenue appeared to be a rarity. Plainly . . . Sheol had been granted a glimpse into Heaven.

Jessica struck out of her front door. She was far more than good-looking; she was a feminine force of gravitating charm. The toned muscles in Jessica's oiled legs screamed *hello* as she slowly stepped down the gray stairs leading from her porch. There was a gap between Jessica's upper thighs, a clear view into tomorrow. Her gear wasn't too ostentatious—however seizing. The men raved; they shouted Jessica's name; these brothers cheered as if they were the Missouri State 6A Cheerleading Champs.

Sarah removed herself from the front passenger seat and took a seat in the rear. The front passenger seat now belonged to Jessica, the new director of affairs.

Mahogany and friends drove down Walton Avenue, listening to "Come On" from Traneen's *Diary* LP on 100.3FM "The Beat". They smiled; they waved good-bye.

A cohesive four, Mahogany and company's first stop would be O'Fallon Park, an inner-city park that was a Mecca for African Americans on Sundays. Well, the park wasn't filled with excitement as rumors favored, and the city police were posted up in the park as if they were protecting the U.S. President.

Regardless of the large police presence, O'Fallon Park had attracted a fair-size gathering of people. Therefore Mahogany and friends took a ride through the park.

Trees, both large and small, balanced the landscape. Green grass, though poorly trimmed, covered much of the park. Neighborhood children ran and played—screaming, shouting, and laughing. Hoochie mommas stared, rolling their eyes at Mahogany and crew. Pants-sagging young men, several of them on cellular telephones, flagged for Mahogany to pull over. She refused and exited the park without sharing a single glimpse back.

From O'Fallon Park to Forest Park, the city was at an all-time low for African-American entertainment. Shopping malls were closed for the evening, and the inner-city streets were gagged by gloom. According to local News media, there had been a major overhaul of the urban community. Jessica interpreted the overhaul as a systematic war on the ghetto Negro.

"Girl, where else can we go?" Mahogany asked Jessica.

Jessica stared at Mahogany's facial expression. "Well it ain't my fault the city's all messed up. Anyway, let's try the Central West End."

"Yeah, that's a cool spot," Sarah said. "My family and I visit it often."

Jessica guided Mahogany into the city's Central West End, a small, cozy division of specialty shops, high-priced office space, eloquent apartments, condominiums, and a multiple of distinguished restaurants. It was all hid within a greenery of trimmed trees, foliage, and colorful, oversized plants. People, each with smiling faces, walked from shop to shop. Some even walked expensive pets. It was a locale to be traversed again, a unique location befitting each of their character.

Leaving the Central West End, Mahogany eased through downtown and historical Laclede's Landing. The four of them came to the conclusion that St. Louis City was a dud this Sunday. They then decided to travel across the "Great Muddy" Mississippi River into East Saint Louis, Illinois. Crossing the Poplar Street Bridge, Mahogany asked, "Hey, you all, what if this bridge happens to collapse while we're crossing it?"

Silence struck the car like a sudden flash of lightning.

"Mahogany, what kind of question is that?" Astarte questioned, grabbing hold of Sarah's arm.

"Hey, y'all, Astarte's afraid of falling into the river," Sarah said.

Jessica looked over her shoulder. Mahogany peered through her rearview mirror at Astarte. Laughter exploded.

Having exited on 13th and Tudor, Jessica directed Mahogany to Lincoln Park. Lincoln Park wasn't a very big park when compared to the huge parks characteristic of St. Louis; notwithstanding, it was East St. Louis' spring and summer cubic zirconia. Scores of African Americans and few whites populated the park. They were of every age. Mahogany and friends figured they'd drove into exactly what they were searching for, a fantastic time.

The aroma of barbecue spurred the air. People laughed and talked, seemingly having a wonderful time. A buffet of exotic and common cars was showcased—not to forget a medley of hoopties. There were two concerts, one on each end of the park. Reggae music banged from one end, and Rap music blurred from the other end. A chain of African-American motorcyclists slowly circled the park, and a bounty of young women exhibited their fleshly goods pleading for rides.

Daisy Dukes, tight Capri pants, and sheer halter tops were the most common types of ladies garments; they were

Scarlet Tears

items of guaranteed attention. The park's community swimming pool was full with shapely young girls and women in thongs and bathing suits. Girls screamed in joy as they tried keeping away from naughty little boys maneuvering through the water. Besides a small showing of law enforcement, there was much more.

In spite of the energetic atmosphere, the park's softball league seemed to be the main attraction. Many people surrounded the baseball field. Jessica said that there were men at the park from all over the St. Louis Metropolitan Area. Fans cheered for their favorite teams. Lincoln Park on Sundays was a melting pot, a network where anything goes. Fun appeared to be inevitable. Lincoln Park had it going on. It was Sunday's "Krunkfest."

Stumbling across a parking space, Mahogany and peers agreed to not render their numbers of communication, but they were willing to receive them. Mahogany parked; she noticed several groups of men and younger boys gazing at her and her friends. Ready to do her thing, Mahogany retracted and locked the convertible roof, turned off the stereo, and informed her friends that it was time to show and prove.

Joining the trail of walking enthusiasts, Mahogany felt a sense of adventure. She was learning a great deal about her race in urban America. Yet Mahogany wondered why her and her friends stuck out like sore thumbs. There was something different, and Mahogany yearned for an understanding. Of so-called higher standards in comparison of those she'd encountered, Mahogany believed her and her friends were a cast of star light being shone upon a stretch of urban darkness. Despite her thoughts, thrill blazed at Lincoln Park.

Mahogany, Jessica, Sarah, and Astarte strolled through the park. Some men whistled; others blurted their desires. Many women snared up their noses; others turned their heads. Little girls waved hello and smiled. Mahogany smiled in return and thought the little girl in pink, snaggle-toothed and short, was adorable.

Little boys gazed, and some asked for loose change. Meeting their request, Mahogany and friends brought smiles to the little boys' faces.

To Mahogany's surprise, a row of female and male wine-heads, probably crackheads, passed one bottle of Wild Irish Rose and a bottle of MadDog 20/20 to one another just feet away from the park swimming pool. The wine-heads sat on the concrete sidewalk against an old, vacant brick building. Some clamored and fussed with one another. Suddenly, a wine-head with a scraggly beard and wearing a dirty gray suit jacket held up a piece of metal to his mouth and flicked a lighter at the end of it. His eyes popped wide open; he peered at Mahogany; Mahogany flinched; the crackhead whistled then flapped his tongue at Mahogany. Laughing, Mahogany and company picked up their pace in the name of a getaway.

"Girl, can you believe this?" Mahogany asked Astarte.

"Those people are insane," Astarte replied, looking over her shoulder. "They're just sitting out here in the open and drinking while children are around."

Sarah continued to smile. "This is incredible," she said with amazement. "I mean . . . I've never seen anything like this before."

"Don't trip, y'all," Jessica uttered. "This is common in the hood."

Mahogany and crew decided to stop and watch the softball game. Her eyes locked on a particular individual, Mahogany found herself attracted to one of the softball players. He gazed at Mahogany and smiled. She smiled back, thoughts of passion setting her afire. This was a challenging moment for Mahogany, a large step towards self-discovery, a crossing into the real world.

Jessica soon toppled across several males that she knew from St. Louis and her old high school, Sumner. She introduced them to her lady friends. Listening to lots of compliments, Mahogany was grateful. She hadn't ever received that much attention before. It was an impressive evening, a day of magical surprises.

Scarlet Tears

The sun began to fade. Mahogany felt that the spirit of the park was changing for the worse. She asked her friends if they were ready to go. Sarah wasn't quite ready to leave. Astarte was more than ready to leave. To Jessica, it didn't make a difference.

Mahogany and Astarte consisted of the majority. So they left the park together, but not without pockets full of fliers, business cards, and whatnots from male admirers.

SEVEN

Monday, June 12, 2000

Her first day on the job, Mahogany peered at the round clock hanging on the office wall. It was one hour before noon, and Mahogany's stomach opposed good feelings. Thoughts of a tasty meal streamed through Mahogany's mind. She and nervousness had been at war all morning, making her introduction into corporate America a tough one.

Poisoned by uncertainty, Mahogany felt unwelcomed at her new place of employment. She questioned her ability to strive in a mid-paced environment, an environment where the color black was on death row.

The only African American who worked in the luxurious hotel's administrative department, Mahogany wanted to learn fast, perform at her optimum. She wanted to prove something to her White counterparts and self, more like make a statement of adequacy. This was a mindset Mahogany did not like, one politely inviting annoyance.

She was hired as a full-time account manager, and a forty-two-year-old White female trained Mahogany. Mahogany's trainer was soon relocating to work at Adam's Mark Hotel in Mobile, Alabama. Mahogany felt friction between her and the trainer, wishing she could erase it all with a click of her heels.

Her new job required managing the interests of the hotel's important clients, clients from a broad spectrum of professions and demands. Mahogany was also to secure new clients by following up on leads and making presentations concerning the hotel's highly ranked catering services, ballroom and banquet amenities, and presidential suites.

Scarlet Tears

Due to an onslaught of negative media attention, the hotel's national offices deemed it necessary to acquire a new, refreshing identity, an image of diversity. Advertising changed to meet their new interests; personnel changed from top to bottom, yet mostly at the bottom. Closer to an optimist than a pessimist, Mahogany believed the hotel was making a move in the right direction.

Several coworkers invited Mahogany out to lunch, mostly White males in supervisory positions. Aware of the importance of playing politics and utilizing a cooperative spirit, Mahogany accepted the invitation. She and six colleagues walked two downtown blocks to Mike Shannon's, a popular, high-end restaurant.

Walking with her coworkers, Mahogany felt a sense of belonging, a belonging to something that the average African American wasn't included or welcomed. Her immediate surroundings brewed such thoughts. There were endless Black people standing on public bus lines. Most looked weary, married to a hard life. None wore corporate attire. From corner to corner homeless people, mostly African Americans of course, wandered the streets. A few of them entertained for coins. Most Whites wore smiles, including those passing by in nice cars.

The sight of a young, professional African-American male was a scarcity; it was as if searching for a penny in the ocean deep. Mahogany judged this as a battered reality; it was a culture shock, maybe even a "pimp smack" to the right cheek. She had been selected into the very world that had conquered her own. Tossed into a foreign arena, an elevated expanse where many Blacks dreamt to explore, Mahogany was a corporate statistic, an effigy in a frying pan.

Led to their reserved seating, the corporate force of seven ordered salads and appetizers. Since lunch wouldn't be long, they chose to eat light. A slew of jokes were aired: dumb blonde jokes, Chinese jokes, Hispanic jokes, Confederate jokes, and African-American jokes. Funny or not, everyone laughed. And Mahogany didn't escape the storm of background-digging inquiries. It didn't matter to Mahogany; her life was as pure as fresh Idaho spring water.

Having survived a lunchtime investigation, Mahogany's first day of work was just about over. The day had been long but productive. She was ready to elude the impudent conservatism and bustle attributable of Downtown St. Louis.

At the very end of her first day of work, Mahogany knew she'd passed Adam's Mark secret summation of acceptance tests. She was now an initiate of corporate America, one that was downsizing. How long would she last?

EIGHT

Nearing the gleam of dawn, Saturday, June 17, 2000, Mahogany had awakened from a dream, one coated with ecstasy. Partly confused, partly excited, Mahogany was growing more interested in men. She'd endured a week long regime of training and being considered inferior by several coworkers. Mahogany wanted to exhale.

With an eight a.m. hair appointment to attend, Mahogany got out of bed, changed the linens, and smothered her nighttime affinity in a cool shower. Curious of the activity associated with her subconscious, Mahogany was flared, the constant thought of men drifting through her mind.

Prepared to depart from home, Mahogany left a note of her planned whereabouts on the kitchen island. It was a family custom to inform each other about one's whereabouts.

Driving north on I-270, Mahogany telephoned Jessica and confirmed directions to the hair salon. From the hoarseness in Jessica's voice, Mahogany figured she was still asleep. Jessica's hair appointment was scheduled for 8:30 a.m. Mahogany doubted Jessica would make her appointment.

Parking in front of Delancy's Stylez Center on Chambers Road, Mahogany hurried inside. She was five minutes late and had already been forewarned that the chief stylist/owner disliked tardiness.

"Girl, you must be Mahogany," a guy said, his hands on his hips and rolling his neck.

Mahogany abruptly stopped; she shook her head up and down.

"Child, I just hung up da phone wit' Jessie asking 'bout you," he continued, looking at Mahogany from head to

Scarlet Tears

toe. "She said you was on yo' way. And, uh, I'm Delancy." Delancy smiled and flipped his right hand in the air.

"Yeah . . . I am Ma . . . Mahogany," she stuttered, caught off guard by Delancy's feminine characteristics.

The other patrons and hairstylists laughed and snickered. Appearing to be in his late twenties, Delancy was comedy relief. He was fair complexioned, maybe five feet, eight inches tall, of medium build, and wore thick black waves. Soft-spoken and seemingly successful, Delancy's hair salon was quite busy for so early in the morning.

"Excuse me, love." He paused. "You don't mind my being gay, do you?" He placed his hands on his hips again, stepped his right foot forward and turned it outwards.

"No, no. . . . I was jus----"

Delancy grasped Mahogany by the hand. "Come on in herr, girl. And relax. You ain't gotta worry 'bout me bitin' you. Honey, Delancy's got uh man. Besides, we kick it up in herr. So have yo' sweet, brown tail a seat."

Laughter fueled the medium-sized, vibrantly decorated hair salon. Mahogany smiled, reading several signs that were posted on the hair salon walls. The sign of most interest read:

PRAY FOR ME . . .
I need the prayer . . .
YOU NEED THE PRACTICE

Thinking of Delancy, Mahogany agreed with the sign. Delancy was one of a kind, in a league of his own.

"I'm sorry if I offended you, Delancy. All of this is sort of new to me."

"Girl, you o'right. Anyway, honey, call me Lance fo' romance." Wearing a long white smock, Delancy snapped his fingers. The hair salon name was pressed on front of the smock, and "SOFT and EASY" on the rear. "So you wanted a French twist, right?"

"Yes, but I'll like to get my hair washed and conditioned, first."

"Dhat ain't no problem, Miss Thangy-thang. Most of dhese heifers come in herr saying . . . 'Lance, all you need to do is just fix my hair. I already washed and conditioned it.'" He imitated. "Heifers always wantin' a damn discount or some credit. Oh cheap ass hookers!" Delancy paused. "Girl, I don't even say nuttin. I just point to da signs."

The two signs read:

ABSOLUTELY **NO** CREDIT!
<u>Including family and friends</u>

ATTENTION
This is a HAIR SALON
NOT a LOAN OFFICE!

Delancy continued, "Anyway, where at did you go to high school, honey?"

"Parkway North."

"Child, you live in West County, I'd suppose."

"Yes. And what high school did you attend, Lance?"

"Da View, baby. Da muthaflippin View."

"Um . . . would that be Riverview Gardens?"

"Sho nuff, honey. And, Mahogany, loosen up. You all uptight and shit. If you a friend of Jessica hip ass, then you a friend of mine. I told you, child, I gotta fine ass man. Trust me . . . we lookin' fo' da same thang, da muthaflipping beef," he said. "You are straight, right?"

"I'm not interested in fornication. But if I was seeking companionship, it would be from a guy."

"Well, damn it man!" Delancy replied, his voice high-pitched. "Da girl done got all formal on me. Check dhis out, Mahogany, you can nevva tell wit' dhese men today. Half of 'em love booty games. Trust me on dhat one, honey." Delancy pumped his chest to the beat on the radio and whispered in Mahogany's ear, "You're not a celibate, are you? If so, I wouldn't want dhese wolves in here to know dhat."

"I am."

Scarlet Tears

"Well, I ain't mad at ya, honey. But if I was packin' what you packin', I'll be doin' just what Juvenile sexy ass is sayin' on dhis song."

Delancy began rapping along to "Back Dat Azz Up" on Q95.5 FM. Way off into it, he demonstrated his version of *backing up azz.* Delancy was a crowd pleaser, setting himself up for an encore.

Mahogany couldn't refrain from laughing. Several tears seeped from her eyes as she laughed away. Delancy touched her heart in a special way. His spirit was embracing, the majestic dove of the high heavens.

It was almost nine a.m., and there was no sign of Jessica. Delancy telephoned Jessica's home again. He told Mahogany she'd left home thirty minutes prior to his call. Mahogany figured Jessica was probably on her way to the hair salon. She then looked out through the glass storefront. "Here she comes," Mahogany said.

Jessica exited the passenger side of a new-looking, black Ford F150, "Harley Davidson Edition." She was wearing tight blue denim shorts, a pink Perrassuco fitted T-shirt, and a pair of shiny fusia, medium-heel sandals that had leather strings wrapped around her lower legs. Jessica was eye candy, hot triple fudge on a mound of vanilla ice cream, the flavor of the month, a BET video vixen. Call it lust, call it a good time and weekend sunshine.

Jessica entered the half-crowded hair salon. Mahogany sensed a difference in her attitude. Jessica was on a new time, seemingly fishing for cash. She had an aura Mahogany had seen before. This bothered Mahogany, because she knew Jessica was capable of making bad moves after bad moves from their college experience. It was a new day, and Jessica was clearly in a present-day consciousness.

"Well, hello dhere, Miss Late Ass, Miss U of H and fine as she wanna be," Delancy greeted. "I just know you got some good gossip to share wit' dhis salon, today. Disrepectin' appointments like dhis yo' joint or sumptin." Delancy rolled his eyes and flipped his hand in the air.

Jessica smiled. She looked at Mahogany and gave her an okay sign. "Lance, boy, you're so crazy. Don't even trip. I got you faded, today." Jessica looked at Mahogany again. "How long has my girl been under the hairdryer?"

"Honey, don't worry 'bout yo' girl. She's my bizness now." Delancy gazed at Mahogany with a smile. "And who is Mister Trucky-truck dhat just dropped you off?"

"Boy, he's just an old friend. And why are you asking me personal questions like that in front of all these people?"

"Oh, yo' ass important now, huh?" he replied. "Anyhow, gimme a hug wit' yo' wild ass."

It appeared as if everyone's eyes zoned in on Jessica. She was dazzling in her new apparel, ass fatter than Bill Gates wallet.

"Hey, everybody, give my girl some big ups fo' graduating from da University of Houst----"

"Lance, don't forget my girl, Mahogany. She graduated, too, from the U of H. And now handlin' thangs down at Adam's Mark," Jessica said, keeping it gutter and lady gangster.

"Well, blow me Jesus!" Delancy blurted out. "We got a twin set of Miss Thangy-thangs up in herr. Give it up fo' 'em, y'all."

Smiling, the patrons clapped. Brothers whistled. However, two females sitting side-by-side sat with frowning faces. Jessica glanced over at them and sneered. She then smiled at Mahogany. Mahogany gave Jessica a menacing stare, praying Jessica hadn't knelt to the pressures of the ghetto.

As everyone enjoyed the "The Delancy Show," time sped along without notice. Delancy was Saturday morning's cartoon, a psychotropic drug that makes one ask for more. The mood in the hair salon was electric, totally pulsating. Customers were in and out. The hairstylists were merry. The weather was perfect, and Friday was payday. Money was circulating, and everybody was seeking harbor from the weekday drag of work and no play. Cellular telephones and mobile pagers beeped, buzzed and rang while the local, commercial Hip-hop and R&B radio stations pumped the latest hit music. Whoa! Thank God for the weekend.

It was three minutes after eleven, and Delancy was done with Mahogany and Jessica's hair. They thanked Delancy, paid him for a job well done, including tips, and prepared to exit the hair salon.

"Hey, Jessie, hold up a minute. I want y'all to come to my swim party at The Rio." Delancy opened a drawer attached to his station and removed two invitations. "Here, y'all. Wit' yo' good-looking asses. Don't miss my muthaflippin party, and y'all know my shit be off da hook."

Jessica looked at the invitation. "Delancy, now you know I'll be there. I only missed your Christmas party because I didn't come back from college." She paused. "July first, hey. We're gone represent. Huh, Mahogany?"

"Yeah, I don't mind going. But where's The Rio?"

"Homegirl, it's over on da East Side. It's some new shit. Dhat muthaflippin club is like dhat, honey," Delancy stated. They walked outside. "It's on Baugh Avenue. Right off Highway Sixty-four. Jessica, all da ballers and fine ass men be at dhis spot."

Jessica smiled, reading the invitation again. Then she said, "Mahogany, are you sure that you don't have plans for July first?"

"None that I can think of."

"What about Sarah and Astarte? Think they'll want to go?"

"I can check with them and see."

"Cool. Delancy, schedule Mahogany and me for the same time on the first."

"Dhat ain't no problem, but y'all asses betta be on time. I'm closin' da shop early on dhat day. Anyway, two people can get in free off each invi. And if y'all ain't tryin' to show no ass and titties—gimme my damn invitations back." Delancy placed his hand on the door handle. "Like I said . . . Lance is fo' romance, and I ain't wit' no muthaflippin half steppin'. Lance parties are known fo' da real muthaflippin deal." He stopped talking. He reached inside his rear pants pocket. "Here. Y'all highly-educated asses take my bizness cards in case y'all need me." Delancy paused. "Again . . . ass and titties."

He opened the door to the hair salon and flagged his right hand goodbye. Mahogany and Jessica laughed. Delancy had given them an awesome time.

NINE

The streets were busy with moving cars. St. Louis was awake. People were everywhere. The weather was lovely, and the city's spirit seemed amiable.

Mahogany and Jessica, having just eaten a foot long steak-and-cheese submarine sandwich from Subway, were stopped at a red light at the intersection of Chambers Road and West Florissant Avenue. Mahogany signaled to make a right turn, her windows and convertible top sealed. Jessica sat gazing at her hairdo in the sun visor mirror, while the stereo played at mid-range.

An older model, candy-painted Buick Regal with shiny spoke wheels and a peanut butter ragtop came to a stop beside Mahogany. Thick smoke gushed from the windows of the Regal.

"Damn, Jessica, what in the h are they smoking?"

"Some of that sticky green."

"Sticky green? What's that?"

"Marijuana, girl."

Rap music boomed from the Regal; the trunk of the regal rattled for mercy. The selection: "3 In the Morning" by the Notorious B.I.G.

Two young males with shiny gold fronts hung out of the passenger-side window of the Regal. They flirted with Mahogany and Jessica, their gold chains bling-blinging in the noon sun. The light signal flashed green; Mahogany and Jessica deserted the regal without play.

Riding south on West Florissant Avenue, Mahogany and Jessica spilled secrets. They didn't waste a single word on the young brothers back at the intersection.

Scarlet Tears

"Jessica, can you believe I had a dream about the guy I said was cute over at Lincoln Park?"

"Are you talking about the one who gave you a flyer and his business card by the barbecue stand?"

"No, not that silly fool, although he was handsome. I'm talking about the one who was leaning against the pearl-colored Escalade with the sun roof and chrome wheels."

"Girl, you're talking about Jazz sexy ass."

"Right! That's his name. And how do you know everybody?"

"Mo, you'll never understand. Being where I'm from, it's important to keep your ear to the streets and know who's who out here," Jessica explained. "Anyway, I hear that brother got mad paper and a bunch of groupies on his team."

"Groupies? Well, maybe so. But I still can't get him off my mind. He was such a gentleman."

"So . . . let's get this correct." Jessica paused. "Mahogany Brown has the hots for a man, now. A brother who I'm positive isn't like your pops."

"Maybe he's not exactly like my father. But I sense something special about him. His business card said something about he was a real estate investor. And the other side mentioned something about a clothing and lingerie store."

"Yeah, he does own a store in Northwest Plaza. It's called Jazz's Women Apparel and Linger----"

"You're right! That's the name of it."

"Girl, look at you." Jessica smiled. "You're all hype and things. Keeping it real, though, it is a bomb ass store. I've shopped there a few times myself. And maybe we should pay him a surprise visit one day."

"I don't know about that. I'd rather call him, first."
"Yeah, you're saying that now. Believe me, you'll learn about these city boys. They do believe in taking a sister's kindness for weakness."

"Well, you're probably right again." Mahogany took a glimpse at Jessica. "I was looking for his card this morning when I was cleaning up my bedroom, but I don't know where I put it."

"Did you check the pockets of the pants you had on at the park that day?"

"No. I'm positive it isn't in them. If so, it's all messed up now. I washed them last night."

"Well that gives you a good reason to drop in his store."

"Uh-uh, Jessica. You know I'll be all nervous. Trust me, I'll find that card. Okay . . . enough about me. And what's up with you and Mister Trucky-truck?"

They laughed, Delancy on the brains.

"Girl, you're silly." Jessica couldn't stop laughing. "Mahogany, I like you like this. Hold up, let me rephrase that. I like the fact that you're loosening up."

"Well, okay then, lil momma." Mahogany playfully rolled her eyes. "That sounds better."

Jessica laughed again.

"Now, to answer your question." Jessica paused. "We're okay as friends, and he's an all right dude. His name is Austin, but they call him Money." Jessica smiled, her eyes flashing dollar signs. "He has his own crib. He owns a record label and a photography studio on Laclede's Landing. He's outgoing. By all means appealing. Smart. Never been to prison. He treats me with respect. And need I say more?" Jessica stared at Mahogany as if she'd been delivered from oppression and poverty.

"Well alrighty then. Sounds like you have yourself a winner, and I wish you, guys, the best of luck. Now . . . have you found yourself a job, yet?"

"I'm still searching, and I've put in a few apps already. Oh, I have an interview scheduled for Tuesday at Cupples Elementary School. That's the school I went to when I was a shorty."

"Well, if nothing comes through soon, my mother said she can get you hired in Physical Rehabilitation at Saint John's Mercy Hospital where she works. With you having a BA from the U of H in Physical Education and being a track

Scarlet Tears

star should easily qualify you for the position. So . . . keep me informed on your job status."

"Mahogany, get ready to make a right into that shopping center coming up. Crystal Nails is just to your right. And please tell your mother I said thanks." Jessica's face expression changed; she'd been tossed back into the world that mattered most. "And I promise to keep you abreast of my job saga."

Mahogany drove onto the parking lot. Parking was tight, because the mini shopping plaza was busy. Mahogany didn't care, though. Her day as of yet had been superb.

Inside the nail salon, the smell of acetone, nail polish, and other beauty chemicals diluted the air. The buzz of small fans, the softness of music, the chatter of woman gossip, and Asian language played a tune devoid of melody. Crystal Nails jumped with business. An awe-inspiring collage of women, young, middle age, and old, purred in splendor.

Mahogany requested a French manicure and pedicure. Jessica preferred neon-orange polish for her manicure and pedicure. Jessica also purchased fake diamonds for the tips of her nails.

Mahogany sat watching her cuticles being trimmed, wondering why African Americans didn't own quality nail salons like Crystal Nails. She heard that Asians dominated the local nail and beauty supply business. This didn't sit well with Mahogany; however, she didn't oppose anyone trying to make an honest living. Mahogany figured those same dollars could have been circulated amongst African-American women, enhancing the local Black economy. Conditions in the Black community were bad enough to make a blind man cry. Mahogany prayed it was all a dream.

Having spent an hour inside of the nail salon, Mahogany and Jessica now had pretty fingernails and toenails. Leaving North St. Louis County, Mahogany drove into the inner city by way of I-70 East. Her destination was Jessica's residence.

"So, I take it you and Mister Man has plans for the evening?"

D. Allen Miller

"And you know this," Jessica said. "I can't wait to go by his studios, tonight. We have dreams to fulfill and . . . . . to experience."

"Okay, and what's . . . . . if you don't mind me asking?"

"I'll give you the full details when I call you, tomorrow, okay."

"You better call, too. Or I'll be blowing up your phone and pager." Mahogany smiled. "Jessica, can I ask you some questions?"

"Go ahead. I don't care."

"Where did you meet Austin? And are you sexually involved with him?"

"Hold up. Didn't know I was on trial. Naw, I'm just kidding." Jessica sighed. "Actually, I know him from high school. When I was a sophomore, he was a senior. And he played on the men's varsity basketball team. Brother's a hooper, too. Oh, and let's not forget that he's smart as hell," Jessica poured it on. "Believe it or not, I had a crush on him then." She took a deep breath. "About ten days ago, I had walked up to High Rollers on MLK to buy some junk food for my little sister and some damn cigarettes for my momma when we sort of bumped into each other. Everything just kind of went from there."

"Girl, don't play with me. Answer question two, please."

"Dang, I was getting there. Losing patience, huh, Mahogany?"

"Uh . . . I'm listening."

"No, we haven't experienced sex. But we've kissed, done a little smooching, and I gave him a massage without his shirt on late one night in his photography studio. There!" Jessica looked at Mahogany. "Are you satisfied?"

"Well, it looks like we need to go and invest in some contraceptives."

"So what are you trying to say, Mahogany? I'm irresponsible?"

"Girl, I just look like this. I know what's happening. Believe that." Mahogany gawked at Jessica. "I just don't want you to end up pregnant without being stable and married. You have too much to live for."

Teary-eyed, Jessica said, "Mahogany, that's so sweet of you. My own momma doesn't tell me stuff like that. And let's not *even* discuss my dad tired ass."

Mahogany parked in front of Jessica's apartment. Jessica reached over and gave Mahogany a hug.

"Well, are you going to ask me what I'm doing, tonight?"

Jessica laughed. "And what might you being doing tonight, Mahogany?"

"Sarah wants me to go out and eat at Culpeppers with her and see a movie at AMC Sixteen on West Olive. She says some of the Rams players will be hanging out that way, tonight."

"Sounds like fun to me. I'm sure she knows since she's a Rams cheerleader. Anyway, don't take any of the Rams players serious if you happen to meet some of them. I know some girls who say they're full of it."

"One last question, Jessica."

"Uh-huh."

"When are you going to invite me in to meet your peops?"

"Uh . . . let's see. How about next Friday after you get off work. I'll prepare a dinner for you and my family. Is that straight with you?"

"Bet. I look forward to it."

"So what shall we eat next Friday?"

"Whatever you cook will be fine, Jessica. I'm not choosy."

"Okay, I know you like seafood. So expect something of that nature." Jessica opened the passenger-side door.

"All right, Jess. And believe me when I say I'll be waiting on your phone call, tomorrow."

D. Allen Miller

"You got that, Mahogany. Bye, girl." Jessica exited the car. She shut the car door, waved farewell, and walked up the paint-peeling stairs that led to the door of her apartment.

TEN

She moaned; she groaned; she took another deep breath. She squeezed him; she flexed her vaginal muscles; her moaning became louder. Wonder was the rapture she was experiencing.

He moaned; he stroked; he dug deeper. The moment was intense, passionate. He howled in delight; he was having the time of his life; he stated he was in love; he even said he was king. Yet . . . was he in total control? Yet . . . was his emotions tainted by elation?

Nearing their zenith, sweat covered their well-conditioned bodies. Zephyr oozed through the barely opened window. The scent of lovemaking rode the night breeze, and ecstasy was the pleasure they embraced.

Then it became midnight; the starry host of heaven spared little light on Mother Earth. Stars were scattered. A quarter moon dangled in the blackness above. The sun was away until morning, and the city streets were alive with drunken and vulnerable souls desirous for fun. This was Saturday night in "The Lou."

The criminal-minded prevailed on the weekends. Senseless murder after senseless murder. Shamefully, Black men were diminishing. When would such apathy ever conclude?

Matters were getting worse in the Black community; moral decay was praising its apex. The same as Jessica and Money rejoiced in their sexual climax.

ELEVEN

Sunday, June 18, 2000

In the semidarkness of her bedroom, Mahogany rested asleep. The curtains and blinds to her bedroom window were closed shut. The most revealing light glimmered from her exotic fish tank; it was occupied with numerous, colorful fish. Mahogany adored the imagery of the ocean deep, using it as a meditative device. Spiritually attuned, Mahogany yearned to keep focus. But pressures from abroad refused to end. Struggle had society in the figure-four leg lock.

Hearing the telephone repeatedly ring, Mahogany rolled over in bed and looked at the digital clock sitting on the nightstand. 12:30 p.m. glowed in red figures. *Damn, I had no intentions on sleeping this late*, Mahogany said to herself. She'd promised Aunt Karen that she would attend church with her that morning. Mahogany had broken her first promise. She then picked up her Sony cordless telephone from its base and answered.

"Girl, are you still asleep?"

"Yeah . . . I was. But I'm up now."

"Mahogany, wake up!" Jessica said. "I'm calling you like I promised."

"That's cool." Mahogany paused. "What's up with you? You sound so full of energy."

"Mo, it's Sunday. Time for Lincoln Park."

"Naw, I'm chilling, today. Tomorrow's the beginning of my second week of training. You know how it is. Just trying to keep my priorities straight."

"It's all good. I got a few things I need to catch up on myself."

Scarlet Tears

"So how was the date last night?"

"Uh, let's see. . . . Emotional! Fun! Uh . . . special. Interesting! And most riveting!"

"Riveting, hey." Mahogany chortled. "Sounds like you really enjoyed yourself. But fill me in on the details."

"Well, we went shopping at the Galleria. We had a candle light dinner at Rossino's. From dinner, we went on the President Casino. And from there, we went to his studios on The Landing."

Spun in her imagination, Mahogany longed for a romantic night out on the town. Jessica's review of her date with Austin was tantalizing, and Mahogany was thirsty for more.

"What did you, guys, do at his studios?"

Jessica sneezed.

"Bless you."

"Excuse me, and thanks. Damn fan! Anyway, we listened to some of his artists' new music. Oh yeah, we need to go to the music store and buy his R and B artist's, named Traneen, CD."

"I'm cool with that. You know I don't mind supporting my brothers and sisters. And I like her song on the radio, anyway."

Jessica cleared her throat.

"Jessica, turn off that fan."

"For what? To burn up?"

Mahogany grinned. "Studio details, please."

"I ain't forgot, Mahogany. I was getting there. Okay," she paused, "we took some pictures of each other in his photography studio. None in the nude, but I did take a few in lingerie, because I'm thinking about entering this modeling conte----"

"Oh God!"

"Well, you asked." There was silence. "Continuing, Austin let me take a few pictures of him in his boxers. I helped him file away some papers. We shared a bottle of Moet. Then we kissed a little, and this time he gave me a massage."

There was silence, again.

"You there, Mahogany?"

"Oh yeah, yeah. My fault."

"Girl, you're tripping."

"Naw, no I'm not. I was just thinking about something."

"Yeah, whatever. I know what the hots feel like."

Mahogany's mind had wandered from St. Louis to The Village in Manhattan, New York, ever drifting in a severe case of heat. A cold shower would be helpless. Mahogany was in a crisis, and male pleasure was the only remedy.

"No sex, right?"

"Girl, naw. It's too early for that."

"I'm getting the truth, I hope. Something is telling me I haven't heard it all."

"Now, Mahogany." She paused. "Why would I lie to you?"

"I don't know. But time will tell."

"I hear you. So, did you meet any Rams players last night?"

"Did I?! Girl, I met three of them. They're some okay guys. Maybe a little cocky, though."

"Girl, you know how money do brothers. What y'all do anyway?"

"Nothing special. Well, at least I didn't," Mahogany said. "We munched on some Buffalo wings with blue cheese dressing, ate salad, and had fries. Um, we talked about our college days and what we want most out of life. You know . . . dada-dada-da. Then we went and saw a movie across the street from the restaurant. Really, it was nothing to brag about. But fun nevertheless."

"Mahogany, what do you mean by 'at least I didn't?'"

"That's Sarah's business. You know NFL players aren't supposed to date team cheerleaders. However, what they don't know doesn't hurt."

"I feel you on that one. So you mean to tell me Sarah left with all three of them? And where was Astarte?"

Scarlet Tears

"Astarte didn't come with us this time. She said her and her family had prior plans. Now, as far as Sarah, I don't know what took place after the movies. She followed them somewhere."

"Mahogany, girl, you know the play. These girls will do anything to be with pro ball players and stars. That's including so-called cheerleaders."

"Like I said, Jessie, I don't know. And I haven't spoken with her today."

Mahogany refused to breathe life into the grapevine. She believed in having loyalty with her friends, although not agreeing with many of their decisions. If the same respect was due Mahogany, the future was anxious to unveil.

Mahogany shared many of the same desires as her friends; she wasn't free from sinning. Mahogany was deeply interested in the unexplored world of mating, seeking the dawn of her first relationship.

"Well, so be it with Sarah. What have you sleeping late?"

"Jessica, I was up until three in the morning reading *The Coldest Winter Ever* by Sista Souljah. Girl, that book had me stuck. Winter is something else."

"Yeah, I've been hearing about that book. But I haven't had the chance to read it yet. So, did you find Jazz's business card?"

"And you know it. But guess where I found it?"

"Uh, in your car?"

"Nope. I found it inside my journal. I had it tucked in the back pages for some reason."

"Lucky you. So what's next?"

"I'm thinking about calling him once I get up and take care of some things. But I don't know what to say."

"Mahogany, please. He can care less about a deep conversation. He's going to be happy as hell with you just calling him. You saw how we represented The Lou." Jessica paused. "Remember . . . he's not a Harvard grad. Just keep it simple. Because these niggas be running from that complex shit. And excuse my French, homie."

"Jessica, what's gotten into you? You know I don't play the N word. And you're getting more ghetto by the hour. Just listen to how you're talking."

"My bad, Mahogany. I did get kind of carried away for a minute."

"Also, I guess you're a Yale Scholar on African-American men, now."

They laughed.

"No, I'm not saying I know it all. But you have to realize most of my friends are dudes. And ninety-five percent of their butts be running from difficult situations, responsibilities, and formal language," Jessica enlightened. "Trust me, Mahogany; just keep it one-two-three. That way, he can always feel like he's in charge. You know that male ego thing."

"Jessica, you are something else. I never knew you were a counselor, better than that, the queen of psychology." Jessica laughed. "You need to give Oprah a call and try setting up a special show. I can read the show's theme, 'Knowing your Black Man: *The Keys of Manipulation*.'"

"Oh, so you have jokes this afternoon," Jessica said.

Tickled, they both couldn't stop laughing.

"Well, check this out. I'm willing to accept your advice, but only if you tell me the truth about last night. I feel, as you always say, 'somebody ain't keeping it real.'"

"Mahogany, nothing majored happened. And if it does, you'll be the first to know. Why are you drilling me about that?"

"Because I'm concerned about your well-being. We're friends, right?"

"Yes, but more like sisters. And you're right. Well, I'ma let you go so you can do yo' thangy-thang. Hey, call me if you happen to change plans."

"All right. I'll do that."

"And yeah, good luck with the phone call."

Simmering, Mahogany's juices bubbled. She could no longer suppress her crave for the opposite sex. The more Mahogany conversed with Jessica, she gained stripes of valor.

Scarlet Tears

Anxiety and doubt was losing ground, their grip slippery with oil. Mahogany believed herself to be a beautiful red rose, ready for the giving. She boiled with passion, and it was time to set it off. The explosion of Ms. Mahogany.

Part Two

The simple-minded and unwise are vulnerable to predators, the same as the good, lonely woman searching for love in all the wrong places.—Anonymous

TWELVE

This was a dream, although Mahogany was awake. It was the cork being unscrewed from her bottle. Gushing, tonic poured from her pores. Smiles of joy paced smoothly, seemingly to never stop. There was no turning back; the awe of new experience was addictive. Into the volatile sea of male and female relationships, where divorce, heartache, and abuse surged rampant, Mahogany had entered. How well would she swim? Would the currents be too powerful? Would the tides be overbearing? Alternatively, would Mahogany ride the waves with stride? Old man clock on the wall would tell it all.

It was Monday; Mahogany was on her lunch break. Caleco's, on the corner of Broadway and Chestnut Street, was the restaurant of choice, a popular restaurant for first acquaintances. The pepperoni pizza and cheese sticks, Mahogany and Jazz toyed with, grew cold; however, warm thoughts of togetherness streamed through the air.

Jazz looked awestruck, seemingly marveled by Mahogany's beauty and purity. Without doubt, Jazz knew he wasn't dealing with Shameika from around the way. Mahogany was born with the finer things in life. She was morally unimpaired, the toast of St. Louis.

Knigel "Jazz" Wennington was twenty-six-years-old with thick black eyebrows. He didn't flex gold teeth, his smile was alluring. Jazz wooed the ladies with his satin-brown skin complexion, his ability to speak well, dimples in both cheeks, and a fine physique. He dressed with class and wore little jewelry.

Jazz was a close six-feet-tall, athletically built, and had natural curly hair. Charisma and strong ambition were his best attributes. Jazz was outgoing and loved traveling. He appeared to be a people's person, the ultimate womanizer. An august saxophonist and pianist while in high school, Knigel earned the nickname Jazz.

Mahogany and Jazz gazed at one another from across the table. Mahogany was titillated. Time-traveling in a perfect world, Mahogany fell in love with the present. The idea of a healthy heterosexual relationship had Mahogany skipping through a fantasyland of absolute love.

Holding Mahogany's hand, Jazz asked, "Mahogany, what most do you desire in a man, the man you've ever yearned?"

"Knigel, I'm so moved by your relationship with word play. Really, it's quite charming." She paused, searching for an answer to Jazz's question. "Uh, you sort of caught me off guard with such a question?"

"Relax, sweetheart, and give it to me as it surface in your mind." He smiled. "A brother like me finds it important to know what his woman long." Jazz leaned over. He kissed Mahogany's hand. "It's my pleasure to keep you merry."

"Oh . . . I'm flattered. However, I like a man with sound goals, a positive mental attitude, a man with self-confidence, um . . . willing to always learn, open to new ideas. Uh, you already have ambition." She hesitated. "A sense of spirituality, intelligent, uhhh . . . let's see, good morals and a touch of class. So, how is that for starters? Think you can handle that?"

"Whoa! Mahogany, you expect a lot from a brother, but I think I can handle your demands. You know, searching for a brother according to your expectations around here is like looking for a needle in a haystack." He paused. "Is it more you're seeking?"

"Yeah, a man who's also health conscious and adore children."

"Well," Jazz smiled, "I honestly think I can serve you well, but that's my judgment of course."

"Okay we'll see about that."

"So, with you mentioning that, I'd suppose I'm still in."

Mahogany gazed at Jazz's lips. "Are you asking me if I want to see you, again?"

"Um, I look forward to it."

"Thank you! You had me worried there for a minute." Jazz took a deep breath; he smiled, probably screaming YES! "Uh, waiter, excuse me. I'd like to pay for our meals."

"Here. Let me help you."

Jazz intercepted Mahogany from reaching inside her purse. "Oh no. Never that. I got you, love. I would feel less than a man to allow you to pay for anything."

Mahogany looked at the time on her watch. "Time sure does fly when you're enjoying yourself. I got ten minutes to get back to work on time."

Jazz's facial expression changed as if what Mahogany said was doleful music to his ears.

Mahogany read Jazz's American Express Gold Card, which bore the name *Jazz's Women Apparel and Lingerie*. This was a plus for Jazz, showing his ability to conduct affairs the American way.

Jazz tipped the waiter and returned his business credit card to his alligator-skin wallet. Subsequently, Jazz offered to walk Mahogany to her place of employment. He tried procuring all the positive points he could obtain, although Jazz was seemingly a natural-born African-American esquire.

Walking east on Chestnut Street, Jazz included a closure to his first impression. Judging Jazz, he lived his life parallel of the "Big Screen." Anyhow, Mahogany wanted to be the jelly atop his peanut butter.

"Mahogany, I meant to tell you earlier that I enjoyed our phone conversation yesterday evening, and I appreciate you having given me some consideration. You know, that kind of makes a brother feel whole being blessed with an opportunity to chill with a wonderful woman as yourself."

"I hear you, Mister Hollywood." They smiled. "No, I'm just kidding, Knigel. Is it okay for me to call you Knigel?"

"Sure. No problem at all. Do yo' thang, love. Besides, beggars can't be choosy."

Scarlet Tears

"Yeah right, Knigel. Being who you are, I'm positive you have plenty of admirers to rid."

"Dig that. A woman who gives orders, but on the sly. Hey, I like that." Jazz stopped walking, outstretched his arms, slightly turned from side-to-side, and gazed at the tall, downtown buildings him and Mahogany were amidst. "Just what I've been missing . . . my queen to this game of chess." He looked at Mahogany. "Sweetheart, you keep talking like that and you'll soon have me turning flips. Really, I adore a strong Black woman." Jazz placed his left hand under Mahogany's chin and held her left hand with his right hand. "Seriously, Mahogany, you're like a breath of fresh air to me, the sacred dove of my heavens," he said. "May it be my duty to keep you happily in love; for the spirit of the stars has whispered to me . . . telling me . . . you're my everything."

Mahogany gazed into Jazz's eyes, searching for sincerity. She believed she'd found it. Tears dribbled down her cheeks. Mahogany was as sensitive as an ice cube in the Sahara Desert, her heart susceptible for love. Jazz wiped away Mahogany's tears with the front, bottom of his soft linen Prada short-sleeve shirt. He then kissed Mahogany on the cheek.

Soft . . . warm . . . stimulating.

"Thank you, Knigel." Mahogany sniffled. "Honestly, I thank you for everything, and I enjoyed our luncheon. And you're single, right?"

"Check this out, sweetheart," Jazz licked his lips, "I have no reason to lie to you. You're my angel." He paused. "Now, I do have a couple of lady friends. However, I'm committed to neither. It's all cordial. But if you'll be my annual valentine," Jazz gently rubbed Mahogany's hand, "I'll put a cease to them both—immediately."

"Well, we'll have to see if you're a man of your word. And you don't have to worry . . . I have patience. So, we'll let it fall where it lay. Deal?"

"It sounds grand to me, my pretty butterfly." Jazz shook Mahogany's hand. "Your every wish is my honor."

"Well, my time is up. I appreciate you walking me to work." She paused. "I'll call you tomorrow during my lunch break."

"Believe me, I'll be waiting."

Jazz and Mahogany waved good-bye. As Mahogany neared the hotel entrance, she heard, "Mahogany, I'm yours for the taking!" Mahogany turned around with a smile. She waved again.

Mahogany was stung by African-American gallantry. On a scale of one through ten, Mahogany gave Jazz an eleven. He was an A+ student in the wonder of love.

On the other hand, Mahogany was aware of love's flip side. She'd witnessed several girls in college lose their focus over men with games. Misery had sharp claws and waited in the crevices of darkness, thirsty to unleash doom. The world over was filled with *Scarlet Tears*; nonetheless, Mahogany was willing to give love a try.

THIRTEEN

With nothing to do, it was Monday night, a night plagued with a constant drizzle. The day had been beautiful, and the city was calm. Mahogany and Jessica talked on the telephone, discussing the pains of the real world and their new beaus.

Life away from college was challenging, though an interesting one. Mahogany had been released into a fast-paced society, a world burden with power struggles, an anticipated depression, threats of terrorism, AIDS, Black-on-Black crime, despair, and the idea of a cashless society. This was just the tip of the iceberg.

Unaware of future dangers, Mahogany sat in the palms of inexperience. Rather if not ignorance was bliss, Mahogany was soon to see. More than often, ignorance only allowed for the use of more Vaseline—a very good screwing distended with agony.

"Mahogany, is he all what he's hyped up to be?"

"Jessica, he's a very nice person. Believe it or not, he reminds me a lot of my father. And he has a lot going on for himself."

"Is that right? Well, I'm happy for you. So when are y'all gone meet again?"

"I don't know, but I'm going to call him tomorrow. I've decided to take it slow with him. You know how it is. I don't want to rush into nothing. After all, this will be my first real relationship if everything goes well."

"Check this out, Mahogany, why don't you invite him to dinner Friday here at my house."

Scarlet Tears

"Are you sure? It's kind of early for that, don't you think?"

"It'll be all good. Anyway, I've already invited Austin to dinner with us. That way, everybody can get familiar with one another."

"Well, if it's cool with you, then it's fine with me. I'll ask him tomorrow when I call him. Girl, hold on for a minute so I can see who this is clicking in."

"Go 'head."

Mahogany removed the cordless telephone from her ear and pressed the flash button.

"Hello."

"Well, hello there. And may I ask what happened to you yesterday?"

"Hey, Aunt Karen. How are you doing?"

"I'm doing all right for a forgotten auntie."

Mahogany smiled. "I'm sorry about yesterday, Aunt Karen. I sort of overslept. And I stayed up all night reading a book. And I know . . . I must put God first."

"Well, at least you have that part right." Karen paused. "What are you doing? And how's the new job?"

"Actually, everything is going great with the job. And I'm on the other end with Jessica."

"Oh, I'm sorry. Tell her I said hello. And why don't you try calling me more often. You know I'm always thinking about you. Seems to me you don't love me anymore."

"No, that's not the case, Aunt Karen. You know I'm crazy about you and Stefaughn."

"I know, Mahogany. Just thought I'd slide that in."

"Hey, how's Stefaughn doing?"

"Stefaughn's doing just fine. He's not around as much as he used to be. Some girl has his nose wide open. Anyway, I'll tell him you asked about him."

"All right, I'll call you later, Aunt Karen. I love you."

"Love you too, baby. Take care, okay."

Mahogany flashed back over to a disappeared Jessica. She called Jessica's name again, preparing to hang up the telephone.

"Mahogany! I'm back. Girl, you'll never believe who just called me."

"Who?"

"Malik from Da Maniaks."

"For real? What are he and the rest of Da Maniaks are up to now that they're overnight stars?"

"He says they're busy as hell out promoting their new LP. And he asked me to go and buy it from the music store. Oh yeah, he also said they're going to be at Streetside Records in the Delmar Loop on Saturday, July first, from eleven in the afternoon until two p.m. doing an autograph signing. He wants us to be there."

"Us, hey? That sounds good. But that's the same day of Delanc----"

"And, girl, they're looking for some new girls to be in their next video. So let's show 'em what's really going on. You feel me, Mahogany?"

"I hear you, girl." Mahogany was tickled at Jessica being overly excited. "So, that makes two CD's we've got to buy. Traneen's and Da Maniaks'. Huh, Saint Louis has been getting busy on the music scene."

"Mahogany, Malik sounded so good on the telephone. I can't wait until July first."

"Jessica, you're something else. So who is it going to be, now? Austin or Malik?"

Jessica laughed. Mahogany often caught her in the spirit of no-good. Jessica was getting loose, and the thought of men had begun to control her life. Jessica stated that she wanted a man with a lot of money, her personal rainbow. Jessica never had a father to teach or show her different. The city streets was her father, the primary school from which she was nurtured.

"Mahogany, I wouldn't do Austin like that, unless he deserved it. Just down right misusing a brother ain't my stee-lo."

"Girl, what's stee-lo?"

"Mahogany, you're going to have to get with the program. Stee-lo . . . you know, like a person's m.o."

Scarlet Tears

"Oh, I see. So you mean mistreating brothers isn't your method of operation."

"There you go, Mahogany. You're getting there."

They laughed at the very different individuals they were, however, sharing a common bond, the preoccupation of early womanhood.

"You know, Jessica, I met all Da Maniaks when they were recording out at Saint's Roller Rink a couple of years ago on summer break. They had some good songs, then. Ormez and I used to talk to each other quite often when I was out there ska----"

"Hmmph! I know you wish you would have given him some play back then."

"No. I wasn't yet focused on relationships. You know, he would just invite me inside the studio part of the skating rink to watch them create and record music. Honestly, he's a real nice guy."

"Okay, I hear you. So have you heard about what happened to one of them?"

"Uh-uh. But fill me in, Miss Channel Five News. And I hope it's not bad."

"Well, you hoped wrong. The one they call Shorty Blu----"

"Yeah, I know Blue. The little, cool one with the sleepy eyes."

"Girl, he's supposed to be in jail for attempted murder."

"You're kidding me. From being around him, the few times I was, he appeared to be real easy going and deep into the music thing."

"Well, that's the way I got it."

"I sure hope that's just a rumor. But if that's true, it's so unfortunate. Just when they done blew up."

"You know how it is. Welcome to da hood, baby. Around here, judging books by the cover went out in the fifties. Shit, every day down here is a damn soap opera. So just know . . . as the world turns, da hood's young gets restless."

D. Allen Miller

Mahogany and Jessica conversed for a little while longer. They discussed love, marriage, money, old age, and eluding Saint Louis. Mahogany was a zealot for the perfect life—the big house with a white picket fence, prosperity, and a family to tend. She would give it her all to obtain the cream of her dreams. Jessica would too, but how was the question.

FOURTEEN

Jazz's night had just begun. He combed the inner-city streets in his Escalade. Thoughts of tax-free money and a good-looking hoochie flooded his mind like a raging river. Jazz knew where to find them both. He was a major figure in the netherworld of Saint Louis.

Light rains and frequent flashes of lightning set the night's tone. None of this was discouraging to a real player, a man who'd been granted a taste of true freedom. The city streets was Jazz's land of dreams come true. He had chips—a lot of chips—and acquired them against all odds.

Arriving at Billiards on Broadway, Jazz cruised around the dim-lit parking lot. He checked to see if he was being followed. Jazz parked, exited the Escalade, and hurried inside from the rain. There, he met his main man, Dread, him practicing on his pool shot.

"Yo, what up, Dread? Ready to get that shiny baldhead of yours bashed in?"

"Nigga, please. You ain't no factor. And you know this, Jazz."

Dread was the backbone of Jazz's empire, the griffin that'd made things fly. He was twenty-eight years old and lion-hearted. Dread went nowhere without his steel, a pocket full of cash, and the desire to sex a new broad. Negativity was his wife, hell's number one whore.

"Let's do a game of nine ball, then, my nig."

"You got dhat, Jazz." Dread racked the pool balls for play, while Jazz hung his Nautica windbreaker.

"Dig this, derrty. I got this new babe, named Mahogany. Man, she's like a crazy case of VS1's." Jazz paused.

Scarlet Tears

"Straight up, Dread, she's serious wifey material, yo. I'm thinking about keeping it real with her, derrty."

"Dhat's on you, Jazz. But I ain't givin' in to none of dhese money-hungry broads." Dread paused, focusing on his pool shot. He made it; then he removed a wooden toothpick from his mouth. "And dhis game's ova." Dread went for the game-winning shot. "Wanna play anutha one, Jazz?"

"Yeah. Good shot, Dread. Bet five hundred I get in yo' ass on this one."

"Bet it is, dhen, pretty boy," Dread emphatically said.

Dread's speech shocked Jazz; he'd never heard Dread call him 'pretty boy' before. Jazz, being the smooth individual he was, reshuffled his deck and said, "By the way, Dread, where is the love, derrty? You have plenty of bread, nice wheels, houses, your mom's out the hood, now. You know . . . it comes a time to try something a little different, derrty."

"Yeah, I feel you on dhat one, Jazz. But it won't be wit' none of dhese scandalous hoes out here." Dread paused. He busted the freshly racked pool balls. His bust was a good one; the one and three ball fell into the two corner pockets. "Jazz, I done seen how dhese niggas be nigga rich today and all fucked up tomorrow dealin' wit' dhese cold-blooded bitches."

"You have a strong point, Dread. But these cats only let women do to them as they let them, derrty." Jazz smiled. He figured he'd landed an uppercut below the belt.

"I hear ya, Jazz. But like I said, I ain't goin' out like dhat. And ain't nuttin you can say to change my mind. So, are you gone shoot or play wit' dhat two-way all night?"

Surprised by Dread's accelerated speech, Jazz peered up from his two-way pager. *What's the fuck wrong with this stupid-ass nigga?!* Jazz thought. Then he said, "You in a rush, derrty?"

"Naw, but you tryin' to cool my shot off. You know we bettin.'"

"Whatever, derrty. Dig this, a lot of these dudes out here got weak game, Dread. I see you being better than the average Joe. Otherwise, you wouldn't be who you are today, derrty."

Dread smiled, seemingly enjoying a pet on the back. Probably self-centered, too. He removed the toothpick from his mouth, again, and started chewing a stick of Doublemint chewing gum. "Jazz, wanna stick of gum, derrty?"

"Yeah, I'll take a stick. But let me finish whipping yo' ass, first. You think you're going to keep winning all the damn time." Jazz paused. He was having a good game and loved winning. "Game, Dread! That puts me up two hundred, derrty." Jazz knew that if he wasn't Dread's source to a better living, he couldn't get away with speaking saucy to him. Dread would have dropped Jazz in his very tracks—never looking back.

Jazz and Dread quit shooting pool. They were under surveillance by a task force of urban P.Y.T.'s, a voluptuous flock of late night call girls.

"Damn, Dread. Girly in them tight light-blue jeans is too fine."

"You got dhat right. And I'll take da short one on da left."

Jazz gestured for the young ladies to come here. They smiled and sauntered right on over. The rest would be easy.

Jazz was a man of risk. Gambling and sex consisted of his everyday rush. His habits were expensive, even suicidal, a scary game of Russian roulette. Overall, Jazz was a better man than the path he'd chosen. He was reared well and had a strong spiritual background. Unfortunately, Jazz had allowed the flowery sins of materialism and instant gratification bribe his heart.

FIFTEEN

Soaked with sweat, Mahogany jumped out of her sleep. She had a fever and her heart tried running away. Mahogany breathed hard; she'd been fighting nightmares throughout the entire night. Demons were the controllers of Mahogany's nightmares, the perpetrators of dysfunction. Mahogany physically fought the malformed creatures in her nightmares—though asleep. It was an after dark date with Satan and its army, a clash with stalking torture.

Where in God's name did that dream come from? Mahogany thought. She looked around her darkened bedroom, gasping for air, desperate for answers. There was nothing but memories from a horrible night's sleep, a clock that said 4:33 a.m. in bloody red figures, and an illuminated fish tank with exotic fish darting back and forth.

Fraught with anxiety, Mahogany thirsted to bury what had just happened. Her nerves racked with fear, Mahogany flung back her bedclothes and rushed into the bathroom. *Good. Nothing strange,* she thought and slowly walked over to the vanity mirror. *Damn, what is this on my face?* There were three, red non-bleeding scars on Mahogany's face, one across her forehead, the other two stemming from each side of her nose. *Baffling. Incomprehensible.*

Scheduled to be at work by eight a.m., Mahogany thought about calling off. She believed the scars on her face would cause too much attention. Yet she was afraid to miss work; it was only her second week on the job. Therefore, Mahogany came to grips with herself and prepared to shower.

The warm water rejuvenated Mahogany as steam seeped out of the shower into the cavity of the bathroom.

Scarlet Tears

Then Mahogany felt a sting. She peered down at her chest. There were matching scars etched across her chest and abdomen. Mahogany panicked, her heart smashing the gas.

Damn, I'm going to have to tell Mom and Dad about this, Mahogany thought. *No, I better not. They'll think I'm going crazy if I explain exactly what happened.*

Finished showering, Mahogany questioned everything—her background, her future, the very present. She wanted understanding, the cause before the effect. Life was changing at a speed in which she wasn't accustomed. So Mahogany decided to contact her doctor. *No, I better not do that, either. He'll probably try prescribing me Prozac*, she thought aloud.

Mahogany dried her body with a white bath towel and returned to the vanity mirror. Surprisingly, the scars on her face were fading away.

Maybe my body is going through some kind of chemical change.

Mahogany wasn't sure if she was coming or going, awake or dreaming. She prayed that it was all an illusion, a short trip through a spiritual matrix. Mahogany pinched herself. "Ouch!" She paused and thought, *Well, I'm definitely awake.*

Inside her bedroom, Mahogany put on her underwear. It was after five, and Mahogany was still sleepy. With spare time on her hands and a mystery to solve, Mahogany figured she'd get caught up in her journal. She was two days behind.

As she wrote, Mahogany felt a sense of relief, however, solving nothing. She demanded answers to what was wrong with her, but the Spirit inside wasn't telling. Life was a journey, one full of twists and turns. PERIOD—Mahogany wasn't exempt from woe.

Seven a.m. crept up on Mahogany before she knew it. She clothed herself, not having enough time to clean her bedroom. Mahogany hated that; she was a young woman of cleanliness. Her scars hadn't quite disappeared yet, but nothing too noticeable. Off to work, Mahogany left home without kissing her mother.

She sped through the neighborhood, hurrying to the interstate. Once on the interstate, Mahogany bobbed and weaved through morning traffic. Horns blew. Tires screeched. Brake lights flashed. People shouted choice words. People threw up the middle finger. Mahogany didn't care; she had to get there.

It was ten o'clock a.m. Mahogany sat at her desk overlooking a list of prospective clients and rubbing her forehead when the light signaled on her desk telephone. She removed the receiver from its cradle and placed it to her ear.

"Hello. This is Mahogany Brown, and how may I help you this morning?"

"Good morning, my dear. You sound very professional on the teleph----"

"Daddy!" Mahogany smiled. "Good morning. Uh, I'm surprised it's you. And what's up?"

"I'm just calling to see if you're okay, honey. Your mother said you left this morning without saying good-bye."

"Yeah, I'm doing great, Dad. I was running behind this morning, and I kind of forgot to tell her good-bye and give her my usual kiss on the cheek. Anyway, I'll be sure to call her at work and let her know that everything is fine."

"That's a good idea, dear. I wouldn't want to keep her worried. Your mom called me here on the job to see if I've noticed anything strange around the house." He paused. "I told her no and asked her why she would ask such a question. She told me she was just wondering. So . . . have you noticed anything strange around the house, Mahogany?"

"No, not at all, Dad." Mahogany hesitated, reflecting on the morning events. "Hmmm, I wonder what Mommy's noticed."

"There's no telling. Anyway, please be sure to give her a call, Mahogany. Believe me when I say she has you on the brains." He paused again. "Sorry, sweetheart, I'm being paged. So continue to have a great day, and I'll see you later."

"Will do, Dad. And you have a nice day, too."

Mahogany hung up the telephone. She called her mother.

"Saint John's Mercy Hospital. This is the obstetrics department."

"Good morning. May I speak to Nurse Brown, please?"

"Mary or Sophia?"

"Sophia, please."

There was a click, followed by listening music.

"Nurse Brown. How can I help you?"

"Good morning, Mom. Are you busy?"

"Well, good morning, dear. I take it you've talked to your dad. And no, I'm not that busy."

"Yeah, I just finished talking with Dad. And I apologize for leaving without my usual kiss on the cheek. I was kind of running behind."

"So I see. Well, is everything okay?"

"Of course, Mom. Why do you ask?"

"Well, I sort of peeped inside your room to see if you were there and noticed it was a little disorderly. That's unlike you, Mahogany."

"Sorry about that, Mom. I was really running late."

"That's okay, dear. I'm just making sure you're all right. We'll discuss a few other things I noticed later this evening. Other than that, have a good day on the job."

Having replaced the receiver on its cradle, Mahogany sat staring at the telephone. Her mother's voice sounded worried. Mahogany didn't know what to think, just hoping that everything was okay.

"Pardon me, Mahogany...."

Mahogany flinched. She looked up.

"Are you okay, Mahogany? Looks like you were gone there for a minute."

"I'm fine, Darla. Besides, what's up?"

"The boss wants you to meet a couple of prospective clients in the front lobby. He says they're interested in renting a banquet hall for a wedding reception. And Barbara is there waiting with them."

Mahogany looked at her watch. It was nearing her lunch break. That didn't matter; lunch could be taken later.

Mahogany got up from her desk, picked up her company notebook and pen, and walked to the ladies room. She looked at her face in the mirror. *Good! They're gone*, she thought. Mahogany scanned her clothing. She appeared neat and presentable. Ready, Mahogany headed to the first floor.

She entered the lobby. It was live, customers criss-crossing in every direction. The floor shined; the fixtures shined; the lights shined. Smiles were everywhere.

There's Barbara, Mahogany said to herself. She took a deep breath and put on a smiling face.

"Excuse me, everyone." The waiting party silenced. They smiled at Mahogany. "Barbara, would these gentlemen happen to be the well-dressed men interested in renting banquet space from us?"

"Why yes they are, Mahogany."

Mahogany and the men in blue suits shook hands.

Barbara continued, "Mahogany, this is Timothy and Samuel McReynold."

"Hello, ma'am." Timothy, the taller and younger McReynold, said.

"Good afternoon. And it's a pleasure to meet you," Mahogany replied.

"How are you, there, ma'am?" Samuel, the older McReynold, asked. He wore silver-white hair and had a gentle voice.

"I'm doing excellent, sir. And I thank you for asking."

"Timothy and Samuel McReynold, this is Mahogany Brown. She'll be your new account representative. Well, I'll let you three talk, and please notify me if you need any help, Mahogany."

"Sure. And thanks a lot, Barbara."

"One! Two! Three!" Timothy counted.

"Surprise, surprise, Mahogany!" everyone shouted, including several other volunteers who were there.

An organized team of five beautiful children, dressed in all white, slowly walked towards Mahogany with smiles and individual gifts. Awed, Mahogany covered her mouth with her hands.

Scarlet Tears

The first child who approached Mahogany was an Asiatic boy. Maybe seven or eight years old, he carried a two-foot teddy bear and a dozen helium-filled silver balloons. The second child, a young African-American girl with long, curly hair and a missing tooth, handed Mahogany a small white cake with a cluster of golden-wrapped candy hearts neatly arranged in the center. A single, lit candle protruded from the cake. Mahogany's eyes became watery, her heart skipping to the tune of love.

The third and forth child were a European boy and girl. They were holding hands, seemingly representing a couple in love, and handed Mahogany two dozens red roses. They were the most beautiful floral arrangements Mahogany had ever seen. She kissed and thanked the boy and girl. They smiled and held hands with the other children.

Mahogany could hear people saying: *Now isn't that sweet. That's so beautiful. She's a lucky woman. How precious!*

Last, an African-American boy, possibly nine or ten, approached Mahogany. He knelt and gestured for Mahogany to untie a gold-colored silk bow from around a tan scroll. Reaching to untie the bow, Mahogany noticed the name McReynold's Florist and Specialty Store on the ends of the ribbon. She gazed over at the McReynolds and smiled.

With the bow untied, the boy unrolled the scroll. He read:

Mahogany,
My beautiful ribbon in the sky, I'm positive that this moment of adoration has caught you by surprise, the very first of many to come. Although early, I can honestly say that I love you. You are an angel. You are the ultimate inspiration. You are my lifeline. Darling, you are my everything, the special woman I have ever yearned. With you, I feel so fortunate. My prayers have been answered, because you are a dream come

true. And with great sincerity . . . will you be the center of my life?

Yours truly,
The chocolate teddy bear

Suddenly, a soft tune played from the glossy Steinway & Sons piano in the hotel lobby. Everyone shifted towards the music. Low and behold, there was Jazz tickling the piano. He, too, was dressed in all white, emotionally singing a self-penned love song, titled "Our Love." Samuel and Timothy walked alongside Mahogany, escorting her closer to the piano.

Observers, many of them holding hands, filled the lobby. Men, women, and children smiled. This was free first-class entertainment, a Broadway extravaganza of first love.

Barbara slid a chair next to Jazz. She indicated for Mahogany to have a seat. Mahogany sat, looking at the circle of smiling faces. It was the Fox Theatre at Adam's Mark Hotel.

Finished singing, Jazz received a hearty round of applause. He leaned over and kissed Mahogany on the lips. Mahogany hugged Jazz and whispered in his ear, "I'm willing if you're willing."

The love show ended. Mahogany asked a bellhop to gather her gifts and carry them to her office. Mahogany and Jazz thanked the McReynolds and the participating children. Off for a moment alone, they walked to Kiener Plaza, a small amphitheater with dazzling fountains. There, Mahogany spent the remainder of her lunch break with her boy wonder.

SIXTEEN

It was evening time, and Mahogany had just arrived home. She walked into the kitchen from the garage. There, Mr. Brown stood pouring himself a glass of Pepsi. Two medium-sized boxes of Imo's Pizza rested on the counter. *Yum-yum*, Mahogany thought.

"Good evening, babe." Mr. Brown leaned over. Mahogany kissed him on the cheek. "I had a real busy day at work, but nothing I couldn't handle. So, I figured I'd kick back for the rest of the evening and enjoy some pizza while watching a good movie." He paused and took a swallow of Pepsi. "Haahh . . . cold and strong. Just the way I like it. Hey, I ordered enough for us all. So dig in when you're ready, hon."

"Will do, Dad. And where's Mom?"

"She just got in, and I believe she's taking a shower. She's supposed to be joining me when she gets out."

"Lovers night, hey?"

"Yeah, if that's what you wanna call it." Mr. Brown smiled.

Mahogany left the kitchen. She headed up the stairs to her bedroom, memories from her nightmares impeding her steps. They were grim recollections that invaded her consciousness without an invitation. Nevertheless, Mahogany swore that she wouldn't allow devilry to ruin her day.

She entered her bedroom, flipped up the light switch, set her purse and a folder of work papers on the bed, and proceeded to open the blinds. Mahogany slowly cast her eyes across the bedroom. Her bed was unmade. The closet door was ajar with open shoeboxes sitting on the floor. Clothing was strewn across the chair, and a glass of grape soda set on

Scarlet Tears

the dresser. Mahogany couldn't believe how she'd left her bedroom. Therefore, she dedicated the remainder of the evening to getting things back in order, but not without enjoying some pizza first.

Mahogany walked towards the bathroom to wash her hands. She stopped, noticing the lid to her fish aquarium was open. A dead fish floated aimlessly with a mutilated body. Mahogany wondered if she'd left the lid of the aquarium open. She also wondered what in the hell happened to her fish. Unable to figure it all out, Mahogany noticed colorless flakes of fish food drifting through the water. That was unusual; the fish would usually consume the food the minute she sprinkled it inside the aquarium. *Something is seriously wrong*, Mahogany thought. She believed someone had been in her bedroom.

The loss of her largest fish, the fish she'd had the longest, saddened Mahogany. A shattered heart, not knowing what to do, Mahogany removed the dead fish from the aquarium with a small fish net. She carried the dead fish, *Stripy*, to the commode, said a short prayer, and flushed it good-bye. Sentimentally attached to the dead fish, Mahogany shed tears of farewell.

Shoot, I need to clean the tank, too, she thought, now looking at her face in the bathroom mirror. There were no scars, just beauty. Mahogany washed her hands and returned to the kitchen.

"Hey, what's up, Momma?" Mahogany spoke. She kissed her mother, who was removing slices of pizza from an Imo's pizza box onto a shiny red dinner plate. "Busy day at work?"

Mrs. Brown scanned Mahogany from head to toe. "How are you doing, sugar? It was rather mild around the maternity ward, today. And what have you getting home so late?"

"Oh, please don't remind me. I was stuck in traffic for almost two hours. It was a six-car accident on the highway."

"You're talking about on Highway Forty, right?"

"Yes."

"Yeah, I heard about that on Majic One-o-five. Three deaths evolved from that accident."

"Momma, don't say that," Mahogany dolefully said.

"Really, that's what I heard on the radio and around the hospital. Why didn't you get off the highway and drive up Ladue Road?"

"Momma, when I say stuck, I mean no movement."

"I thank God I wasn't jammed up in traffic like that. Are you going to eat some pizza, dear?"

"Now you know better." Mahogany removed a plate from the cabinet. "Imo's is my favorite." Mahogany looked at her mother. "Oh yeah, I won't be home this Friday evening, because I'm invited to dinner at Jessica's."

"Jessica's?" Sophia asked. "Exactly what do you and Jessica have going on? It seems like that's all who you know. Anyway, do you still associate with Astarte and some of the other girls you went to high school with? You know that city can get a little rough, Mahogany."

"Yeah, that's true. However, I'm not in the city as much as you think. Then, too, Astarte is deep off into her own thing. And Jessica and I have great comradeship."

"I hear you talking," Mrs. Brown said, walking towards the kitchen exit.

"Hey, Mom."

Mrs. Brown stopped and turned around.

"Before you join Dad, did you happen to go in my room, today?"

Mrs. Brown hesitated before responding. "As a matter of fact, I did. I fed your fish, because when I peeped inside your bedroom, I noticed all the little fish attacking the big fish. So I figured they were hungry. Why? Is anything wrong?"

"Are you serious, Momma? No wonder Stripy was all nicked up. I wonder what got into my fish this morning." Images from Mahogany's nightmare burst into her mind— partying, parading, bringing the blues.

"I don't know, hon. But that was some strange sh. . . . if you know what I mean. The whole while you were away for

Scarlet Tears

your senior year in college your fish never carried out in that manner. Then there was this weird noise coming from your bathroom. Sort of sounded like light footsteps." She paused. "But maybe that was just my mind playing tricks on me."

"Oh, so that's why you were inquiring if Dad and I had noticed anything strange around the house."

"Yeah, you can say that," Mrs. Brown replied. She left the kitchen.

Mahogany stood in front of the patio door, eating a slice of pizza. Thoughts of Jazz were more seizing than her mother's accounts of the morning. She decided on a time to sneak her gifts up to her bedroom from her car. The sun was setting, and Mahogany saw a squirrel run down from a tree in the backyard. She smiled and tapped on the glass.

SEVENTEEN

Friday, June 23, 2000

True love, Jazz discovered, had a voice. It was revealing, removing the fog from around Jazz's heart. He'd asked for the perfect woman. So appeared Mahogany. But would Jazz remain free of the pitfalls akin to lust and desire?

Jazz and Austin sat on the sofa in the living room of Jessica's apartment. They'd become acquainted, engulfed by the spicy aroma from Jessica's cooking. Then Jessica's mother exited her bedroom into the living room. She was shapely, sexy in a fitting black skirt and matching top.

Goddamn, she's fine, Jazz thought. *Look at that walk and them thunder hips.* Jazz looked at Austin, whose eyes were fixed on Jessica's mother.

The lady was foxy, hotter than a Mexican-grown habanera, the spark of an erection.

"Hi!" she said sassily. "See something y'all like?"

"Uh, yeah, oops . . . I mean how are you, Miss Francis?" Austin said.

"Please," she paused, "call me Girlie if you don't mind." Wearing long microbraids, Ms. Francis stood with her hands on her hips. She flashed the boys a smile then stared at Jazz. "And who are you, handsome?"

Jazz bounced to his feet. "Hello, Miss Girlie. I'm Knigel, but you can call me Jazz." Jazz reached for Girlie's hand; he kissed it.

"Thank you, Knigel. But I prefer a hug."

Jazz and Girlie hugged. He loved her perfume, her softness, her tight squeeze, her large breast resting against his chest. Girlie then hugged Austin. Jazz sat, gazing at Girlie's rumpshaker, fantasizing a steamy moment of pleasure.

"So, do I still have it for a forty-year-old lady?"

Jazz and Austin peered at one another. "Of course, Miss Francis. I mean Girlie," Austin answered.

Girlie gazed at Jazz, her thick tongue easing across her pearly whites. Her eyes cast downward towards the center of Jazz's body.

Holding his breath, nervously excited, Jazz thought, *Oh shit! Please don't tell me she's doing this.* Just naturally, Jazz's hand landed on his crotch. "Uh, by all means, Girlie." Jazz paused, sexual thoughts making a raid on his cool. He peered down at Girlie's glossy pink toenails that hung out the tip of her black slippers. *Hell yeah*, he thought, his penis stout like King Kong. "Better yet, you're enticingly gorgeous."

"*Whew*, boy." She smiled; she slanted her eyes. "That's an interesting way of putting it. And I thank you, both." She paused, cupping the bottom of her breast and pushing them up with gentle care. "Well, I'ma run in here with the girls for a second and see if Momma can feed all of me something delicious."

Girlie strolled out of the living room. Both Jazz and Austin's thoughts shuffled close behind with their eyes glued on the jelly, the great mounds of joy.

No wonder Jessica is so damn fine, Jazz thought.

****

"Well, hello there, Miss Ladies. Y'all got it smelling good up in here. The music is jamming, and I take it you're Mahogany."

"Yes, ma'am. And good evening, Miss Francis. I've been eager to meet you."

"And I've been eager to meet you, myself. You know, Jessica's always bragging on you. And why don't you stop by more often."

"Will do, Miss Francis."

"Girl, call me Girlie. You make me feel and sound like a grandmomma calling me Miss Francis."

Mahogany eased into a smile, wowed by the cordiality characteristic of Jessica's mother.

"Momma! Now why are you wearing that?" Jessica clamored. "You know we have male company over."

"Well excuse me!" Girlie rolled her eyes. "I thought I was the momma here." There was silence, music playing in the background. "I take it you're just jealous, child. Besides, Knigel and Austin seemed to not have had a problem with it," she added. "And where did y'all find their good-looking asses at? Maybe they can teach these tired-ass men my age a thing or two about dressing, smelling good, and taking care of self."

"Momma, you're crazy." Jessica looked at Mahogany. "Girl, please excuse my mother. And don't pay us any attention. This is how we do it up in here."

Listening to Jessica, Mahogany felt relieved, saved from the flames of uncertainty. She thought trouble was about to explode, fists were about to be thrown. Clearly, Mahogany wasn't used to daughter and mother speaking to each other as if they were broads at a catfight.

"Mahogany, are you considering getting married?"

"Maybe in the future. Why you ask, Miss Francis?"

"Momma, can we finish up here? We can talk girl talk another time."

"Okay, Miss Smart Ass," Girlie said. "And where's your little sister?"

"She's next door with Fee-Fee. I told her I'll save her a plate in the microwave."

"Y'all excuse me. I'ma take a plate now and go eat in my bedroom. As good as those boys look in there, y'all can use some privacy." Girlie prepared her a dish of food, poured herself a cold glass of Fanta orange soda, sung along to the song on the radio, then left for her bedroom.

"Jessica, you and your mother act more like sisters than mother and daughter. Do you like that?"

"Um, it's all right. But it does have it ups and downs."

Scarlet Tears

****

"Could one of you gentlemen please open my bedroom door? My hands are full."

Jazz sprung to his feet. "Sure thing, Girlie." He quickly stepped over to the bedroom door. He opened it. Girlie sauntered inside, her hips brushing against Jazz's nature. Jazz liked that. Okay . . . he damn loved it. He took a look inside Girlie's bedroom.

There was a queen-sized bed surrounded by sheer black curtains. The bedspread and pillowcases were leopard print. A pair of steel handcuffs hung from one bedpost, and a small black leather whip hung from the other bedpost. Two lithograph pictures of naked humans hung on opposite walls. One of the pictures displayed a muscular, brown-skinned man carrying a brown-skinned woman into a pyramid. The other picture displayed an orgy around a swimming pool with drops of blood leaking from a cherry moon. *Talk about DEEP! Way down below the surface! That haunted place where intimacy has no boundaries.*

A tube of Joy Jelly and burning yellow and green candles set on the dresser. A pair of red, five-inch stilettos set on top of a sheer red negligee in a chair. Spiked bracelets and neck collars and an issue of *Playgirl* set on top of the 19" color television. Seemingly, Girlie played for keeps. And Jazz's imagination needed capturing.

Girlie set the tray of food on the dresser. Her napkin fell on the floor. She bent over and picked it up from the carpeted floor. She turned around towards Jazz. They gazed at one another.

"Oh, I'm sorry." Girlie paused. "I was just making sure. . . ."

"I know. It, it, it's okay," he stuttered.

Biting her bottom lip, Girlie winked at Jazz. She wiggled her tongue, and Jazz's penis stood taller than the Washington Monument.

"You can close the door now, Brother Knigel."

108

Talented

****

Mahogany and Jessica set the dining table for dinner. Jessica lit two long candles that stood in the center of the dining table.

"Come on, let's go and get them," Jessica said to Mahogany.

They walked into the living room. Jazz and Austin sat gazing at them.

"Y'all ready for some good cooking?" Jessica asked. She extended her arm to Austin. Mahogany followed suit with Jazz. Together, they walked into the dining room. Jazz sat across from Mahogany. Austin sat across from Jessica.

"I want to let the both of you, pretty ladies, know how much I appreciate this occasion," Jazz said. "And dinner sure does look and smell good."

"Thanks, Knigel. And hopefully you'll enjoy my cooking," Jessica replied.

There were grilled boneless steaks, grilled jumbo shrimp, grilled boneless chicken breasts, heated cherry tomatoes, green stuffed olives, grilled bell peppers, fresh pineapple, lime wedges, grilled corn on the cob, zucchini, and grilled mushrooms all marinated in a special marinade with Spanish herbs and spices.

"Whoa! Candlelight, 'ey. I'm digging this. And whose idea was this?" Austin asked.

"That's Mahogany's idea," Jessica answered.

"An educated, romantic dame with a sweet touch of class." Austin paused. "I'm feeling that."

Mahogany sat smiling; her words were few. Jessica asked Jazz to pray over the meal. Austin gawked at Jessica. Jessica smiled in return. Jazz prayed.

"That was a nice prayer, Jazz. Are you religious?"

"Thanks, Jessica. And I do have a religious background."

Scarlet Tears

"Good. And eat as much as you want, everybody. There's plenty. This is our moment of love and friendship," Jessica said, gazing at Jazz out the corner of her eyes.

"Man, this grub looks delicious. Looks like it's from a five-star restaurant," Austin said, filling his plate with food.

"Yo, how about a toast to a long-lasting friendship and a future paved with abundance," Jazz suggested.

"I'll toast to that," Jessica said.

"Me, too," Austin and Mahogany said together.

"Cheers!" they all said, tapping their glasses of cold Sprite.

Jessica sighed after taking a swallow of Sprite. "We'll try for wine next time."

Everyone laughed.

"Why are you so quiet, Mahogany?" Austin inquired. "Are you feeling okay?"

"Yes. Just savoring the moment. And thanks for asking." Mahogany smiled.

Jazz looked at Austin. He took a bite from his corn on the cob. Jazz looked at Austin again.

"Oh, Mahogany, guess what?"

"What, Jessica?"

"I got the job at Cupples Elementary. I start training the second week of August. So let your mom know I'm straight."

"Great! I'm so glad to hear that. Give me five, girl."

"Congratulations, Jessica. It's always a treat to see my beautiful sisters excelling in this male-dominant world. Seriously, I wish you further success," Jazz said. He bit a piece of steak from his kebab. "Ooh-wee! Tender. And it tastes better than it looks."

Austin stared over at Jazz, his facial expression saying *Now what is this nigga trying to prove! Simp ass motherfucker!*

Seemingly, Jessica loved the occasion. Her and Jazz connected eyes throughout the affair. Mahogany sat quietly, slowly eating piece by piece.

EIGHTEEN

Saturday, June 24, 2000

"Yo, Stef."

"I'm listening, Dread."

Dread turned down the stereo.

"You stay loyal like you've been, and nigga, I'ma have you crazy rich." Stefaughn sat smiling. "Fo' real though, Stef, I'm feelin' yo' work ethics, derrty. Nigga, you uh soldier! Welcome aboard, derrty." Dread smiled, more in love with the ghetto than the American penal system. He felt the hood was his, dilapidated homes, chaos, and all.

"Thanks, Dread. But I ain't nothing until I get one of these."

"What? A SL Five Hundred, derrty?" Dread glanced over at Stefaughn.

"Damn right, Dread! This is the type of load ladies love."

"Yeah, it has its advantages, but dhese hoes out here will go crazy ova any nice car. Anyway, you keep doin' what you doin', and in six months I'ma introduce you to my man out in Saint Charles who can make it happen fo' you. But you gotta keep it on da low." Dread paused. "We got uh deal?"

"Deal it is then, Dread. Trust me, you ain't seen nothing yet."

"Yeah, dhat's what I like to hear. Uh nigga focused on the prize."

Having just exchanged four-and-a-half-pounds of cocaine for $50,000 at "The Horseshoe," (Ashland and Herbert Street) Dread and Stefaughn styled east on Natural

Scarlet Tears

Bridge. Dread knew he was driving the wrong car, tumbling in fool's play. In St. Louis the authorities wasn't comfortable seeing young African-American men driving $100,000 sports cars. Old money and perpetual racism, the so-called big foot that kept the Black men down, dominated St. Louis.

Stefaughn had made a decision to associate with the underworld. The everyday influence of ghetto stardom was apparently too alluring. He wanted to be like the rest of his homies, having a nice car, a flock of jezebels, fancy jewelry, loads of urban wear, and a counterfeit sense of authority. The hood was king!

"Hey, Dread, UGK some cold muthafuckas, ain't they?"

"Nigga, you see I'm still bumpin' dhey shit."

"Turn that back down for a minute," Stefaughn said. "Check this out, Dread. I got a cousin who just graduated from the University of Houston. She lives out in Creve Couer with my aunt and her pops. Man, Dread, my cuz is finer than a muthafucka! I swear if she wasn't my cousin I'll be at her ass."

Dread laughed; he adored foolishness.

"Anyway, I think she's the type of woman you should try settling down with. She's already used to having things, Dread."

"What's her name?"

"Mahogany, Dread. Mahogany."

A bell signaled in Dread's mind. He immediately recognized the name and other familiar characteristics he'd heard about Mahogany from Jazz. Dread couldn't believe what he'd just heard. He was certain there was only one Mahogany Stefaughn could have been talking about.

"Naw, Stef. You kiddin' me. Nigga, you ain't got uh cousin wit' it goin' on like dhat."

"I'm for real, Dread. I went to her graduation last month. She got a good ass job downtown at Adam's Mark. You ought to let me introduce you to her. I'm telling you, Dread, you'll like her."

Dread sensed that Stefaughn was ambitious, wanting to be the king of the city overnight. He'd been poisoned by the love of money, and Dread possessed the ladder that Stefaughn wanted to climb. This was advantageous, the power to manipulate events.

"Stef, my nig, you uh real nigga. I'm glad I met you. And yeah, I can use uh broad, well uh woman, like yo' cousin. I'd like fo' you to hook us up when you get da chance."

"Nigga, you ain't said nothing but a word. As a matter fact, let me see your cell phone. I bet she's at the crib."

Dread turned off the stereo. He handed Stefaughn his cellular telephone and activated the telephone speaker system in his car. Dread wasn't thinking friendship. Honor was dead, assassinated a long time ago.

"What's up, cuz! This me. Stefaughn."

Dread's heart pumped faster. He gripped the steering wheel.

"Hey, what's up, Stefaughn. I can't believe you're calling me."

"I know, I know, this is only my second time calling you since you've graduated. I'm sorry, but I've been real busy, cuz."

"Doing what, Stefaughn?"

"I got this lil gal I'm kicking it with. Th----"

"Yeah, I heard."

"Okay, I know you talked to Mom's. Anyway, I've been busy searching for a job, too. So come on, cuz, you know how it is."

"Whatever! I hear you talking, Stef."

"Listen up, cuz. What are you doing later on?"

"Not a whole lot. Why?"

"I got somebody I want you to meet."

Dread tapped Stefaughn on the arm. "Don't say my name," he lip talked.

"Who?"

"One of my best friends. Oh yeah, he's also looking forward to promoting some concerts. Mom told me you were in the market for renting space for a variety of events down at Adam's Mark. So what's up?"

"Stefaughn, how old is your friend?"

"He's in his late twenties, cuz. Why you ask?"

"I'm just checking. Because I'm sure nobody your age is trying to rent space from Adam's Mark."

"I feel you on that one, cuz. But don't let age fool you when it comes to the hood."

"Well, since you insist. And we're going to keep this on a business level, okay."

"Yeah, yeah, that's cool."

"Okay, I can meet you at your house by six o'clock. I need to come see my auntie, anyway."

"No. Let's not meet at my house."

"Well, we can mee----"

Dread whispered, "Tell her Dave and Busters in Earth City?"

"How about Dave and Busters in Earth City?"

"Yeah, that's a nice spot to hook up. Besides, that isn't far from my house. I'll have one of my friends with me if you all don't mind."

"Hell yeah, cuz! You know me. It ain't nothing like meeting a new honey. Hey, how is Jessica doing?"

"I thought you said you were chilling with a woman, now. Stefaughn, you had better slow down. It's too dangerous to be promiscuous. Anyway, Jessica's fine, and we'll be there at six. So don't be late! And no, I'm not bringing Jessica."

"All right, I'll see you at six, cuz."

"Bye, crazy."

Stefaughn pushed the end button on Dread's cellular telephone. "What I tell you, Dread. Believe me when I tell you things, derrty." Stefaughn sat back in his seat, smiling away. "You're going to feel my cousin. I'm down with you, Dread. I'm down."

Dread looked at the clock inside of his car. "Nigga, gimme five."

"It's all good, Dread. I just want you to be all right. We can all use a good woman like my cuz. I feel I owed you that for all you've done for me. And I'ma continue to take care of my business out here, Dread. We gone do this. We gone do this, homie."

"I see you real serious 'bout yo' thing, Stef. Dhen on top of dhat, you uh real ass nigga. Dig dhis, derrty . . . I was gone sell you uh quarter bird and front you one. Just being honest, my nig, you bigga dhan dhat, now. So I'ma take yo' sixty-five hundred and front you uh whole chicken. And just pay me fifteen-five as soon as you get it. Nigga, dhat's uh bird fo' twenty-two. You ain't gone beat dhat 'round dhis neck of da woods, especially on da front tip, derrty."

"I appreciate that, Dread."

"When you finish dhat, I'ma front you two chickens. But I gotta have twenty-six uh piece fo' 'em, Stef. You should be all da way on yo' feet after dhat." Dread stared at Stefaughn, feeling close to him. Stefaughn reminded Dread of himself when he was younger.

"Fo' sho, Dread. I should be able to buy my own two chickens after all that. And why is your name Dread?"

"Back in da day, I used to rock dreadlocks."

"Oh, I see. And how much did those diamonds and gold teeth hit you for, Dread?"

"Damn, Stef, what's up wit' all dhese questions, derrty?"

"Oh . . . my fault."

"'Ey, Stef. Check dhis out. We gone stop by Asher's on Kingshighway and St. Louis Avenue and buy us sumptin fresh to wear. When we finish shoppin', you can put dhis here chicken in yo' bag and walk to da crib, since it's only two blocks from yo' pad. Dhat way, won't nobody in yo' hood be tryin' to put two and two tegetha."

"That's a good idea, Dread. 'Cause if my neighbors saw me hop out of something like this, the first thing they'll run and tell my mom is I'm selling dope. I wanna keep everything on the DL, you know."

"I'm tellin' you , Stef, you gone eat in dhis game. But you gotta stay focused and always keep it real wit' uh nigga." Dread stared over at Stefaughn. He didn't smile. Stefaughn

Scarlet Tears

stiffened, looking serious. "And call my brutha-in-law when you get home. I want you to tell dhat nigga I'ma holla at him late on tonight. I'ma do sumptin special fo' dhat fool, since he hooked me and you up. I been promisin' it to his jive ass."

"I got you covered, Dread. And believe me . . . it don't get no realer than me. That's why Bruce decided to go ahead and hook us up."

"I feel you. And I'ma pick you up over Bruce and my sister's crib at five-thirty."

Having arrived at Asher's Clothing, Dread and Stefaughn entered the store. Dread was an appreciated regular at Asher's. They even addressed him by his nickname. He'd spent thousands of dollars buying Mauri alligator-skinned shoes, Versace clothing, Avirex and Divoucci leather coats, and more. The storeowner and the sale clerks were smiling, their minds probably shouting *ching-ching*.

NINETEEN

Dread and Stefaughn zipped down the interstate, listening to Rap music. Dread had prepped Stefaughn to call him Tony. As a man of deceit, he didn't want Mahogany to know his real name. Still, Dread drove trying to picture Mahogany in his mind. She was a force he longed to see.

Dread knew that Jazz only associated with beautiful women. Why Dread would risk ruining his relationship with the very man who was responsible for his lavish lifestyle was imprudence. Dread was only being himself, conspiring with his mentality.

Five minutes late for their six o'clock arrangement, Dread and Stefaughn drove in front of Dave and Busters. Dread asked Stefaughn to go inside and see if his cousin had arrived. Dread sat in his car looking at himself in the rearview mirror. His goatee was well trimmed, but a small pimple on his right cheek annoyed him. Dread rubbed his finger across the pimple when he suddenly heard Stefaughn informing him that Mahogany was inside.

"Okay. Wait fo' me right dhere while I park," Dread hollered from the car.

His car parked, Dread walked towards Dave and Busters. He paid close attention to his every step, figuring he was suave, a true ladies man. Dread and Stefaughn met, gave each other dap, and proceeded inside.

The atmosphere was vibrant, busy with flashing lights, dings and buzzes from arcade games, and cheery human voices. Everyone now acquainted, Dread invited the crew to dinner. The wait for dinner was an estimated thirty minutes, so they all decided to shoot a few games of billiards until their names surfaced on the waiting list.

Scarlet Tears

"So, Tony, what do you do for a living?" Mahogany asked.

"I, I own uh couple of... of beauty salons in da city," he stammered. "And I'm par, part owner of uh liquor store."

Bending over and focusing on a bank shot, Mahogany said, "Oh really."

Dread couldn't keep his eyes off Mahogany's derriere; it appeared inviting, soft and juicy in tight Girbaud jeans. He now understood why Jazz was falling in love with Mahogany. There was genuine mystique about Mahogany that inspired men to better themselves. She was living encouragement, a heavenly spirit enchanting all those she encountered.

"Good try, cuz. But no cigar. And this shot's for you, Astarte," Stefaughn said. "Cross corner, eight."

Mahogany and Astarte booed Stefaughn after his lousy shot. Everyone started laughing.

"Oh, y'all gone boo a brother because he missed." Stefaughn began laughing himself.

"You's a bum, Stefaughn. Your shot, Astarte," Mahogany said.

"Yeah, let's see what you're going to do, Astarte," Stefaughn playfully said.

"You'll see," Astarte replied, seemingly confident in her game.

"Damn, Stef. Look like homegirl is uh pool shark," Dread uttered, wondering if he was speaking good enough English. "Good shot, Astarte." Dread also wondered where in the hell had Mahogany and Astarte been hiding. They were extremely gorgeous. Fresh. Focused. Down-to-earth. Well-mannered.

"Our game. Way to go, Astarte," Mahogany said.

"We have a table ready for Mister Wennington and party," a female voice said across the P.A. system.

Dread's eyes opened wide; his heart thumped; he turned from side-to-side. The face of Knigel "Jazz" Wennington was the image he didn't want to see. Dread slipped behind a shield of strangers. This was his worst nightmare.

"Did I just hear Wennington?" Mahogany asked, looking around.

"I think that's what they said," Astarte replied.

Stefaughn racked the pool balls.

"Here we are, ma'am." A tall White man said as he approached the waitress standing by a set of glossy wooden stairs. "We're the Wenningtons."

Dread took a deep breath. He relaxed and returned his attention to Mahogany. Again, Dread had trouble trying to keep his eyes off Mahogany's ass.

"Hey, Stefaughn, are you going to church in the morning?"

Stefaughn looked over the pool table at Dread. They both grinned. "I'ma try my best, cuz. Why? Are you going?"

Dread knew the answer; it wasn't his business to tell. Stefaughn had strayed away from God, now a member of self-destruction.

"Yeah, I'll be at your house in the morning. I really enjoyed you guy's choir the last time I attended services."

"Is that right, cuz?" Stefaughn smiled.

"Yo, you go to church, Astarte?"

"Why sure, Stefaughn. I sing in the choir at my church."

"Straight up," Stefaughn said, gazing at Astarte. "I bet you have a pretty voice."

Astarte smiled. No comment.

"How about you, Tony? Do you attend church?"

"Unfortunately not, Mahogany. But it is on my to-do list."

Dread was proud of himself for not mispronouncing unfortunately.

"Is it safe to have all those diamonds in your mouth, Tony?" Mahogany asked.

"It's all right. I don't see it as uh problem."

"So, how long have you been promoting concerts?"

"I've been doin' it now fo' 'bout three years," Dread answered, uncomfortable with being the subject of an inquiry. Nonetheless, he was charmed by Mahogany's symmetry.

Scarlet Tears

"Who are some of the acts you've brought to town?" Astarte asked.

"Donnell Jones, Eight Ball and MJG, Outkast, Kevon Edmonds, uh . . . David Hollister, Too Short, and uh few more."

"Any female acts?" Mahogany questioned.

"Yeah, I've brought Eve to town, Trina, and Gangsta Boo."

"Do you do all of this alone?"

Dread felt like he was on trial. "Most of it, Mahogany. But I do have uh few partners here and dhere."

"That's good," Mahogany said. "There's nothing like team work."

Well, the conversation continued, and the group of four was eventually called for a dining table. The outing was going smooth, everyone having a super time. It was a friendly date of smiles and risky business. Hot wings and pasta alfredo were the dishes ordered. Desert was avoided. From dinner to video games, Dread, Stefaughn, Astarte, and Mahogany lost themselves in amusement. More than happy, Dread covered the entire expense; he was enthusiastic with having brought joy into the life of Jazz's number one sweetheart.

At the end of the date, Mahogany promised to mail Dread a price list, FAQ sheet, and a list of available dates for renting ballroom space at Adam's Mark Hotel to the address he provided. Stefaughn tried acquiring Astarte's telephone number. He was unsuccessful. Astarte said she was appreciating the single life. Stefaughn looked embarrassed. He didn't say another word. They parted, both parties going their separate ways.

TWENTY

Tuesday, June 27, 2000

The city was ablaze with excitement, everyone scrambling to the nearest music store. Nelly's debut release, *Country Grammar*, was the fire that burned.

Saint Louis had not undergone such music enthusiasm in a very long time. Nelly and his Midwest flavor had captivated the entire nation. He was Hip-Hop's new poster boy, just what the music connoisseurs in New York City had been fishing for, a well-appreciated breath of fresh air.

It was lunchtime, and Mahogany had just purchased a copy of *Country Grammar* from Downtown Music. Unexpectedly, thoughts of Stefaughn flashed in Mahogany's mind. Stefaughn didn't attend church services, Sunday. In fact, he wouldn't even return Mahogany's telephone calls. An optimist, Mahogany hoped all was well.

The day had been busy on the job. Mahogany was growing tired, but a passionate thought of Jazz was the fuel she burned. Mahogany had not spoke with Jazz since Sunday after church, the day he left for Texas. Jazz told mahogany he was visiting Texas to attend two lingerie fashion shows, one in Dallas and the other in Houston. He wasn't expected to return until Sunday, July 2nd.

Preparing to leave her office, Mahogany dropped a package in the outgoing mailbox located near the exit of the office, the very package she had promised Dread.

TWENTY-ONE

It was electric! Saturday, July 1, 2000, was sizzling with emotion. From the South Side to the North Side, everybody was animated with excitement. From the East Side to the West Side, everybody was galvanized with excitement. From University City throughout St. Louis suburbs, everybody was stimulated with excitement.

Da Maniaks' promotional campaign was going great; the city over was infected with Hip-Hop fever.

Delancy, a local celebrity, had generated a strong buzz concerning his party, the late night bash that would bring the noise. It's where everyone would converge, lose themselves, pop XTC pills, and celebrate into the wee hours of the morning, the acknowledgment of a city on the move. *It was party time! It was party time!* WITHOUT FAIL, *it was party time!*

"Remember, y'all, like I said before . . . ass and titties!" Delancy ordered. "And bring y'all swimsuits if y'all thinkin' 'bout getting' in da pool." These were the last words Mahogany and Jessica heard from Delancy as they left his beauty salon. They had been inspired to go ahead and show "The Lou" what their mommas gave them: ass of wonder, slim waistlines, appealing legs, and nice round breast. There was a statement to make.

As it approached eleven o'clock a.m., Mahogany and Jessica hurried to meet Sarah and Astarte at Shell Gas Station on the corner of Skinker and Delmar Boulevard. Mahogany didn't want Sarah and Astarte waiting around parked in a Mercedes. She knew the city was dangerous, although early in the day. Crime and St. Louis were in love, and if one was caught snoozing—he or she would certainly lose. So be it!

Scarlet Tears

"Damn, it's packed out here!" Jessica exclaimed. "I don't see them, anywhere."

"Girl, where am I going to park? I didn't think it was going to be this crowded."

"I don't know, but we'll find somewhere to park. Hey! There's someone pulling out over there. Hurry up! Hurry up, Mahogany!"

Mahogany sped up, an attempt to secure her a parking space.

SKURRRR! squealed the tires from an emerald green Corvette, its top down. The crowd silenced. Everyone looked in the direction of the loud, shrilling noise.

"Damn, Jessica! I thought we were hit," Mahogany said. She took a deep breath, the wits being scared out of her.

"Stupid ass, idiots!" Jessica yelled, gawking at the two men foolishly smiling inside the new convertible Corvette, their gold teeth gleaming in the summer sun.

"Jessie, no!"

"Girl, screw them!"

"Sorry 'bout that," the driver of the Corvette said. The passenger inside the Corvette continued to smile and waved hello. The brothers were young, apparently getting money, and still in need of a parking space.

Mahogany parked on Skinker across the street from Shell Gas Station. She and Jessica exited the car. They jaywalked across the busy street onto the gas station parking lot, causing even more commotion. It wasn't intentionally; their good looks commanded attention.

"There they are, Jessica."

"It looks like they're the main attraction."

Sarah and Astarte sat inside Sarah's electric-blue Mercedes Compressor, talking to a host of admirers. The top of Sarah's car was down; her and Astarte were wearing shades.

Mahogany and Jessica eased their way through the enthusiastic crowd. They approached Sarah's car from the rear.

"Well, it seems to me as if you, girls, have it going on," Mahogany said.

Sarah and Astarte turned around. They joyfully screamed.

"There you, guys, are. I was hoping you, both, would make it," Sarah said.

"What's up, Mahogany and Jessica?" Astarte spoke.

"What's up! What's up!" Jessica rapped.

Sarah and Astarte exited the car. They looked and smelled lovely.

"How long have you, all, been waiting? And are you allowed to park here?" Mahogany asked.

"About fifteen minutes. And nobody hasn't said anything so far regarding us parking here," Sarah replied. She looked around. "It's not like we're blocking an entrance or anything. But I'll go inside to check if it's okay."

"Girl, I like y'all's hairstyles."

"Thanks, Astarte," Mahogany and Jessica said.

Sarah let up the roof to her car. She activated the alarm. They then walked inside the gas station and asked for permission to leave Sarah's car on the parking lot.

"Yeah, y'all cool. It's to da good," the middle-aged attendant permitted. He did not remove his eyes from Sarah's silicone bust. "Anytime for you." He smiled, displaying his gold fronts.

"I thank you," Sarah said. She winked her eye and shook her boobs. They all laughed and exited the gas station.

Now walking on the sidewalk down Delmar Boulevard, towards Streetside Records, Mahogany and friends discussed the local music industry, elaborated on Delancy's nearing party, and shared details about what they had planned to wear to the party. The weather was beautiful and "The Loop" was pulsating with merriment.

"I heard some people back there say they hadn't made it, yet," Astarte said.

"Oh, so that's why the News and everybody are holding down the corner. They'll be coming in from that way," Jessica uttered.

Mahogany, Astarte, and Sarah looked at Jessica like *duh*!

Scarlet Tears

Suddenly, there was the whoop of fast-approaching sirens and blaring horns. The crowd shifted towards the noise. "That's them! That's them!" people yelled.

A caravan of St. Louis Police Department motorcycles and squad cars, SUVs with Da Maniaks painted on them, and white stretched limousines cruised down the street through the cheering throng of fans. Da Maniaks and other men and women hung out the roofs of the limousines and SUVs tossing promotional T-shirts, bandanas, and hats into the screaming swarm of Maniak lovers. It was like the NBA, *fantastic*. Totally exhilarating! Da Maniaks, along with Nelly, was the new urban voice of the Midwest. They were stars who had risen from the clutch of the ghetto. These boys were the *down-down babies* of The STL.

"Malik!" screamed Jessica, waving her arms as Da maniaks passed by.

Mahogany, Sarah, and Astarte were too reserved to shout, however waving hello and displaying winsome smiles.

"Watch out, y'all!" Astarte said.

A stampede of yelling children, adolescents, young adults, and parents carrying toddlers on their shoulders chased close behind the caravan. They were coming from every direction. Some carried roses. Others carried stuffed animals, posters, and CDs. This was shocking to Mahogany; she had never experienced anything like it before. Rap music was powerful, unbelievably influential.

Now parked in front of Streetside Records, a brigade of bodyguards and law-enforcement officers cleared a path from Da Maniak's limousine into the music store. It was a struggle trying to maintain the energetic crowd. The crowd screamed and cheered.

Walking through the excited crowd of fans, Da Maniaks smiled, shook hands, signed few autographs, and shared a kiss or two.

"I love y'all!" somebody screamed.

"Choose me, please," a young lady in a tight body suit plead.

"Maniaks, you're the best!" a little White boy yelled.

"Y'all CD is da bomb!" Mahogany heard someone say from the rear.

Cameras clicked and flashed. People waved signs throughout the crowd. A neon-green bra and matching G-strings flew through the air. The press loved it, capturing every moment.

It was at least twenty minutes before Mahogany and friends would make it inside the store. Luckily, Jessica knew one of the private bodyguards who suddenly walked outside of the music store for a smoke. Jessica, being the belle chose she was, got the bodyguard's attention with ease. He worked his magic, and off into the store Jessica and company went.

Inside the music store, Mahogany and crew were embraced. They shared kisses with the stars. Ormez and the rest of Da Maniaks complimented Mahogany and her friends. Blushing away, Mahogany and crew smiled as if their smiles were permanent.

Mahogany and Ormez were ecstatic to see one another. Yet the moment did not allow for an extensive conversation. The Rap group was busy greeting fans and signing autographs. Therefore, Mahogany gave Ormez and the group's manager, each, one of her business cards and encouraged them to give her a call regarding a concert. Mahogany and Ormez locked eyes; there was a message sent.

Jessica and Malik talked privately for a moment. There is no telling what they discussed, and Jessica would probably never tell the truth. Astarte and Sarah, both, made a lasting impression. Needless to say, Astarte wasn't interested in *part two*.

Mahogany and her friends were asked to be in Da Maniaks' next music video. Saturday, July 1, 2000, would be a special entry in *A Life to Remember.*

TWENTY-TWO

The Rio was alive with beautiful women, the hottest music, and well-dressed brothers who were nicely groomed and aflame with diamonds, platinum, and gold. The club was packed. Peace had not been broken. Smiles were on most faces. The dance floor was busy, bodies bouncing and wiggling to the ass-shaking tune.

Hot wings, Moet, and Cristal were seemingly the crowd's favorites. The picture line was at least twenty-people long; everybody tried making a fashion statement. The indoor temperature was comfortable, yet heat was just around the corner. Mahogany could hear men, along with a few women, talking about how fine she and her friends looked.

Mahogany and friends walked out onto the club's private terrace. The outdoor swimming pool sparkled under the golden half moon. The night sky was starry, appearing only an arm's stretch away. Sexy babes in exotic bathing suits filled the illuminated swimming pool. Mahogany counted six men in the swimming pool, their bodies fit. They were playing keep-away with a beach ball from the ladies. The ladies screamed and tried getting the beach ball, just what the fellows desired.

Scores of fully-dressed brothers surrounded the deck of the swimming pool like flies on shit, many of them bragging out loud how they'd sex the young babe of their choice. The indoor and outdoor disc jockeys were having a ball. The club was hype, everyone appearing to be enjoying him or herself. It was the party of the year, a ghetto fiesta of African-American phenomenon.

Guessing, the owner of the nightclub and the waiters were the happiest of everyone, their cash registers and pockets overflowing with green.

Mahogany and friends walked back inside the club. They saw Delancy.

"Hey, now! *Looky-looky!*" Delancy said, the music pumping. "Y'all heifers got it goin' on! And I love the muthaflippin' outfits. Huh, y'all representin' much ass and titties!" Delancy paused and asked Jessica to turn around. "Good God, Jessie! Yo' ass plump like uh pumpkin on steroids. Girl, let me see you wiggle that thang like uh salt shaker."

Mahogany, Astarte, Sarah, a flock of women who were following Delancy and Jessica started laughing. Delancy was in the spotlight; there was no holding back. He was the life of the party, the *Mr. Goodbar* under the influence of alcohol.

"Cut it out, Delancy," Jessica said.

Slowly rotating his neck, Delancy had his hands on his waist and rolled his eyes. He replied, "Jessie, I ain't playin' wit' you. C'mon and shake uh lil sumptin. C'mon, shake that thang. The hell wit' that pretty shit! Girl, it's time to get krunk!"

Everyone continued laughing. But Delancy was serious with Jessica, nonetheless, his intentions good. In ghetto terminology—*Delancy was off da chain, doing it WAY BIG.*

"All right. Just because it's you, Delancy."

Jessica dipped, shook her tail feather, dipped again, and wiggled her tail feather. *Oh Jesus!*

Watching Jessica dance, Delancy and few other brothers in close proximity cheered Jessica on by saying, "Dip, baby, dip. C'mon, Jessie . . . dip, baby, dip."

Charged, Jessica dipped the night away. She made the boys pop their collars, made the boys wish Jessica was on top.

Delancy thanked Mahogany and Jessica for attending his party. He inquired about Astarte and Sarah. Sarah and Astarte seemed to like Delancy. His ability to inspire laughter was irresistible. He was the women's choice of an exalted friend, the esteemed answer for joy.

Brothers liked Delancy, too. Because wherever Delancy was, if not with his boyfriend, there was a herd of honeys nearby. Call him gay, call Delancy a beef lover, but never call him lame.

Wanting to see more, Mahogany and friends roamed throughout the lavishly designed nightclub. From the main floor, to upstairs, then back outside near the swimming pool, Mahogany and crew found a super time. Fun was everywhere, rocking the night away.

Mahogany and friends took some pictures, enjoyed hot wings and fries, and met brother after brother. Jessica had a few drinks; she was now wired for *the nasty*, the late night whatever.

Ready to dance, Jessica grooved to the DJ's mixture of R&B and Rap music while standing near the dance floor. Mahogany grooved, too. Yet she felt her groove wasn't as smooth as Jessica's. Sarah was aroused, and Astarte was amazed. They were experiencing the inner city's number one weekend passion, kicking it at the nightclub, possibly meeting someone hot for the night.

"There are four cute dudes over there," Jessica said, pointing in the direction of the DJ booth. "C'mon, let's ask them to dance."

Mahogany stalled; she had never before asked a person to dance. Sarah and Astarte also stalled.

"Well, are y'all coming?" Jessica asked Mahogany, Sarah, and Astarte.

"Oh yeah," Sarah answered.

Mahogany and Astarte followed suit.

"Yo, yo, yo, ladies," a voice said through the nightclub speakers. Music continued to blare from the speakers. "Yeah, I'm talking to you, four lovely ladies," the DJ said.

Mahogany and friends all looked at one another. They smiled and put their hands on their faces. They were abashed, now in the spotlight with hundreds of people staring at them. Mahogany gazed at the illuminated red exit sign, which hung next to the DJ booth, it appearing as a neuroleptic. She yearned for invisibility.

The DJ continued, "How y'all, sexy ladies, doing, tonight? Yeah, it's me, DJ Big Pimpin' from One Hundred Point Three, 'The Beat'. Don't be ashamed now, looking as good as y'all looking." The music stopped. "Where you, ladies, from?"

"West Side!" Jessica uttered.

Other West Siders in the nightclub cheered in support.

"Okay, hold up, hold up, everybody," the DJ said to the crowd. "And where the rest of y'all from?"

There was a break of silence. Mahogany, Sarah, and Astarte looked at one another, again.

"We're from Creve Couer," Sarah blurted in proper English.

The crowd laughed. Sarah looked around, her faced flushed with red.

"It's all good, baby," the DJ said. "We appreciate you coming out and kicking it with us, tonight. And remember . . . *I wanna be yo' man*," he toyed on the microphone.

Music came blasting through the speakers, again.

"Y'all ready to make some noise?" the DJ yelled through the speakers to the entire crowd.

"HELL YEAH!" the crowd roared.

"Okay, somebody . . . everybody . . . *screeeeam*!"

The crowd screamed; they screamed some more; the roof was on fire; they didn't need no water; just let the motherfucker burn.

"I like that, I like that," the DJ said. "Well, y'all continue to enjoy yourselves, and I'ma keep this thing krunk like a real DJ is supposed to do." He paused. "And for all of y'all who ain't getting' yo' party on, I suggest you get it pimpin', *big baaaaaby*!" He paused again, the music pounding away. "Yeah, I'm the hit man, DJ Big Pimpin'. The rawest DJ in this part of the land. And Delancy, wherever you are, you're the man, my brother. You got 'em traveling all the way from Creve Couer—and looking good as uh mutha!" The music pumped hard like an old Run DMC concert, more energetic than L.L. Cool J performing "Rock Da Bells." ""Yo, everybody, Delancy's the biggest playa in the house, tonight. Kudos, my brutha. And let's give it up fo' him, y'all, by making some noise."

The crowd cheered. The crowd screamed.

"I can't hear youuuuu," the DJ said.

Talk about krunk, talk about loud, this crowd was wild. Hands waved in the air, and people rooted and roared as if they were sounding the alarm.

Moving along, Mahogany, Sarah, and Astarte followed Jessica to where the four guys were standing.

"Can some sisters get a dance?" Jessica asked. "Since y'all standing here like y'all need some attention."

Quickly, the four brothers agreed to dance.

Joining the crowd on the elevated, large wooden dance floor, Mahogany and company blended in perfect. Everybody appeared to be doing his or her own thing. Mahogany danced, wondering if her groove was cool. She looked at Sarah and sniggered. Sarah was three beats ahead of the song that was playing. And no, she wasn't high off drugs.

****

"What's your name?" Jessica asked her partner, his hair wavy like the Atlantic Ocean.

"Brandon. But the ladies call me Big-D."

Please don't let him be one of them, Jessica thought. "Well," she paused, "is that right?" Jessica took one step backwards and peered down at Brandon's genital. "And what's the D for?"

"There's only one way to find out, but I think your eyes done already answered that." Brandon smiled, gazing at Jessica's breast.

I wonder if he's really packing, Jessica thought aloud. "Oh, that's the cut right there."

Scarlet Tears

"Shake it Fast" by Mystikal rumbled from the large speakers. Within seconds, the dance floor was crammed with people—sardine style.

Now is a good time to see if this nigga's shit is big, Jessica continued to think aloud. She turned around backwards and brushed her rumpshaker against the self-acclaimed big dick figurant, Mister Heavy Down Yonder. Jessica slowly rolled her tail of wonder against Brandon. She was the tease of a lifetime, carefully sensing for "The Beef." She sensed and sensed. Finally, Jessica felt something, an erection of some sort.

"Work that thang!" Brandon ordered with pleasure. "Work it, lil momma!"

Jessica laughed inside; she had Brandon just where she wanted him. Flirting with the far side, Jessica turned around and faced Brandon. She smiled. *I aught to take you for everything you got,* Jessica thought, gazing into Brandon's eyes.

It was getting warm on the dance floor, bodies bumping bodies, folks getting down in their weekend best. Jessica continued gazing into Brandon's eyes. She rubbed near his crotch. *Well, maybe it's on the other side,* Jessica assumed. Brandon kept dancing, seemingly caught up in a fantasy. He was being sexually raided, too excited to take a stand. Therefore, Jessica explored new territory. She rubbed his upper inner thighs. Still . . . no beef!

The whole while, Jessica continued gazing into Brandon's eyes, her mouth partially open. Brandon slowly closed his eyes, drifting into la-la land like a little baby. He kept dancing, though helplessly offbeat. Jessica and her mother shared common traits; they enjoyed pulling pranks and altering the minds of men.

Fuck it! Jessica silently said. She rubbed directly on Brandon's heartland. BINGO! She'd found beef, nevertheless, baby beef. His eyes still closed, Jessica stared at Brandon in disbelief. Disappointed, frowning, Jessica silently exclaimed: *You little dick, motherfucker! And you have the nerves to call yourself "Big-D." You tiny dick, bastard! Poof! Yeah, disappear with your sorry ass! Ole lame!*

Rudely, Jessica deserted the dance floor. She looked back. Her and Brandon met eyes. Jessica reasoned he would figure it out.

Well, so much for the notion that only White and Chinese men have tiny peckers; size obviously didn't discriminate.

****

"Come on, y'all. Let's go see what's wrong with Jessica," Mahogany said to Sarah and Astarte.

They excused themselves from the dance floor.

"Jessica, is everything okay?" Mahogany asked.

"Girl, yeah. Y'all have a seat."

"Good. I was tired of dancing, anyway," Astarte said.

"Okay, Astarte, you were only out there for two songs," Sarah objected. "You couldn't possibly be that exhausted."

"Why did you leave that guy out there standing on the dance floor, Jessica?" Mahogany asked.

"Girl, can you believe that trick asked me to go home with him?"

"Are you serious, Jessica?" Mahogany asked. "The guy I was dancing with was very respectable."

"Mine was too," Sarah added.

"How about yours, Astarte?" asked Mahogany.

"I guess he was all right. We shared very few words."

"Y'all, don't start tripping," Jessica said. "That ain't the first time it happened, and it probably won't be the last. C'mon, let's go see what's happening out by the swimming pool."

The party was at its climax. And Delancy was right: HIS PARTY WAS OFF DA HOOK.

The midnight air was cooperative. The outside temperature was ideal. Columns of smoke rose into the night sky from The Rio's barbecue grills. The smell of barbecue drifted through the air. Women and men danced on the terrace, some ladies in two-piece bathing suits. *Ass and titties* were shaking all over the place.

****

Looking at the screen on his digital camcorder, Dread noticed Mahogany and Astarte standing with friends. He was surprised. Dread figured The Rio was the last place he'd ever see Mahogany. He got excited, considering Mahogany's presence in a nightclub as good fortune.

Dread handed the camcorder to his friend. He tried seeing if he knew the other two women with Mahogany and Astarte. Nothing surfaced, yet one of the two looked familiar. Dread excused himself from his friends and approached Mahogany from the rear. He tapped her on the shoulder.

Mahogany turned around. "Tony. What's up, man?" Mahogany and Dread hugged one another. "I didn't know you were here. Is Stefaughn with you?"

"Naw, I'm wit' uh couple cats from 'round my way." Dread stepped back from Mahogany. He looked at her from top to bottom. "Goddamn, Mahogany! I knew you was beautiful, but I ain't know you had it like dhat."

Mahogany blushed. "You're so crazy, Tony." She smiled, again. "Just know this is only for tonight."

"Hi, Tony."

"I'm sorry. What's up, Astarte?" Dread gazed up and down at Astarte. "You uh good-lookin' sumptin yo' self. Betta yet, all of y'all are."

"Thanks!" they replied.

"Oh, by the way, this is Jessica," Mahogany said.

"Nice meeting you, Tony," Jessica kindly said, shaking Dread's hand. She gazed at Dread's diamond-studded Rolex watch.

"And this is Sarah."

"Hi. It's a pleasure to meet you," Sarah said.

Dread smiled and nodded his head hello as he shook Sarah's hand. He wished he could spend a night with them all.

"So, did you receive the package I sent you?"

"Yeah, I got it Thursday from my mailbox."

"Well, what do you think about it? Did it answer all of your questions?"

"Of course. But I'ma look over it, again. And I was gone call you at work, Monday. Try makin' some plans, you know. And thanks fo' sendin' it so fast."

Mahogany told him he was welcomed.

Dread did not want to discuss business. He had sex on the brains. The tight-fitting clothing Mahogany and friends were wearing was erotically appealing. Dread's eyes wandered from woman to woman. He was hypnotized by Mahogany and company's beauty. Dread licked his lips, imagining explicit acts. If there was a price Dread could pay to make his dream come true, he was more than willing to bear the expense. Dread even thought tips.

****

Man, he favors this cat named Dread, Jessica thought.

****

Inside The Rio, patrons were still arriving. The Da Maniaks were now in the house, besieged by groupies and neighborhood friends. The nightclub was jammed pack. Management seemed as if they did not care about the fire hazard. Everyone was spending: admission, valet parking, drinks, tips, pictures, food, and more. Money ruled!

"Yo, ladieees, we got Mister Jazz in the house, the owner of Jazz's Women Apparel and Lingerie. But that's just for starters, ladies. Y'all take it easy on him, now," DJ Big Pimpin' announced, the music rumbling through the nightclub like a rip-roaring tidal wave. "Yo, Jazz, throw it up fo' me, *playa*."

Jazz raised both his arms in the air, his bracelet and watch glistening like glitter. He smiled and pointed at the DJ. Jazz appreciated the warm welcoming, clicking his mind over

Scarlet Tears

into player mode. He walked through the nightclub's interior, speaking to all those he knew. There were handshakes, hugs and kisses from a stream of women. Several women asked if they could take a picture with Jazz. He didn't mind; he was at play. There was no better feeling than being the heartthrob of total desire. Jazz ran into a good friend, The Rio's owner, Stivey. Jazz and Stivey walked outside by the swimming pool, looking forward to gazing at a few, shapely young tenders.

"Damn, Stivey! She's thick as hell!"

"Where at, Jazz? Which one are you talking about?"

"Right there, that fine muthafucka coming out of the pool."

"Yeah . . . righhht . . . righhht." Stivey paused, rubbing his beard. "Jazz, these young girls are a beast these days." Stivey, in his late thirties, was a very popular businessman in the Black community, a big spender who couldn't get enough of young women.

"Man, it's some bad ass chicks out here. Delancy be bringing them out like never before."

"I feel you on that, Jazz." Stivey tapped Jazz on the arm. "But check out them four, lil sexy broads talking to that dude they call Dread."

Instantly, Jazz was displeased, encountering a sordid state of affairs that left a sour taste in his mouth. His heart crushed by a pound of rocks, Jazz felt lifeless, terribly unresponsive. He'd blundered upon a tainted awareness, a picture more depressing than the MLK and JFK assassinations. *How? How? No! Nooo!* a quiet voice grieved in Jazz's head. His soul was upside down, dark and gloomy. Oh, how Jazz wished he could turn back the hands of time, to have never met Dread, to even leave him dead.

"You all right, Jazz?" Stivey asked. "You don't look the same, my brother."

"Uh, I'm cool." He paused. "Yeah, I'm straight. Just tripping off how fine these babes are out here." Jazz was locked in on Mahogany, destructive thoughts assaulting his rationality like the Mexican Mafia.

"Yeah, the one standing off to the side in the black Capri pants is a foxy sumptin." Stivey paused. "That girl is sumptin special, and the one talking to dude ain't short stopping either."

Jazz agreed with Stivey regarding the young lady in the black Capri pants, Jessica. However, he wished he could make Stivey eat and shit his words regarding Mahogany. She was the one "talking to dude."

"Jazz, you happen to know any of them?" Stivey asked, looking at Jazz's face.

"Naw, but I've seen them around before."

"Ooh-wee! That White girl is strapped like a sister," Stivey uttered, watching Sarah bend over and pick up a napkin she'd dropped.

Jazz was speechless, wishing Stivey could somehow disappear. He was on pussy patrol, unruly thoughts stealing his cool. Jazz tried placing the pieces together in his head. Without facts, it was impossible. Yet, Jazz knew Dread was aware of a young woman, named Mahogany.

Jazz could not figure it out for the life of him why Mahogany was at The Rio in the first place. Her standing with Dread was an episode in his existence that riddled his heart, a scene from the Living Dead. This boy needed answers, and he determined to acquire them quickly. Absolutely nothing would deter him!

"Hey, Jazz, I gotta run inside for a minute and take care of a few things," Stivey said, looking at his buzzing pager. "Besides, the pool closes in twenty-five minutes, and I'ma talk to you a lil later."

Good, Jazz thought. "All right, that's cool. I'll make sure I holler at you before I go, bro."

Stivey's sudden departure was a personal celebration. Jazz deemed their conversation as somewhat noteworthy, yet more of a disturbance. Anyway, Jazz could now transform into the private detective he yearned to evolve. He decided to keep his distance from Mahogany and Dread. They would remain under tight scrutiny. No matter where Mahogany and

Dread would possibly traverse, Jazz was going to follow. There was no escaping the ALL-SEEING EYE.

Maintaining his cover, Jazz moved to a distant location on the terrace. He found the perfect opening between a thinning outside crowd. Jazz's vision was keen, comparative to that of a hawk. Although he didn't want his heart to ache from more agony and distress, Jazz made a commitment to see it all. Deep down inside, Jazz wanted to make his presence felt, spoiling any plans Dread and Mahogany may have had.

Mahogany's tight pastel-blue shorts and medium-heel sandals outraged Jazz, but the devil in Jazz fretted to remove Mahogany's every garment for his own selfish exploitation. Jazz dwindled into an animal state. Just the sight of Dread speaking with Mahogany was infuriating.

How dare this wanna-be, bitch-ass, punk motherfucker try playing me! Jazz thought aloud. *I made you, nigger! All right, I got something for your ass! You wanna fuck with me! I ain't giving yo' dumb ass shit else! Sorry ass, nigga! Get it how you can, bitch!*

On the brink of rage, Jazz burned out of control. Jazz wished death on Dread. He would make certain of Dread's death if he could prove Dread had betrayed him. This was the dark side of Jazz, a desperado of jealousy.

Maybe God is trying to tell me something, Jazz wanted to believe. *My making it back from Texas a day early has to be for a purpose.* He sought closure, swaying from negative to positive; however, Jazz remained exactly where he started—clueless!

Mahogany was Jazz's number one, the goddess of his heart. Despite the spirit of love, 12:00 a.m., July 2, 2000, marked the beginning of devil's play.

PART THREE

Consequences of Sin
Every day is a conflict
My future destroyed
Unruly and without wit
Disconnected, I'm torn
Tumbling in agony
My life ablaze in torture
By consequences of sin
It's never I'll win.

                        Anonymous

TWENTY-THREE

Friday, July 7, 2000

Cocaine was scarce in St. Louis; its absence had both sides of the Mississippi River's underworld in a state of depression. "Drought" season was looked upon with disfavor, except by the few whose supply of cocaine hardly ever dwindled. It was a crisis, a time when theft, robbery, and murder notoriously escalated. Tempers were short. The bills were due, and account receivables were up for collection. No excuse would do!

Although six days had elapsed since Delancy's party, it was still the hottest subject on the young African-American scene. The life of the party was seemingly immortal, along with Jazz's ever-growing frustration. Jazz's behavior became anti-social; he wanted nothing to do with anyone, except Mahogany. Jazz thought the world was against him. That was as far from the truth as elephants have wings. In actuality, Jazz's unawareness and ill thinking were the creators of his pique, the negative influence of bad decisions. Emotionally rattled, Jazz was in quicksand.

Having paid Jazz a surprise visit at his lingerie store in Northwest Plaza, Dread asked, "Yo, Jazz, dhat still ain't come in, yet?"

"Naw, man. I don't know what's up with them peops down the way," Jazz said with a low voice. He looked away from Dread. "I took that to them, but the shit still ain't made it, yet."

Dread stared at Jazz as if he was trying to read his mind. "You got uh idea when sumptin will break? You know it's come up time, Jazz. The city is dry."

Scarlet Tears

"As of now, Dread, I don't know anything. The minute I hear something I'll be sho to get at you."

"Is everything cool between us, derrty? You seem uh lil uptight, my nig."

"Yeah. Everything's copasetic, Dread." Jazz paused, staring directly into Dread's eyes. "You know I don't like having this conversation at the store."

"I feel you on dhat, Jazz. But I've been tryin' to call and page you. But for some reason, you won't call back. You know . . . dhat ain't like you, Jazz."

Jazz thought, *Boy, do this nigga have some nerves. Sneaking around my bitch like it's all good.*

"Feel me on this, derrty," Jazz retorted, looking around the store to make sure there was nobody near to hear what he had to say. "You owe me nothing, and I don't owe you anything. I'm about done with the streets, anyway. So, it might be good for you to begin your own thing, Dread." Jazz paused again. "No harm meant, derrty."

Dread hesitated before responding. His facial expression said this was the last thing he wanted to hear. It was a silver dagger to the heart. Dread had no out-of-town connections, and he was dedicated to distributing death. To purchase narcotics from local drug dealers would decimate Dread's profits. He wasn't admired by many—or trusted. Dread was known as a villain. He would allow nothing to ruin his lifestyle. NOTHING!

Dread had grown up in the Darst-Webbe Housing Projects, a human pigsty of twenty-four hour violence, hopelessness, broken elevators, graffiti-scribbled walls, neglected automobiles, shattered glass, and murdered dreams. Not only was it poverty with an insane attitude, but living death with bitterness. Dread knew nothing else besides drugs, scheming, and robbery, and he had no desire to reform his thinking. Dread was a product of morbidity. There was no turning back, and the line had been scratched.

"Oh . . . you fo' real, derrty?" Dread's eyes became watery. "All right . . . it's like dhat, dhen. It's cool. Yeah . . .

I'll see ya later, Jazz. See ya later, homeboy," Dread dolefully uttered. He then exited the store.

Jazz took a deep breath; he had made a very courageous move. Jazz thanked God for matters settling peacefully in his store. There were only two customers in the store at that time, but they were towards the rear of the store with a sales clerk. It was a moment of relief.

Wondering what Dread was thinking, Jazz pondered his decision to brush Dread off. Jazz even weighed the possible consequences of his choices. He was somewhat nervous, fully aware of Dread's unbalanced apperception. Howbeit, Jazz was not afraid; he had been involved with Black-on-Black drug wars twice before.

Jazz reasoned: *Let it fall where it lies.*

****

Speeding down I-70 East—like the madman he was—Dread blasted his stereo, listening to "Jealousy Got Me Strapped" by 2Pac and Spice 1. Dread felt estranged, contemplating an array of violent acts. Jazz had cut his purse strings. To Dread, this was a threat on his well-being. He didn't like that; he didn't like feeling disengaged.

He thought, *Jazz must be penalized.*

****

Inside Jazz's Women Apparel and Lingerie, Jazz talked on the telephone with Mahogany. He was falling deeper in love. He wanted nothing more than Mahogany. Jazz wanted to be Mahogany's only friend, her sole source of dependence. Weakening to Mahogany's mystique, Jazz had begun thinking marriage. Mahogany was a priceless woman, the very one Jazz longed to support and adore. To live happily with Mahogany, Jazz knew it would require sacrifice. Separating himself from the buffoonery of the netherworld would be challenging, the greatest test of his life.

Scarlet Tears

"Mahogany, if it isn't too much of a hassle, why don't you stop by here when you get off work." Jazz paused; he made a gesture to a sales clerk that he'd be right there. "I want you to see the store, and maybe we can grab a bite to eat."

"That's fine. I'll get there as soon as I can. I've been looking forward to seeing your store, anyway. I've heard so much about it."

"All right, I'll see you shortly, love. And drive safe, sweetheart."

"Sure thing, Jazz. Byyye," Mahogany said with a sweet tone of voice.

TWENTY-FOUR

The more Dread thought about Jazz and Jazz's sudden, early retirement from the streets, the more he became exasperated. Recollections of poverty had begun enveloping his mind as if they were a coat of bull thistles. Everything was uncontrollably annoying, ever driving Dread nuts. Dread was steaming like lava, losing all self-control; he was a living time bomb.

Dread stopped by a liquor store off Goodfellow and Natural Bridge Road to purchase a pint of Crown Royal and a box of Phillie's blunts. This would only heighten his already extreme agitation, carrying him further into the abyss of unreasonable thinking. Nothing mattered to Dread. The only thing that concerned Dread was maintaining his image; he cherished being the head of Joneses.

Driving south on Goodfellow, while smoking a spliff, Dread disregarded most traffic signals. He was in a rush to his eldest sister's house on Chamberlain, his stash house. It's there he grabbed a nickel-plated, Army edition .45 caliber Desert Eagle, three pounds of highly potent marijuana, and his last kilo of cocaine. Dread had not long ago received three pages for narcotics: one page for three pounds of marijuana, another page for half a kilo of cocaine, and the last page for half a kilo of crack cocaine.

Dread exited his sister's house with a blue duffel bag. He got inside a 1995 Oldsmobile Delta 88, feeling it was important to ride low profile. Dread was *higher* than Heaven. His destination was Beacon Street, the North Side's one-way avenue of carnage and mayhem. Beacon Street, an artery of the Walnut Park community, wasn't to be taken lightly. Chaotic nonsense swamped the streets like dope fiends

Scarlet Tears

buying crack on the first of the month. *Murder, murder, murder* was the cry of its chant.

Waiting for the traffic signal to turn green at the intersection of Union Boulevard and Natural Bridge, Dread drank from his bottle of Crown Royal. He thought: *Damn! I hate I paid that soft ass nigga all his money this week! Soft ass nigga got me fucked up!* Dread took another swallow of "ignorant oil." He looked at the clock on the vehicle's dashboard; it displayed 4:13 p.m. Dread felt invincible, however, wishing the traffic signal would hurriedly turn green. He had a collection of serious issues to tend, issues that zipped in and out of his thought process.

Looking at his whiskey, Dread decided to gulp the remainder of it. He removed the bottle from his mouth. Something inside Dread's head signaled him to look to his right. It was Dread's unlucky day. Two White undercover DEA agents wearing dark shades set in the next lane smiling and waving at Dread. Dread could not believe what he'd encountered. The agents looked familiar. He gaped into the clean-shaved agent's face. Images of prison bars instantly flickered through his mind. Dread hoped this was an illusion or maybe a bad dream; he wanted fucking out of it.

Befuddled by paranoia, Dread slowly looked to the traffic signal as it turned green. He was afraid to touch the accelerator, his right foot glued to the floor. *Just cool out, Dread. Just cool out. It's only the weed and drinking. Take it easy, Dread. This ain't real,* Dread thought aloud. He then peeked out the right corners of his eyes. He hoped the black Chevy Impala had disappeared. It was still there. Dread knew it was trouble. Thoughts of elusion came roaring.

Deciding to go ahead and proceed, Dread tried lifting his foot to the accelerator. It was a struggle, his foot seemingly filled with lead. His situation was intense. Dread looked over at the agents, again. They gestured for him to proceed. People inside cars behind Dread and the undercover agents began blowing their horns. The agents paid the noisy horns no attention; they were busy watching their bobber, Dread. It was fishing season.

Dread eased away from the intersection. He tried maintaining control. It was impossible, his right foot trembling on the accelerator. Dread's arms quivered on the steering wheel; his eyes wandered; his heart skipped beats. Dancing at the disco, Dread's car bobbed and weaved like the St. Louis Rams scoring a touchdown.

Whoop-whoop! sounded the siren from the agents' car as they trailed Dread with flashing headlights. Dread cruised along, hoping God would somehow intervene. God was taking too long, so Dread took matters into his own hands. He stepped on the accelerator, the front end of his car jumping into the air. The engine roared. There was a chase. It was *Dragnet 2000* on Union Boulevard, adrenaline pumping faster than the U.S. government spending the taxpayers' hard-earned dollars. Off to the races they sped.

Dread's high was evading him. He grew more afraid as seconds ticked. He'd barely escaped two, would-be fatal accidents, and it was still early in the chase. Nearing a busy cross street, Bircher Boulevard, Dread figured driving straight through it would be too dangerous. There were oncoming traffic and vehicles waiting at the traffic light. Dread saw no more use for his vehicle. So he thought about trying it on foot. Dread just wanted away, far, far away. Within inches of smashing into a beige Toyota Camry, Dread came to a screeching halt. Heads turned from every direction, except for two, pretty little Hispanic girls standing on the back seat of the Toyota Camry playing with small dolls. Dread's life flashed in front of him. It was burning in Hell.

He opened the driver's side door. Dread hopped out. He left the duffel bag, running as fast as he could. Air shot into his nostrils. His eyes were wide open. Dread dashed through traffic, fright riding his back. Tires squealed. Horns honked and blew. People yelled curse words. Others screamed. And cars crashed. Everything was sudden and crazy. Dread ran. Dread flew. Dread lost his right shoe. It was an evening of *hubbub* and *hoodoo*.

"Freeze! Stop now, you Black bastard!" one of the agents yelled.

Scarlet Tears

Dread looked over his shoulder. He measured the distance between the agent and himself. Dread figured the agent would have been further away. His heart kicked in overdrive. His lungs gasped for more air. His high was in submission. Dread tried running faster, his arms flopping up and down.

"I said freeze, you Black motherfucker! Or I'll shoot!"

Dread played deaf. Fuck the agent and his order. He kept fleeing with one shoe on and jeans sagging. Dread was winded; his mouth was dry; his body was overheated; sweat was everywhere. Dread could smell his fright. He was a running duck. *Quack! Quack!*

POW! POW!

"Ahhh!" Dread screamed. "I'm hit!" The loud gunshots stunned Dread. They blitzed his mind. Now fifty or so feet inside a residential neighborhood, Dread tumbled to the concrete. He was dazed, his heart damn near busting through his chest.

Dread felt a knee drop into his back. "Why did you scream, you Black punk? I ain't shoot ya."

Dread felt a combination of punches to the rear of his head, his face banging against the pavement.

"Thought you were gonna get away, didn't you, you Black son-of-a-bitch!" the agent bellowed.

"Quit punching that damn boy like you done lost yo' damn mind!" Dread heard a woman say. He turned his head so he could see the woman. She was an elderly Black woman. There was hope.

The punching ceased. People exited their homes left and right. They started gathering around the scene, many of them exclaiming their disapproval of the agent's actions. It was an awful sight, the slave master beating the shit out of his runaway slave all over again. Dread prayed the people would rescue him.

The agent handcuffed Dread and got off his back. He stepped away from Dread. The large crowd of people complained louder. The agent drew his pistol from his holster. He pointed his left index finger at the tumultuous crowd.

"This is a fair warning! Please—do not step any closer. Or I'll be forced to shoot!" The agent was serious, his face flushed with red.

The crowd of onlookers stopped dead in their tracks, their faces filled with astonishment. Silence stood bold.

"Clear an opening! Clear an opening! Police!" ordered from out of nowhere. It was the agent's partner. "Bobby, is everything okay?" He paused to catch his breath. "I thought I heard your voice a ways back."

"Yeah . . . I'm all right. And you probably did hear me a minute ago," Bobby, the agent who handcuffed Dread, replied. "Some of the people in this crowd made a few threatening remarks. I just gave 'em a warning." Both of the agents stared into the crowd. "Anyway, is back up on the way?"

"Fuck, you pigs!" someone yelled from the back of the crowd.

"Disband now, you people!" the second agent ordered, his hand on his gun. "Or the all of you can go to jail."

"Yeah right!" the same voice yelled from the back of the crowd.

"Enough is enough, big mouth. And step to the front if you're big and bad," the second agent said, squeezing the butt of his gun.

Nobody replied.

"Bobby, backup should be pulling up in a minute," the second agent said, looking down at Dread. "The city police have already secured the scene where this piece of trash hopped out of his car." He stared at the crowd, still holding his firearm in his right hand.

"Did you find any contraband besides the open alcohol?" Bobby asked the second agent.

"You fucking right I did. I found enough to throw his ass away for life."

"Did you corroborate the find with pictures?"

"Of course. I took several of the contraband inside the car. Then I took two pictures of the vehicle's exterior, both front and back."

The agents gawked down at Dread's bloody face. Dread had heard the worst he could hear; he wished he was dead. Dread silently asked God, *Where are You when I need you?* He paused. *I swear if You save me on this one, I'll never do anything wrong again.*

"My gosh, Bobby. What the fuck happened to him?"

"Hold on, here comes back up," Bobby said. He returned his gun to its holster. "Okay, let's clear it out, ladies and gentlemen."

"Ain't that about a bitch," a lady voice said from the crowd. "It's ladies and gentlemen all of a sudden."

Bobby continued in a calm voice, "The show is over, now. This is official police business. Please return to what you were doing before any of this occurred." He paused. "Everything is fine. We've just taken another bad guy off your streets. We have this under full control. And please . . . have a great day."

The agents chuckled.

The crowd of irate spectators began to disperse. Some of them shouted derogatory remarks with their backs turned towards the agents. Dread hated this sight. He felt defeated, incredibly hopeless.

"Again, Bobby, what the fuck happened to him?"

"The fucking jerk was running and fell on his damn face. Then he resisted arrest when I tried handcuffing him. So I had to use necessary force to restrain him."

The officers giggled. Dread lay on the ground slowly shaking his head in disagreement.

"I bet you won't try that, again," the second agent said to Dread. "Come on, let's get this bum to his feet so we can search him and take his ass where he belongs."

"Where would that be, Sharp?" Bobby asked.

"A cage."

"Exactly. A steel cage at that," Bobby said, staring down at Dread. "You fucking animal!"

They searched Dread and found a small sandwich bag of marijuana. Agent Bobby read Dread his rights—as if he ever had any in the first place—and placed him in the back seat of an assisting DEA agent's undercover vehicle. Dread stared through the tinted car window. The arresting agents jotted down notes and talked to one another.

A short while later, Dread received medical attention for his bruised face, which came out to be minor. Afterwards, the DEA agents drove Dread to the DEA headquarters on Forsyth in Clayton, Missouri, for processing and interrogation. His car was towed, and his day had ended.

As for the DEA, it was a fun day fishing for largemouth bass, a wonderful day for a night of good drinking.

Bad boy, bad boy, now whutcha gonna do?

TWENTY-FIVE

Nearing the DEA headquarters, Dread gazed into the partially cloudy, blue sky through the rear window of the undercover car. He longed for a sign of God; occasional tears dribbled down his cheeks. The tears irritated the cuts in his face, but not more than his frightening predicament. Dread continued wishing for a divine blessing, a miracle, an angel of freedom. He wouldn't receive one; therefore, Dread figured he must do what he had to do. Anything would be considered. Anything!

Now inside the DEA headquarters, Dread completely humbled himself. He'd been through the cooperation process before. Dread knew what type of spirit the agents mostly admired: A STONE COLD SUCKER! The DEA craved for valuable information and a tin man, someone they could scare half to death. Having Dread apprehended they'd have even more. Dread was afraid of prison and was well aware of the unjust sentencing practices characteristic of the federal judicial system. He didn't want to play any games; the agents' every wish would unequivocally be his command. Once again, Dread was prepared to tap dance; he wanted to make it on Broadway.

"It's chilly in here," Dread said, quivering in his chair. He looked at the tall walls of the interrogation room, more nervous than Anne Frank and her family being turned over to the Gestapo. "Don't y'all think?"

"One thing for sure, it feels damn better in here than it does out there," Agent Bobby said with a stern face.

Dread's quivering intensified; his teeth chattered like a drum roll.

Scarlet Tears

"Okay, Dakar, I want you to relax and be very straight up with us. We can only help you if you effectively assist us," Agent Sharpinsky said.

"Yes, si, si, sir," Dread stammered, rubbing his arms.

"Now, are you sure this is what you want to do?"

His eyes stretched open and holding his arms tight against his body, Dread shook his head yes. He hadn't any interest in becoming a martyr for the desolate brave.

"Because I don't want any bullshit out of you, Dakar," Agent Sharpinsky uttered, staring directly into Dread's eyes.

"I un, understand, Mi, Mister Sharpinsky." Dread paused. "Ca, can we hu, hurry up s, so I ca, can get dhis o, over wit'? I, I'm r, real cold."

"Well, before we discuss anything further, I'm going to bring in our superior, Mister Harlington, to briefly speak with you regarding your situation and a custodial interrogation."

"Oh, u, uh, I di, didn't know M, Mister Har, Harlington w, was st, still around," replied Dread.

"Man, you boys never seem to learn a lesson. When are y'all gone realize this is our game?" Mr. Sharpinsky shook his head at Dread. "Anyway, you, fellows, keep the peace in here while I run and get Mister Harlington."

Agent Sharpinsky exited the interrogation room with a smile on his face. Dread was aware of the good cop-bad cop strategy the agents were using. Although cold, his face sore, Dread felt a little better.

"Well, look what we have here, Mister Dakar Sanford, a.k.a. Dread," Mr. Harlington said, closing the door behind him. He walked towards Dread and shook his hand. "So we meet again, my boy." They smiled at one another. "I hear you've been busy, and I see you've purchased yourself some new, expensive teeth within the previous five years. Business must be going great, my boy."

Deemed a fair man, Mr. Harlington was an adversary of nonsense. He was in his early fifties and acclaimed as an important figure of the DEA. Mr. Harlington wore confidence and was looked upon as a role model of great service to his country. He stood six feet, three inches tall, was in excellent physical condition, had dark blond hair and grayish-blue eyes, and was a soft-spoken intellect.

"How y, you doin', Mi, Mister Harlington?" Dread spoke, still trembling with chills.

"I'm doing fine, son." Mister Harlington looked at his agents. "Hey, will somebody try getting this man a jacket? It's our duty to keep our friends comfortable." He smiled at Dread.

Agent Bobby Datino left the interrogation room to retrieve a jacket for Dread. If he'd had his way, Agent Datino rather saw Dread fully decay in prison.

"Well, let me see here," Mr. Harlington said, looking at the arrest report. "Damn, son, what were you thinking about riding around with a half kilo of crack cocaine along with a Desert Eagle? You know . . . this carry a lot of time in the federal system." He paused and cleared his throat. He stared at Dread. "Then you were drinking while driving. You resisted arrest. You wore no seat belt. You had a quarter ounce of cannabis on your person. You attempted to elude federal agents. Your driver's license is invalid, and you have a warrant out for your arrest for other traffic violations. Then on top of that, you have criminal history." Mr. Harlington paused again. He looked at everybody around him. "Dakar, I'm not concerned with the minor stuff, but it is quite extensive. I also believe a good rest in federal prison will do you some justice. And may I ask you a question, Dakar?"

"Ye, yes. G, go 'head."

"Since I've last seen you, you don't look the same. Are you using a bit of dope, yourself?"

"N, naw . . . just uh l, lil we, weed and dr, drinkin'." Dread held down his head and apologized. He'd begun feeling sorry for his self. Soft as cotton, a pup for attention, Dread had been stripped of his manhood.

Agent Datino returned to the interrogation room with a dark-blue jacket. "Excuse me, gentlemen. Let me help our friend here with his new jacket." Standing behind Dread,

Agent Datino held up the jacket while Dread slid his arms through the arm sleeves of the jacket. "There. Feel better, Dakar?" He patted Dread on the back.

Dread looked at Agent Datino and rendered a phony smile.

"Guess what, Dakar, this jacket doesn't look bad on you after all," Agent Sharpinsky said. "How does it feel to wear a jacket with DEA written all over it, an astute power of law enforcement?"

The greatest sucker of all time, the buster of 2000, Dread sat feeling ashamed. Nevertheless, Dread overlooked the agents' comedic remarks and joined the circus. He wanted away and exonerated of his criminal actions.

"Well, before anyone says another word, Dakar, I suggest you go ahead and read your Miranda rights and everything else on this voluntary statement. If you understand them and agree to cooperate with us then please sign your initials next to them," Mr. Harlington explained. "Once you finish that, you may go ahead and sign your name at the bottom. I want honest and complete details, Mister Sanford."

Dread read the entire voluntary statement before writing a single letter, although he didn't have a thorough understanding of criminal law or a high school diploma. Yet, Dread did earn his GED while doing state prison time in his early twenties. Suddenly, he thought about passing on the whole ordeal, something telling him to have an attorney present. Disregarding his hunch, Dread went along with the agents' plan, especially since him and Mr. Harlington had prior relations.

The situation was overbearing. Dread figured if he'd back out now he'd insult the agents' intelligence, thereby, inflaming them with anger. Dread didn't know what to do. He just wanted to return to his world, a consciousness that didn't require such strenuous thinking.

"Well, Mister Sanford, I see that you're still a smart man," Mr. Harlington said. "We welcome you aboard once again."

The three DEA agents exchanged handshakes with Dread.

"Okay, we are going to start taking some notes and recording everything as of now, Mister Sanford," Mr. Harlington informed. "We're going to ask you some questions, and you answer them correctly as possible. If you aren't aware or contain any knowledge about any particular person or crime we may mention, please inform us that you're not. Also, please feel free to share with us any information you may deem helpful to our duty." He cleared his throat, again. "Mister Sanford, I'm making no promises regarding vindication, especially with this being your third felony. But I'll do the best I can. And if you can reel us something in of great magnitude it will definitely be to your advantage. And yes, your previous successful cooperation will be considered.

"Now, I want to make a note on this recording that you have personally volunteered to cooperate with the DEA in the War on Drugs without being compelled to do so. Do you understand and agree with everything I, Jeffrey Harlington, just said, Mister Dakar Sanford?"

"Yes sir. I agree," Dread replied, feeling warmer.

Did Dread fully understand all of the terminology Mr. Harlington was using? *HELL NO!*

"Let's proceed, gentlemen."

"Do you agree with possessing a half of kilo of crack and a Desert Eagle nine-millimeter at the time of arrest, Mister Sanford? And if you do, who were you preparing to sell it to?"

Dread stared intently at Agent Sharpinsky, who was conducting the interrogation, and Agent Datino. He searched his brain for the correct answer. Then he thought, *Man, I wonder what happened to the rest of it and the nine thousand dollars I had in the glove box. The less drugs the better, though.*

Dread answered, "Yes. If dhat's what da . . . da report says." Dread paused. "I was preparing to sell it to DeMarco Little on Beacon Street."

Scarlet Tears

Agent Datino and Agent Sharpinsky smiled; they were as crooked as the bell curve and seemingly loved playing with snitches.

The agents continued to question Dread about a variety of local drug dealers, serious crimes, and murders. Dread told them mostly everything he knew; he even told lies. With his voluntary cooperation, Dread had incriminated himself. There was no way out. Dread would have to ride the tide as long as it took. He was no longer his own man. Dread was now the property of the DEA. They could use him as they saw fit. Dread was without courage and loyalty to his world. He was the premier snitch of St. Louis—*the pope of betrayal.*

"We've been questioning you now for over an hour, Mister Sanford. And you're doing a fantastic job, my boy. Would you care for a snack?"

Dread smiled, enjoying the good news. "Yeah, I can use uh bite to eat, Mister Harlington. And thanks."

Mr. Harlington exited the interrogation room to fetch his high-powered informant a bite to eat. He enjoyed a late evening news update with an old friend, *Dread the Telltale.*

Well, it was time for a commercial break.

Dread yielded some very substantial information; he'd connected a matrix of dots. Dread was the *great simplifier,* the Don of snitching. He was doing well, leaking information like a faucet sprouts water. The Drug Enforcement Agency would have to call the local water company to repair Dread's broken valve; he was letting it flow like Niagra Falls.

"All right, Dread, break time is over. Let's get back down to business," Mr. Harlington said. "And remember, you're doing a great job, son. You are paying your community a splendid service by aiding us in the riddance of bad people. I'm certain that the D.A.'s office is going to love and appreciate your cooperation." Mr. Harlington turned his attention to Agent Sharpinsky. "Let it roll, my friend."

"Okay, Mister Sanford, now tell us about your supplier, those who you possibly supply, and any out-of-state illegal drug trafficking you're aware of." Mr. Sharpinsky rubbed his nose.

Dread stalled before responding, a light blinking on in his mind. This was pressing.

"Come on, Dread," Mr. Harlington said forcefully. "Give it to us. This is very important. We really need to know this."

Dread gazed into Mr. Harlington's piercing eyes as he spoke, sensing Mr. Harlington's desperation for his forthcoming information. A silent voice informed Dread to immediately bargain for his freedom. It was now or never.

"Check dhis out. I think I need uh attorney present to give y'all dhis info. I honestly think it's worth my freedom." Dread paused to look at all the agents' faces. "I'm positive I can get y'all some serious drug dealers if y'all gimme da chance. I proved to y'all last time dhat I could get y'all man."

"You think you're clever, huh, Dread? That's a pretty bold move coming from a scum who's in a shit load of trouble."

"Calm down, Bobby. Let me handle this," Mr. Harlington asserted. He then gestured Agent Sharpinsky to stop the recording by sliding his right hand across his throat. "You listen, and you listen to me well, son. You don't control anything here. This is my city. I know practically everything that's going on out there in those streets. Son, you aren't the only snitch we have. I've given your dope-pushing ass a chance before, and you went right back to doing the same damn thing. Boys like you think this thing is a joke."

Agent Datino smiled in the background. Dread prayed to catch him alone in the nearest alley, particularly at night.

Mr. Harlington continued, "But I'm willing to bargain with you, because time is of grave essence regarding what I'm about to present." Momentarily, Mr. Harlington broke away from his lecture. "You see these, here."

Dread was astounded by the pictures he was viewing, however delighted by the beauty of Mahogany.

"As you can see, I'm already aware of your ties. Both you and Mister Wennington have been under a thorough federal investigation. And, son, I can assure you that I can have your ass convicted at will. The fucking laws are in our favor." Mr. Harlington's face was red. "So, let's cut out the bullshit and keep it straight with one another. You understand me, Dakar?"

"Yeah, I get da point," Dread softly said, his tail stuck between his damp ass.

"Here's a deal," Mr. Harlington uttered. He placed a boilerplate agreement for informants and an ink pen on the table. "If you're willing to make a phone call to Mister Jazz Wennington and to those you were getting ready to deliver those drugs to, I'm willing to let you roam free for a while to take care of some things." Mr. Harlington stopped pacing the shiny tiled floor. He looked at Dread. "But know . . . the show doesn't stop here. It's some unfinished business you're going to have to take care of out there for me. Believe me, Mister Sanford, I'm doing you a favor. And the D.A. is probably still going to want at least two years in prison out of you." He paused. "Hopefully, you'll learn something different."

Dread thought, *That ain't a bad deal. I can leave shortly. I'll get my car back. I can get my money straight. I'll be able to settle all my business. Have a whole lot of sex. And these textbook punks will supply me with everything I need. Shit, if it comes down to it, I can handle two years.*

"All right, you got a deal, Mister Harlington. I'm your man to bring down Jazz, his out-of-town connections, and whatever else you need me to do."

The DEA agents cheered; they'd scored a game-winning touchdown. Everything unfolded as they desired. Dread was predictable, the king crab of the polluted seas.

Dread skimmed through the agreement, possessing a fractured idea of what he was preparing to endorse. Dread just hoped Mr. Harlington would honor his word; he relied on blind faith. Dread was eager to depart the DEA's Clayton offices, his mind on a wayward mission.

Dread signed the agreement. The agents then escorted Dread out of the interrogation room into a private area in the facility. The sign on the new door read: CONVICTION CITY. There were only three chairs in the private room, a square table, and a black telephone, nicknamed "Conspiracy." Every conversation used on Conspiracy was logged and recorded.

Dread first called and implicated the three individuals that were awaiting him and his goods of destruction. Dread was a professional liar and schemer; he'd incriminate Earth's entire population if it was necessary and achievable. Dread was at a crossroad he'd stumbled upon before. The central theme of Dread's existence was *better him than me.*

A living horror story, a true Uncle Tom, Dread needed stopping. He could benefit from a new outlook on life. He needed an upcoming date with death or a boxing match with Mike Tyson when he was in his prime. Dread was a malfunctioning tellurian and incapable of fixing. THE BOY WAS HOT!

"All right, Mister Sanford, you're doing a spectacular job. How about we keep the ball rolling." Mr. Harlington smiled.

"Yo, Dread. . . ."

Dread, now soaked with sweat, turned to look at Agent Datino. He felt pathetic.

"Before you pick Conspiracy back up, have you ever thought about opening up a school for training informants? Boy, you're damn good at it."

Everybody burst into laughter, including Dread. Dread knew he, himself, was something awful.

Standing helplessly by Conspiracy, Dread's ass got tighter, embarrassment giving him a stiff one. Dread was Homie the Clown; he even felt that he was pitifully inadequate, a feeble pathfinder of self-destruction. Dread was ridiculous, without values, and a foe of racial pride. The *hell* with African Americans, Dread's afflictive actions portrayed. He was long lost, only worried about petty issues and immediate gratification. Dread was unaware of many things, nonetheless, concerned with nonsensical matters. He didn't believe in the popular saying of *do the crime, do the time.*

"Now, let's get to the grand finale," Agent Sharpinsky said. "You're the man, Dakar! You're the man!"

"Excuse me, Mister Sharpinsky. I need Jazz's business card out of my wallet. He's at his store right now, and I don't know da number by heart."

"Sure. No problem, partner. Here. Catch!"

Dread caught the wallet, his hands trembling. Dread couldn't believe what he was about to do. He'd rather rob Jazz than send him to prison forever. Unfortunately, Dread had brokered a deal with the DEA; it was Jazz's ass—or his. YOU CHOOSE!

"Is it in there, buddy?" Agent Sharpinsky asked. "If not, I can extract it from his file."

A file? Damn, these people want this boy for real, Dread thought aloud.

"Here it is." Dread paused. "Okay, y'all ready fo' dhis?"

The agents smiled, gave Dread a thumbs up, and slid on their listening headphones. It was going down!

While dialing Jazz's Women Apparel and Lingerie, Dread silently prayed that Jazz would be gone for the day. Then Dread realized it wouldn't have mattered, because the federal agents would have asked him to call Jazz on his cellular telephone. Dread was in a jam; there was only one way out. FULLY COOPERATE!

"Hello. Jazz's Women Apparel and Lingerie. This is Mahogany. And how may I help you?"

Dread became tongue-tied. His eyes widened. It was the unexpected, a swallowed golf ball.

"Uhh . . . yeah . . . Mister Wennington, please," Dread tried disguising his voice.

"Sure. Can you hold, sir?"

"Yeah."

"Hello. I apologize for the wait. This is Mister Wennington."

Dread hesitated before speaking.

"Hello. Is anyone there?"

"Yeah, what's happenin', Jazz? Dhis Dread."

"Okay, what's up, Dread?" Jazz said, his voice sounding like he didn't feel like being bothered.

"Yo, Jazz . . . I'm sorry 'bout earlier, man. I was just trippin' fo' real. You know, derrty . . . I just been havin' thangs on my mind lately. On e'erythang, Jazz . . . I'm down wit' you fo'ever, derrty."

"That's cool, my brother. It's good to know that. That definitely makes me feel a bit better."

"Anyway, Knigel----"

"Knigel? Man, what's up, Dread? You haven't called me by my first name in over a year. You okay, derrty?"

"Yeah, I'm straight, Jazz. What I'm callin' fo' is . . . 'bout some work, Jazz. Man, you can't back out on me now. A nigga need it fo' real, derrty."

"Yo, Dread, you tripping on this phone. You know I don't play that. I told you, man, I'm finished with that life. Besides, I'm at work. And people are coming in the store as I speak. But check this out, I'ma call you later or maybe some time tomorrow. And on everything, Dread, don't be calling this store like this, derrty."

"All right, Jazz. I'll be waitin' on dhat call. Don't leave me hangin', my nig."

"Yeah, I hear you, Dread."

****

Jazz replaced the telephone on its cradle, deeply bothered by Dread's conversation. Dread had Jazz stretched out like a limousine, experiencing a day without the sun. Ingrained ripples of difficulty zigzagged through Jazz's body. His thoughts were twisted. Jazz wished Dread would vanish out of his life. Dread was a problem he couldn't solve, a pestering gnat. Jazz smelled something fishy brewing, but he hadn't befriended his sixth sense. Therefore, a skunk appeared as a cat. *Choo-choo*, trouble steamed down the Chicago line.

Scarlet Tears

****

"Hey, that's a job well done, my boy," Mr. Harlington said. He and the other agents gave Dread a round of applause.

Dread felt disgusted, the food in his esophagus nearing regurgitation. He wanted to scream, petitioning the coward within to flee. White power, ignorance, and the U.S. Federal Sentencing Guidelines were overpowering. Dread couldn't bear the pressure.

"Hold your head up, Dakar. You're only being who you really are." Agent Datino chuckled. "Can't you see that?"

This was hot butter poured on a bald scalp. Dread was set afire, but he couldn't do a damn thing but accept the truth. His integrity had been bought for pennies on the dollar—just like Judas Iscariot.

"Take it easy on him, Bobby," Agent Sharpinsky said. "Dakar's a wonder to the world." They laughed. "Our world that is."

"Hey, Dread, do you want to keep on that jacket? I must admit . . . you look damn good in it."

Dread felt defenseless, subject to authority. He was now a puppet to the very power that considered him three-fifths of a man.

"Okay, let's not get out of hand, gentlemen. It looks like Dakar is getting misty eyed," Mr. Harlington said. "It's getting late, and I'm ready to move on."

With tears coasting down his dark-brown cheeks, Dread asked, "Have I done enough fo' tonight?" He sniffled. "Dhat's four people I've called, along wit' all da information. Dhis ain't right."

The DEA agents were pitiless; they'd seen and heard it all before. Having sympathy for snitches was like America's national debt being zeroed. NEVER!

"Mister Sanford, it'll all be over soon. Within an hour or two, you'll be riding around in that pretty Mercedes of yours. You can call up a pretty lady or two, even make a little money. Oh, yeah, we're going to give you your Delta Eighty-eight back, although it's in your sister's name." Mr.

Harlington paused. He handed Dread some napkins from his rear pants pocket. "Son, you have nothing to be ashamed of. It's nothing wrong with playing the game to win. Snitching has been going on forever. It's the rule of the land, my boy. Unfortunately, you're on the other side of the fence. Anyhow, I'm certain you have a nice stash of cash somewhere, so go out and have yourself a night of fun."

Dread's spirits brightened, thoughts of freedom caressing his unhappiness.

"Wai-Wai!" Agent Datino uttered.

Dread gave him a *fuck you* stare.

"Well, Dakar, you've earned yourself a stay on the streets. But when you talk to Knigel, tonight or tomorrow, you're going to need to wear a wire. We need a little more on him. Maybe we can catch him mentioning drugs or possibly speaking about an illegal transaction. Even better . . . we catch his slick ass red-handed," Mr. Harlington prepped Dread. He signaled for Agent Sharpinsky to give Dread a concealable electronic listening device. "Dakar, be sure to notify us if anything's getting ready to go down. We like to catch things on film, and we're counting on you. Here. You now have all of our cards."

"Hey, cheer up, son. You're getting ready to go home." Mr. Harlington shook everyone's hand and congratulated each person on a great day's work. It was just another day at the office, a good old-fashioned game of cat-and-mouse. "All right, boys, y'all can handle it from here. I'm going home to wifey."

Although a very rigid man, Dread felt Mr. Harlington was considerably fair. Conversely, he knew Mr. Harlington was married to America's justice system and all its depravity. It was his fantasyland, a barbarous world of corruption.

TWENTY-SIX

Saturday, July 8, 2000

Dread was experiencing sexual fission for the second time when his cellular telephone rang. It was an enjoyable, early morning with two, female African-American exotic dancers, more like an explicit act involving the devil and his temptresses. This was more than a striptease; it was demonic passion at its apogee. Everything was considered. *Just like Daddy,* the harlots whispered.

Dread picked up his cellular telephone off the almond-colored nightstand that set next to the king-sized bed and stared at the incoming number on the telephone screen. *Damn, this Jazz. Why in the fuck now,* Dread thought.

"Go 'head," Dread said to the tattoo-covered nudists. He paused to moan. "Y'all keep doin' what you doin'----" He moaned again. "I think I, I ca, can make it."

The exotic dancers rejoiced, their minds seemingly focused on supreme pleasure. They fondled Dread's very soul, purposely committing sex crimes. Was it graphic sex? Rapture? Feel free to call it whatever. The wanton experience was mind-grasping, an addictive exploit of immorality's grandest fulfillment.

Dread's orgasm was on the verge of exploding, although six times the impact. He was propped on all four, his rear end slightly lowered. One of the exotic dancers rested on her backside between Dread's legs. She entertained Dread's dangling, 10" anaconda inside her warm mouth. Her thick, fleshly lips wrapped snug around Dread's *tummy toucher.* The sexual act was intense, explosive, even indicting.

Scarlet Tears

The second temptress' performance was a triple X act of sexual sin—too graphic for explanation. Fascinated, plagued by lust, Dread was somewhere every man yearned to be.

"Yo, what's ha, happenin', Ja, Jazz. Why s, so ear----" Dread almost shouted in extreme delight. "Wh, why so early, de, derrty?"

"Damn, what's the fuck going on, Dread?" Jazz paused. "Are you all right?"

"Hel, hell yeah. Jazz!" Dread replied, feeling his penis being sucked with more aggression. "I'm j, just chi . . . chillin' w, wit' uh cou, couple of Pink Sl, Slip's finest."

The double dose of human erotica asked Dread to rest on his backside. They now licked and sucked on Dread as if he was the prince of Saudi oil. They gazed into Dread's squinting eyes, gently sliding their long, colorful nails all over his anatomy. Dread squirmed, his chest rising and falling. The cosmetically enhanced eyes of the exotic dancers were practically hypnotizing, stimulation of an impious sort. They were amazing fantasy dolls, everything one could desire in a threesome.

Caught in a jam, on the verge of screaming YES, Dread pumped his chocolate serpent inside one of the dancers' mouth.

"Oh shit!" he blurted, yelling for mercy. "I love you, bitches!" Sperm-filled semen rushed through his thick shaft, shooting into the exotic dancer's mouth. The dancer sucked tighter, jerking her head to increase intensity.

Finished licking Dread's testicles, the healthier of the lewd Jezebels quickly hopped on top of Dread's penis. This girl was eager for a quick thrill ride. She wanted whatever little action she could enjoy before Dread's stubbornly long penis would deflate. Swiftly inserting Dread's mushroom-shaped rod into her heated love tunnel, baby girl pounced and popped that pu-nanny.

Her partner of subjugation licked Dread's nipples, her tongue long, hot, and moist. Dread bucked. Dread barked in ebonics. Dread lost all fucking control. Damn, *the good feelings rolled.*

De-energized, Dread was wooed asleep. His cellular telephone lay on the floor. Colors of seduction drifted through Dread's subconscious, whilst demons of disgrace grinned in the sexually contaminated mist. He was in a deep sleep, his flaccid penis lying to the side. This was Lucifer's play at six in the morning.

****

"Yo, Dread! Pick up the phone!" Jazz shouted through the cellular telephone.

"*Jaaaazz.*"

"Yo, who is this with your sexy ass voice?"

"Your dream comes true."

"Goddamn, you sound good, girl." Jazz paused, listening closely. "Seriously, though, who is this?"

"It's me, Miss Taffy, boy."

"Oh shit! What's up, love? I know my nigga is kicking it up in there."

"And you know it. But his ass is out like a light."

"Shit, I can imagine why. Who else is there with you, love?"

"Caramel."

"Oh, for real? How did Dread pull that shit off?" Jazz's imagination ran wild. "Y'all still got some energy for me?"

"Show you *righhht*," Ms. Taffy seductively said.

"Damn, I love your voice, girl. But do me a favor."

"I'm listening."

"Wake Dread up for a minute so I can holler at him. It's important, love. And I'ma get back with you and Caramel on some freaky shit a lil later. Cool?"

"Yeah, I hear you, Jazz."

"C'mon, Miss Taffy. You know I can't take you and Caramel."

Scarlet Tears

"Well, we'll see about that. And my number is the same." Ms. Taffy gave Jazz a kiss through the telephone. "*I miss youuu.*"

****

"Damn! My fault, derrty. A ni, nigga been up all night," Dread wearily said. His cellular telephone signaled low power. Dread gazed at Caramel licking the thick nipples of Ms. Taffy's breast. Both Ms. Taffy and Caramel were fun girls, apparently firm believers of *if a trick got his, then it's time to get ours.* GOOD GOD ALMIGHTY! The libertine angels of sodomy French kissed. They caressed one another. It didn't matter whether if they were rapacious whores, because Dread saw them as a tantalizing duet of thrill and sensation.

"Whatever, Dread. Them hoes done laid yo' black ass out."

They both laughed.

"Man, you got dhat right. Anyway," Dread paused. He wiped his hand over his mouth, "what got you dhis morning?"

"I'm calling you like I said I would. So get up and get ready, derrty. We need to talk."

"Bet, dhat ain't no problem. Oh yeah, I ran across Lil Salvador from Brooklyn when I was at da Pink Slip last night. He said he got dhat fo' you."

"Shit, it's about time. His phone number isn't the same, though."

"Don't trip. I got it. Said he's been tryin' to page you."

"Whatever. By the way, where are you?"

"Downtown at da Courtyard Marriot on Market."

"Nigga, you doing it up this morning."

"You know how it goes, Jazz. Gotta escape sometimes to keep from cryin'," Dread uttered, his eyes fixed on Ms. Taffy and Caramel's lesbian activity.

"Right, right. But dig this, Dread. It's twenty-seven minutes after six. How about meeting me at Uncle Bill's on South Kingshighway in an hour and a half?"

"I'll see you at eight dhen, my nig."

"And be on time, Dread. Because I got a few more places I gotta go to."

"I'm at you, Jazz. I'll be dhere."

Removing himself from the sex-polluted bed, Dread thought about rejoining his one-thousand-dollars prostitutes in their homoerotic drama. He wanted to provide a flash of oral sex, but the possibility of acquiring some narcotics was more intriguing. A pair of gorgeous exotic dancers was easily obtainable as long as cash was readily available. So Dread took a warm shower instead. Then he blandly excused himself from Satan's harlots.

It was seven-thirty a.m., and Dread exited the hotel's crowded parking lot in his shiny, black SL 500. While driving to Uncle Bill's, Dread considered wearing his wire and contacting the DEA. *Naw, I'll use this nigga to get my money all the way straight, first. Then I'll set his pretty-boy ass up,* he planned. Dread knew he, himself, was a backstabbing, two-timing, double-crossing, no-good scoundrel, the greatest rogue of deceit.

He'd been up all night smoking ganja, drinking champagne, gossiping about nonsense, and spending stacks of cash at topless bars. Dread needed some rest, a new line of thinking, and an ass whipping: the kind of ass whipping when one was told to remove all clothing and be lashed by a fist-full of flexible green switches; the type of ass whipping when one figured he'd never catch his breath again; the kind of ass whipping when it hurts to be seated. Maybe then, just maybe, Dread would establish a sense of connectedness to his people.

Driving onto Uncle Bill's parking lot, Dread noticed Jazz sitting inside of his crystal-white Lexus LS430 and flashed a peace sign with his right hand. Jazz returned a peace sign. Truthfully, there was no peace with Dread. Real friendship was fiction.

Scarlet Tears

Dread parked. He got out of his car. Jazz walked towards him, well groomed, nicely dressed, and looked fresh. Dread smiled, though it wasn't genuine. His body begged for rest, but the crab in him lived for sham.

****

"Good morning, Jazz." Dread paused. He gave Jazz some dap. "Goddamn, dhat bitch look good, derrty." Dread gripped the crotch of his pants. "When did you put dhem new shoes on dhat bitch?"

"A few days ago," Jazz answered, simultaneously thinking, *Look at this grown ass nigga! This nigga will never pass go.*

"Fo' sho. Let's do dhat."

Dread and Jazz entered Uncle Bill's. The aroma of freshly cooked breakfast foods stirred hunger. Jazz and Dread looked for an available table and took a seat. They ignored the menus. Uncle Bill's was a regular, early morning stop. Breakfast favorites were already set.

They ordered breakfast. Jazz and Dread met eyes while sitting across from one another. There was silence, and Jazz's stare didn't say he was a happy camper. Dread appeared defenseless, therefore receptive. Messages resonated. Dread placed a straw in his mouth.

"Excuse me fo' uh sec, Jazz. I gotta hit da bathroom."

Jazz said nothing. He drank from his chilled glass of water and thought, *Sissy can't stand the heat when it's hot, with his tired ass.*

****

Dread made sure he was inside the men's room alone. He entered the restroom's single stall and reached inside the front, left pants pocket of his baggy jeans. Dread removed a folded piece of aluminum foil. Uncomfortable and experiencing fatigue, Dread decided he'll reward himself with a chemical uplift, a wake up.

Dread thought about stripping naked. That's how cocaine made him feel. It was a ritual of freedom and glee. Dread wasn't in the comfort of his home or a hotel room, so he unbuttoned his jeans and let brother long john enjoy some hang time. Dread was dealing with bizarrerie, a habit he couldn't shake. The pressure from the DEA irritated him, leading Dread deeper into a chasm of discord.

He bit the straw, shortening it into an appropriate size for snorting cocaine. Dread jones for a fix, an instant with Jolly Roger. He carefully unfolded the aluminum foil, his eyes widening. Licking his lips, Dread separated a line from the small pile of sparkling white cocaine with his straw. Ready for liftoff, Dread snorted the line of cocaine through the straw. *"Ahhh,"* he uttered. He closed his eyes and stroked his penis. Dread imagined himself drifting amongst the starry and planetary host of Heaven, a dazzling tryst with the Most High.

Dread floated on cloud nine with his eyes closed, holding the small piece of aluminum foil in one hand and stroking his penis with the other hand. Suddenly, he thought he heard something. His eyes flashed open. He focused on hearing. Dread stood frozen, his dick still in is hand. He thought he heard something again. *Shit! The DEA is following me,* he thought. *But damn, that might be Jazz.*

Dread was paranoid, thwarted by a ruse. Mother cocaine influenced fun and games.

Next, Dread thought he saw something, his eyeballs slowly rolling from side-to-side. "Shoo!" he murmured; his ears popped. "Get away from me!" Dread quietly ordered the ghost. He was way out there, now coasting in Seventh Heaven.

This time Dread really did hear someone enter the men's room. He peeked through the crack between the stall door and the stall wall. A short, red-haired, middle-aged White man wearing bifocals whistled a cheerful tune. Dread thought he felt something crawling on his leg. "Oh shit! Get off me!"

The whistling stopped.

Scarlet Tears

"Go 'head, now, and get off me!" Dread shouted again.

"Hey, are you okay in there?" the red-haired man asked from outside the stall.

Busy brushing away imaginary critters, Dread didn't reply. He then peeked through the crack again, noticing the red-haired man had stooped to see under the stall. Dread thought he felt something crawling on his back. He jumped up and down; he yelled at whatever was on his back to get off. He quieted. He breathed hard. Then he demanded, "Get off me I said! I ain't goin' to jail!"

"My God, you're totally nuts in there," the red-haired man shared.

Dread suddenly heard the men's room door open and close.

Inside the dimly-lit stall, Dread started brushing his shirt and arms off again, now combating a new set of imaginary bugs. He'd forgotten about Jazz in the dining area of the restaurant, and his appetite had faded. All of this was inspired from a blast of *good girl*, a pale whore that would soon vanish.

Having spilled the remainder of the cocaine, Dread glared down at the floor. The cocaine dissolved in what appeared as a tiny pool of urine. His spirit saddened. Dread looked . . . and looked . . . and looked. *Man, she's gone*, he silently mourned.

Returning to his fractured senses, Dread thought about Jazz. He quickly pulled up his underwear and pants, flushed the aluminum foil and straw down the toilet, exited the stall, walked to the face bowl, and washed his hands. Dread looked into the dull mirror placed above the elderly face bowl. He inspected his face. *Damn, I gotta get myself together.*

****

Dread returned to the dining area. He took a seat at the table. While eating, Jazz looked up from his meal. He peered into

Dread's eyes. They were red, signaling problems and uneasiness.

"How long our brea----" Dread sneezed. "Damn! My bad." Dread peered up into Jazz's eyes. He sniffled and quickly glared down at his steaming breakfast. "Has breakfast been out long?"

"For about four minutes." Jazz paused. "Yo, you cool, derrty?"

"Yeah. I'm str, straight. J, Just feelin' uh l, lil weary dhis mor, mornin'," Dread responded. He sniffled again.

"Your ass wore out from them freaks. One thing I've learned is to appreciate some good rest." Jazz inserted a forkfull of cheese omelet into his mouth. "And what took you so long in the restroom?"

Dread hesitated before answering. "I ain't tryin' to spoil yo' breakfast, but since you asked . . . I had to do da number two."

Jazz didn't buy Dread's reply. He saw and sensed much more.

"Damn, sorry to hear that," Jazz said, his mouth full of food. "Dread, are you going to eat or play with those eggs and pancakes all morning?" Jazz swallowed. He smiled and rubbed the bottom of his nose with his thumb.

****

Dread didn't like the idea of Jazz rubbing his nose. He believed Jazz was teasing him, removing his veil without permission. This was an insult. Dread sat trembling, desperate for another fix. He struggled trying to gather himself, his spirit searching for cover. Jazz's radioactive waves were too much. They stung with a surge—more like a critical mass—the spark that would detonate a chain reaction of hostilities.

"You s, see. . . . It, it, it's fu, funny, huh," Dread stuttered, his tongue numb and lips fleeing in opposite directions. Jazz's nose-rubbing had pissed Dread off, and small beads of sweat set on the tip of his nose.

Scarlet Tears

"Naw, derrty. I just figured you were hungry." Jazz looked like he wanted to laugh.

"Anyway, wh . . . what d, do you wanna t, talk 'bout?" Dread asked. He felt weird, yet the anger in him grew rapidly. Looking around, Dread noticed other patrons looking at him and Jazz. This was a breakfast engagement Dread wanted to evade.

"We're mature men, right, Dread?"

Dread shook his head yes.

"Hold on. Let me get Salvador's new number before I forget." Jazz placed his fork on his plate then unclipped his two-way pager from his belt.

Dread unfastened his cellular telephone from his braided leather belt, scrolled through its memory for Salvador's telephone number, and placed the cellular telephone in front of Jazz. Personally, Dread had no desire to say another word.

After storing Salvador's telephone number in his two-way pager, Jazz thanked Dread and re-clipped his two-way onto his belt.

"Dread, I want to briefly discuss Mahogany with you."

Ah shit! I be damned! Dread said to himself. His heartbeat increased. His left hand twitched.

"It's nothing personal, derrty. Better yet, let's go sit inside my ride."

****

Having paid for breakfast, Jazz and Dread sat inside Jazz's luxurious foreign automobile. Dread's nose continued to run. Jazz offered him some Kleenex which was inside of his glove compartment.

"Right on, derrty," Dread said.

Jazz's Lexus LS430 featured a powered moonroof, cream-colored, heated leather seats, and wood paneling of a soft, golden hue described as bird's-eye maple. Gadgets were everywhere. The sumptuous styling of the LS430's cockpit was awesome, and the engine was unbelievably quiet. Dread was in Lexus Heaven.

"Dread, if I wasn't considering marrying Mahogany, I wouldn't even approach you with this. I'm the first to admit that I love her." Dread gazed out the passenger window while listening. "I haven't discussed you to Mahogany, and I don't intend to. I figured you and I could settle this like derrties. I'm aware that you're feeling her, Dread. That's all good, though. You got that right, derrty. But as real niggas, it's about respect." Jazz paused. He made sure Dread was awake. "Saint Louis might be a big city, but the circles we fuck with is sort of small, my nig. There's nothing going on in this city that niggas like you and I ain't gonna find out about."

"Yeah, I feel you on dhat, Jazz," Dread replied. "But I ain't feelin' yo' br, broad like that. An, anyway, I thought we were g, getting' ready t, to talk dope."

"Don't trip. We'll get there. But between you and me, let's keep it love like, derrty."

"Love like? N, now I know you ain't tr, tripping off no p, pussy, Jazz. You got me f, fucked up, man. But I'm w, wit' dhat if it's g, gone make you f, feel better. And I was only sc, screamin' at yo' broad 'bout promtotin' some concerts at her g, gig, derrty." Dread paused. "It w, wasn't like I w, was goin' behind yo' back. I had been meanin' to tell you I met her." Dread paused again. "On e'erythang, you sh, shouldn't be worried 'bout her 'cause sh, she's a g, good broad, homie."

Yeah right! Nigga please! Jazz thought aloud. He felt pressure, aggression towering, then remembered it was a full day he had planned. "I'm sure she'd appreciate the compliment, Dread," Jazz said. He turned up the blower to the A/C. The temperature outside was already eighty-four degrees. "Well, that's that, derrty. So let's move on." Jazz paused. "As I told you at the store, Dread, I'm leaving the game alone. It's been one, derrty. A nigga can't last forever out here pushing ki's. We're fortunate to have lasted this long." Jazz extended his arm to give Dread some dap, his diamond bracelet sparkling in the sunlight shining through the moonroof. "Later on this evening, I have a little work

Scarlet Tears

I'ma give you on the love tip, derrty. It's yours. You don't owe me anything. So expect a call from me around six. You should be up by then."

****

Dread's spirit brightened with joy. Jazz's cessation was the most beautiful words he'd ever heard. Acquiring some free drugs was a moment to rejoice, and Dread knew Jazz was a hefty giver. A smile enlivened Dread's face. Also, a part of Dread didn't want to collapse Jazz's empire for the DEA. He figured there just had to be another way. Dread was being stretched out of normality, pressured by both good and bad.

TWENTY-SEVEN

Everything was moving along fast; time had purchased itself a pair of roller skates. Jazz had fallen in love, and marriage was the theme he'd adopted.

Now sailing west on Highway 40, Jazz listened to the soothing tunes of music great, Kenny G. His thoughts were intense sentiments of affection, an exaggerated excitement of love's mystery. He enjoyed the infancy of adoration, the beginning stages of passion; it was all a dream of idealistic romance, a medieval tale of chivalry.

Thank God for woman, Jazz sung to himself.

Throughout the course of the previous week, Jazz had been studying his romantic compatibility. To his surprise and delight, he'd embarked upon the perfect match—Mahogany. Mahogany was a Taurus, born May 2, 1978. Jazz was a Capricorn, born December 25, 1974. He was a Christmas baby, a God-gifted present from Santa Claus. Ho! Ho! Ho! The ladies loved him.

Exiting on South Lindbergh, Jazz drove to Plaza Frontenac, Saint Louis's shopping center for the wealthy, rich, and famous. It was shopper's paradise, a dwelling where the word price was ignored.

He walked inside of Tiffany & Co., an elegant jewelry store. A pretty, stylishly dressed White female sales representative approached Jazz. Her smile was golden. The tone of her voice was pleasing. She was a magnet, the kind of woman a man could never tell no.

"And your name, sir?"

"Knigel," Jazz answered with a smile.

"Let me guess. You're searching for a woman's ring."

Jazz paused before responding. "That's correct."

"Would it be for a birthday present, engagement, or wedding?"

"An engagement."

The sales representative smiled and congratulated Jazz. "Do you have a particular type of ring you're interested in, Knigel?"

"Well, her magical birthstone is an emerald, but I'm more interested in a solid, clear diamond. From there it's pretty much whatever catches the eye, ma'am."

"I take it she's a Taurus."

Jazz shook his head yes.

"My mother is a Taurus." She paused. "I must admit that they're great women. Oh, by the way, my name is Dolly."

"Dolly as in Dolly Parton?" Jazz asked. He focused in on Dolly's breast. *Well, they're nice, but not Dolly Parton's,* he thought.

The saleswoman smiled as she followed Jazz's eyes. "Okay, let me show you these, Knigel." Dolly unlocked one of the store's glass jewelry cases and removed a dark-green, velvety ring tray. "These are some of our favorite designs in eighteen karat gold. And those on the left side are brilliant cut solitaires." She paused, looking at Jazz. "They're really some super rings. I'm sure she'll be happy."

Jazz carefully examined the left side of the ring tray. "Can I see the third one from the top, please?"

"Certainly. That is a gorgeous piece."

Dolly removed the scintillating ring from the ring tray and handed it to Jazz. Holding the beautiful ring, Jazz imagined how it would appear on Mahogany's caramel finger. The image was beyond compare; it was the ring of choice. He flipped over the price tag.

"I really like this one. Will you tell me more about it, please?"

"Sure," Dolly replied, retrieving the diamond ring from Jazz. She slid it on imitative, dark-green, velvety ring finger. "Its colorless diamond is the most popular style of cut, which is the brilliant cut, a round stone with fifty-eight facets.

The solid diamond weighs three, point twenty-six carats, and it's a VS1. The band is eighteen karat white gold and a size six." She paused. "Overall, it's really a fabulous solitaire."

"Yeah, something is telling me this is the one," Jazz said. He glanced at the other rings, again. "What if it's the wrong size?"

"That's no problem. Just bring it back, along with your fiancée, and we'll gladly size it up for you." Dolly smiled. "Is her ring finger near the size of mine?"

"Yeah. They look about the same."

"Well, it'll probably fit her. I wear size five-and-three-quarters."

"Fine. Go ahead and ring it up, please."

"Okay, I'll wrap this up real nice and pretty for you. And would you like to see if you'll qualify for one of our finance plans?" she asked. "It'll only take a few minutes."

"No thank you, Dolly. I'll pay six thousand in cash and charge the remainder on my credit card."

"Fantastic!" Dolly replied. "You must really love this woman. She's very lucky, I'd say. However, our jewelry comes with a great warranty."

Dolly explained the warranty. She polished the ring and wrapped it. The ring cost a whopping $22,158.39 with tax. This was kid's play to Jazz. His total assets were worth well over three million dollars.

Leaving from inside Plaza Frontenac, Jazz returned to his Lexus LS430 on the busy parking lot. Once inside his vehicle, Jazz started the engine. He lowered the windows, allowing the heat to escape. Jazz then dialed information on his cellular telephone. He wanted the telephone number or an automatic connection to Ruth's Chris, a leading, upscale restaurant in Downtown St. Louis.

Now connected with the restaurant, Jazz arranged for a private candlelight setting. Reservations were for seven o'clock p.m. Jazz was preparing the stage for a romantic outing, a dreamy night of wooing and poetic rapture. To the apex of his ability, Jazz thirsted to unleash his innermost. Love had scooped Jazz in its glory. Jazz was in a lofty castle, a

Scarlet Tears

mental state of magnificence and grand beauty. Everything had become perfect; error was extinct. It was an exalted feeling Jazz prayed would always last.

Anyhow, it was approaching noon, and Jazz had promised his daughter he'd spend some quality time with her that day. This was a Saturday Jazz had taken off from all business. Life was twofold, both personal and business. Jazz was aware of such, and he knew that a balanced life paved a sacred path for a merry heart. Jazz was definitely changing for the best.

Driving south on Tower Grove, in South St. Louis City, Jazz conducted a U-turn and parked in front of his daughter's home. From the 1800 block to the 2600 block, Tower Grove was a tranquil street, spoiled with greenery and well-maintained brick houses, condominiums, and apartments. He called inside and informed his daughter's mother that he'd arrived to pick up his daughter. Jazz was asked to step inside for a moment, because his daughter wasn't prepared to depart. Therefore, Jazz exited his car and headed for the concrete stairs leading to the front door of the home, a situation he often tried avoiding.

The door opened.

"Yeah, don't trip," Dina, the mother of Jazz's daughter, said. "I know it looks good."

Jazz agreed with Dina, gazing at her oiled, creamy soft skin and glossy lips.

"Oh, so you just gone stand out there?"

Awed by the beauty before him, Jazz entertained recollections of he and Dina's sexual escapades. His heart functioned to a new drum. Dina was totally irresistible, a persuasive force of womanly satisfaction. She was ghetto fabulous, the sweet taste of banana taffy. Many of times, Jazz tried peeling Dina from his thoughts, but she was invincible—unable to conquer. Irrefutably, Dina was the cream and secret thrill that married men chased, the ones with pockets full of cash.

Stepping inside of Dina's home, Jazz stood there, his penis enlarging. He could not abstain from gazing at Dina's pulchritude. Dina stood five feet, three inches tall. She had one hand on the front door doorknob and the other on her hip. She wore a sheer lime-green matching G-string and bra; her toenails and fingernails were the same color.

"Goddamn, Dina! Baby, what's up with this?" Jazz smiled. "So you're going to do me like this, huh?"

"Nigga, please! You know you miss this shit."

Jazz could only laugh as he peered down at the bulge in his pants. "Yeah, he misses you. But you still ain't right." He held both of Dina's long, braided ponytails in his hands. "What's up with the Native American look, the long eyelashes, and the green contact lenses?"

Dina closed the front door. "Some shit I know you like. So don't play, nigga. And do you ever forgive? I've told you I was sorry for the dumb shit I did. Besides, I was young as fuck." She gazed at Jazz's lips. "Gimme a kiss, stranger."

Jazz wanted to refuse, but Dina's amatory majesty, lustrous-brown skin complexion, kiwi-strawberry fragrance, and comeliness were capturing.

"Whew, them lips of yours are still softer than ever," Jazz uttered, gripping Dina's juicy ass cheeks. "Damn, I can't keep doing myself like this." He let go of Dina's butt cheeks, yet she continued to grip the hump in his pants. "Let go of my dick, baby. A brother is trying to get himself together. And where is Lil Jazz?"

"She's in the bathtub. And don't you have the nerves. Nigga, you know you can't take this pussy," Dina retorted. "So, quit stunting like you're all that." Dina reached for Jazz's penis, again.

Damn, I still love this crazy ass broad. I knew I shouldn't have come in, Jazz argued with himself.

Sexually aroused, Jazz tried smothering his resistance. He desired Dina, gazing at the thickness of her bulging, shaved vagina. Dina's G-string didn't bear privacy. The holiest of holiest would have never said no. Dina was more than a *Georgia Peach*; she was even more than a *dyme piece*; Dina was a walking hurricane, the hydrogen in an H-bomb . . . BOOM!

"So, what's up, Jazz? Are you gone let a bitch get hers or what?" Dina asked with both of her hands on her hips.

"Girl, yo' ass is something else," Jazz said as he pulled Dina closer to him, allowing her to kiss and lick on his neck. Dina's breath was warm, so exciting. Jazz slowly rubbed Dina's soft, curvy buttocks.

"Hold on for a second, Jazz." Dina yelled and told Knyla, Jazz's daughter, to go straight into her bedroom once she exited the bathroom. "Baby, are you ready for this?"

"Of course. But I must tell you something important."

"Uh-huh! Hell no! Tell me when we finish."

"Dina, wait a sec," Jazz stressed. He quickly stepped back from Dina's sexual attack, suddenly noticing two new tattoos on her lower legs. "Seriously . . . what I'm about to say is very important." Jazz paused. He stared into Dina's eyes. "First of all, my love for you has never wavered. But both of us have always been on two different times. No, I'm not claiming to be an angel, but what you did was the ultimate," he said. "Hold your head up, sexy. What's done is done. I've been forgiven you for that, and I'll never stop supporting you and my shorty as long as I'm able. But anyw----"

"Hold up a minute. I just wanna ask two questions, nigga."

"I'm all ears, Dina."

"One, you always talk that shit about we're on different times. Then why in the hell do you keep fucking me?" She paused, crossed her arms across her chest, and poked out her lips. "Two, if you've forgiven me, then why can't we get back together?"

"Like I said, Dina, I still love you, and I always will. And yes, your sex is the greatest. But things will never be the same if we get back together."

"Boy, you're full of shit. And you got some strong ass nerves coming up in here stalling me. Niggas be praying to suck this pussy, let along fuck it."

"I feel you on that, Dina." Jazz smiled, his eyes refocusing on Dina's breast and vagina. "Honestly, I just considered myself keeping it real with you."

"Yeah whatever! Nigga, I see what you're staring at. Anyway, go ahead and finish." Dina rolled her eyes. "I wanna hear you out on this one."

"I'm preparing to get married."

Dina's breathing came to a halt. "Uhhh, run that by me, again."

"I'm making plans to get married, so I'm trying to do right, Dina. I'm sure you understand."

Dina looked into Jazz's eyes with a deadly stare. "You're preparing to marry me, right?"

"Come on now, Dina. Don't do me like this."

"Quiet, nigga!" Dina quickly raised her hand in front of Jazz's face, gesturing for him to shut up. "What bitch are you trying to marry?"

"She's not a bitch, Dina. And you don't know her."

Dina removed her contact lenses. Tears welled in her eyes.

"Dina, I apolog----"

"Motherfucker, you mean to tell me you gone defend another bitch in my house!" Tears streamed from her eyes; the pitch of her voice increased. "How are you going to do me like this, Jazz? As much as I've stood by your side, nigga. We've been dealing with each other since high school," she sobbed. "That's almost nine years, Jazz. Nine whole fucking years, nigga." Sniffling, she cried intensely. Seemingly, life was no more. "You know I love you," her voice quivered. Tears were now pouring from Dina's eyes like a waterfall. "And I've honestly been waiting on you." She burst into a howling cry.

"I know, Dina. And come on, baby, and stop crying." Tears welled in Jazz's eyes. "I'm so sorry about everything, Dina. And I promise to always help and take care of you." He attempted to wipe away the tears from Dina's face.

"Nigga, get yo' goddamn hands away from me!" Dina exclaimed, smacking away Jazz's hand.

"Okay now, Dina." Jazz stared at Dina's red, mean eyes. "Let's keep the peace, here, please?" he said calmly. "Just give me Knyla, and I'll leave."

Jazz was completely aware of Dina's temper tantrums; they were tools she had used many times before.

"Motherfucker, get yo' fake ass out of my house before I stab yo' bitch ass!" Dina yelled, now the queen of ghetto rage. She took off towards the kitchen. "My daughter ain't going nowhere with yo' sorry ass!"

Jazz placed his hand on the front door doorknob. "Come on now, Dina. Cut it out, girl. Knyla has nothing to do with this. Besides, my mother is waiting to see her."

Dina stopped instantly in her tracks. She picked up a ceramic saltshaker off the glass dining table and flung it at Jazz. By inches, it missed his face and crashed into the front door; bits and pieces shattered everywhere.

"The hell if she doesn't has anything to do with this! And fuck you and yo' momma! You ain't *never* taking my daughter 'round none of them bitches! Get out!" she screamed at the top of her lungs.

"Dina, take a chill pill. What in the hell is wrong with you? We can talk this out, girl. And leave my mother out of this."

"Punk, I ain't talking shit out with you! I said get out!"

Jazz heard Dina yank open a drawer in the kitchen. Utensils clatterred. Goose pimples appeared on his arms. Suddenly, Dina came after him with two, shiny butcher knives. Jazz's eyes grew larger. He stormed out the front door and dashed to his car.

"Trick, don't call here no more nor come by with yo' pussy sucking ass! And I hope you and yo' bitch die in a car wreck!" Dina yelled while standing in the doorway.

Terribly bad, the ghetto needed love, too.

Standing outside of his Lexus on the driver's side, Jazz shook his head in disgrace. Dina had temporarily lost her mind; nothing mattered anymore. Jazz knew that she was optimistic of reuniting with him, yet he couldn't keep his magic stick out of her slip & slide.

He stood gazing at Dina's gorgeous body through the glass screen door. She still held the knives in her hands.

Shit, when will her fine ass ever get over the hump of acting like a damn fool, being so fucking ghetto? Sex isn't everything, but damn . . . that shit is good, Jazz thought aloud.

Knyla, staring out her bedroom window at Jazz, waved good-bye. With plaits and ribbons hanging from her head, she shared the prettiest smile. Jazz knew that Knyla's grandest dream was for him and Dina to get married so they could live happily together as a family. She was her father's angel, Daddy's baby girl.

Jazz waved at Knyla, tears seeping from his eyes. Knyla was his only child and best friend. Through her smile, Jazz could sense the pain in Knyla's heart. He became confused, questioning becoming engaged with Mahogany. Jazz wanted to give his daughter the all of him, and Knyla craved for his everyday affection.

If I could put aside pride, Dina, Knyla and I could live a good life, Jazz thought, now sitting inside of his car. *After all, Dina has always been there for me through thick and thin, even with her sleeping with my father. Shit, she was only seventeen.*

TWENTY-EIGHT

"Hello."

"Hey, what's up, baby?" Jazz asked.

"Oh nothing. I'm just looking forward to you picking me up this evening."

"Mahogany?"

"Yes, I'm listening."

"Can you be ready by three o'clock instead of five? I've made plans for you to meet my mother."

"Yes, I can be ready by then," she said. "So, how has your day been going?"

"Busy, busy, busy."

"Is that good or bad?"

"That's a good thing, love. Three o'clock it is, then."

"Okay, I'll be waiting, Knigel."

It was four minutes after one o'clock p.m. when Jazz ended his telephone call with Mahogany. Dim visions of Knyla fired at his calm. Jazz had planned to take Knyla shopping and out for lunch. He'd also planned a trip to Six Flaggs Over Mid America and an evening movie for Sunday. Well, it wouldn't happen that way. If Knyla was depressed, Jazz was depressed. He knew that his predicament with Dina needed to be reconciled, *fast.*

Jazz decided to have his car washed, although it was already shining. He stopped at a car wash not far from Dina's home. While waiting to have his car washed, Jazz called Lil Salvador, an attempt to get a feel for his mindset.

"Yo, what's popping, derrty?"

"This Jazz?"

"Fo' sho, derrty. It's been a while, Salvi. Everything copacetic?"

Scarlet Tears

"Fo' cheesy, my neezy. Just been hangin' tough on this side of da bridge."

"I got your new digits from Dread. He said you said to get at you."

"Hell yeah, my neezy fo' pleezy."

Jazz laughed. "Hold up, derrty. What's up with all this neezy and cheesy lingo? You been out to the West Coast or sitting around listening to Snoop Dogg all day?"

"A little bit of both. Naw, I'm just kiddin'. Anyway, you know how it go, Jazz. Niggas always changin' in this ga-heezy."

"I hear you, derrty. So, when can I holler?"

"Let's say Tuesday. Uh, about two in da afternoon. And I been tryin' to get at you, my neezy. But somehow I could never get through."

"Yeah, that's cool, Lil Salvi. And I'll call you around one to make sure it's to the good, derrty."

"Fo' cheezy, Jay-sneezy."

"All right, stay up, derrty."

Talking to Lil Salvador, an East Side hustler, had become an adventure. Lil Salvador was a money-getting whoremonger with dark, long hair. He fluently spoke Spanish, and the women in his small community of eight hundred citizens praised him. Lil Salvador was twenty-four years old and the father of twelve children by nine different mothers. Salvi was the preeminent *beef slinger* of his poverty-stricken community, the male whore of Babylon.

Notified that his car was clean, Jazz glanced at his platinum-cased, casual Perrelet watch with gold rotary hands. An hour had passed since Jazz first arrived at the small car wash. He paid for the car wash and tipped the three young men who washed his car. Although associated with the underworld, Jazz was a gentle, yielding fellow.

Jazz thought about driving home and freshening up before traveling to Mahogany's house. He decided different; that would have made him late for his three o'clock arrangement. Jazz examined himself and figured everything was fine. Besides, he wanted Mahogany to see his house, his palace of pleasure.

It was seven minutes to three o'clock p.m. when Jazz arrived in front of Mahogany's house. He was impressed by the engrossing beauty of Mahogany's neighborhood, a community that was a taste better than his. The trees were healthy, trimmed, and green. All the lawns were well maintained. Quietness resonated through the community, except for the colorful birds' evening songs. There was no debris, anywhere. All the neighbors wore smiling faces. It was a wooded, stress-free community filled with heavenly characteristics, a duplicate of *Pleasantville.*

Jazz dialed inside and informed Mahogany that he was waiting outside of her home. Mahogany asked Jazz to come inside, because her parents wanted to meet him. She assured Jazz that it would only be for a few minutes. Jazz felt obliged to acquaint himself with his possible, future parents-in-law, an occasion he had recently imagined.

"Good evening, Knigel," Mahogany said, holding open the front door to her home. "And please come in."

"Good evening, love. And you're prettier than ever. Oh, and thanks for the excellent directions." Jazz leaned over and kissed Mahogany on the cheek.

"No, I thank you for being able to follow directions. And you look very well, yourself." Mahogany shut the front door.

"I appreciate the compliment. But we're gonna stop by my home, first, so I can get prepared for our date. I've been on the run since early." He paused. "That's if you don't mind."

"Of course not, Jazz. I'm all yours this evening. Come on . . . follow me, so I can introduce you to my parents. I've told them all about you."

Jazz walked behind Mahogany, gazing away. "I must admit I'm a very lucky man."

Leading Jazz by the hand, Mahogany looked back and flashed a smile.

"Mom . . . Dad, this is Knigel Wennington. And, Knigel, this is my mother, Mrs. Brown. And my father, Mister Brown."

Mr. Brown stared at Jazz from his recliner then stood to his feet and shook Jazz's hand. "How are you, Mister Wennington? And it's a pleasure to meet you, for I've heard a lot of terrific things about you."

"It's a pleasure to meet you, too, sir. And I've also heard a lot of good things about you."

"Well, hello there, Knigel," Mrs. Brown said as she stood up from her his-and-hers recliner. She shook Jazz's hand. "You certainly appear to be everything my daughter said you were."

"I will accept that as a compliment, ma'am. Therefore, I thank you, and I'm delighted to meet you."

Encouraged to speak proper English, Jazz wanted to land a good first impression. He knew that Mahogany's parents didn't acquire their upper middle class status and their exemplary possessions through mediocrity and self-defeating behavior. Unquestionably, Mr. and Mrs. Brown was a set of parents Jazz desired to call his mother and father-in-law. They were a team of love, the exact picture Jazz had mentally drawn of him and Mahogany.

For nearly five minutes, Mahogany's parents and Jazz conversed in the family room, discussing their occupations, college life, and long-term goals. Supposedly, Mahogany was upstairs adding final touches and feeding her angelfish and GloFish.

"All right, I'm all ready, Knigel."

Jazz stood up from the cream-colored leather couch and expressed his farewells to Mr. and Mrs. Brown. Mahogany kissed her parents good-bye and gestured for Jazz to follow her.

"Excuse me for a minute, son. Before you leave, I want to share something with you."

Jazz turned around. "Yes sir, Mister Brown."

"If you all don't mind, I'm going to share this with Mister Wennington amongst the all of us." Mr. Brown paused. He muted the television with the remote control and walked closer to Jazz. He removed his eyeglasses. "Knigel, you're preparing to exit this home with my pride and joy. You're the first to have ever done this. This is my only child, and she's sacred to me. With this in mind, my son . . . I ask that you take great care of her while she's in your company." Mr. Brown firmly placed his left hand on Jazz's shoulder. "I know that you know my daughter's an invaluable gem, therefore defend and treasure her as if she's the last." Mr. Brown dolefully looked at Mahogany. "Take care, sweetheart. And please be safe, you all."

Mahogany smiled at her father. A tear seeped from her right eye. True love flowed, depiction of a wonderful feeling.

"I fully understand you, Mister Brown. And I promise to share with Mahogany the best of me."

Mrs. Brown couldn't handle anymore. The moment was a dramatic eve of loving-kindness. She covered her face with her hands and walked off to the hall bathroom. Mrs. Brown was apparently heartsore, maybe even afraid of the word "promise."

Walking down the driveway, Jazz said to Mahogany, "You, guys, are a very close family. And both you and your mother are quite sensitive. So, this really is your first time dating someone. Without a doubt, my dear . . . you are a rare breed, a beautiful young lady who I'm honored to know."

Mahogany looked Jazz in the eye. "Why thank you, handsome. And I appreciate you opening the door for me. Gentlemen rule, I'd surmise."

"My pleasure, my caramel-covered strawberry."

"Hmmm, sounds delicious," Mahogany replied. She blew Jazz a kiss.

Before driving off, Mahogany and Jazz waved at Mr. and Mrs. Brown standing in the huge family room window, their smiles half-mast.

"This is a fascinating car you have, Knigel. It's so you. So, are you crazy about foreign luxury cars? Because my father sure is."

"Yeah, I favor foreign luxury cars over American luxury cars. There just seems to be more to them."

"It definitely rides nice. Sort of feels like my father's Q Forty-five."

"I thank you, love."

"You know, to be age twenty-six, you've acquired quite a bit. I'm positive that's inspirational within itself."

"Yes, it has its highs and lows, but certainly more highs. Really, it's not all that difficult to obtain nice things if a person knows how to go about achieving them. Everything's a system of requirements. Meet the requirements, and in most cases, it's yours."

"Sounds logical. And you speak with so much confidence. I like that in a person. College taught us that having self-confidence was a prerequisite towards becoming successful."

"Oh, no doubt. Without it, a person is destining for failure."

"Tell me about your parents, Knigel."

"Well, my mother and father is age forty-two. They're presently separa----"

"So, your parents were only sixteen when you were born?"

"That's perfect math, Mahogany." Jazz smiled.

"I'm sorry for interrupting. But please finish."

"That's okay." Jazz smiled, again. "They're currently separated. My father is an electrical engineer for AmerenUE. My mother is an in-house accountant for Ralston-Purina. They both acquired their secondary education here in Saint Louis. Uh, let me see . . . my mother is very humble, thoughtful, sensitive, love listening to the oldies, not very outgoing, and for some reason don't have many friends. Now, to explain my pops, I'll sum it up in two words. Overly adventurous."

"Interesting. I'm eager to meet them."

Coasting along, Mahogany and Jazz continued to brief a variety of subjects. They were compatible, two hearts but one love. Jazz valued this with all his heart and did not intend on allowing Mahogany to meet his father any time soon. His father was a scar in his life, the opposite of a California dream. Howsoever, Jazz understood the significance of forgiveness. He, too, was a member of flawed humanity.

Having made it to his home in Paddock Forest, a hilly suburban subdivision in Florissant of St. Louis County, Jazz slowly drove up the driveway. He pushed a button on the control panel. The door to the right side of his two-car garage began to rise. The exterior of Jazz's house was built with brown brick. The front yard was well manicured and perfectly landscaped. Paddock Forest was a hidden middle-class locality of beautiful houses and winding, clean streets, a lofty center of Black Pride.

Jazz and Mahogany entered the house.

"Whoa! Look at this," Mahogany said. "The inside of your home is gorgeous. It must have cost you a mint. And who's the decorator? I'd love to meet her, for there's such creative excellence here."

"'Her' died with yesterday. You're looking at him."

"Did you really? If so, your taste is unusually phenomenal. In person, I've never seen a home decorated with such splendor. I'm sure your next venture is the start-up of your own interior design consulting firm."

"Great idea. But not me."

"It was only a compliment. Anyway, can I see the rest of your home?"

"For sure. Follow me."

Jazz gave Mahogany a tour of his home. She adored every square foot of it. Jazz was an aesthete, infatuated with the colors of royalty, precious arts, collector's items, and odd furnishings. With Jazz, Mahogany had found herself a woman pleaser, her personal amusement park. Jazz was stimulating, the encouragement women desired.

"Oh, look at this. I'm sure your daughter hates to leave her bedroom. It's like a fun center in here."

"Yeah, this is her hang out when she's here. I enjoy her being out here, too."

"So when can I meet her? I know she's adorable," Mahogany stated while gazing at a picture of Knyla.

"I'd made plans for you to meet her, today. But her mother wasn't having it."

"Baby's momma drama, hey?"

"No, not really. But that's another story. Hey, feel free to roam as you please. I'm going to hop in the shower and change for the evening."

"Okay, thank you!"

Her personal tour having ended, Mahogany decided she'd wait in Jazz's library/study room, the thinking quarters of his budding empire. It was a place where Mahogany would learn more about Jazz, the molding of his thoughts. Inside of Jazz's chambers, there were two modern computers; a fax machine; a paper shredder; common office supplies; two antique desk lamps; a set of filing cabinets; beautiful, stained hardwood furniture and shelving; maps; a globe; a film projector; a telescope and more. It was an ideal atmosphere for the construction of a master plan, and there was a broad variety of interesting books.

Jazz possessed books concerning the world's conspiracy theory, spirituality, Greek philosophy, Egyptian philosophy, health, poetry, business, self-help, effective writing, politics, world history, psychology, including two types of encyclopedias and four different dictionaries. Jazz was sharp-witted, a young loner of wisdom. Earth and its heavens was Jazz's playground, the learning center of his divine journey.

"Oh, here you are. I've been searching all over for you."

"Finders keepers, losers weepers," Mahogany said, reading a collection of poems by Jazz, titled *Purple Butterfly*.

"Do you like any of them?"

"No, I downright love them. Your poems are so crafty, original, filled with emotion." She paused. "How long have you been a poet?"

"I've been writing poems and short stories, now, for about three years."

"Why haven't you had this published? I know a lot of people who would cherish your works."

"It's coming, love. It's coming. But I think we better get a move on it, because time is in a hurry, today."

Mahogany laughed. "Well, you sure look nice and exquisite." She paused. "How about a kiss?"

Jazz hesitated, his facial expression bearing confusion. "Uhh, I just didn't hear the word kiss, did I?"

"Yes, I asked for a kiss. So how about it?" She eased up to Jazz.

Jazz loved Mahogany's gentle, spontaneous aggressiveness. It set him afire. Jazz embraced Mahogany and kissed her with a passion more intense than Michael Jordan's love for basketball. He dreamt of a bed stop, an occasion to make love all day and all night long.

"Oh, my God. Let me slow up," Mahogany said. "I don't know what just came over me."

Feeling the warmth of Mahogany's body temperature, Jazz said, "Yeah, I think we both are a little excited."

"Can I share something with you, Knigel?"

"Certainly. Consider me as your vault of secrets."

"How sweet. Nonetheless, I think I'm falling in love with you," she confessed. "I have these queer feelings that keep giving me the butterflies. But I enjoy it when they strike me."

They were the words Jazz yearned to hear.

"That's some good news, I believe. And that makes two of us with odd, but pleasing feelings. But let's get out of here so you can meet my mother."

Jazz's mother lived only ten minutes away from him in Black Jack, an adjacent community to his own. Black Jack, North St. Louis County, was a nice suburban subdivision with homes ranging from $99,000-210,000. It wasn't Paddock Forest or Barrington Downs, an upscale African-American inhabitant with lush everything. Yet, Black Jack was a safe, distinguished neighborhood in its own fashion.

"Well, this is my mother's pad."

Scarlet Tears

"This is another fine neighborhood," Mahogany stated, looking from house to house. "I didn't realize so many African Americans were living this good in Saint Louis. All you hear about our people is negativity."

"Yeah, there's a purpose and reason behind everything. But I'll fill you in on that one a while later. Right now, it's all about us."

"I agree. And how about another kiss?"

They kissed, such an act of affection becoming standard.

Walking up to the front door of Jazz's mother's house, Jazz and Mahogany held hands. They shared trust; they shared effort; they shared sincerity; it was reciprocity at its finest.

"Well, hello, my son," Jazz's mother spoke. She then hugged Jazz. "And this must be Miss Mahogany. Because you look exactly as my son described you . . . beautiful."

"Hello. And thanks, ma'am."

"Well, I'm doing just fine, y'all. But let's get something straight right away, doll." Jazz's mother paused with a smile. "Call me Claire and nothing more. And what would you like for me to call you, dear?"

"Mahogany."

"Okay, Mahogany. Give Claire a hug," she said. "You're an attractive, young something. You remind me of myself when I was your age."

"Thanks, Claire."

"Knigel, where's my granddaughter?"

"You might need to discuss that with Dina. I tried. But things didn't go as planned."

"Oh lord! Who knows with that chic. You can tell me later. So, what's on you, guys, agenda for the evening? You both sure look nice in your clothes."

"We're going to enjoy some dinner, and from there, it's wherever the stars lead us."

"Well, I sure hope you, both, enjoy yourselves. It's always fun and exciting in the beginning."

The day was developing for the best. Jazz was getting everything completed in a timely fashion. Mahogany was Jazz's inspiration, the revolution of his sometime porous behavior. From Jazz's observation, Mahogany and his mother were going to get along fine. He watched them closely as Mahogany and Claire became acquainted. Jazz was aware of his mother's signals of disapproval. There weren't any. There were plenty of smiles and spontaneous laughter, the sign of a future to be.

Jazz looked at the time on his Swiss-made Patek Philippe dress watch with special cut baguette diamonds. He suddenly remembered to contract Dread. It was five, thirty-eight p.m., and Jazz wanted Dread out of his life. Jazz politely excused himself from Mahogany and his mother. He walked into the garage. There, Jazz called Dread via cellular telephone and obtained what he'd promised Dread.

"Dhis Dread."

"You woke, derrty?" Jazz asked.

"Yeah, yeah. What up, Jazz?"

"Just keeping my word, Dread."

"Damn, I had uh good sleep."

"I feel you, derrty. But here's the dealy. It's five, forty-three, and I need to see you at S-two in twenty minutes. No later, derrty. So get a move on it."

"I'm on dhat. See ya in twenty."

Jazz raised the garage door. He exited the garage with a rolled-up, brown paper bag in his hand. The voices of children playing echoed through the warm air. Both the sun and winds were friendly, complementing a sensational day. Jazz tucked away the brown paper bag in his car and walked back into the garage. He lowered the garage door and re-entered the kitchen. The aroma of microwave butter popcorn streamed into his nostrils.

"Excuse me for a minute," Jazz said. "I'm going to make a quick run, so do either of you need anything back from the store?"

"No. I'm fine, son."

"How about you, Mahogany?" Jazz asked.

"No thank you."

"I'll be right back, love. And, Mom, keep my angel smiling."

"Boy, go where you have to go. It's ladies time, anyway. You're disturbing us. Isn't that right, Mahogany?"

"Yes. Mothers know best."

Jazz smiled at his sweetheart. Mahogany was so special to him. He left, now traveling to meet Dread. Exciting thoughts of Mahogany were constant. She was the spark who had ignited his soul. Jazz was illuminated with joy, caught up in the rapture of love, his heart slowly turning cartwheels. Everything seemed faultless. Life was merry. Jazz had found someone new, someone he deemed an angel, someone he wanted to hold in his arms for life all time.

Turning onto the parking lot of Popeye's Famous Fried Chicken at the junction of Lucas and Hunt Road and Halls Ferry Road, Jazz noticed Dread walking inside of the restaurant. Jazz didn't blow his horn, an attempt to not attract any attention. He parked next to Dread's burgundy Chevy 1500 and called him on his cellular telephone.

"Yeah."

"I'm out here, derrty."

"Okay. In a minute. 'Ey, don't forget to call Lil Salvi."

"Did that already, derrty," Jazz said. He ended the telephone call.

Popeye's Famous Fried Chicken wasn't crowded. Dread soon exited the fast food restaurant carrying two bags. There was a smile on his face, and he was wearing a Sean John sweat suit. Dread looked fairly fresh, three times better than that morning.

Abstaining from the obvious, Jazz stepped out of his car as Dread opened the driver's side door to his pickup truck. Jazz handed Dread the brown paper bag and walked inside of the restaurant. The handoff went smooth, easy as one-two-three. Jazz ordered some spicy chicken and buttermilk biscuits. He was playing it all the way through.

****

Driving south on Halls Ferry Road, through Jennings, Dread aimed for the inner city, the abode of disorder and ruptured thinking. It was where Dread felt most comfortable. He picked up the brown paper bag and read the message Jazz had printed on it: *Thanks for everything, especially your staying true to the game. Be easy, derrty. And soon find a better way in life. Every book has an end.*

Dread appreciated the message but gave it no true consideration. He was only interested in the bag's contents. Dread opened the bag. It was 1.5 kilos of cocaine inside of the bag, given free as a token of Jazz's appreciation.

That nigga Jazz really is a good dude, Dread thought. *There ain't another nigga in the city who would have did this. Damn, I hate to pop that boy off. Fuck it, though. Better him than me.*

Dread was a lost case, a foot soldier of disgrace. He was happy, running free with a license to "ball" and destroy African-American life. Dakar Sanford was a vermin, the ophidian of dissolution. So . . . say hello to an ugly situation—the very face of Revelations 12:9.

TWENTY-NINE

"I'm back, Ma. Where's Mahogany?"

"I don't know. She left here walking a short while after you left," Claire yelled from the rear of the house. "She's pretty steamed right about now. I had to tell her a thing or two."

"Okay, you're kidding me, right?"

Claire walked into the living room. "Tricks are for kids, son."

"Surprise, Knigel!" Mahogany uttered from behind the front door. Her eyes and lips were now enlivened with cosmetics.

"Well, looky-looky. And, Ma, this must be your work?" Jazz reasoned, gazing at Mahogany's face.

"Yes, you know me. Just figured we'd have a little fun while you were out."

"It all looks good on you, baby."

"Thank you," Mahogany said. "I was unsure if you'd like it or not."

"If my mother supports it, then you can best believe I love it. She knows me better than anyone."

Jazz brought everything to a conclusion. It was time for him and Mahogany to depart. Jazz felt his greatest. Dread was now a thing of the past.

"I smell chicken, but maybe I'm just hungry," Mahogany said, sitting in Jazz's car.

Jazz hesitated before responding, thoughts of his previous drug deal racing through his mind. "Do you? Maybe I need to hurry up and get to the restaurant so you can get your grub on."

"Okay, let me fasten my seat belt, first."

Scarlet Tears

"That wasn't to be taken literally, Mahogany."

"I know, I know. I'm just having fun."

Yes, Saturday, July 8, 2000, was monumental. The date was off to a good start. Mahogany and Jazz were great together, companions in a grand love scheme. No doubt about it.

Arriving in front of Ruth's Chris, Jazz and Mahogany were assisted by the restaurant's valet. They walked inside the restaurant, holding hands. Confirming reservations, Jazz and Mahogany were led to their private setting. It was seven o'clock sharp, and Ruth's Chris was alive with business—big-timer style.

Time had lost its meaning; love was the power that is. Mahogany and Jazz gazed at one another through the glow of burning candles that set on their table. The reflection of the candles' flames danced through the sparkling glasses of water. It was a classic, private outing of sincere affection. Mahogany and Jazz wanted one another for nothing more than who they were as a person. Seemingly, nothing could break them apart.

Having decided what to order, the match from Heaven placed their order with the waiter. They, both, had an appetite, and the aroma of fine foods was teasing. However, the special feel of love kept hunger in its cage.

"Knigel, do you want more children?"

"Yeah, I wouldn't mind having a son. That's one of my desires. Why do you ask?"

"I was just wondering."

"Is it that you want children?"

"Yes, I wouldn't mind in the future."

"Mahogany, tell me . . . please . . . exactly how do you feel about me."

"Is that a question or a command?" Mahogany smiled.

"Is it fair to say that it's a mixture of the two?"

"Well, since you insist," she said. "I think you're an excellent thinker, well-mannered, the ideal man and very understanding. But I do believe there's a side of you you're keeping from me. And don't ask why. It's just a hunch I have."

Damn, I knew she was figuring that, Jazz thought. He took a deep breath. "It's a joy to hear those words, and I feel the same about you. But I don't believe you're hiding anything from me."

"Of course I'm not. That wouldn't be fair."

"Pardon me, Mister and Mrs. Wennington. Here's dinner as ordered. And be careful of the plates. They're very hot."

"Whew! It smells good and looks delicious. And thank you, sir," Jazz said.

The waiter finished serving dinner. He smiled and excused himself.

"Mister and Mrs. Wennington, hey. That doesn't sound bad," Mahogany said.

"It does have a ring to it. Maybe that's telling us something."

"We shall see."

Jazz and Mahogany put a damper on speech. It was time to eat. Dinner consisted of steaks, barbecue shrimp and more. It wouldn't take Jazz and Mahogany long to get full, one steak was actually enough for them both.

Jazz reached across the dinner table for Mahogany's hand. He asked Mahogany to listen carefully as he read her a poem:

Mahogany,
Our brick road is golden,
It's covered with red rose pedals,
There's a wind as gentle as cotton,
And my love is happily ablaze,
A love growing deeper and stronger,
Therefore . . . inspiring these happy days;
Truthfully, so beautiful . . .
Is the Sweet Land of Love;
Doves are soaring,
Maneuvering through the cloudless heavens,
Blooming is our every tree,
Because wonderful is the beauty in we;
O', how magnificent . . .

Scarlet Tears

Is the Luscious Land of Love;
We are the perfect pair,
A couple everlasting,
Romance will be our bond,
The power of our magic wand,
We'll live to understand,
To always hold each other's hand,
Hereby, it's blessed . . .
Our union of woman and man
Amazing and so divine . . .
Is the Majestic Land of Love;
Darling,
There is a holy place,
A God-given home,
I pray we forever embrace,
It is . . .
The Glorious Land of Love;
Now kneeling in your presence,
Acknowledging you're my queen,
I raise my hands to a lofty star,
Wanting to always be where you are,
So, Mahogany . . .
With me wholeheartedly adoring you,
Will you please marry me?
Will you let my dream come true?

Mahogany was touched, stroked, floating in fantasy. She cried, gazing into the eyes of her proposing king.

"Knigel," she paused, "I wonder what my parents would think and say about this, although my heart is your heart."

"It's okay, Mahogany. I'm sorry if I've startled you."

"Yes, I'm a little surprised, because it's so early. And will you please stand up, my favorite poet in the whole wide world. I need a hug."

"My pleasure, love. I didn't think my proposing to you would trigger such an emotion."

"How could you not? It's one of the most important questions a woman could be asked."

"I understand, love."

Jazz and Mahogany stood hugging one another.

"You know, it's been only three weeks we've been spending time together," Mahogany said. "But I do feel very close to you. It's like we belong together."

"I agree, baby. You couldn't have said it any better."

"Yes . . . I'll marry you."

"Thank you, Mahogany. Thank you, love. You've just made me complete."

Jazz hugged Mahogany tighter. She cried in his arms, baptizing the occasion in the name of love.

"Excuse me, Mister and Mrs. Wennington, is everything fine?" the waiter asked.

"Yes it is. We're just sharing a moment in union," Jazz answered, tears slowly dribbling down his cheeks.

"Do you mean union as in marriage proposal?"

Jazz nodded yes, softly rubbing Mahogany's back. Mahogany lay her face against Jazz's neck, wetting his neck with tears. She was love-shocked.

"Well, congratulations to you, both. I look forward to this day, myself," the waiter commented. "Gosh, I can feel the love in this room."

"Thanks a lot, partner."

"All right, I'll check back in a while. Have fun!"

Jazz gave the waiter a thumbs up. He reached into his front pants pocket and removed the ring case. "Hold up for a minute, Mahogany."

Mahogany let go of Jazz. She stepped back.

"A proposal wouldn't be official without the ring." Jazz flipped open the ring case.

Mahogany smiled, gazing at the sparkling diamond ring. She then looked at Jazz, reflections from the candles' flames grooving on her pupils. "It's so beautiful. And it must have cost you a fortune."

Scarlet Tears

Jazz removed the ring from the case and placed it on Mahogany's ring finger. It fitted perfectly. Mahogany hugged Jazz, again.

"For better or for worst, I'll always stand by your side," Jazz uttered.

"I love you, Knigel. And you can best believe I'll be the best wife I can possibly be. I understand troubles may come, that relationships have rainy days." She paused. "However, I'll keep my head high, knowing that the morning sun will rise again. I love you, Knigel. And I don't ever want to lose you."

"I believe you, sweetheart. And I promise to be the best—and only—husband you'll ever have and desire. Honestly, I thirst to keep you smiling, to keep you inspired, to keep you focused on your goals."

THIRTY

Monday, July 10, 2000

When Dread woke in the morning, his head ached. He looked at the mirror-covered ceiling in his bedroom and for a moment could not remember where he was. Dread raised himself to sit on the side of the oval-shaped bed, massaging his temples. His clothes and tennis shoes were lying across the floor. The tennis shoes were still laced. A Colt nine-millimeter set on the nightstand, along with a wad of cash and an ounce of cocaine. The light was on in his bedroom. Dread had no recollection of taking off his clothes or what took place the day before. Firing his handgun was the last thing he remembered. Dizzy, naked, Dread was three lives away from death. His breath was atrocious, associated with the *dragon family*.

Finally realizing where he was, Dread thought about what to do with his hangover. He figured drinking a cold glass of water or making his self regurgitate would do the trick. Dread passed on them both and lied back down, saliva stains on his pillow. His head was spinning like a Ferris wheel, distorting his picture of reality. Dread was off to a bad day.

Ring . . . ring, the home telephone rang. Dread wished it would stop ringing, yet he reached over and answered the telephone.

"Good morning, Dakar. It's ten, thirty, and it sounds like you're still asleep. I've been calling your cellular phone all morning. You know, Dread, sleepers accomplish nothing. You're still with us, aren't you?"

"I'm sorry, Mister Harlington. Yes, sir, I'm still in. I've been workin' on somethin' over da weekend. Gimme two or three hours, and I'ma call you back wit' some good info."

"Well, Dread, the boys and I will be looking forward to that call. We're ready to roll. Yahoo!"

Lethargic and unhappy that he couldn't live his own life, Dread removed himself from bed. He waddled to the bathroom, stumbling over his Nike tennis shoes. Inside the bathroom, Dread caused himself to vomit. It was a funky mess; however, he immediately felt relieved, the dark clouds absconding.

Dread's head still hurt. Howbeit, it was time to produce. And no—*Dread wasn't footloose.* He was committed to the DEA and responsible for condemning Black life, although the individuals he was targeting were already involved with self-destruction. Who knows? Jail has saved many lives. Snitching was double-faced, a product of the Holy Bible.

****

Leaving work for her lunch break, Mahogany met Jessica at Houlihan's inside Union Station, downtown, on Market Street. Union Station was an extravagant facility, a wonder of St. Louis. The grandeur of its architecture was commanding. It was a major tourist attraction, energized with a broad variety of shops and popular restaurants.

"Mahogany, it's too crowded in here. Let's go upstairs and eat."

"That's cool, but I sure had a taste for some popcorn shrimp," she said. "Jessie, the unbelievable happened Saturday night."

"Exactly what could be so unbelievable, Mahogany?"

"Knigel proposed to me. Can you believe it?"

"Girl, whatever!"

"I'm serious, Jessica. Look at my ring. It was so romantic."

Jessica gazed at Mahogany's sparkling diamond ring. "That's a very nice ring, Mahogany. I take it you said yes."

"Yeah, I said yes. I honestly think everything will be fine."

"You don't think it's too soon?"

"I thought about that, but I'm all in now."

Going up the escalator, Jessica looked Mahogany in the eyes. "Well, congratulations, Mrs. Too Soon. I can't believe you, girl. You're so naïve, and do you know anything about his background? And what do your parents think?"

"As far as I know, his background is excellent," Mahogany replied, stepping off the escalator. "And I haven't discussed this with my parents, yet. But I'm thinking about telling them, tonight." Mahogany paused and stared at Jessica. "You're not mad at me are you, Jessica?"

"Girl, naw. And excuse me if I sound like a hater. Remember, honey, we're friends for life."

"I was just checking."

"However, Mahogany, I truly think you're moving a tad too fast. And what has Jazz done to you to win you over so quickly?"

"Too fast! Jessie, look who's talking. Only Lord knows what you and Austin possibly did in that studio. Sooner or later the truth will surface." Mahogany smiled.

"So, I guess it's tit for tat. Come on, let's order something from here."

"Chinese food. . . . Yeah, that's cool. But never tit for tat, Jessie. Anyway, Jazz hasn't done anything to me. He's just a great person and a charismatic gentleman. And I think my parents really like him."

"Well, if you like it I guess I have to love it. I'm waiting, though."

"As they always say," she paused, "different strokes for different folks."

"Yeah, must be nice," Jessica replied.

****

Scarlet Tears

Ready to show and prove, Dread poured himself another glass of cold water and swallowed an aspirin. He was determined to rid his headache. Dread then helped himself to a piece of cold chicken from inside the refrigerator. He laughed at himself, knowing he was losing his mind.

He picked up his cellular telephone off the kitchen table and called Lil Salvador. *Fuck it. I gotta start somewhere,* Dread thought.

"The real deal! Holla at me."

"Salvi, what's poppin', derrty?"

"These hoes, dominoes, and gettin' that dough. So, are you in or fleein', Dread. Holla at ya b-zoy."

"Nigga, I'm in. You know I love some East Side pussy, and my middle name is dough."

"Act like it then, Dre-heezy, and hit that bridge."

"I'm wit' dhat. But check it out, Salvi. Anybody cool over dhere on da work? It's dry like uh mutha over here."

"Yeah, I know a couple of lames with some shi-zit. What you talkin' 'bout?"

"Eighteen hard, derrty. Dhat'll be cool until da weekend when our shit gets in. I wanna check it out first if dhat's all right. So I'ma have uh crackhead or two wit' me."

"I can make that happen, and I trust you, Dread. Y'all been good to me. What time you screamin', Dre-sneezy?"

"In 'bout two hours, derrty."

"You got that. Hit me on da h-zorn when you're re-zeady."

"Fo' sho, derrty," Dread said, preparing to disconnect the call. "'Ey, Salvi."

"Yo, what it is, Dre?"

"You talk to Jazz, yet?"

"Yeah. I suppose to get at him tomorrow."

"Dhat's cool. I was just checkin', derrty."

The telephone call ended. Dread wasted no time contacting his family, the DEA. He gave the DEA Lil Salvador's information and arranged with them to bust him. Dread was to meet the DEA soon. He was disgusting, an undercover crime fighter for inadequate reasons, the ugly scab of evil's sore.

There were thousands of Dreads in the Black community across America, those partially responsible for the systematical demise of Black fathers. Howbeit, when would Black men, those associated with nonsense, ever learn and stand up as productive leaders of their communities? Until then, their becoming scarce would never end.

"I'm glad you were able to make it down here, Dakar. Time is ticking, so let's get right down to business." Mr. Harlington looked away. "Excuse me, Mister Sharpinsky, could you prep Dakar for Conspiracy? I'm going to go ahead and lock this bum up we got in the other room. He's interested in playing games with us. It's time to cash in."

Dread was at the DEA headquarters. He was ordered in to help complete planning for the special operation. No details would be withheld; this was serious.

Dread's expertise added the final touches. Mr. Harlington was a foe of faulty intelligence, however, a lover of minority betrayal. This was the ax that chopped down the Black man's progress tree. *Despicable!*

"All right, Dakar. Everything is set. You can now place the phone call. But remember, we need him to mention Jazz and anything about distributing or buying narcotics," Agent Sharpinsky said. "We're counting on you." He winked his eye at Dread and gave him a thumbs up.

There Dread was again, standing at Conspiracy with his tail stuck deep in his rotten ass. Dread was a mangy mutt, far from a competent, uplifting pure breed.

"Salvi it is. Talk to me."

"Dhis yo' boy, Dread. I'm hittin' you back like I said I would. You got dhem eighteen hard for sale, Lil Salvi?"

"Nigga, you know my work. It's thirteen, five in dead presidents, though. Brothers ain't got it like y'all do over there. Think you can handle that?"

"A done deal, derrty. I'll meet you out in front of da Pink Slip in thirty minutes."

Scarlet Tears

"Oh, hell naw, Dre. Meet me at my sister's in the projects. It's safer there."

"You talkin' 'bout where me and Jazz came da last time?"

"Yeah, the same sp-zot, Dre. Hey, are you coming through with Jazz, tomorrow? We suppose to get up around two o'clock."

"I don't know, Salvi. It all concerns on what I'm doing."

"All right then, Dre. Peace out!"

Dread replaced the receiver on its cradle and took a seat in a wooden chair. He held his head down, shaking it from left to right. Dread wanted everything to be over.

Walking into Conviction City, Agent Sharpinsky said, "Boy, does that guy speak fancy. Why in the hell does he put a z in every damn thing? Sure can't wait to meet his slick ass."

"Good job, Dakar. You're starting to ace this thing. Care for a drink or snack?" Mr. Harlington asked.

"No thanks. But what about da money?"

"Don't worry about that. We got that covered. Just keep your cool, son. And let's go fishing for some trophy fish," Mr. Harlington said. He turned to exit Conviction City. "Hey, there's no better feeling than seeing another one bite the dust."

"Hee-haw! I second that," someone blurted from the hallway.

Dread recognized the voice. He maneuvered to see Agent Datino standing in the corridor. "Oh please naw. Not you, again."

"Dakar, save it! I wouldn't miss this for nothing in the world."

"Yeah, I can imagine why," Dread returned. *Fucking redneck,* he said to himself.

It was time for the big show. It was time to bring down the walls. The DEA from the Eastern District of Missouri created a task force with the DEA of the Southern District of Illinois and MEGSI (Metropolitan Enforcement Group of Southern Illinois). Dread and the DEA from the

Eastern District of Missouri cruised down the interstate in unmarked cars, preparing to enter Illinois. The agents were confident, geeked like young students on a field trip. Dread was nervous, still wondering why God hadn't intervened. The agents loved Dread, well, his substantial assistance.

With Blacks implicating one another, the so-called *War on Drugs* was a breeze. The agents adored an easy day on the job; they played smart, not hard.

Now across the Poplar Street Bridge, Dread and the DEA of the Eastern District of Missouri met with the DEA of the Southern District of Illinois near the Gateway International Raceway, three-and-a-half miles from the point of interest. The agents' adrenaline was pumping, kicking out gallons by the seconds. They loved nothing more than a raid, a manhunt, and exertion of power over inexperienced, powerless Black men.

"Hey there. How are you doing, Mister Harlington. It's a pleasure to be fighting crime with you, again. Nothing beats making our world a safer place."

"I'm doing just fine, Lieutenant Wolfe. And I agree that there's no better feeling than bringing down the scums in society. They're an abomination to our value system," Mr. Harlington said. He exchanged handshakes with Lieutenant Wolfe. "Boy," he looked around, "you and your crew sure do look well-prepared for this mission."

Dread sat listening in the back seat of an unmarked car.

"Yeah, we're quite enthused about this one. Oh, let me introduce you to the leading officer at MEGSI." Lt. Wolfe and Mr. Harlington walked over to a tan SUV with tinted windows. "Captain Harlington, this is Captain Gannett of MEGSI. And Captian Gannett, this is Captain Harlington from the Saint Louis branch of the DEA in the Eastern District of Missouri."

"I'm thrilled to meet you, Captain Gannett. You and your group have really been making some noise. And you're a lot younger than I suspected. However, I commend you on the fabulous job MEGSI is doing."

Scarlet Tears

Captain Gannett removed his dark shades. "It's a pleasure to meet you, too, sir. And thanks for the encouragement." They shook hands. "On behalf of MEGSI, I want you to know that we honor this opportunity to work with you and your agents."

"No problem, Captain Gannett. You appear to be a fine fellow. So I hear you and your group is extremely familiar with this neck of the woods."

"Yes we are, Captain Harlington. And I assure you our best effort. Salvador and the rest of the hooligans he hangs around is a growing mob of thugs we've been studying, gathering information on, and watching for approximately five months, now. The make up of their community increases their stay on the streets. Reason for . . . we have no Black agents, besides a list of exhausted informants, who can penetrate the nucleus of their community. Obviously, we stick out like sore thumbs," Captain Gannett explained. "I tell you . . . the tiny village is a closely-knitted hell drowning in illegal activities. You name it, and it's there. From the mayor on down to the smallest children, they're all committing serious offenses. It's really a disgrace."

"Go ahead, tell me more, Captain. This is interesting."

"What we've been missing is what you have. That's someone who can rub elbows with the major players in Brooklyn. Salvador Henry is a great place to start according to our intelligence. He's an influential street icon who has deep ties with local police and politicians. He and the rest of the thugs buy their way out of everything. Hopefully . . . this mission will mark an end to that shit."

"Is everything he's telling me correct, Lieutenant Wolfe?"

"He's right on the money, Captain Harlington. But that's just for beginners. I'll tell you more about Little Las Vegas, later. Right now, let's review the info you faxed us and overview this map for positioning. We cannot fail on this mission. There's too much at stake." Lieutenant Wolfe paused. "With that in mind—it's time to get busy."

D. Allen Miller

Dread listened on, not allowed to exit the car. He sat next to an African-American undercover agent who was assigned as his partner in crime. The DEA didn't want to risk exposing their hand before the buy; precautions were crucial. Dread trembled with jitters as the undercover agent he sat next to counseled him. They sat in a blue, 1998 Nissan Maxima. The agent said it was seized from a former drug dealer. That's exactly how the Feds flexed, capturing drug dealers with their own cars, kind, testimony, money, and drugs. It was the biggest racket known to humanity. Nevertheless, the blind couldn't see.

Dread was afraid of federal prison. There was where a number of his enemies dwelled. The BOP was an eerie system of indifferent institutions that seemingly housed inmates forever. Prison was a perilous place, overcrowded with treacherous, deceitful, scheming malefactors. Homosexuality was becoming the norm. Gobbledygook suffocated progress. There was no guarantee of returning home. Dread knew this and had heard many horror stories about cooperating inmates, *snitches*, designated to the same institution with those they helped convict. Unmerciful violence was reality. Dread was petrified of this. Therefore, Lil Salvador and Jazz had to go!

THIRTY-ONE

Dread and the undercover agent waited in the parking lot of Lil Salvador's sister's apartment. They were late, waiting on Lil Salvador to arrive. Small children were running around everywhere. Loud music blasted throughout the government housing project. Empty beer bottles rolled across the parking lot. Graffiti-covered plastic trash bins were turned over on the sidewalk, and uncut grass maimed the landscape.

Lil Salvador was on his way. Dread had just spoken with him on his tapped cellular telephone. He had given the DEA full consent to whatever they wanted to do. Both Dread and the undercover agent were wired for sound, ready to make it happen.

"Uh-oh! Dhat's him pullin' into da parkin' lot," Dread said. "Remember, you my homie. And you wanna buy a quarter ki hard. But let me do all da talkin'."

"I got you, Dakar. But try and keep everything in the open, so I can capture it all on the camera attached to my belt." The undercover agent paused. He handed Dread a small paper bag of marked money. "Is he by himself? And don't forget the code word, expensive. That's the signal for the raid."

"Naw, it's anotha head in da front seat. And I ain't forgot da code word. Trust me . . . I know what to do. All right, play it cool. Dhey pullin' up on da side of us."

"Yo, what's cookin', Saint Lou?" Lil Salvador said. He exited a black 1998 Cadillac Seville with chrome wheels.

"Da same ole, same ole, derrty. What it be like?" Dread replied, stepping out of a fairly new gray Chevy Malibu.

"It ain't shit. Just livin' by da pager. And nigga, what happened to thirty minutes?"

"I got tied up for uh sec, and I was waitin' on my derrty to show up. He wanna buy a quarter ki hard. Think you can take care of dhat, too?"

"Yeah, it shouldn't be a problem. I think my sister's nigga got that inside the crib. But it's gone cost him seven g's. C'mon, let's go inside. I think I saw some narcs a few minutes ago."

Dread paused; he took a deep breath, nervousness invading. "'Ey, Salvi, is it cool my nigga come in? He got seven on him."

"As long as he's straight, it's to da good," Salvador answered. He took a toke from his joint. "Dre, you wanna hit this?"

Dread passed on the marijuana and signaled for the undercover agent to exit the car. Lil Salvador was in for a huge surprise. He had just invited in the DEA. His ass was grass, burnt toast on a Monday evening. There would be no butter, no jelly, nothing easing the pain. Hoodwinked, Lil Salvador was in a Venus flytrap. The entire area was swarming with U.S. Marshals, the DEA, and MEGSI, all ready to sting.

"Damn! I just know they ain't fucking, again. They were fucking when I left," Lil Salvador complained, leading his friend, Dread, and the undercover agent into the dining room.

A woman's moan sounded from upstairs. Then there was a male voice asking whose it is. Something bounced steadily against the floor upstairs. "Stroke it! Stroke it, Big Daddy!" the woman uttered.

"That chubby ass fool must have had took some Viagra. Y'all excuse them, and let's make this quick," Lil Salvador continued. He then asked everyone to hold tight while he goes upstairs.

The undercover agent looked around, noticing roaches that weren't afraid of light. These bad boys were bold and healthy. Apparently, they had been around for a long time. Roaches and government housing were allies; they abetted one another in the psychological art of human degradation.

"Yo, bro, what's yo' name?" Lil Salvador asked as he stepped off the last stair. He was holding a large Ziploc plastic bag in his left hand.

"Who? Me?" the undercover agent asked.

"Yeah you."

"Gr, Gregg."

"You all right, my brother? You seemed a lil nervous when I asked you that. And let's do this, y'all. My boy said I can serve those additional nine ounces."

"I'm solid, my brother," the undercover agent retorted, his eyes roving from the Ziploc plastic bag brimmed with narcotics to the gun handle sticking out of Lil Salvador's front pants pocket. Perspiration quickly appeared on the undercover agent's forehead.

Dread didn't like what was taking place. He sensed danger and wished he was wearing a bulletproof vest.

"Gregg, I hope you don't mind yo' package being half soft and the other half hard," Lil Salvador said, staring at the undercover agent as if he was trying to make a read. He set the Ziploc plastic bag of cocaine ounces on the glass dining table.

"Yeah, he's cool wit' dhat," Dread butted in. "And here's my money fo' mine."

"Kelton, come over here and help me count this," Lil Salvador asked his friend who was still getting high.

Kelton walked to the table, smoke expelling from his nostrils. He looked at the undercover agent and Dread. His eyes were red like fresh strawberries. The undercover agent began making sudden movements, seemingly losing his cool. Kelton kept his eyes on the undercover agent, though keeping quiet.

"Do y'all wanna weigh this shit up? I got a scale in da clo-heezy. And what happened to da crackhead who supposed to test this P-funk?" Lil Salvador asked.

"Nigga, you know I trust you. So it whuttin no need for uh dope fiend. Besides, derrty, Jazz wouldn't be fuckin' wit' you if you was shady."

"I feel you, Dread." Lil Salvador looked at the undercover agent. "And where's yo' scrilla, playa? So I can count everything up."

The undercover agent removed a wad of one hundred dollar bills from his pants pocket. He withdrew five of them. "Must be some good stuff, because it's expensive," he said.

"Yo, Dread, where ya man from? He sounds more like a working man than a baller."

"He's from my hood, Salvi. He's just uh lil more on da educated side. You know, one of dhem low-key hustlers."

"Is that right? It's a cold world out here, Gregg," Lil Salvador warned. He set his gun on the glass table, took a seat and began counting the money.

"Hey, do y'all hear that?" Kelton asked. "It sounds like a helicopter flying right over us."

Dread rubbed his hand across his face. "Damn, Kelton, dhat must be some good ass weed you hittin'." Dread paused. "I don't hear nothin'."

Suddenly, something rammed against the rear door. Trembles ripped through the apartment building. Maybe it was an earthquake. Then there was a loud bang, again. Kelton took off for the front door. Lil Salvador sat froze with his hand on his gun. He stared at Dread and said, "You muthafucka!"

"Get down on the floor, now! Right now, goddamn it before I shoot!" a man yelled wearing full raid gear. "This is a fucking raid!"

A swarm of law enforcement agents flooded the apartment. The smell of marijuana hung in the air, and dense smoke from Kelton and Lil Salvador's spliffs fogged up the apartment. The terrifying image of the small army of bloodthirsty agents, their large caliber weapons drawn, was chilling. A wrong move by anybody would have spurred disaster, reflecting the Battle of Wounded Knee, the heinous massacre of a small group of Native Americans by the United

States Army. The days of government-lead cruelty was only a tick away, the Black community its target.

Lil Salvador kept still, his hands in the air. He stared at Dread and the undercover agent. Salvador then peered into the pitch-black barrel of the leading agent's .45 caliber Glock and slowly rolled out the chair onto the floor.

Dread, standing next to the undercover agent, sunk to his knees with his hands in the air. His body shivered. Wavering images of retaliation zoomed in and out of his mind. Several agents ran upstairs, and another agent dashed after Kelton. Kelton had now made it out of the front door.

"Freeze, you sapsucker!" Dread heard someone yell in front of the apartment. Looking out the front door, Dread saw Kelton stop and drop to the ground. There was a wall of law enforcement outside the apartment with deadly weapons and a barking canine. More than likely, marijuana had Kelton a few steps slow, even lost in a damaged state of Heaven. Kelton was forced out of his fantasy, a vision of a getaway. Lying flat on the grass, Kelton's tears watered the earth.

Gregg, too, was on the floor. He smiled at Dread. Dread didn't like that, wanting to spit in the undercover agent's face. Shit was fucked up!

Soon, Tasmine, Lil Salvador's sister, and her boyfriend were escorted down the stairs wearing handcuffs. Tasmine was practically naked. She had on a silver bra and panties set. Dread gazed at Tasmine from the floor, wishing he could fondle her perky round breast. Tasmine had a slim waistline and a Brazilian complexion. She was a work of art, the fantasy of a White man's dreams. Tasmine and her overweight lover, who was wearing orange boxers, were ordered to lie flat on the floor.

"Jesus Christ! Whose ass is that?" a tall White agent, DEA written across his chest, said as he entered the apartment's front door. "I mean let's cover this girl up with something. We can't just have her lying on the floor like that."

All of the crime-fighting agents laughed.

"Okay, boys, let's search this dump in and out," Lt. Wolfe said. "And will somebody please run a nationwide check on this blob wearing orange boxers. Here's his I.D."

The agents searched the apartment up and down, along with the assistance of two drug-sniffing canines. They eventually found two kilos of cocaine hydrochloride with an estimated street value of $144,000, sixteen pound of marijuana, drug paraphernalia, $137,000 in drug money, two scales for weighing drugs, four automatic weapons, false identification, and the narcotics associated with the controlled buy. The seizure of such contraband, along with relevant conduct and possible criminal history, would easily secure life sentences under the U.S. Federal Sentencing Guidelines in the Southern District of Illinois.

Ooo-wee! Their asses is out, Dread thought.

"Well, do I have good news," a DEA agent said. "This chunky boy in orange boxers is wanted in the Eleventh Circuit for murder and drug charges. His real name is Lloyd Fleming, a.k.a. Big Boy. He's from Fort Lauderdale, Florida, and has been on the run for seven months, now."

Big Boy looked at Dread, tears coasting down his cheeks. He knew he could now kiss freedom goodbye--forever.

"Well, isn't that fortunate. Birds of a feather certainly flock together," Lt. Wolfe said. He then gave Captain Harlington five.

Kelton was brought back into the apartment. He wore handcuffs and was told to lay face-first on the floor. The agents had found a half-ounce of "black tar" heroin, $2,600 in drug proceeds, and a .380 semiautomatic handgun on his person. Kelton was Fed bound, in trouble deeper than deep.

There was only a single option available for the four arrestees to ever see daylight again. That was to sell their very souls to the U.S. government. The United States government wouldn't settle for anything less. The walls must come falling down.

Lil Salvador was raised to his feet. Urine had darkened the color of his light-blue jeans. Lil Salvador was escorted towards the rear door of the apartment. He looked back at

Dread before exiting the apartment. *How could you do this to me?* his facial expression asked.

Dread held his head down, unable to keep looking at Lil Salvador. At that instant, the spikes of betrayal gouged years from Dread's life. Dread thirsted to remain on the streets, and he silently said, *It's better him than me.*

Black man, Black man, when will you ever win? This was the pleading wail of the ancestral brave, the untamed lions of African descent.

Dread was then raised to his feet and taken outside to an awaiting car. He could not believe how many people were outside watching the drug bust. Dread felt embarrassed, unfit for nothing. He looked up into the sky. There was a helicopter hovering over the scene. A small group of children stood near the car where Lil Salvador sat. They were waving and crying.

Really, it was a disappointing day for the small children of Brooklyn, Illinois, America's first chartered all African-American municipality. Lil Salvador was one of the only individuals in the entire community who would always lend a helping hand, his money, and provide quality recreation for the children, regardless if the chips were up or down. Local citizens looked upon Lil Salvi as a sign of hope, although he was affiliated with madness to the utmost degree. Lil Salvador's behavior was typically confusing, jammed in a crossfire between good and bad. Dread knew all of this, but nothing mattered when it came to his fractured life.

Two deputy U.S. Marshals also escorted Tasmine, who was now clothed, and Big Boy from the apartment in handcuffs to a waiting prisoner van. Older women and men of the community, those who had probably been secretly calling the drug tip hotline with concerns about drug trafficking and violence in their neighborhood, held their hands up to their face in disbelief. Regrettably, Tasmine was guilty by association.

As Tasmine was loaded onto the white, tinted-window van, a woman who favored Tasmine ran towards the van. The woman looked sad, now waving goodbye. A small boy and girl who looked as if they were Tasmine's children stood next to the woman. They were also crying and waving goodbye. Apparently, these children had no steady father; all they had was their Mommy. Tasmine was now being hauled away like a piece of livestock, fear and distress written across her beautiful face.

Witnessing the arrestees' agony, the impounding of their vehicles, and the federal and state agents' blatant disrespect of the African-American community, Dread figured an early voyage to his grave—and that's without a coffin and funeral—wouldn't be a bad idea. Being burned by misgivings, the Holy Voice within Dread shouted with ire: *Look at the difficulty you're causing, the very indecency you're promoting. No one has ever done this to you. Why not accept your responsibility?*

The arrests of Lil Salvador and Kelton capped a five-month investigation by the DEA of the Southern District of Illinois and MEGSI. Salvador and Kelton were now facing extreme federal gun and drug trafficking charges within one thousand feet of a protected location. They would be compelled to *sing, sing, and sing.*

Arresting Tasmine and Big Boy was a huge bonus, two more reasons to cheer at the suburban pub that attracted members of law enforcement, defense and prosecuting attorneys, and court employees. The power structure dominated, them ever supporting the extinction of indigents and the feeble. The agents all lit large cigars. It was a remarkable day hunting African Americans.

THIRTY-TWO

Tuesday, July 11, 2000

It was five minutes before one p.m., and Mahogany stood in the lobby of Adam's Mark Hotel. She had been rewarded with an early day off from work with pay. As of yet, Mahogany's job performance was superb. She had been bringing in new business by the herds.

Gazing out the hotel's huge, shiny glass window, Mahogany saw Jazz driving under the front pavilion. He was driving his Cadillac Escalade. Mahogany exited the hotel through the revolving door, happier than a preacher at Sunday's tithing.

"So, how have your day been going, Casanova?" Mahogany asked, closing the passenger side door of Jazz's SUV.

"Oh no, please don't call me Casanova." Jazz smiled. "That Italian brother had some serious sex issues."

"Duh! And like you don't with all of your good looks and success."

"I take it I'm on trial," Jazz said.

"Yes, you are. But in my court. So express your repentance by giving me a soft, juicy kiss."

"Show you right. I'm guilty."

They kissed. Jazz then asked Mahogany to ride in her car. Mahogany didn't mind, submitting to Jazz's every known desire. She guided Jazz into the hotel's parking garage. There, they exchanged vehicles. Mahogany even offered to drive, anxious to lower the convertible roof. St. Louis was on a spree for beautiful weather.

Scarlet Tears

****

Jazz looked down at his watch and gave Mahogany directions to Big P's Car Wash on the corner of Natural Bridge and Red Bud. He thought Mahogany's car was dusty, in need of special treatment.

Big P's Car Wash was one of St. Louis' most popular hand car washes, the North Side's stomping ground for ghetto hoo-ha, thrills, and guaranteed replenishment from boredom. Big P's was an everyday action movie, extolled for its unusually great surprises. Regardless of the excitement that surrounded Big P's, it was a car wash known for cleaning cars very good.

Now at the car wash, Jazz said, "Go ahead, sweetheart, and take a seat in the waiting lobby. They have air in there. Trust me, you're all good with me."

Mahogany smiled as she walked away from Jazz. The scent of her perfume was pleasing. Mahogany was turning heads left and right. Jazz liked that; Mahogany was his woman trophy.

Wondering what Lil Salvador was doing, Jazz called him on his cellular telephone.

"My nigga, Jazz, what it be like, my neezy?"

"Just taking it easy like real players do."

"I can ride with that, playboy."

"You're a fool, Salvi. Anyway, are you ready to get at me, derrty? I told you I was gone call you before I cross the bridge."

"Yeah, I'm ready. I got the whole twenty-five g's for you."

"Damn, Salvi! You're tripping, derrty. Phone check, my nig."

"Oh, my bad. Well, I got that and wouldn't mind doin' it again if it's cool."

"We'll discuss that when I get there. And I'm nowhere from you. So don't get lost. I should be there by two, fifteen. It's one, thirty-seven now."

"'Ey, don't come by my sister's. I'll meet you at the Platinum Club or inside my uncle's joint."

"Either one is cool with me, but I got my gal with me. So we have to make it quick, derrty," Jazz said.

"I can understand that. And what type of car are y'all in?"

"I'll be in a gray, convertible Mustang. And if you can, how about meeting me at Venice Mobil Gas Station?"

"All right, I take it you comin' across the McKinley Bridge?"

"Yeah. Two, fifteen, derrty."

"Fo' cheesy, my neezy."

Jazz walked inside the waiting lobby. Mahogany sat watching television. Jazz sat next to Mahogany and kissed her on the cheek. Mahogany blushed.

"So, you're stealing kisses, now, hey?"

"Actually, I thought I was lending you one. That way I'd get two in return," Jazz replied.

Mahogany giggled. She gave Jazz two kisses. They sat for a while discussing one another. Jazz was notified that Mahogany's car was clean. He footed the expense, and they left on their merry way.

Waiting at the traffic light, at the crossroads of Salisbury and Broadway, Jazz and Mahogany held hands. They were happily engaged, one in the same. Mahogany's car was spotless, showroom status all over again. The convertible roof was lowered, and they where listening to "I Wanna Know" by Joe. The lovemaking ballad was comforting, just what the love doctor prescribed. The mood was romantic, a dreamy instant of sweetness.

Mahogany informed Jazz that she'd discussed their engagement with her parents. Jazz was relieved and delighted to know that Mahogany's parents mostly supported the decision. However, Mahogany's parents encouraged them to practice patience. Mahogany and Jazz were wafting in visions of their wedding day, smiling in the castle of love.

The light having turned green, Mahogany proceeded to the McKinley Bridge, a ragged, historic bridge connecting Saint Louis, Missouri, to Venice, Illinois. Venice was a small town, mostly African-American, stifled by political disorder and crime. "This bridge sure does looks old. And why are the streets so battered on it?"

"I don't know. It's been like this for a long time. I hear it's privately owned, but in the process of being closed until further construction. And can you believe we got to pay a toll on the Illinois side?"

"Tell me you're kidding." Mahogany paused. "Jazz, did you feel that?" She paused again. "This bridge is moving."

"Yeah, I did. But be careful approaching the lanes ahead. They're real narrow, and you might want to drive in the outside lane. The middle is a little dangerous."

"Are you sure? It looks like we might fall off in that nasty river if we drive on the outside. And turn off that radio so I can focus."

Jazz laughed. "Watch out, Mahogany!"

Mahogany screamed.

"Damn, that was close. I'm glad you said something. Why in the hell. . . . I'm sorry. Why haven't someone removed that from the street?"

"Beats me. And I'll hate to see somebody run that over."

"You got that right. And can you imagine how the car sounds that lost its exhaust system?"

"Mahogany, you're a county girl. How do you know what that was?"

Mahogany smiled. "Uh-huh, you figured I was just a woman who knew how to drive. Maybe even a suburban klutz."

Jazz leaned over and kissed Mahogany again, his right hand resting on her thigh. "To do so would spark my demise."

"Correct. So, that means you're going to love me, respect me, and compromise with me until death do us part?"

"Certainly. You couldn't have said it any better."

"This is one filthy river. I could never eat a fish out of it."

"I hope you wouldn't. I'm sure they're blind, finless, and one step away from being retarded."

Mahogany and Jazz laughed.

"Here. Toss this fifty cents in the coin collector when you get up there," Jazz instructed.

"Boy, do they have some nerves. If they had any self-respect, they'll be paying us fifty cents for crossing this shabby bridge."

"I agree, baby."

"Baby? Ooo-wee! Today must be my lucky day," Mahogany said.

Having paid their toll, Mahogany and Jazz advanced through the tollgates into Illinois. They were excited in love, looking forward to all the sweet blessings of matrimony.

****

"Yo, dhat's dhem, right dhere."

"Oh, yes it is, Dread. We got Mister Slippery Ass, now. Along with that gorgeous woman he's riding with," Agent Sharpinsky said, more excited than a young child at the arcade.

"Believe and you shall receive. That's why in God we trust," Captain Harlington enlightened, his Masonic ties shining through like points of light. "Make sure you've got him crossing state lines on film, and we'll secure a copy of the bridge's film a little later. Mister Datino. . . ."

"Yes, sir."

"Call Agent Templeton and let him know the culprit is quickly approaching. And I'll contact Lieutenant Wolfe from my phone."

Both telephone calls were successfully made to the members of the task force on standby. Everybody was in position to perform his or her best, eager for some action. Agent Datino, Agent Sharpinsky, Captain Harlington, and Dread sat in an unmarked car with side and rear tinted windows on the bridge's employee parking lot. The joy of catching their man was a feeling untold.

Captain Harlington turned and looked at Dread in the back seat. "Dakar, you're sure enough the man, my main man."

"Okay, Mister Harlington."

"Are you okay, son? It seems like you'd be happy, for you're earning yourself an extension on the streets."

"Yeah, I'm cool, Mister Harlington."

Dread wasn't cool at all, envisioning Mahogany doing time drew flames beneath his feet. Dread wasn't comfortable with the decision he'd made, ever praying Mahogany would be dismissed from prosecution. Mahogany looked so happy and beautiful while driving her car. She was unaware of the poison she'd swallowed. Only if she knew, her fairytale was due for a twist. The greatest test of Mahogany's life had awakened from the dead.

"Dakar, are you sure Jazz don't know about yesterday's bust?" Mr. Harlington paused. "Lil Salvador better be on top of his game, or he and his sister can start preparing for a life behind bars."

"Trust me, Jazz hasn't got da news. Y'all did good by lettin' Salvador and his sister right out. And I told you he'd be ready to cooperate," Dread replied, living by the U.S. Army's slogan: **BE ALL YOU CAN BE!**

****

Driving onto the small filling station service lot, Jazz felt something funny. He looked around the depressing vicinity for abnormal activity and law enforcement. He noticed none.

Jazz noticed Lil Salvador stepping out of a white, four-door Pontiac Grand Am. Jazz then asked Mahogany to raise and lock the convertible roof, to turn on the A/C, to pop the trunk, and to park next to a gasoline pump so he could fill-up her car with premium fuel. Mahogany gave Jazz a suspicious look, but she refused to ask any questions. She just followed the plans of her dearest.

Lil Salvador approached the rear of Mahogany's car with a small bag tucked under his armpit. "What it be like, brother Ja-zazz?"

"You know me, derrty . . . maintaining and always thinking of a master plan," Jazz answered. He gestured Lil Salvador to drop the bag in the trunk.

"Yo, who is that pretty ass broad you flossing with? Does she have a sister? Shit, the little man needs love, too."

"She's my gift from above, the queen of my everything."

"Damn, you talk like y'all married, Jazz."

"Put it like this . . . we're soon to be."

"Well, congratulations. And come on, man, with the pump. You know you gotta pay first over here. You're in the gutter, Jay."

"Thanks for the reminder, derrty." Jazz smiled. "And watch this trunk while I step inside to pay for gas. But don't close the trunk."

"Do yo' thing, playboy. I got you."

Jazz walked inside the service station. He looked back at Lil Salvador. Lil Salvador was giving someone the okay sign. Jazz felt a funny feeling, again. He disregarded it, though, and purchased snacks and gas.

"Damn, Jazz, what's up with all the bottle water and snacks?"

Jazz set a case of bottle spring water and a see-through grocery sack of potato chips and cookies in the trunk of Mahogany's car. He then set the black bag of money inside the grocery sack. "I'm trying not to be too obvious."

"Shit, I knew that. Anyway, can a brother keep his hustle on? Just front me one more kilo, and I'll be cool. After that, I'll start buying my own weight."

Jazz looked across a large field of small weeds and rubbish at a lone car. He peered closer, unable to detect anything fishy.

"Salvi, I got some shit, but I've been chilling lately. Anyhow, I'll call you on Thursday, and we'll go from there. But listen up," Jazz paused, "what goes on between you and me stays between us. No Dread—nobody. And thanks for pumping the gas."

"I understand. And you're welcome, player. I take it yo' gal likes Joe."

"Yeah, she does."

"That shit sounds good coming through the trunk. I might need to go and buy that CD."

"That wouldn't be a bad move. The ladies love Joe."

"All right, Ja-zazz, I'll be waiting on that phone call. And y'all be easy, pla-zayer."

Jazz and Lil Salvador shook hands. Jazz wasn't very sure of Salvador. He had changed as of late. However, business between Jazz and Lil Salvador had been quite profitable. Lil Salvador cherished the ghetto life, while Jazz only used the hood to fulfill his fantasies and increase his net worth.

Driving away from the service station, Mahogany asked, "Knigel, who was that guy pumping the gas? I saw him give the guy he was riding with an okay sign through my side rearview mirror when you walked inside of the gas station. He looked sneaky."

"Oh, naw. That's my man, Lil Salvi. I've known him for a few years, now. He plays softball with a local team over here."

"I was just wondering. And no, I wasn't insinuating anything. Hey, when are you going to take me to one of your softball games?"

"Make a right, here. And that's the ice cream stand I was telling you about right over there to your left. So, are you going to be busy Thursday evening? I got a softball game at seven o'clock at Fairgrounds Park. I'd love to bring you along."

"No. I won't be busy. I can't wait. Can we invite Jessica?"

"Indeed, Mahogany. Indeed."

Mahogany and Jazz drove onto the popular ice cream stand rock-covered parking lot, now listening to Donnell Jones.

"Dang! Look at the dust we've stirred up. I forgot that about this parking lot. I haven't been over here since my other softball friends got picked up by the Feds," Jazz said.

"Don't worry. It's only a car. And the wind will probably blow most of it off once we get back on the highway."

Jazz and Mahogany exited the car. They walked up to the order window of the ice cream stand, named John's Drive-in. Jazz and Mahogany were deep into one another. Their new love was overpoweringly addictive, tasty like the banana split and pineapple malt with extra crushed pineapples they had ordered.

While walking back to Mahogany's car from the ice cream stand, Jazz noticed a red Dodge Intrepid with dark tinted windows parked next to a telephone booth behind the small grocery store across the street from John's Drive-in. Jazz became nervous, observing another tinted-window vehicle slowly cruising up a side street.

"That's the undercover five-o parked across the street," a young woman said, wearing gold rings on every finger and large hoop earrings. "That's the same car I saw when they busted Rusty and 'em."

Jazz panicked, nearly shitting on himself. Something told him not to deal with Lil Salvador. Mahogany's statement about Lil Salvador appearing sneaky suddenly rushed through Jazz's mind. Jazz didn't know what to do, but he didn't want to frighten Mahogany. Therefore, Jazz just went ahead and sat in Mahogany's car, uncomfortable with being on foreign turf. Jazz's appetite had fled.

"Are you okay, Knigel? It seems like something heavy is on your mind."

Jazz didn't reply, his attention in chains. Mahogany started the engine of the car.

"Knigel, what's the matter?"

"Oh . . . nothing. Ju, just got lost in thought for a second," he said sluggishly.

"Man, you had me worried there for a minute. So, are you going to eat your ice cream?"

"Uhh . . . who me?" Jazz asked, staring out the passenger window of Mahogany's car at the Dodge Intrepid parked across the street. Jazz also noticed that the tinted-window car that was slowly moving down the side street had parked on side of the road. Jazz wished for a disappearing act, an outlet to the abode of absolute spirituality. Magic was the power he coveted.

"Knigel . . ." Mahogany called.

He didn't respond.

"Knigel, please tell me what it is that's on your mind." Mahogany touched Jazz on the arm with her pineapple malt and turned up the A/C.

Jazz rubbed his arm. He slowly turned towards Mahogany, still speechless.

"You look sick, Knigel. And your ice cream is melting." Mahogany paused, gazing into Jazz's eyes. "What are you staring at out there? A ghost?"

Jazz didn't reply; he was horror-struck, visualizing everything he'd acquired and accomplished burning in flames. Leaping five minutes into the future, Jazz mentally visited his worst encounter with law enforcement. Such a vision stole Jazz's essence as if a thief in the shadows of the night. Mahogany drove off the parking lot. She made a right turn, heading towards the McKinley Bridge.

"Have I done anything wrong, Knigel?"

"No . . . no you haven't," Jazz answered, resting his aching head on the headrest. He closed his eyes, afraid to look in any rearview mirror. Jazz prayed to that which was in Heaven, pleading for forgiveness of his transgressions and a second chance to make better decisions.

God was listening. But would He/She save Jazz? Would God save Mahogany? Would God save them both? Or would God let the dice roll and stop where they lay? Just hopefully . . . they wouldn't land on craps.

THIRTY-THREE

"All of a sudden, you just stopped talking to me. And I apologize if I said or did something wrong," Mahogany said. "Hey, I wonder what's going on up ahead. There's a police roadblock in front of the tollbooths. I hope nobody has been hurt."

Listening to Mahogany, Jazz nearly fell unconscious. He refused to open his eyes, hoping it was all a big dream. Jazz felt disgusted, disappointed with his self. He could not believe what was taking place. Mahogany was fully ignorant of Jazz's felonious activities; she never thought once that Jazz was associated with wrongdoing.

"Put on your seat belt, Knigel. Just in case this is a random police check."

Jazz said nothing. Jazz didn't move. Jazz kept his eyes closed, sweat flowing through his pores.

"Oh shoot. They're walking towards the car. No problem, though. I'm straight." Mahogany let down her window.

"Good evening, ma'am. My name is Lieutenant Wolfe from the DEA. And we're aware that this vehicle has been used in the commission of a crime. Therefore, will you please put your car in park, shut down the engine, give me your keys, and hand me your identification."

Another member of the DEA knocked on the passenger window of Mahogany's car. Jazz looked; he was spiritless.

"Unlock the door and slowly step out of the car, sir," the agent ordered.

Mahogany and Jazz looked at one another with expressions of fear. Next, they did what they were told.

"Thank you, ma'am. And do you mind if we search your car and trunk?"

"No. I don't mind, sir. Go ahead." Mahogany turned around as gestured. *Damn*, she was handcuffed.

Lieutenant Wolfe gazed at Mahogany. He smiled. "I appreciate your cooperation, ma'am. And we'll try and make this quick. Stay put, though."

Leaning forward against Mahogany's car, Jazz was spread-eagled. The agent searched Jazz, and a wall of backup police officers guarded the perimeter. There was no contraband discovered on Jazz's person. However, following necessary procedures, the agent handcuffed Jazz. Humiliated and frightened, Jazz leaked a twin set of tears from the far corners of his eyes. Then, looking around at all the faces of the bystanders and McKinley Bridge employees, Jazz bowed his head as he was escorted to a waiting squad car.

"I'm going to go ahead and conduct a nationwide computer check on him and her for any outstanding warrants while you, guys, search the vehicle," the agent said, looking through Jazz's brown leather wallet.

****

Dread observed the scene from the rear seat of the vehicle he was stashed in, very unsatisfied with his self. Dread felt like a reject as he witnessed the shame and confusion disfiguring Mahogany's face. In his heart, Dread wanted nothing to happen to Mahogany, but the coward in him wasn't brave enough to defend her innocence. With the malady Dread had orchestrated, he was prearranging severe repercussions for himself. Ominous signs of terror had been keeping Dread awake at night and worried by day.

****

Sitting in the front seat of an unmarked squad car, its windows rolled up and engine turned off, Jazz dolefully peered at the DEA agents searching Mahogany's car. They immediately went to the trunk and pulled out the black bag of money. Mahogany stood outside of her car, conservatively dressed and crying. She looked inside the car where Jazz was temporarily detained in incredulity. Jazz wished he could make it all go away, and tears continued seeping from his eyes.

Jazz was becoming savagely angry with law enforcement. They'd locked him in a vehicle with no air and its windows shut. It was a humid ninety degrees outside, therefore warmer inside. The handcuffs Jazz was wearing were on too tight. With Mahogany witnessing everything, Jazz felt dethroned, lesser than a man. He wanted to burst into rage. *But for what?* He asked himself.

****

"Well, we found nothing more inside the car or the trunk. So what do you want to do with them, Captain Harlington and Lieutenant Wolfe?"

Mahogany stood listening to the agents, terribly displeased with Jazz. Salty-tasting tears continued streaming from her eyes into her mouth and on her clothes.

"Actually, I vote to let them go for now, and we'll re-arrest them once formal charges have been secured here in the Southern District. We have more than enough evidence to validate a conviction. That way, we can put them both under tight surveillance and monitor their every phone call," Mr. Harlington paused. He looked at Lt. Wolfe. "I'm certain there's more to this over on our side of the river, and Mister Wennington is now prone to make a lethal trail of mistakes."

The agent standing next to Mahogany smiled at her. She didn't return the favor.

"Okay, remove Knigel from the squad car so we can take a set of evidentiary shots of him, Miss Brown, and her car," Mahogany heard Lt. Wolfe say.

Mahogany and Jazz had their pictures taken by an assistant federal agent with a Polaroid camera. Onlookers stood and watched. Mahogany didn't know what to say, there yearning the love of her mother and father.

Allowed to leave until further notice, Mahogany and Jazz stopped to pay their bridge toll.

"Homegirl, I wish you and yo' man the best of luck," a dark-skinned, chunky attendant with a pierced nose said. "And keep yo' head up, my sister."

Mahogany thanked the lady attendant and asked her to discard her and Jazz's thawed ice cream treats. Mahogany then proceeded across the dilapidated bridge. She asked Jazz, "Why come you never told me that you sold drugs? And why would you use me to promote your unlawfulness?" she sobbed.

Jazz tried explaining. He apologized and apologized. "Seriously, Mahogany, you have nothing to worry about. They haven't caught me with no drugs or selling any drugs. And I'm going to hire the best attorneys my money can buy if they try prosecuting us. Believe me . . . we're both fine."

"*Us?*" Mahogany asked. "Why not hire an attorney immediately? And please don't include me in your foolishness. I know nothing and would like to keep it that way."

"I understand where you're coming from, Mahogany. But I promise you them officers were only trying to persuade us into making some bogus statements against ourselves. You know . . . the panic squeeze."

"Knigel, are you serious?" Mahogany looked at Jazz with skepticism. "Just listen to what you're saying. Get a grip on it! They found a bag full of marked money in my trunk. Do you honestly think they just suddenly chose to establish a roadblock in front of a toll bridge? Please . . . think for a chance. You're losing me. And I'm sure your so-called friend at that gas station was a part of setting you up."

Jazz was wordless, shocked by Mahogany's frankness.

PART FOUR

My people are tortured; my people are confused; my people are struggling, and many won't change. Therefore, you may find me burdened at my resting place by simply following my long trail of tears.—D. Allen Miller

THIRTY-FOUR

Wednesday, July 12, 2000

Wake up, Mahogany. Wake up, a soft, breezy voice whispered to Mahogany in her sleep.

Again, Mahogany was experiencing nightmares, nail-biting encounters with the scoundrels of death. Mahogany tried awakening, but she was captured in a far-out dream, a mind-bending struggle with Erebus. This particular nightmare was life-threatening, a deadly subconscious duel between righteousness and sin. Sin was screaming victory, drowning righteousness in a contaminated pool of lamb's blood. Desperately, Mahogany wanted out of her dream. She tried moving her limbs and opening her eyes. Horribly, Mahogany's soul was shackled in torture.

Buhn-buhn-buhn-buhn-buhn, the alarm clock in Mahogany's bedroom signaled. Her eyes flashed open. Her body remained stiff. She tried to scream. Nothing. The subconscious battle for Mahogany's soul was violently severe, bleeding into the physical realms of existence.

As if a heavy object had been removed from atop her, Mahogany suddenly began gaining control of her muscles. The first rays of the morning sun slashed through the window into Mahogany's bedroom, freeing her from the hardship of Beelzebub.

Coated with perspiration, Mahogany hurried from her bed. She noticed an unfamiliar odor in her bedroom. Everything was strange, seemingly akin to the paranormal. "Shit! You fucking chair!" Mahogany exclaimed, having bumped the big toe of her right foot on the leg of a chair in

Scarlet Tears

her bedroom. She dropped to the floor and squeezed her throbbing toe.

Mahogany sat on the floor, questioning God about a series of issues. She needed answers, rescuing from tribulation. Mahogany was undergoing the downside of worldly experience, the unsightly faction that played for keeps.

As the pain decreased in her toe, Mahogany stood to her feet and limped into the bathroom. She needed to urinate, therefore hurrying to the toilet. While urinating, Mahogany felt a tingle down below. She thought, *Damn, I wonder what's causing that. I drink plenty of water, and I'm still a virgin.*

Mahogany peered down at her genitals and noticed a small spot of blood on the outer surface of her vagina. *This can't be*, she thought. *I just came off my menstruation last week.* She paused. *Something is really happening to me.*

Mahogany looked inside of the toilet bowl, stunned by what she saw. The toilet water was crimson, the color of Jeffery Dahmer's human stew. Mahogany wondered if she had been attacked by demons, violated while asleep. She thought about Satan, the manufacturer of horror, and his/her death grip on society. Evil was a runaway train, and the good was its target.

I must contact my doctor this time, Mahogany thought. *Maybe he can replenish me with some answers. If I don't find out what's going on with me, I'll soon be in a psychiatric hospital. And what is the fucking deal with these puzzling nightmares?*

Mahogany wiped herself, flushed the toilet, and ambled to the bathroom mirror. She wanted to take a shower, yet decided to inspect her face, chest, and abdominal section for scars.

Jesus Christ! Look at me! Am I cursed or what? Mahogany said loudly, staring at thick, deep-red bruises on her face. She lifted up her T-shirt. *Shoot! Not again!* Mahogany cried out and rushed to the shower. However baffled, however emotionally offset, entropy psychologically attacked Mahognay like a wild pack of hyenas.

Undressed and waiting for the shower water to turn warm, Mahogany scrolled through her things-to-do list in her mind. Although burden by unexpected issues, she figured her day would be relatively easy. She reached in and placed her hand in the shower water. The water was warm, so she entered the shower. *Sss-ouch!* she exclaimed, feeling a stinging sensation in her back.

Mahogany extended her left hand over her shoulder. She felt a pack of fresh scars. Overpowered by fright, Mahogany quickly showered so she could call the family doctor. Against breathing life into the idea of bad luck, Mahogany figured a black cat had crossed her path somewhere. Shit, strange shit, had started happening too fast.

Mahogany dried herself and examined her backside through a silver hand-held mirror while standing with her backside facing the large mirror hanging over the face bowl. There were six, non-bleeding scars diagonally stretched across the top of her back. Mahogany fell deeper into distress. She didn't know what to do or what to believe; she just wanted resolution. Mahogany then wrapped the orange dry towel around her waist, took a seat on the bed, and called her doctor.

"Hello. Doctor Powell speaking."

"Good morning, Doctor Powell. This is Mahoagny Brown, and I apologize for calling you at home so early."

"You're okay, Mahogany. And please tell your parents I said hello. Other than that how can I help you?"

"Uh, I desire that we keep this conversation between us, Doc. What I'm about to tell you is very personal."

"Yes, I understand, Mahogany." He paused. "So let me have it, please."

"I've been experiencing extreme nightmares as of late, and they're unlike normal nightmares. I'm actually interacting with these nightmares . . . physically."

"Exactly how long have you been having these nightmares? And please try explaining them."

"No more than a month, and I've had them twice. As far as explaining the nightmares, I can't remember everything.

But the creatures I be fighting are very ugly, aggressive, slimy, and relentless. And let me finish."

"Sure, Mahogany. Please continue."

"Each time I awaken from these dreams, my midsection and face are disfigured with red scars. They never bleed, though. And it literally seems like I be trapped in my nightmares, struggling for survival. Oh yeah, my back has scars on it, too. And I noticed post spotting this morning while using the bathroom. So, do you have any answers, Doctor Powell?"

"Mahogany, I'm trying to make a diagnosis, but your situation is fit for a psychiatrist and a psychologist. Even consulting with an exorcist wouldn't be a bad idea. I have contact numbers for them all if you're interested."

"Yeah, that sounds about right, and I'll take the numbers just in case."

"Are you presently okay, Mahogany? And do these scars cause any pain or any other abnormal symptoms?"

"No, they don't hurt. But the ones on my back stung when I showered a minute ago. They're very noticeable, slightly puffy, and appear out of nowhere," she said. "However, the last time this happened the scars disappeared within one and half hour after I noticed them."

"Mahogany, I've heard something like this once before, maybe twelve years ago. From the explanation of your occurrence and condition, along with me knowing you, it sounds like the scars could be stigmata."

"Stigmata? What's that?"

"Dear, I'm not an expert on religion or spirituality, but I'll try giving you a brief description of what it is. And please . . . try remaining calm, Mahogany. I do believe you'll be fine." He paused. "Well, according to Christian tradition, stigmata are bodily marks or pains comparable to those of the crucified Jesus Christ. Individuals with stigmata are said to be of divine favor." He paused again. "However, some psychologists believe that the individuals who so-call receive the unexpected scars are experiencing hystero-epileptic attacks. That's exaggerated experiences through temporary loss of consciousness associated with inhaling, consuming, or injecting chemicals."

"Hey, you're not thinking I'm using drugs, are you, Doc?"

"Oh no. Of course not, Mahogany. I'm certain that you're better than that, and I apologize if I somehow offended you."

"That's okay, Doctor Powell. I think I'll do some research on stigmata. I just hope I'll be okay, because I really don't want my parents worrying about me. They have enough to deal with in their own lives."

"Mahogany, I promise to keep this call confidential, but I am going to make a record of it. And I'll forward you the telephone numbers once I get to the office."

"Thank you, Doctor Powell. And can I call you back in two hours to update you on my condition?"

"Absolutely, Mahogany. I'll be looking forward to the call, and I'll definitely be at the office by then. Now regarding other things about you, I would like to schedule you in for an appointment so I can give you an early check-up and a physical. Is that fine with you, Mahogany?"

"Yes sir, Doctor Powell. And I'll be sure to call your offices in two hours."

"Take care, Mahogany. And thanks for calling."

Partially relieved, Mahogany removed the burgundy sheets that covered her mattress. She placed them in the dirty clothes bin, fed her fish, and prepared for work. If need be, Mahogany considered concealing her scars with her mother's cosmetics. Nothing would stop Mahogany; it was live or die.

Almost eight o'clock a.m. and having replaced the linens on her Beauty Rest mattress, Mahogany entered the bathroom to examine her face and body again. She was happy, though amazed, her scars had nearly disappeared. Driving to work would now be a bit easier.

Finishing up with her hair, Mahogany thought about Jazz. She was disappointed with him, howsoever, wishing him the best. Marrying a drug dealer was hari-kari, purpose

Scarlet Tears

defeating; nevertheless, she had practically fallen in love with Jazz.

Prepared for work, Mahogany walked down the stairs and told her mother good-bye. Mahogany's mother was bathing, unable to receive her ritual kiss on the cheek. Ready to face the challenges ahead—if any—Mahogany left for work.

Barely making it to work on time, Mahogany clocked in through the hotel's touch-screen employee computer. She waved hello and smiled at a host of coworkers before riding the elevator up to her office. Mahogany felt good, preparing to make final arrangements for Nelly's upcoming concert at Adam's Mark Hotel.

She sat at her desk, reading incoming E-mail and two hard-copy internal memorandums that were placed in her office message box. Routine duties were a bore, the ABC's of her occupation. Mahogany would spend the next two hours on her job responding to E-mail, reviewing files, gathering data, and making follow-up telephone calls to prospective clients. Wednesday, July 12, 2000, was a day Mahogany felt like losing herself in her job responsibilities.

Nearing her lunch hour, Mahogany dialed 314-265-JAZZ. She couldn't refrain from thinking about Jazz, regardless of her dissatisfaction with his hustle.

"Good morning, love. I was wondering if you were going to call me. I've seriously been thinking about you, and I'm very sorry about yesterday. Yet something's telling me you're not accepting my apology."

"I take it you took a look at your caller I.D., but never mind that. Do you have an attorney, yet?"

"Actually, I just got off the phone with him. He wants me to call him back at two o'clock."

"Well, what does he think? And who is he?"

"He didn't have a whole lot to say at this time, just that he wish everything would have happened on this side of the river. He said the Southern District of Illinois wouldn't be an easy fight if they decide to charge me. And his name is David Greenblum."

"Sounds like bad news. Therefore, I better secure an attorney for myself."

"You'll be fine, Mahogany. Don't pester yourself with this situation. Remember . . . we have a wedding to plan."

"I'm sorry, Knigel. But I have some more phone calls to make. So I'll call you later if you don't mind."

"No problem, love. But be sure to call me back. I got a few things I need to tell you."

"Okay, will do."

Hearing the word marriage irritated Mahogany. Jazz was number one on Mahogany's shit list. She couldn't understand why Black men and Black Women happily sold death to one another, destroying themselves for temporary highs and tickets to prison. The Civil Rights Movement of the mid 20th century was being trampled on, more like spiked in a coffin. Mahogany hoped that her race would wake up and abstain from self-destruction. But as far as she could see, it appeared as if the sun would never rise again for many African Americans. Black life was criticized as lazy, undesirable, purposeless, inappropriate, and substitutable at the power structure's round table. Getting first hand experience, Mahogany believed that Blacks, especially Black men, were facing the point of no recovery.

Remembering to contact her doctor, Mahogany informed Dr. Powell that she was feeling okay and that her scars had vanished again. Nonetheless, Mahogany wrote down the telephone numbers on a yellow pad that Dr. Powell provided. She passed on the exorcist's telephone number, caring not to relive *Poltergeist.* Mahogany then scheduled a doctor's appointment for two weeks away.

Serious issues were arriving in Mahogany's life faster than a speeding F-117 stealth bomber. Mahogany couldn't detect the severity of her new experiences, yet she knew that they weren't peaches and cream.

Pondering her freedom, Mahogany avoided leaving work for lunch. She chose to order a fresh Caesar salad and a turkey sandwich with melted cheese on rye bread from the

Scarlet Tears

hotel food menu. Waiting for her lunch to be delivered from the main floor kitchen, Mahogany called Sarah Warrenberg.

"Hello, this is Sarah."

"Sarah, what's up? I'm glad you answered the phone."

"Hey, what's happening, Mahogany? Girl, I was just thinking about you."

"I'm doing okay, just trying to make it through a day's work. Anyway, is your father home?"

Sarah hesitated before replying. "Yeah, but he's about to return to work. Why? What's up?"

"Sarah, you'll never believe what I'm about to tell you."

"I hope it's not bad. I say that because my father is an attorney. Come on. Tell me."

"You must keep this to yourself, and I haven't even told my parents about this."

"Okay, I'm listening."

"Yesterday, both Knigel and I were stopped by plain-clothes agents in Illinois for illegal drugs. They only found money, though."

"Drugs? Tell me you're kidding, Mahogany. I figured Knigel was above that type of lifestyle, especially with all the good things you've said about him."

"Yeah, me too. And I'm serious, Sarah. This isn't a playing matter."

"I'm sorry to hear this, Mahogany. So, are you all right?"

"I'm making it, taking it one day at a time. But it does worry me," she said. "Now of course, I didn't know what was going on. But, anyway, he was set up by some guy from Illinois. And, unfortunately, we were driving my car."

"Oh gee! This doesn't sound good. I think I better get my dad on the phone."

"Hold up, Sarah. I don't know what to say to him. Girl, I haven't spoke with him since you guy's summer picnic in ninety-eight at Malcolm Terrace Park."

"Mahogany, please. Say exactly what you said to me. Believe me, he'll understand."

"Okay, I'll give it a try, but I was hoping you would explain it to him first."

"I'll talk to him about it later. Hold on."

There was silence . . . and more silence.

"How are you, Mahogany? It's good to hear from you. So, how can I help you?"

"Hello. I'm doing fine, Mister Warrenberg. And it's a pleasure to hear your voice."

"Well, I thank you. And please call me John."

"John, I was stopped yesterday with my fiancé in Venice, Illinois, by the DEA. There was marked money found in the trunk of my ca----"

"Excuse me, I take it your fiancé is maybe distributing illegal narcotics and was probably set up by some informant working with the DEA to save his own back pockets. Funny, but cooperating with law enforcement is a common thing to do these days. The Feds are locking these guys and gals up for a long time, sweetheart."

"That sounds about right, but I had nothing to do with any of it. This might sound crazy, but I didn't even know my fiancé was a drug dealer."

"I understand, Mahogany. Believe me, I've tried, heard, and studied several cases like this before. And you're doing the right thing by contacting an attorney, because these types of situations often get ugly. Hey, you haven't talked to anyone about this, right? That's including the police."

"No, I haven't. You and Sarah are the only ones."

"Great! Keep it that way. But what about your parents?"

"I'm sorry, but I'm afraid to tell them."

"Uh, that's a tough one, Mahogany. They may need to be informed about this, especially if the Southern District of Illinois decides to file charges. With me knowing majority of the players over there, I'm sure they will. Human life means nothing to those guys."

"Oh God! What now?"

"Well, give me the name of your fiancé, the time this occurred, and a phone number to contact you. Within an hour or two, I'll know exactly what's going on. I've got connections like that, Mahogany. And keep calm, okay. A dear friend of my daughter is a dear friend of mine. Together, we'll get to the bottom of this."

Listening to Mr. Warrenberg's deep, self-assured voice, Mahogany was enthused with a sudden burst of confidence. She felt empowered, ready for whatever. John Warrenberg was known as St. Louis' legal eagle. However, fear had found a home in Mahogany's heart. She wished her legal troubles, along with Jazz, could be quietly swept under the rug.

Dream on, Mahogany. Dream on, the ghosts of the federally prosecuted silently uttered.

THIRTY-FIVE

"Yo, what's shaking, derrty? You don't know uh bro no mo'?"

"Naw, Dread. You got me mistaken, man. I didn't recognize you in this bucket. What it be like, Dread?" Stefaughn asked and walked closer to the car Dread drove.

"Ain't nuttin new, playa. Shit ain't gone change. Crack done killed da hood. Hop in, derrty."

Stefaughn hesitated, seemingly wanting to do different. Even so, he got inside the light-blue Ford Tempo. The Ford Tempo was a decade old and partially rusty with dark-blue cloth seats that had many burnt cigarette holes. The interior smelled like a pack of crackheads who'd been awake for nine days chasing cars and pulling scams. And from Stefaughn's facial expression, he wished he'd never seen Dread.

"Man, Stef, I've been tryin' to holla at you, you dig. But you won't even call uh brotha back. What's da deal, derrty?"

"Go ahead and drive off, Dread. This ain't a cool spot to be sitting. A brother is dirty, and the po-poes been on a mission lately."

Dread pulled away from the curb.

"Nigga, what you doin' dhis far west on Page? You know dhese cats ain't havin' no newcomers settin' up shop. Dhis uh dangerous move, Stef. You playin' wit' fire, derrty."

"Naw, it's all right, Dread. I got everything under control. Plus, I know a few of these cats from my early childhood. Oh yeah, I lost the pager. I got a new one, though."

Scarlet Tears

"Dhat whutz wrong. I knew sumptin was goin' on, and I hear you're fuckin' wit' uh lil dame ova dhis way, named Rochelle." Dread paused. "Wit' her sexy ass!"

"How do you know that, Dread? Bruce don't even know about this one. But, yeah, that's who it is. She's cool. A fun girl, Dread. You feel me?"

"I hear you, playboy. Da streets talk. And on e'erythang, be careful, Stef. 'Cause dhese broads up fo' da two-eleven."

Stefaughn paused before replying. Dread's statement had seemingly struck a nerve.

"Make a right, right here, Dread. That way we can just circle the block. Some of my best customers are on their way to get at me. And thanks for the scoop, Dread."

"Say, Stef. . . ."

Stefaughn turned and looked at Dread. "Yeah, what's up?"

"You got dhem ends fo' yo' boy? It's been uh while, derrty. Uh nigga need to make uh move. I'm countin' on dhat, Stef. You kinda got me held up, derrty."

"I got some of it, Dread. But don't trip, because I'll have the rest in five days. That's what I was doing when you pulled up on me. Getting that dough, Dread."

"Are you fo' sho, Stef? You seem uh lil uptight, derrty."

"Seriously, I got you covered, Dread. Anyway, I hate to tell you . . . but somebody did steal a lot of my shit when I fell asleep over the last girl's house I was dealing with. I'm still trying to track her brother down. The word is he got me, Dread." Stefaughn turned and looked at Dread again. "You ain't mad, are you?"

"Damn, Stef! Man, I thought you knew betta. Nigga, you can't be leavin' shit ova no bitch's crib. Dhat bitch was probably in on it." Dread shook his head in disagreement, his voice becoming stern. "Dhis serious, derrty. I need dhem ends, my nig. Straight up!" Silence stood. Stefaughn looked as if he'd been spooked by the ghost of hell. "So how much you got, Stef?"

"Uh, uh, I got about sixty-eight hundred right now, Dread. And I also got five ounces I'ma have cooked up. That way, when I finish selling them, I'll have just about what I owe you, if not all of your bread," Stefaughn tried bargaining. "I'm sorry, Dread. That's why I left my old girlfriend alone, man."

"Yeah, I hear you, derrty. Just gimme da sixty-eight hundred and da ounces. And when you come up on four g's just get at me, derrty. On e'erythang . . . get at me, Stef."

"Okay, Dread. I need you to drop me back off where you picked me up at, so I can run to my stash spot and grab the loot. The candy is put up at my crib," he said nervously.

Returning to the location where Stefaughn was picked up, Dread asked Stefaughn to hurry back. Dread was peeved, steaming like a raging bull. Apparently, Stefaughn sensed this; he appeared suspicious, committed to a wary look. Dread didn't smile nor did he render comforting words. There was one thing Dread wanted—his money.

Stefaughn exited the car, probably wishing like hell he could pay Dread then go on his own. Stefaughn wasn't a troublemaker, far from a bad guy. He was just addicted to the ladies, trying to get his piece of the American pie.

Well, Dread sat waiting. Twenty minutes had elapsed. There was no Stefaughn. He'd disappeared behind the decrepit apartment building to never return again. Dread's heart beat faster, almost pounding out of control. Dread hated this, violence fueling his mind.

THIRTY-SIX

Fortunately, tornadoes were uncommon in St. Louis, limited to a few once in a blue moon. The twisters were mostly unsubstantial and short-lived, therefore, hardly ever feared. However, Thursday, July 13, 2000, Mahogany felt like she had been violently rattled by a whirlwind and mauled by a typhoon. Mahogany's sun was bleeding agony, weakened by terrifying darkness.

It was four o'clock p.m., and Mahogany had been informed by John Warrenberg that the United States Attorney's Office of the Southern District of Illinois sought indictments for both her and Jazz. Mahogany wondered if Jazz was aware of the judicial development. The load of living was getting too heavy.

Waiting for the traffic signal to turn green, Mahogany lost sense of herself. She was mute, daydreaming of a life away from society. Everything seemed false, memories of nothing. Seriously, Mahogany feared the future.

Beep-beeeep! a horn sounded.

"Move your ass, sister," a young White male yelled from his car.

Suddenly hearing the loud horn from the vehicle waiting behind her, Mahogany looked at the traffic signal. The light was green. She stepped on the accelerator and progressed forward onto I-64 West. While driving up the highway ramp, Mahogany heard her cellular telephone ring. She answered it.

"Mahogany, what's the deal, baby? Are you and Jessica still coming to the softball game, tonight?"

"I'll have to see, Knigel. And it looks like it's going to rain. Right now, I'm on my way home from work. Hey, have you heard from your attorney?"

"Yeah. We talked this afternoon."

"So you're aware that we're in trouble?"

"Mahogany, I've asked you not to worry about this. Even my attorney thinks you'll be fine. He said it's all normal procedures for them to file charges on everybody who was present during the current offense. Trust me they'll drop the charges on you."

"Knigel, this is a serious matter, and I don't have time to be running in and out of a courthouse. I haven't even been on my job for ninety days, and how in the world do you think I'm going to tell my parents about this?"

"I understand everything you're saying, love. But as I've said before . . . don't flip out on me. I'm sure we'll be fine. And most important, I need you."

"I hear you, Knigel. But you've put me in a situation I'm very uncomfortable with. Believe me, I've never done anything wrong in my life."

"And I'm sorry, I'm sorry, I'm sorry. So can we talk about this later? And do you want me to come and pick you up for the softball game? It's scheduled for seven o'clock. That'll be here before we know it."

"Yeah, that's a good idea. Because I don't feel like driving back into the city. And why don't you call Jessica for me. My cell phone battery is about to go ahead, and I didn't bring my adapter."

"No problem. What's her number?"

"You know the area code. Five, three, four, twenty-one hundred."

"All right, I'll call her. Then I'll call you back at your house in an hour."

"Okay, bye, Kn----"

Mahogany's cellular telephone became disconnected, its battery powerless."

****

Although worried about his judicial concerns, Jazz tried using the power of positive thinking. He'd read several books by Napolean Hill and other authors of success books. They all supported positive thinking.

"The Francis residence."

"Hello. Is this Jessica's mom?"

"Yes. And who would you like to speak to?"

"This Jazz, and can I speak with Jessica?"

"How are you doing, handsome?"

"I'm doing okay, Miss Francis. And where did you get that sexy voice from?"

"It's a gift from God, honey. And that ain't the. . . . I'd better not say that. Hey, I told you about calling me Miss Francis."

"Sorry about that. So, is Jessica home?"

"Hold on. She's right here, Knigel."

"What's up, Jazz? What have you calling?"

"I'm chilling, Jessica. And I'm calling for Mahogany."

"Yeah, speak as you may, then."

"Mahogany wanted to know if you would like to go to my softball game with us, tonight, at Fairgrounds Park."

"Of course. Where's Mahogany?"

"She's on her way home from work. And she asked me to call you because her battery went out on her cell phone."

"Oh, I see. But yeah, I'd love to go. So what time should I be ready?"

"Well, the game doesn't start until seven, and it's almost four, thirty now. So I guess around a quarter after six, unless you want to ride out to Mahogany's with me."

"Yeah, come pick me up so I can ride along. That way, I can see Mahogany's parents."

"Bet. I'll be there in thirty to thirty-five minutes."

"Okay, I'll be ready, and I hope it doesn't rain," Jessica said.

"Yeah, me too. Then it'll probably hold off until later on."

"All right, I'll see you in a little bit."

Scarlet Tears

Every since Jazz first met Jessica, he'd grown a deep respect for her. Jessica was diverting, a diamond in the rough. Jazz then stopped by Rally's on Goodfellow and purchased a large order of seasoned French fries and a large strawberry soda. Jazz wanted more to eat, but didn't want to tire himself from eating too much. He thought about his softball equipment and uniform, remembering he'd placed everything in the trunk of his car.

Jazz played for the St. Louis Heat, an urban softball force of sluggers and well-skilled defensive players. Jazz enjoyed playing softball and all the local attention the sport attracted. In St. Louis softball was a joy magnet. Hoards of attractive women supported the sport. It's where the urban giants performed their best, entertaining the male-seeking babes of The Lou.

Still sitting in his car on Rally's parking lot, Jazz listened to the stereo and enjoyed his seasoned French fries and strawberry soda. Suddenly, thoughts of justice and more serious issues tackled Jazz like a Sumo wrestler.

I wonder what Dread crazy ass is doing. I know that fool will knock off Lil Salvador ass for a few g's. But damn I hate to fuck with that nigga again, Jazz thought aloud.

The sky darkened. Clouds shifted in a hurry. Jazz wanted the sun to dominate the evening. Thursday evenings at Fairgrounds Park was the "greatest show" in St. Louis. But more than anything, Jazz couldn't wait to flaunt Mahogany and Jessica; they would be the flame of the evening festivities.

Jazz drove away from the fast-food restaurant to Jessica's home, wondering what she was wearing for the evening. It was a breezy eighty-three degrees, and the sun was playing hide-and-go-seek with the light-gray clouds. Honestly, if there was no Mahogany in Jazz's life, it would certainly be Jessica.

Parked in front of Jessica's home, Jazz dialed inside and informed Jessica of his arrival. He asked if he could come inside to change into his softball uniform. Jessica approved his request. Jazz figured by the time he'd made all his rounds, it'll be time to play softball. There was no time to misemploy on Thursday evenings; it was show time.

"Good evening, Jazz," Jessica heartily said, stepping to the side to allow Jazz inside her home.

"What's up, Jessica?" Jazz replied. "Girl, don't you look lovely."

Jessica smiled. "Thank you. And you're a cutie, yourself." She paused. "Go ahead on upstairs. You already know where the bathroom's at."

Jazz advanced up the stairs. He looked back and witnessed Jessica standing in the doorway. She was slowly rubbing her buttocks, looking at Jazz's vehicle. Jazz's car was a show stopper, *and so was Jessica's rear view.*

Jessica wore a red Adidas mini catsuit with a pair of hip-hugging, white denim shorts. She had on a pair of red-and-white short-heel sandals. Jessica's hair was tied to the rear, partially hanging down her back. She also wore a matching gold anklet and bracelet, along with a diamond-faced watch and a pair of diamond earrings. Her body was oiled, and her perfume was sexually stimulating.

Jessica turned around. Her and Jazz met eyes. Jazz dropped his Reebok duffel bag. "Oops! I'm sorry. I was ju . . . just uhh. . . ."

"It's cool, Jazz. The feelings are mutual," Jessica said. She smiled. She slowly glided her tongue across her top lip.

Jazz's penis enlarged, seeking friendship. He was in disbelief, questioning his next move. Howbeit, Jazz regained his composure and continued up the staircase. He could hear Jessica snickering.

Now inside the bathroom, the bathroom door closed, Jazz undressed. He still had an erection, making it difficult to put on his jockstrap. Therefore, Jazz removed his toothbrush and toothpaste from inside his blue duffel bag and brushed his teeth in front of the bathroom mirror. He placed his left hand on his extended penis, still brushing his teeth with the other hand. Jazz slowly stroked his penis, imagining Jessica.

****

Scarlet Tears

Jessica went inside her bedroom and called her boyfriend to let him know that she'd planned to spend some time with Mahogany and that she wouldn't be returning home until after nine p.m. Austin, Jessica's boyfriend, had been spending a lot of money on Jessica as of late; still, he wasn't overly possessive. Austin was understanding, busy producing music. He wouldn't be free until after nine p.m. *Perfect timing*, Jessica thought.

Jessica exited her bedroom, suddenly seeing her mother open the bathroom door. Ms. Francis had on a black brassiere, a black thong, and a pair of black slippers—nothing more.

"Good lord, baby! Ooo-wee! The Creator sho know He blessed you. Just look at that thing," Ms. Francis said, gazing at Jazz's manhood.

Jazz didn't say a word. He smiled.

"Momma!" Jessica shouted. Ms. Francis flinched, quickly shutting the bathroom door. "What are you doing? Jazz is in there."

"Shit! Girl, I didn't know. You should have said something. And don't be scaring me like that," Ms. Francis retorted. "When he gets done, bring me the cotton balls and my nail kit from under the sink. I got plans for tonight."

Jessica didn't respond. She figured her mother must have adored what she saw. And at that point, Jessica's imagination ran wild.

Minutes later, Jazz exited the bathroom wearing a gray-and-green softball uniform. He asked Jessica to call Mahogany and enlighten her that they were on their way. Jessica okayed Jazz's request, however, staring at the huge lump in the center of his fitted pants. *Damn Jazz is packing*, Jessica thought.

"Hello."

"Hello, Mahogany. I'm calling you for Jazz to let you know we're on our way."

"Okay, I'll be ready by the time y'all get here, but it's sprinkling out this way. Hey, you know Friday, July twenty-eighth, is Nelly's concert at our hotel. I'm in charge of the event. So you know you're all good, right?"

"Yeah, I heard about it, and you know I'm coming."

"All right. So is Jazz inside by the phone? Or is he waiting in his car?"

"Hold on. Here he is." Jessica handed Jazz the cordless telephone.

"Hey, love," Jazz said.

"Knigel, whatever you do, don't tell Jessica about our judicial concerns, okay."

"Most certainly, and we'll be there shortly."

Jazz ended the telephone call. He handed the cordless telephone to Jessica and told her he was ready to depart. Jessica was excited, eager to ride in Jazz's Lexus LS430. She told Jazz to go ahead and walk down the stairs while she get something for her mother.

Now riding through the city, and preparing to get on the highway, Jazz and Jessica couldn't keep their eyes off one another. Jazz occasionally gazed at Jessica's juicy thighs, and Jessica endlessly stared at the hump in between Jazz's upper legs. Jessica craved Jazz, especially the hump of beef in his pants.

Jessica loved Jazz's car, complimenting it several times. Jazz thanked Jessica, telling her how gorgeous she was. Their conversation grew warm, nearing extremity. Suddenly, a light rain began to fall just as Jazz drove onto the highway. The sky was getting darker, lightning flashing within the clouds. Jazz turned on the windshield wipers as the rain fell faster.

****

"Well, there goes the game for tonight," Jessica said.

"You're right, and I'ma get off this highway before traffic gets loco. Hey," Jazz handed Jessica his cellular telephone, "call Mahogany so I can let her know the game is cancelled and it isn't any use of us driving all the way out there in this weather."

Scarlet Tears

Jessica followed Jazz's instructions, unable to keep her eyes off him.

Mahogany answered the telephone.

"I'm sorry, dear, but the game is cancelled. And the traffic out here on this highway is getting crazy, so I'ma go ahead and take Jessica back home. Then I'll call you later."

****

Jazz exited the interstate at Big Bend Boulevard, going north. Jessica had no intentions on returning home so soon, seizing the instant as an opportunity for obscenity. Jessica looked around, and then told herself, *Fuck it! You only live once. And God forgive me, because I got to do this.*

Jessica leaned over and softly kissed Jazz on the cheek. Then she slowly wiggled her tongue against Jazz's neck. Jazz moaned, gripping the steering wheel. Jessica raised Jazz's shirt. She began licking his right nipple and gently rubbing the hump in his pants. Jessica discovered that the hump between Jazz's legs was pure muscle; there was no cup inside of his jockstrap. Jessica's body temperature increased, her vagina flooding with moisture. The feeling was powerful; the feeling was arousing; Jessica and Jazz were one step from exploding.

****

Jazz was amazed, nervousness taking control. Jazz's arms trembled as he tried steering his vehicle. The warmth and moistness from Jessica's mouth were pulse-quickening, along with the sight of her pretty hand and colorful, long nails. Jazz was set aback, his penis on a rampage.

HOT! SEXY! UNBELIEVABLE!

As the rain continued to descend, Jazz and Jessica's passion inflamed. They lusted for one another, forgetting all about the pains associated with life. Everything was for the moment, and they were interested in the gusto, the maximum of feeling. Jessica unsnapped and unzipped Jazz's pants. She reached inside his jockstrap, liberating his pride and joy. Jazz's penis was thick, banana-shaped with a mushroom top.

"Ooo-la-la! Look what momma found. I can feel it in me already," Jessica passionately said.

Jazz thought of his male organ as a collector's item, good dick without batteries.

Jessica asked Jazz to lift up. She slid down his pants, making matters more suitable for enjoyment. Jessica enveloped the large head of Jazz's penis with her mouth, her silver dog tag rubbing against his jumbo testicles. She rolled her tongue around its surface. Jessica's mouth was warm, melting ice cubes at Lido Beach. Jazz's mind went astray, thanking God for promiscuity. Cherishing the moment, Jazz slowly drove a maze of side streets. Jessica was rapidly developing the new love of his life, the perfect wife/whore.

Jazz couldn't take it any more. Jessica's oral sex was dynamite. He exploded into her mouth, moaning away. Jessica squeezed the head of Jazz's penis with her powerful jaw muscles. She swallowed, stroking Jazz's penis. Jazz quickly pulled over. He screamed. He yelled how it felt. Jazz cursed in delight. He'd been victimized, mugged in the name of ecstasy. Really, Jessica was the good wife's worst nightmare.

Jazz figured since Jessica's oral sex was so marvelous, then experiencing sexual intercourse with her would be mind-blowing. Woman . . . man's everything.

"Jessica, let's ride out to my house for a while," Jazz suggested as he pulled up his pants.

Jessica couldn't respond. She was busy spitting out the window. Jessica wiped the outside of her mouth with a napkin. "Whew! Well, that was that. And burning out to your spot sounds like a good idea." Jessica looked at Jazz with a smile. "So, are you straight?"

"Am I straight?" Jazz paused. "Hell yeah! I'd be lovesick without you from now on." Jazz placed his right hand on Jessica's left thigh, gently rubbing it up and down. Jessica looked into the small mirror built into the passenger sun visor, moisturizing her lips with a cherry lip salve.

Scarlet Tears

As Jazz drove to his home, the sky continued falling from day. Light thunder rumbled, and the sun rarely glowed from behind the shifting clouds. Drizzling showers fell from above, mellowing the evening, hallmarking a special occasion.

Twenty-five minutes had elapsed since Jessica serviced Jazz with her extraordinary gift, and they'd finally arrived at Jazz's home. Jazz noticed an unfamiliar car parked not far from his house. He didn't bother, his mind far deep in images of pussy.

"Jazz, you have a nice place. It's a shame you live alone. I can see a family enjoying this house and neighborhood," Jessica said, drying her feet on the doormat.

"So, are you trying to tell me something?" Jazz kissed Jessica on the lips, softly squeezing her ass cheeks.

"If I am a part of the family . . . then yes."

"It's coming, Jessica. And you've given me something to think about," he said. "You're welcome to walk around if you want to. There's food and juice in the kitchen, and the bathroom is right around the corner, there. The remote control to the TV and the stereo is on the sofa in the entertainment room. So make yourself at home."

****

Jessica had planned to do just that, wishing Austin had a home like Jazz's. While Jazz went to prepare for a bath, Jessica entered the guess bathroom to rinse out her mouth. She opened the cabinet beneath the vanity and found a new bottle of Scope original flavor mouthwash. Jessica removed the plastic safety wrap from around the bottle, opened it, and poured herself a capful. She gargled twice, admiring the yellow and light-blue color coordinated bathroom.

The kitchen was the next stop, the place where Jessica poured herself a cold glass of fruit punch juice and removed a bag of Lay's plain potato chips from a cabinet. Jessica left the kitchen with her evening snack and strolled into the entertainment room. She took a drink from her glass of juice. Jessica placed the glass of juice and potato chips on a round glass cocktail table that set in front of the white leather sofa. She then lit the black cherry candle positioned in the center of the cocktail table with a black candle lighter. Next, Jessica kicked off her short-heeled patent leather sandals. She removed her denim shorts and jewelry, except for her gold anklet. Jessica also removed the white tie from the rear of her head, allowing her hair to hang freely. Jessica had on nothing but her mini catsuit, more provocative than words can explain. Jessica turned on the television with the remote control. She changed the channel from ESPN to BET. Jessica had found home.

Wondering what type of music Jazz listened to, Jessica walked over to the tall, black CD stand that stood next to the Kenwood stereo. After a quick browse, Jessica removed Sade's "Lovers Rock" LP and placed it inside the five-disc CD changer. Jessica turned the volume down on the television, turned the volume up on the stereo, pushed play, and sat on the sofa with her legs and pampered feet stretched across the sofa. Jessica was ready for Jazz's every desire; her mission was to enslave his fantasy.

****

Minutes later, Jazz walked into the entertainment room. He gazed at Jessica relaxing on the sofa. Jazz wore nothing but a pair of dark-blue Dolce & Gabanna silk boxers, a diamond-studded bracelet, and a pair of Dolce & Gabanna house slippers.

"You've made yourself at home, I see," Jazz said.

He leaned over the edge of the sofa and kissed Jessica on the forehead and neck. Jessica tilted her head, her hair nearly touching the floor. She rubbed her breast nipples that pressed against her catsuit like Hershey Kisses.

"Jessica, you're charmingly dangerous." Jazz gazed at the thick print between Jessica's partly spread legs.

"Would that be true? I think I can say the same about you. And I love your place. It's so you and me." Jessica smiled.

"You're still hinting. But guess what? . . . You're more than welcome here." Jazz kissed Jessica again. "And what do you know about Sade? I figured you were a hip-hoptress," he teased. "Stand up, please." Jazz extended his right arm, aiding Jessica from the sofa.

"So, you're unfamiliar with a diversified woman, I'd suppose. A real woman who can satisfy you in a variety of ways."

Jazz stepped back from Jessica, marveled by her award-winning physique. "Jessica, I'm feeling you, and it's a damn shame how fine you are. Girl, a brother couldn't take seeing you and Serena Williams together." Jazz paused, shaking his head. "And yeah . . . I'm not familiar with a diversified woman. So teach me everything I need to know."

"You're lucky. I enjoy teaching. But putting in a sex flick would intensify the lessons," Jessica replied. She gazed at Jazz from head to toe.

"You for real?"

"Ain't no shame in my game. I love pornos, and Mahogany didn't tell me you lifted weights."

Jazz turned on the DVD player with the remote control, suddenly remembering there was adult pornography already inside the disc tray.

"Believe it or not, Mahogany and I haven't crossed that line, yet." Jazz pulled Jessica close to him. He began sucking on her neck and kissing on her ear.

Jessica moaned and rubbed Jazz's back.

"You smell so good, Jazz," Jessica softly said. "What cologne are you wearing?"

Jazz refused to answer, far into a sex zone.

Jessica raised Jazz's head from her neck. She looked intensely into his eyes, her arms wrapped around his neck. "Jazz. . . . No, Knigel sounds better. Can I say something, first?"

Gazing at Jessica's gloss-coated lips, Jazz shook his head yes.

"I feel like you're enjoying me. And yes, it's about to go down. I also feel like you've always wanted me, and I'm promising you a good time." She paused without smiling. "But know this, Knigel. I really care for you, even more than Austin. And I want to give you the greatest time of your life. I hope this is the beginning of our union to be, and I know I can keep you happy." Jessica kissed Jazz. "Keeping it real, I want you for me—and only me." She kissed Jazz again, but longer and more passionate. "So let's get this party started."

Jessica parted from Jazz and picked up the stereo remote control off the cocktail table. She went to song six on the CD and ordered Jazz to have a seat in a white bentwood chair. Jessica replaced the stereo remote control on the cocktail table, studiously gazing at Jazz. The selection had an energetic African tone, spurring Jessica to move in rhythm to the drumbeat.

"Je----"

"Shhh!" Jessica uttered, her right index finger placed against her lips. "Relax, sexy. And welcome to Jessica's private show. Oh, and there's no touching on your part."

Jazz didn't say another word, overtaken by Jessica's appeal. As the song progressed, Jessica alluringly danced. She aroused Jazz with lap dances and a few subtle moves of her own. Jessica was incredibly flexible, twisting and bending into seemingly hurtful positions. Jazz was charmed and astonished by Jessica's muscle control. Her legs appeared powerful, prompting Jazz to feel a little insecure. Jazz would not back down, though; the occasion was a desire come true.

"You enjoy that, sweetie?"

"Jazz was overwhelmed, speechless. Anyway, he nodded yes.

The song ended. Jessica turned her backside to Jazz and asked him to stand and slowly unzip her mini catsuit. Staring at Jessica's *Apple Bottom*, jitters struck Jazz like a high-speed automobile accident. He longed Jessica's permanency, everything she had to offer.

"There you go, sexy. You're all unzipped, now."

"No, you're not finished. I thought you wanted to learn a few things. So peel it off. It's stimulating to have my clothes removed by my man."

Scarlet Tears

'My man,' Jazz thought aloud. "Jessica, I don't know if I'm going to be able to handle you. You're so consuming." He smiled. "Tell me . . . what are you doing to me? You'll probably think I was bullshitting if I told you I wanted you to stay."

"A great idea, but currently too risky. All that can be easily fixed, though. And yes, I'm being a little treacherous. But I think y'all men like us that way. It keeps y'all weird thinking butts on your toes."

Jazz removed Jessica's mini catsuit. Jessica wasn't wearing any underwear.

"Uh, hmm, I agree. But it's painful finding out that your woman is cheating."

Jessica kicked her mini catsuit from beneath her feet. She eased her backside against the front of Jazz's body. "Thank you, big boy. And are you calling me a cheater?"

"I'll let you answer that."

Jessica chuckled. She reminded Jazz of her mother, enchanting men with fascinating properties.

"Okay, enough wit that. And caress my breast while whispering some freaky shit in my ear, but keep brushing your dick against my ass," she instructed. "I like the way it feels inside of your silk underwear."

Again, Jazz was speechless.

"Uh, are you still with me? I'm not hearing you."

"Yeah, I'm with you, baby. I'm ju, just in dreamland."

Jessica reached back and grasped Jazz's penis. "Why aren't you all the way hard?"

"Don't trip. It'll get there. Trust!"

"Naw, don't you trip. Here, I'ma help it." Jessica stepped forward. She picked up her glass of juice off the cocktail table. "Just chill while I do my thing, okay."

Jessica knelt down on the carpeted floor. She slid down Jazz's silk boxers, held his half-limp penis with her right hand and inserted it into her mouth. Jazz loved the feeling. He could feel his penis inflating. Jessica removed her mouth from around Jazz's penis. She placed his dangling penis inside the glass of fruit punch juice and licked his balls. Jazz hadn't experienced such a tactic before. Yet it was working. Jessica removed Jazz's dick from inside the glass. His wood was now as hard as a brick. She stuffed as much of Jazz's dick in her mouth as possible, dick deep down her throat. That was all she wrote. Sparks flared like breakaway lightning. Jazz's penis stood firm, geared for plowing the darkest valleys.

Jazz was well alive, making Jessica moan throughout the entire sexual affair. Tears of delight seeped from Jessica's eyes as Jazz delivered nice, firm strokes of fulfillment. He brought a missionary zeal to his lovemaking. Jessica had his heart. She had an immense zest for sex, an uncontrollable desire for its energy. It was the golden egg witches yearned.

Jazz believed there was no better feeling than enjoying sex with a fresh, inner-city snapper, a sumptuous African-American delicacy. Up and down, with a hump in his back, Jazz performed like a yo-yo. He was in and out, doing it like a pro. Jessica's nature blew heat, well massaged by the pussy masseur.

Well, Jessica was far from just being a receiver; she let it loose, *every damn bit of it*. Jessica rode Jazz like an Indian in rage, the power of sex driving her insane. Sweat covered her body like a layer of baby oil.

They moaned one another's names, often shouting in mercy. Jessica was elated, proud to have not been cheated with a *wam-bam-thank-you-ma'am*. Jazz was thrilled, on fire like a wild blaze.

Exploding like a volcanic bomb, both, Jessica and Jazz hollered in perverted passion, their hearts and thoughts tangled in ecstasy. Whether if it was betrayal, deceit, treachery, mischief, or disloyalty—Jazz and Jessica were sold on one another, hoping their bond would last for a lifetime. The double-dealing of friendship, the very thief of serenity. Nonetheless, sensation was better than infidelity.

"I'm sleepy, Knigel. Are you?"

"Yeah." He took a deep breath. "You know I am." Jazz wiped his forehead and nose clear of perspiration. He smiled. "Continuing to have sex with you is going to require some additional training." He paused to catch his breath. "You're a workout, baby."

"Yeah, yeah, yeah, make me feel good. You know you're the man. And what time is it?"

Jazz looked at the clock on the stereo. "Seven, fifty-two."

"Damn, we had sex for an hour and something. And that flick ain't went off yet," Jessica said, looking at the TV screen. "Shit, he's pounding her ass."

Jazz could only shake his head, praying Jessica would instantly fall asleep. The telephone suddenly rang. Jazz looked at the caller ID sitting next to the telephone.

"Guess who it is?"

"Don't tell me. Mahogany," Jessica replied.

"Yep. Should I answer it?"

"No! You don't even know what you're going to say. That's what's wrong with men. Y'all don't think before y'all act."

"Okay, mother."

Jessica and Jazz smiled. She sat between his legs on the sofa, watching *Ghetto Booty USA.*

"I wonder if she's called my house."

"Call your mother and see," Jazz said.

Jessica pushed star sixty-seven and called home.

"The Francis residence. How can I help you?"

"Momma, this me. And quit answering the phone like that. You sound like a secretary, and have Mahogany called looking for me?"

"Yeah. Twice as a matter of fact. Where are you?"

"I'm over a friend's house. What did you tell her?"

"I told her I thought you were with her, because you and her man left here together."

"Okay, that's cool. We couldn't make it to the game. It got rained out. And I'll give Mahogany a call."

"All right, you have your key, don't you? Because your sister is staying over to Danielle's until Sunday night. Danielle is going to drive her and Amber to go swimming in the morning. And I'm waiting on Rufus to come and pick me up."

"Oh lord! Not Rufus again." Jessica paused. "Yeah, I have my key. But I won't be returning home until morning. You be careful, and I'll talk to you later." Jessica replaced the receiver on the cradle and turned to Jazz. "So there you have it, Knigel. I'm yours for the rest of this rainy night."

"That's fine with me." Caressing her stomach, Jazz kissed Jessica's neck. "But do you think Mahogany will ride out here looking for us?"

"Boy, naw. She'll never suspect us of being together, especially if you call her with all the right words," Jessica said. "Knigel, you're rubbing my belly as if I was carrying your child."

"Uh-oh. That's deep."

Following Jessica's suggestion, Jazz called Mahogany from his cellular telephone. Jazz told Mahogany that he'd dropped Jessica off over one of her female friend's house in the inner city and that he'd been busy in a business meeting. After one lie, there followed another. Jazz even bored himself with so many fibs, wondering if Mahogany was buying them at all. Last, he told Mahogany that he would see and call her the next day.

Sequentially, Jessica called Austin and pushed star sixty-seven again. She rid him for the night with hyperbole. Jazz and Jessica were frauds, fabricating pretext. They then returned their attention to one another. Jazz led Jessica into the bathroom in his master bedroom so they could bathe together in the Jacuzzi. A short while after bathing, Jazz and Jessica skipped round two and fell soundly asleep.

THIRTY-SEVEN

Saturday, July 15, 2000

Mahogany felt good; she hadn't been terrorized by demonic nightmares. Her night's dreams were pleasant, therefore, inspiring a spry attitude.

It was nine, thirty a.m. Mahogany's parents called her to breakfast. Cooking breakfast for the family was a sporadic weekend pastime for Mr. and Mrs. Brown. Together, they ate French toast, scrambled eggs with cheese, fried Polish sausage and sliced fruit. The subject matter of morning dialogue was work and vacationing. Mahogany continued to withhold the introduction of her judicial situation.

Considering going to church the next morning, Mahogany excused herself from the breakfast table. She had eaten all the food on her plate. Mahogany went upstairs to wash her hands and brush her teeth. She had already bathed, appearing fresh and vivacious.

Thinking about Karen and Stefaughn, Mahogany called their house.

"Hello," a voice murmured.

"Who is this?" Mahogany asked.

"It's me, Stefaughn."

"Why are you trying to disguise your voice? Lady problems?"

"Yeah. How do you know, cuz?"

"I don't know. A lucky guess maybe. And are you going to church, tomorrow?"

"Yeah, I'm going. Are you?"

"Yes. And I'm thinking about spending the night down there. That way I won't be rushing in the morning."

Scarlet Tears

"That sounds like a good idea, cuz. We need to spend some time together, anyway, so I can get you caught up on everything."

"Well, I'll be there around six this evening. And make sure you're there to let me in."

"All right."

"Before you hang up, let me speak to my auntie."

"Sorry, cuz. Mom isn't here. She's gone to the grocery store. You can try catching her on her cell phone, though."

"Maybe I'll do that, but you just have your butt there at six."

"Trust a brother, cuz. I'll be here. I'm a changed man, now."

"And what inspired your sudden change?"

"Predicaments and circumstances, cuz. You know how it is."

"Well, we'll talk about it when I get there. And how's Tony doing?"

"That's a novel within itself, cuz. And his real nickname is Dread. Like I said, we'll cover everything when you get here."

"Dread? Now that's scary. I'll see you at six, then."

Mahogany ended the telephone call. She wondered why Dread would lie about his name. Also, Mahogany hadn't heard from Jazz or Jessica. She wondered why.

Refusing to contact Jazz via telephone, Mahogany planned to pay Jazz a surprise visit at his lingerie store. Yet she called Jessica at home; Jessica wasn't there. Mahogany figured she'd try again later.

Using the next hour for packing a small travel bag, choosing what dress and shoes to wear to church, Mahogany prepared for departure. She placed her cellular telephone and keys in her purse then put on her sunglasses and endeavored for her car.

On her way to the garage, Mahogany set her travel bag on the kitchen floor. She walked to her parent's bedroom. Standing outside of her parent's bedroom, the door closed, Mahogany listened. Mr. Brown was breathing hard. Mrs.

Brown encouraged her husband to pump harder. Mahogany placed her hand over her mouth. She giggled and walked away from the door.

Mahogany left a brief note detailing her plans and whereabouts on the kitchen island counter. Mahogany was out the door, off into the summer winds.

Searching for a decent parking space at Northwest Plaza, Mahogany prowled the parking lot. She wished she had a handicap sticker or sign to place on her dashboard. Finally, Mahogany drove up on a car backing out of a good parking space.

Entering the mall, Mahogany was immediately subjugated by the aroma of Auntie Annie's Pretzels. Unable to bypass the small food stand, Mahogany purchased a regular pretzel with caramel dip and lemonade. From there, she scrambled her way through the crowded mall, targeting Jazz's Women Apparel & Lingerie.

Walking into her fiancé's store, Mahogany noticed Jazz assisting a middle-age White woman near the rear of the store. Looking from the outside in, the woman appeared to be enjoying Jazz's presence much more than the lingerie. Jazz was a great salesman, always focused on retail's main objective. Hereby, Jazz found it beneficial to befriend his often flirtatious patrons. That is what he once told Mahogany.

Ready to eat her pretzel, Mahogany sat near the checkout counter. She was hidden from Jazz's view by a full rack of designer summer blouses. Mahogany tried listening in on the verbal exchange between Jazz and the woman. Her attempt was unsuccessful, deferred by an employee, Leslie.

"What's up, Mahogany? You come to work, today? I'm sure we can use your help after a while. Saturdays get hectic after two, and you did a good job the last time you were here."

"I don't mind helping if you, guys, need me. And what's up with you?" Mahogany dipped her pretzel in the plastic container of caramel.

"Not a whole lot, girl. Just trying to meet this month's sales quota. Sisters love a bonus."

Mahogany chewed a piece of pretzel. "I second that."

Jazz suddenly approached the checkout counter. He asked Leslie to ring up the items belonging to the woman he'd been assisting. Jazz told the woman thanks and handed her a store brochure.

"So what wind blew you in this afternoon, Mrs. Wennington?"

"Uhh, let's see. It wasn't the north or the south, and it sure wasn't the east or west wind. I think it's called a wondering about Knigel wind."

Mahogany and Jazz laughed. Mahogany and the White female patron stared at one another.

"I take it you're asking me why I haven't called since Thursday."

"Correct. And follow me if you don't mind," Mahogany said.

Mahogany and Jazz walked to the rear of the store, directly in front of the dressing rooms.

"Did you recognize that woman you were just helping from somewhere?"

Jazz took one last look at the woman before she exited the store. "Naw, I think that was my first time ever seeing her. Why?"

"I can almost promise you that was one of the two lady agents at the bridge. Believe me, that's why she just hurried out of here. We noticed one another."

"Well, what can she do? I haven't done anything wrong. Everything is legit here."

"No, I wasn't thinking that. I just want you to be a little more aware. Okay, honey," Mahogany said. She fed Jazz the last of her pretzel.

"I'm with you, baby. Come on. Follow me to the cash register, so I can see how she paid for her items. Hopefully, she paid with some type of plastic or a check. That way, I can have her name checked out."

"Are you sure if that's legal, Knigel?"

"Ah, she'd never know."

"If you say so."

Jazz walked behind the checkout counter and asked Leslie how the patron paid for her items. To his dismay, the woman paid with cash. That eliminated a trace.

"Uh-oh! It's that time. They're about to start pouring in," Leslie said. "The ladies are 'bout to get fresh for the clubs tonight."

Just as Leslie announced, customers entered the store one after another. Jazz, Mahogany, Leslie, and Carrie, Jazz's only White employee who'd just ended her break, went to work. They sold merchandise as if a buy-one-get-one-free sale was in progress. Why Jazz would jeopardize everything by continuing to deal narcotics left Mahogany confused. There was something more Mahogany yearned to learn about Jazz, and she would dig until treasure was found. Jazz was on Mahogany's hit list.

Jessica, her mother, and a heavyset man wearing nice clothes entered the store. The man appeared older than Jessica and her mother, and he was completely bald. Mahogany waved at them from the rear of the store. She was assisting a lesbian couple.

****

Immediately, Jessica spotted Jazz. She strutted into his view. Jessica was provocatively dressed—as usual. Her mother was, too.

"Jessica, what's up?" Jazz peered to the rear of the store. "I'm surprised to see you."

"Good. I hope you like surprises. And how about," Jessica held up three fingers, "days in a row. Last night was even better than Thursday night."

"Hold that thought, Jessica," Jazz nervously said. "I need to run this smaller size over to the checkout real quick." He paused. "Oh yeah, take a look to the back."

Jessica looked to the rear of the store. She figured Mahogany was too green to catch on to anything. Regardless, Mahogany was a barricade, preventing Jessica from fully obtaining her greatest desire. Jessica then refocused on Jazz. She blew him a kiss.

****

Jazz felt pressured, moisture sitting in his armpits. His anxiety became obvious, grasping the attention of Leslie. *Please, Jessica, just keep your cool. We'll work this out, baby. Patient, patient, Jessica,* Jazz thought aloud.

****

Mahogany walked towards Jessica. "Hello, Jessie," Mahogany said with excitement. "Girl, I'm so glad to see you. I've been calling you like crazy. Have you been receiving my messages?"

"Girl, naw. I've been on a mission, lately," she rudely replied.

"Jessica, are you okay? You don't sound like yourself."

"Uh-huh. I'm fine. How about you?" Jessica stared at Jazz.

"Why are you looking over there? Have one of the employees upset you?"

"Don't trip, Mahogany. It'll be settled."

"Girl, I haven't seen you this bothered since you and that one chick got into an argument in the cafeteria at college."

"It'll be all right like I said, Mahogany. And what dragged you out, today?"

"I just figured I'd come down to help out at the store. There was nothing else to do," Mahogany answered. "And why did you use the word 'dragged'?"

"Oh, so you're offended, now. Girl. . . ." Jessica looked at her mother across the store. "So are you going to speak to my momma or what?"

"Jessie, you're on one, today. Stress isn't good for you. And I'ma let you get that off this time, because I'm in a professional environment. Whether if you're aware of that, who knows." Mahogany walked away from Jessica, heading towards Jessica's mother. She stared back at Jessica. "Holla when you get yo' mind right, homie."

Bitch, please! You don't even sound right trying to talk like you're from the hood, Jessica silently countered.

****

Jazz didn't know what to say or do. He peered at Mahogany near the dressing rooms and thanked God Jessica didn't get completely out of hand. Jazz was so nervous he damn near left the store. He could not believe how Jessica was behaving. If pressure bust pipes, then Jazz's main artery was in a thousand pieces.

Soon, Jessica, her mother, and the heavyset man approached the checkout counter. The bald, heavyset man paid nearly a thousand dollars for women clothing and accessories. Jessica's mother stood rubbing the man's back, and Jessica winked her eye at Jazz. "Call me," Jessica whispered, holding her left hand up to her ear and mouth like a telephone.

THIRTY-EIGHT

It was an extremely quiet morning in the inner city. Even the birds sounded shallow. There wasn't a breeze, just stillness. Everything appeared exhausted. This was strange for the inner city, one plus one equaling four. According to the signs in the air, midnight had rolled into the day.

Six o'clock in the morning, Karen was awakened by the telephone. The assistant pastor of her church called requesting that she arrive at church by seven, thirty a.m. so she could teach Sunday school. Karen agreed, forever pleased to cover for a spiritual colleague.

Having only an hour and a half to arrive at church on time, Karen hurried to prepare herself. She awakened Mahogany and Stefaughn, excited to lead Sunday school.

Seventeen minutes had passed, and Karen hadn't seen or heard Stefaughn moving around. She returned to his bedroom. He was asleep, happily in love with his pillow.

"Boy, get up! You're not missing church, today," Karen said.

"All right, all right . . . I'm woke," Stefaughn uttered. "I'll be ready." He reached over and picked up the telephone receiver.

****

Dread removed the bedclothes from over his head. He rubbed Rochelle's breast as she talked on the telephone.

"Hey, baby. What have you calling so early?" Rochelle asked.

Dread sneezed. There was silence.

"Who was that?"

Scarlet Tears

"Stefaughn, that's my son sneezing with his scary butt. He always run in here throughout the night talking about he be dreaming." Rochelle snorted. "You know how he is."

Rochelle listened on the telephone. Dread licked her breast, happy he'd found his man.

"I ain't doing nothing. And what's up with all these early morning questions? If you were here you wouldn't have any questions." Rochelle signaled for Dread to stop licking her breast, her nipples hard like tiny cannon balls.

"Thanks for the reminder, but I hadn't forgotten," she said to Stefaughn. "What time do you have to be at church? And what church do you attend?" Listening, Rochelle looked at the small digital clock on the dresser. "That'll be around seven, thirty. And I heard Rhema was a good church. But why so early?" She listened some more. "Well good luck. And I'll be ready at one o'clock to go eat. Maybe my kids and I will go with y'all next week."

Rochelle ended the telephone call. Dread heard everything he wanted to hear. He'd been searching for Stefaughn, in desperate need of his cash. Stefaughn was apparently afraid and lacking funds, placing himself in harm's way. Rochelle was unfaithful, doing whatever to pay the bills. So scary, so widespread, just reality.

"Yo, Rochelle, I gotta bust uh move," Dread said. "Take dhis fifty spot, and I'll call you later."

"Fifty!" she retorted. "Oh, so you're into that hit and run shit, too?" She paused. Dread grinned. "That's cool. And you know you love this pussy. But handle yo' business."

Completely dressed, Dread left without cleaning himself. He crossed the street in front of Rochelle's apartment and quickly entered a car with Indiana license plates. Dread hurried to the nearest telephone booth, a professional at knavery.

"Yo, what up, derrty. Showtime! You know who he be," Dread said.

"Straight up! How's the clock looking?"

"Dhat muthafucka tickin' as we talk."

"Enough said. Get here!" the guy on the other end said.

Excited in the name of evil, Dread sat back in the car he was driving and snorted two lines of cocaine. He was charged, completely away from sanity. Although paranoid, Dread safely drove to pick up his main crony in crime, a heartless scab.

****

Meanwhile, Karen, Mahogany, and Stefaughn were just about prepared for church. Karen's home smelled good, enlivened with quality perfume. There wasn't any time to prepare a good breakfast; therefore, everyone ate Hostess powder and coconut donuts and drank cold milk.

"Hey, it's five after seven. Are y'all ready in there?" Karen asked. "I want to make it to church a little early, so I can go over a few things with the senior pastor."

"Yeah. We're ready," Stefaughn answered.

Within minutes, they left. Everyone was in a great mood, ready for God.

****

Driving on Cass Avenue, Stefaughn and family neared The Rhema Church. "Yeah, look at da lil punk, now. Thinkin' God gone erase all his problems." Dread paused. "Just like uh sissy, runnin' to church."

"Hurry up, Dread. Put yo' mask on. I'll drop all three of 'em with this nine if you want me to."

"Naw, not dhis time. Killin' dhem hoes by uh church will attract da Major Case Squad. Just knock Stef. Dhat way won't too many people give uh damn."

"Word up! Let me toot this button real quickly, then ease up on them fools, Dread. Stef's a dead man."

The individual charged himself with heroin. He slid on a black ski mask and black gloves. He kept his nine millimeter in his shoulder holster, however, cocking his chrome .45 revolver. "Everything looks good, Dread. Let's do this."

Dread eased away from his parking spot, caring less about his surroundings. He drove down the street as if everything was normal. Both Dread and his partner were skilled murderers, eliminating their own kind.

"We got this lame, now, Dread," the gunman said. Dread drove up on Stefaughn and his family from the rear. "Well, he can say hello to my new friend."

Squealing, the car came to a sudden stop. The masked gunman quickly exited the car, his gun blazing. Stefaughn, Karen, and Mahogany were shell-shocked, ducking and placing their hands over their heads. Stefaughn was hit, now holding his stomach.

"POW! POW! POW!" sounded the large caliber weapon, its chamber emptying.

Mahogany ran screaming. Karen stood in total shock. Two other individuals who were standing in front of the church ran inside. Stefaughn rested on the concrete sidewalk, blood pouring from his wounds.

Dread and the gunman escaped the scene. They cut a quick left on a side street. They were crazed, experiencing the rush of cold-blooded murder. This was a fatal drive-by attack, a violent shooting spurred by urban psychosis.

****

On bended knee, Karen cried. She gazed at her son, bearing the pains of tragedy. "Who did this to you, Stefaughn?" she sobbed uncontrollably. "Tell me! Tell me, baby! Please don't die!"

Stefaughn couldn't yet respond, the heat from the bullets burning his soul. He'd been shot nearly point-blank range, twice in the chest, twice in the stomach, and once in his left thigh. The other bullet missed. Images of death set still in Karen's mind; her son's eyes were devoid of fight.

****

Her face drenched with tears, Mahogany ran back to where Stefaughn lay flat on his backside. She struggled to utter a single word, fear having grasped her tongue like a pair of C clamps. Mahogany dropped to her knees, placing Stefaughn's right hand between her palms. His hands were bloody and cold. This was a sad morning, a day without sunshine.

"I . . . feel . . . st . . . stiff, M, Momma," Stefaughn stammered, blood pouring from his bullet wounds. "It, it's . . . h . . . hot, Mo----"

Mahogany cried harder. Karen cried harder. The three of them were colored in blood.

"Will somebody help us?!" Karen begged in desperation, drunk in despair.

"Just hang on, ma'am. Help is on the way," an elderly man yelled from the east parking lot.

A crowd encompassed the scene. The clergy and church members were now down on their knees next to Karen and Mahogany. Police cars hurried to the scene, sirens wailing. Nobody knew what to do, fear and disbelief strangling all thought. This was far past a simple gunshot, a simple wound. A stream of blood leaked from the curb onto the street, and death danced in the air.

"D, don't . . . l, let me . . . die, Momma," Stefaughn gasped, blood seeping from the left corner of his mouth. "It h, hurt. . . . H, help me."

"Hang on, baby," Karen cried, tears dripping into her son's blood. "Help is on the way."

Everyone in proximity hugged one another and sobbed. They prayed, asking God to sustain Stefaughn's life. Suddenly, Stefaughn's head leaned over towards Mahogany. His eyes were open, yet no movement, no life. Mahogany screamed, feeling Stefaughn's spirit withdraw from his body. Fifteen minutes had passed, and there was still no ambulance.

"Come on, Lord! Where are you?" Karen pled, looking into the dull sky. "Tell me my baby ain't dead!" She paused, gazing at Stefaughn. "He's alive, isn't he, Lord? Isn't he?" Again, Karen stared into the morning heavens.

Scarlet Tears

With their sirens wailing and lights flashing, two ambulances arrived. The paramedics hurried from the ambulances and ran to where Stefaughn lay with several police officers. After checking Stefaughn's vital signs, he was pronounced dead on the scene. Stefaughn's violent death was a mental blow to his family, to the church congregation, to humanity. He was considered a happy, fun-loving young man by everyone. His term on Earth had expired, now resting in a perpetual sleep.

Searching for clues, the police asked questions, No one really knew anything, except for a partial description of the vehicle used in the crime.

"I can't believe my baby is dead," Karen stood to her feet and hollered. She pulled her hair. She jumped up and down in agony, under attack by grief. Paramedics rushed Karen to Barnes-Jewish Hospital along with her son.

Congregants of The Rhema Church and local citizens held hands in a moment of prayer. Next, they sang gospel songs to the Man/Woman upstairs. Everyone yearned to overcome, longing for a brighter day. Stefaughn's murder was the blackening of a tired eye, a strong reason to unite against foolishness. Good versus bad was on the way; an end to senselessness had been summoned.

Mahogany was emotionally riddled, torn apart by the plight of her race. Helplessly lost, Mahogany cried everyone's tears. Witnessing Stefaughn's death, Mahogany felt bereaved. Life began seeming so unfair, so worthless. Mahogany couldn't understand what was wrong with the Black race. She figured in her neighborhood such a brutal, heinous act would have never occurred. It is there . . . she wanted away.

Mourning the death of Stefaughn, life for Mahogany and The Rhema Church would never be the same.

THIRTY-NINE

"Are you sure you don't want to go for a ride, Mahogany. We can stop by Denny's or Steak and Shake and grab a bite to eat."

"No, Knigel. I just want to relax so I can try pulling myself together," she said. "I've been talking to police and at the hospital all day with my family. Besides . . . it's almost midnight."

"It's whatever you want, love. And how is your mother and father taking all this?"

"They're taking it pretty hard, especially my mother." Mahogany took a seat in Jazz's entertainment room, reaching for the television remote control on the cocktail table. "My mother didn't want to leave the hospital, but visiting hours were over. So her and my dad decided to stay at my aunt's house so they could return to the hospital and pick up my aunt in the morning."

"And how are you since you wouldn't talk to me in the car?"

"I apologize, Knigel." She paused. "Anyway, I'm okay."

"Well, that's some good news. And, again, I'm very sorry about what took place this morning," he said. "Can I help you with anything?"

Mahogany scanned through the television stations. "I wouldn't mind taking a warm bath and try getting some sleep. So do you have a long T-shirt I can wear?"

"Plenty of them," Jazz replied. He kissed Mahogany on the forehead. "Make yourself at home while I go and get your bath water star----"

"Hold up, Knigel. I want to discuss something with you regarding what happened today."

"I'm all ears, love. Is it okay if I sit next to you?"

"Ha-ha. Boy, I told you I was all right."

Jazz sat next to Mahogany. He gazed into her eyes and said, "I love you, Mahogany."

"Okay, we'll get to that later. But check this out." She paused again. "I think I have an idea of who's responsible for my cousin's murder."

"Tell me you're shitting me."

"No. I honestly think I do."

"Fill me in then."

"Last night, Stefaughn and I discussed his personal life. He kept saying he was in debt to this guy, named Tony. But Tony's real nickname is Dread----"

"Who?" Jazz interrupted.

"Tony or Dread. What? Do you know him?"

"Just keep going. I want to make sure of something first."

"Well my cousin wouldn't say how much he was in debt or why he owed the guy. But I do have an idea, because Stefaughn was unemployed and I noticed all types of new stuff inside his bedroom when we were talking last night. Items I know his mother wouldn't dare purchase."

"I think I'm familiar with that line of business."

"Yeah . . . you are. Anyway, I've met the guy, named Dread twice before. Once at Dave and Buster's in Earth City and at this nightclub, called The Rio."

"Dave an----"

"Hold up. Let me finish," she said. "Dread drove a convertible Mercedes and claimed he wanted to promote some concerts at Adam's Mark. But he never followed through with his claims. All talk and no show." Mahogany paused. "In so many words, Stefaughn informed me that he was afraid of this guy and didn't trust him or the dude's brother-in-law, anymore. I believe that's why he was in the process of reuniting with God."

"Did you tell the police all this?"

"No. I want to speak with my aunt, first. She may know something I don't know."

"Okay, I've heard of a cat, named Dread. And I know several dudes, named Tony. Oh yeah, I think Dread does drive a Mercedes. Did you see the shooter's face?"

"No. They had on ski masks. And it all happened so quickly. I ran the minute I realized what was actually going down." She hesitated. "Reflecting back, I could tell that the shooter was a Black male with dark eyes and maybe five feet, ten inches tall."

"I don't know Mahogany. I've heard some foul things about Dread. And how would someone know to catch your cousin going to church that early in the morning?"

"Now that's a good question, especially since Stefaughn wasn't attending church on a regular basis. Then, too, we were going to church extra early because of his mother. Either they were watching us or got tipped off."

"Now you're talking."

"There's only one person I know of that my cousin talked to last night, and that's this girl, named Rochelle. She lives on Page. And we were supposed to pick her up after church so we could go and eat."

"Babe, that's worth investigating in my book. And you said you met Dread at Dave and Buster's, right?"

"Yeah, you were at work that day. It was a business meeting. My cousin insisted that I meet the guy."

"Oh, I see. Uh-huh, if I was your family I'd start with that chick, Rochelle. It just sounds like a Saint Louis classic."

"What do you mean by that?"

"Dudes be meeting these sheisty broads, thinking they're all that. But the whole time the broad is only out for the money. Meaning . . . anything goes, including setting up cats to be robbed."

Mahogany shook her head in disgrace. "The little I've seen and learned about the inner city is terrifying. It all seems like a fiction movie. You know . . . this big ass story tale. I had no idea people were actually doing all of these crazy

Scarlet Tears

things. I mean . . . you hear about it, but seeing is believing. And why did you choose to sell drugs?"

"Uh, now that's a super long story. Let me go and get the Jacuzzi started and a T-shirt, then I'll have the story abridged by the time I return."

Jazz got up from the sofa. Mahogany stared at Jazz from the rear. Something told her Jazz knew more than he claimed. Thirsty, Mahogany got up from the sofa and walked into the kitchen. She pulled open the refrigerator door. There was a variety of drinks.

Mahogany removed a plastic container of Florida-Style Sunny Delight from the top shelf inside of the refrigerator. She walked towards the sink to obtain a clean glass from the dish rack that set next to the sink. Looking in the sink, Mahogany noticed a glass with a colored lip print on its brim. She picked up the glass out of the sink and smelled the lip print.

This smells just like that cherry stuff Jessica be wearing, Mahogany thought. *Well, it could be from his mother.*

Overlooking the lip print on the glass, Mahogany poured herself a glass of Sunny Delight. She replaced the plastic container inside of the refrigerator and returned to the sofa in the entertainment room. Mahogany busted into laughter. On television, Fred Sanford stood arguing with Esta.

Wanting to get more comfortable, Mahogany removed her earrings and watch. She dropped one of her earrings in front of the sofa. Mahogany reached down to pick up her earring and noticed a silver item sitting on the carpet by the edge of the sofa. She picked up the silver item and her earring. Mahogany then read the reverse side of the silver item. She flipped it over and read the front side:

Jessica Francis
"Ms. LEGS"
11-29-1977
Conference USA

This was more than a coincidence; it was fact-finding, a secret unveiled in an instant. Mahogany temperature soared; her cool fled. She was on the brink of detonating.

"Knigel!" she screamed, ambulating back into the kitchen.

Jazz ran into the entertainment room. He stopped dead in his tracks. Mahogany stood in his pathway with the glass from the sink and the metal identification tag in her other hand.

"The truth!" she ordered, tears streaming down her cheeks.

"Uh . . . uh . . . I can explain, Mahogany."

"Tell me it isn't true, Knigel!" she yelled. "You've been with my friend, haven't you?"

"Mahogany, please stop shouting. I can explain."

"Well explain, Knigel! Explain!" Mahogany cried harder. Her lips and cheeks trembled.

"I . . . I can only say that I love you." Knigel held down his head. "And there's nothing serious between Jessica and me." He paused. "She asked to come over the day my game got canceled, and I figured everything would be okay."

"Okay, why is her dog tag off, Knigel?! Why, Knigel?! Answer me!"

"Okay, okay, just relax, babe. All we did was kissed."

Mahogany slung the glass she was holding. It crashed into a framed wall mirror, exploding into a thousand bits of sharp-edged glass. The wall mirror shattered. Jazz appeared frightened.

"Mahogany, no more! Or you'll force me to call nine-one-one."

"Oh, Mister Drug Dealer running to the police, now. Ain't that some shit!" Mahogany uttered, staring at Jazz's stupid face expression. "You're already in trouble. And you know what? You'll never be the man my father is! I hate you, Knigel! I hate you!"

Mahogany stalked over to the cocktail table and grabbed her belongings. She knocked over the glass lamp that set on the end table. It broke into large pieces of pointed glass.

Mahogany then placed Jessica's silver dog tag in her pants pocket.

"Where are you going, Mahogany? It's too late to leave here without your car."

"Too late my ass, you whore!" Furious, in rage, Mahogany was 666. "Don't worry about me, you unfaithful, dope-pushing, no-good bastard!" She removed the engagement ring from her finger and threw it on the floor.

"Why are you calling me names, Mahogany? You're losing me. And let me drive you home, please."

"Yeah, I've lost you! And kiss my ass!" Mahogany yelled and stormed through the foyer leading to the front door.

"Mahogany!"

The front door slammed. Working things out with Mahogany was beyond remedy.

Light rains drizzled from above. Looking around, there wasn't any motion in Paddock Forest. The huge houses stood bold beneath the midnight sky. Dismal from betrayal, Mahogany walked the silent, misty streets. Tears seeped from her eyes; heartbreak slowed her every step. Mahogany could not control the pain. In a million years, she would have never thought of Jessica backstabbing her. They'd come a long way as friends. In retrospect, Mahogany now understood why Jessica was behaving in such a strange way at Jazz's Women Apparel & Lingerie. She figured the sex must have been good; however, the mystery puzzle was now assembled.

Mahogany walked through the wooded neighborhood, talking to self. Her clothing was soaking wet, sticking to her skin. It didn't matter, though. Mahogany felt that life was hell.

A car stopped.

"Pardon me, miss. Is everything okay?" an older, White female asked. "And would you like a ride?"

"No thank you, ma'am. I'll be okay. But how do I get to the main road?"

"You just follow this road until it comes to an end. Then you make a left on Lakeside Hills and follow it to

Partridge Run. Swing a right on Partridge Run and follow it to Parker Road, which is the main road. Anyhow, I'll be more than happy to give you a lift, dear. Trust me I've been where you are before."

"Thanks a lot, ma'am. But I'm fine. And I appreciate the directions."

"Well okay, hon. Can't say I didn't try. And please be careful."

As the lady drove off, Mahogany waved good-bye. Twelve minutes later, Mahogany had made it to the main road. She crossed the street, wishing she'd brought her cellular telephone. Mahogany located a pay phone on the lot of an Amoco gas station. She removed several coins from her purse, inserted them into the coin slot, and dialed a number.

"Hello."

"Daddy, come and get me," she sobbed.

"Baby, what's the matter? Are you okay?"

"No. Knigel is no g---"

"Did that nigga put his hands on you?"

"No. I'll explain everything when you pick me up."

"Then why are you crying? And where are you?"

"It's just a matter of everything." Mahogany sniffled, the moist night air streaming through her nostrils. "I'm at Amoco on Parker Road and Three Sixty-seven in North County."

"I know where that is. But isn't it. . . ." He paused. "That was your mother wanting to know if you were okay. Is it raining out there?"

"Yes, but I'm all right. Just hurry and bring me my night bag from the guest room in Aunt Karen's house."

"Will do, honey. And something told me to keep my cell phone on. You know I usually turn it off at night."

"Okay. Hurry, Dad."

Standing in the night drizzle, the night winds increasing discomfort, Mahogany refused to step inside of the gas station. Patrons, stopping for gasoline, continually asked Mahogany if she was fine. Unable to stop crying, Mahogany

Scarlet Tears

handled the situation as best as she could. This was a gloomy moment in time, the pouring of *Scarlet Tears.*

FORTY

Tuesday, July 18, 2000

Karen had been released from the hospital. She was okay, but life was quite different now. Her words were few and empty as she grieved the sudden, vicious lost of her only child. Karen longed for answers, the reason behind it all. She was God's soldierette, married to her Faith. Yet, Karen felt like she'd been handed over, delivered into the hands of Satan.

    Karen was prescribed a medication to help cope with her situation. She refused to use it, yearning the facts that led to her son's death. Karen searched Stefaughn's bedroom, prowling for a simple clue. She found nothing, except for a lot of new clothes and two gold necklaces with medallions. Her find sparked wonder but offered no answers. However, Karen firmly believed that if one seeks one shall find.

    Burdened and having made general funeral arrangements, Karen spread the information via telephone and E-mail. She waited on Sophia to arrive, so they could continue planning the funeral. Karen decided to rest for a while. She was catching a headache, growing tired of everything.

****

Mahogany was at work, working on a solution to her personal woes. She was bothered, needing someone to lean on. Mahogany decided to call Jamie, her roommate from college. Jamie was not at home, but her father gave Mahogany her work telephone number. Insisting that she speak with Jamie, Mahogany called her at work.

Scarlet Tears

"J.F. Chemical. How can I help you?"

"Jamie Hightower, please."

"Sure. Can you hold?"

Waiting to hear Jamie's voice, Mahogany doodled on a scratch pad.

"This is Jamie."

"Surprise!"

"What's up, Mahogany?" Jamie said with excitement.

"Too much to mention. And how's the new job?"

"I really like it, especially the pay."

"That's good. I'm happy for you."

"Mahogany, I was just speaking about you last night when I bumped into Gale at the seven o'clock movie. She wanted to know if I'd heard from you. Anyway, I told her you were doing fine since we last talked a month ago."

"Yes, I'm surviving, and that's special of her to ask about me. But I do have some bad news."

"Oh, I hope everything is okay."

"Well . . . Stefaughn, my cousin from the graduation. . . ."

"Yes, I remember him."

"He was murdered right before my eyes."

"Are you serious, Mahogany?"

"Unfortunately, yes."

"I'm so sorry to hear that. So when is the funeral?"

"This Saturday at noon."

"I want to come and support, Mahogany. Can you pick me up from you all's airport Friday evening if a flight is available?"

"Of course. And I apologize for the bad news."

"Mahogany, you owe me no apology. That's what true friends are for, being there for each other regardless of the sitation."

"Thanks, Jamie."

"Well, give me the phone number to where you're at, and I'll call you back with my flight information."

Mahogany gave Jamie her work telephone number, her home telephone number, and her cellular telephone number. She ended the telephone call and returned to her duties. Mahogany always enjoyed speaking with Jamie. Jamie reminded Mahogany of herself: thoughtful, understanding, and loyal.

It was approaching one p.m. Mahogany had bypassed lunch. She sat and keyed Jessica a letter on her office computer:

7/18/2000

To Jessica:

What have we here? It's dreary outside, not a beautiful summer day. That explains exactly how I feel. Nonetheless, I'm positive you weren't expecting a letter from me with your "dog" tag enclosed. You'll never guess where I discovered it. Yep . . . you're right—over at my ex-fiancé's house. So, what's your definition of a friend? Oh, don't bother to share your faulty explanation. I already know your definition: A SLIPPERY SNAKE!

Regardless of what you are, I sincerely wish you well. Hopefully, you and Knigel will learn values and live happily ever after. I'm pulling for you guys. So please . . . smile for me.

Staying true,

A REAL WOMAN

P.S. I'm sure you're aware of what happened to my cousin; it's been all over the news. Unfortunately—that wasn't. . . .

Mahogany printed the letter, placed both it and Jessica's dog tag inside an envelope, added postage, and addressed the envelope. She dropped the envelope inside of the office outgoing mail bin, experiencing a sense of relief. She returned to her desk and noticed the extension light blinking on her office telephone. She answered it.

"How are you, Mahogany? This is John Warrenberg."

"I'm making it, but matters could be better. Anyway, how are you, sir?"

"I'm just fine, but I have both some good news and some bad news. And that's the order I prefer to give it to you. So are you ready?"

Mahogany took a deep breath. "Okay, let me have it."

"The good news is I've spotted several loopholes in this case, putting you in a better situation than Knigel. The rule states that the burden of proof lies on the prosecution, and I can't possibly see them proving that you knowingly associate with illegal activities, unless there is something you haven't told me," he said. "Well, I'm sure this situation has been causing you a world of difficulty. Mahogany, just continue trying to relax and let me work my magic. I'm seriously working my pants off for you. Now, do you have a pen and a piece of paper near? Because you need to record the information I'm preparing to tell you."

"Go ahead. I'm ready."

"Your arraignment is scheduled for Monday, July thirty-first, at nine a.m. You have to be at the United States District Court in East Saint Louis, Illinois. Its address is seven hundred Missouri Avenue. And you're to go in front of Magistrate Holcombe." He sneezed. "Pardon me, Mahogany."

"Bless you."

"Thanks. However, I advise you to dress conservatively and have as many friends and family members there as possible. We have to make a strong statement of support, because you're being charged with a serious crime. But not to worry, for I'm sure they will let you remain free on your own recognizance," he stated. "This is all procedure."

"Okay, I've written all that down, but I don't understand a few of these words."

"Never mind that. I'll have my secretary to fax you everything I've just told you in detail. And a good book to purchase for understanding legal terminology is *Black's Law Dictionary*."

"Hold up while I jot that down."

Mr. Warrenberg paused; then he said, "Be sure to purchase the latest edition which is the Seventh. It's highly enlightening. Now . . . the bad news. Your fiancé is buried in trouble, and the federal judicial system is a lot harder to beat than the state. I've talked to a few people about this matter, and it's typically ugly. Well, for my staff and me to continue working on this case, I'm definitely going to need half of what I would normally charge for such a high-profile case. That's fifty percent of forty thousand dollars." He paused. "I'm willing to accept so little because you're a friend of the family, and I want to see you walk away from this horrible ordeal like the champ you are. This probably sounds like a lot to you, but it's requiring, and will continue to require, a lot of energy and strategy trying to get things to work in our favor. Believe me . . . it's no easy fight over there in the Southern District of Illinois."

"Okay, I understand, Mister Warrenberg. I just want out of it. I haven't done anything wrong."

"I'm certain you haven't, dear. But the system plays by different standards. I'm sorry, Mahogany. We just have to go through the motions."

"Now raising that type of money will definitely have to include my parents. So I guess I'll sit down with them this evening and explain everything," Mahogany said. "Will it be okay if they call you?"

"Absolutely not a problem and I'm looking forward to speaking with them. Take down my cell number if you don't mind."

Mahogany wrote down the cellular telephone number. She provided Mr. Warrenberg with her office facsimile number. A sign of hope tingled in her heart; nevertheless, it was impossible to expunge her fear of unchartered waters.

FORTY-ONE

Friday, July 21, 2000

Mahogany was granted a day off from work. Everyone on her job had been expressing his or her sympathy over the loss of her cousin.

It was early, the city blessed with a beautiful day. Mahogany and her mother were on their way to pick up Karen. They had arranged to speak with Rochelle. Rochelle did not mind, hoping to learn the mystery behind Stefaughn's death.

Mr. Brown had also taken the day off from work. He was at the bank ordering a cashier's check to pay Mahogany's attorney. Mr. Brown wasn't happy with the decision, because he'd briefed Mahogany's situation with four other criminal attorneys who'd basically offered the same information and services, but for a significant lower fee. However, Mr. Warrenberg had won Mahogany's trust; therefore, he was the chosen candidate.

Everyone was prepared for the funeral. Karen, her church administration, Wade Funeral Services, and Sophia had organized everything in a professional, timely manner. In hours, Stefaughn would be lowered six feet deep into the earth.

Mahogany would have to pick up Jamie from Lambert St. Louis International Airport at 8:30 p.m. They had a lot to discuss. This wasn't the normal Friday; it was a blue day, one fraught with severe issues.

Having picked up Karen, Mahogany and her mother arrived at Rochelle's apartment. They were dazed by the exterior of the apartment building. Once they entered the

Scarlet Tears

apartment building, Mahogany, Karen, and Sophia noticed trash scattered across the corridors, writing on the walls, and large holes in the corridor walls. The smell of mold and dirty diapers spoiled the air. The small doors to the private mailboxes were broken, some only attached by a single hinge. There was below average lighting throughout the apartment building, and yelling voices sounded through the corridors. The facility had condemned written all over it, yet human life existed behind every closed door in the building. Mahogany and family were afraid for their lives. Anyhow, they refused to turn away, seeking just a single clue or partial answer leading to Stefaughn's murder.

Knock-knock-knock. . . .

"Who is it?" a woman said from the other side of the door.

"It's me, Stefaughn's mother," Karen replied.

Rochelle opened the door, her smile charming with two gold teeth. Rochelle was cute, but clearly into the hood of things. She welcomed everyone inside the apartment, her twin daughters holding onto her shapely legs. The twins were sucking their thumbs. It was picture time, a precious reason to smile.

"Hi! I'm Karen, Stefaughn's mother. This is my sister, Sophia, and her daughter, Mahogany."

"It's nice to meet y'all. Please have a seat."

Mahogany and family looked around, surprised by Rochelle's clean, cozy, well-decorated apartment.

"Rochelle, I really appreciate you allowing us to come speak with you. It's nice people like you who make life special."

"Really? Thanks a lot, Miss Karen. Anyway, this is Salina, the oldest of the twins, and she's Katina, the youngest. LeRon, my son, is upstairs over to my friend's. So what's the deal?"

"Excuse me for a second," Mahogany said. "Aren't they beautiful, Momma?"

"Yes. Two of the prettiest little girls I've ever seen."

"You people are so nice." Rochelle paused. "Just like Stefaughn was."

Suddenly, a roach sped across the removable tray of a high chair that set in the small living room. Mahogany became uncomfortable, again. She had to itch.

"Don't let that bother y'all. I've been trying like hell to rid those things. That's why I hate I lost Stefaughn, because we were making plans to relocate to a better neighborhood with better apartments."

"That's a first," Karen said. "Stefaughn was presently unemployed."

"Uh, are you sure? He told me he had a job."

"Well, maybe you can tell me something I don't know. He lived with me and hadn't had a job in the last four months."

"Although we hadn't been dating very long, he was never broke. And he was real freehearted. Actually, he was the one who gave me the down payment for the furniture we are all sitting on."

"Are you serious?" Karen asked.

"Uh-huh. That's why I don't understand how someone could kill him like that."

"Whoever is responsible for his murder will be brought to justice, sooner or later. Nobody can escape karma," Sophia said.

"What's karma?" Rochelle asked.

"Cause and effect. You know . . . reap what you sow either in this life or the next life."

"Oh yeah. You got that right, ma'am," Rochelle uttered. "So you're the Mahogany Stefaughn always bragged about. Girl, you must be a swell sister."

"I guess I'm okay. But I still have some growing to do."

"Huh, that makes two of us, then."

"Rochelle, did you know that we were going to church extra early the morning my son was murdered?" Karen asked. "I'm aware that you all had plans for dinner at one o'clock that day." Karen paused. "But don't mistake me; I'm certainly not accusing you of anything."

"No, I didn't think that. And yeah, I knew y'all were going to church early that morning. He called and told me. But I promise you I didn't tell anybody y'all were going to church that early. Truthfully, I fell right back to sleep."

"I believe you, dear. But is there anything you would like to share with us regarding my son?"

"I'll say this much," Rochelle paused, "I honestly believe he was selling drugs on the DL."

"The DL. What's that, baby?"

"The down low, Aunt Karen," Mahogany said.

"Oh, some ole street talk," said Karen. "But why you say that, Rochelle?"

"Because a few times I saw him with a little too much bread for a man who only worked a regular job. Then sometimes he would have to leave when his pager go off. Just little signs like that tell a story. At least I believe."

"Well, I searched his bedroom, and I didn't find a pager or a lot of money." Karen paused. "Isn't that something? You never know what's going on in this world."

"Wait a minute, y'all. I have to answer the phone." Rochelle set the twins in their play pin. She walked into her bedroom.

Rochelle was a loud talker, easily heard in the living room. Her apartment was small.

"Dread, I told you I was chilling," Rochelle said.

Mahogany eyes widened, quickly gesturing for her family to keep quiet. They listened closely to Rochelle on the telephone.

"Just like I told you the other day, I ain't finna let no' men use me. You showed me what you were about Sunday morning. Gone fuck my brains out and leave me wit' fifty lousy dollars," Rochelle continued. "Boy, I got three damn mouths to feed around here, plus my own. Then bills on top of that. And you know better than I know—welfare ain't enough."

A bell dinged inside Mahogany's head, the mystery unraveling. She whispered to her mother and Karen that there was something important she needed to share with them and to let her take charge of the conversation when Rochelle re-entered the living room.

"Okay, Dread, I gotta go. My babies are crying in the other room. When you feel like paying me what I'm worth, then you can hit this again. See, we enjoy the finer things in life, too. Like Gucci, Fendi, and all them good things. Until then—keep fiending."

Mahogany heard the telephone slam.

"Y'all couldn't hear me in there, right?" Rochelle asked.

Mahogany, Karen, and Sophia all looked at one another. "No. Not me," they said.

"Good! That was one of my stupid friends."

"Yeah, we all have a few of them. So you're not by yourself, Rochelle," Mahogany said.

"I sure can tell you ain't from the city, Mahogany. You talk almost like a White girl."

Silence leaped onto the stage. Mahogany thought what to say next. "Rochelle, I was talking with Stefaughn the night before he was murdered, in which he called you that night. He said the reason he'd slacked up coming over here was because it wasn't safe anymore," Mahogany said. "Why do you think he said that?"

"Beats me. He never told me that."

"Okay, the morning he was killed, you're for sure nobody else knew we were going to church on your behalf?" Mahogany asked.

Rochelle gazed at Karen. "Check this out. I'ma say this much. I did have a male friend over that Sunday. But he and Stefaughn don't know one another that I know of. My friend was asleep when me and Stefaughn talked early that morning. Hell, you might as well say I was, too," she said. "Other than that, it's nothing else I can tell y'all." Rochelle walked to the front door. She opened it. "Okay, it was nice meeting y'all."

309

"It was nice meeting you, too, Rochelle," Karen said. "And we appreciate your time."

"Be good. And take special care of those angels," Sophia said.

"Will do, miss."

"Hopefully, we'll meet again, but on a better note."

"Yeah, okay, Mahogany. And I'll talk to y'all later."

Mahogany and family exited the apartment building, delighted to have escaped alive. Mahogany stared back at the shattered glass doors of the apartment building. She felt sorry for the twins, wanting to do something special for them. Notably, Mahogany had enough problems of her own and was hot on the demon's trail.

Once inside her mother's car, Mahogany explained everything she knew leading up to Stefaughn's murder. It all made sense to Karen and Sophia, perfect addition. Nonetheless, there were two individuals who carried out Stefaughn's murder, and neither of their faces was seen. The puzzle was yet solved.

FORTY-TWO

It took Mahogany precisely twenty-seven days to rid herself of Jazz, eleven hundred eighty-five days for Jessica, but twenty-one short years to lose her favorite cousin. Also, there remained one dark spot in Mahogany's life, a ruthless foe of productivity.

However, it was the day of Stefaughn's funeral, a day foreshadowed with grief, pain, and anguish. The Rhema Church was full to capacity. Everyone was dressed in his or her finest. The flower arrangement surrounding Stefaughn's elegant wooden casket was beautiful. A portrait of Stefaughn set on a shiny brass tripod. Many wept in sorrow, deeply disappointed by the premature loss of a young soul filled with potential.

Mahogany and her family sat together, consoling one another. Karen was dressed in black, her face concealed beyond a veil. Family and friends mourned, listening to the wailing organ. The mood was sad, forty rainy days and nights.

The assistant pastor rendered a heartfelt prayer, marking the opening of the ceremony. He read a Scripture. The church's choir sung a hymn. Sensitivity and sniffling increased. Next, Mahogany and family were introduced to read letters and poems from themselves and distant friends. The funeral director then spoke a brief passage. Things were progressing along smoothly, one step at a time.

St. Louis Metropolitan Area's local R&B songstress, Traneen, was directed to the flowery platform to sing a solo. Traneen appeared confident as she ambled to the platform in her wine-colored, partially fitted dress. She was becoming, unique with a wavy, low haircut. Rumor was that the House of God was the foundation of her stardom.

Scarlet Tears

As Traneen began to sing, Mahogany looked over her shoulder. She noticed two black males walking into the sanctuary. They were ushered to seats two rows behind the last row of seats that were reserved for the family of the deceased. The people in the row were asked to sit closer. They shifted. The two Black males took a seat.

Turning back towards the singer, Mahogany thought, *Now I know that isn't who I think it is.* Mahogany glanced over her shoulder again. She and one of the Black males locked eyes. Signals flared. *No! This guy is too strong. Come on, God, please keep it peaceful.* Mahogany was paranoid, losing focus.

Jamie seemed to have noticed something wrong with Mahogany. She kept whispering, asking if everything was all right. Mahogany denied being uneasy.

Listening to Traneen's powerful, soulful, heart-grasping voice, women began shouting; many wiped tears from their eyes; some called on the Lord; and others shook their heads, lamenting. It was a shallow moment, Heaven's spirit moving through the soloist's voice.

Karen slowly began leaning forward. She appeared devoid of life. The singer's voice seemed to be too much, consuming souls at bay. All guilt was cornered, staring into the pitch-black barrel of God's judgment. Conversely, individuals hurried to Karen's rescue. Prayers flew into the warm air begging for God's help. Suddenly, Karen told family and friends that she couldn't take any more of the singer's song. She then asked for a glass of water.

Someone signaled Traneen to cut it short. Mahogany was unsettled, staring at Jamie covering her face with her hands. "Jamie, are you okay?" Mahogany asked.

Jamie moved her hands from her face; her facial expression clearly stated that she wasn't well.

Curious of the strange men seated behind her, Mahogany couldn't concentrate while reading her obituary. Mahogany scribbled a message on her obituary; she handed it to her mother. Sophia read the message. She gazed at Mahogany. Neither said anything. Sophia excused herself from her family, saying that she had to use the ladies room. Curiosity maimed the cat.

Moving along, Bishop Rainwater, the widely-revered spiritual leader of Faithful Central Bible Church in Inglewood, California, and the Great West Forum delivered a twelve minute, ardent speech. He was the visiting minister and a very close friend of, both, the deceased's family and the senior pastor. Bishop Rainwater was brilliant, his speech hitting home. He reminded the audience that the greatest revenge was forgiveness and nothing reflected God more than kind words, positive thinking, and love. He also stated that evil's day of destruction was quickly approaching and that anything ungodly couldn't evade God's punishment. In closing, Bishop Rainwater said Stefaughn was now in God's care.

The church choir sang another selection. The eulogy was next, and the senior pastor gave it. His sincere tribute brought back the tears, especially when he said, "Stefaughn, I want you to know . . . if I could decorate the night firmament, I'd carefully position you as the brightest star."

There would be no open-casket parting view. Yet, there was a recessional, the committal, and finally the benediction.

Mahogany noticed the two, well-dressed Black males standing outside the church talking with others. She quietly asked Karen to take a good look at them.

Peering through her veil, Karen said, "Hey, I know the shorter one. That is Stefaughn's close friend." Karen entered the white limousine.

With everyone inside the limousine, conversation regarding the two males ceased. Investigating Stefaughn's murder belonged solely to Mahogany, Karen, and Sophia. They were drove to St. Peter's Cemetery. Stefaughn was no more, but an image confined to memory.

FORTY-THREE

It was late evening, and Stefaughn was tucked away in his grave. The last of family and friends were just leaving Karen's house, having enjoyed a fine dinner.

"Well, sis, are you going to be okay? I'll stay with you, Momma, and Daddy if you want me to."

"We'll be fine, Sophia," Karen said. "Y'all journey on home, and I'll drive Momma and Daddy out to your house before I take them to the airport, tomorrow."

"Are you sure? Because it's not a problem. We have to take Jamie to the airport, too."

"I'm sure, and thanks for everything," Karen answered.

They all embraced one another, allowing the occasion to tighten the family's bond. Sophia and family, along with Jamie, departed for Creve Couer. Everybody was jaded, hoping that they would never experience such hardship again.

As time continued to tick, Karen's parents fell asleep. They were in their early seventies, refusing to remain awake after ten, thirty p.m. It was now eleven, twenty-two, and Karen couldn't fall asleep. So she got out of bed, slid on her house slippers and robe, and walked to the guest bedroom.

Barely opening the guest bedroom door, Karen saw that her parents were asleep. Karen smiled; she hadn't seen her parents in six months. From there, Karen entered the kitchen, obtaining a port glass. She removed two ice cubes from an ice tray, dropping them inside of the port glass. Next, Karen removed a cigarette lighter from the kitchen utility drawer, then she returned to her bedroom. Karen set the port glass on her bedroom dresser. She lit a tall, slim peach-colored candle. Karen placed the burning candle next to an 8 x 10 photo of Stefaughn that rested on the dresser.

Karen turned off the bedroom light, set an armchair and a footstool in front of the dresser, and turned on the slow jams. She kept the radio volume low. Sequentially, Karen

315

Scarlet Tears

knelt down on the right side of her bed and removed a gray shoebox from beneath it. Karen lifted the top off the shoebox and removed a fifth of Courvoisier XO Imperial. Karen yearned to go there, that place in space where burdens held no weight. It was a dwelling place where Karen often chilled in her younger day. This moment was planned, Karen's secret way of saying farewell.

Karen walked over to the dresser, opened the cognac, and poured herself a half glass. She put on a pair of dark shades, took a seat in her armchair, propped her feet, and let the good times roll. Karen sipped and sipped, both crying and smiling. She was out there, riding Heaven's slow lane.

Karen began talking to someone, the ghost of good feelings. The expensive cognac was doing its job, taking Karen to wonderland.

"You were my wings, boy," she slurred, gazing at Stefaughn's picture. "You know I love you. Come here and give Momma K uh kiss." Karen paused, imagining herself being kissed. "Now that's my son . . . sweet as can be." Karen took another sip. "Hahhh," she exhaled, "just soothing the soul, Stefaughn. That's all I'm doing. . . . Kicked back like uh champ. Momma K ain't letting go, baby. Oh yeah . . . somebody's got to pay," she continued to slur, tears trickling down her cheeks. "You's uh winna, Stefaughn . . . and don't let nobody tell you nuttin different. You are special . . . my ebony rock." Karen paused again. "Well, I ain't gone keep you all night. So try and get some good sleep, baby. . . . 'Cause me and you got some bizness to finish!" she shouted. "Okay . . . just let me know if you need anything. I'll be right here, sugar-sugar."

FORTY-FOUR

Sunday, July 23, 2000

Karen couldn't open her eyes, but she could hear. She hadn't seen her parents all-day. Then there was a knock on her bedroom door.

"Kay, are you in there?" Karen's father asked.

Listening to the bedroom door squeak, Karen sensed that it was opened slowly. Then she heard shuffling footsteps coming towards her.

"Maggie Sue, you need to see this. Looks like ole Karen done backslid," Karen's father said loudly.

"Oh, let me see what you're talking 'bout," Maggie Sue replied from outside Karen's bedroom. "Well, if the sun ain't shining. Our baby sho feeling the blues." She paused. "So, are you just gone stand there or do something, Robert Joe?"

"Oh shoot! Get out of the way, Maggie Sue," he advised. "Karen. Hey, Karen!" Robert Joe tapped Karen on the shoulder. Karen's left finger wiggled. Her head flopped to the right, away from her dad. "Well, she's alive, Maggie Sue. But this girl is as drunk as a skunk. And it smells like a tavern in here."

"Oh, never mind that. She's going through something, Robert Joe. Go 'head . . . wake the child up, you ole joker. And it's no wonder we haven't eaten all day."

"If she drank that whole bottle by herself, then she probably won't get up. Look at her . . . still got her shades on."

Robert Joe vigorously shook Karen.

Scarlet Tears

"Robert Joe, you gone shake the life out of her. And watch out for that glass by your foot."

"Well, you said to wake her up. Make up your mind, Maggie Sue."

Karen reached up to remove her shades. She glared at her dad. "What, what, what? I'm okay."

"Are you sure, Kay? You sure don't look good. And your eyes are red just like the devil," Robert Joe said.

"You get out of the way, Robert Joe. You ole fool!" Maggie Sue ordered.

"Seriously, I'm fine," Karen uttered, getting out of the chair. "I apologize for you, guys, seeing me like this." She paused. "It's just one of those days."

"We understand, Kay. Just get yourself together while your daddy and I run in the kitchen to prepare something to eat," Maggie Sue said, picking up the glass off the carpeted bedroom floor. "I'm sure you're hungry."

"Yeah. What time is it?"

"It's after noon, Kay. And your phone has been ringing all morning. Anyway, we called Sophia, and they're all doing fine," Robert Joe replied.

Karen was embarrassed. Her intentions were to drink responsibly and say farewell to her son in her own unique way. She had planned to awaken early and prepare breakfast for her parents. Nonetheless, Karen cleaned up her bedroom, bathed and brushed her teeth, and enjoyed a hearty breakfast that her parents prepared.

Karen tried remembering her night's dream; she could not. But there was one thing for sure, Karen wanted to search Stefaughn's bedroom again. As a result, she got up from the kitchen table, briefly chatted with her parents and wandered into Stefaughn's bedroom.

This time, Karen would search thoroughly. She wasn't in a rush, targeting every inch in Stefaughn's bedroom. Karen searched under Stefaughn's bed; there was nothing. She searched in between his mattress and box spring, finding six Hip-hop magazines. Karen combed through Stefaughn's dresser and chest drawers, only to discover clothing and a bunch of female telephone numbers written on torn pieces of paper. She found nothing in his pillows, nothing lying under anything.

Karen tried figuring when and where did Stefaughn purchase the gold jewelry that set on top of his dresser. Besides a small gold necklace she had bought him years ago, Karen had never seen Stefaughn sport jewelry. She pondered everything while sitting on the edge of Stefaughn's bed. Some things were beginning to make sense. Karen didn't want to believe her son was dealing drugs, but the signs were appallingly informative.

Karen got up from the bed, beginning the last part of her search. She examined the curtains, the windowsills, and the baseboards. Again, Karen came up empty. Rummaging through a box of DVD's, Sega cartridges, and music CD's, Karen found nothing. Off into Stefaughn's closet, Karen went searching. She had been searching and examining items for forty minutes; Karen seriously wanted to solve the mytery. Piece by piece, Karen removed items from the closet. Every item was scrutinized and then thrown in a pile on the floor.

"Hey, Kay!" Maggie Sue yelled from the living room. The television volume was loud. St. Louis Cardinals was playing Atlanta Braves. "Do you need some help in there? It sounds like you're ransacking the place."

"No. I'm all right. Thanks anyway."

Feeling on the inside pocket of an orange Nautica winter coat, Karen suddenly felt something abnormal. She reached into the pocket and pulled out a stack of money amassed between two rubber bands. A note on top of the money read:

$8,500
Owe Dread $7,000 more
Need to get quick!

This find was the proof Karen sought. Her already sunken heart sank even lower. *Why in the world would he want to slang dope?* Karen thought. She tossed the money on the bed, continuing her search. Karen felt something in one

Scarlet Tears

of the coat's outside pockets. She reached into the pocket and removed the pager she had been informed about. The black pager had a folded white piece of paper secured between its clip. Karen turned on the pager to see if it worked. It beeped. She removed the piece of paper from the clip's grasp and unfolded it. It read:

To Do List

1. Find a job
2. Go back to church
3. Help Rochelle and her kids
4. Start back studying for school
5. Stay away from Bruce
6. Never sale drugs again
7. See if I can borrow enough money from family, along with job to pay Dread. Also pawn jewelry and sale my videodisks and cartridges to get up Dread's money.
8. Tell Mahogany to don't deal with Dread and his real name.
9. **Dread's numbers are saved in pager and Mahogany has his address.

After reading the to-do-list, Karen slid it into her skirt pocket. Tears began streaming from her eyes, goose bumps covering her arms. *Now I know Dread ain't killed my baby when all he wanted to do was pay him,* Karen thought aloud, slowly losing control of self. She checked the pager to see if any communication numbers were stored in it; it was. Karen was near solving her son's murder, reminding herself to contact Mahogany. She wanted a solid conclusion to the ferocious occurrence that took her son's life, therefore, continuing to search the last few items in Stefaughn's closet.

Having searched the entire closet, except for the empty-appearing top shelf, Karen left from the closet to obtain a red crate sitting on the floor next to the wooden chest of drawers. She picked up the crate, carried it to the closet, set it on the floor upside down and stood on top of it.

Karen noticed a short stack of books sitting on the back of the shelf. She slid the books closer to herself, finding a small cardboard box behind the books. Karen slid the stack of books to the side and reached for the small cardboard box. After obtaining the cardboard box, Karen stepped down from the crate. *This box sure is heavy to be so small,* she thought. Karen sat on the side of her son's bed, removing balled up newspaper from inside the cardboard box. Under the newspaper, Karen discovered a new box of bullets and a used .38 snub-nosed revolver. Karen was surprised, wondering all sorts of things.

Leaving the contents in the cardboard box, along with placing the bundle of cash inside of it, Karen placed the small cardboard box under Stefaughn's bed. She walked over to the dresser and looked into the dresser mirror. Karen dried her face. She was vexed, losing grip with God.

Exiting Stefaughn's bedroom, Karen closed the door behind her and walked into the living room. "Momma and Daddy, are y'all finished packing? It's about time we get out of here and head out to Sophi's."

"Yeah, we're ready. Just watching this ball game and waiting on you, Kay. And did you find what you were looking for?"

"Yes and no, Momma," Karen replied. "Anyway, I'll be ready in five minutes."

Karen went into her bedroom to freshen up and change blouses. It didn't take long. Karen had a new agenda to complete. She contacted Sophia to let her know that her and their parents were on their way. From there, Karen loaded up her loaner car, and off they traveled.

FORTY-FIVE

Darkness was riding in, and Mahogany and Karen were just leaving Wal-Mart. They had recently left Lambert St. Louis International Airport, seeing Jamie, Mr. and Mrs. Dooley off to their destination. The day appeared long, a minute lasting one hundred twenty seconds.

Now inside of Karen's car, Karen said, "Mahogany, I don't feel the same without Stefaughn. I probably won't get a good night's rest until his murderers are captured. Every day, all day, that's all I think about."

"You're not alone, Aunt Karen. And when are you going to get your car back from the dealer?" she asked. "I sure like yours better."

"Sometime this week. It's just a loaner. Anyhow, the police said they think they have the car that was used in my son's murder, but there was little or no evidence. Guess what? The car was scorched," Karen said. "As many murders happen in this city, they'll probably never solve Stef's murder."

"Well, let's continue to think optimistic, Aunt Karen. I believe if the church and we put up a reward for information leading to his murder, it'll probably speed up the process." Mahogany paused. "And maybe we should go ahead and tell the police what we know."

"Yeah, that ain't a bad idea, but I want you to read something for a minute."

Karen handed Mahogany Stefaughn's to-do-list from inside her skirt pocket. Mahogany read it, bursting into tears. "Who's Bruce?"

Tears streamed from Karen's eyes. "That's the boy who attended the funeral with Dread. Whew! I just hate the name Dread. No good sapsuckers!"

"You mean to tell me the one you said you know standing outside?"

"Uh-huh. Ain't that some BS! And I wouldn't put it past him being a part of killing my son. He looked disturbed, anyway. Huh . . . Jesus sho got a way of exposing the guilty."

"Well, Aunt Karen, let's stick to what we know." Mahogany paused, returning the paper to her aunt. "Dread is definitely involved. It's too obvious."

Karen didn't respond, revenge whispering in her ear. She was angry, hot like fire.

"Are you okay, Auntie?"

Karen shook her head yes. "Hey, give me that boy's address and his numbers if you still have it. I'ma go ahead and turn all the info we have over to the homicide detective handling my son's case."

"Uh, I think I left my address book in the house. But hold up; let me see if it's in my purse." Mahogany scrambled through her purse. "Naw, here it is." Mahogany wrote Dread's information on a piece of yellow paper from her small note pad. She handed it to Karen and began drying her face with a napkin.

"Thanks, Mahogany. And I appreciate you taking the time out to help me with everything," she said. "You know, Mahogany . . . I kind of wish you were my daughter. I once was pregnant with a little girl, but I lost her at birth. And that was when I learned I couldn't have any more children."

They'd made it back to Mahogany's home.

"I didn't know that, Aunt Karen. And I'm sorry to hear that. You don't have to thank me for helping you. It's my pleasure, Auntie. And do you need me to do anything else?"

"No, except for give me a hug, and try to get a good night's sleep. Oh, there's one more thing. Try keeping what I showed you to yourself. I don't want you and Sophia involved in this at all. Besides, you have enough to deal with already."

"If you say so, Aunt Karen. And just call me if you need me."

On her way home, Karen thought about driving by the address Mahogany had furnished. She was familiar with the name of the street and zip code. However, Karen passed on that idea and hurried home.

Once having made it home, Karen called Sophia to let her know she had safely arrived. It was ten o'clock p.m., and Karen wasn't very comfortable with her home anymore. Nonetheless, she would allow nothing to scare her away. Karen entered her bedroom, changing into a pair of fitting blue jeans, a small T-shirt and tennis shoes. Karen pinned her hair to the rear, put on a blue jean cap, and placed her driver's license and forty dollars in her rear pants pocket. She looked at herself in the bedroom mirror. *Yeah, I can still pass for a young tender.*

Karen hadn't worn a pair of pants in a very long time, adhering to a religious code. Apparently, Karen had stepped out of her religious bubble, rejoining the worldly way of things. Her son's death was a strain, sifting spirituality through its sieve. Karen sought one thing—*the big payback.*

Wearing a pair of plastic gloves, Karen returned to Stefaughn's bedroom. She removed the revolver and bullets from the cardboard box, loaded six bullets into the revolver's chamber, and placed the gun inside a purse with a towel in it. Karen exited her home, off into the lethal night.

Chaos and St. Louis were in love, stepping on the innocent, threatening the welfare of everything good. Karen's new decision was a dare; she had entered a scavenging game of bloodthirst.

Now driving down the quiet street where Dread lived, Karen slowly cruised by his home. She noticed two cars in his driveway, a Mercedes Benz and an Oldsmobile. Lights were on inside of Dread's house. There was no movement on the street, and Karen was growing nervous. Therefore, Karen parked five houses down from Dread's house on the opposite side of the street, praying for God's protection.

The moon was full, and the night sky was clear. Karen suddenly spotted two rabbits dashing across a yard. She smiled, marveled by the beauty of life's little ones. Karen

Scarlet Tears

chose to take the law into her own hands, possessing minimum faith in the city's police department. With her "iron" in her purse, Karen was the new sheriff in town, patrolling the very dangerous night shift. She had found her man, awed by a falling star. Funny, Karen had planned for Dread to descend in the same fashion, burning from the heat of *Ms. Trusty*.

To her surprise, Karen noticed Dread exiting his house—and alone. She sunk down in the seat, observing Dread rubbing his nose while walking to his Delta Eighty-eight. Dread entered his car, started it, backed out of the driveway, and drove the same direction Karen's car was faced. Karen took a deep breath, unsure of the decision she'd made. Still, Karen started the car, following Dread from a distance.

She followed Dread four neighborhood blocks from his home. Dread drove onto the parking lot of a twenty-four hour Schnuck's grocery store. This was a good thing, an opportunity for great stationing. The parking lot was nearly empty of cars, however, cluttered with shopping carts.

Parking two car spaces over from Dread, her driver's side door facing the driver's side door of Dread's car, Karen looked at the clock in her loaner vehicle. She shut off the engine. The clock displayed 12:09 a.m. Karen was far from a professional hit man, having allowed retaliation taint her thinking. Howbeit—*she was all in.*

Waiting for Dread to return to his car, Karen quickly thought of a plan. She carefully overlooked the dim-lit parking lot and its surrounding area, searching for law enforcement, cameras, and human eyes. Karen saw neither, but she figured there was a camera somewhere. So be it. Karen's heart was beating fast, beads of sweat gathering on her arms. Karen hoped she wouldn't be seen committing the ultimate crime. Thoughts of imprisonment scratched her brain. None of it really mattered anymore; Karen was in the passion of revenge.

She peered over at the grocery store and noticed Dread exiting the grocery store with a bag. Headlamps suddenly flashed on from a parked car. Karen stiffened, her eyes shifting from side-to-side. As Dread crossed the street in front of the unbusy grocery store, the red car drove off. Karen thanked God. She hadn't noticed the White male sitting in the red car. Quickly, Karen removed the revolver from her purse and tucked it in her jeans. She placed her T-shirt over the revolver.

Before Dread got too close, Karen exited the car. She left the door unlocked and the keys in the ignition. Karen walked to a narrow, metal enclosure, a parking lot pen for placing shopping carts. It set to the near rear of her car and the front of Dread's car. There were two shopping carts at the rear of the enclosure. Karen acted as if she was trying to pull them apart. She could hear Dread's footsteps getting closer. The footsteps stopped.

"Pa, pardon me. Do you need some help, miss?"

Karen rapidly spun around, removing the revolver from her waist. She pointed it at Dread's head, cocking the firing pin. Dread's eyes grew big; his knees trembled.

"Stefaughn says he's waiting on you," Karen said, slowly stepping towards Dread and lowering the gun at his chest. She held the gun steady, feeling the rush of revenge. Her cap was pulled down just above her eyes, strings of hair swaying in the night, soft winds.

"Hold up! I'm sorry about Stefaughn, miss. Please don't shoot! I can ex----"

POW! POW! POW! POW! POW! POW!

Karen quickly unloaded the weapon, bullets ripping through the grocery bag into Dread's abdomen and chest. He screamed like a bitch, yelling for mercy.

Karen hurried inside her car. The coast appeared clear. She drove away from the scene as if nothing happened. Dread lay facedown on the asphalt. It was quiet, and so much for a nighttime snack.

FORTY-SIX

Saturday, July 29, 2000

Mahogany slept late, exhausted from the day before. It had been her busiest day on the job, nevertheless, a very exciting day.

The Nelly concert went successfully, taking place in front of a sold-out crowd. The Adam's Mark Hotel made tons of money from liquor sales and the concert itself, placing Mahogany in a position to receive a hefty bonus.

Mahogany and Jessica had crossed paths at the concert. They refused to speak to one another. Jessica rolled her eyes. Mahogany didn't care, just wishing Jessica would mature. Mahogany had also bumped into Jazz. She avoided his every stunt, his every attempt to repair their relationship. Jessica and Jazz were mere crumbs beneath Mahogany's feet. She wanted to step on them, sweep them up, and toss them into the nearest trash can.

Sarah and Astarte also attended the concert. They had a splendid time. Mahogany provided them with special attention and more.

****

Karen was in the process of relocating; she wanted out of St. Louis in a hurry. Karen was deeply saddened with everything—including herself. Although she had cleaned and tossed the revolver used to kill Dread in the Mississippi River, Karen continuously relived the moment in her mind. It was arduous to shake, an eternal scar.

Scarlet Tears

There was limited media coverage regarding Dread's murder. Only a small article surfaced in the St. Louis Post-Dispatch. He was said to have been high on drugs, and cocaine was found on his possession. A gun was also located in his vehicle, said to have been used in several murders. Dread's murder was considered drug-related, therefore tossed into the swallowing sea of oblivion.

FORTY-SEVEN

Monday, July 31, 2000

Despite all the hardship Mahogany had been experiencing, there was still a single impediment to confront. It would be her first day in federal court, a frightful moment in her journal.

As Mahogany waited for the magistrate to enter the courtroom, she looked at her codefendant, Jazz. Mahogany was dismayed, afraid, and unbelievably embarrassed—plunged into a quandary. The dimly lit courtroom had a chilling effect, intensifying paranoia to extreme degrees. None of the European court employees smiled; it was strictly business. Mahogany was in a heraldic, conservative environment, the judicial halls of dread and doom. She thirsted to escape, tortured by the unexplored.

The courtroom was full with Mahogany and Jazz's family and friends. Mahogany appreciated the support, but couldn't remove the daggers of fear from her heart. Anticipating the near future, Mahogany began sweating and crying. She looked at the White female prosecutor with dark hair, searching for relief. The prosecutor, U.S. Attorney Fedora Crockwell, stared at Mahogany. There wasn't a smile. Ms. Crockwell was known as a kick-ass prosecutor, the gladiator of putrid justice. Mahogany cried more . . . and more . . . and more.

Mahogany's attorney, John Warrenberg, tried comforting her. He told Mahogany it was only an arraignment, an initial step in her criminal prosecution. After hearing the charges, Mahogany's attorney told her to enter a plea of not guilty. Mahogany understood, still unable to stop crying. Mahogany gazed out into the gallery, meeting eyes with her mother. Sophia, too, was crying.

****

Witnessing everything taking place, Jazz felt ashamed and disappointed with his self. In his heart, he only wanted the best for Mahogany. Jazz refrained from crying, being what he thought a man should be. Mr. Brown looked at Jazz with a death stare.

As the magistrate entered the courtroom from behind the bench, everybody was asked to stand. Once the magistrate took a seat, everybody was asked to be seated.

****

Mahogany was asked to approach the bench with her counsel. While approaching the bench, she felt her legs getting heavy, nearly shuffling. The situation was mentally-draining, a spooky ride on the dark side. Mahogany didn't know if she was coming or going.

Sitting up high in his black robe, wearing a pair of reading glasses on the brink of his pointed red nose, wearing his short spread of silvery-white hair groomed to the rear, Magistrate Holcombe read the charges: "That from on or about July the eleventh, two thousand, within the Southern District of Illinois, Mahogany Brown, defendant herein, did knowingly and intentionally combine, conspire, confederate, and agree together with each other and others known to the grand jury to commit the following offense against the United States of America," he said. "You are being charged in a one count indictment. Count one charges you with conspiracy to distribute five kilograms or more of cocaine hydrochloride, a Schedule Two controlled substance, in violation of Title twenty-one, United States Code, section 841 (a)(1) and 841 (b)(1)(b); all in violation of Title twenty-one, United States Code, section 846. The penalty for violation of section 841 (b)(1)(b) is a mandatory minimum of five years and a maximum sentence of forty years," Magistrate Holcombe said emphatically. "So, how do you plea, Miss Brown?"

Mahogany paused before answering; she tried to grasp an understanding of what all was said. Hearing "forty years" was paralyzing.

"Not guilty, Your Honor."

Once Magistrate Holcombe finished his colloquy, Mahogany returned to her seat. She wondered why Magistrate Holcombe didn't express any compassion. Mahogany's tears were useless, openly expressing vulnerability.

****

It was Jazz's turn to be arraigned. He would have to answer to a long list of drug-related counts. Matters didn't appear favorable for Jazz, especially from the confident, stern expression on the prosecutor's face. Nevertheless, Jazz pleaded not guilty to all the charges drawn against him.

To Jazz's disbelief, Magistrate Holcombe ordered for him to be detained until further notice. Jazz was drawn out to be a flight risk, and the prosecutor insisted that Jazz's *notorious street influence* would be harmful to her witnesses. By design, Jazz was painted as a threat to society.

Jazz turned to his attorney, demanding answers. He could not believe what was happening. But an order was an order. Jazz was then handcuffed by a United States Marshal.

Suddenly, a voice blurted from the gallery, "Gimme my daddy back! Now!"

Jazz looked over his shoulder. It was Knyla, standing and crying. She appeared prepared for war, frustrated in her father's pain. Everyone was awed, captured by the unbelievable. Dina ordered Knyla to have a seat and be quiet.

As he was steered out of the courtroom, Jazz shouted, "I love you, Knyla! Keep strong! And they can't keep me forever!" Tears dribbled down his cheeks. Life for Jazz was at its worst.

"Okay, we'll see about that, tough guy," one of the U.S. Marshals said and jerked Jazz by the arm.

Jazz didn't say a word; he stood bold, strong in his pride. Yet he was agonized, his naked soul covered by a coat of thistles. Now in the bullpen, a stuffy group of tiny holding cells in the basement of the federal courthouse, Jazz rested his head in his hands. Fear and rage zigzagged through his body. Jazz sensed that he would be railroaded, never to receive fairness. Away from what he considered a kangaroo court, Jazz wondered what exactly he could do.

Fortunately, Mahogany was allowed to leave on her own recognizance. In the Southern District of Illinois, this was a sign of a favor for a favor. *No one ever received something for nothing in the Southern District.*

Jazz sat on the cold concrete floor of the lifeless middle holding cell. He peered up at another detainee.

"I can tell you're mad as hell. I see it in yo' eyes," a tall, thin African-American male said, his presence timid. "What? They did it to you, too?"

Jazz remained quiet, emotionally decimated. He figured he'd ransomed his soul for zilch. Jazz was numb; he was confused, an intelligent brother trapped in the royal empire of untamed power.

Staring into the faces of those he was caged with, Jazz believed himself at a designed disadvantaged. He detected hopelessness in the eyes of the other detainees. Listening to the conversations of others, Jazz grew sick on the stomach. He dreamt of jailbreak, an overthrow of authority, that the men he was detained with would shut up and stand up.

FORTY-EIGHT

Wednesday, August 2, 2000

Inside the federal holding facility, annexed to St. Clair County Jail in Belleville, Illinois, the air was stiff; the mood was dull, and yesterday's debris was scattered across the facility. It was five a.m., and the desolate, poorly-lit social bay stunk with human stale and mold. The entire annex was a pigpen, the Feds' breaking grounds of psychological war.

Fomenting unrest throughout the forty-man annex, pressured water jolted from a dilapidated shower on the upper tier, and Lloyd "Big Boy" Fleming snored like a two-ton grizzly in cell thirteen.

"Put a lid on that fat fucker!" someone yelled from inside of a locked cell.

Sitting at the small desk inside cell seventeen, Jazz shook his head in disgust. He was awake writing a letter, and Jazz was very disappointed with his bunkmate. His bunkmate was a forty-year-old pastor who was awaiting sentencing for secretly adding the date-rape drug, GHB, in the drinks of women and young males. The pastor would then drive the victims across state lines to private locations and have nonconsensual sex with them. Keeping one eye open, Jazz couldn't sleep well.

Jazz was a zealot for freedom, believing freedom was only moments away. He was incapacitated by the "hope bug." Having finished writing his letter, Jazz decided to proofread it:

Mahogany,
 It's nearing sunrise, and I've been awake all night gazing into the starry, night sky from the tiny window in my

Scarlet Tears

cell. The moon is very bright; the stars are twinkling, and my spirit is blue. Nevertheless, I'm always thinking of you. Someday, sweetheart, I know we'll overcome our temporary distress. I'm solemnly praying for the both of us, and I dearly apologize for all the drama you're experiencing. It kills me softly to see you cry. You're a wonderful woman, the apple of my eye. Although we've been divided by circumstance, I still love you and wish you eternal happiness. Again . . . I'm so sorry, and I miss you like crazy. Well, this isn't a clever attempt to invade your emotional barriers. I'm well aware of the pain I've caused you. I respect and honor you, Mahogany. You are the joy I thirst, the perfect dozen red roses. You see, I can't believe what I'm going through; it appears to be a nightmare, one I'm finding difficult to escape. If I could click my heels and make a wish, I'd request that our Heavenly Father start all over with humanity. We are so imperfect, especially me. I never wanted to cause you a single problem, yet irrational thinking has a way of keeping me on a leash. Mahogany, you couldn't possibly fathom what I'm subjected to. Life in "the belly of the beast" is worse than the hottest hell. My environment is quarrelsome, an atmosphere bombarded by self-hate, corruption, human neglect, homosexuality, and faded dreams. It's so painful to witness the condition of Black brothers. We're seemingly lost, deeply in love with bad decision making. Yes, there's a purpose behind it all. Regardless, I know there's a brighter day ahead. And I wouldn't wish imprisonment on anyone except those who violate children and women. Moreover, I've been shackled and dragged naked into a dark world, the burning inferno of judicial iniquity. However, I strive to sustain, to win at all I do. I'll never give in to despair. I will fight until the end, because I will someday emerge again. This presumption is logically foreseeable. Dear, I feel as if I've been stoned, blood pouring from my distress. My well running dry, I'm seeking the perfect advice. I'll admit that I cried yesterday while under my single, little blanket, and I'm still crying inside. It hurts to be away from loved ones, especially you, Momma, and my daughter. I've never experienced anything

like this before, and I miss my liberty with a passion. I feel as if I'm buried alive, slowly approaching a miserable death. The mood is cold, and my predicament can drive a sane man into insanity. Oh God . . . will you help us? Well, I won't keep you much longer, and I was elated to learn that you weren't ordered to be detained. Jail is no place for an angel like you. You are marvelous, the darling I've ever longed. Believing in us, let's keep the faith as a team.
Sincerely,

Knigel
P.S. I live to become the Moses of my people.

FORTY-NINE

Monday, February 26, 2001

Jazz disturbed the idle and simple-minded; he'd become an opponent of the federal judicial system. Most of the other inmates at the county considered Jazz too smart for his own good, a damn fool for going to trial.

Jazz looked upon those who disagreed with his actions as mentally unstable. He often paid them no attention. Jazz was hungry for quick results, remedy that never surfaced and wishes apparently extinguished. He was in a legal quagmire, fighting with very limited resources. Regardless of his plight, Jazz was in until the end. He had no desire to sell out his fellow brother. Jazz's attorney also believed him to be a damn fool, because he'd pleaded with Jazz to fully cooperate with the U.S. government and law enforcement so he could receive a favorable sentence. Jazz put to use the Sixth Amendment of the U.S. Constitution and enjoyed the right to a speedy and public trial. Unfortunately, Jazz wasn't blessed with an impartial jury. An all White jury found him guilty on his third day of trial. After seven months of throwing rocks at the U.S. government, Jazz concluded that he was born guilty, hated because of his rich, golden hue.

It was one o'clock p.m., and Jazz sat on a steel bench staring at the dull, yellow brick walls of the holding facility. Majority of his fellow inmates were mesmerized by Rap videos on BET. Jazz refused to surrender to the norms of his environment. He believed and knew there was a better way to spend his time. Thinking in the future, Jazz had grown exhausted with the all the law books his mother and attorney had sent him. The federal judicial system and law

Scarlet Tears

enforcement didn't play by the established rules. New rules occurred as the game continued.

Suddenly, a middle-aged, African-American woman with long, reddish-brown microbraids opened the mechanical door to the annex. She was the inmates' favorite correctional officer.

"Mail call!" she announced.

All forty detainees scurried near the door, happy to see their lady Santa Claus.

While standing in the gathering, his orange jumpsuit too large, Jazz said to himself, *Damn, I'm starting to act like everybody else, desperate for mail.*

"Knigel Wennington times two," the correctional officer called. After receiving his correspondences, Jazz looked at the front of the envelopes. He smiled, expressed sympathy for those who didn't receive any mail, and returned to his cell.

Uh, I'll read the one from Jessica first. Then I'll read Mahogany's, Jazz thought aloud.

He removed the letter from the envelope. He sniffed the letter, stimulated by the fresh, fruity fragrance. Jazz unfolded the letter. There were pictures of Jessica, and they put a smile on Jazz's face as he fantasized about the past. He read:

Dear Knigel,

I've been thinking about you, wondering why you never told me you were in trouble at first. I wish I could help you, and I apologize for haven't written earlier. But I'll continue to accept your phone calls. And why don't you call more? You've been gone for almost seven long months, and I've only spoke with you twice.

Baby, I wish you the best, and I want you free. Jail is no place for a man like you, so please do what you have to do to come home. I'm with you, and I'm willing to help you through this. Don't hesitate to call if you need me. I promise to write when I can, and I'm making plans to visit you next week. So let me know if I'm still on your visitor's list. Everything is fine with me, and I'm enjoying my job. Also, I will send you a money order with my next letter. I love you, Knigel, and I miss you. We were meant for one another.

No, Mahogany and I will probably never be friends again. Months ago she wrote me this crazy letter. So what! I did what I did, and that's that. I'm positive she'll get over it.

Guess what, Knigel? I caught my mother and Austin sleeping together around Chrsitmas. My mother thought I was gone out of town with a couple of my friends, and Austin did too. We'd canceled the trip at the last minute for personal reasons. Yes, that really crushed me, but I had a feeling that they wanted one another. He always talked about my mom, and she always asked about him. I still love my mother, but I don't fool with her or Austin anymore. It's over!

P.S. I'm waiting to hear from you, and be sure to save my new address on the envelope. I'll be moving there this coming weekend. Stay strong, my Black king, and keep your head up. By the way, I'm seven months and two weeks pregnant with your shorty.

Love, Jessica

After reading the postscript of Jessica's letter, the bottom fell out of Jazz's stomach. He rubbed the top of his head and shouted. Jazz felt dead, sealed in a coffin.

He removed Mahogany's letter from the envelope. There was no special fragrance. No pictures. Proceeding, Jazz read:

A New Day

When it feels as if your sun is setting, reach deep within and trust the promised sun of tomorrow. It is there . . . Heaven's joy will embrace you.—Mahogany Brown

To Mr. Wennington,
I received your letter, dated August 2, 2000. I enjoyed reading it; it was very thought-provoking. I even cried, because I could feel your pain bleeding through that letter. At that time, I wasn't in a position to respond. I pray that you

understand why. Nonetheless, I've read it over and over, and I can almost remember it verbatim. You're an excellent writer, and you express yourself very well. I encourage you to never stop writing. It's your calling.

It's good to know that you desire to remain both productive and optimistic. Those are revered symbols of true manhood. Knigel, I treasure you for the genius you are; you are not a failure because of what has occurred. It's just another stage in life, an opportunity to better you. I will always wish you good health, success, and joy. Really, you are a remarkable person, and I admire you with all my heart.

Everything is fine with me, patiently accomplishing my every goal. I'm attending services again with the Jehovah's Witnesses, but I'm not sure how long it will last. Actually, I'm trying to find myself spiritually, because I'm awful fortunate to have received immunity. I didn't tell the government anything about you. As you know, I didn't know anything illegal about you. I just told them what happened the day we got stopped by the McKinley Bridge; therefore, I'm positive my written testimony didn't harm your defense.

Knigel, life is the ultimate learning experience. We all have so much to live for. Time isn't to be wasted, but spent wisely. I do believe you will agree. Also, I will always keep you in my prayers. You definitely didn't deserve receiving a 456 month prison sentence. I was shocked when I learned of that. Occasionally, I will write you, sincerely desiring that you pull through this. In my heart, I don't believe you'll have to serve your entire sentence. I've heard rumors about federal parole being reinstated. Think positive, Knigel. Jehovah never forgets those who strive to correct themselves, especially in His name.

Although times may be hard, opportunities will always be available for you. You're more than the average Joe. I appreciate all the sweet things you done for me, and I can never forget you. I forgive you for all the bad decisions you made in regards of us, and I ask that you please forgive me for tearing up your house. We are only human, aiming for perfection.

D. Allen Miller

Oh yeah, I'm being considered for a promotion at my job. They have already increased my pay, and I've won employee of the month two months in a row. Remember, Knigel, nothing outperforms a smile and a happy heart, and you'll always be my "Teddy bear."

Well, I care not to burden you with a book for a letter; hereby, I'm signing out. Take care and develop your best.

Cherishing life,
Mahogany Brown

P.S. I've been experimenting with poetry lately. Your poetic works is the source of my inspiration. I hope you enjoy the poem I've enclosed, and I pray that everything is working out for your mother.

The Poem of Inspiration

In the past of yesterday
There was encouragement
In the presnt of today
There is benevolence
In the future of tomorrow
There will be opportunity
And in the glory of ourselves
There is suffering's remedy

In the sky of kinder means
There is consolation
In the dark of simple dreams
There exists countenance
In the waters of Eternal Love
There thrives productive development
And in the smile of gentle hearts
There subsist in is happiness.

By: Mahogany Brown 2/14/2001

The 1776 GUIDE
FOR PENNSYLVANIA

by DIANA BURGWYN

HARPER COLOPHON BOOKS
Harper & Row, Publishers
New York, Evanston, San Francisco, London

THE 1776 GUIDE FOR PENNSYLVANIA. Copyright © 1975 by The 1776 Guide, Inc. All rights reserved. Printed in the United States of America. No part of this book may be used or reproduced in any manner without written permission except in the case of brief quotations embodied in critical articles and reviews. For information address Harper & Row, Publishers, Inc., 10 East 53d Street, New York, N.Y. 10022. Published simultaneously in Canada by Fitzhenry & Whiteside Limited, Toronto.

First HARPER COLOPHON edition published 1975.

LIBRARY OF CONGRESS CATALOG CARD NUMBER: 75-27195

STANDARD BOOK NUMBER: 06-090420-8

75 76 77 10 9 8 7 6 5 4 3 2 1

Cover Painting:
  "Reading of Declaration of Independence in Philadelphia", Courtesy of: H. E. Harris Stamp Co., Boston, Rendering by: John William Nutter.

Composition & Art:
  H.R. Sims Enterprises, Abington, MA
  Robert Casey, Art Director

Production:
Burtram J. Pratt

To Virginia Bortin,
with love

ACKNOWLEDGMENTS

A book of this kind depends heavily on the cooperation and expertise of local historians, representatives of the travel industry, and residents who take a particular interest in the city or town in which they live. Many such people have contributed generously of their time and knowledge to THE 1776 GUIDE FOR PENNSYLVANIA. Space limitations prevent us from acknowledging them all, but special gratitude is due the following:

David M. Adams, Colonial York County Visitors and Tourist Bureau
Bicentennial Women '76
George C. Brewer, Erie County Historical Society
Mrs. A. Newton Bugbee, Lehigh County Historical Society
Cumberland County Tourist Council
Louis DeV. Day, art consultant
John Feldman, historian, University of Pennsylvania
E. Wilmer Fisher, Washington Crossing State Park
Winifred Q. Fothergill, Cape May County Art League
Gary Fulton, Chester County Tourist Promotion Bureau
Germantown Historical Society
Gettysburg Travel Council, Inc.
Drs. Charles Gladfelter, Robert Bloom and Robert Nawrocki, Gettysburg College
Chryst W. Groff, Pennsylvania Dutch Tourist Bureau
Martha Hermann, French Azilum, Inc.
Hershey Foods Corporation
Historical Society of Pennsylvania
Mrs. R. L. Hoffman, Bucks County Historic-Tourist Commission
Independence National Historical Park
Paul Lauer, Luzerne County Tourist Promotion Agency
Muriel Lichtenwalner, author
Tom Linn, author
John Logue, Keystone Automobile Club
John Ward Willson Loose, Lancaster County Historical Society
Miki Mahoney, researcher
Donald R. Mathewson, Division of Economic Development, Delaware
John C. McIlhenny and Nancy Hammer, Fairmount Park Commission
Marjorie Paschkis and Helen Tomkins, Fellowship Farm
Alan Perkins, Drake Well Park
Pennsylvania Historical and Museum Commission
Philadelphia Convention and Visitors Bureau
Lynn Poirier, Bucks County Historical Society
James F. Ponder, Bethlehem Chamber of Commerce
Selma Rabinowitz

John Reed, Valley Forge Historical Society
Partrick M. Reynolds, Bureau of Travel Development, Commonwealth of Pennsylvania
Ruth Salisbury, Historical Society of Western Pennsylvania
Mayron Shoemaker, Endless Mountains Association
Frances St. John, Valley Forge State Park
Roger Steck, Cumberland County Historical Society
Margaret Tinkcom, former historian, Philadelphia Historical Commission
Robert J. Wise, Pocono Mountains Chamber of Commerce

Photo Credits

Lawrence S. Williams, Inc., Photography; The Free Library of Philadelphia; Maris/Senel, Bucks County Historical Tourist Commission; Hess Commercial Studios, Atlantic City; Atlantic City Convention Bureau; Mr. Greg Ogden; Pennsylvania Historical and Museum Commission; Lebanon Valley Tourist Bureau; Allentown Lehigh County Chamber of Commerce; Pennsylvania Dutch Tourist Bureau; Moravian College; Pocono Mountain Vacation Bureau; Historic Bethlehem Inc.; Hershey Foods Corporation; Mel Horst; Pennsylvania Department of Commerce; Frank Brown, Photography; Gettysburg Travel Council, Inc.; Ziegler Studio; Wyoming Historical & Geological Society; Luzerne Tourist Promotion Agency; Greater Erie Chamber of Commerce; Drake Well Museum; Tourist & Convention Bureau, Allentown, Pa.; Pittsburgh Convention & Vistors Bureau, Inc.; George D. Hetrick; The Henry Francis Du Pont Winterthur Museum; Beaver County Tourist Promotion Agency; Philadelphia Museum of Art; Fayette County Development Council

Finally, gratefulness beyond measure to H. James Burgwyn, who shared in the dream and helped shape the reality of this book.

The 1776 GUIDE FOR PENNSYLVANIA

Contents

	Page
Acknowledgements	iv
Preface	vii
About This Guide	viii
Excursion 1 – Colonial Philadelphia	1
Area Map	2
Historic Location Map	4
Historic Insight	15
Excursion 2 – Benjamin Franklin Parkway & Fairmount Park	23
Historic Location Map	24
Historic Location Map	30
Excursion 3 – Germantown	39
Historic Location Map	40
Historic Location Map	44
Excursion 4 – Valley Forge & The Brandywine	55
Historic Location Map	56
Historic Location Map	64
Excursion 5 – Pennsbury, Fallsington & Washington Crossing	74
Historic Location Map	75
Area Map	80
Historic Location Map	81
Historic Insight	85
Excursion 6 – Doylestown & New Hope	89
Historic Location Map	90
Excursion 7 – Batsto, Atlantic City, Cape May & Lewes	101
Historic Location Map	102
Historic Insight	114
Excursion 8 – Malvern, Trappe, Fagleysville, Pottstown, Boyertown, Douglassville, Baumstown, French Creek, Hopewell & St. Peters	116
Historic Location Map	118
Historic Insight	125

Excursion 9 – Lancaster, Strasburg, Ephrata, Reading, Kutztown & Allentown	127
Area Map	128
Area Maps	140
Excursion 10 – Bethlehem & The Poconos	150
Area Map	151
Historic Location Map	152
Historic Insight	158
Historic Location Map	160
Excursion 11 – Hershey, Harrisburg & Carlisle	163
Area Map	164
Historic Location Map	165
Historic Location Map	166
Excursion 12 – Gettysburg & York	181
Historic Location Map	182
Historic Insight	192
Historic Location Map	194
Excursion 13 – The Wyoming Valley	201
Area Map	202
Historic Location Map	204
Excursion 14 – Erie, Waterford & Titusville	213
Historic Location Map	214
Excursion 15 – Pittsburgh & Old Economy	227
Area Map	228
Historic Location Map	230
Historic Location Map	231
Historic Location Map	232
Area Map	233
Historic Location Map	245
Area Map & Public Facilities	246
Tourist Promotion Agencies	248

PREFACE

Pennsylvania is a lot more than Independence Hall and the Liberty Bell and the Betsy Ross House.

For instance, do you know where...
- the first capital of the U.S. was located?
- the first written protest against slavery in the New World was recorded?
- Daniel Boone was born?
- the first medical school in America was started?
- the nation's huge Centennial celebration was held?
- our giant oil industry had its beginnings?
- classical music was first heard in the colonies?
- Federal troops assembled for the first test of our government's ability to enforce law?
- the oldest "White House" still standing in the U.S. is located?
- the turning point of the Civil War occurred?
- the first American pretzel was twisted and baked?

The answer to all of these questions is: PENNSYLVANIA. Or, more specifically: York, Germantown, Baumstown, Philadelphia, Fairmount Park, Titusville, Bethlehem, Carlisle, Germantown, Gettysburg, Lititz.

The purpose of our little quiz was not to stump you, but rather to introduce you to the facts and fun that are described in the pages of **THE 1776 GUIDE FOR PENNSYLVANIA.** Indeed, so much diversity exists within the 45,000 square miles of the "Keystone State", second of the original thirteen colonies, that this book cannot pretend to be more than an introduction. It has been written, of course, with 1776 as a prominent theme and hence emphasizes those areas that were of particular significance during the Revolution. But it was written also with the vacationer in mind, the family, the foreign visitor — people who want to combine museum-going with lake swimming, battleground tours with fine eating, the study of colonial ironmaking with treks into those areas that remain of our nation's precious wilderness.

Pennsylvania, more than any other state, was the product of the dreams and work of one man. William Penn made it the setting for his "Holy Experiment", where men and women of differing faiths, political beliefs and places of origin could live in peace and equality. In large measure this was the same philosophy upon which our nation itself was structured. For this reason, Pennsylvania is all the more fitting a place to celebrate the United States' 200th birthday. Here we can study our nation's past, observe its present, and contemplate its future.

D.S.B.

ABOUT THIS GUIDE

THE 1776 GUIDE FOR PENNSYLVANIA contains fifteen one- and two-day excursions which hopefully will be of value not only to visistors but to natives of the state. Thirteen of these use Philadelphia as the starting and return point. The last two, which are in the western part of the state, are best planned with Pittsburgh as base.

For each excursion we have prepared a suggested itinerary with leading sites given in order of easy visiting, car routings, and some thoughts on recreational activities. By studying each excursion before setting out, you will be able to plan an enjoyable visit, eliminating those sites that do not interest you and perhaps adding some others.

A heading called "Historic Insight" appears after the list of sites in certain of our excursions. These vignettes are vital to the understanding of the particular excursion and should be read in conjunction with it.

THE 1776 GUIDE FOR PENNSYLVANIA does not encompass all of the state, since space limitations make adequate coverage of such a vast area impossible. Rather, we have given fuller coverage to fewer locales, especially those that are relevant to our Bicentennial celebration. You may be surprised to find one excursion that features New Jersey shore resorts and a number of museums and homes in Delaware; within easy reach of Philadelphia, these are favorite visitor attractions.

We have tried to give accurate information on prices and visiting hours for all sites discussed. THE GUIDE suggests, however, that you check these out before embarking on any excursion, for they are always subject to change.

Local tourist offices, listed at the back of the book, will be glad to answer questions and provide you with additional information.

EXCURSION 1

Colonial Philadelphia

Tradition dies hard, especially in Philadelphia. Visitors often think there are only two things to see in connection with the American Revolution. First is the Liberty Bell which they assume, quite logically, was cast in celebration of American independence. It wasn't. It hung in the tower of the old State House for fully 25 years before the birth of our nation. Second is the Betsy Ross House where we all can picture the widowed flagmaker creating "Old Glory" with a few snips of her scissors. In truth, say historians, she never lived at this charming little house, may never have created our first flag!

Philadelphia is both a living monument to the colonial period and a treasurehouse of Revolutionary history. THE GUIDE offers you a glimpse into that richness. Plan, if you can, to spread your sightseeing over two days. Best means of transportation is your own two feet.

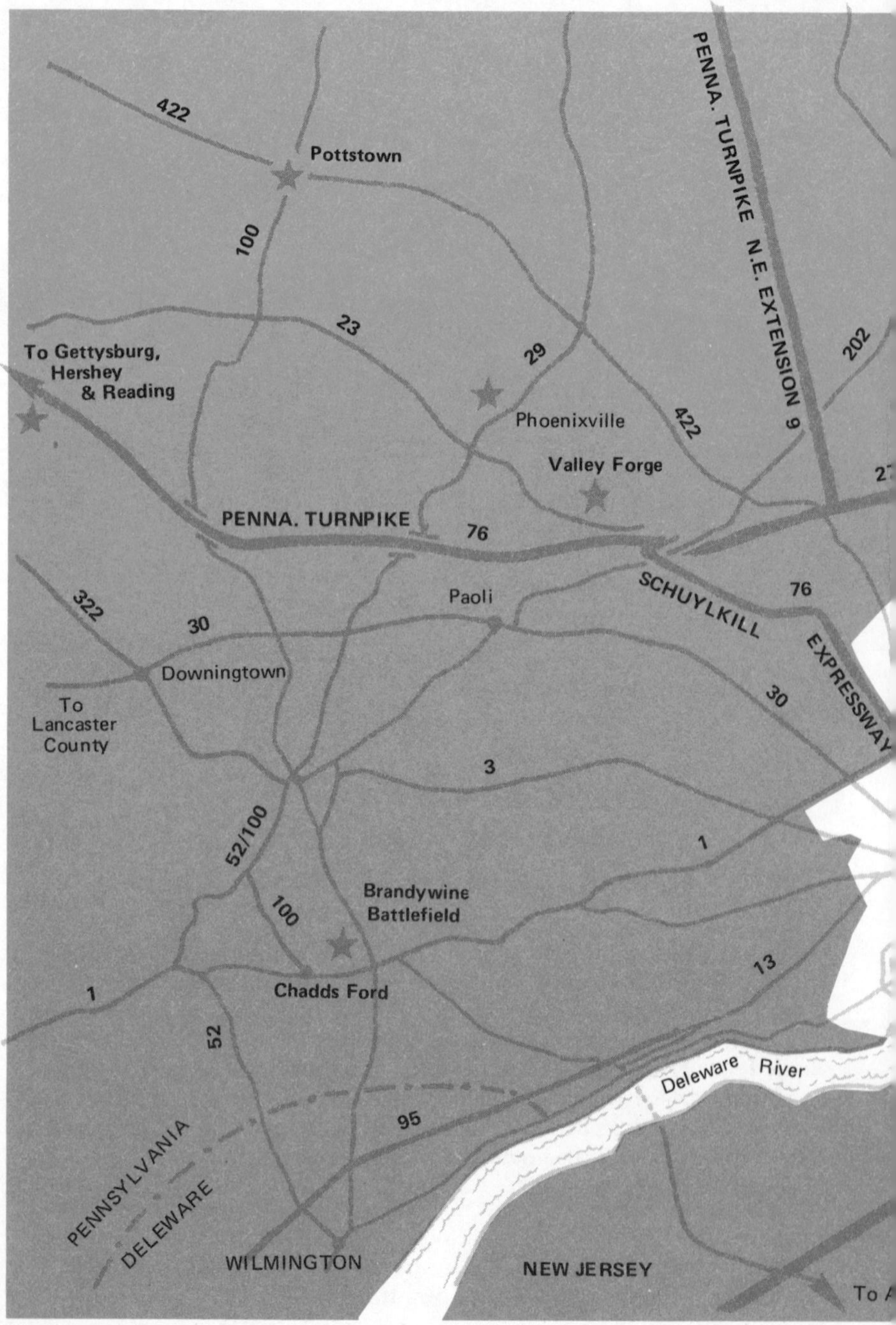
422
Pottstown
100
23
To Gettysburg,
Hershey
& Reading
29
Phoenixville
PENNA. TURNPIKE N.E. EXTENSION 9
202
422
Valley Forge
PENNA. TURNPIKE
76
SCHUYLKILL
76
EXPRESSWAY
Paoli
322
30
Downingtown
To
Lancaster
County
30
3
52/100
1
Brandywine
Battlefield
100
Chadds Ford
13
1
52
Deleware River
95
PENNSYLVANIA
DELEWARE
WILMINGTON
NEW JERSEY

Philadelphia Area

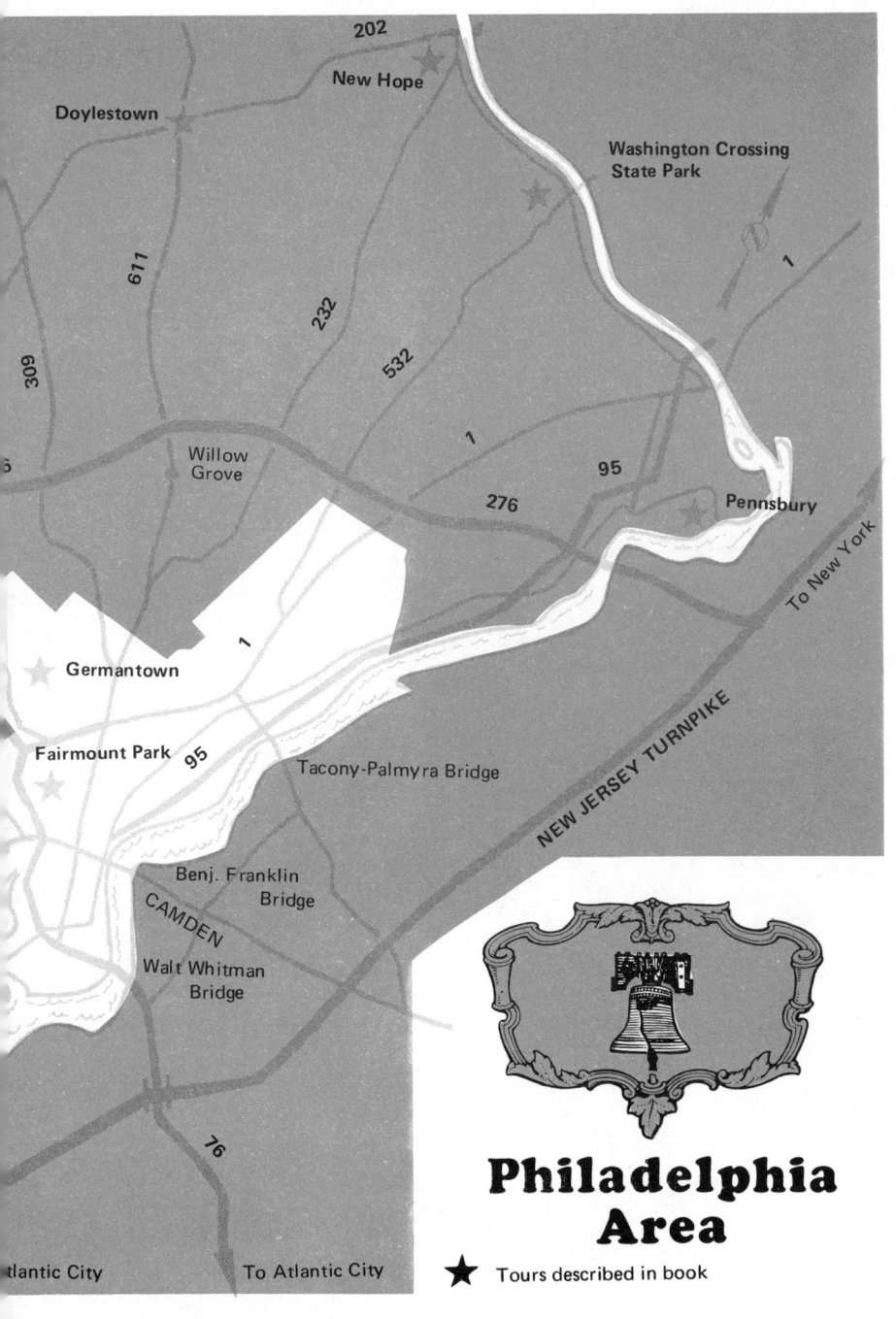

★ Tours described in book

HISTORIC LOCATION MAP

Downt

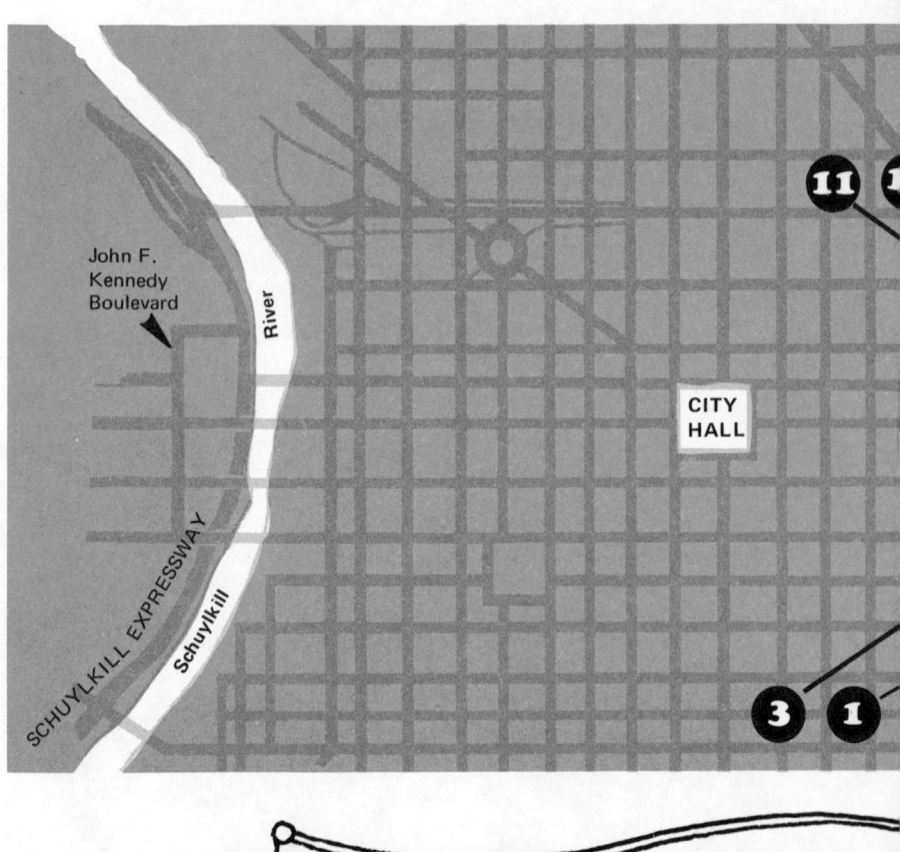

30th St. · 26th St. · 25th St. · 23rd St. · 22nd St. · 21st St. · 20th St. · 19th St. · 18th St. · 17th St. · 16th St. · 15th St. · BROAD ST. · 13th St. · 12th St. · 11th St.

John F. Kennedy Boulevard

Schuylkill River

SCHUYLKILL EXPRESSWAY

CITY HALL

(1) Pennsylvania Hospital
(2) Congress Hall
(3) Independence Hall and Liberty Bell
(4) Second Bank of the U.S.
(5) Carpenters' Hall
(6) Pemberton House (Army-Navy Museum)
(7) Todd House
(8) Bishop White House

wn Philadelphia

10th St.
9th St.
8th St.
7th St.
6th St.
5th St.
4th St.
3rd St.
2nd St.
Front St.
Delaware Ave.

Rte. 95

0 16 17 13 15 14 12

2 4 7 5 9 8 6

Spring Garden St.
Callowhill St.
VINE ST.
Benjamin Franklin Bridge
Race St.
Arch St.
Filbert St.
MARKET ST.
Chestnut St.
Walnut St.
Locust St.
Spruce St.
Pine St.
Lombard St.
South St.

(9) Powel House
(10) Benjamin Franklin "archeological dig"
(11) First Bank of the U.S.
(12) City Tavern
(13) Christ Church
(14) Museum of the Fire Department
(15) Betsy Ross House
(16) Friends' Meeting House
(17) U.S. Mint

5

COLONIAL PHILADELPHIA

You'll find that the sites described below are within easy reach of each other as well as the shops, restaurants, theaters, movies and hotels of center-city. If you don't want to walk to all the destinations, use SEPTA, the city's transportation system (DA 9-4800).

Center-city and the old colonial area slightly to the east are only a short cab ride from 30th Street, the central train terminal. Philadelphia Convention and Tourist Bureau at 1525 John F. Kennedy Boulevard (864-1976) and the new tourist center being erected by the National Park Service at 3rd and Chestnut will tell you everything from where to see President Cleveland's jawbone (at the Mutter Museum, in case you're wondering) to where to find rest rooms. One of the best books out on Philadelphia is John Marion's *Bicentennial City,* Pyne Press, 1974. For special tours of the old city, call Centipede at KI6-2968, whose guides are well versed in things colonial. Another useful number — WE7-1212 for the weather.

And now our excursion, in order of visiting.

1 **Pennsylvania Hospital,** 8th and Spruce. This world-renowned institution was founded in 1751 by the enterprising Dr. Franklin along with Dr. Thomas Bond.

Walk into the lobby of the hospital's main building (Pine Building at 8th between Spruce and Delancey) to see its most treasured work of art: the painting "Christ Healing the Sick." It was created by Swarthmore-born artist, Benjamin West, who as a boy learned about the mixing of pigments from local Indians. He gave this painting to the hospital in 1817, after which the Board of Managers put it on display, charging admission. Total raised: $25,000.

Pennsylvania Hospital was a pioneer in the treatment of the mentally ill. Its surgical amphitheater, oldest in the states, utilized a glass skylight that provided natural light for operations. The hospital also has the oldest medical library in the nation. Here leading American physician Benjamin Rush was associated. Rush tried to save lives during the terrible yellow fever epidemic of 1793, but his technique of purges and bleeding might have killed as many as he cured. Said Rush: "I have resolved to stick to my principles, my practices, and my patients to the last extremity. I will remain, if I remain alone."

The hospital can be visited from 8:30 a.m. to 5 p.m. daily; free.

② Congress Hall, 6th and Chestnut, where George Washington took the oath of office for his second term as president, attired in a full suit of black velvet with black stockings and diamond knee buckles, his powdered hair gathered behind him in a black silk bag. In these halls Washington delivered his farewell message to Congress, John Adams was sworn in as second President, and the Bill of Rights was amended to the Constitution.

Completed in 1790 as the county court house, this building looks much today as it did when Congress met here during Philadelphia's position as U. S. capital. On the first floor members of the House of Representatives met, sitting in studded leather chairs at semi-circular rows of mahogany desks. In the south alcove they smoked or had a glass of madeira at recess. The room is authentic down to its venetian blind tapes and wooden spitting boxes. Upstairs in a smaller, more elaborately furnished chamber with a great eagle painted on the cove, the Senate met. The small dais in this room has an exquisite crimson canopy.

Open daily, 9 a.m. – 5 p.m.; free.

③ Independence Hall, between 5th and 6th on Chestnut. The old State House, now known as Independence Hall, was almost torn down in the early nineteenth century. The city of Philadelphia purchased it in 1818 to save it from the developers, and a visit by the elderly Marquis de Lafayette, great Frenchman who had come to our aid during the Revolution, sparked the move to restore this great national treasure.

After World War II the hall became the focal point of a huge restoration project known as Independence National Historic Park. The once shabby area, now considered the "most historic square mile in America," is a lovely, grassy section, the precious old buildings either restored or their former location indicated by low brick walls and identifying plaques. All buildings in the Park are free. Some, but not all, are described in this excursion, and we have chosen others that are not part of the Park.

So much history has occurred in Independence Hall, from the years of the provincial government (when visiting Indians are said to have lit festive bonfires within its walls) on through the first workings of our national Constitution, that you would do well to pick up some literature and take a guided 20-minute tour (free) from the East Wing.

The story of the Liberty Bell (which traditionally was housed inside the Hall but for the Bicentennial has been moved outside to its own pavillion) fills a good-sized brochure. For starters, the bell was cast in London in 1751 to commemorate the freedom given 50 years before to the citizens of his province by William Penn. The words inscribed upon it, "... and Proclaim Liberty thro' all the land to all the Inhabitants thereof" from the Bible were thus strangely prophetic. The bell cracked in testing, was recast in Philadelphia by Pass and Stow, summoned the citizens to the State House yard on July 8, 1776, to hear the Declaration read and, according to tradition, cracked yet again in tolling the death of Chief Justice John Marshall in 1835.

Highlight of your tour will probably be the Assembly Room where both the Declaration and Constitution were signed. Note the silver inkstand used for signing and the chair painted with a rising sun from which Washington presided over the Constitutional Convention. You'll also find the Long Room, which could accommodate 500 guests for dinner, a most impressive sight.

Learn more about Independence Hall at a dramatic hour-long sound and light show ("The Nation is Born") presented free of charge outside the Hall in Independence Square at 9 p.m. Tuesday through Saturday during the summer. It's a most enjoyable – if somewhat overblown – production, with the clopping of horses, actors' voices taking the part of our founding fathers, and prisms of light focused on the silent old buildings.

Personnel at Independence Hall will tailor events and hours to the number of Bicentennial visitors, so check them out at MA7-1776.

Likely hours are 9 a.m. to 5 p.m. daily except from July 1 to Labor Day when the Hall should be open 8 a.m. to 8 p.m. Free.

Second Bank of the U.S.

④ Second Bank of the U.S., 420 Chestnut St. Housed in one of the most beautiful examples of Greek Revival architecture in the nation is an important new portrait gallery featuring works by Revolutionary and Federal artists.

The building, completed in 1824, was designed by William Strickland. It was the center of a bitter controversy between President Andrew Jackson and the Whigs over the nation's banking policy. Jackson won and the Bank lost its charter. Though its financial past is only a memory, you can visualize the excitement of the banking floor whose vaulted ceiling springs from Ionic colonnades. Sumptuous new period furniture serves as backdrop for the art.

Among the gallery's finest holdings is the largest number of works by Charles Wilson Peale in any one place. Peale, a leading colonial portraitist and well-lived gentleman, married three times and had 17 children; he died at age 86 while courting his fourth wife. George Washington posed for four of the Peales in 1795 (Charles, two sons and a brother — all artists): particularly impressive was the study by son Rembrandt, age 17.

Open 9 a.m. — 5 p.m. daily except New Years, Christmas; free.

The Famous Rising Sun Chair

5 **Carpenters' Hall,** Chestnut below 4th. There were no professional architects during the colonial period, but so-called master carpenters were in actuality both architects and builders.

Founded in 1724, Carpenters' Company of Philadelphia is the oldest builders' organization in the U.S. and its place of business, begun in 1770, still is owned and maintained by the Carpenters' Company. So private a group was this that when Thomas Jefferson wrote for a copy of its book of rules, prices and patterns, he didn't get it; members were faced with expulsion if caught showing the book to an outsider — even if he was a former president.

The perfectly proportioned Georgian building of Flemish bond (red stretcher bricks alternating with glazed black headers in a checkered pattern) achieved its greatest hour as scene of the First Continental Congress (1774) which, after the British had closed the port of Boston, met to resist oppressive British policies. The 55 delegates adopted the "Declaration of Rights and Grievances" written by Pennsylvanian John Dickinson.

Open 10 a.m. to 4 p.m. daily; closed holidays; free.

6 **Pemberton House** (Army-Navy Museum), Chestnut below 4th. Housed in a replica of the 18th century home of a Quaker merchant is a museum devoted to Army and Navy history from 1775 to 1805. (For the history of the Marine Corps visit New Hall on the same block.) It's tailor-made for the young ones in your family because of the do-it-yourself exhibits, some of which are quite imaginative. "Try Your Hand at Maneuvering for a Sea Battle" is one; with switches you can control the ship's rudder, trim its sails and assume a southern wind. There is also a recreation of the gun room of an 18th century warship and a clearly illustrated depiction of the combined land and naval action at Yorktown that brought the Revolution to a close.

Open daily, 9 a.m. to 4:45 p.m., closed Christmas, New Years; free.

7 **Todd House,** northeast corner 4th and Walnut. This charming home is one of the few houses open to the public that illustrates middleclass life in colonial Philadelphia. Dolley Todd lived here from 1791 to 1793 with her attorney husband who perished in the 1793 epidemic, as did their baby. Dolley moved on to a more elegant way of life as wife of a future President: James Madison. Ironically, before the house was restored it was occupied by a luncheonette; above the entrance hung a sign advertising Dolly Madison ice cream.

Note the location of the house at the end of the street, with the entrance and a center hall on the side of the house (a peculiar feature of "end of row" houses in Pa., N.J., and Del.)

Open every day, 9 a.m. – 5 p.m.; necessary to make reservations on day of visit; free.

8 **Bishop White House,** 309 Walnut St. Here the long-time rector of Christ Church, Dr. William White, resided for 49 years. The house, built in 1786-87, has been beautifully restored. An archeological excavation of the drain under the house and the use of a detailed oil painting of the study helps recreate the interior. Bishop White entertained many persons prominent in the state and the nation in his cosmopolitan abode which had 12-foot high ceilings and an inside "necessary" (such facilities usually were in the garden at that time).

See the Bishop's sermon box with sermons written in his own hand, his eyeglasses, the cigar burns on the fireplace mantel, even an apple corer.

Open Mondays through Fridays by tour only at 11 a.m., 1 and 2 p.m.; tickets through First Bank, Visitors Bureau, Free.

Powel House

9 **Powel House,** 244 South 3rd. This home of Samuel Powel, last Mayor of Philadelphia before, and first after the Revolution, is one of the outstanding Georgian-style mansions in the U.S. It was almost demolished for commercial purposes back in 1930 but was salvaged literally in mid-wrecking, parts of it already having gone to leading museums.

Note the signed Gilbert Stuart painting and the massive tea chest in the parlor, the staircase of Santo Domingo mahogany, and the Waterford chandelier (c. 1790), piano, French harp, and gilt-framed mirrors of the second floor drawing room.

John Adams described one of Mrs. Powel's mouth-watering suppers as: "... a most sinful feast again! Everything which could delight the eye or allure the taste; curds and creams, jellies, sweetmeats of various sorts, 20 sorts of tarts, fools, trifles, floating islands, whipped sillibub..."

House can only be seen by guided tour, though advance notice is not necessary. Admission: $1 adults, 50¢ children 12-16, 25¢ children 6-12.

Open Tuesday-Saturday, 10 a.m. to 4 p.m., Sunday 1 to 4 p.m. Closed Mondays and major holidays.

10 **Franklin Court "archeological dig"** between 3rd and 4th Streets at site of Benjamin Franklin's home (south side of Market). Ben Franklin is Philadelphia's favorite son and one of America's all-time heroes.

He left his mark as a leading scientist — inventing bifocals, the Franklin stove, the lightning rod, the burglar alarm, a musical instrument called the glass armonica for which Mozart composed. He was an astute political leader, largely responsible for the French alliance so vital to our Revolutionary victory. He was a businessman, a fund raiser par excellence, the vital force behind Philadelphia's first circulating library, insurance company, university, hospital, gazette, learned society. Deeply human, he stressed the life of prudence and plain tastes while indulging in the finest wines and women, entering a common-law marriage and fathering an undetermined number of illegitimate children. He wrote the best autobiography of the colonial period, was an inveterate literary hoaxer, and showed no hesitation in offering his advice on any subject from "Fish and Visitors stink in three days" to "The having made a young Girl *miserable* may give you bitter reflections, none of which can attend the making of an old Woman *happy*." When Ben Franklin died in 1790 at age 84, 20,000 mourning Philadelphians followed his cortege to Christ Church.

And now at Franklin Court where he lived while not abroad during a 25 year period, the results of an "archeological dig" may be seen underneath a see-through plastic bubble. The actual house is not being renovated because records are not precise enough as to specifications, but you'll be able to see wells, pottery, and other relics being dug up. Stainless steel is used judiciously to show the size or angle of a one-time roof or stairway. Other houses that Franklin owned on Market Street will, however, be restored.

Independence Hall, Mall Behind

11 **First Bank of the U.S., 120 S. 3d St.** In 1791 Secretary of the Treasury Alexander Hamilton supported the creation of a central bank for the U.S. Modeled after the Bank of England and chartered by the Congress, it opened for business in Carpenters Hall, then moved here to its own building. After the bank's 20-year charter was allowed to expire in 1811, Stephen Girard bought the building, took over the staff, and called it Girard Bank which it remained until his death.

French-born Girard had been a ship's captain. A strange man, his life was filled with personal tragedy and altruistic deeds (he helped finance the U.S. during the War of 1812 and was the biggest benefactor Philadelphia ever knew).

The handsome building now houses an exhibit on the history of the Treasury Department and the Constitutional battles over money. The great rotunda with its giant dome has been restored.

Open 9 a.m. to 5 p.m. daily; closed Christmas, New Year. Free.

12 City Tavern, 2nd Street and Moravian (between Chestnut and Walnut). Taverns of colonial days weren't mere taprooms; they were centers of business, social and political life where big events happened and were celebrated or mourned, as the case warranted. Now the most famous of them all, City Tavern — John Adams called it "the most genteel one in America" — is being reconstructed for the Bicentennial with colonial-style food and drink.

Opened originally in 1774, City Tavern was the gathering place for the Continental Congress. the Constitutional Convention and the Federal government of the 1790's. Its board of directors represented the town's elite. The tavern's healthy food and hearty drink inspired some stirring, if occasionally unprophetic, toasts. Example: "May the collision of British flint and American steel produce that spark of liberty which shall illuminate the last posterity." (Thomas Paine, 1774).

13 Christ Church, 2nd above Market. William Penn's Pennsylvania was built upon respect for the individual worth of its citizens. In no area was this respect more vibrantly expressed than in the freedom to worship.

The age, beauty and diversity of Philadelphia churches is remarkable. In these pages we have space to describe only a few, but THE GUIDE urges you to see many more — Mikveh Israel (Jewish cemetery), Old St. George's (Methodist Church), Old St. Joseph's (Roman Catholic), St. Peter's (Episcopalian), Old Pine (Presbyterian), Mother Bethel (African Methodist) — each faith has its own colonial tradition here.

Christ Church

According to a clause in Penn's charter of 1681 from King Charles II, as soon as 20 residents of the city so desired, a minister would be sent them by the Bishop of London. Christ Church was founded in 1695; it is the oldest Anglican (now Protestant Episcopal) church in Philadelphia. Fifteen signers of the Declaration of Independence worshipped here, seven of whom are buried either in the churchyard or at the separate burial grounds at 5th and Arch. George Washington attended services here, resplendent in a rich blue Spanish cloak faced with red velvet, his conveyance a dazzling cream-colored coach. Note the font, sent over from England, at which Penn himself was baptised.

This building, erected 1727-54, of red brick with a slender white steeple — the latter financed by a lottery — is a gem of Georgian architecture.

Open 9 a.m. to 5 p.m. daily, services every day; free.

14 **Museum of the Fire Department**, 149 N. 2nd (at Quarry St.). This is the oldest continually active fire department in the country, and its museum is full of the lore and paraphernalia of fire fighting.

Men on duty will tell you about the old wagons, the history of the department, and the present-day two-way fire radio dispatch system. There's a comprehensive exhibit of engines from 1799 on, some with beautiful brass fixtures. See the most elegant engine of them all, the 1804 "Spider Hose Reel"; also note the leather buckets for water and the brass poles on which the men slid from third floor dormitory to first floor when an alarm was sounded. The kids may complain about seeing old houses or churches, but you won't hear a whimper here.

Open daily except Monday, 10 a.m. to 4 p.m.; closed some holidays; free.

15 **Betsy Ross House**, 239 Arch. On June 14, 1777, Congress resolved "that the flag of the United States be 13 stripes, alternate red and white, that the Union be 13 stars, in a blue field, representing a new constellation."

George Washington is said to have drawn the design of the first American flag with six-pointed stars, after which a committee of Congress went to the home of Betsy Ross at 239 Arch Street. The widowed flagmaker suggested five points as being more artistic and easily made with one clip of the scissors.

Historians still enjoy arguing over whether it really happened this way. In any case, the charming Betsy Ross House remains one of Philadelphia's most beloved landmarks.

Open 9:30 a.m. to 5:15 p.m. daily except Christmas; free.

16 **Friends' Meeting House**, between 3rd and 4th on Arch. On a plot of land donated by

Central Philadelphia

William Penn to the Society of Friends was erected the oldest Friends' meeting house still in use in the city and the largest in the world. Constructed in 1804, its austere, hand hewn wooden benches — softened now with yellow cushions — and unadorned interior reveal the simplicity inherent in this religion.

Thanks to William Penn, himself a lifelong convert to the Society of Friends (commonly called Quakers), Philadelphia was a major refuge for these people who were persecuted and even jailed in Europe for their beliefs. Their faith, resting on the word of God as spoken to the human soul, requires no formal church, no priest. As every man is his own priest, fellow Quakers are addressed as "Thee" and "Thou."

The Friends earned a proud place in Philadelphia and for many of the colonial years were the dominant force in trade, charity, finance, education, politics and business, adopting such advanced precepts as equality to women and abhorrence of slavery. Because they were pacifists, there was resentment among other groups toward Quakers, and in 1775 they withdrew from active participation in the government of Pennsylvania. Later, their influence gradually waned. Friends who joined the cause of independence were disowned by the Society of Friends and formed their own group, the "Free Quakers."

See a documentary film at the meeting house and exhibits of old clothing, Bibles, etc. Buried in an unmarked grave on the meeting house grounds in accordance with Quaker custom is William Penn's close friend and secretary, James Logan.

Open 10 a.m. to 4 p.m. daily; free.

17 **U.S. Mint**, 5th and Arch. Philadelphia has been producing U. S. coins since 1792, the first being half dimes made by hand from silver plate belonging to George Washington. In the museum area of the nation's largest mint, you can see the first coining press of that year. A self-guided audiovisual tour explains the process of melting, casting, pressing, cleaning and inspecting coins.

Don't miss Peter, the eagle. Early in the 19th century he adopted the Mint as his home and became its mascot. When he died after catching his wing on a flywheel, his Mint friends had him mounted so that he is still with us today. It is thought that Peter was the model for the eagle on the U.S. silver dollar (1836-39).

Open 9:00 a.m. to 3:30 p.m. Monday to Friday, closed holidays; free.

William Penn Statue Atop City Hall

Historic Insight...

Fifty-Five Men Seek a System of Government

It was May 1787. Fifty-five of America's finest men — men whom Thomas Jefferson called "an assembly of demigods" — had arrived at Philadelphia's State House. Their purpose: to create a form of government that would bring unity to their disunited states.

This was the same State House that had seen momentous events eleven years before. Ben Franklin, now an old man, had been present then, too ... Summer, 1776; The Second Continental Congress. Fighting already had broken out with England and George Washington declared commander-in-chief of the Continental forces, but still the colonies had not formally declared their independence from the mother country. Not an easy pronouncement. There was heated discussion, but eventually a committee under 33-year-old Jefferson had prepared a statement of strength and beauty. It was adopted July 4, 1776, and signed by 56 delegates August 2. "Yes," said John Hancock in affixing his signature to the Declaration of Independence. "We must all

15

hang together or, most assuredly, we shall all hang separately."

And now, May 1787, the war was over and the colonies a nation, but the Articles of Confederation that had been intended to govern that nation were not working, and anarchy threatened. George Washington was presiding officer. Some of the expected delegates didn't show up, fearing loss of state independence. (Patrick Henry was among the missing. "I smell a rat in Philadelphia," he said.) When seven states were represented, proceedings began.

Over half the men were lawyers, their average age 42. They represented wealth, property, business, scholarship. Aside from abolishing the Articles of Confederation, they didn't agree on what would be best for their foundering nation. A few wanted a monarchy, Alexander Hamilton a strong central government, and George Mason a strong state government. In the middle was James Madison, 32, a scholar and theologian. ("Compromise, compromise, compromise," he urged, and without this spirit there would have been no final product.)

For 17 weeks they worked and argued. The exact words exchanged behind closed doors during this tense period were not revealed to the public for 60 years for fear of upsetting its repose. Finally, agreement was reached on the Constitution of the United States, a document that — as was recently proved — still works, with a President and a Congress balancing each other and the Supreme Court and judges watchdog over both and guardian of the people's rights. When on June 21 nine states had ratified the document, it became effective.

After it was all over, Franklin met a woman outside. "Well, Doctor, what have we got — a republic or a monarchy?" she asked. "A republic, madam," he answered, "if you can keep it."

* * * * *

The Philadelphia of these momentous days was not quite the "greene countrie towne" that William Penn had envisaged. Rather, it had become a metropolis — the largest, richest and most beautiful of the nation. As befitted the capital of the insurgent republic (1775-83) and of the new nation (1790-1800) it had a concentration of brilliant minds that never again was equalled. So many national "firsts" took place here that one hardly knows where to begin the list — daily newspaper, scientific society, law school, volunteer fire company, art academy, botanical garden, hospital, and mint, to name a few.

The city was helped by its location as a large freshwater port and by the rich agricultural terrain surrounding it. It was aided, too, by the incentive of its inhabitants — people of varied faiths and nationalities who, in the tradition of William Penn, had freedom to worship and work as they desired. But despite its sophistication and wealth, Philadelphia continued for a large part of the colonial period to exhibit a sober spirit. Commented Dr. Alexander Hamilton, who in 1744 wrote one of the best travel accounts of colonial days, "Never was a place so populous where the gout for publick gay diversions prevailed so little." He complained that the women kept "att home" all day and that he could not see them, "therefore I cannot with certainty enlarge upon their charms." Hamilton attributed Philadelphia's sobriety to the "rich, obstinate, stiff-necked Quakers."

As the Revolution approached and Quaker influence declined, life became more as Dr. Hamilton would have it. Theatrical entertainment was popular, horse racing had come in along with dancing and balls, and drinking — hearty before — had become heavy now. After 1750, social life in Philadelphia was elaborate, even brilliant, and home furnishings were sumptuous.

Strangely, during the worst time of the Revolution for Philadelphia — when the British occupied the city for nine months in 1777-78 — life was at its gayest. Many more Americans sided with the British than sometimes is realized, and these people (most of them wealthy) took enthusiastic part in British revelry. There was, for instance, the farewell put on for General Howe when he was recalled from Philadelphia to England. They called it the "Meschianza." Gaily decked barges floated along the river front, and queens of beauty presided over a four-acre lawn attended by knights on fine steeds. In a ballroom festooned with some 80 huge mirrors, a midnight supper of 1200 dishes was lit by as many wax candles. Outside the lawn blazed with illuminations, fountains spouted fire, and the rush and roar of rockets filled the air.

It was the same season that General Washington's men were tramping shoeless and hungry through the icy fields of Valley Forge.

While You're Walking Around . . .

. . . you'll be able to read different stories in the architecture of old Philadelphia. Some streets are charming in their intimacy, others impressive for their massive homes and broad sidewalks. You will come upon unexpected walks and ways, alleys, gazebos, children's playgrounds with a sculpted kangaroo or a frog. And don't be surprised if a resident who's outside polishing the brass of his 150-year-old home invites you in for a look. (Philadelphians are friendlier than you might expect.) Remember that you needn't limit yourself to walking in the daytime hours; as sun sets in old Philadelphia the street lamps shed a lovely, pinkish glow on the streets and homes.

The best known of all the small residential streets is Elfreth's Alley between Arch and Race, Front and Second Streets, which has 33 homes, some dating from the early 1700s, making it the oldest continually occupied residential street in America. During a festival held generally every first Saturday of June, homes and gardens are open to the public.

The homes on Camac between 12th and 13th Streets date from the early 1800s. Note that some of them display plaques denoting membership in fire insurance companies, the oldest of which (Philadelphia Contributorship) was begun in 1752. Also on Camac Street, you'll see several of the so-called "busy-bodies," an arrangement of three mirrors at the second floor window which enabled residents to look down from inside and see what was going on at their doorstep or in the street. Shutters of the 18th century were usually paneled on the first floor for protection and to keep out dirt and smells emanating from the street. (Don't forget, farmland was close by, and pigs occasionally ran up and down the streets which were not always free of garbage. Take note of the houses displaying plaques of black iron with a blue shield in the center, for these are certified by the Philadelphia Historical Commission as being of historical or architectural interest and maintained in their original state or restored to it.

For a different kind of dwelling, see the "Father, Son and Holy Ghost" houses on Iseminger Street between Camac and 13th, so designated because they have only one room to each floor; usually the kitchen is in the basement. These homes, lived in by artisans, date from the first half of the 19th century.

Clinton Street between 9th and 11th dates from the 1830s-1850s. In its grand homes lived the Wetherills, Lippincotts, Reppliers, and other of Philadelphia's leading families. You'll see a lot of decorative iron work on these buildings which are of Greek Revival design with temple-like doorways. At 9th and Clinton is one of the city's few remaining watering troughs for horses. Of stone and often quite lovely, these items of miniature statuary have different inscriptions ("A merciful man is merciful to his beast," reads this one).

The "Society Hill" section directly south of Independence National Historic Park is loosely bound by Walnut and South, Front and 7th Streets. Originally the area had nothing to do with society as we know it but derived its name from the Free Society of Traders which purchased a part of this section from William Penn. An active renovation since the 1950's has seen the restoration and construction of some 1,000 homes, and a large number of prominent Philadelphians have moved there.

Washington Square between 6th and 7th is a particularly fine part of Society Hill. It started out as one of William Penn's five squares, then became a potter's field where Revolutionary soldiers and victims from the yellow fever epidemic were buried. Ringing the square are some of the nation's best known publishing houses (Lippincott, Saunders, Lea and Febiger, etc.), a famous library, the Athenaeum, housed in an elegant building of Italian palazzo design, and Federal houses with delicate trim. Today modern high rise apartment houses and their accompanying townhouses stand alongside these old landmarks.

On the site of the Penn Mutual Life Insurance Company at 6th and Walnut was the old Walnut Street prison where criminals, Tories, prisoners of war, and debtors were jailed. Here Robert Morris, wealthy merchant who helped finance the Revolution, was jailed as a debtor — the victim of unwise land speculation; George Washington came to dine with him in prison. In its courtyard the new nation's first manned balloon flight went up in 1793 with Pierre Blanchard seated in its basket; Blanchard carried with him a message from George Washington which he delivered upon his descent in Glassboro, N.J.

Penn Mutual has just built an annex whose glass elevator will whisk you to the top for a unique view of the city. Notice how this annex of concrete, steel and glass rises from behind the facade of a 19th century building (a marvelous edifice of Egyptian Revival design with columns of tulip design and oft repeated scarab insignia); such architecture was inspired by Napoleon's conquest of Egypt. This is a fine example of the fusion of old and new that is Philadelphia at its best.

Society Hill

MORE ABOUT PHILADELPHIA

Colonial Philadelphia, important though it is, is only one part of this large and varied metropolis. The following sites are all within easy reach of center-city and the colonial area. You'll not be sorry you stayed that extra day — or week — to see some of them.

Center City

Academy of Music, Broad and Locust, whose fine acoustics (owing to a basement well) show off the rich sound of the Philadelphia Orchestra; *Chinatown,* between 9th and 11th, Arch and Vine, where you can indulge your tastebuds in all kinds of Pekinese or Cantonese specialties; *City Hall,* Broad and

Market, a fascinating building costing $24 million, atop which stands a 26-foot statue of William Penn; *Historical Society of Pennsylvania,* 1300 Locust, repository of priceless books and manuscripts as well as historic items like the wampum belt the Indians gave Penn; *Masonic Temple,* Broad and Filbert, with an amazing representation of architectural style from Corinthian, Italian Renaissance, Gothic and other periods as well as momentos from the first masons on (Washington was one, so was Franklin); *Pennsylvania Academy of the Fine Arts,* Broad and Cherry, oldest art school and museum in the U.S. with paintings by masters like Peale and Thomas Eakins; *Rittenhouse Square,* between 18th and 19th at Walnut Street, named after colonial astronomer David Rittenhouse and until the 1930's the most prestigious residential area in Philadelphia (art and flower shows in summer); *Rosenbach Collection,* 2010 Delancey Place, treasures of antique furniture, silver, paintings, rare books; *Walnut Street Theater,* 9th and Walnut, oldest theater in continuous use in U.S., newly renovated; *The War Library,* 1805 Pine, memorabilia of Civil War, including life masks of Abraham Lincoln.

North Philadelphia

Chapel of the Four Chaplains, 1844 N. Broad, interfaith chapel in memory of four religious leaders of differing faiths who gave their lives to save others on a sinking World War II ship; *Edgar Allan Poe House,* 530 N. 7th St., where the gloomy master lived with his tubercular child-bride and wrote "The Raven;" *Progress Plaza,* Broad and Girard, center for prominent black Philadelphia businesses.

South Philadelphia

American-Swedish Museum, 19th and Pattison Ave., deals with the accomplishments of the Swedes in America (there's a lovely candle-lit Santa Lucia fest each December); *Gloria Dei,* Delaware and Swanson, oldest church in city and a treasured landmark, house of worship for the Swedes who preceded the first English settlers by over 40 years; *Italian Market,* 9th and Christian, open air market with lusty personality and goodies from kale to kohlrabi, snails to scaloppine; *Stadiums* — Spectrum, Phila. Veterans and John F. Kennedy, all at Broad and Pattison, largest sports complex in nation; *Tinicum Wildlife Preserve,* W. 86th and Lyons Ave., marshland and haven for wildlife.

West Philadelphia

John Bartram's House and Garden, 54th and Elmwood, America's first botanical garden, home of a great naturalist and close friend of Franklin; *Civic Center Museum,* 34th and Civic Center Boulevard, crafts from around the world, model ships, musical instruments, other exhibits excellent for young people; *Institute of Contemporary Arts,* 34th and Locust, part of University of Pennsylvania and a center for op, pop, avant garde, etc; *University Museum,* 33rd and Spruce, also part of the University of Pennsylvania, its subject civilization — from jewelry of Bible-age Egypt to stone artifacts of Austrailian bushmen.

THINGS TO DO IN PHILADELPHIA...

JOHN WANAMAKER PHILADELPHIA

Tradition, in Philadelphia, is not necessarily all "Colonial" and "Revolution". One notable exception is in its second century, 115 years old — impressive, enduring, exciting.

Among America's greatest merchants was John Wanamaker of Philadelphia. He began on a modest scale in 1861, expanded rapidly, and, in 1911, completed the impressive building (now a designated historical structure) which stands firmly at the cross roads of Center City on an entire block bounded by 13th, Market, Juniper, and Chestnut Streets.

Here you will find merchandise, both usual and unusual, gathered from the world over, plus unique extras: one of the world's great concert organs, and the magnificent 8-story Grand Court. Presiding here in cool bronze elegance, is the celebrated Wanamaker Eagle, progenitor of the state-wide slogan "Meet me at the Eagle". (You can't come to Philadelphia and not say it at least once!)

Fine shops and boutiques ... the superb, spacious Crystal Tea Room with food and service reminiscent of a bygone era ... organ recitals in the Court at regular intervals. And — if you arrive at store opening you can hear the Wanamaker Store open with a bugle call! (13th and Market; daily 10 AM to 6 PM, Wednesday 10 AM to 9 PM; 215–422-2000).

Among its twelve stores (in four states), that in King of Prussia Plaza will be of interest to visitors making the pilgrimage to Valley Forge.

The NewMarket at Head House Square. A full-city-block of international shops and restaurants overlooking the Delaware River. Outstanding modern glass architecture, sculptured waterfalls and reflecting pool, open courts, a glass elevator, colorful promenades are combined with restored colonial buildings in this specialty center of award-winning design. Built on the site of a late 1700's marketplace, which includes historical Head House Square, NewMarket reflects the affluence and charm of Philadelphia's famed Society Hill and also, a cosmopolitan atmosphere. Bright awninged terraces, glass kiosks, umbrella-studded plazas are reminiscent of Europe. There are several fine restaurants at NewMarket, as well as smaller pubs and bistros. Specialty shops offer goods of outstanding quality from around the world, ranging from fashionable clothing to fashion housewares; sporting goods to gourmet foods; ethnic crafts to plants and flowers. Key historical buildings include the Bake House (oldest structure in the center dating back to 1787), the Harper House, and the Ross House, where General George Washington is said to have visited on several occasions. The primary award-winning new structure at NewMarket is The Glass Palace, a banner-and-plant-lined promenade of shops reached by a wooden footbridge from the Second Street Entrance. Permanent NewMarket exhibits include mid-18th Century artifacts and specimens retrieved from a formal archaeological "dig" at the site. Monthly events and seasonal celebrations include concerts on the Water Plaza, flower shows, Christmas and July 4th programs, and international food festivals.

NewMarket is open seven days a week. For event information call: WA3-6032.

The Old Curiosity Shop, 1621 Sansom Street, Philadelphia. An incredible collection of Nostalgia, Ephemera, Documents, Antiques. Nothing like it, anywhere.

America's Most Famous Shrine, The Liberty Bell • Independence Hall, Philadelphia

EXCURSION 2

Statue of Benjamin Franklin
at Franklin Institute

Benjamin Franklin Parkway & Fairmount Park

Benjamin Franklin Parkway

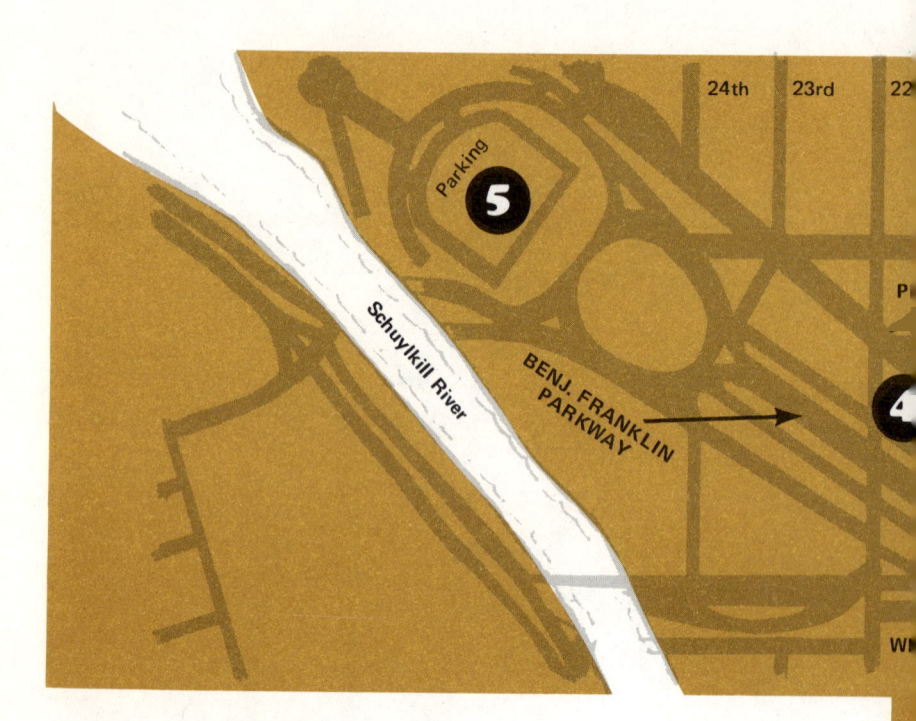

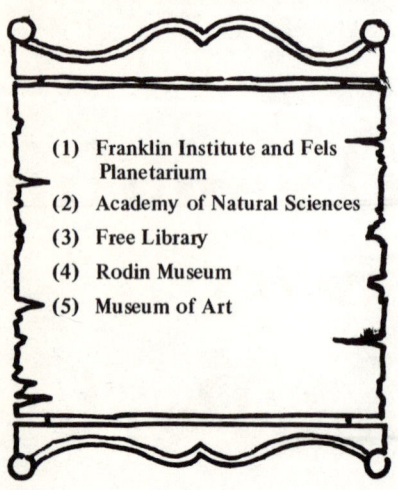

(1) Franklin Institute and Fels Planetarium
(2) Academy of Natural Sciences
(3) Free Library
(4) Rodin Museum
(5) Museum of Art

JOIN, or DIE.

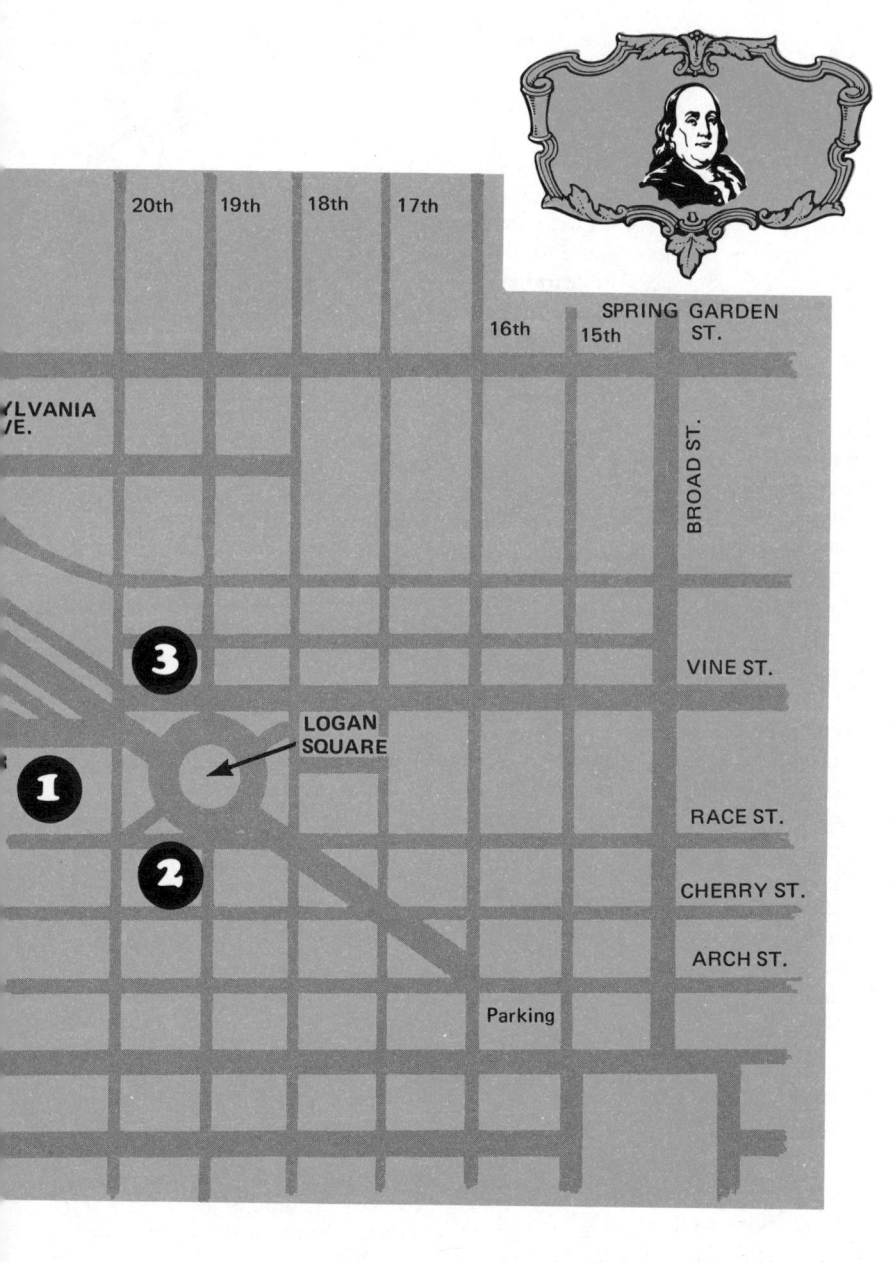

HISTORIC LOCATION MAP

BENJAMIN FRANKLIN PARKWAY

Philadelphia's Benjamin Franklin Parkway has more palaces of learning per square foot than any other city in the world. They're not tired old institutions with dull exhibits, but fascinating repositories of information where you can see a Buddhist temple hall, greet a 100-million year old dinosaur, and learn from the movement of a four-story high pendulum about the earth's rotation.

The Parkway leads into Fairmount Park, a giant recreation center of some 4,000 acres which offers everything from sculling to siberian huskie races, open air concerts to Japanese tea ceremonies. People even get married on the grassy slopes of this largest municipally owned park in the world. Our sightseeing will focus on several mansions that stand intact from colonial days, each with a unique personality.

Choose among all these according to your tastes, but do plan to spend a day in this fine area of Philadelphia.

Benjamin Franklin Parkway: Philadelphia's Champs Élysées

The Gallic appearance of the Benjamin Franklin Parkway, which leads from center city to the East and West River Drives into Fairmount Park, was not accidental. Begun in 1907, the Parkway was a means of bringing old world elegance to the new, and two of the buildings that rose upon it actually were duplicates of ones in Paris.

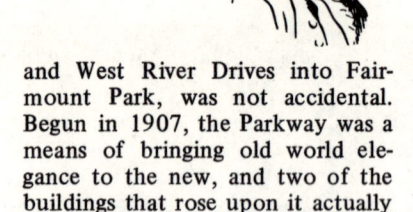

After eleven years of work and $22 million in expenses the old blocks and houses had been swept away, replaced by an eight lane avenue that is rather difficult to drive if one is not familiar with it. Upon the open stretches were erected imposing buildings of classic style surrounded by statuary, fountains and plantings. All this is quite a contrast to the rest of Philadelphia which has a more narrow, crowded look. Some of the impressive views of the Parkway museums have been marred by recent construction, but still it's hard to eclipse the sight of the Art Museum on a clear night, its soft buff color enhanced by subtle floodlighting. Parades, concerts, a Festival of Fountains in summer, flea markets — all these find an ideal setting on Philadelphia's Benjamin Franklin Parkway.

Parkway Excursion

You can easily reach the Parkway museums on foot from center city. SEPTA also provides good service, including the "A" bus which travels along Broad Street and turns onto the Parkway. Best of all is the "Cultural Loop" bus; for 50¢ you can go from town to all the museums described in this section, plus the zoo, getting off and on as much as you like during the day for that price. The Loop runs on a daily basis in spring and summer and on weekends in fall and winter. Call SEPTA for specifics (DA9-4800).

All the museums listed below are closed on major holidays.

1 **Franklin Institute Science Museum and Fels Planetarium**, 20th and Parkway. Named in honor of Philadelphia's most inventive scientist, the 152 year old museum and associated private research laboratories do Dr. Franklin's memory proud. The museum is a push-button, do-it-yourself heaven that turns young people on. They love to walk into the human heart 15,000 times the size of their own, find out what their weight would be on the moon, see the demonstrations of man-made lightning. Among the Institute's prize possessions are a Focault Pendulum hanging four stories high which is illustrative of the earth's rotation, and a printing press believed to have been Franklin's.

At the entrance facing the Parkway is the Fels Planetarium whose 45 minute shows take you into the world of sun, stars and distant planets.

The Franklin Institute is open Mondays through Saturdays, 10 a.m. to 5 p.m., Sundays noon to 5 p.m.; closed Mondays September through March. Admission: adults $2, students 12 through college $1.50 and 5 through 11 $1.25,

Central Library, Logan Square

senior citizens $1, children under 5, 50¢. Planetarium is 50¢ extra; shows every afternoon except Monday and some evenings. Call LO4-3838.

② Academy of Natural Sciences, 19th and Parkway. If you'd like to meet Dina, the huge Hadrosaurus dinosaur, see an important shell collection, or learn about recycling and hashish, visit the Academy of Natural Sciences. Our nation's first natural history museum (founded 1812), the Academy has a lot of imaginative exhibits, particularly the 35 groupings of stuffed animals in their native Asian or African setting. If you prefer the live variety, there are farm animals who put on a show of sorts. The Academy is not just for viewing; it has sponsored some major scientific expeditions such as Admiral Perry's to Greenland. You can bring a few of its wonders home, too, via the purchase of a preserved sea horse or, perhaps, a fossilized shark tooth.

Open 10 a.m. to 5 p.m. Mondays through Saturdays, 1 to 5 p.m. Sundays. $1 adults, 50¢ children and senior citizens. (Look for possible increase in 1976.) Phone: LO7-3700.

③ Free Library of Philadelphia, Logan Square (19th and Vine). The central library of Philadelphia's large branch system is known for its Rare Book Collection which has cuneiform tablets of 5,000 years back, a notable collection of Dickens memorabilia (see his pet raven stuffed in 1841), three centuries of children's books, and the colorful Pennsylvania German manuscripts known as "fraktur".

The Library also has a significant collection of theatrical items, letters of every U.S. president, orchestral scores and automobiliana. There are changing exhibits in the marble entrance hall and special events including chamber music (8 p.m. Wednesdays, November through March), children's concerts and story hours, movies and art shows. A rooftop cafeteria leads to an attractive outdoor eating and reading area.

Open Mondays through Thursdays, 9 a.m. to 9 p.m., Fridays from 9 a.m. to 6 p.m., Saturdays 9 a.m. to 5 p.m., Sundays during academic year, 1 to 5 p.m. Rare Book Collection open 9 a.m. to 5 p.m. Mondays through Saturdays all year. Free. Call: MU6-3990.

"The Thinker"

④ Rodin Museum, 22d and Parkway. A gift to the city of Philadelphia by an admirer of this master French sculptor, the Rodin Museum houses the largest collection of Rodin's work outside Paris. The museum is filled with bronzes, drawings and prints — a pensive, quiet oasis whose spirit is revealed in the entrance where "The Thinker" broods. Note the many sensitive studies of hands.

Administered by the Museum of Art, the Rodin Museum is open daily Tuesdays through Sundays 9 a.m. to 5 p.m. A pay-what-you-wish policy is expected to be in effect during 1976.

5 **Philadelphia Museum of Art,** 26th and Parkway. The Art Museum building of buff colored Minnesota dolomite is itself a treasure of art. Of adapted Greek design with Ionic colonnades, it covers ten acres. Ninety-nine steps lead to the entrance (take heart; there is also a street level entrance.)

Inside are thousands of paintings and pieces of sculpture, as well as rooms and buildings from around the world which have been reconstructed in their entirety. See an eleventh century Romanesque cloister, magnificent tapestries from the Palazzo Barberini in Rome, enormous Calder mobiles, and collections of Dutch, French impressionistic and Italian religious art. A major American exhibition is being planned for April through October 1976. You can even see the wedding dress worn by society girl-turned actress-turned princess Grace Kelly, and a costume worn at that wild colonial fete, the Meschianza.

Buy lunch in the cafeteria and eat on the terrace on a summer afternoon, participate in summer folk dancing outside, see 150 varieties of azaleas behind the museum in May, attend Sunday afternoon concerts in the Van Pelt Auditorium in winter, and buy art reproductions in the shop.

Unfortunately for those visitors who come to Philadelphia in 1975, the museum closed in April for extensive renovation, including air conditioning throughout.

The re-opening is scheduled for February 1976, at which time longer visiting hours may be initiated (seven days a week and five evenings) with a possible pay-what-you-like policy and free tours. Call PO3-8100 for specifics.

Philadelphia Museum of Art, Benjamin Franklin Parkway

Fairmount Park

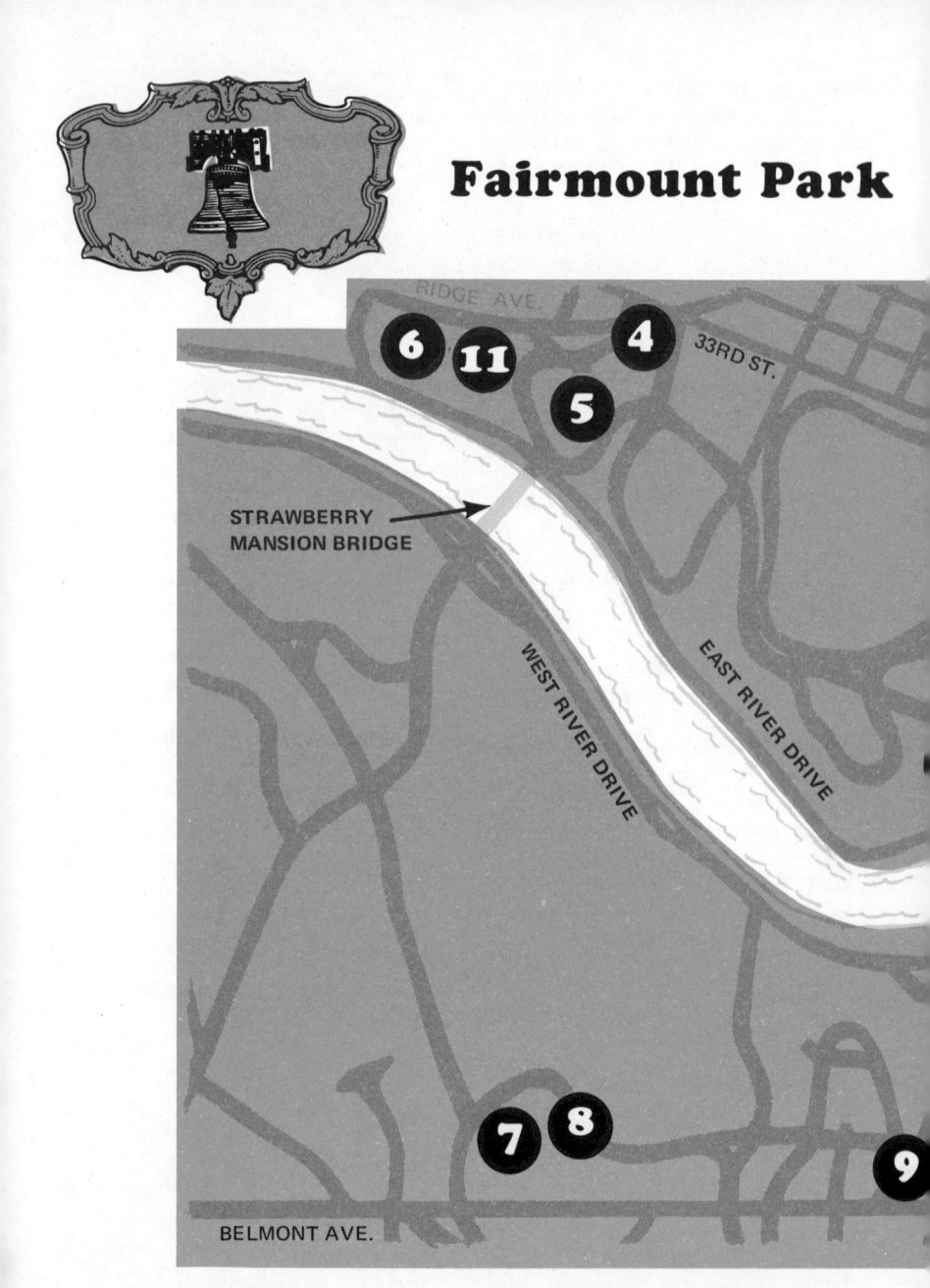

STRAWBERRY MANSION BRIDGE

RIDGE AVE.
33RD ST.
WEST RIVER DRIVE
EAST RIVER DRIVE
BELMONT AVE.

HISTORIC LOCATION MAP

ART MUSEUM

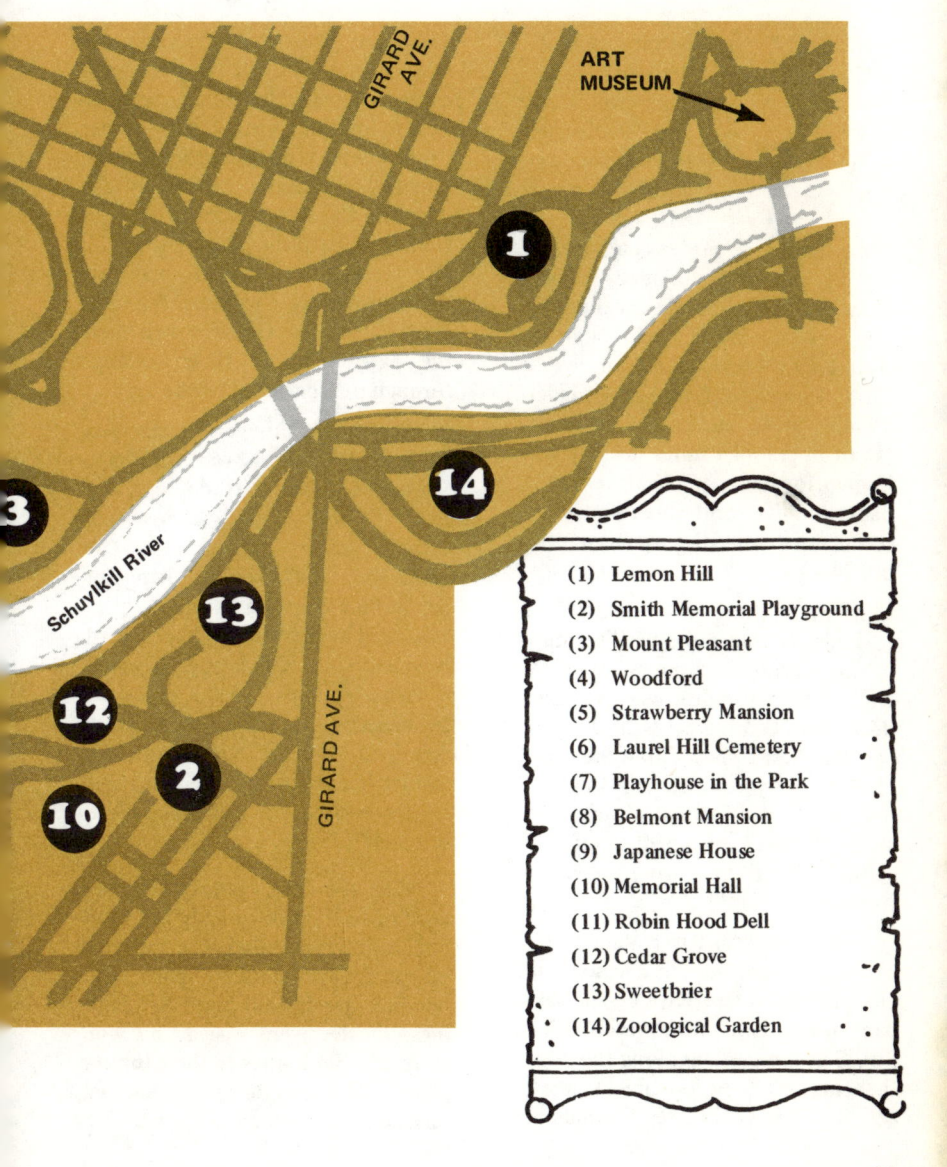

GIRARD AVE.

Schuylkill River

GIRARD AVE.

(1) Lemon Hill
(2) Smith Memorial Playground
(3) Mount Pleasant
(4) Woodford
(5) Strawberry Mansion
(6) Laurel Hill Cemetery
(7) Playhouse in the Park
(8) Belmont Mansion
(9) Japanese House
(10) Memorial Hall
(11) Robin Hood Dell
(12) Cedar Grove
(13) Sweetbrier
(14) Zoological Garden

FAIRMOUNT PARK
Setting for Colonial Splendor

The city of Philadelphia that grew up along the Delaware River became quickly crowded – a far cry from the ample gardens and breathing spaces that founder William Penn had envisaged. The Schuylkill, however, remained virgin land; its river banks provided a cool, lovely spot where well-to-do Philadelphians could escape in summer. (Even in colonial times the city was known for its muggy heat; it was "a pain to live and breathe here" complained one disgruntled visitor in 1744.)

Many of those who could afford to build on the Schuylkill's ample banks were merchants wealthy from Indian trade, western land deals and commerce with Europe and the West Indies. Often they had close professional ties with England and sent their sons abroad for study. Some remained staunchly faithful to Britain during the Revolution.

The Schuylkill River Valley first became a park in 1812 when the city purchased five acres on the east bank for Philadelphia's waterworks. Strolling the gardens along the river then became a fashionable Sunday activity. Ten years later Fairmount Dam was created to increase the water supply. But as the park grew more accessible to the average citizen, it lost its appeal for the estate owners who were disturbed by the swampy conditions caused by the dam and the commercial enterprises that were intruding on their exclusive terrain. As a result, many of them moved to the more "salubrious" milieu of Germantown, and the park acquired their holdings through purchase and bequests.

The biggest thing ever to happen to Fairmount Park was the 1876 Centennial, 100th birthday party of these United States. Almost ten million visitors thronged to the event which reflected the change of our nation from an agrarian to an industrial economy. They heard President U.S. Grant speak, gaped at the telephone and the typewriting machine, ate their first banana, examined Queen Victoria's embroidery, and studied the hand and the torch of the as yet incomplete Statue of Liberty.

With the 20th century the park continued to grow quickly and a bit haphazardly, but always in the style of an English country park with winding roads and natural plantings. Battles were waged and won to return old homes to their former glory. (At least one of the colonial mansions had taken on a less lustrous life as beer garden, speakeasy, dairy farm, and headquarters for ladies of doubtful virtue.) Mechanization continues to threaten the serenity of the park's remaining wilderness, but various organizations work to protect this precious area. And precious it is, not only for its beauty but its history — a history that takes us back long before white men sailed up the Delaware, to the days of the Lenni-Lenape Indians who carved out a life amidst this sylvan splendor.

Fairmount Park Excursion

Though Philadelphians use their park frequently, they tend to take it for granted. Visitors, on the other hand, are often startled to find all this loveliness within the city limits.

For information on special events, recreational facilities, transportation and sites within the park, call Fairmount Park Commission at MU6-1776, Ext. 81204 or 81216. The Convention and Visitors Bureau at 16th and the Parkway is stocked with maps and brochures. A recently published book on the

**Benjamin Franklin National Memorial
Four Times Life Size**

park is Esther Klein's *Fairmount Park,* Harcum Junior College Press, $3.

Those who want to pedal the 15 miles of scenic paths in the park can rent bikes behind the Art Museum at the old Aquarium; call 765-9075. Canoe, rowboat and sailboat rental is handled by the East River Canoe House located south of Strawberry Mansion Bridge on the East River Drive (BA8-9336). By the way, Philadelphia is considered to be the "sculling capital of the world", and high school, college and club races are held along the Schuylkill during spring and summer. The graceful shells are stored at the Victorian structures that make up Boat House Row, of which East River Canoe House is part.

Many of the sites listed in the excursion that follows can be reached on SEPTA's #38 bus. Still a fair amount of walking is necessary between sites. If you take your car instead, be prepared for the fact that many of the houses have no street addresses; directions have to be given by monuments and bridges. The Park Guards are a helpful group if you happen to get lost. Another possibility is to arrange a guided tour of some of the colonial mansions through the Art Museum; call PO3-8100 for information on prices, etc. Note that not all houses are open the same days and that all are closed on legal holidays.

In our excursion we cover first the six sites on the eastern bank of the river and then we cross Strawberry Mansion Bridge to the west bank for #7 on.

① Lemon Hill. One of the park's architectural gems, Lemon Hill was built by wealthy merchant Henry Pratt on land that had been owned by Robert Morris. Morris, an unfortunate patriot through whose efforts the first bank on American soil was founded, ended up in debtors' prison after some unwise land speculation. (Said he in a poignant note to Alexander Hamilton, "I am sensible that I have lost the confidence of the world as to my pecuniary ability, but I believe not as to my honor or integrity.") Pratt acquired the property in 1799 at a sheriff's sale and built the present house in 1800. His gardens and greenhouses were famous.

The most unique feature of the Federal style house is its elegant oval salons on all three floors, each with two curving and matched fireplaces.

Open 11 a.m. to 4 p.m. Thursdays and the second and fourth Sunday of July and August. 50¢ adults, 25¢ for those under 12.

② Smith Memorial Playground, Reservoir Drive near 33d and Oxford. This delightful house and playground are open only to children under 12, except if in a family group. The gift of a local philanthropist, it contains a "village" with small-scale cars and fire trucks to "drive", parking meters, gas pumps, angle and parallel parking. There are some 6½ acres of playground equipment including a basketball court and a giant ten-child-wide slide. When it snows, the playground provides sleds, flying saucers, hot chocolate and cookies, all free of charge. If you have a child not over five years old whose birthday occurs during your Philadelphia stay, you can reserve a room in the main building for a party on any Saturday from 1 to 4 p.m. (call PO9-0902); bring your own decorations and refreshments.

Grounds open 9 a.m. to 5 p.m. daily except Sundays; building open 1 to 4 p.m. daily except Sundays; closed holidays. Free.

③ Mount Pleasant. This mansion had some pretty wild owners. It was designed and built in 1761-62 by John Macpherson, a Scotch sea captain who'd made a fortune during the French and Indian War preying on enemy ships as a "legalized pirate". He was wounded nine times in battle, with an arm "twice shot off".

Benedict Arnold, the proud Connecticut soldier who turned traitor, purchased it for his beauteous society bride Peggy Shippen, daughter of Chief Justice Edward Shippen. The two never occupied it, however. Arnold's plan of giving West Point over to the British was exposed, Mount Pleasant confiscated, his possessions sold publicly and Peggy ordered to leave Pennsylvania. Arnold's co-conspirator Major John André who had masterminded the Meschianza fete in Philadelphia didn't have it so easy; he was hanged for his part in the affair. History has never been sure whether Peggy was part of the plot or innocent bystander. A grim footnote to the tale is that Peggy and Arnold were seen after their move to London, standing in Westminster Abbey before the newly built crypt of Major André.

The Georgian structure is a majestic and harmonious one of utter symmetry. John Adams called it "the most elegant country seat in Pennsylvania". Its woodwork alone is worth a visit, as is the Chippendale furniture. Note the shortness of the beds (people then were shorter than we are and slept sitting up) and the outbuilding that has been turned into a museum of colonial household items and toys.

Open 10 a.m. to 5 p.m., Tuesdays through Sundays; 25¢ adults, 10¢ those under 12.

**The Japanese House
Fairmount Park**

④ Woodford. Built in the 1750s, this home became the property of William Coleman — merchant, lawyer and judge. Benjamin Franklin said that he had "the coolest clearest head, and best heart, and exactest morals of almost any man I ever met." The handsome house is known for its William and Mary, Queen Anne and Chippendale furni-

35

ture. It was the scene of Tory gaiety during the British occupation of Philadelphia.

Open 1 to 4 p.m. Tuesdays through Sundays; closed August. Free.

5 **Strawberry Mansion.** This largest of the park mansions takes its name from the exceptionally fine strawberry plants that were grown by an early inhabitant from roots imported from Chile. The original house was burned by British troops searching for Congressional records during the Revolution, and the present mansion was begun in 1797 by a Quaker judge.

Note the Empire parlor with its collection of Tucker porcelain, the exquisite music room, and the antique toys that fill the attic.

Open 11 a.m. to 5 p.m. Tuesdays through Sundays; adults 50¢, those under 12, 25¢; closed January.

6 **Laurel Hill Cemetery**, 3822 Ridge Avenue. The tombstones, monuments and mausoleums of this cluttered Gothic-style cemetery were so popular a visiting place during the early 19th century that tickets were issued in order to limit the size of the crowds.

Buried here are David Rittenhouse, famed colonial astronomer and clockmaker, and, perhaps, Charles Thomson. Thomson, scholar, good friend to the Delaware Indians, and Secretary of Congress for 14 years, died at age 97 and was buried at his ancestral home in Bryn Mawr. Years later the agents at Laurel Hill decided that having Thomson in their cemetery might be good for business, so they engaged his rather unprincipled nephew to carry out a transfer of resting place. After a stealthy night's work, during which the plot was almost discovered by a farm hand, the body was dug up and removed to Laurel Hill where a splendid monument soon appeared. Rumors floated around for years that in his haste the nephew had taken up the remains of a slave instead of his illustrious uncle.

7 **Playhouse in the Park.** The delightful air conditioned playhouse presents shows in the round from spring to fall (call GR7-1700. The #38 bus from town will take you directly there.

8 **Belmont Mansion.** Next door to the Playhouse is *Belmont Mansion*, open for dinner in summer.

The latter is worth seeing not only for its excellent skyline view of Philadelphia but because it, too, dates from colonial times. Call 879-9646.

9 **Japanese House**, Lansdowne Drive off Belmont Avenue. For a total change of pace — indeed, of century and continent — see this authentic replica of a 17th century Japanese scholar's home, surrounded by native gardens, walkways and a pond.

Its architecture is a beautiful blend of the practical (it is built on stilts to prevent mildew in a wet climate like that of Japan) and the symbolic (the curving path to the door is intended to keep out evil spirits which supposedly travel in a straight line.) Kimono-clad guides will show you around, and they frequently hold a 2 p.m. tea ceremony.

Open 10 a.m. to 5 p.m. Tuesdays to Sundays. Admission: 25¢. A call to the Fairmount Park Commission can be helpful as schedules tend to vary with the season.

10 Memorial Hall, 42nd and Parkside. This is the only major building still standing of the 200 created for the Centennial celebration. A massive granite structure surmounted by a glass and iron dome, it displayed Philadelphia's collection of art and sculpture from around the world and continued to do so until the Museum of Art opened in 1928.

The building serves now as a recreation center, headquarters of the Park Commission, and site of a fall harvest show. There is a fascinating large-scale model of the entire Centennial exposition in the basement of Memorial Hall which you can see by appointment (call MU6-1776, ext. 81216).

Tours by appointment only through Art Museum (PO3-8100).

You'll see large curved benches close by the Hall. They are known as "whispering benches" because if you sit at one end and whisper, your voice can be heard at the other end.

11 Robin Hood Dell, George's Hill near 52nd and Parkside. For almost half a century Robin Hood Dell has been offering free summer concerts under the stars in a natural amphitheater setting, with the Philadelphia Orchestra and guest soloists. The problem was that fickle Philadelphia weather. Now a new Dell is being constructed on George's Hill which will allow for open air concerts accommodating 10,000 in good weather and closed-cover concerts seating 5,000 in bad. It is expected that the first concert in this new location will be in June of 1976 after which a seven week summer festival will ensue. At the same time the old Dell at Huntingdon Pike and Ridge Avenue will be utilized for other Bicentennial activities.

Philadelphia Department of Recreation at MU6-1776 can provide further information.

New Robin Hood Dell, Fairmount Park

12 Cedar Grove. This Fairmount Park mansion was moved, stone by stone, from another location (Frankford). It is unique in that five generations of one early American family lived here, and the furniture they purchased reveals the changing styles. A simple but elegant stone farmhouse, this Quaker residence shows the warmth and comfort of country living. The great kitchen is its most interesting room. Note the "breakneck" stairs, called such because there is no banister between the parents' bedroom and that of the children in the attic.

Open 10 a.m. to 5 p.m. Tuesdays through Sundays; 25¢ adults, 10¢ children under 12.

13 Sweetbrier. Samuel Breck who came to Philadelphia from Boston after the Revolution to escape heavy taxes built this fine home, the first in the park to be a year-round residence rather than a summer place. In it he entertained many distinguished guests, both American and French. Breck lived here for almost 40 years until his daughter died, a victim of the "river disease" (possibly typhoid).

Note the south drawing room whose windows look across the river — the furnishings delicate and graceful, revealing French influence at its best.

Open 10 a.m. to 5 p.m. Mondays through Saturdays; closed July. 25¢ adults, under 12, 10¢.

14 Zoological Garden, 34th and Girard Avenue. Not surprisingly, we have another American first here, opened in 1874. This fine zoo houses over 1,600 mammals, birds and reptiles. Some of its highlights are: a Hummingbird House where the tiny, brightly colored birds fly free among the flowers, ferns and waterfalls as they would in the tropics; a New Reptile House which has an electronic rain forest thunder shower to make the snakes feel at home; a 20 minute, one mile long Monorail Safari, narrated aerial trip above the tree tops. The zoo is known for the longevity of its inhabitants and for the successful breeding of rare and endangered species.

Open every day from 9:30 a.m. to 5 p.m., later on Saturdays and Sundays from May through October; closed major holidays. Adults $2, children 2 to 11, 50¢, under 2 free. Hummingbird House is 25¢ extra and Monorail Safari is $1.25 for adults, 75¢ for children. Call 243-1100.

The Zoo is the last stop on the Cultural Loop bus, so you might include it on your visit to the Parkway museums.

**Fairmount Park
It's 8000 Acres Make it The
World's Largest
City Owned Park**

EXCURSION 3

Merion

Germantown

Today's excursion takes us to two communities whose rich history goes back almost three hundred years. Merion and Germantown, each founded by a group of Europeans seeking religious freedom in William Penn's colony, were in those early years little more than woods whose trails were known only to the lightfooted Indians.

Today, a mere half hour from each other and about the same distance from the center of Philadelphia, both are full of rewards for the visitor. Unfortunately, most of the sites listed are not open every day of the week, nor all day, and you may have to do a bit of juggling. Consider spending a Saturday morning in Merion and the afternoon in Germantown.

Merion
HISTORIC LOCATION MAP

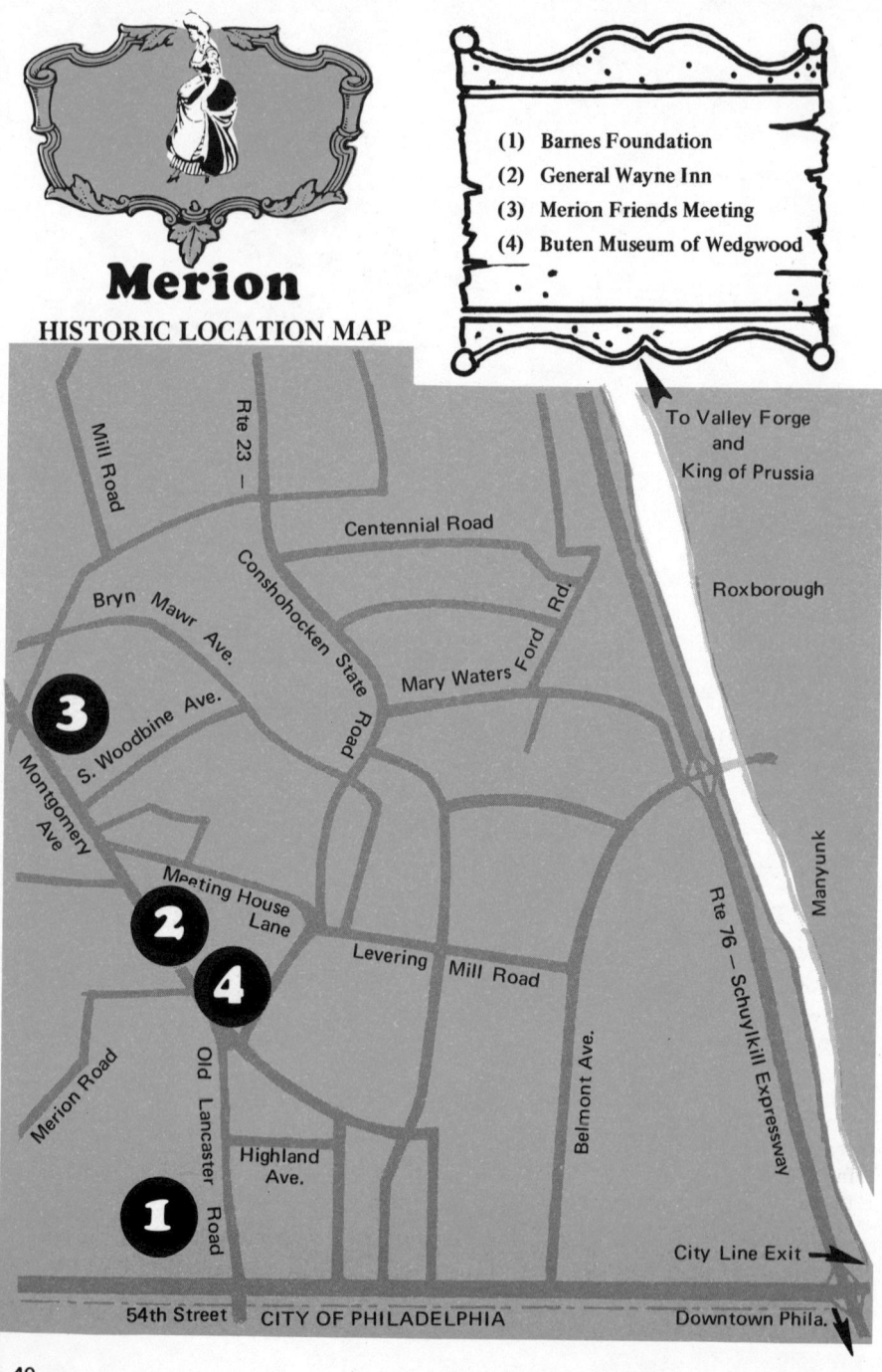

(1) Barnes Foundation
(2) General Wayne Inn
(3) Merion Friends Meeting
(4) Buten Museum of Wedgwood

MERION
Welsh Quakers Build A New Home

In May of 1682 a group of Quakers from Merionethshire, Wales departed from Liverpool for Pennsylvania in search of religious freedom. After a 12-week journey they arrived at Chester, Pa., and proceeded up the Delaware River. During the first weeks they lived in caves befriended by the Lenni-Lenape Indians.

William Penn had agreed to sell these hardy folk a tract of 40,000 acres, later referred to as the "Welsh Tract". The area was forest then and the Quakers had to live amidst wild animals; they contributed a shilling apiece toward stamping out the most vicious beasts, known as wolverines. Of the yeoman farmer class, the new colonials gradually cleared the land, created settlements and gave Welsh names to their fertile townships.

Merioneth, now Merion, was the closest of these settlements to the city of Philadelphia. The pious Welsh Quakers held their first gathering for worship here in a tent fashioned from a sail of the ship that had borne them to these shores. Then they began to build a permanent structure. And permanent it was. You can visit it, worship in it today.

Merion Excursion

Merion is easily reached from town by car (out the Schuylkill Expressway to Route 1 South and west on Route 30), by train via Penn Central, or on the #44 bus. The first stop on our excursion is where you will want to stay longest, for it is a treasurehouse.

1 Barnes Foundation, N. Latch's Lane and Lapsley Road, Merion Station. Dr. Albert C. Barnes who made his fortune in the drug argyrol (for throat congestion) established an endowment of $10 million in 1922 for an institute of fine arts, using his collection of masterpieces of painting and sculpture in connection with courses of instruction. During his lifetime the eccentric, fiercely opinionated gentleman kept his holdings closed to the public (and even to artists whose work or tastes he deplored). After a 19-year court battle a Pennsylvania judge ruled that the Barnes Foundation must open its doors to all.

It was worth the wait. Barnes' collection, said to be worth more than $250 million, is one of the finest in the world, particularly in the French modern school; it contains 200 works by Renoir, 100 by Cezanne, 65 by Matisse.

Barnes Foundation is open Fridays and Saturdays from 9:30 a.m. to 4:30 p.m., and Sundays from 1 to 4:30 p.m.; it is closed holidays and July and August. Admission is $1; no one under 12 admitted. Only a certain number of guests can visit each day so you would be wise to write in advance for a reservation, though if you come early enough you might get in without one. Phone: MO 7-0290.

Gen. Anthony Wayne

② General Wayne Inn, 625 Montgomery Avenue. In the original section of this historic old inn, General Anthony Wayne and his officers are said to have eaten a meal of "generous pot pies with beet greens, corn and beans" in 1777; the following evening George Washington and the Marquis de Lafayette arrived for supper, remaining overnight. From this inn Ben Franklin handled colonial post office matters, and three quarters of a century later Edgar Allan Poe showed up to pen verse and scratch his initials on a window pane.

Said to be the oldest continuously operated restaurant in North America, the General Wayne has served colonial specialties from "ambushed asparagus" to "snickerdoodles", from "jambalaya pandowdy" to "whaler's toddy".

Open for lunch and dinner. 11:30 a.m. to 2 a.m. Tuesdays through Saturdays, 4 to 10 p.m. Sundays (dinner only); closed Mondays. Reservations are preferred: MO 4-5125.

③ Merion Friends Meeting, 615 Montgomery Avenue. It is said that William Penn attended services here and addressed the members of the meeting; however, he spoke in English to the consternation of the Welsh Friends who did not understand a word!

This oldest house of worship in Pennsylvania, dating to c. 1695, was enlarged in 1712. One of its founders was Penn's physician on the ship "Welcome". Men and women worshipped together and children were placed upstairs in the "gallery"; the word "balcony" was not used by Friends since it had connotations of the theater which they abhorred. The overhead portion was used as a schoolroom. Both Quaker and Indian children studied here, though separately. Outside in unmarked graves Welsh Quakers and Lenni-Lenape Indians lie side by side.

Visitors are welcome at Sunday meeting for worship at 11 a.m. You can ask to see the house at other times by calling 642-9202 or by asking the manager of the General Wayne Inn.

④ Buten Museum of Wedgwood, 246 N. Bowman Avenue. This museum features Wedgwood ceramics as produced by the famed British potter Josiah Wedgwood and his successors, from 1759 on. The basic varieties of this magnificent art form are earthenware or pottery, porcelain, and stoneware. Some 10,000 items are on exhibit, and Wedgwood purchases can be made at the sales desk.

The museum is open from 2 to 5 p.m. Tuesdays through Thursdays, October through May; a gallery talk is given regularly at 2 p.m. Free.

The Tavern, 261 Montgomery Ave., Bala Cynwyd. Excellent food and cocktails at reasonable prices. Courteous service, pleasant surroundings. Dancing, too, at this popular spot. ■ *(215) 664-3082*

WHILE YOU'RE THERE . . .

Merion is the entrance to the "Main Line", Philadelphia's lovely and prestigious suburban district. Some people think it just grew that way naturally, but actually it was deliberately conceived by the Pennsylvania Railroad which in the latter part of the 19th century encouraged its executives to purchase their estates in the towns established along the tracks. (The tracks run all the way to Chicago, although the social Main Line ends at Paoli.)

This is fox hunting country, the home of the "horsy set". If you have time, you'll enjoy visiting the dignified campuses of Quaker-founded Haverford and Bryn Mawr colleges, Devon's horse show and country fair in May, and, in Radnor, a most historic church. Located on Valley Forge Road, St. Davids Church was built in 1715 by Welsh Episcopalians. It is the final burying place of Anthony Wayne and was immortalized by Longfellow in a poem: "What an image of peace and rest is this little church among its graves . . . "

GERMANTOWN
Center of Industry

Almost three centuries ago a small band of 13 families established Germantown, having fled The Netherlands and the Rhineland because of religious and economic unrest. Within a quarter of a century they were followed by large numbers of Germans who gave the area a decidedly Teutonic character.

Artisans and craftsmen, these settlers established trades — working as weavers, tanners, millers, shopkeepers, doctors, carpenters, butchers, tailors and tavern keepers. William Rittenhouse set up the first paper mill in the British colonies and Christopher Saur made Germantown a center for the publication of books, pamphlets and newspapers in German. The main road, now Germantown Avenue, which had been an Indian trail leading to the interior of the state, was transformed within a hundred years into a road with comfortable homes living either side for about a mile north and south of the market square. The terror of yellow fever and the desire to escape Philadelphia's summer heat brought many prosperous Philadelphia merchants to settle here, thus attaching the little town more firmly to the fortunes of the city.

Germantown Avenue was the first road to be listed in the National Register of Historic Places.

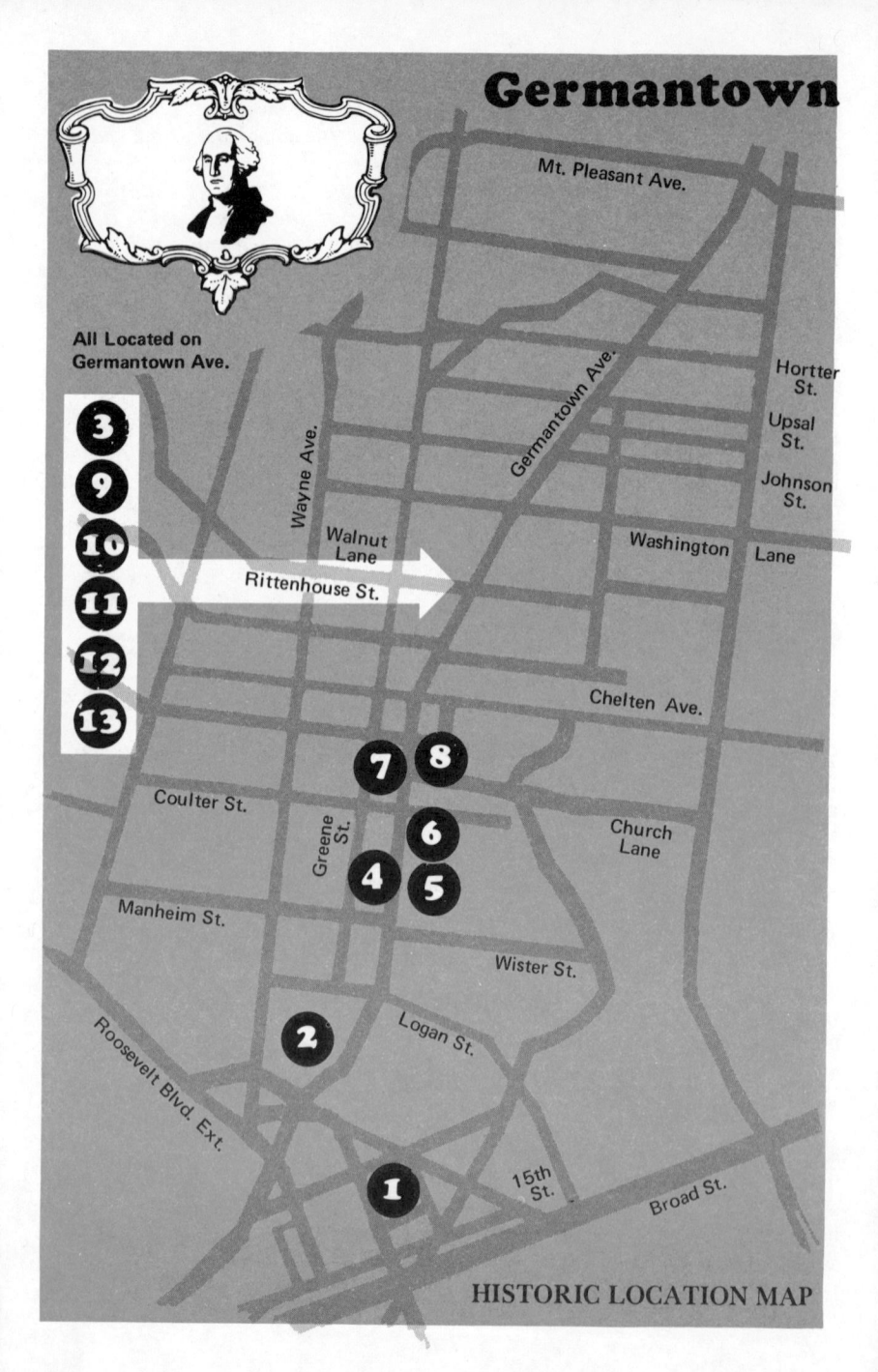

Germantown

Mt. Pleasant Ave.

All Located on Germantown Ave.

3
9
10
11
12
13

Hortter St.
Upsal St.
Johnson St.
Germantown Ave.
Wayne Ave.
Walnut Lane
Rittenhouse St.
Washington Lane
Chelten Ave.
Coulter St.
Greene St.
Church Lane
Manheim St.
Wister St.
Logan St.
Roosevelt Blvd. Ext.
15th St.
Broad St.

7 8
6
4 5

2

1

HISTORIC LOCATION MAP

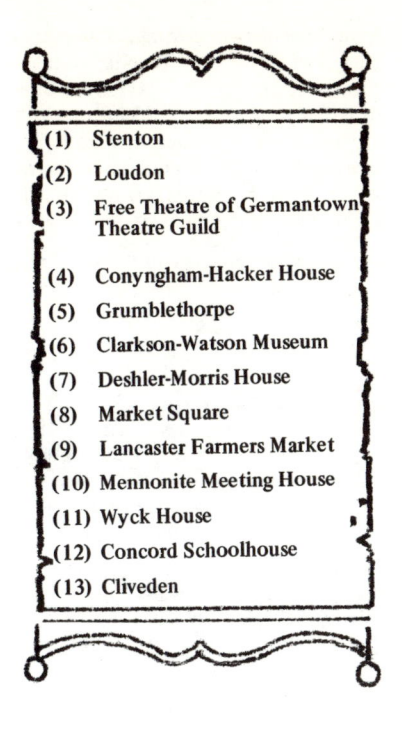

(1) Stenton
(2) Loudon
(3) Free Theatre of Germantown Theatre Guild
(4) Conyngham-Hacker House
(5) Grumblethorpe
(6) Clarkson-Watson Museum
(7) Deshler-Morris House
(8) Market Square
(9) Lancaster Farmers Market
(10) Mennonite Meeting House
(11) Wyck House
(12) Concord Schoolhouse
(13) Cliveden

Germantown Excursion

Germantown can be reached from center-city Philadelphia by train on the Reading or Penn Central lines, by #23 trolley, or by car via the Schuylkill Expressway West.

It's a hodgepodge of old mansions, businesses, factories, high rises, and unexpected shopping malls featuring everything from kite shops to outdoor bread and cheese lunches a la francais. Don't let the rundown appearance of Germantown discourage you from seeing the fine sites. Actually, the area is undergoing something of a renovation, and a large number of vital young people have moved here.

You can see most of the historic sites, except for Stenton, by staying close to Germantown Avenue. House schedules and prices may change in 1976, so before setting out check with the Germantown Historical Society (VI 4-0514) or with Cliveden (VI 8-1777); the Society has walking tours of the colonial houses every spring. The National Park Service is planning an information center at 5448 Germantown Avenue. A word of advice: This listing is a particularly full one; you'll benefit most by choosing from among the sites rather than trying to see too many.

1 **Stenton,** 18th and Courtland. Stenton was the country home of James Logan who followed William Penn to America and for 50 years served as agent to the Penn family and secretary of the province. It was he who gave reality to the founder's dream. So completely did the Indians trust Logan that they were frequent guests at Stenton, camping out on the grounds for as much as a year at a time.

His fortune made in fur trading and land investments, Logan married at age 40, and bought 500 acres of forest land, and designed and built this beautiful home. Like Cliveden, Stenton has Revolutionary associations; in fact it was the only Germantown house to be used as headquarters by both British and American commanders — by George Washington on his way to the Battle of the Brandywine and by Sir William Howe at the Battle of Germantown.

A renowned scholar, Logan developed the finest collection of books in the American colonies, now at Philadelphia's Library Company. The second floor room that may have housed this collection extends along the whole front of the house. See the completely paneled parlor with handsome Delft tiles around the fireplace, the Logan family furniture, paintings and porcelains. The children's room has a fully furnished, three-story doll house built into the wall.

Open Tuesdays through Saturdays, 1 to 5 p.m.; 50¢ adults; 10¢ children under 12; guided tours only.

② Loudon, 4650 Germantown Avenue. The original part of this imposing Federal house was built c. 1801; later other parts were added. Five generations of one family lived here. The interesting brick-floored kitchen in the basement has the richness of an English or early American tavern with its generous fireplaces, pots and utensils.

Open Tuesdays and Thursdays 1 to 4 p.m.; 25¢.

③ Germantown Theater Guild Free Children's Theatre, 4821 Germantown Avenue. Award-winning adult casts perform professional children's theater here, including puppet shows and dance. Admission is free but advance reservations are needed.

Performances October through May, Saturday and Sunday afternoons. Call 849-9799 a few weeks before you would like to attend, if possible.

④ Conyngham-Hacker House, 5214 Germantown Avenue. This 18th century house, now the museum of the Germantown Historical Society, has furnishings from the 17th through 19th centuries which reveal the change from the austere to the lavish to the downright cluttered. It is one of a cluster of four houses on this block belonging to the Society, one of the more active orgnaizations of its kind in the nation.

All these houses are open Tuesdays, Thursdays, and Saturdays, 1 to 5 p.m.; 50¢ adults and 25¢ children, combined admission.

⑤ Grumblethorpe, 5267 Germantown Avenue. This house, built in 1744, was jokingly given its Dickens-like name by a member of the Wister family which owned it. It was the summer, and later year-round, residence of prosperous Philadelphia merchant John Wister. The stone was quarried on the property and the woodwork came from the trees of "Wister's Woods". The summer kitchen of this cozy house has barely changed through the centuries, and its cupboards are full of interesting items. During the Battle of Germantown, Grumblethorpe was occupied by the British whose General Agnew was wounded and died here.

Open Tuesdays through Saturdays from 2 to 5 p.m.; 50¢ adults, 25¢ children to 15; under 15, free. Closed holidays.

⑥ Clarkson-Watson Museum, 5275 Germantown Avenue. Another part of the Germantown Historical Society, this museum is unusual because it displays everyday garments of local residents in the 19th century. You'll see fine silks from Paris, simple Quaker attire and children's outfits. Thomas Jefferson lived here during the yellow fever epidemic of 1793.

See #4 for hours and price.

Philadelphia Light Horse Trooper

7 Deshler-Morris House, 5442 Germantown Avenue. George Washington came here from Mount Vernon during the same epidemic. He liked this fine house so much that he took it again the following summer, bringing Martha and her two grandchildren along. Since he carried out his presidential duties while here, it is sometimes termed the oldest "White House" still standing. The house was also headquarters for the British command after the Battle of Germantown.

Now refurnished in colonial style, the Deshler-Morris House, built in 1772, features fine painting, beautiful woodwork and marble, a Delft tile fireplace, oriental rugs, and an oddly shaped tearoom overlooking the lush rear garden.

May close briefly for additional renovation; check out schedule. (Property of National Park Service.)

8 Market Square, Schoolhouse Lane and Germantown Avenue. Laid out in 1704, this center of community activity housed Germantown's market, firehouse, jail and stocks. Indian delegations going to Philadelphia from further inland broke their journey here, and linen sellers and weavers offered their wares for sale.

The site is far different now but still interesting, with a huge Civil War monument surrounded by a fence made of bayonets.

9 Lancaster Farmers Market, 5942 Germantown Avenue. On Tuesday and Friday mornings at around 5:30 a.m. this building comes to life as farmers unload their fresh produce and bring it into the stalls. It's a marvelous place to visit at lunch if you are touring in Germantown. Stop at the dairy counter behind which stand pink-cheeked Pennsylvania Dutch country girls in their starched aprons and bonnets; they sell cottage cheese so fresh you'll never want a supermarket variety again. Perch at Bassett's ice cream counter and have a dip of English plum or pumpkin. There's no end of delicacies, from snow peas so tender you can eat them raw to baked shoefly pie. By 2 or 3 p.m. the place is picked clean.

10 **Mennonite Meeting House.** 6119 Germantown Avenue. Some of the original settlers of Germantown were Mennonites (often called "German Quakers") who established the first Mennonite meeting in America in 1683. Later many of them moved westward to Lancaster, York and Harrisburg. This tiny meeting house, built in 1770, is furnished with the original pews, and the service is much like it was two centuries ago. The minister in those early years was the same William Rittenhouse who built the paper mill referred to earlier.

The Mennonites hold a particular distinction in that they were instrumental in writing and signing the first recorded protest against black slavery in the New World in 1688, before even the Quakers took an official stand against it. Their document read in part: "There is a saying that we shall doe (sic) to all men like as we will be done ourselves; making no difference of what generation, descent or colour they are. And those who steal or rob men and those who buy or purchase them, are they not alike?... have these negers (sic) not as much right to fight for their freedom as you have to keep them slaves?" In the meeting house is the communion table on which that document supposedly was signed.

Services held Sundays from 10 a.m. to 12 noon. Tours Tuesdays through Fridays, 10 a.m. to noon, and 2 to 5 p.m.; free.

11 **Wyck House,** 6026 Germantown Avenue. The oldest standing house in Philadelphia, Wyck was a Quaker farmhouse occupied by nine generations of one family. Its original section dates from the 1690's.

Open by appointment: VI 8-1690.

12 **Concord School House,** 6313 Germantown Avenue. This one-room school was first used in 1775, the only heat via a fireplace and light from candles. See the dunce cap, the old books and desks, the cannon fired every July 4 and the patchwork quilt that warmed the teacher. Education was considered a privilege back then, and tuition was $1.50 for each quarter in 1797.

No regular hours; ring bell for custodian or ask someone at Kirk and Nice (first funeral parlor in America) at the corner for the key. Free.

13 Cliveden, 6401 Germantown Avenue. The outstanding Georgian-style home that miraculously survived the Revolutionary battle remained in the hands of the Chew family until recently. An event of much distinction here was the gala for Lafayette on his triumphal return to the U.S. in 1824.

Note the simple and balanced lines of the architecture, the elegant entrance hall, the pieces of furniture signed by important 18th century craftsmen.

Open every day but Christmas, 10 a.m. to 4 p.m. Special musical performances are given at Christmastime and refreshments served as they were 200 years ago. Admission $1.25 adults, children under 12 and students, 50¢. Guided tours only.

WHILE YOU'RE THERE . . .

If you would like to spend more time in this area, Chestnut Hill further north is one of the most beautiful and distinctive sections of Philadelphia. In addition to walking the streets and seeing the fine homes, you'll enjoy the Woodmere Art Gallery whose collection is housed in a onetime private mansion with priceless furnishings; the elegant little shops on "The Hill" along upper Germantown Avenue; the Morris Arboretum, a 175-acre estate of exotic and native plantings; and Pastorius Park which, in addition to being a favorite romping spot for Chestnut Hill's friendly canine population, is the setting for free outdoor concerts in summer. Call Chestnut Hill Community Association for specifics (CH 8-4250).

Fairmount Park wends its way out here, too, taking on a craggy, wild look along the banks of the winding Wissahickon (the word is Indian for "catfish creek"). Its beauty has inspired many to poetic raptures, including Poe and Whittier. In colonial days thriving mills were built up here, including William Rittenhouse's paper mill; nearby, in a simple whitewashed home was born his great-grandson David, famed astronomer and clockmaker. The Wissahickon also has inspired some religious fanatics; here in 1694 Johann Kelpius and 40 followers established themselves in a cave and awaited the millennium, expected in 1700.

You'll love walking in this area, fishing, horseback riding, gazing at the 12-foot tall limestone statue of Indian chief Tedyuscung which crouches on a huge jaw of granite. Valley Green beside the creek on Valley Green Road is a lovely, 126 year old restaurant serving three meals a day, every day.

Colors of the Philadelphia Light Horse Troop

49

CHESTNUT HILL SHOPPING . . .

Chestnut Hill Shopping: "The Hill" is the happy result of an extensive redevelopment program in this charming community. The quadrant teems with imaginative shops and fronts on Germantown Avenue (bi-sected by the #23 Trolley — touch of nostalgia). Shop numbers, in parentheses, refer to the Avenue. Ample parking, free to shoppers with updated ticket. From Philadelphia Suburban or 30th Street Stations, 30 minutes via Penn Central.

The Male Room (7918) If you're gift hunting for a man, be sure to wander through this imaginative maze of male oriented gifts.

M.G. Maloumian & Sons (8009) dealers in Oriental rugs . . . new, used, antique. A fascinating visit. Chestnut Hill Development Group.

Diane Bryman Carpets (8038) Karastans for wall-to-wall installation . . . odd-size remnants . . . also finest orientals from the East . . . find it all here in "Carpet Heaven".

It's a Small World (8042). This is where you'll find beautifully designed furniture, clothing, toys and accessories to delight children of all ages (and their mothers). A very unusual and engaging collection. (215) 247-7929.

Carr Ford rents Fords by the day, week, or month. Roomy Campers, too. *(215) 242-3300*

Wedel, Inc. (8201) harbors the type of ski fashions and equipment seen from Vail to Gstaad. Also, women's sportswear of the same caliber.

The Back Door (8316 R): Pottery, woven goods, delightful old pieces . . . all in a tidy woodworking shop.

Chestnut Hill Stationery (8335) has *everything* in office supplies.

Concept Natural Foods, 3 East Gravers Lane. Health books, current files on nutrients and vitamins. Whole grains, raw milk yogurt, raw nuts, dried fruits, honey ice cream, organic meats and eggs, herbal teas, juices. And a full line of vitamin, mineral, and protein supplements. (215) 247-3215.

Joseph Condello's Son, Inc. (8405). Traditional men's clothing and furnishings. Three generations of Condellos have served the Delaware Valley area. (215) 247-1676.

Gilbert Stuart Studio (8407) is a charming atelier specializing in Philadelphia prints, oils, watercolors, and graphics, framed and unframed. Also, an attractive assortment of frames, wall decor and the whole gamut of art supplies.

Barbara Russell Designs (8400) for Bicentennial needlepoint. You can stitch an heirloom of her registered Franklin Court Collection from the archeological finds of Ben Franklin and his neighbors. If your mood is contemporary, see the best in modern design.

The Kitchen Korner, Inc. (8420) is Gourmet Heaven. This shop specializes in imported and domestic cookware, copper things, bakeware, kitchen gadgets, gifts. Their sign says "the most complete cookware store in the Philadelphia area". We don't doubt it. (215) 242-2866.

The Linen Closet (8425) carries a complete line of bath and bed linens (monogrammed if you like) and features exclusively designed Bicentennial towels and placemats.

Rita Coyne (8438) has the knack of knowing just how a gracious and conservative woman wants to be dressed. Her established "mark of good taste" is apparent in everything in her shop. Fashions for daytime and evening. Half sizes, too. And charming coordinated accessories. (215) 247-0313.

Cubby Hole (8441) Separates in junior sizes ... tops, pants, skirts (215) 247-1716.

Wm. A. Kilian Hardware Co. (8450) carries a complete line of hardware and garden supplies. Worth a stop to see this grand oldtime hardware store.

Mary P. Fretz's 21 West, 21 West Highland Avenue. This is a landmark restaurant tucked away in a petite mall, featuring fine Continental cuisine. Served in the charming Garden or Meissen Rooms. You may also order cocktails in the piano-bar Swan Room.

Lunch and dinner Monday through Saturday. Sunday dinner from 2:00 to 8:00 p.m. It's wise to reserve. (215) 247-8005.

Helen Siki, Inc., 5 East Highland Avenue, says her clothes are for the "Special Woman". Translation: you don't see these fashions everywhere.

The Frigate Book Shop, Inc., 16 East Highland Avenue, is one of the country's most outstanding book marts. Books, cards, games mailed anywhere in the world. (215) 248-1065.

George Robertson & Sons (8501) Originally (1777) an historic Inn owned by Henry Cress. During the Revolution it became a hospital for American troops. Today this gracious building contains a riot of beautiful flowers (freshest blooms in the whole area, says Mr. Robertson, proudly). Also ceramic, silk, bone china flowers. Fascinating cachepots, ingenious holders.

Nana, Ltd. (8504) is a fresh and colorful boutique for infants through juniors. Hand-smocked toddler dresses, mod denims, bright ginghams. A haven for mothers, grandmothers, teens — they all come out smiling.

Sylvia Shop (8505) is where you go (exclusively on THE HILL) for the Philadelphia woman's favorite ... that wonderfully wearable imported "Kensington Suit". (215) 247-3689.

The Leather Bucket (8506) is where you'll want to spend some time absorbing the past. This shop has 18th and 19th Century English and American furniture, antique fireplace equipment, and Silver, among which you will find beautiful Old Sheffield Silver. Anything selected here will bear the stamp of history — long after the Bicentennial.

Chestnut Hill Cheese Shop (8509). If cheese is your dish, visit this specialist in the world's great cheeses. Exotic gourmet foods ... French copperware and cookware, too.

The Bootery (8511) is all set for weary "Tourist Feet" (one can take only so many cobblestones in stride). Head for Chestnut Hill's popular shoestore when you can't go on. Huge variety.

Dorothy Bullitt (8514) legendary Philadelphia fashion for women in a charming shop on "THE HILL".

Depot 8515 — Steaks, Prime Ribs, Lobster, (Salad Bar), Entertainment, Dancing.

Miriam Leshner's (8521) special focus is delicate lingeries. But she's also awfully good on blouses, skirts ... just about everything in the feminine fashion orbit.

Elaine Cooper's charming shop warrants a stroll up Evergreen to the Hill House (201 W.). Miss Cooper, third generation jeweler and certified gemologist, American Gem Society, offers a sensitive selection of rare antique and contemporary pieces. Custom design and intuitive counsel in gemcraft.

Actually, just listening to Miss Cooper on her fascinating and esoteric subject will give you a new concept of the lore, and lure, of gemcraft down through the ages. (215) 242-1457.

Sports & Specialties (8615) handles the "total look" in women's (men's too) sportswear. Colorful, imported sweaters. Accessories, gifts, even Wagner spices and teas.

Hill Hardware (8615) is where Philadelphians flock for really fine garden furniture. Rope hammocks, too.

L.T. Muench (8620). Well-dressed Philadelphia men shop here for the *natural* look in clothes. Enormous selection (largest in Philadelphia area, they say). Odd sizes, too.

McNally's Tavern (8634) has the bright green door. Sandwiches, soup, brew.

Crossing Over to
PHILADELPHIA'S MAIN LINE

Philadelphia's Main Line contains two of the most prestigious liberal arts colleges in the nation: Bryn Mawr for women and Haverford for men. In recent years these two Quaker-founded institutions have developed an exchange program that almost amounts to a merger; in fact, undergraduates can live in dorms at either campus. At Haverford, chartered in 1833, is Founder's Hall erected that same year, a fine example of colonial Quaker architecture. Bryn Mawr's 95-acre campus is Gothic in style. Among its many illustrious graduates is Katherine Hepburn, Class of 1928.

HARRITON, the beautiful mansion at Old Gulph and Harriton Roads, Bryn Mawr, was the home of Charles Thomson, the highly honored Secretary of the Continental Congress, from 1774 until his death in 1824.

Harriton is one of the oldest surviving houses in America. The present property of 16½ acres was part of a 600 acre grant by William Penn to Rowland Ellis, a Welsh Quaker, in 1682. In 1704 Mr. Ellis built a 2-story manor house which he named "Bryn Mawr" after his ancestral home in Wales. In 1719 the property was sold to Richard Harrison, Jr., a Maryland Quaker, who changed the name to "Harriton" and, for years, operated a thriving tobacco plantation there. His daughter, Hannah, married Charles Thomson in 1774 and thus the home passed to her husband.

Harriton restoration will be completed in 1976 and will contain magnificent 18th Century antiques.

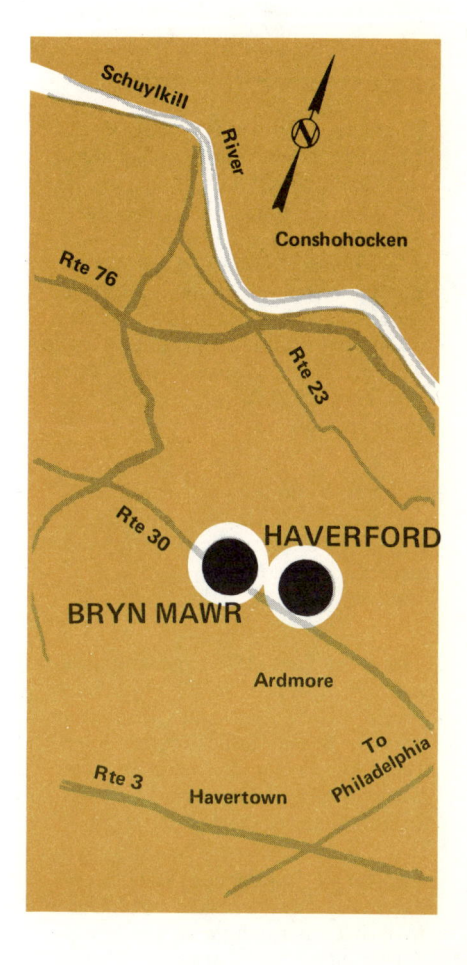

BRYN MAWR SHOPPING...

Lilly Pulitzer, 24 North Merion Ave., Bryn Mawr, famous for colorful hand-screened floral and animal print fabrics. Ladies apparel, children's clothing, "MENS STUFF" and myriad boutique items.

Page & Biddle Mini Mall, 1038 Lancaster Avenue, Bryn Mawr. **Page & Biddle** itself has unusual gifts in a bright, gay, colorful atmosphere, with garden and terrace furniture by **Molla.**

TEA ROOM open daily for luncheon 12:00 to 2:00.

Whichcraft, Bryn Mawr Mall, Morris Avenue, Bryn Mawr. Complete craft and art supplies. Decoupage is **big** here. Instruction in many crafts. Saturday morning classes for children (their finished masterpieces, each week, include macrame, stained glass, plastercraft, needlepoint, rug hooking and decoupage). The attractive young owners, Pam and Hunter McMullin, would love to have you drop in.

Suky Rosan, one of the shops in the unusual **Page & Biddle Mini Mall,** featuring gowns — bridal and evening, specializes in reasonable fashions by talented young American designers. Suky, a well known Philadelphia fashion commentator, has a sixth sense about what's right for her customers.

Richard Stockton, descendant of the Signer of The Declaration of Independence, founded the famous quality gift and card shop at 851 Lancaster Avenue, Bryn Mawr.

Anthony Rowley's Frog Pond fascinates the Mini Mall customer from 6 to 60. Authentic reproductions in miniature scale 1" to the foot. Doll house furniture and accessories, craftsmen's kits for the amateur. Nostalgic doll houses old and new. Paper goods for parties.

The Pear Tree, 857 Lancaster Avenue, Bryn Mawr: Colorful kaleidoscope of Spanish rugs, Baccarat crystal, Spode and Herend china, Leitz binoculars, Farmington Cook Book, status stationery by Mrs. John Strong. (215) 525-0101.

The Small Indulgence, Inc. is prepared for your smallest indulgence to doing up a whole house. Fascinating gifts, fine antiques, full decorating service. 24 North Merion Avenue, Bryn Mawr 19010.

EXCURSION 4

**General Washington Statue
Valley Forge**

Valley Forge & The Brandywine

Today we stop first at the most famous memorial to our American Revolution, Valley Forge, where thousands died though no battle was fought. Next we travel through Chester County to the Brandywine River Valley whose idyllic beauty has enthralled generations of poets and painters – and whose battlefield was stained with patriots' blood. Excursion 4 can be made in one day, but THE GUIDE recommends that you allow two.

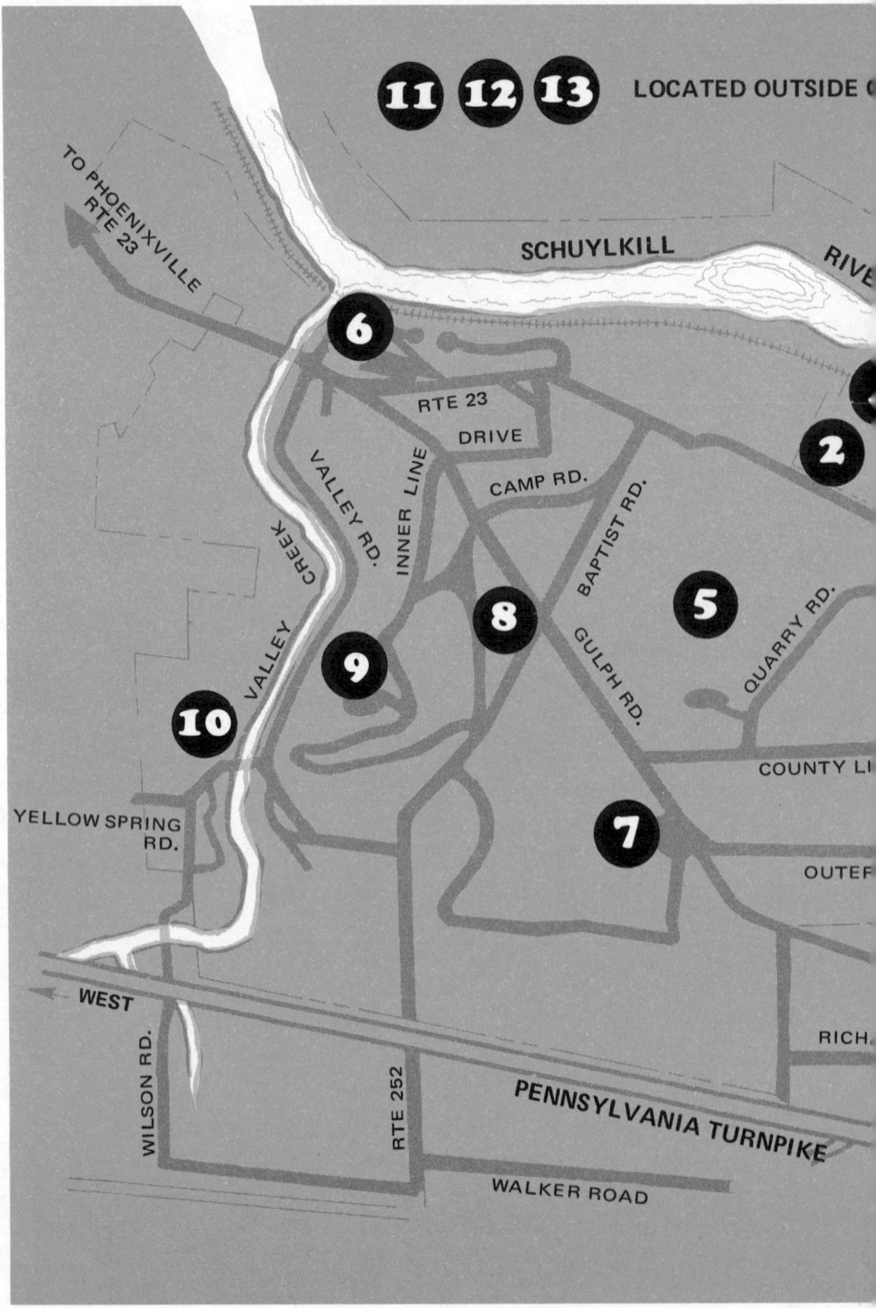

11
12
13
LOCATED OUTSIDE
TO PHOENIXVILLE
RTE 23
SCHUYLKILL
RIVE
6
RTE 23
DRIVE
2
CAMP RD.
VALLEY RD.
INNER LINE
BAPTIST RD.
CREEK
5
QUARRY RD.
8
VALLEY
9
GULPH RD.
10
COUNTY LI
YELLOW SPRING RD.
7
OUTEF
WEST
WILSON RD.
RTE 252
RICH.
PENNSYLVANIA TURNPIKE
WALKER ROAD

VALLEY FORGE

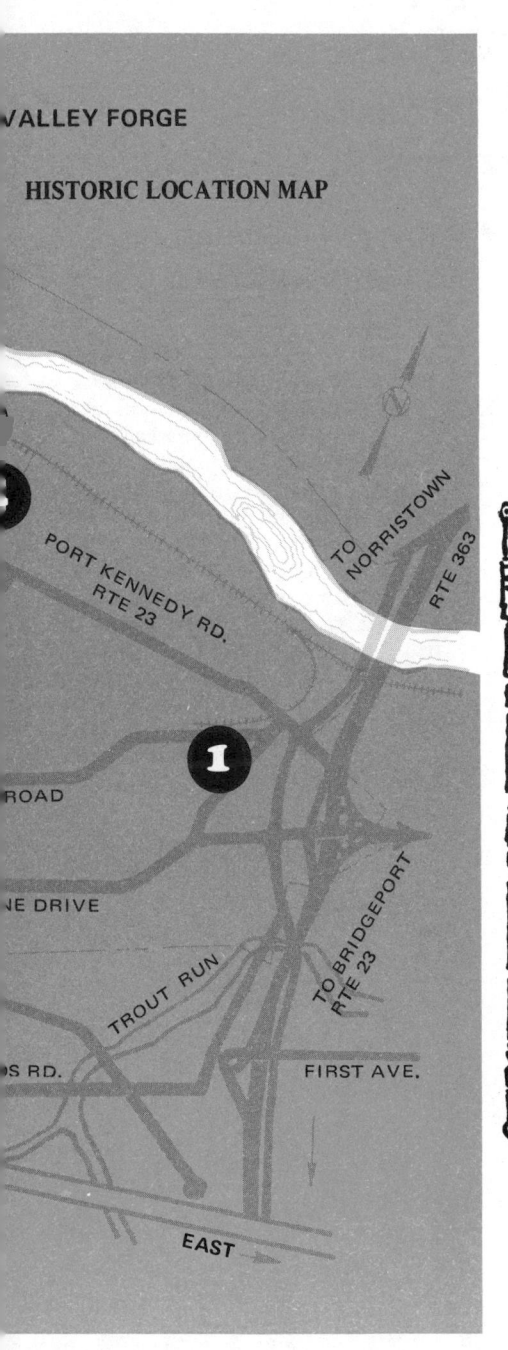

HISTORIC LOCATION MAP

Valley Forge Park

(1) Reception Center
(2) Washington Memorial Chapel
(3) Memorial Bell Tower
(4) Museum of the Valley Forge Historical Society
(5) Grand Parade
(6) Washington's Headquarters
(7) National Memorial Arch
(8) Camp Schoolhouse
(9) Mt. Joy Observatory
(10) General Knox Covered Bridge
(11) Freedoms Foundation
(12) Mill Grove
(13) Valley Forge Music Fair

VALLEY FORGE
A Bleak Winter,
A Springtime
of Renewed Hope

"To see men without clothes to cover their nakedness, without blankets to lie upon, without shoes (for the want of which their marches might be traced by the blood from their feet), and also as often without provisions as with them, marching through the frost and snow, and at Christmas taking up their winter quarters within a day's march of the enemy without a house or hut to cover them until these could be built, and submitting without a murmur, is proof of patience and obedience which, in my opinion, can scarce be paralleled."

If you visit Valley Forge in spring or summer, particularly during the early May days of pink and white dogwood, you'll probably find it difficult to imagine the scene described by the Continental troop's commander, George Washington. Yet his words, written in December of 1777 to the President of the Continental Congress, were not exaggerated. Though not one real battle took place on Valley Forge grounds (there had been a skirmish with the British prior to the encampment), over 3,000 of the General's men died as a result of their privations and suffering here. It was a time when men's courage was tested — a time, in retrospect, of triumph.

George Washington did not have a pleasant season himself that winter. Having been defeated at the Brandywine and Germantown in an attempt to stop the British march on Philadelphia, he was held in low esteem by some. Congress had fled to York, Pennsylvania, and soldiers were deserting the army in droves. But in Philadelphia, as we've said, life couldn't have been better — for the British and their sympathizers, that is. Here young officers were having a gay season watching cock fights, putting on amateur theatricals, and filling their cups at such spots as the City Tavern and the Bunch of Grapes; many a pretty Tory maid rustled her skirts alluringly, hoping to win a husband from their ranks.

Washington chose Valley Forge for winter quarters because it was near Philadelphia and could be easily defended, lying between two

Revolutionary Cannon At Valley Forge

ridges of hills covered by dense forest. The forge itself, built on a plot of land given by William Penn to his daughter, had been burned by the British.

The Continental Army marched into the forge on December 19, 1777, after a week's journey, faced with the need of building some 900 huts for shelter. Food and clothing were painfully sparse and local farmers had already lost much of their produce to the British. The sentries had to stand on their hats to keep from freezing, and stomachs were soothed with tasteless "fire cakes" from the outdoor ovens. (Wrote one soldier in his diary, "The Lord send that our Commissary of Purchases may live on Fire Cake and Water 'till their glutted Guts are turned to Pasteboard!") It is said that General Washington, concerned about this poor fare, ordered a cook to provide a good meal for the men. The cook didn't have anything on hand but tripe, peppercorns and scraps — the result being Philadelphia (after his home town) pepper pot soup.

Hopes began to rise at springtime with news of the treaties of alliance and commerce with France, recognizing American independence and spelling out defense of each other's trade on the high seas. Supplies were organized on a better basis, and General Baron Frederick von Steuben, a German officer who had joined the Revolution, drilled the army into an efficient fighting machine. So much did the men's health and spirits improve that on St. Patrick's Day Washington himself had to quiet a fight between troops of Irish descent and New Englanders.

On June 18, 1778, Philadelphia was evacuated by the British and one day later George Washington departed Valley Forge with his men, forced to leave behind 2300 of the sick and unequipped.

Only one grave of all the men who died there that fierce winter is identified with a gravestone.

Valley Forge Excursion:

The entrance to Valley Forge is at the corner of Routes 363 and 23, about two miles from the Valley Forge interchange on the Pennsylvania Turnpike. Partially restored to its original appearance as a military camp, this State property is a "must" stop in any Revolutionary tour. It is accessible by bus from Philadelphia (call Grey Line Motor Tours at LO9-3666) and local motels (call Valley Forge Tours, Inc. at 265-6446).

The park is easily traversed and all sites can be reached over 20 miles of well paved roads; allow a few hours for a comprehensive visit. Parking, picnic areas, pedestrian and bridal paths and a snack bar all are available.

Some of the park's highlights are listed below; buildings can be visited free of charge from 9 a.m. to 5 p.m. every day unless otherwise indicated.

1 **Valley Forge Reception Center.** You'll receive a map here and see a movie on the encampment which will plunge you right into that frigid December of 1777.

2 **Washington Memorial Chapel,** sometimes called ''The American Westminster''. Its lectern is the only monument at Valley Forge to a British soldier: Major General Edward Braddock, who was Washington's commander in the French and Indian War. Note the exquisite wood carving in the Pew of the Patriots, the statuettes of Continental soldiers in the choir stalls, and the brilliantly colored windows which depict the origins and early history of our nation.

Chapel is open daily from 8 a.m. to 5 p.m.; services every Sunday morning. Attractive items are sold in the Log Cabin Gift Shop behind the chapel; open from 10 a.m. to 4 p.m.

3 **Memorial Bell Tower.** This houses the carillon of 58 bells, the largest of which (b flat note) weighs 8,000 pounds. Concerts every day.

4 **Museum of the Valley Forge Historical Society.** Its collection of Washingtonia and other military relics of the Revolution is considered one of the nation's best. See Washington's battered field tent, the original Commander-in-Chief's flag with its six-pointed stars, and two of the twelve priceless silver cups which were Washington's only luxury in Valley Forge (they were later used at Mount Vernon). Also on display is a check for $120,000 given to the Marquis de Lafayette by Congress in partial payment for his services and expenditures during the Revolution. The brave French aristocrat became like a son to Washington during their shared travails at Valley Forge and the Brandywine.

Museum is open weekdays 9:30 a.m. to 4:30 p.m. in winter and 9 a.m. to 5 p.m. May through September, Sundays 1 to 5 p.m.

5 **"Grand Parade".** Here troops were drilled by Baron von Steuben and news of the French alliance was celebrated. The only identified grave at Valley Forge is here: that of Rhode Island soldier John Waterman.

Baron Von Steuben

6 **Washington's Headquarters.** This is where he lived from Christmas to June of 1778. See his office, reception room, bedroom and kitchen. This building is thought to be largely original. Martha Washington joined her husband in February of 1778 and stayed until June; you'll see her sitting room. The first public celebration of Washington's birthday was held in this house.

7 **National Memorial Arch.** The huge granite arch, which honors the officers and private soldiers of the Continental Army, is the only monument on Valley Forge grounds erected by the Federal government. It was designed by Paul Cret.

8 **Camp Schoolhouse.** According to legend, this building was used early in the 1777-78 winter as a hospital and later as a schoolhouse where illiterate soldiers were taught to read and write. It is being restored, though historians still differ as to its age and use.

9 **Observatory, atop Mt. Joy.** Seventy-five feet high, this steel skeletal structure with wide flights of steps leading to the top offers an excellent view of the valley.

There are many other sites of interest in Valley Forge, including the reconstructions of the primitive soldiers' huts, outdoor bake ovens and field hospital; the likeness of "Mad" Anthony Wayne, considered to be a particularly fine equestrian statue; and the gravestone of a luckless soldier who paid with his life for stealing a neighboring farmer's chickens. "Living History" demonstrations are given of cooking, spinning, weaving, candle dipping and the like, and there is a working farm.

10 As you leave Valley Forge, look for one of Chester County's picturesque covered bridges; situated west on Route 23, the **General Knox Covered Bridge** was built in 1865.

WHILE YOU'RE THERE...

11 **Freedoms Foundation** is just two miles outside of Valley Forge. This ultra-patriotic educational institution, meticulously landscaped, features a statue of Washington at prayer, flags of all the states, and a collection of doorsills, bricks and stones from the homes of the 56 signers of the Declaration of Independence.

Free of charge, open Monday – Friday, 9 a.m. to 4 p.m.

12 High on the banks overlooking Perkiomen Creek, also just a few miles from Valley Forge, is **Mill Grove, the Audubon Wildlife Sanctuary.** Built in 1762, Mill Grove is the only existing authentic home in this country of renowned ornithologist and artist John James Audubon. Furnishings are early 19th century, modern murals tell the story of his life, and the attic has been restored to a studio and taxidermy room. The wildlife preserve surrounding the house can be traversed via a six-mile trail, rich in floral and bird life. You can even dig for minerals in the "mine dump" area.

Haitian-born, Paris-educated Audubon came to this locale in 1804 at the age of 19. He soon became known as something of a strange bird himself, roaming the woods in satin pumps and silk breeches in search of feathered creatures. Tongues were silenced, however, when in 1838 Audubon's folio edition of *Birds in America* with its startlingly realistic studies of wildlife sold to 161 subscribers at $1,000 a set.

No charge, open daily except Monday, 10 a.m. to 5 p.m.; closed Thanksgiving, Christmas, New Years, but open Monday legal holidays.

13 Should you plan your stay at Valley Forge so that you have an evening here, you might enjoy an in-the-round performance at the 2750-seat, all-weather **Valley Forge Music Fair.**

The Peacock Inn Restaurant (Routes 202 & 363) is the oldest building in the King of Prussia area. Built circa 1708, it was originally known as the "Pawling House". The Inn, with its charming colonial atmosphere, offers American cuisine prepared in the unique "open fire" method of our forefathers.

Bar and restaurant open 7 days a week from 11 a.m. Reservations suggested. (215) 265-5566.

THE BRANDYWINE
War Comes to a Peaceful River Valley

*"Speak to your lover, meadows
No one can hear,
I lie, as lies yon placid Brandywine,
Holding the hills and heavens in my heart
For contemplation."*

So wrote Sidney Lanier, American poet of Civil War days. Lanier was not alone in his love of this land, for sparkling Brandywine Creek and the valley which surrounds it have invited many admirers through the years — the most famous today being the remarkable Wyeth family now in its third generation of painters.

In our time Brandywine Creek is a mere trickle, but during the colonial era floods and ice rendered the ford here so hazardous that it became necessary in 1737 to provide ferry service. The prosperous, largely Quaker-populated river valley remained untouched by the Revolution until the fateful day of September 11, 1777, when General Washington attempted in vain to halt Sir William Howe in his march toward Philadelphia. Here the Continental Army's 12,000 troops fought bravely but, being no match for the British 18,000, were forced to retreat to Chester, then to Germantown. Some 1,000 American men died on these once peaceful fields, within sight of two Quaker houses of worship.

Chadds Ford, locale of this significant Revolutionary battle, occupies the east bank of the Brandywine; the battlefield will be our final destination. On the way we will see many other places of interest amidst a panorama of ancient mills, 300 year-old oak trees, Quaker meeting houses, barns, graveyards and mushroom-growing houses.

If your trip is not limited timewise, you could find no better way to become acquainted with the Brandywine than by canoeing its lazy currents on a warm day. There are eleven miles of nearly continuous waterway on the stretch from Lenape, Pa. to Rockland, Del., and the entire trip would take about eight hours. One access point is at Lenape Park at Route 52 (#3 on historical map), a popular amusement park. Another is at Brandywine River Museum (5) which is described in some detail later; the museum sells a guidebook written especially for people who choose to go the canoe route.

The Brandywine
INCLUDING CENTREVILLE DEL.

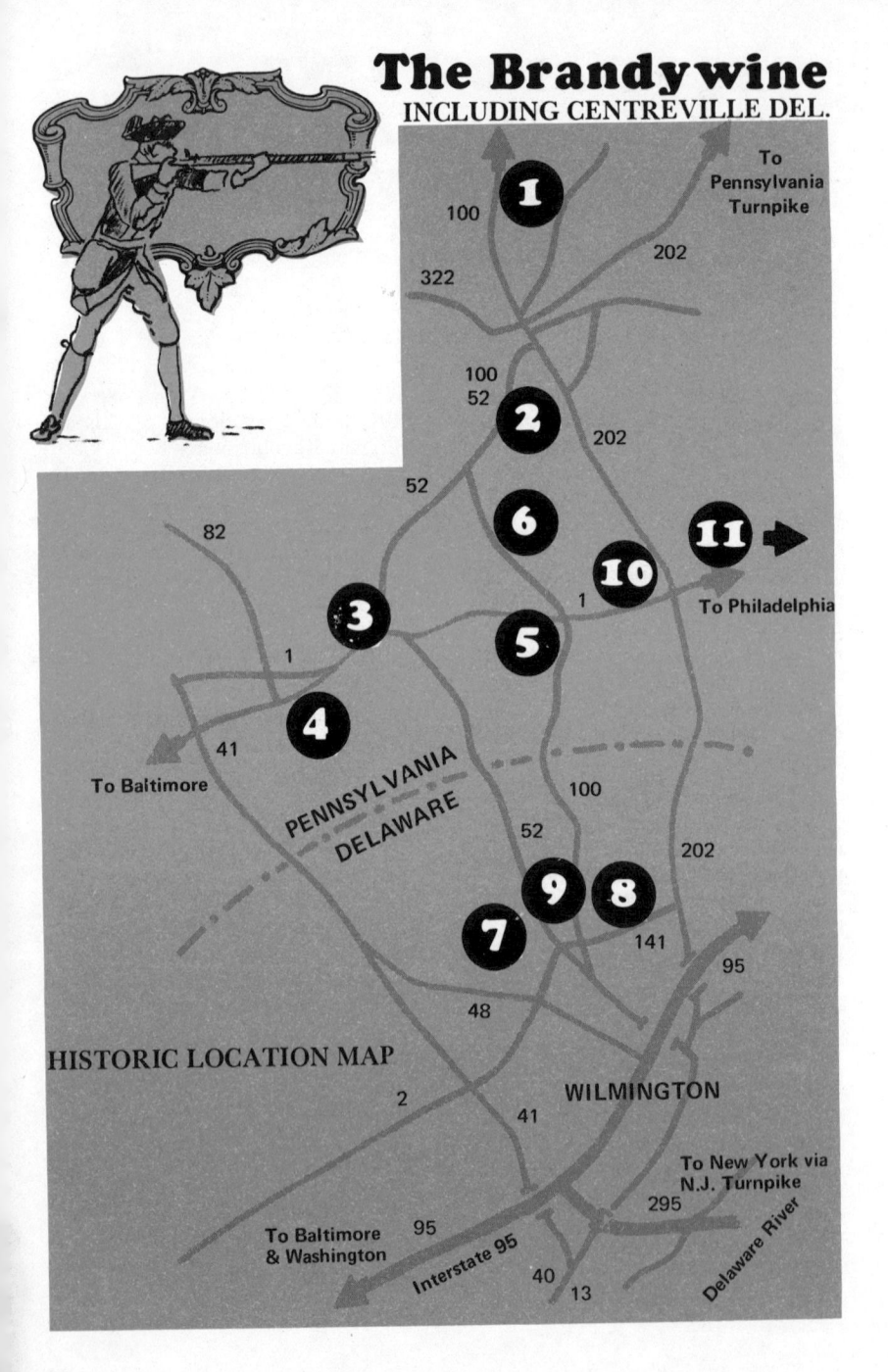

HISTORIC LOCATION MAP

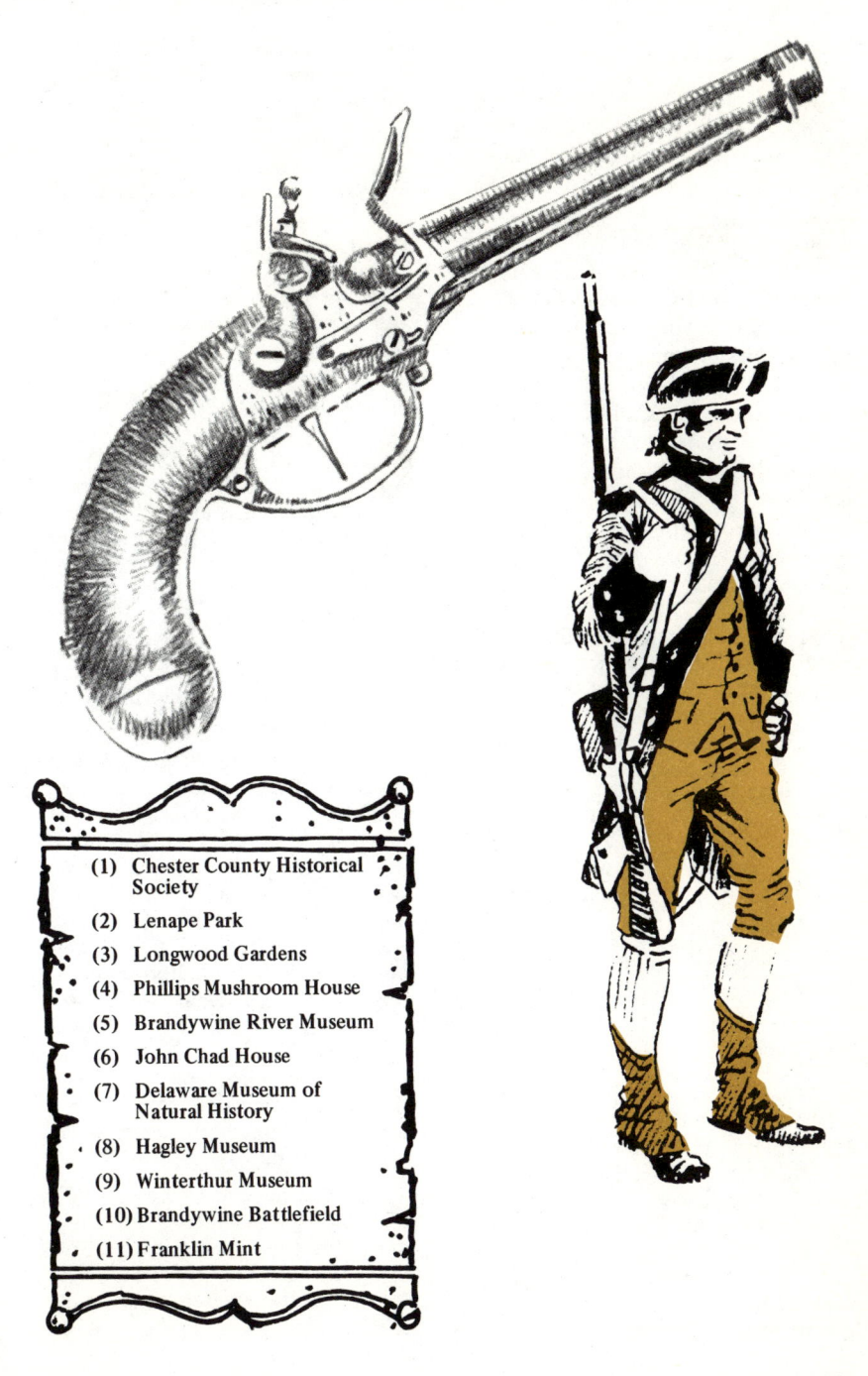

- (1) Chester County Historical Society
- (2) Lenape Park
- (3) Longwood Gardens
- (4) Phillips Mushroom House
- (5) Brandywine River Museum
- (6) John Chad House
- (7) Delaware Museum of Natural History
- (8) Hagley Museum
- (9) Winterthur Museum
- (10) Brandywine Battlefield
- (11) Franklin Mint

Brandywine Excursion:

If, however, you're a bit less rugged (or more pressed time-wise) let's continue by car from Valley Forge. Route 202 South will take you to the county seat of fertile rolling Chester County: West Chester. This town, setting of West Chester State College, had the more dubious distinction in Civil War days of being publishing headquarters for "The Jeffersonian", one of the few northern newspapers to sympathize openly with the southern cause.

1 At 255 North High Street is located the **Chester County Historical Society**, one of the finest of the state's local museums. The building's facade, dominated by an intricate arch, was designed by Thomas U. Walter who also created the town's neo-Greek Chester County Courthouse. (Wings and dome of the Capitol in Washington, D.C. are probably Walter's best known work.)

The Chester County Historical Society features a number of excellent exhibits, both in the High Street building and in houses of historic interest owned by the Society. (Ask about the David Townsend House, the Hopper Log House, and the Brinton House which was built in 1704 and has 22 inch-thick walls.) Among the exhibits: country kitchen, general store, dolls and dollhouse, Conestoga wagon, early fire fighting equipment, farming tools, furniture — Chippendale, Queen Anne, William and Mary, etc., and pottery and pewter items by local artisans. The society has, too, an extensive library.

It is free to visitors, open Mondays and Tuesdays 1 to 5 p.m., Wednesdays 1 to 9 p.m., Thursdays and Fridays 10 a.m. to 5 p.m., closed August.

2 Moving along Route 100 to Route 52 South, we come to **Lenape Park**, a good place for a swim, picnic, or a ride on the antique merry-go-round.

3 Just off Route 52 South on Route 1 at Kennett Square is the American answer to Versailles: the du Pont estate of **Longwood Gardens**. Since the beauties of Longwood warrant a leisurely visit and are best seen in the bright sunlit hours, THE GUIDE suggests you make an overnight stop at a nearby motel or inn, then move on to the estate the next morning.

In 1701 William Penn conveyed the tract of land that is now Longwood to a fellow Quaker, George Pierce. One of the first skirmishes in the Battle of the Brandywine took place on its grounds, and almost a century later "long wood" became a station of the Underground Railroad, sheltering black slaves who were fleeing the South. In 1906 the 1,000 acre estate was acquired by Pierre S. du Pont, whose family fortune had been made in gunpowder. Now it is a non-profit foundation, open to the public every day of the year.

There is no end to Longwood's horticultural wonders, both in greenhouses and outside: rare orchids, a water lily garden whose South American water-platters have raftlike pads that can hold up to

150 pounds, fields of scarlet poinsettias at Christmas, an elaborate setting of six pools patterned after a Florentine Renaissance villa.

Perhaps most remarkable of all are the illuminated fountains; half-hour displays are given from the observatory terrace Tuesday, Thursday and Sunday evenings, from mid June to the end of August (9:15 p.m. in June and July and 8:45 in August). If you have the chance to attend a performance at the open-air theater don't miss it; a vine-covered stone wall serves as backdrop, hemlock trees as wings, and jets of water rising six feet in the air as curtain. After the show (Gilbert and Sullivan, Shakespeare, ballet, musical comedy) fountains from a sunken garden are illuminated in rainbow colors. The audience usually expresses its delight by "ahs" and "ohs" at each new color combination. It all adds up to a magic evening.

Admission to Longwood, on weekdays, is $1.00 for adults, 50¢ for children 6 to 12, pre-schoolers free; Saturdays, Sundays and holidays $1.50 for adults, others same as weekdays. Outdoor gardens are open from 9 a.m. to 6 p.m., conservatories from 10 a.m. to 5 p.m. For information on performances, special events, call: 388-6741.

For special bus trips to Longwood Gardens from Philadelphia and return, call SEPTA: DA9-4800.

4 Kennett Square's landscape features numerous mushroom nurseries with darkened interiors. This industry was started innocently enough some 75 years ago by two local hot house operators who, finding there was a lot of waste space underneath their carnation benches, decided these dark, humid areas might be good for growing mushrooms. Indeed they were — Kennett Square has become "the mushroom-growing center of the world". Visit **Phillips Mushroom Museum** on Route 1 just north of Kennett Square if you'd like to see these "snow apples" taking form.

Open daily 10 a.m. – 6 p.m.; $1 adults; 50¢ children 7-16; under 7, free.

5 And now we move on to the heart of the Brandywine, whose history and spirit are most vividly revealed in its **Brandywine River Museum**. Located on Route 1, west of Route 100 in Chadds Ford, it is housed in a restored grist mill, built originally in 1864. The courtyard of the rugged red brick structure is paved with 100 tons of Belgian block, and the hand-hewn beams of its art galleries are supported by huge pillars of oak, poplar or fir.

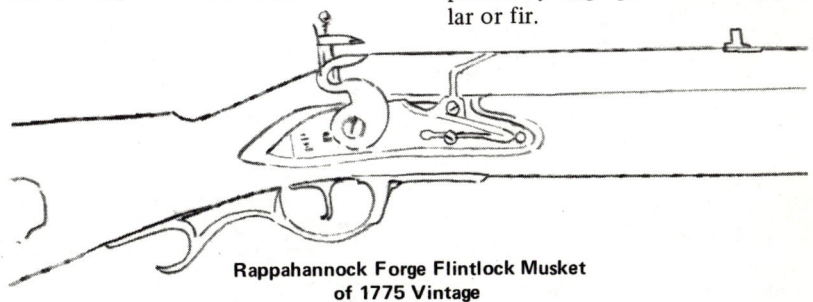

Rappahannock Forge Flintlock Musket of 1775 Vintage

The museum has a national reputation for its exhibits of sculpture and painting, particularly the permanent gallery devoted to the Brandywine tradition. That tradition dates back to illustrator Howard Pyle whose student N.C. Wyeth was father to Andrew and grandfather to James; all have delighted in the changing splendors of their river valley and the character of its people. You can buy reproductions of their work in the museum. Many will doubtless be familiar to you — "Christina's World", the well known Jamie Wyeth study of J.F.K., the gallery of family portraits.

Watch also for chestnut roasting in the courtyard of the museum on winter weekends, medieval plays there in warm weather, and concerts in spring and fall on Sunday afternoons ("On the Brandywine").

The museum is open daily from 9:30 a.m. to 4 p.m.; $1.50 for adults and 50¢ for children. For information call 388-7601.

Brandywine River Museum

6 That the old grist mill housing the Brandywine River Museum is standing at all is a victory for a local conservation effort known as the Tri-Town Conservancy of the Brandywine. Among its other successes in rescuing priceless landmarks from the bulldozer is the **John Chad House** on Route 100. This was the homestead of the ferryman from whom Chadds Ford took its name; the house and its springhouse, both newly restored, also have been painted by Andrew Wyeth.

7 **Delaware Museum of Natural History,** Route 52, north of Wilmington. This scientific house of wonders contains three exhibit halls. The Hall of Mammals has as its highlight a large open African waterhole scene depicting some of Mt. Kenya's wildlife inhabitants. Shells are featured as food, barter, decoration, utensil and religious item in a second hall; one section studies the formation of pearls. The Hall of Birds contains examples of extinct and vanishing species, as well as the largest known bird egg in the world, weighing 27 pounds.

Open Wednesdays through Saturdays, 9 a.m. to 4 p.m., Sundays 1 to 5 p.m. Adults $1.25, children 75¢.

8 **Hagley Museum,** 3 miles north of Wilmington. From the earliest colonial times water-powered mills of many types flourished along the Brandywine. On the property of the du Pont powder mills, begun in 1802, has been established the Hagley Museum whose purpose is to preserve and interpret the story of Brandywine industry. On the 185 acre property are powder, flour, paper, iron and textile mills, a reconstructed wooden water wheel, and a section from an 18th century Delaware grist mill. In a mid 19th century machine shop a series of models demonstrates the steps used in manufacturing black powder when it was the world's only explosive.

Open Tuesdays through Saturdays and holidays (except for Thanksgiving, Christmas and New Year's when closed) from 9:30 a.m. to 4:30 p.m., Sundays 1 to 5 p.m.; free.

9 **Henry Francis du Pont Winterthur Museum**, Route 52, north of Wilmington. This world-renowned museum houses a collection of American decorative arts from the 17th through the early 19th century. In a great county house (once the residence of the late Henry Francis du Pont) are almost 200 period rooms and thousands of objects, ranging from the smallest accessory to building facades. The vast array of treasures make up a fitting tribute to our nation's tradition of craftsmanship and architecture. The gardens are worth a visit in themselves, encompassing 2½ miles of exquisite colors and scents.

Winterthur's schedules and prices are rather complex, the regular tours requiring advance reservations; you can also see certain rooms and the gardens without reservations during specific times of the year. THE GUIDE suggests that you either write to the museum at Winterthur, Del. 19735, requesting a brochure with all this information, or call the reservations office at (302) 656-8591.

10 One mile east of Chadds Ford along Route 1, **Brandywine Battlefield** is now a state park. Only two cannons remain to remind the visitor of the Revolutionary battle,

Interior — Winterthur Museum

but the homes used as headquarters by Washington and Lafayette are open for touring. Washington occupied the commodious abode of the Rings, a Quaker family with ten children. The house is frequently referred to as "Ring's Tavern". Mr. Ring never did take out a tavern license and he was fined ten pounds in 1802 for "maintaining a tippling house". Lafayette used another smaller Quaker home, that of Gideon Gilpin. Gilpin lost so much property in the war that he, too, was forced to open a tavern (unlike Mr. Ring he did it legally); for this, however, and for his pro-Independence sentiments he was disowned by the local Quaker meeting.

The Ring home has been reconstructed on the original site. It contains authentic period furniture as does the smaller Gilpin house whose massive stone walls date from 1745. In each, figures have been placed which represent leading characters of the historical pageant; there is even a captured Hessian soldier sitting in leg irons in the ice house near the Ring home. See the huge sycamore tree where Lafayette rested while his battle wounds were being dressed.

On special holidays Colonial regimental musters are presented in full dress with fife and drum and musket drills.

The park is open, free to visitors, daily throughout the year, 8 a.m. to dusk during the summer and 8 a.m. to 4:30 p.m. the rest of the year. The two houses are open from 10 a.m. to 5 p.m. daily from May 30 to Labor Day and on weekends during the rest of the year.

Marquis DeLafayette

11 If there is some time left in the afternoon, you might drive east on Route 1 to a prosperous young business enterprise: the **Franklin Mint** near Media. Free weekday tours (9-10:30 a.m. and 1-3 p.m., each tour a half hour) provide an intriguing lesson in the process of coin- and medal-making at this largest private mint in the world; its Museum of Medallic Art is open weekends as well, noon to 5 p.m. Franklin Mint struck the nation's first gold coin when the precious metal went on sale the end of 1974.

Baltimore Pike will take you back to center-city Philadelphia.

BRANDYWINE SHOPPING...

Barn Shops. Between Chadds Ford Inn and the Brandywine Battlefield (so set back from the scurry of U.S. Route 1 that many rushers-by never find them) are the Chadds Ford Barn Shops, a serene community of craftsmen and specialists. ■

■ This community, quietly prospering on green lawns under mature trees, is housed in more than 15 enticing shops built into a warren of carefully adapted old barns and outbuildings.

■ It is an almost "secret" place, unique in the Delaware Valley, that friends delight in showing to visiting friends — so resolutely uncommercial that the shopkeepers have turned to spending a large part of their "publicity" budget on improvement of the surroundings.

■ Here is the delightful **Collector's Cabinet,** with exotic seashells, rare butterflies, minerals and fossils from around the world; the refreshing **Milkhouse,** a quaint snack shop with Belgian waffles, icecream, sandwiches and beverages — and the **Wooden Shoe,** with exquisite Holland Deflt, fine pewter and crystal.

■ Here is the **Battle Creed Pottery,** the home of a potter preoccupied with quality pots — and the **Pennyfeather Shop,** with unusual gifts for all nature lovers; everything to bring songbirds to your garden all year. Here also is the **Turk's Head**

Bazaar with a collection of rustic metalware and 18th century reproductions; and **Gerrity-Pesce Photography** with environmental art on unique barnwood mounts.

In **The Silver Shop** Douglas Verity makes cloisonne enamels on silver, an art lost in time. Here are nature's ageless beauties — fine stones handset in silver, at backwater prices. Here too are little silver treasures, young when Queen Victoria was young — and new silver pieces to be had for a few dollars.

Crum Creed Leather shares the Silver Shop. Two discriminating craftsmen produce classically styled leather goods, handbags, light luggage, belts and various smaller items.

At the **Fudge Drum** (quality candies) Jim Case makes delicious creamy fudge on the premises.

Richard McCabe-Murray, Route 1 near the entrance to the Brandywine River Museum, is a specialist in 18th Century Americana.

An appointment is advised. (215) 388-7562.

The Red Fox Inn, Toughkenamon, Pennsylvania, 5 miles south of Longwood Gardens on US Route 1. Public 18 hole Golf Course, Restaurant and Motor Lodge. (215) 768-2232.

SEVENTEENTH CENTURY CENTREVILLE, DELAWARE

Land grants in this lovely area date back to 1687. Such families as Chandlers, Baileys, Todds, Hollingsworths, and Greggs flourished in a number of traces and businesses.

Formerly a community of large, rich farms, it was also the hub of splendid Inns and Taverns, catering to the many travelers who came to advance their fortunes in the luxuriant countryside.

Drovers stopped over here en route to Wilmington to load the boats for the trip up the Delaware River to Philadelphia. Artisans and shops began to open up and prosper in 1821. And in 1840 to 1850 there was a notable religious development. Friends Meetings were established at Centre Grove and Lower Brandywine. Methodists, Mormons, Presbyterians, Plumerites and Episcopalians all held services. The first public meeting place was established in 1842 and was named "Centreville Hall".

Today Centreville is an alive and active community, carrying on the old traditions of craft and commerce. The huge farms, the lusty Taverns have gone, But the spirit, beauty and charm remain — here 1776 and 1976 relate.

Buckley's Tavern at 5812 Kennett Pike, Centreville, Delaware.

Luncheon, Tuesday through Saturday. Super shrimp salad. Wise to reserve. Cocktails and liquor store open Monday through Saturday.

The Lampshade, at 4810½ Kennett Pike, behind Buckley's Tavern, does just what you would expect ... beautifully. Cut-out custom shades, traditional and modern, are designed to your order and hand painted.

The Jolly Needlewoman, 5810 Kennett Pike (Route 53) in historic Centreville, Delaware, is the ultimate goal for needlepoint and crewel "buffs". Mrs. Anne Bennethum, nationally known designer, directs this haven of original hand-painted custom design. Select finest raw materials, imaginative accessories. When your masterpiece is done bring it back (or send it) to be hand finished by staff professionals. Custom kits, lessons. ■

Visit, write, or call Mrs. Bennethum for delightful new needlepoint ideas. (302) 658-9585.

La Cocina. In Centreville, Delaware, on Route 52, you'll find LA COCINA, a cook's tour of culinary needs and attractive serving pieces.

■ This versatile shop is geared for every level of cookery, backyard to *haute cuisine.* Stocks range from larding needles to copper *au gratin* dishes to authentic oriental woks.

Two walls are hung with accessories culled from around the globe, all to help you in preparing a feast. Wine lovers will find every amenity.

If you're an *average* cook (and you want to put your best foot forward) you'll find the wherewithall amongst the bright imported enamelware, colorful pottery and porcelain.

LA COCINA has everything needed to raise cookery to art. We think most any cook will find a stop here worth her (his) time. 5808 Kennett Pike.

■ If you've ever wondered how people get on the Best Dressed List, one sure answer lies midway between Winterthur Museum and Longwood Gardens, in Centreville, Delaware ... **Frances Boutique.** Beautifully turned out women of the First State have been coming to **Frances** for years for their superbly simple wardrobes. Clothes for daytime, sports, and evening. Lovely lingerie and accessories. You'll find **Frances'** sign at the Centreville crossroads. ■

10:00 to 5:00 Monday through Saturday. (302) 652-0816.

The Shop of Four Seasons. While you're in historic Centreville, The Guide heartily recommends a stop at the **Four Seasons Gift Shop.** Elegant and traditional atmosphere, even to the staff in their long-skirted dresses. Hand painted Herend porcelain, Tiffany Silver, beautiful crystal stemware and serving pieces are appealingly displayed with lamps, decorative accessories, and unusual gifts. Wander into the Solarium with its lighted ceiling, shutters, mirrors, palms. Then downstairs to view all the amenities for leisure living, including tabletop treasures, and cachepots. Gift wrapping is deluxe, beautiful silver boxes, tied with festive bows. What we liked best of all ... browsing is encouraged. (302) 656-2414. ■

Marjorie Speakman, Shield's Shopping Center, Greenville, Delaware, would love to show you her "Fairyland" collection of children's clothes, unusual toys. ■

Stop in or call (302) 658-3521.

The Wilmington Country Store will revive your morale, instantly, if you have reached the state of "wilted traveler," or even if you haven't. Attractive, well-designed sportswear for men and women. Route 52, 2 miles south of the entrance to Winterthur.

Bootiful Shoes, 4003A Kennett Pike, Greenville, Delaware, is an ultra bootery with a dashing assortment of shoes, handbags, jewelry, and interesting accessories.

Go Tell Aunt Rhody is a "must" for anyone with a children's gift list. Old-fashioned and unique toys, young books and records, imaginative room decorations. 4003 Kennett Pike, Greenville, Del.

Books, Inc., 3826 Kennett Pike, Greenville (near Wilmington), Delaware, is one of those rare stops not only for the true book lover but for all those whose hobbies include Art, Gardening, Needlework, Gourmet (and Practical) Cooking. A wide range of all this, plus many interesting books from overseas. Best-sellers, of course, both hard cover and paperback. And a delightful Children's Room, lined to the ceilings with specially selected reading for The Young (302) 652-3209.

Historic **Dilworthtown Inn** and **Country Store** (1758) are restored to their original elegance.

The Inn (11 mini dining rooms with fireplaces) serves luncheon Monday through Friday 11:30 to 2:30; Dinner 5:00 to 10:00 Monday through Thursday, 5:00 to 11:00 Friday; Saturday, Sunday 3:00 to 9:00. Reserve (215) 399-1390.

The Country Store and **Gift Shop** has original works (and reproductions) of local well-known artists (Wyeth, Robert Goodier), bird lithographs, handmade quilts, Armatale mugs. (215) 399-0253.

At Dilworthtown Village, ¼ mile off Route 202 on Old Wilmington Pike.

EXCURSION 5

Pennsbury
Fallsington
Washington Crossing

Today our destination is the scenic country along the Delaware River. Here we shall visit William Penn's country estate; so artfully reconstructed is Pennsbury that one can feel his presence, his personality throughout. After another stop at the colonial village of Fallsington, we go on to the state park that commemorates the crossing of the Delaware by the Continental Army on Christmas Day 1776 – a battle that some historians feel constituted George Washington's "finest hour".

Pennsbury Fallsington

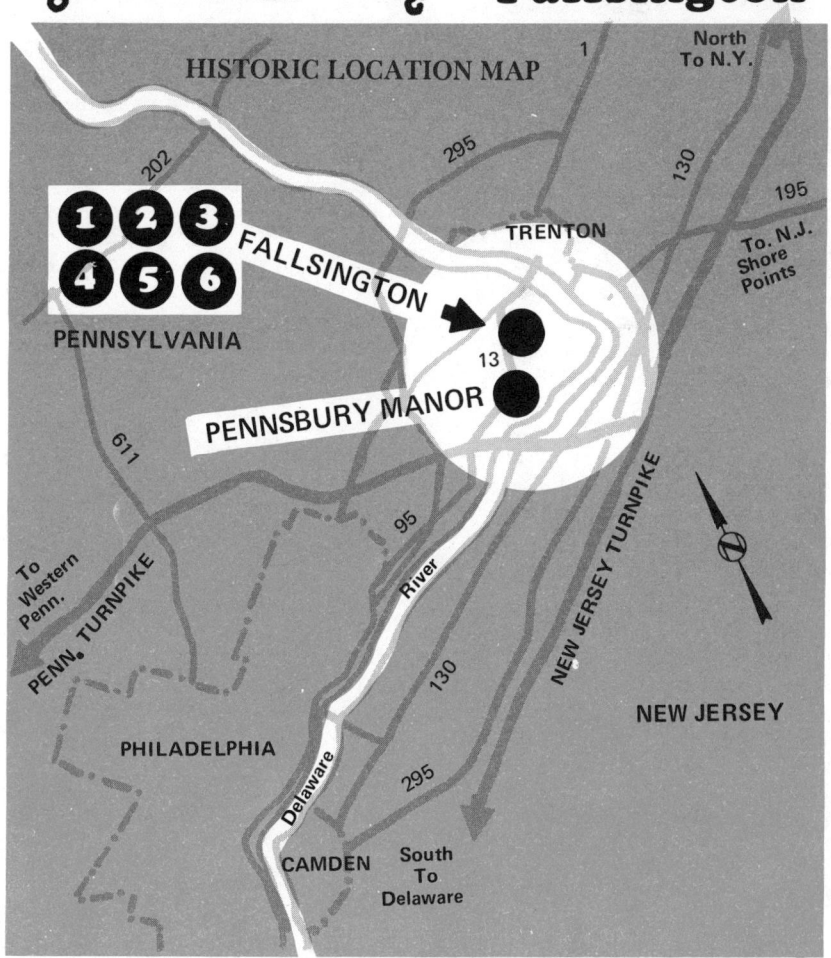

FALLSINGTON
1. Gillingham Store
2. Burges-Lippincott House
3. Moon-Williamson House
4. Friends Meeting Houses
5. Schoolmaster's House
6. Gambrel Roof House

HISTORIC LOCATION MAP

75

PENNSBURY
Dream House
in The Wilderness

Introduced as a young man to George Fox who founded the Quaker religion, William Penn embraced this faith and adhered to its tenets throughout his life. When he left England for American shores in 1682, having been given a land grant by King Charles II in payment of a family debt, Fox's words were uppermost in his mind: "My friends that are gone and are going over to plant, and make outward plantations in America, keep your own plantations in your hearts with the spirit and power of God, that your own vines and lilies be not hurt." In this manner Penn created Pennsylvania, named after his family by order of the King. This was his "Holy Experiment"; here he offered lifelong friendship to the Indians, a refuge to the persecuted of every sect, and a just and humane system of government.

But there was another side to William Penn — a side revealed in Pennsbury, his country manor. For he was also an aristocrat, a handsome, athletic, courtly gentleman, son of an admiral. He doted on good food and wine and admired well-built women and ships. This was a man of possessions — Tamerlaine, sire of famous American race horses; exquisite Jacobean and William and Mary furniture; and, above all that famous barge, manned by coxswain and six oarsmen, which transported him the 25 miles between Pennsbury and Philadelphia. "Above all dead things," admitted William Penn, "I love my barge."

Located in the wilderness, Pennsbury was of necessity self-supporting, with several outbuildings to supply the various housekeeping needs. But it went far beyond mere necessity. To maintain its 8,400 acre grounds, the best English and Scotch gardeners were hired. Inside a vast retinue of servants, attaches and slaves kept the place in order (Quaker strictures against slavery did not come until later), and the steward ordered butter from Rhode Island, rum from Jamaica, candles from Boston, and madeira from England. Here, in the style of an English lord, Penn entertained foreign dignitaries, colonial governors and, of course, his friends the Indians. All this did not go unnoticed by the citizens of Pennsylvania who, by paying a required annual fixed rent or "quitrent", helped keep him in this fine style.

Pennsbury was built between 1683 and 1700, and William Penn made it his home for two short but happy years, from 1699 to 1701. He had hoped to remain at Pennsbury for the rest of his life. However, threats to his colony's charter and financial worries which eventually landed him in a debtors' prison forced him to leave this home on the Delaware. William Penn returned to England in 1701, never to return, and his beloved manor fell slowly into ruin.

PENNSBURY EXCURSION

Pennsbury has been meticulously reconstructed on its original foundations at the cost of $200,000. Penn's own detailed instructions were of much help, as was a massive excavation effort. The manor was refurnished so completely that it contains the largest collection of 17th century antiques in Pennsylvania. The acreage is not what it was in Penn's day, nor is the view; but Pennsbury is still a most impressive sight. If you're driving take U.S. Route 1 or 13 north, and follow state signs for Pennsbury, which is located in Morrisville.

The manor is open weekdays from 8:30 a.m. to 5 p.m. and Sundays 1 to 5 p.m. from April through October; from November through March it is open 9 a.m. to 4:30 p.m. weekdays and 1 to 4:30 p.m. Sundays; closed Christmas, New Years, Easter, Thanksgiving. Hours are subject to change. Adults, 50¢; children under 12 free. Phone: 946-0400.

Picnicking is allowed in the pavillion area, where you likely will be joined by some chattering guinea hens. The blossoming apple trees in spring are lovely as are the later damask roses.

Our tour of Pennsbury begins with the outbuildings which you will reach on foot before coming to the house itself.

The Arms of Penn

1 **Tool House.** This has been rebuilt and now is being refurnished with colonial-style tools.

2 **Ice House.** Here ice blocks, cut from the frozen Delaware, were stored in sawdust to cool foods and beverages in summer.

3 **Plantation Office**, headquarters for the plantation manager.

4 **Smokehouse**, where meats were cured by subjecting them to dense smoke.

5 **Bake and Brew House.** This has a 2,200 gallon tank for ale, the favorite drink of Penn's time. The ovens were so vast that it took days to heat things up.

6 **Herb and Vegetable Garden,** thick with the odor of thyme and rosemary, with rows of eggplant, beans, horseradish, all the other vegetables that Penn found in America or imported from Britain.

7 **Boat House**, on the river and containing a replica of Penn's barge.

8 **Manor House.** William Penn's abode is a harlequin of a house, half white painted board and half brick, its porch stretching the entire length and looking out over formal gardens. It is situated now, as it was originally, 15 feet above high water and 150 yards away from the river.

The spirit of Pennsylvania's founder is immediately apparent upon entering the Great Hall where the Penns received guests. Here, as elsewhere in the house, the furniture is solid and massive. The window hangings are of crimson brocade and the floors of random width pegged oak. Over the mantel of the fireplace is displayed the Penn family coat-of-arms. In the parlor a lantern clock without hands strikes the hour. See the room where Penn powdered his wig and the wainscotted dining room with refectory table and imposing Dutch chairs where banquets were held. Above the dining room is a guest room with canopied four-poster bedstead; its highboy is an original Penn piece, as is the heavy carved chair in wife Hannah's parlor. The living quarters of daughter Letitia are elegant, William Penn's more modest. Admiral Penn's portrait is on the second floor landing.

9 **Stable.** Horses are in the stable and goats and sheeps in the adjoining shed.

HISTORIC LOCATION MAP
PENNSBURY

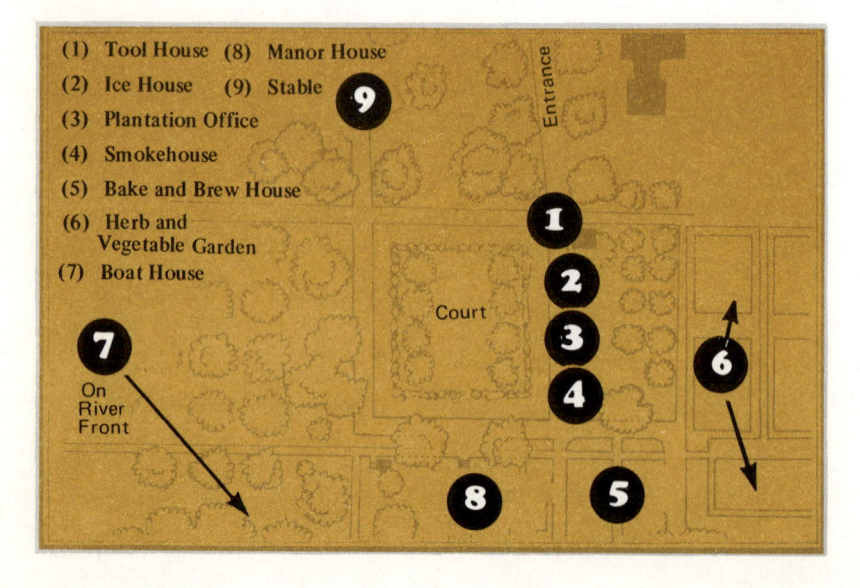

(1) Tool House (8) Manor House
(2) Ice House (9) Stable
(3) Plantation Office
(4) Smokehouse
(5) Bake and Brew House
(6) Herb and Vegetable Garden
(7) Boat House

7 — On River Front

FALLSINGTON
Village of The Past

Only four miles distant from Pennsbury Manor is the charming colonial village of Fallsington. Here William Penn arrived by horseback to worship at Falls Meeting, established in 1683. Over 25 pre-Revolutionary buildings still stand (unfortunately the old meeting is not among them). Most were built by friends and followers of Penn, and some of the private ones still are inhabited by descendents of the original families.

FALLSINGTON EXCURSION

Fallsington is located northwest of Pennsbury just off Route 13. The houses we will tour are within a half block of Meetinghouse Square. A fine time to visit is the second Saturday of October which is Fallsington Day, when residents in costume demonstrate colonial crafts, foods, etc.

The quiet village, incorporated in 1953 as a non-profit corporation, is open from March 15 to November 15, Wednesday to Sunday, 1 to 5 p.m. cost for adults is $1, students 25¢, children under 12 free.

1 **Gillingham Store.** A fire destroyed the old country store in 1910; it was replaced by the present building which is the corporation's headquarters and gift shop.

2 **Burges-Lippincott House.** Built in 1780, this house has "one of the most beautiful doorways in Bucks" (County), a delicate carved fireplace and stairway with a unique wall-banister. The entire Historical Fallsington, Inc. project was born when Burges-Lippincott House was put up for sale and possible destruction.

3 **Moon-Williamson House.** Of log construction with traces of Swedish influence, it is believed to be the oldest house in the village. Two ancient sycamore trees, perhaps 300 years old, flank the front door. The house was owned by a "joyner" and cabinet maker.

4 **Friends Meeting Houses.** After the original Friends place of worship was destroyed, another was built in 1789 and now is a community center. Facing it is yet another meeting house, this one built by the Hicksite Quakers. (In 1827 there was a schism within the Quaker faith, resulting in two separate branches, Orthodox and Hicksite.)

5 **Schoolmaster's House**, dates from 1758.

6 **Gambrel Roof House**, erected in 1728, was a girls' boarding school in the early 1800s and now is an apartment house.

Washington Crossing

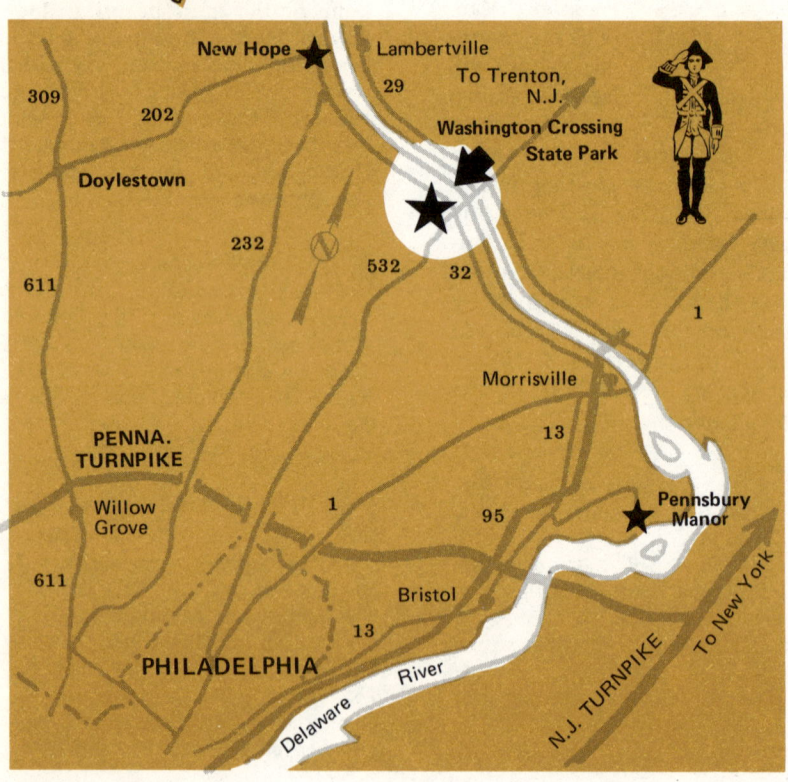

(1) Memorial Building
(2) Old Ferry Inn
(3) David Library
(4) Bowman's Hill Tower
(5) Bowman's Hill State Wild Flower Preserve
(6) Grist Mill
(7) Thompson-Neely House

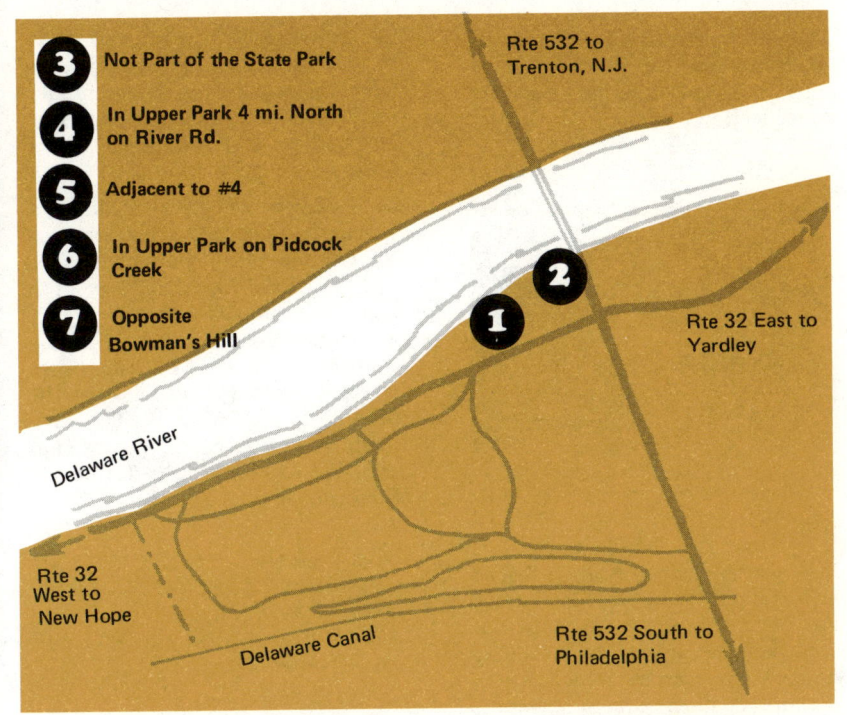

Map legend:
- **3** Not Part of the State Park
- **4** In Upper Park 4 mi. North on River Rd.
- **5** Adjacent to #4
- **6** In Upper Park on Pidcock Creek
- **7** Opposite Bowman's Hill

Map labels: Rte 532 to Trenton, N.J.; Rte 32 East to Yardley; Delaware River; Rte 32 West to New Hope; Delaware Canal; Rte 532 South to Philadelphia

WASHINGTON CROSSING STATE PARK

Hallowed Ground

The spot where George Washington crossed the Delaware, now the focus of a 500 acre state park, is hallowed ground to America. Its setting, especially in warm weather, is bucolic and peaceful. Ducks swim back and forth, little realizing that 200 years ago an army of men crossed the same waters with far less ease and an almost impossible mission.

WASHINGTON CROSSING EXCURSION

To reach Washington Crossing from Fallsington, go out U.S. 1 to Route 13 north, through Yardley, to the intersection of 532 and 32. The park is open 365 days a year from dawn to dusk. Park buildings are open from 9 a.m. to 4:30 p.m. daily November 1 to March 1, and 9:30 a.m. to 5 p.m. daily March 1 to November 1; closed election days, Thanksgiving, Christmas, New Years. Free except where indicated.

The park is divided into a lower and upper section, separated by a few miles; both are described here, the upper section beginning with #4.

1 **Memorial Building.** To the north of this keystone-shaped building, erected 1959, is a statue of George Washington looking out over the river from atop a slender spire. Steps near by lead down to the point of embarkation. Inside, on the stage of the auditorium is a full sized 12 foot by 21 foot exact copy by Robert Williams of the famous painting WASHINGTON CROSSING THE DELAWARE. The original done in the 1830's by Emanuel Leutze is in the New York Metropolitan Museum. Popularity of this work is easy to understand, for it is a vivid, stirring rendition of the event. Unfortunately, its inaccuracies have invited an equal share of criticism: wrong type of boat, flag depicted before America had that particular flag and the Napoleonic stance of Washington, hardly appropriate under the circumstances. The ridicule stemmed, too, from anti-German sentiment in this country, during and after World War I. Leutze, a German, produced this work in Dusseldorf and used the Rhine as his model for the Delaware. Rumor went so far as to suggest that he employed a German washwoman as the model for Washington's head. In all probability he worked from the Houdon bust.

Also, in the Memorial Building, a 15-minute descriptive narration of the encampment is presented every half hour. On Christmas Day at 2 p.m. large crowds gather to watch the annual live re-enactment of the crossing when two Durham boats traverse the river with about 30 prominent Delaware Valley residents dressed in colonial garb. Theatrical producer St. John Terrell has been playing George for many a year.

A movie "WASHINGTON CROSSING THE DELAWARE", narrated by the late Chet Huntley, fills in any historical gaps you may have at 1 and 3 p.m.

2 **Old Ferry Inn.** In this restored house of native stone on the north side of Route 532, it is believed that Washington ate his evening meal on December 25 before crossing the Delaware. You can buy snacks and gifts here. A 50¢ admission charge entitles you to visit this house and the Thompson-Neely House further along. A short distance north of the inn is a 40 foot replica of a Durham boat, the type built by local ironmaster Robert Durham. Originally intended for carrying iron ore down river, these graceful vessels transported the Continentals' 2400 men over to the Jersey shore.

3 **David Library of the American Revolution.** A fascinating stop in Washington Crossing (not part of the State Park) is this superb research library and audio visual center housing over 2,000 original letters and documents on the American Revolution. Its inspired and generous founder, Mr. Sol Feinstone, has donated the David Library to the United States Government, thus assuring it will be free to visitors forever.

Among its more frivolous but intriguing items is a letter penned by Washington to Annis Stockton, a vivacious Princeton poetess, in response to one of her poetic tributes. "You see, Madam", he wrote in part, "when once a woman has tempted us and we have tasted the forbidden fruit, there is no such thing as checking our appetite, whatever the consequences may be".

There is some question as to whether such remarks constituted a love letter or a mere flirtation, but in any case, this was a far cry from the Washington who crossed the Delaware.

The David Library, in its lovely rural and historic setting, is open Monday through Friday, 10 a.m. to 5 p.m. Special film presentations pertaining to the American Revolution can be arranged for groups by appointment: (215) 493-6776, P.O. Box 48, Washington Crossing, PA 18977.

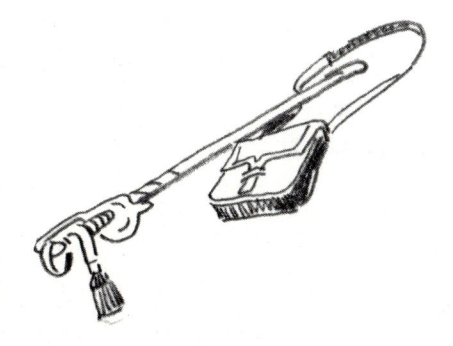

④ Bowman's Hill Tower. Washington used this hill as a lookout post from which to watch the river for redcoats. In 1930 a stone observation tower was erected here. If you climb the 121 steps to the top you'll be rewarded with a magnificent view of the Delaware and surrounding countryside.

⑤ Bowman's Hill State Wild Flower Preserve. Adjacent to the tower is a 100-acre sanctuary for native flowers, trees, shrubs and ferns. You can't picnic here, but do enjoy the beauty; there is always something in bloom from March to November and the spring displays are particularly fine. A newly added Platt Bird Museum houses an extensive collection of birds, nests and eggs.

⑥ Grist Mill, along River Road on Pidcock Creek. This is where the local miller ground the grain for Washington's army. It is being restored.

⑦ Thompson-Neely House. A bit further along the river opposite Bowman's Hill is the "House of Decision", so called because in its cozy kitchen with vast fireplace and exposed wooden rafters, Washington and his officers planned the famous attack of Trenton. Eighteen year old James Monroe, later to be our fifth President, was among these men. The rooms of this 18th century farmhouse have been authentically furnished. Every year on Washington's birthday colonial-style gingerbread is baked in the oven and served warm to visitors. Sheep and lambs graze in the nearby pasture, and a road leads over the canal to the graves of the unknown soldiers of the Continental Army.

WHILE YOU'RE THERE

If you enjoyed a simple picnic lunch in the wooden setting of Pennsbury, now is an ideal time to treat yourself to a bit of luxury. Washington Crossing Inn at Routes 352 and 32 is a delightful restaurant and guest house dating in part from 1778. Should you have the time to extend your excursion by one day, stay overnight at the inn and drive the next morning to Princeton, New Jersey.

Princeton is a town rich in culture, beauty and Revolutionary history. The scene of a decisive American victory on January 3, 1777, it also was the new nation's capital from June to November 1783. Here on October 31 of that year news was received of the Treaty of Paris ending the Revolution.

Throughout its history the town has been greatly influenced by its prestigious Ivy League men's college, Princeton University, founded in 1746 (it has been co-educational since 1969). Also here is the Institute for Advanced Study where Albert Einstein spent his last years.

The Greater Chamber of Commerce at 44 Nassau Street can help you plan your time. Don't miss a tour of the university; this can be arranged through a campus guide (phone: 452-3603). Its highlights include: Firestone Library, containing papers of John Foster Dulles, Bernard Baruch, Woodrow Wilson and Adlai Stevenson; University Art Museum whose exhibits range from the ancient Greek to the contemporary; Nassau Hall where the Second Continental Congress met in 1783; the Putnam Sculptures, one of the largest modern outdoor sculpture showcases in the nation with works by Picasso, Calder and Lipchitz, and the McCarter Theater, a professional repertory theater company which presents classical and modern dramas, concerts and ballet (call 921-8700).

The house called Morven (erected 1701) belonged to one of the signers of the Declaration of Independence and was British general Lord Cornwallis' headquarters in 1776; now it is the official residence of the Governor of New Jersey. At Rockingham State Historic Site eight miles outside of Princeton was Washington's headquarters in the latter part of 1783; here he wrote the famous "Farewell Orders to the Armies." The state of New Jersey has maintained it as a museum with ten rooms of period furniture.

Eating in Princeton is good, too – the Peacock Inn and Nassau Inn having traditions that go back to colonial times.

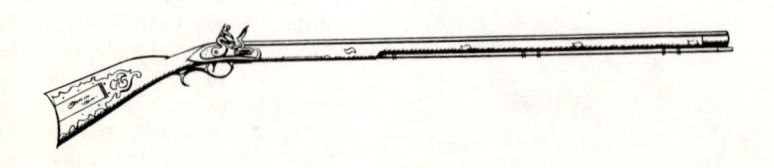

Historic Insight...

The Painting by Emanuel Leutze

Washington Crosses The Delaware

December 1776, The Americans had been fighting for barely six months and already the Revolution seemed to be lost, with defeats in Long Island, Fort Washington and Fort Lee. Washington's men had barely any clothes on their backs, Congress was apathetic in appropriating desperately needed funds, and citizens were lukewarm, if not downright negative, to the cause of independence. Even Washington was low. "The game is almost up," he wrote to his brother on December 18.

A month before, the General and his troops had made a humiliating retreat across New Jersey. Encamped along the Delaware River, the 2400 men were hungry, filthy, ill, cold and depressed; they looked, said one viewer, like a "flock of animated scarecrows". Their last chance, it seemed, was to take the enemy in winter quarters at Trenton. Here, Colonel Johann Rall headed a brigade of Hessian mercenaries. Rall was a competent officer, so sure of victory that he refused even to fortify the city, choosing instead to concentrate on holiday drinking. His commander-in-chief, General Howe, was engaged in an equally frivolous pursuit — gambling with his blonde mistress in New York.

Washington knew that once the river had frozen over, the British — who, unlike the Continentals, had virtually no boats — would be able to move men and artillery directly across the Delaware and take Philadelphia. This must be prevented or the Revolution would be over and Washington himself would face personal disgrace. On December 23 he wrote to his generals: "Christmas Day, at night, one hour before dawn, is the time fixed for our attempt on Trenton. For heaven's sake, keep this to yourself, as discovery may prove fatal to us. Dire necessity will, nay, must, justify attempt." That same day, an order was sent to all troops to prepare and keep on hand a three day supply of cooked rations. Aware of his men's low morale, on Christmas morning Washington had copies passed out of militiaman Tom Paine's stirring words written only days before by the light of a campfire on the head of a drum: "These are the times that try men's souls ... The summer soldier and the sunshine patriot will, in this crisis, shrink from the service of his country, but he that stands it now deserves the love and thanks of man and woman."

When darkness fell, it was time to bring out the graceful black Durham boats which had been hidden behind Malta Island. Colonel Glover and his seafaring men of Marblehead, Mass. began to board. Wrote one of Washington's men in his diary, "It is fearfully cold and raw and a snowstorm is setting in. The wind is northeast and beats in the faces of the men ... but I have never heard a man complain. They are ready to suffer any hardship and die rather than give up their liberty." On preparing to enter the boats, many of the shoeless men, some with old rags tied around their feet, left bloody footprints in the snow.

The crossing began. Soldiers huddled in the boats, trying to hold on to their tricornered hats as the river swirled and ice threatened to overturn their overladen vessels. So difficult a journey was it that they arrived at the other side near 3:00 a.m., a full three hours behind schedule. On the shore, Jersey residents — finally angered by Hessian looting of their property — helped haul the boats ashore in the floating

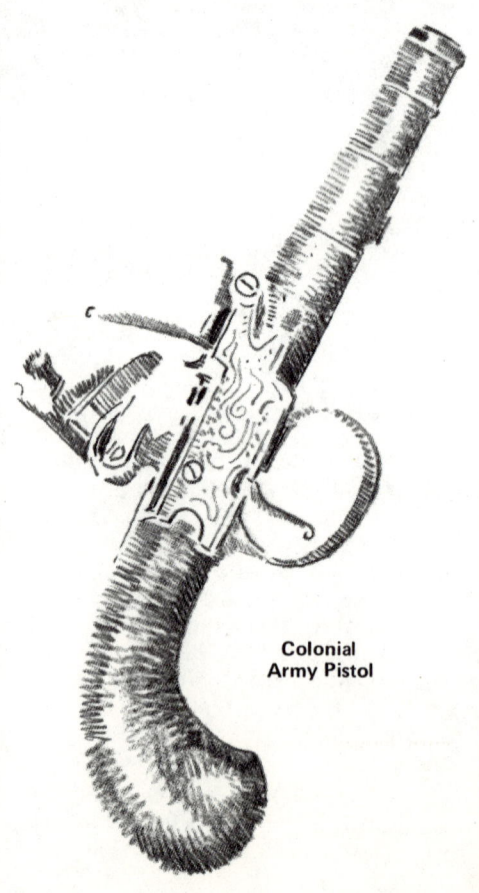

Colonial Army Pistol

ice. Reported an officer of the landing: "I have never seen Washington so determined as he is now. He stands on the banks of the river, wrapped in his cloak, superintending the landing of his troops."

After 3 a.m. the advance began, Sullivan's wing going along the river road and Greene's inland. As they marched, General Greene sent a message to Washington that the muskets were wet and could not be fired. Replied their commander: "Tell your men to use the bayonet. The town must be taken." In fact, many of the men had no bayonets.

Meanwhile in Trenton, a holiday celebration had been going on since Christmas Eve, thanks to local Loyalist hospitality. Colonel Rall had partaken of a gay supper and was so intent on his card playing that he crumpled in his pocket, unread, a note warning of the American approach which had been scribbled by a Pennsylvania farmer and left at the door. Rall retired very late and not very sober.

At the juncture of King and Queen Streets the Continentals went into action, pushing the surprised Hessians back on every side. Victory was theirs within two hours, and with hardly a fatality in the American ranks. "This is a glorious day for our Country," said Washington, riding down King Street. With their prisoners, the Americans crossed over the ice-choked Delaware, taking the Hessians to Philadelphia where they paraded them through the streets with captured arms and colors behind them. Once again the victors recrossed the Delaware, and marched back to Trenton.

After his victory at Trenton, General Washington went on to another brilliant success. A British force of 5500 under Lord Cornwallis marched to Assumpinck Creek, in the hope of blocking the Continentals' approach to Princeton, but the General moved his men out and around the British and headed toward town by a back route — rags wrapped around the gun carriage wheels so as to muffle the sound. The battle took place outside Princeton at dawn on January 3, 1777 and ended with Washington chasing the defeated British into the college town. Exhausted, the victorious Americans then took up winter quarters in Morristown.

It had been a totally unexpected series of defeats for the British, a warning that the Continentals were an army to be reckoned with. Among the British dead was Colonel Rall; he was found with the unread letter of warning still crumpled in his pocket.

Almost five years later in a Virginia town along the Chesapeake, a victory dinner was held after Yorktown, ending the war that had made America a nation. As was customary, George Washington proposed a toast to the defeated General, Lord Cornwallis. Replied the British commander, "When the illustrious part your Excellency has borne in the long and arduous contest becomes a matter of history, fame will gather your brightest laurels from the banks of the Delaware rather than those of the Chesapeake."

THE GUIDE RECOMMENDS...

Lahiere's Restaurant, 11 Witherspoon Street in Princeton, offers superb French cuisine, sensitive service, backed by one of the finest wine cellars in Central New Jersey. 20,000 bottles of imported wines kept under constant temperature control.

For reservations, call (609) 921-2798. Closed Tuesdays.

Forsgate Country Club, located at Exit 8A of the N.J. Turnpike, is a fine dining and 36-hole golfing facility. Dining areas are open to the public without membership fee. Ideal for business groups, weddings and private parties.

Reservations suggested. Call (201) 521-0070. Or write to Jamesburg, New Jersey.

Palmer Square, in the heart of Princeton, will appeal to browser and serious shopper alike. Here on Nassau Street, facing Princeton University, you'll find book shops, smoke shops, clothing, gift and jewelry shops. And art galleries. When you can't go on, drop in at the famous Nassau Inn which has been refreshing travelers for 200 continuous years.

Down the street from **Morven** is another historic building, the 1776 home of Jonathan Deare, now **The Peacock Inn.** Fine cooking, cocktails, lodging, all under the delightful supervision of Agnes and Chuck Swain. 20 Bayard Lane, (609) 924-1707.

A unique store... **Princeton University Store,** 36 University Place.

Thompson-Neely House, Washington Crossing

EXCURSION 6

New Hope and Ivyland Railroad

Doylestown
New Hope

No area of Pennsylvania holds more appeal for the visitor than does Bucks County, famed for its river scenery, legendary art and theater colony, antique shops, restaurants, and venerable age. Indeed, the 200th birthday of many Bucks County homes already has come and gone. Today we visit two favorite towns in the central part of that county, first Doylestown and then New Hope.

A word of warning: On summer weekends it seems like the whole world has converged on New Hope. Go on a weekday if you can, or during spring or fall. In the winter you won't be able to take that famous mule-drawn barge ride, but the town will have shrunk in size by thousands and you'll find out who the *real* residents are.

Doylestown
New Hope

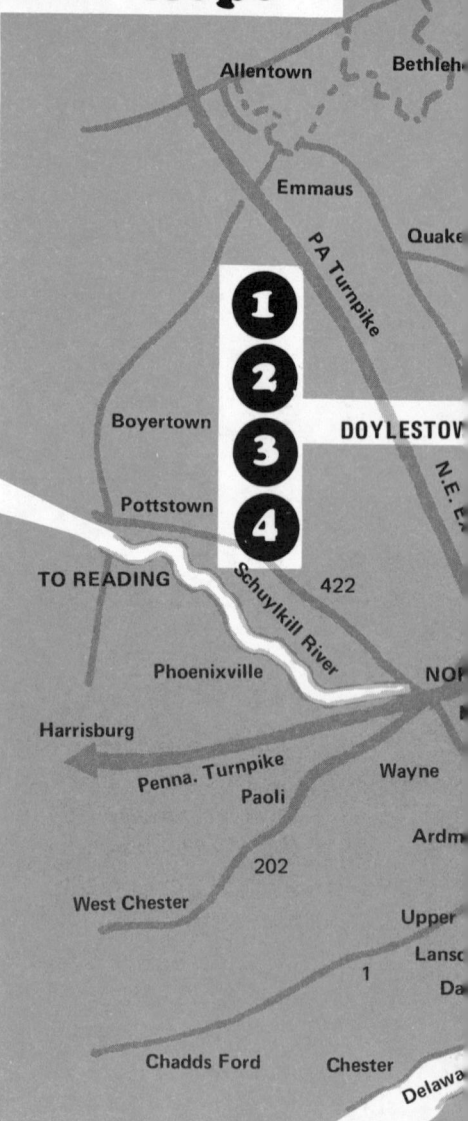

DOYLESTOWN

(1) Moravian Pottery and Tile Works
(2) Fonthill
(3) Mercer Museum of the Bucks County Historical Society
(4) The National Shrine of Our Lady of Czestochowa

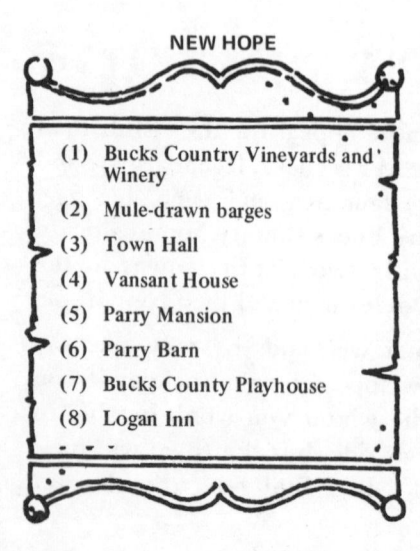

NEW HOPE

(1) Bucks Country Vineyards and Winery
(2) Mule-drawn barges
(3) Town Hall
(4) Vansant House
(5) Parry Mansion
(6) Parry Barn
(7) Bucks County Playhouse
(8) Logan Inn

HISTORIC LOCATION MAP

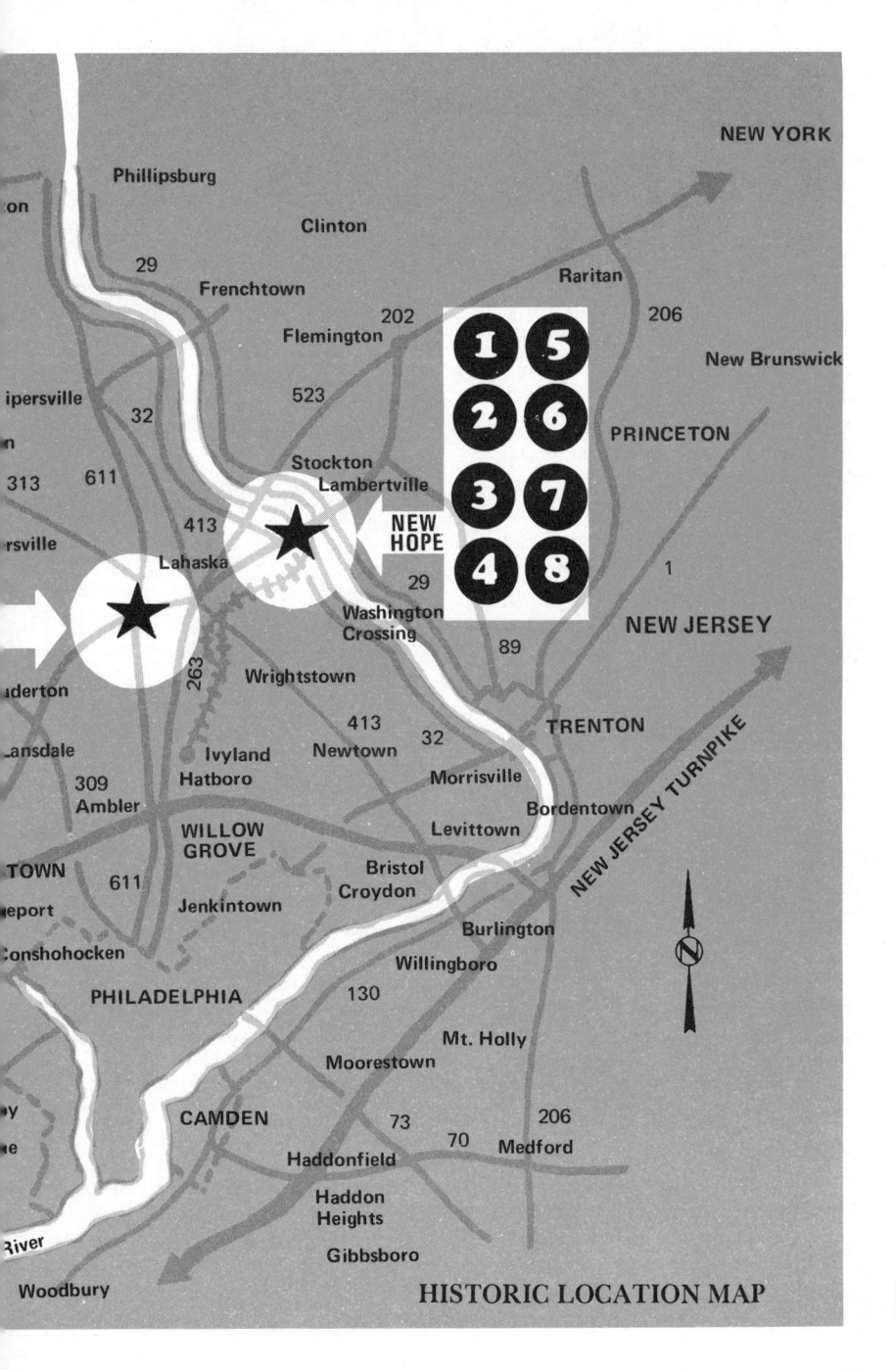

DOYLESTOWN
Heritage of an Artist

Doylestown, the country seat of Bucks County, was part of William Penn's original land grant from England's King Charles II. Not yet a town during the Revolution, it was, however, an important stagecoach stop between Philadelphia and Easton, Pa., and it had a bustling tavern at the intersection of two roads. The Continental Army is believed to have encamped there on June 20, 1778, having marched from Valley Forge. Their hope was to overtake the British who had evacuated Philadelphia and were fleeing to New York. On this hot summer evening George Washington slept overnight on the lawn of a local home while his army rested nearby. The next day they left to cross the Delaware at New Hope, and on June 28 the Americans faced their foe at the terrible battle of Monmouth, NJ.

An unhurried, attractive town with tree-lined streets and old frame houses, Doylestown is renowned today for the remarkable heritage of a native-born artist, Henry Chapman Mercer (1856-1930). A man of immense learning, Mercer held the position of curator of American and prehistoric archeology at the University of Pennsylvania. He was as well an anthropologist, historian, ceramicist, ecologist, horticulturalist, author and architect. And he was rich. Mercer designed and built three castle-like structures in Doylestown which reveal both his genius and his eccentricities. We shall visit all three today.

DOYLESTOWN EXCURSION

Doylestown can be reached from center-city Philadelphia by car via the Schuylkill Expressway west to the Pennsylvania Turnpike, the Turnpike east to Willow Grove Interchange, and Route 611 into town. Greyhound and Trailways buses also go to Doylestown as does the Reading Railroad.

1 **Moravian Pottery and Tile Works,** East Court Street and Swamp Road (Pa. Route 313). Henry Chapman Mercer's chief artistic mission was to save for the world the moribund techniques of Pennsylvania German pottery-making. His decorative tiles were so fine that they won for him the grand prize in the St. Louis World's Fair. Mercer was hired to produce these for such varied enterprises as the Capitol building in Harrisburg (he created 400 tiles depicting the history of the state), a gambling casino in Monte Carlo, the Rockefeller home in Pontico Hills, N.Y., and a Washington, D.C. press club. In the Moravian Pottery and Tile Works, whose design shows the influence of Mercer's architectural research in the Yucatan, these beautiful objects were made.

The works fell into ruin some years after Mercer's death but have been restored, and tiles are now made there using his original methods. Conducted tours explain the ceramic process and the history of this art.

Open Wednesdays through Saturdays 10 a.m. to 5 p.m., Sundays noon to 5 p.m.; closed Thanksgiving, Christmas. Adults $1, children 4 to 18, 25¢; family groups $2.

2 **Fonthill, East Court Street** (adjacent to Site #1). Begun in 1908, this stone and mortar castle was bachelor Mercer's home. Fonthill is straight out of a Gothic novel, with turrets, vaulted ceilings, winding staircases and eerie lighting effects (Mercer was, in fact, a writer of Gothic tales). The structure has many different levels and startling changes in the size and shapes of rooms. Tiles, naturally, are a focal point, being set into floors, ceilings, walls and furniture; even the brightly colored red roof is of tile. Some of the inside tiles were of Mercer's own making and others (from his collection) of Moorish, Persian, Spanish and Delft origin.

Fonthill's visiting schedule is in the process of change. For information, contact the Bucks County Historical Society, Pine and Ashland, about a mile away (phone: 348-4373).

Adults $1; children over 12, 50¢; under 12, 25¢.

3 **Mercer Museum of Bucks County Historical Society**, Ashland and Pine Streets. In 1897 Dr. Mercer began collecting early American tools, machinery and artifacts from such sources as junk heaps, attics and country auctions. By 1914 his collection was so great that he had to build a museum to house it. The result was this immense building, the first ever to be made of reinforced concrete. (Architects predicted scornfully — and incorrectly — that it would come tumbling down over its creator's head). Mercer spent two years on the project, with the help of a dozen day laborers and a horse named Lucy.

Mercer Museum of Bucks County

to 5 p.m.; closed January, February, all legal holidays. Adults $1.50, students 75¢; under 6 free.

④ The National Shrine of Our Lady of Czestochowa, Iron Hill and Ferry Road. A short drive from the Mercer Museum, this shrine is located on a picturesque tract of 250 acres. Comprising a basilica and monestary, it is the counterpart of a 12th century shrine in the town of the same name in Poland. The American version was established in 1953 by the Pauline Fathers and is still maintained by them. All are welcome to this lovely shrine every day at no charge. Note the extensive use of stained glass windows.

Over Labor Day weekend (and also the following weekend) the shrine is the site of an annual Polish Festival and Country Fair. Thousands take part in this well planned event which features polka bands, balalaika music, dancing and Polish foods galore — kilebasa, columbki, kishkies and babka, for a starter. There are many amusements for children.

$2 per car admission; call 343-0600 for details on scheduling.

One of America's most unique museums, this showcase displays over 33,000 priceless items of Americana (dating mostly between 1700 and 1820) including dugout canoes, cider presses, conestoga wagons, carpenters' tools, ship models, gallows, glassblowing tools, musical instruments, a whale boat, and a cabinetmaker's shop. The rooms are arranged around a five-story open section where such items as looms, cradles and sleighs are suspended in mid air, creating an amazing effect. Winding stairs take you from gallery to gallery.

Mercer Museum is open from March through December, Tuesdays through Saturdays from 10 a.m. to 5 p.m. and Sundays from 1

NEW HOPE
From Mill Town
to Artist's Colony

The town that is now New Hope was founded in 1710 by John Wells who operated a ferry at this location. His business was bought out by a man named Coryell, owner of the ferry across the river in New Jersey, and for a time the town took on the name of Coryell's Ferry. When in 1790 a wealthy local businessman, Benjamin Parry, rebuilt his gristmills which had burned down, he optimistically dubbed them New Hope Mills. Eventually this became the name of the town as well.

New Hope's location is a strategic one. The Old York Road, which ran through the town, was a main artery between Philadelphia and New York (a three day trip in colonial times). With the creation of the Delaware Canal in the early 19th century – its main purpose being the transporting of anthracite coal from mines in the Lehigh Valley to the city markets of Philadelphia and New York – New Hope took on even more significance.

As the century turned, three young artists, drawn by the isolation and beauty of this rolling country, came here to paint. An art colony evolved and, by the early 1930s, New Hope and environs had become a favored residence for leading figures in entertainment, letters, finance, and law. Among these settlers were Oscar Hammerstein, S.J. Perleman, Pearl Buck and James Michener. In 1939 the New Hope Mills were converted into the Bucks County Playhouse which rapidly became an entertainment center, and restaurants and shops of all kinds were added. The sleepy little hamlet had become a lively "in" place. Too lively. Today only Michener remains of the old crowd. Those who can afford the untouched fields and placid streams (highly paid athletes in the main) move to Upper Bucks County.

And New Hope is left to the tourists. But it is well worth seeing, steeped as it is in colonial history, in the bygone era of canals and barges, in its own peculiar charm. Unfortunately, that charm is realized most completely when we tourists have left and the ancient houses decorated with lovely iron grillwork stand quietly on empty, uneven brick sidewalks.

NEW HOPE EXCURSION

New Hope is a short drive from Doylestown going east on U.S. Route 202. There is so much to do here in the way of historical sightseeing, shopping, entertainment and gourmet eating, that you would do well to choose from our listing before you set out. Once again THE GUIDE recommends an overnight stay in this area if you want to see all of New Hope and explore some of Upper Bucks as well.

Plan to park your car on the street or in a lot as soon as you enter New Hope (after seeing Site #1). Most of the places you'll be visiting are clustered around Main Street and the blocks that slope down to it from the west.

① Bucks Country Vineyards and Winery, U.S. Route 202 (three miles west of New Hope). Winemaking is not nearly as common as antique selling in these parts, so take advantage of this enjoyable place before entering New Hope proper. The Bucks Country Vineyards and Winery is located on a farm which had been granted to a local resident by William Penn in 1717. Here wines are produced from French-American hybrid varieties of 100% American grapes. Tour the cool wine cellars and sample free wines in the tasting room. There is also a wine museum, the first of its kind in the state which explains early American successes (and failures) with the grape.

② Mule-drawn barges, New Street. The Delaware Canal from Bristol up to Easton, Pa. was one of three canal systems in the state. Built between 1827 and 1832, it remained operational until 1931 by which time the railroads had made it obsolete. At its heyday around 1862, from 2500 to 3000 large flat boats and barges were traveling the Delaware Canal. They could carry a load of 100 tons and were towed by horses, mules or a combination of both (four, six or eight to a team) who walked along the towpath. Two men usually were on board, one as steersman and the other as mule team tender; they switched positions regularly without stopping the boat by pole-vaulting across the water. Cooking was done on a tin-plated stove, and at times the steersman was required almost simultaneously to steer, cook and serve meals. At the front of each boat there was a man who was hired to blow a horn when they came to a bridge or lock. Canal folk took great pride in the notes of warning they could produce in this fashion, some of them gaining local renown for their lung capacity.

The Delaware Canal is the only continuously intact remnant of the great towpath canal building of the early and mid 19th century. Today that era is recreated delightfully in an hour-long trip along the Delaware Canal on awning-covered barges drawn by a pair of mules. As the boat glides along the still water of New Hope and surrounding countryside, the bells on the mules jingling rhythmically and the overhanging trees surrounding you in cool shade, you may find yourself wondering whether airplanes were such a good invention after all.

Schedule: April and from day after Labor Day through October, Wednesday, Saturday and Sunday 1, 3, and 4:30 p.m.; May to Labor Day, daily except Mondays, 1, 3, 4:30 and 6 p.m.; closed November 1 - April 1; open all holidays during season. Admission: adults $1.50, children under 12, 75¢.

For information on schedule and prices call 862-5206.

(If you prefer a train to a barge and an engineer to a mule, go to the New Hope and Ivyland Railroad at 32 West Bridge Street. You'll be treated to a one hour, 14 mile scenic trip to Buckingham and back on a Victorian era steam train.)

3 **Town Hall**, Corner of Main and Mechanic. This building was erected in 1790. The town council has met here since the borough was incorporated in 1837, and the building serves also as a tourist information center on travel, shopping, etc.

Open every day but Monday after 11 a.m.

4 **Vansant House**, northeast corner of Mechanic Street. Built around 1743, this is probably the oldest house in the borough, and it carries "battle" scars from the Revolution. (Legend has it that a British soldier stationed across the river fired on Vansant.) It is privately owned.

5 **Parry Mansion**, southwest corner Main and Ferry Streets. This house, owned originally by Benjamin Parry of New Hope Mills, was built in 1784 and has been restored by the New Hope Historical Society. The life style of five successive generations of this wealthy businessman's family is authentically depicted here. Charming to the last detail, its earliest furnishings are in late 18th century style and other decor is Federal, Empire and late Victorian.

Parry Mansion is open May, June, October and November on Fridays and Saturdays from 11 a.m. to 4 p.m. and Sundays from 2 to 5 p.m.; from July through September, open Wednesdays through Saturdays from 11 a.m. to 4 p.m. and Sundays from 2 to 5 p.m. Adults $1.

6 **Parry Barn**, Playhouse Plaza on Main Street. Local painting, arts and crafts vary widely in quality. Some of the best is displayed in this building maintained by the New Hope Historical Society.

Open Mondays through Saturdays 11 a.m. to 5 p.m., Sundays 1 to 5 p.m.; free.

7 **Bucks County Playhouse**, South Main Street. In a remodeled late 18th century gristmill on the Delaware River is located one of the nation's earliest and most famous summer theaters. The playhouse recently went through a financial crisis, closed, and was rescued by a group of Bucks County residents and other interested people. Now reopened, it presents a variety of entertainment in the spring and fall (concerts, Shakespeare, rock opera, showings of old films); in summer the theater is leased to a New York equity company which puts on mostly Broadway favorites.

For schedules, call 862-2041.

8 **Logan Inn**, 10 West Ferry Street. This old inn, part of which dates from 1727, has had a colorful history with numerous name changes. The current one is related to James Logan, William Penn's secretary who was instrumental in laying out the township in which New Hope is located.

Logan became such a good friend to the local Lenni-Lenape Indians that a ceremonial name-exchanging ceremony was held between him and a redskin chief named "Wingohopking". The latter, having become "Chief Logan", made an impassioned speech of brotherhood under a tree on the premises of the inn. It is for him that the inn was later renamed, rather than the original Logan — a lovely tribute to a friendship that, sadly, was sullied by Penn's own son Thomas. (He was responsible for the notorious "Walking Purchase" in which Indians were cheated out of thousands of acres of prime lands.)

George Washington is said to have visited Logan Inn on at least five occasions, and later guests have included the Raniers of Monaco.

A Word for Antique Buffs

For those who are interested in antiques, the towns along State Route 179 and U.S. 202 west toward Doylestown offer an abundance of buys from the truly unusual to the frankly phony. Among the quality stores are the Pink House on Ferry Street in New Hope (18th and 19th century French and English furniture, porcelain and American quilts); Joseph Stanley, Route 179 (17th, 18th and early 19th century English furniture, porcelain and Delft); Rowland's on U.S. 202 in Buckingham, south of New Hope (a large stock of rareties including pottery and porcelain); and Ronley at Limeport, three miles north of New Hope on State 32 (unusual lamps). On Aquetong Road in New Hope is the workshop of the nationally known Japanese cabinetmaker, George Nakashima, and on Route 202 is Peddler's Village in Lahaska, offering shoppers everything from gourmet cookware to houseplants, clogs to train lanterns.

WHILE YOU'RE THERE . . .

Bucks County's 616 square miles have some of the finest old stone houses still remaining from colonial days and 13 picturesque covered bridges. The views in the upper section of surging hills, rock upheavals, plummeting waterfalls and 500 foot high palisades are exhilarating. One way to see the unspoiled areas is by hiking; you can walk along the romantic towpath that stretches between river and canal all the way from Bristol to Easton 50 miles away. Cyclists have a 40 mile bike path linking nine state and county parks. If you're less athletic, the drive upriver from New Hope is lovely, with hardly a roadside stand or signboard all the way to Easton. In its parallel course with the river the Delaware Canal appears and disappears at your side; stop along the way for a picnic.

The Bucks County Historical – Tourist Commission located in lower Bucks has put out an excellent brochure entitled "Highways of History" which has three separate tours of the county with descriptions of over 100 sites of historic interest. Among these are several dating from Revolutionary times. Stop in or write for this brochure if you can plan a longer stay in this locale. Address is One Oxford Valley, Suite 410, Langhorne, Pa. 19047.

The area also offers many places of contemporary interest, such as the home of novelist Pearl Buck, located in Dublin. Only recently opened to the public, it contains a large number of art objects from her home in China and the desk at which she wrote <u>The Good Earth</u>. Children particularly enjoy "Ringing Rocks" in Bucks County Park, 3½ acres of trap rock which produce bell-like sounds when hit by a hammer.

Finally, of course, there is Bucks County dining. The area is justifiably renowned for its many fine restaurants — some of them located along the river, many rich in history; often they offer overnight accommodations as well. Space limitations prevent THE GUIDE from a complete listing, but here is a sampling to whet your appetite. Be sure to make reservations and don't go on a Saturday evening in summer if you can help it; dining will not be leisurely then nor the food at its best.

Chez Odette on River Road in New Hope is a French auberge run by a Martinique lady whose musical comedy background includes the role of Bloody Mary in <u>South Pacific</u>. River's Edge, across the Delaware in Lambertville, is a one-time grist mill; the restaurant overlooks a patio where flowers bloom in abundance and partridges and pheasants roam freely. Lambertville House was established in 1812; General U.S. Grant and President Andrew Johnson slept here even if Washington didn't.

If you wish to spend your evening in Doylestown, try Conti's Cross Keys Inn; the old section on Easton Road looks much as it did 200 years ago. Also on Easton Road is The Water Wheel Restaurant, once a grist mill which supplied corn for Washington's troops during the Revolution. Nearer to Philadelphia at Newton is Temperance House. When this structure was built in 1772 it was a tavern and schoolhouse in one. A few decades later the citizens turned teetotalers; hence its name. Today, however, imbibing is once again the practice.

If your travels have taken you upriver, you might go to Lumberville whose ancient stone and wood houses are among Bucks County's most picturesque. The Black Bass Inn is particularly well known; it started out over 200 years ago as a resting spot for river travelers. Inland and further north is the Pipersville Inn in the town of that name. The present structure was built in 1894 on the ashes of Piper's Tavern where Benjamin Franklin, General Anthony Wayne, and the Marquis de Lafayette once dined.

Bucks County Covered Bridge

Black Bass Hotel, Route 32, Lumberville, Pennsylvania, first opened its doors in 1745. European Country Inn atmosphere.

Monday to Saturday: Lunch 12:00 to 2:30; Dinner 5:30 to 10:00. Sunday Dinner 1:00 to 8:00. (215) 297-5770.

Bucks County Vineyards and Winery. Located on U.S. Route 202 (three miles west of New Hope).

Open Monday through Saturday 11:00 a.m. to 6:00 p.m. Closed Sundays. Bus groups must reserve. R.D. 1, New Hope Pennsylvania 18938 (215) 794-7449.

Logan Inn, Ferry Street, New Hope, Pennsylvania, is New Hope's oldest building. Since 1727 it has provided the traveler with fine food, drink, and lodging. The same pre-Revolutionary Country Inn warmth and hospitality exists today.

Open 11:30 a.m. to 2:00 a.m. (215) 862-5134.

The Golden Door Gallery in historic Parry Barn at New Hope is an intriguing stop for the art "buff" and collector. A particularly fine selection of paintings, graphics and sculpture.

Peddler's Village, Lahaska. There are those who say "if you don't do another thing in Bucks County, do Peddler's Village." It's a whole new world of shopping in an old world setting. Unusual things to wear, to use in your home, to give as gifts.

Forty-two shops open 10:00 to 5:00 daily, Friday until 9:00 p.m., all year round. Most shops also open Sundays.

New Hope and Ivyland R.R. Station at New Hope

EXCURSION 7

Batsto·Atlantic City Cape May·Lewes

There is hardly a more invigorating tonic than the ocean — especially for the foot-weary, fact-filled Bicentennial traveler. This excursion takes you across Pennsylvania's eastern border to a Revolutionary ironmaking center in New Jersey and then to two popular shore resorts, Atlantic City and Cape May. Finally we proceed by ferry to the southern tip of Delaware where, at Lewes, one of our nation's first settlements was established.

With an overnight stay in Atlantic City, you can see the main points of Cape May and Lewes on your second day, returning to Philadelphia the third. Sun worshippers and boardwalk pacers probably will want to spend longer. Summertime is, of course, the most popular season for the seashore because of the swimming, but the other seasons can be equally — if not more — delightful, thanks to greatly increased elbow room.

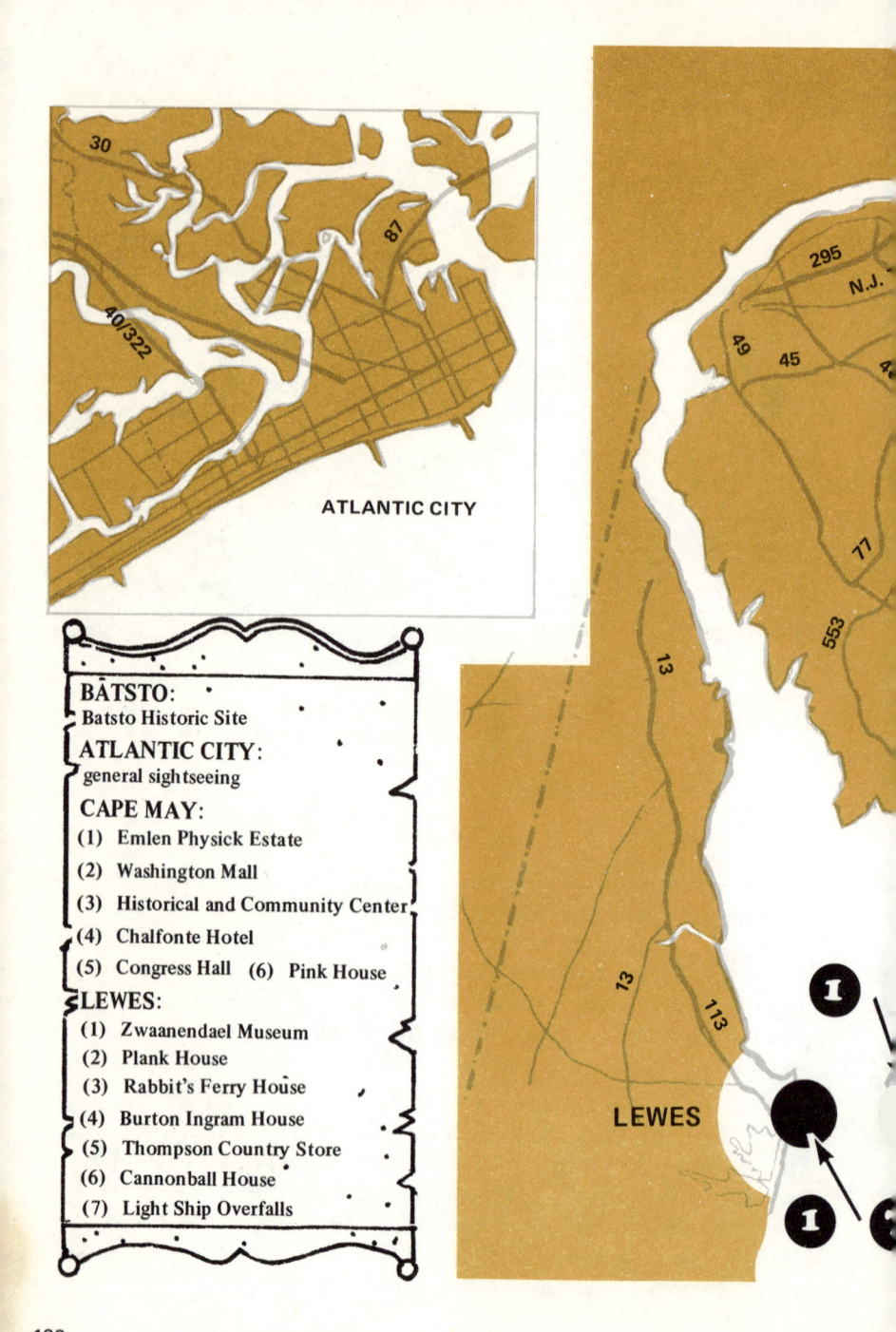

ATLANTIC CITY

BATSTO:
Batsto Historic Site

ATLANTIC CITY:
general sightseeing

CAPE MAY:
(1) Emlen Physick Estate
(2) Washington Mall
(3) Historical and Community Center
(4) Chalfonte Hotel
(5) Congress Hall (6) Pink House

LEWES:
(1) Zwaanendael Museum
(2) Plank House
(3) Rabbit's Ferry House
(4) Burton Ingram House
(5) Thompson Country Store
(6) Cannonball House
(7) Light Ship Overfalls

LEWES

Batsto, Atlantic City, Cape May & Lewes
HISTORIC LOCATION MAP

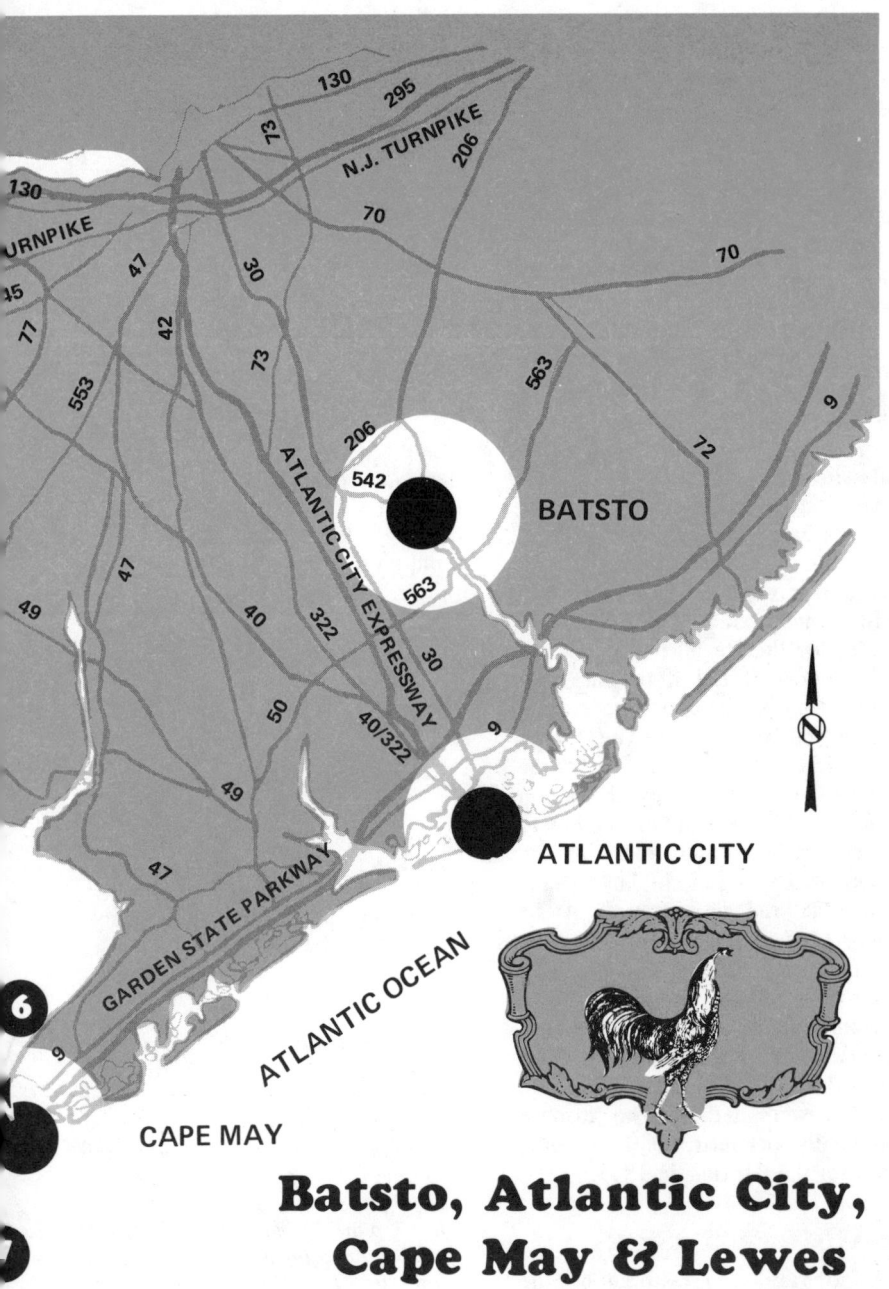

BATSTO: Iron for The Revolution...

In 1766 an iron works, the Batsto Furnace, was erected by Charles Read, distinguished lawyer and Supreme Court Justice. It was one of a chain of four southern New Jersey ironworks. Four years later, Batsto (the word means "steam bath" in the Dutch and Scandinavian tongues) was acquired by Colonel John Cox of Philadelphia, an ardent patriot. Under his direction the furnace cast cannon and cannon balls for the Revolutionary Army. So important did it become that the men working here were exempt from military service. The British hoped to burn Batsto but were prevented from this by the legion under Polish general Pulaski. Batsto also furnished munitions for the War of 1812 and, in later years, manufactured glass as well. At its height it was a community of nearly one thousand people. Among the ironworks' products was a fence around Philadelphia's Independence Square and the cylinder for John Fitch's fourth steamboat. With time and newer methods the furnace gradually declined, its fires going out for the last time in 1848.

BATSTO EXCURSION

Purchased and restored by the state of New Jersey, Batsto Historic Site is located on R.D. 1 in Hammonton, New Jersey. The Wharton Forest which surrounds it comprises almost 100,000 acres with swimming, camping, picnic and cooking facilities, fishing, a children's playground, and three rivers for canoeing.

From Philadelphia, take U.S. Route 30 across the Benjamin Franklin bridge, go south to New Jersey's Route 542 (Hammonton) and seven miles east on 542.

You can walk the grounds at Batsto free of charge, but the buildings are open to visitors only when accompanied by a guide. There are almost 30 points of interest, including the ironmaster's mansion, ice house, village store, grist mill, mule barn, blacksmith shop, pig slaughter house, water tower, carriage house, threshing barn, sawmill, spy house, workers' cottages and church burial grounds.

Open from 10 a.m. to 6 p.m. daily from Memorial Day to Labor Day; the balance of the year, open weekdays 11 a.m. to 5 p.m. and on Saturdays, Sundays and holidays as follows: 11 a.m. to 6 p.m. during Daylight Savings Time and 11 a.m. to 5 p.m. Standard Time. Guide service including admission fee is $1 for adults 18 and up, 25¢ those 6 to 17, under 6 free.

ATLANTIC CITY: Carnival Town U.S.A.

Atlantic City is a slice of Americana, a glittering monument to man's ceaseless search for amusement.

Geography has played a vital part in its success. The coastal curve shields it from devastating northeast storms and the Gulf Stream comes near enough to temper its winter climate. Before the mid 1800s, however, Atlantic City was undiscovered, an isolated island known as Absecon. When the potential of its mild climate and fine sandy beach was realized, a railroad was constructed from Camden and the city laid out.

The boardwalk, that five-mile long, 60 foot wide steel and concrete construction overlaid with pine planking, was the joint conception in 1870 of a local hotel man and a train conductor. The next milestone was the invention of a rolling chair along the boardwalk. First intended for invalids, it then was adopted by sedentary tourists; man-pushed chairs of the past have been replaced by propane-powered ones. In 1895 the picture postcard emerged on the scene. Introduced by a resident who had picked up the idea in Germany, these became a local, then a national, fad. At this time also, the manufacture of salt water taffy developed into a thriving industry. (This confection — children's delight and dentist's nightmare — has nothing to do with salt water.) Atlantic City showmanship achieved its height with the creation of the amusement pier, the first in 1882 and four others following it. These structures, whose spindly legs extend well into the Atlantic surf, offer a mind-boggling number of attractions, including vaudeville shows, ferris wheels, chambers of horrors, art centers, name bands, miniature golf, movie houses, water sports, concerts, cafes and aquariums.

Lucy the Elephant soon emerged on the scene; made of a million pieces of heavy wood and 65 feet high, she was placed in nearby Margate City where she still stands. Never a place to do things on a small scale, Atlantic City erected a Convention Hall and Municipal Auditorium on the boardwalk between Georgia and Mississippi Avenues. Said to be the largest hall of its kind in the world, it seats 41,000 and in winter becomes an ice-skating rink, football gridiron and steeplechase course. Today, Atlantic City's biggest claim to national attention is probably that four-day extravaganza in early September when Burt Parks and company come out on stage with tearful eyes to sing that hymn to beauty: "Here she comes, Miss America."

ATLANTIC CITY EXCURSION

THE GUIDE does not list specific sites in Atlantic City because it is the sea and sun that are its specialties rather than its history.

Walking the boardwalk is certainly as delightful as any of the man-made amusements invented by Atlantic City to tempt you — and it's free. There are benches all along its length if you want to rest; some face the boardwalk for uninterrupted people-watching (a favorite Atlantic City pastime) and others face the sand and sea. During off-hours — late at night and in the early morning when the hot dog stands and pizza parlors are closed — the sound and scent of the ocean reach you unhindered. Bicycle riders are in their element from 6 to 10 a.m. every morning when, without hindrance of traffic lights, they are free to peddle the length of the boardwalk.

As you walk or ride, you'll see bingo games, shooting galleries, auctions, palmreading establishments, frozen custard stands, and shops that sell everything from Chinese Ming vases to New York ready-to-wear. Some of the most elegant dress shops are located in the first floors of the old hotels, most of them rundown now but still with hints of their onetime opulence.

Beaches are open from Memorial Day to October 15; you can rent cabanas, beach chairs and umbrellas, or charter a fishing boat. Some 16 million visitors come to Atlantic City each year, and in summer you'll find it hard to stake out a patch of beach. (Nearby Ventnor, Margate and Longport are a bit quieter.) After Labor Day crowds are less of a problem, with the exception of big convention gatherings, the Easter Sunday parade, and, of course, the Miss America pageant. During the winter Atlantic City caters to elderly visitors who come here for their health, as well as to business and professional people taking off-season vacations.

The invigorating climate will no doubt enhance your appetite. Seafood restaurants are many and good, ranging from the simple decor of Dock's Oyster House to the elegance of Knife and Fork Inn.

The amusement piers are: Steel, Garden, Central, Steeplechase, and Million Dollar. By the way, if the street names seem familiar to you, it may be because you recognize them from the game "Monopoly".

Atlantic City Racetrack is located 14 miles northwest of town at the junction of Black Horse Pike and U.S. 40 in McKee City. There is harness racing in June - July and thoroughbred racing in August - October.

Jitney service within the city makes transportation easy. If you wish to take the bus to and from Philadelphia, New Jersey Transit has direct service. From Batsto by car, go east on Route 542 until it connects with Route 9, then go south on Route 9 to Atlantic City.

Fun at Atlantic City

CAPE MAY:
Farewell Victoriana...

The Victorian town that saw Presidents Lincoln, Pierce, Grant, Buchanan and Harrison dabbling their toes in its salty surf first came to notice in 1801, when the local postmaster advertised in a Philadelphia paper. "The subscriber," he wrote, "has prepared himself for entertaining company who use sea bathing, and he is accommodated with extensive house room, with fish, oysters and crabs and good liquour." In reality, according to one visitor, the accommodations consisted of one large room, partitioned off with sheets into two rooms at night, men sleeping on one side and women on the other. The first guests carried old clothes in their carpetbags to wear as bathing suits. Mixed bathing, though permitted, was carefully chaperoned.

These primitive conditions were rectified, and it was not many years before the Cape (named after Cornelius Jacobsen Mey who sailed past it in 1623) had become a favorite watering place for the rich, the powerful, the elite. On spacious verandas of massive, gingerbread-trimmed hotels they sat and rocked, engaging in small talk — and in talk of national import. Incidentally, it was here that the young Henry Ford lost a beach race in 1903, having to sell his car for railroad fare back to Detroit.

This glory lasted for about a hundred years. Then, gradually, the 20th century began to encroach on the dean of New Jersey's shore resorts. Next to the sedately genteel rooming houses and the time-honored hotels arose newer, flimsier structures. The honky-tonk atmosphere of nearby resorts infiltrated the quiet, and society began to favor more exclusive spots. Victorian splendor has not by any means left town, however, Cape May's residents recognize — both with a sense of nostalgia and an eye to economics — that it is precisely this old-time flavor which gives the town its special charm. Particularly now, there is a nationwide urge to relive our romantic, gracious past — a past exemplified by Cape May. Many visitors actually prefer to stay in the older hotels with the fewer conveniences. They prefer to shop in the pseudo-Victorian stores instead of the huge complexes. Indeed, it seems as if America has a new need of Cape May which may help to save its treasures of history.

CAPE MAY EXCURSION

From Atlantic City take the Garden State Parkway south directly into Cape May, where the Atlantic Ocean meets Delaware Bay. (On the way there are 14 shore resorts; located on narrow islands, these are strung together like beads.)

Cape May has the largest concentration of Victorian structures in the nation. The old area of town has been declared a Registered Historic Landmark, and new construction there is subject to stringent regulations as to style. If you walk along Beach Drive, you'll see rows of rambling three and four story frame hotels. They are especially treasured because others of the old landmarks have been razed, due largely to the increasing cost of fire insurance. Note the diversity of the architecture — free improvisations on the Greek, Gothic, Renaissance, Queen Anne, Italianate — and the exquisitely detailed porches. Some of the private homes feature raised platforms on the roofs; on these "widows' walks" once stood the wives of whalers, hoping — sometimes in vain — for the return of the ships carrying their men. And if you think rooming houses are by definition modest structures, take a look at the impressive Victorian Mansion on Columbia Street. Tours of some of the Victorian houses are given one day in spring, summer and fall. Call the Cape May County Art League at 884-8628 for information.

While enjoying the beach and ocean, you'll probably want to try your luck at finding a "Cape May diamond". These semi-precious stones, popular in jewelry, are a curious feature of the area. Usually colorless or varying shades of yellow, they range from pea- to walnut-size and are composed of almost pure quartz which has been ground by thousands or even millions of years of weathering and abrasion by the sand.

Among Cape May's Victoriana, here are a few sites you should not miss:

1 **Emlen Physick Estate**, 1048 Washington Street. Emlen Physick, a grandson of the "father of American surgery" and himself a physician, lived in this showplace with elaborate English-style garden. Built in 1878, the estate was saved recently from extinction and extensively restored by the Mid Atlantic Center for the Arts. Note the massive chimney and the textured leather wall coverings of this 16-room house.

Open summer months from 10 a.m. to 1 p.m. Tuesdays and Thursdays, 10 a.m. to 4 p.m. Wednesdays and Fridays, 1 to 4 p.m. Saturdays; closed Sundays, Mondays, rest of year. $1.00. Hours subject to change.

Housed in the carriage house of the estate is the Cape May County Art League (its address is 1050 Washington Street). This first county art league in the nation (1929) has excellent exhibits and classes in oil, water color, pottery, photography, weaving, silk screen, and in subjects as varied as puppetry and dog obedience training.

Open from 10 a.m. to 5 p.m. Tuesdays through Sundays in summer, and from 1 to 5 p.m. Wednesdays through Sundays in other seasons; closed January. Free.

2 **Washington Mall**, Washington Street. Though some of the shops in this three-block area have a pseudo-gingerbread look, they provide an enjoyable area for browsing and souvenir hunting. For a bit of lunch, stop at the gourmet delicatessen. Constructed in 1971, Washington Mall is closed to cars for part of its length. You can pick up a "jeep tour" of Cape May here.

3 Historical and Community Center, 407 Lafayette Street between Bank and Jackson. Originally a church (Presbyterian), then a community center, this lovely edifice was built in 1853. The onion-shaped dome reveals a strong Byzantine influence. Summer theater performances are given here; check the Chamber of Commerce for details.

4 Chalfonte Hotel, Howard Street off Beach Drive. This fine old hotel, erected in 1876, prides itself on generations of ownership by one family. Guests love the wide porch, the maze of narrow corridors within, the home-baked spoonbread. The cook has been in the kitchen for 50 years and her daughter for 25; a third generation is being trained to follow in their footsteps.

The Chalfonte is open from June until the week after Labor Day, though you can visit it until the end of September.

5 Congress Hall, Beach Drive and Perry Street. An inn since 1816, this venerable structure has been host to more than one vacationing president. The massive architecture and imposing white columns are offset by an air of delicacy, of architectural lightness in the trimmings.

Open in summer.

6 Pink House, 33 Perry Street. One of the former owners of this 1878 house decided to show off its detail work by painting it a luscious shade of pink. You can't see the interior except during the house tours, but the first floor features an antique shop.

WHILE YOU'RE THERE...

If you have the time to continue around the tip of southern New Jersey, you'll find additional historical sites in Cape May Point, such as the Atlantus, an experimental ship made of concrete during World War I, and the British Sloop of War Martin, wreckage of a vessel that blockaded Delaware Bay in the War of 1812. In the town of Cape May Court House there is the Jonathon Hand Building, home of a captain in the War of 1812, the Historical Museum of Cape May County which has ship models, whaling tools, etc., and another fine old home, the Alfred Cooper House.

The Pink House

DELAWARE: "Fighting Blue Hen's Chickens"

Known to Dutch traders since it was discovered by Henry Hudson in 1609, the Delaware Bay was an area coveted by many, including the original Indian settlers, the Dutch, Swedes and English. The land eventually came under English domination, and a favor owed the Penn family brought it into the possession of William Penn. He first set foot in the New World at the Delaware town of New Castle in 1682. Delaware remained part of Pennsylvania as its so-called "Lower Counties", but tensions developed and it was granted its own assembly. The area achieved complete sovereignty at the outbreak of the Revolution.

Delaware counts among its citizens Caesar Rodney of the midnight ride and John Dickinson whose magnificent writings earned him the title, "Penman of the Revolution". The tiny area entered the struggle for independence wholeheartedly, with the burning of the portrait of King George III on Dover's The Green at a turtle soup fest. It also furnished troops to the war — the most fierce and professional of the Continental Army — who became known as the "Fighting Blue Hen's Chicken". (This name derived from a strain of fighting cock — the blue hen, now the state bird — bred here and carried by the troops.) There was only one confrontation on Delaware soil, at Cooch's Bridge, which was more a skirmish than an actual battle, serving to delay the British march on Philadelphia. However, British war vessels menaced the coastline during these Revolutionary years, and there were spirited battles between the Royal Navy and the infant American fleet. After occupying Philadelphia, the British entered and captured Wilmington in September 1777.

In 1787 the U.S. Constitution was ratified in Dover, making Delaware the first state in the Union. Centered at the crossroads of the eastern seaboard, Delaware has become a mercantile giant. This industrial destiny was sealed as early as 1802 when French émigré E.I. du Pont started black powder mills on the Brandywine.

LEWES: Phantom Ships and Sunken Treasure

The first settlement on Delaware soil was that of the Dutch in 1631. Thirty-three men, chiefly from the town of Hoorn, came to the mouth of Delaware Bay, establishing a whaling station and settlement they called Zwaanendael ("Valley of the Swans"). On land purchased from the Indians they erected a dwelling, storehouse and cookhouse, all surrounded by a palisade. Unfortunately, they were killed by Indians and the settlement destroyed in the "Tin Pipe Massacre" of 1632. The Dutch, however, later became the predominant force in the area for about nine years.

The town which now stands at Delaware's southern tip, Lewes (pronounced Lewis), is one of narrow streets and aged cypress-shingled homes. Treacherous sand dunes outside the harbor have claimed their share of ships, and stories of sunken treasure abound — including a bargain made here with pirate Captain Kidd.

The town, established by the British under the direction of William Penn, did valiant service throughout the Revolution, bearing the brunt of the menace to shore and shipping from British vessels and privateers in the bay. During the War of 1812 the town survived British bombardment through a clever scheme. First they fooled the redcoats as to their number (in actuality only about 500) and then collected British cannonballs to return enemy fire.

LEWES EXCURSION

The sole connection between the southern terminus of Garden State Parkway and the state of Delaware is by a lovely **40 minute ferry trip between Cape May and Lewes. The ferry leaves and returns frequently on a daily basis and costs $6.50 for both car and driver, plus $2 for each passenger over 6. For the schedule call 886-2718 in Cape May.**

Should you wish to see Lewes' sites by bus rather than on your own, tours leave from Angler's Motel daily from June to September. Call 645-8864 for schedule and price.

And after your sightseeing, take some time, if you can, for swimming, boating or fishing in the bay and ocean. Cape Henlopen State Park, just east of Lewes, is an ideal setting for camping and picnicking.

1 Zwaanendael Museum, intersection of Kings Highway and Savannah Road. In 1931 the state of Delaware celebrated the 300th anniversary of the founding of the first Dutch settlement on Delaware soil. To commemorate this event, the state erected the richly ornamented Zwaanendael Museum, a small-scale adaptation of a wing of the ancient Town Hall in Hoorn, Holland. Inside the Dutch Renaissance building you'll see a model of the 1631 settlement, artifacts from 17th century Hoorn, fragments of pottery from Indian and colonial sites near Lewes, and a set of stoneware given by a Revolutionary War hero and governor of Delaware to his daughter on her marriage to a future governor of the state. The maritime and military history of Lewes is beautifully covered in this museum. One exhibit deals with the bombardment of Lewes by the British during the War of 1812.

Open Tuesdays - Saturdays, 10 a.m. to 5 p.m., Sundays 1 to 5 p.m., closed Mondays and legal holidays. Free.

Zwaandael Museum

The Lewes Historical Society is an active organization, responsible for the restoration and maintenance of several sites. A number of them are clustered at 3d and Shipcarpenter Streets (#s 2-5) and two others are located near the canal at 1812 Memorial Park (#s 6-7).

All can be seen for a combined admission price of $2.50 (50¢ if seen singly), from June 15 to Labor Day, Tuesdays through Saturdays, 10 a.m. to 5 p.m.

2 **Plank House.** Built in 1700 or earlier, this is the oldest building in the area and was probably used as a dwelling.

3 **Rabbit's Ferry House.** The small farmhouse was built in the early 18th century with additions made later.

4 **Burton Ingram House.** Built c. 1800, this is typical of architecture in this fishing village.

5 **Thompson Country Store.** An oldtime country store, it sells many items, proceeds of which go toward Historical Society projects.

6 **Cannonball House,** now known as Lewes Marine Museum. This is the last remaining Lewes house to bear the scars of British attack in the War of 1812. It contains a number of marine artifacts and has a landscaped garden.

7 **Light Ship Overfalls.** In service until recently, this 108 foot ship, built in 1939, originally guided ships into Boston Harbor.

WHILE YOU'RE THERE ...

Instead of retracing your steps back through the New Jersey area, you could with sufficient time drive northward in Delaware, returning full circle to Philadelphia. Dover, the state capital since 1777, was laid out around its lovely Green according to instructions of William Penn. Visit the Hall of Records, housing such documents as the Royal Charter granted by King Charles II to James Duke of York for the Delaware territory. Unfortunately, the estate of Caesar Rodney burned down, but you can see his burial place at the town's Christ Church. Near Dover is the childhood home of John Dickinson.

The town of Odessa has two handsomely furnished colonial homes open to the public: the Corbit-Sharp House and the Wilson Warner House. There are, too, numerous privately owned 18th and 19th century homes. Continuing northward, New Castle, the state's colonial capital, appears with its old homes and cobblestone streets much as it did 200 years ago. Visit the Old Court (State) House, now a museum, the Amstel House Museum, and Old Dutch House (considered to be the oldest dwelling in Delaware).

Near the town of Newark is Cooch's Bridge where Delaware's one Revolutionary confrontation took place. A new observation tower on Iron Hill near Washington's lookout offers an excellent view of the entire area from Elkton, where the British landed, to Wilmington. Here, at the Cooch House, the Stars and Stripes supposedly was first unfurled in land battle. Finally we reach Wilmington which bears many signs of its Swedish, Dutch and British heritage, and has been a center of industry for all its history. You'll enjoy seeing Old Swedes Church, consecrated in 1699. Rodney Square where the Delaware leader's famous ride is immortalized in a statue of horse and rider, and Fort Christina, site of the first permanent European settlement in Delaware. Slightly to the north of Wilmington are the excellent museums discussed in Excursion 4: Winterthur, Hagley and the Natural History Museum.

The state's rich history is, in truth, all out of proportion to its small size, and you will find a stay here well worth your while. There are fine areas of recreation and beauty. For swimming, try Rehoboth, Silver Lake or Dewey Beach. Further information is available from the Delaware State Visitors Service at 45 The Green, Dover.

Cooch's Bridge Battle Monument

Historic Insight...

Caesar Rodney Monument

A Patriot's Choice

July 2, 1776: It was late afternoon of a steaming, rainy day. A thin, pale man arrived in boots and spurs as the members of the Second Continental Congress assembled in the ground floor meeting room of Philadelphia's State House to take the vote regarding independence. He was a strange man in appearance, this Caesar Rodney of Dover, Delaware. John Adams once called him "the oddest looking man in the world... his face is not bigger than a large apple." Now, mud-spattered and soaking wet, a green silk handkerchief covering the lower part of his face, Rodney hardly looked to be the man who would decide a

114

people's future. But his role was just that crucial.

Caesar Rodney was a member of the Congress from Delaware, at that time considered to be the "Lower Counties" of Pennsylvania though it had its own assembly. Involved at home in the affairs of his colony, he had not been present at the beginning of the proceedings here in Philadelphia. However, when the Delaware representatives were seen to be divided in their sympathies during the preliminary vote, a messenger had been dispatched requesting Rodney's presence — the hope being that he would vote in favor of independence, thus breaking the deadlock. A unanimous decision, felt Jefferson and others, was necessary if the cause was not to be weakened. Aside from Delaware, those other states which opposed or were indifferent to independence (South Carolina, New York and Pennsylvania) were expected to join the majority vote.

Rodney had started out at midnight. He rode all night, amidst thunder and lightning, on the 75 mile stretch between Dover and Philadelphia. The journey was not an easy one, for he suffered from a dangerous malady: cancer of the face. It was to hide this disfigurement that he wore a face handkerchief. Only in England, Rodney had been told, might a cure be effected. By voting for independence and against England, he would forever deny himself that opportunity for British medical help.

But Rodney's convictions were stronger than his fears. When it came his turn to vote in Philadelphia, he rose and said: "As I believe the voice of my constituents, of all sensible and honest men, is in favor of independence and my own judgment concurs with them, I vote for independence." The vote being unanimous, our people's 169-year old tie with the Mother Country was severed.

The midnight ride of Caesar Rodney had not been in vain.

EXCURSION 8

Hopewell Village

Malvern Trappe Fagleysville Pottstown Boyertown Douglassville Baumstown French Creek Hopewell St. Peters

Japanese gardens, pioneer heroes, ironmaking communities and plush Victorian resorts — these are some of the ingredients of today's excursion. We cover several quaint old towns, laden with history and within ten or fifteen minutes of each other by car. This is too full a schedule for one day, so plan either to stay overnight in the area and continue sightseeing the second day, or eliminate a site here and there according to the weather and your particular interests.

SOUTHEASTERN PENNSYLVANIA: Ironmaker to a Nation

The colonial settlers in America were fortunate in having both rich natural resources and the ability to put these to good use. Recognizing that it was both costly and time-consuming to import their iron tools and household items from Europe, they decided to produce their own iron. Among the earliest of such industrial enterprises were those at Falling Creek, Virginia, and Saugus, Massachusetts. By the end of the 18th century, southeastern Pennsylvania had become the center of the nation's ironmaking industry, turning out stoves, farm machinery, all kinds of household utensils, and the necessities of war: cannon, shot and shell.

The hundreds of communities developed for this purpose consumed about one acre of trees a day for fuel, which meant they had to be located in rural areas near a supply of timber. Thus they tended to be somewhat isolated and self-sufficient, encompassing all the residents' needs. Each was presided over by an ironmaster who, in fact, often ruled with an iron fist and became quite wealthy in this trade. Characteristically he employed 50 or 60 men as vs. the one- or two-man operations typical of other businesses.

Many colonial ironmaking industries flourished until the middle 1800s when the Bessemer process, which used anthracite coal instead

Colonial Hopewell Furnace

of the more expensive charcoal, was developed, making the old coldblast charcoal-burning furnaces obsolete. Too, with the coming of railroads it became easier to move the necessary materials to the city foundries than it was to move a large work force out to the isolated old ironmaking communities. Unable to compete, the colonial ironworks ceased operation.

Today's excursion, varied though it is, has iron as its unifying theme. At Hopewell Village iron was made, at Pottsgrove Mansion an ironmaster lived in elegant style, and to this same area George Washington traveled during the Revolution's darkest days in order to have repaired the machinery of war.

117

Malvern to Saint Peters

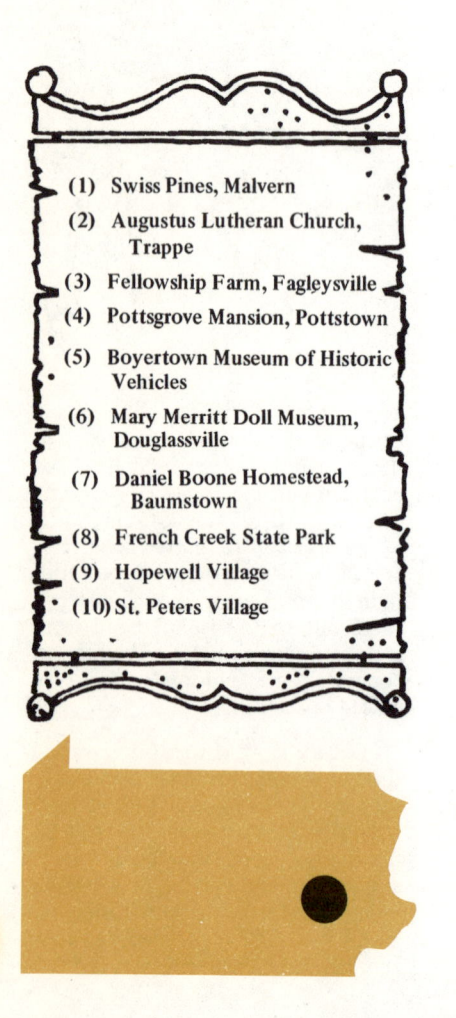

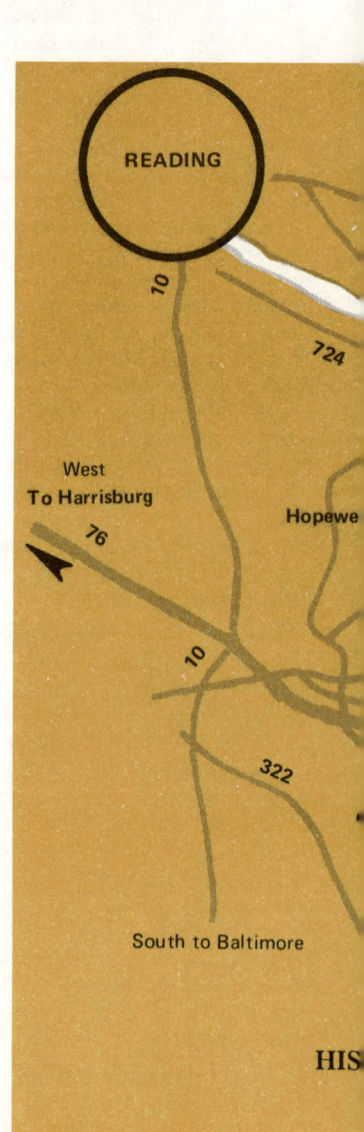

(1) Swiss Pines, Malvern
(2) Augustus Lutheran Church, Trappe
(3) Fellowship Farm, Fagleysville
(4) Pottsgrove Mansion, Pottstown
(5) Boyertown Museum of Historic Vehicles
(6) Mary Merritt Doll Museum, Douglassville
(7) Daniel Boone Homestead, Baumstown
(8) French Creek State Park
(9) Hopewell Village
(10) St. Peters Village

READING

724

West
To Harrisburg

76

10

Hopewe

322

South to Baltimore

HIS

TRAPPE FAGLEYSVILLE, POTTSTOWN, BOYERTOWN, DOUGLASSVILLE, BAUMSTOWN, FRENCH CREEK & HOPEWELL

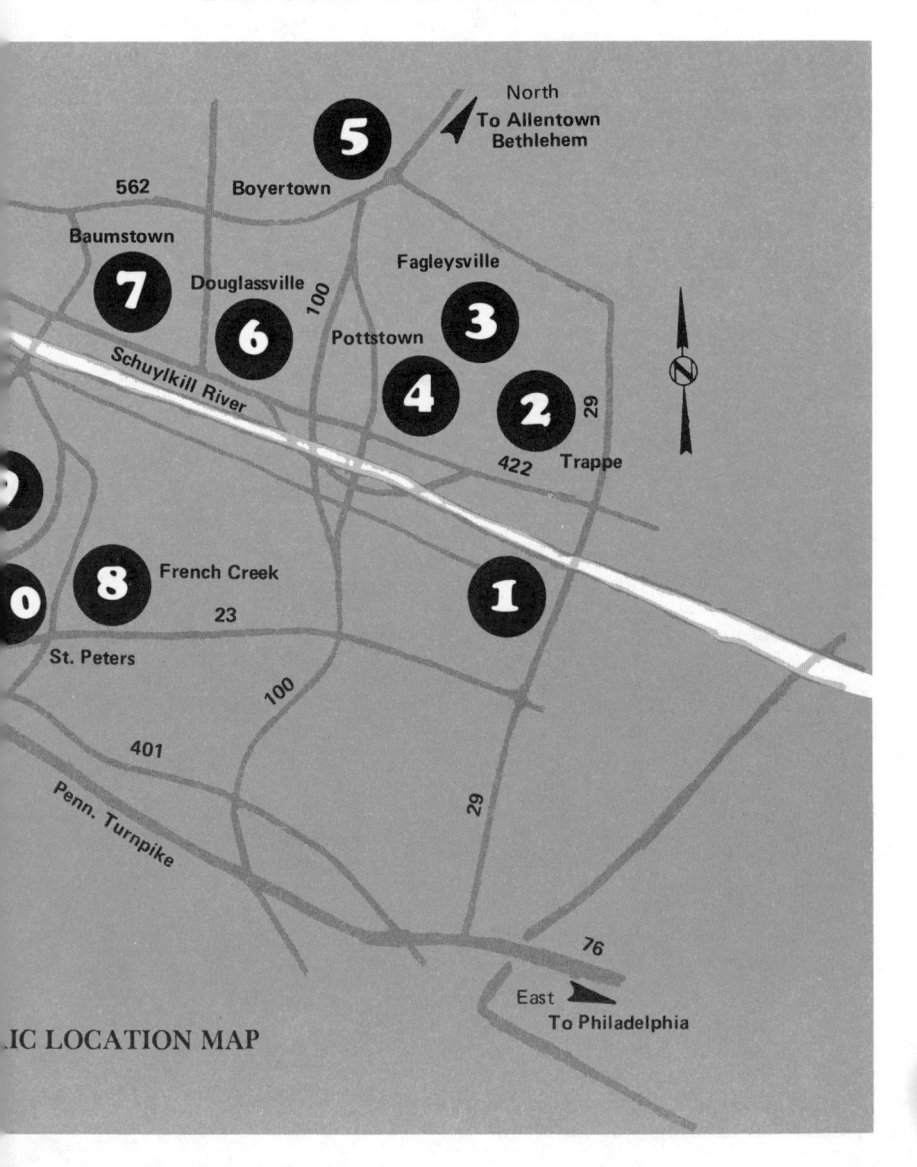

LOCATION MAP

EXCURSION 8:
MALVERN TO ST. PETERS

1 **Swiss Pines,** Charlestown Road, RD 1, Malvern (a few miles outside of Phoenixville). This first stop on today's excursion will take about a half-hour by car from center-city Philadelphia. Go on the Schuylkill Expressway to Route 202, north on 202 toward Paoli to Route 29, north on 29 to Charlestown Road and turn left here.

Swiss Pines, a 300-acre garden and wildlife sanctuary, was once the estate of wealthy druggist William H. Llewellyn. Now open to the public and associated with the Academy of Natural Sciences in Philadelphia, it is a delightful refuge. Two Japanese gardens are particularly unusual. One, the Zen, has no trees or bushes but is an abstract configuration of pebbles and large rocks explaining the cycle of life. The other, the Shukkel, is of pure white sand raked into a pattern representing Japan's natural landscape. There are also rose and rhododendron displays, a Polynesian garden, a sunken herb garden with over 130 culinary and aromatic varieties, and over 100 heaths and heathers. Every spring and fall hundreds of migrating geese and ducks join the permanent winged residents here for rest and food.

Open Mondays through Fridays, 10 a.m. to 4 p.m., Saturdays 9 a.m. to 12 noon; closed December 1 through March 15 and Sundays and holidays. Free.

2 **Augustus Lutheran Church,** 717 Main Street, Trappe. Route 29 north and left on Route 422 will take you to the town of Trappe and the Augustus Lutheran Church. Built in 1743, it is the oldest unaltered Lutheran church in America. The building was made of local stone with hand-hewn timbers and hand-forged nails, hinges and doorlatches. The old altar is still in place as are the original pews. Note the cut-out balcony railing with its fanciful heart pattern.

The fine old place of worship was founded by Dr. Heinrich Melchoir Muhlenberg, patriarch of the Lutheran Church in America, who is buried in the adjoining graveyard with his son John (Peter) beside him. It was Peter Muhlenberg who, as pastor of a church in Virginia during the Revolution, concluded his farewell sermon with the words: "There is a time for all things: a time to preach and a time to fight — and now is the time to fight!" He stepped from the pulpit, threw back his ecclesiastical robes and revealed the uniform of a Continental soldier.

Services will be held here on Sundays from June 13 to September 12, 1976, at 10:30 a.m. The building may also be open to visitors during the week and Sunday afternoons.

③ Fellowship Farm, RD 3, Sanatoga Road (near Swamp Pike), Pottstown. This 25-year old rural training center in human relations, devoted to the cause of peace, is located right on the grounds of what 200 years ago was Camp Pottsgrove. The staff at the center welcomes visitors to see its films, learn more about this locality, view the garden and longhouse which are devoted to the world of the American Indian, and study materials on the Underground Railroad.

Open Mondays through Fridays, 9 a.m. to 5 p.m.; ask about special weekend events.

A Bedroom at Pottsgrove Mansion

④ Pottsgrove Mansion, Route 422, Pottstown. Thomas Potts was a partner in the first iron furnace in Pennsylvania at Colebrookdale. Son John expanded the family's ironworks to nine furnaces and, in 1752, began to build lovely Pottsgrove Mansion. Shortly after its completion he turned his attention to establishing the first town in Montgomery County, now called Pottstown. In the tradition of the pioneer iron forge, Pottstown today has some 70 modern industries, including the fabrication of structural steel.

John Potts' Georgian-style home of sandstone with 24" thick walls drew colonial visitors from miles around to view its grandeur. Even today it offers impressive proof of the comfort and style to which some early ironmasters were accustomed. Pottsgrove is said to have been visited many times by George and Martha Washington, and local lore suggests that Martha stayed here in 1777 while her husband and his troops rested four miles away at Camp Pottsgrove.

Note the large central hallway, the overmantels, corner cupboards, cushioned window seats, beautiful Philadelphia Chippendale furniture and flower and herb garden. A very spacious house, Pottsgrove was none too big for Potts' 13 children, several of whom made the family name even more prominent during the Revolution.

Daylight saving hours, Tuesdays through Saturdays, 8:30 a.m. to 5 p.m., Sundays 1 to 5 p.m.; in winter, Tuesdays through Saturdays 9 a.m. to 4:30 p.m., Sundays 1 to 4:30 a.m.; closed Mondays and most holidays. Admission: 50¢, children under 12 free with adult. Guided tours of about 40 minutes; a wait is sometimes necessary.

⑤ Boyertown Museum of Historic Vehicles, Reading Avenue and Warwick Street, Boyertown (north of Pottstown). You'll find every kind of transportation imaginable here with emphasis on vehicles produced locally from the mid 1800s to the 1920s. Sleighs, buggies, firetrucks, Conestoga wagons, doctors' wagons, even a 1922 Daniels touring car with solid pewter radiator, are on display. At an annual event, Duryea Day (Saturday before Labor Day), there is an antique and classic auto meet.

Open Mondays through Fridays 8 a.m. to 4 p.m.; June - August also open Saturdays, Sundays, 1 to 4 p.m.; closed holidays. Free.

6 Mary Merritt Doll Museum, RD 2, Douglassville (on U.S. Route 422). This is a Lilliputian paradise of over 1500 rare and beautiful dolls made between 1725 and 1900. There are 40 miniature period rooms furnished, papered and inhabited by dolls of the appropriate time. You will also see miniature china and tea services, furnished dollhouses, and even a hospital where antique dolls are repaired and refurbished.

Open Mondays through Saturdays, 10 a.m. to 5 p.m., Sundays and holidays 11 a.m. to 5 p.m.; closed Easter, Thanksgiving, Christmas, New Year's Day. Adults $1; children 12 and under, 50¢.

(For this admission price you can also visit the Merritt Museum of the Pennsylvania Dutch just across the drive, which has old drugstore lamps, Currier and Ives prints, a replica of a Victorian garden, cigar store Indians, and Stiegel glass; same hours as Doll Museum.)

7 Daniel Boone Homestead, a mile north of Route 422 at Baumstown. No folk hero more completely captures the imagination of the American school child than Daniel Boone: frontiersman, Indian fighter, wagoner, blacksmith, hunter, surveyor. His experiences as an Indian captive, his escape in time to warn Boonesboro of an impending attack, the way he was swindled out of tracts of land he himself had cleared — these make for dramatic fare that has no need of Hollywood's embellishments. Though Daniel Boone's name is most closely associated with the Yadkin Valley of North Carolina where the family moved in 1750, this spot on the eastern frontier is where he was born to Quaker parents on November 2, 1734. Here Daniel learned to hunt, trap and shoot accurately the Pennsylvania rifle given him on his twelfth birthday.

Boone's actual birthplace was a primitive log cabin which no longer exists. In its place is a more substantial two-story house erected sometime in the 18th century. (It is possible that Boone's father built part of this house before the family's departure.) The restored building offers a vivid picture of life on the Pennsylvania frontier and has simple, crude furniture and housewares. Nearby are a blacksmith shop, stone smokehouse, barn and log cabin.

The homestead is part of a 600 acre sanctuary of the Pennsylvania Game Commission. Fishing and picnic areas are available. The community of Baumstown consists of scattered houses occupied mostly by workers employed in the steel mills across the river at Birdsboro.

Open April – October: weekdays 8:30 a.m. to 5 p.m., Sundays 1 to 5 p.m.; winter: weekdays 9 a.m. to 4:30 p.m., Sundays 1 to 4:30 p.m. Adults 50¢; children under 12 free.

8 French Creek State Park, RD 1, Elverson (a few miles south of Birdsboro). This lovely 7,000-acre area is the closest place to Philadelphia for camping. It has a clean, protected beach, fine swimming, fishing, boating, and forest cabins and campsites. You can eat a picnic meal sitting on the massive boulders right in the middle of the creek or use the grills and open fires for cooking.

The park is open all year and is free; no reservations. If you visit during the week, you'll find fewer crowds than on weekends, especially in summer.

9 Hopewell Village National Historic Site, RD 1, Elverson. The village, surrounded by French Creek State Park, is located six miles south of Birdsboro on Route 345. Founded by Mark Bird in 1770, it was a leading ironmaking community where 65 men worked, many of them living in company-owned homes. Its output through the years was impressive: over 80,000 stoves alone in 138 different patterns; these were shipped as far as Boston. Hopewell also supplied cannon and shot for the Revolution, and Bird himself joined the militia as a colonel. The ironworks existed until 1883 when it could no longer remain competitive. Fortunately, the National Park Service began a massive renovation effort in 1938, and now the village is a superb representation of what Hopewell was like from 1820 to 1840.

Allow about 90 minutes for this tour and start first at the Visitor's Center which shows a 10-minute slide presentation; taped narrations at various of the sites fill in details about life in the community. You'll see the charcoal hearth, water wheel and blast machinery, blacksmith shop, casting house, spring house, whitewashed tenant homes, sturdy ironmaster's house, barn housing the horses and mules who transported products to market, etc.

Hopewell is open daily from 9 a.m. to 5 p.m.; closed Christmas, New Year's; free.

There are special events such as demonstrations of home crafts like fireplace cooking, summertime wagon rides, and lovely programs one evening in July and one in August when all personnel are in colonial garb and the village lit by candles. For specifics, call (212) 582-8773.

10 St. Peters Village, slightly south of French Creek State Park. Since 1731 the Knauer family has held the land that comprises St. Peters Village. The town itself originated with the discovery of black granite on the west side of French Creek in the mid 1800s. To accommodate the needs of his quarry workers, Davis Knauer built homes for them, a general store, post office, bread and pretzel bakery, barber shop, cigar factory, boarding house, and even a pool room. In 1868 he started construction of the French Creek Falls Hotel with low mansard roof, dance pavillion and park, and bridges and boardwalks over French Creek Falls. The lovely setting and charm of the area were such that St. Peters became a favorite spa for Philadelphia's gentry. Knauer also built the "Sowbelly Railroad" from Phoenixville to his village, facilitating travel to this Victorian haven. Now rebuilt, the village features numerous small shops selling quilts, pottery, candles, dolls, black granite jewelry, cider, molasses, etc. Craftsmen make most of their wares right in the shops and give demonstrations of such arts as bird carving, quilling and chair caning. The hotel has been restored to its oldtime opulence and has a restaurant, an early American tavern, and a Bavarian beer garden which resounds to the sound of lively band music.

St. Peters does not portray the authentic history of the area the way Hopewell Village does, but it's fun.

Shops open daily: Tuesdays through Fridays, 10:30 a.m. to 5:30 p.m., Saturdays 11 a.m. to 6 p.m.; Sundays 12 noon to 6 p.m.; closed Mondays unless legal holiday.

Historic Insight
False Alarm at Pottsgrove

September 1777: Indian scouts for the Americans stood at two lookout points, unable to see clearly because of the endless rains that had made Camp Pottsgrove a swamp. General George Washington's army, having arrived here from defeat at the Brandywine, was battle-weary and, as usual, lacking in food and clothing. The scouts, hearing the sucking of horses' hooves in the wet mud and seeing dimly the red of uniforms, shouted out through the fog that the dreaded redcoats were coming. Had these blurred figures indeed been the British, the Americans would have been trapped. But the Indians were wrong about the color. The uniforms were, in fact, not red but maroon — the maroon of allies. Under the direction of General Casimir Pulaski, a group of superbly trained, well equipped Polish troops from Warsaw had come to the aid of the colonials. The two armies did not speak each other's language, but words were not needed for this was a reunion of brothers. Almost as an omen, the sky began to clear.

George Washington had been in this remote camp at the appropriately named Swamp Creek since September 17, having come here to plan future strategy for his bedraggled army and to have cannon repaired. But this ironmaking country was not entirely receptive to the Continentals' plight. Largely Quaker and Mennonite, many of the people were against war — any war — on religious principles, and those in favor of it were less enthusiastic in the face of recent defeats. Too, the poor summer crops would not serve their own, let alone a starving army. The women, however, seeing the desperate plight of the soldiers, took pity on them and convinced the town to come to their aid with large sacks of rye flour and the construction of an oven. The aroma of fresh-baked bread spread all over the camp, and as the loaves emerged, the men grabbed them and wolfed them down steaming. Soon the farmers began to barbeque sheep, calves and oxen for the soldiers.

With the arrival of Pulaski, Washington decided that his army could afford to continue the fight. His troops, fortified with food, rest and military reinforcements, left by the "Great Road" (later Route 422). Passing the church of Heinrich Muhlenberg, the men stopped one by one to talk to the renowned old Lutheran pastor. Many of them had known him all their lives, had been christened by him. Muhlenberg, tearful, could not answer their words of confidence, for he feared the hardships that lay ahead. And he was right. Valley Forge was soon to come."

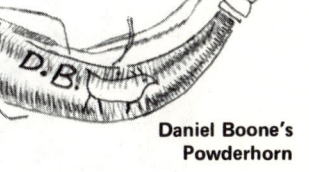

Daniel Boone's Powderhorn

Coventry Forge Inn, Route 23, Coventryville (Pottstown), would have delighted General Lafayette. Superior French cuisine in pre-Revolutionary setting. Excellent wine cellar.

Dinner, reservation only. Closed Sunday. (215) 469-6222.

St. Peters Village, 1 mile off Route 23 at Knauertown. Iron, first in the United States, was forged here for General Washington's armies. Marvelous restoration of Victorian quarry town on scenic French Creek Falls, old crafts shops, Pennsylvania's oldest winery, elegant dining, home of the "Whoopie" pie.

Open year round. (215) 469-6277.

French Creek Sheep and Wool Company. This working sheep ranch, in the rolling hills of northern Chester County, turns out just about the finest sheepskin coats in the world. The owners, Eric and Jean Flaxenburg, with their staff of Pennsylvania Dutch craftsmen, produce these quality coats in a beautiful 18th century stone barn.

This company also designs various types of sportswear which is made up in British and Irish tweeds. And while you're there, don't overlook their superb natural grease-wool sweaters which are spun from the fleece of their own Corriedale sheep.

The 18th century setting, the glorious rural environs, and the quality craftsmanship compliment each other so successfully that the results — marvelous, classicly styled sheepskin coats — are seen on the best-dressed backs everywhere (their world wide shipping list would stagger you).

How to reach **French Creek Sheep and Wool Company:** Morgantown Exit off Pennsylvania Turnpike, East on Route 23 to Route 345. Turn North, drive three miles and look for the sign.

Hours: weekdays 9:00 to 5:00. Weekends: 12 noon to 5:00. Phone (215) 286-5700.

Daniel Boone Homestead, Baumstown

EXCURSION 9
Pennsylvania Dutch Country

Lancaster Strasburg Ephrata Reading Kutztown & Allentown

What is the traveler to make of a people who shun electricity and modern attire and still use a horse and buggy for transportation? THE 1776 GUIDE introduces you to the Amish, as well as other groups among the so-called Pennsylvania Dutch who together contributed much to America's history, folk art and gastronomy. Our two-day excursion takes you into the heartland of the rich Pennsylvania Dutch farm country where you'll meet the original "plain and fancy" folk.

- (1) Strasburg Railroad
- (2) Eagle Americana Shop and Gun Museum
- (3) Dutch Wonderland
- (4) Pennsylvania Farm Museum of Landis Valley
- (5) Wheatland
- (6) Lancaster County Historical Society
- (7) Fulton Opera House
- (8) Robert Fulton Birthplace
- (9) Hans Herr House (10) Old City Hall
- (11) Evangelical Lutheran Church of the Holy Trinity (12) Rock Ford

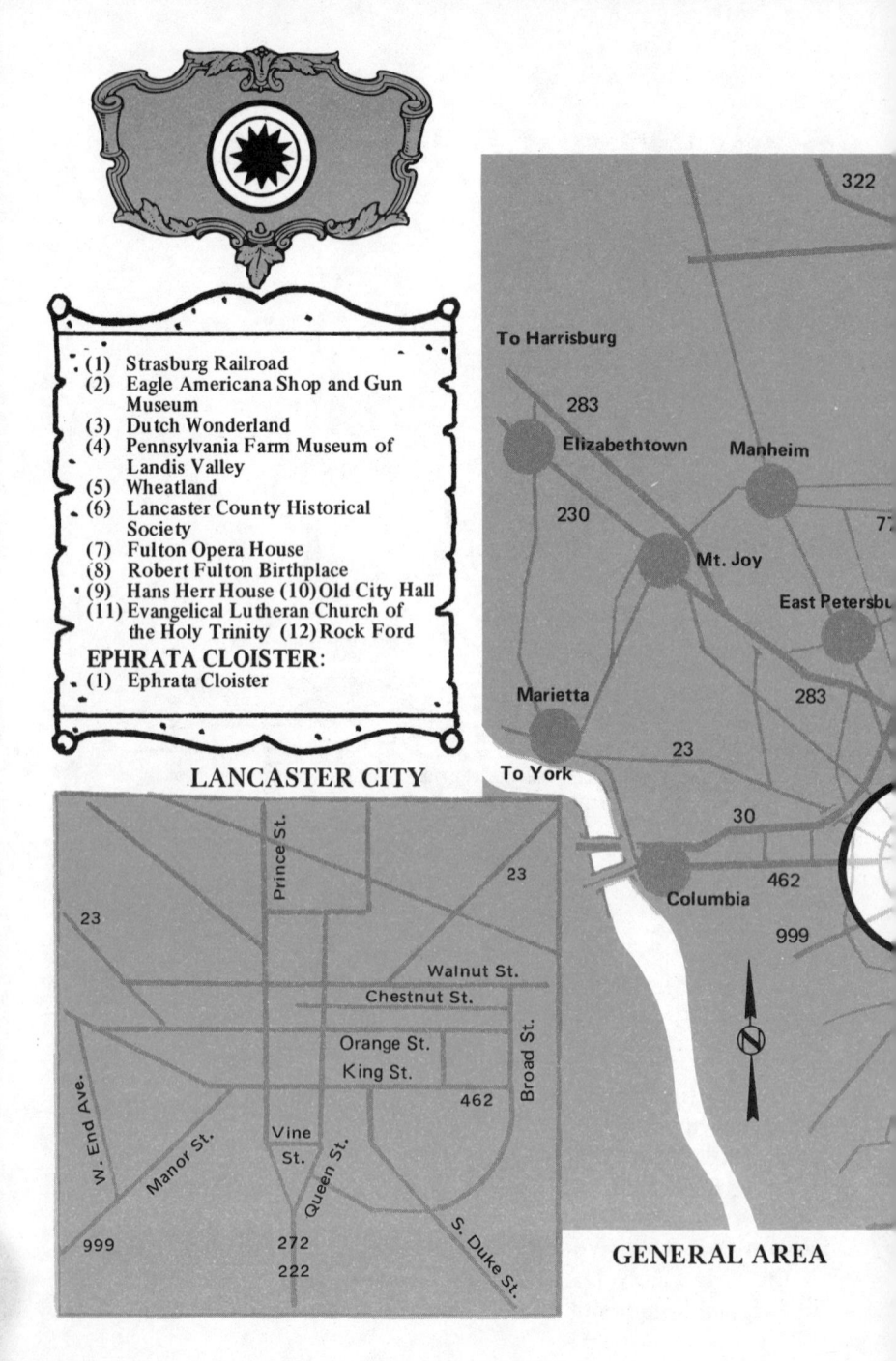

EPHRATA CLOISTER:
- (1) Ephrata Cloister

LANCASTER CITY

GENERAL AREA

PENNSYLVANIA DUTCH COUNTRY

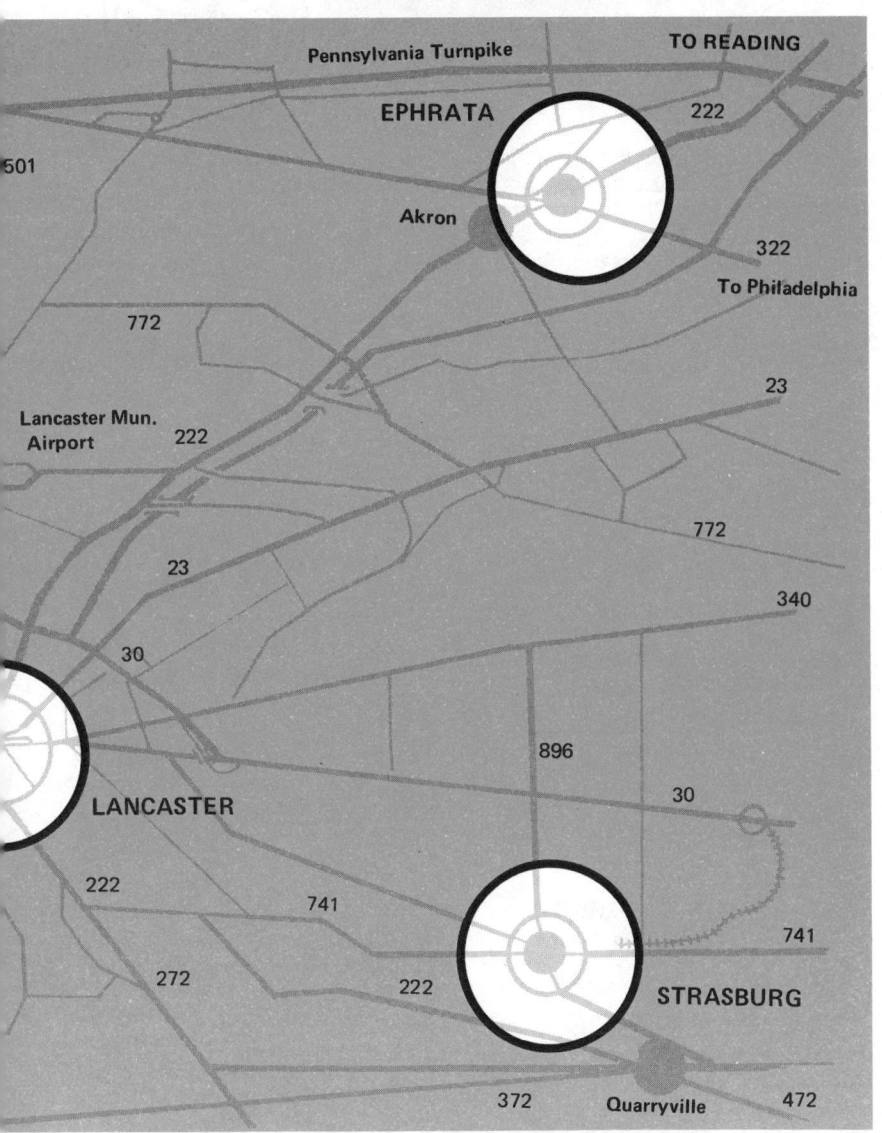

Lancaster, Strasburg & Ephrata

129

WHO ARE THE PENNSYLVANIA DUTCH?

The Pennsylvania Dutch are not Dutch, nor are they of Dutch heritage. Rather, they are descendents of various German religious sects who settled in the area around Lancaster between the late 17th and early 19th century. The incorrect nomenclature stems both from the word "Deutsch", meaning "German" (which in their dialect was "Deitsch" and sounded much like "Dutch") and from the fact that many of these people came to the colonies by way of Holland. Once here, they held tenaciously to their language, gradually taking on a good number of English words.

There are certain characteristics which can be said to be typical of the Pennsylvania Dutch. They are a thrifty, hard working, prompt, God-fearing people, a people who show great charity to each other and a pacifist attitude toward others. But there are vast differences among them. One means of division is according to the terms "plain" and "fancy" or "gay".

The plain Dutch, from the Anabaptist tradition, are mostly Mennonites and, to a smaller degree, Dunkers and Brethren. Within the vast spectrum of Mennonite thought the most conspicuous sect is the Amish. Little touched by modern America, the kindly Amish live quietly according to their religious precepts, making the land prosper with age-old methods of farming. You'll see no TV antennas, no telephone wires, no signs of electricity in their homes, nor do they wish to be photographed. Transportation is via trim, open "courting" buggies for the unmarried and dignified closed ones for families. The bearded, long haired men wear broad rimmed hats and somber, buttonless garments, and the women are attired in calf-length, solid colored frocks, aprons and bonnets. Formal education is rudimentary and conducted in their own schools.

In contrast, the gay or fancy Dutch are a much larger group comprising such religious faiths as the Lutherans, German Reformed, Moravians and Schwenkfelders. Their life style, dress and culture cannot be distinguished from most of America's, and they value education highly, insisting on a university-trained clergy. The gay Dutch love color and use hearts, tulips, peacocks and other cheerful motifs to decorate barns, toolchests, hooked rugs, pottery and baptismal certificates. Contrary to popular belief, their so-called "hex" signs never were intended to ward off evil spirits but are simply decorations.

The division of plain and gay is somewhat arbitrary, just as is the statement that the plain people live to the south of the Pennsylvania Turnpike and the gay to the north. Modern ways of life have intruded on even the most devout of sects, and every once in a while an Amish boy or girl will leave the church literally and figuratively, taking off in a T-shirt behind the wheels of a brightly colored car. More frequent are the compromises — for example, farm machinery purchased because it is a necessity but a television denied because it is a luxury. Too, there are those who have capitalized on their own uniqueness, utilizing tourist interest for commercial gain — a very understandable attitude in our travel-oriented nation.

Whatever their particular life style, the Pennsylvania Dutch preserve much of what is best in traditional American values. In seeing their way of life, the visitor feels a sense of both familiarity and strangeness — and, perhaps, a bit of envy.

LANCASTER: Home of The Conestoga Wagon and The Kentucky Rifle

The largest inland town in the nation, Lancaster was laid out in 1730. Next to Philadelphia it was the most important town of colonial Pennsylvania, thanks largely to its craftsmen and merchants who made and sold goods for western development.

It was to the craftsmen of Lancaster County that the colonies owed the Conestoga wagon. Specially designed to prevent displacement of cargo on rough and sloping roads, these 3500 pound vehicles could carry a five-ton load in their curved boxes. A breed of powerful, large black horses also was developed here to pull the wagons in teams of six. The Conestoga wagons were vital in the transporting of provisions for battle. During the French and Indian War Lancaster provided Benjamin Franklin with its horses, wagons and provisions for use by General Braddock on the march against the French at Fort Duquesne. Too, in the big move westward the wagons were employed to carry freight across the mountains; the trip between Philadelphia and Pittsburgh took three weeks.

Another local skill of major import was gunmaking, the chief product being an astoundingly accurate weapon often inaccurately referred to as the "Kentucky Rifle". This industry proved so vital

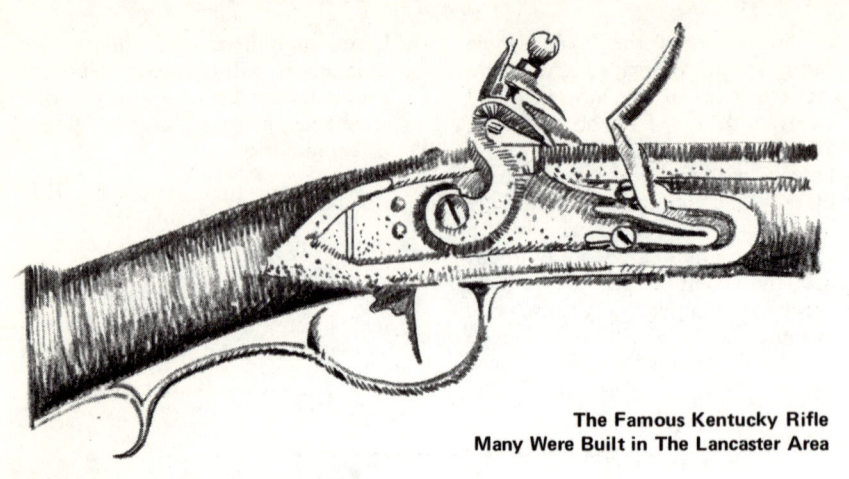

**The Famous Kentucky Rifle
Many Were Built in The Lancaster Area**

during the Revolution that it was taken over by the Continental Congress. The Pennsylvania rifle was particularly successful in situations where the conspicuous redcoats were too far off to fight back with their own inferior weapons. Noting the fear it inspired among the enemy, General Washington took to camouflaging his musketeers in the butternut brown of riflemen.

Lancaster rallied early to the cause of independence, offering its men as well as its weapons. In May 1775 the town organized two companies of riflemen, some of whom went to Cambridge to join Washington's Continentals where they made quite an impression with their rugged appearance and deadly marksmanship. Later, when British general Howe entered Philadelphia in September 1777, the Continental Congress paused in Lancaster to hold a session in the courthouse on Centre Square before continuing to York, Pa.

After the war Lancaster offered itself as a suitable place for the U.S. capital, asserting that "there is no part of the United States which can boast of more wagons and good teams than ourselves. We have five public buildings ... 678 dwellings and about 4,200 souls." The offer was turned down, but Lancaster did serve as State capital from 1799 to 1812.

One of the nation's first institutions of higher learning was established in Lancaster in 1787. This was Franklin College, named after that supreme fund-raiser and philanthropist Benjamin Franklin (he gave 200 pounds toward its founding). Later it merged with another institution, becoming Franklin and Marshall College.

Lancaster was the first town in the nation to be reached by a macadamized road. The 60 mile stretch from Philadelphia known as the Lancaster Turnpike was built between 1792 and 1794. This was the beginning of the vast turnpike movement in the states and a further boon to Lancaster's strategic importance.

LANCASTER EXCURSION

Coming from Philadelphia, take Route 30 or the less crowded Route 340. (Traveling on the latter road you will come to one of the most enthusiastically photographed signposts in America: the town of Intercourse. Contrary to popular impression, the name relates merely to its geographical location.) Picturesque though Route 340 is, try to avoid it on Sundays when many residents are out with horse and buggy; car traffic is both hazardous to them and an invasion of privacy on the Sabbath.

If you desire to see the less "touristy" areas of rich farmland, take some of the side roads off into surrounding country. There are several working farms open to the public, one of the best being the 71 acre Amish Homestead, three miles east of Lancaster on Route 462.

For specific information on the entire Pennsylvania Dutch area, try the Mennonite Information Center just outside Lancaster on Route 30 East or the Pennsylvania Dutch Tourist Bureau Information Center at the junction of U.S. 30 and Hempstead Road. Four-hour sightseeing bus tours are available through Conestoga Tours and Dutchland Bus Tours, Inc. both in Lancaster.

And don't end this excursion without sampling some local food. Pennsylvania Dutch cooking has earned quite a reputation — with good reason. It is hearty, tasty, rich in butter, economical, substantial in quantity, and fraught with calories. Meat and potatoes are eaten three times a day as are home-baked desserts; at dinner "sweets" (fruits) and "sours" (pickled vegetables) are combined in large number. Even soup is rich and with lots of filling in it — noodles, butter balls, even pretzels and popcorn. Obviously, the Pennsylvania Dutch love to eat. To borrow a phrase which often is attributed to them: "Kissin' wears out, cookin' don't!"

There are numerous restaurants specializing in Pennsylvania Dutch food in the area covered by our excursion. Among those in the vicinity of Lancaster are: Plain and Fancy Dining Room on Route 340 east of town, Willow Valley Farms Restaurant south of Lancaster on Route 222, Groff's Farm to the west in Mount Joy, and Miller's Dutch Smorgasbord east of Lancaster on U.S. 30.

For a special treat, mingle with the localities at the various Farmers Markets. Here you can buy the freshest of produce, homemade crafts, and specialties such as homemade shoofly pie. The town of Lancaster has two Farmers Markets; Central is open Tuesdays and Fridays, Southern on Saturdays. Central has been operating since colonial times.

This is a particularly full excursion, so choose from among the sites or plan a full two days in Lancaster and environs.

The Strasburg Railroad

1 **Strasburg Railroad,** Route 741 in the town of Strasburg. Established during the first term of President Andrew Jackson, the Strasburg Railroad's coal-burning steam locomotive gradually lost its business to trolleys and buses but was salvaged as a hobby and tourist attraction. Painstaking care has been given to maintaining the authentic turn-of-the-century aura with pot-bellied stoves in each car for heating and coal lamps for lighting. Even the East Strasburg station, an ornate Victorian building dating from 1882, has been reassembled to complete the setting.

Your trip will be nine miles long, to Paradise, Pa. and return, with a stopover at a picnic grove.

The railroad operates frequently from 10 a.m. to 5 p.m. on a daily basis during the summer months; check with the railroad (717-687-7522) for the modified winter, spring and fall schedules. Cost: $2, $1 for children under 12.

Ask while there about seeing the excellent state-operated Railroad Museum of Pennsylvania, also located on Route 741.

2 **Eagle Museum,** west of Strasburg on Route 741. Housed in the Herr Mill (erected in 1740 and one of the nation's oldest mills) is a remarkable collection of American weapons — in particular, the Pennsylvania rifle. You'll also see exhibits of early glass, china, iron, tin and wooden articles, as well as toys, coins and bottles.

Museum is open April - June and September - October, from 10 a.m. to 5 p.m. weekdays and 10 a.m. to 7 p.m. Saturdays and Sundays; July - August daily 9 a.m. to 8 p.m., November, weekends only, weather permitting. Adults $1, children 6-11 25¢ with adult.

③ Dutch Wonderland, just east of Lancaster on Route 30. This is an entertainment park with assorted rides for children, a wax museum, food, gift concessions, and nearby campsites and cinema.

Daily 10 a.m. - 8 p.m. Memorial Day weekend - Labor Day; Saturdays (10 a.m. - 6 p.m.) and Sundays (noon - 6 p.m.) only on Easter and Memorial Day weekends and in September and October. General admission $1.75; package ticket (includes all but monorail) $4.50.

④ Pennsylvania Farm Museum of Landis Valley, 2451 Kissel Hill Road, off U.S. 272 (about five miles north of Lancaster). This carefully maintained complex of 30 farm buildings and related exhibits depict 19th century farm life in the fertile Pennsylvania Dutch area. The original Landis homestead is a typical colonial farm of brick, c. 1815. Nearby is a small home of similar style which housed the widowed mother of a Landis son who inherited the house. Both are furnished with original items dating back to 1815-50. Other buildings include a schoolhouse, barn, and print, saddle and blacksmith shops.

Open Mondays through Saturdays 8:30 a.m. - 4:30 p.m., Sundays noon to 4:30 p.m. Closed election days, Thanksgiving, Christmas, New Years and Easter.

⑤ Wheatland, 1120 Marietta Avenue on Pa. Route 23, Lancaster. The only U.S. president from Pennsylvania was James Buchanan who held office just before Abraham Lincoln, striving unsuccessfully to maintain a balance between the free and slave-holding states.

Born near Mercersburg in 1791, Buchanan was the son of a Scotch-Irish farmer and merchant. He graduated from Dickinson College and practiced law in Lancaster. Buchanan once stated that he'd "never intended to enter politics... but as a distraction from a great grief which happened at Lancaster when I was a young man... I accepted a nomination." (This grief was a broken engagement to the daughter of the owner of the Cornwall Iron Mines; she mysteriously died soon afterward.) Buchanan remained a bachelor, entering the White House at age 65.

Wheatland is a lovely mansion, built around 1828 and restored to its pre-Civil War appearance with broad lawns, some original Buchanan furniture, china and silver. Guided tours are given by women in period dress.

Open April through November, from 9 a.m. to 5 p.m. Mondays through Saturdays, 10 a.m. to 5 p.m., Sundays, last tour at 4:30. $1 adults, under 12 free.

⑥ Lancaster County Historical Society, N. President and Marietta Avenues. This library and museum are filled with 200 years of Lancaster history.

Open Tuesdays - Fridays from 1 to 5 p.m. and Saturdays 10 a.m. to 5 p.m.; free.

⑦ Fulton Opera House, 12 North Prince Street, Lancaster. This structure, erected in 1852, has served a number of purposes: political convention site, hospital and armory during the Civil War and theater for performances by the "greats". Concerts, operas and dramas are still presented here in Victorian splendor.

Daily tours at noon from June through August except Sundays; inquire for schedule during rest of year. 90¢, under 12, 30¢.

8 **Robert Fulton Birthplace,** south of Lancaster on Route 222. While noted primarily for his invention of the steamboat, Fulton was also a talented designer of firearms and an artist of miniature portraits. Fulton memorabilia may be seen here in his refurnished birthplace.

Hours are subject to change but generally extend from 9 a.m. to 4 p.m. weekdays except Monday when closed; Sundays 1-4 p.m.

9 **Hans Herr House,** off Route 222 south, Lancaster. This was the home of Bishop Herr, one of the first Mennonite settlers in the area. The Mennonite Historical Society only recently saved this structure — a fine example of medieval German architecture — from the ravages of time.

Open Mondays through Saturdays 9 a.m. to 4 p.m.; $1; children 7-12, 50¢; under 6 free.

10 **Old City Hall,** W. King Street at the corner of Penn Square. The red brick building, erected in 1795, is an excellent example of Pennsylvania colonial architecture. It is being restored as the "Heritage Center of Lancaster County Museum".

Hours not yet available.

11 **Evangelical Lutheran Church of the Holy Trinity,** northeast corner of E. Mifflin and S. Duke Streets. Lancaster's oldest house of worship, erected 1761-6, shows the influence of Christ Church in Philadelphia. In addition to regular Sunday services, there will be daily guided tours. The church organ was built c. 1770, and its case still is used.

12 **Rock Ford,** three miles south of Lancaster on Rock Ford Road off Duke Street at Williamson Park. Built around 1793, Rock Ford was the Georgian-style mansion of General Edward Hand, Irish-born Revolutionary War commander and member of the Continental Congress. Hand saw a great deal of battle, including the Trenton, White Plains and Princeton confrontations, and he was present for the surrender at Yorktown. His home is open to the public with its original furnishings; the restoration of neighboring outbuildings is now taking place.

Open 10 a.m. to 4:30 p.m. weekdays and from noon to 4 p.m. Sundays from April - October. $1.50, 50¢ children 6-12, under 6 free; combination admission ticket with Wheatland $2.50.

EPHRATA CLOISTER: The Life of Piety

One of the more remarkable examples of early religious communities in our nation was that of the Seventh-Day German Baptists, a monastic group of German Protestants who settled in the Pennsylvania Dutch country during the 1730s. Their settlement, Ephrata, reached its height around 1750 when there were some 300 members. Under the leadership of the eccentric mystic, Conrad Beissel, these men and women sought to serve God in medieval fashion through lives of austere self-denial and pious simplicity. All property was shared as was the work, and celibacy was a requirement for the inner circle; a married group of householders was allowed to live in special quarters.

Even the physical surroundings were planned so as to teach the good life. Halls were narrow to symbolize the straight and narrow path and doorways low to teach humility through stooping. The single men and women lived apart, one to a cell, each cell being four floor boards wide with a small window. Narrow wooden ledges too short for complete repose served as beds and wooden blocks eight inches long as pillows. Garments were white, flowing and simple, and shoes were made of wood and hide. Daily schedules, too, were firmly fixed: From 9 p.m. to midnight the brothers and sisters slept; from midnight to 1 a.m. they prayed; from 1 to 4 a.m. again they slept; the remaining hours were spent in labor and devotions, the Bible being the only rule of faith and discipline. Charity to the poor was the Sunday responsibility.

Yet this ascetic life was not devoid of beauty and creativity. Music was important to the order as a means of exalting the mystical life, and Beissel wrote many hymns. To enhance their vocal abilities the members followed special dietary laws. In 1746 the brothers and sisters, as "a religious discipline to castigate the flesh" and a testimonial of filial esteem for their leader, copied with quill pen and ink about 500 hymns, mostly by Beissel. Excelling in the calligraphic art of *Frakturschriften,* the sisters produced many magnificent hand-illuminated songbooks and inscriptions, some of which still exist.

Ephrata also became known for its printing. The community press was, in fact, the third in America, its most ambitious undertaking being the translation and publication in 1748 of the 1200 page *Martyrs Mirror.* Printed for the Mennonites, this was the largest book to be published in colonial America.

Ephrata Cloister was self-sufficient in almost all regards. The members made their own building materials, utensils, furniture, cloth, and did their own farming, basket making, carpentry. Their arts and crafts showed both skill and refinement of taste. Although pacifist by creed, they responded with generous assistance to the sick and wounded of Washington's army after the Battle of the Brandywine, when some 500 soldiers were brought here for nursing. The buildings which served as hospital on Mt. Zion had to be burned afterward to arrest the spread of camp fever. (A monument in the cemetery marks the graves of the soldiers who died here.) Even the celebrated print shop came into special use, turning out Continental money during the British occupation of Philadelphia. It is said that during one low point of the war, Washington's troops took apart copies of *Martyrs Mirror* to make wadding for their rifles.

Ephrata began to decline after the Revolution due to a lessening of interest in the monastic life and lack of effective leadership. However, the society was not officially dissolved until 1934.

EPHRATA EXCURSION

Beautifully restored by the State, the neat complex of immaculate, weathered buildings that comprise the Ephrata Cloister are located at 632 West Main Street at the intersection of Routes 322 and 272. From Lancaster go north on Route 272.

This 24-acre museum in the midst of the rich Pennsylvania Dutch farmlands is a place of unique and stark beauty. Among the surviving buildings are Beissel's log house, the sisters' house, the chapel, the alms and bake house and three cottages. You'll see Ephrata's third printing press, bought in 1804, which is still operational, as well as original furnishings and examples of the fine handiwork done by the group.

A lovely event is the *vorspiel*, a historical pageant with related choral music, mostly by Beissel. This is presented every Saturday evening from the last Saturday in June through the Saturday of Labor Day weekend; there are also two Sunday performances, the last Sunday in July and the Sunday of Labor Day weekend. Pre-performance candlelit tours of Ephrata Cloister are given from 6:30 p.m. to 8 p.m. with craft demonstrations from 7 to 9 at which time the *vorspiel* begins. Cost is $3, $1 for those 6 to 11, under 6 free.

If you happen to be in Ephrata on a Friday, the Green Dragon Auction Market off Route 272, about two miles from the Cloister, has all kinds of delectable produce indoors and out, with auctions and livestock sales.

Your day thus far will have been a very full one, and an overnight stop outside of Ephrata is suggested.

READING: Industrial Center

Reading, the unofficial "capital of the Pennsylvania Dutch land" was settled by William Penn's two sons Thomas and Richard, who named it after their home in England.

A military base was established here in the French and Indian War and, in 1758, Reading furnished General John R. Forbes with "fifty-six good Strong Waggons" plus "freeholders who have the English and German tolerable well." (Already there were so many Germans here that it was a handicap not to know that language.) When the Revolution came, the Berks County residents threw their support to the Continentals — partly because they had so little kinship with the English rulers in either customs or speech — sending companies of infantry to Massachusetts. Reading was used as a depot for military supplies, its forges and furnaces turned out cannon for the army, and British and Hessian prisoners were held in a camp in the area.

The town's industrial development was spurred by the skilled German craftsmen plus the area's location which featured canal and railroad transportation. Today nearly 700 factories continue the old tradition, producing everything from pretzels to steel, cough drops to letter boxes.

Contemporary writer John Updike was born in West Reading and uses the locale a good deal in his books. He once remarked, "I find there is a sense of human richness here. Puritanism didn't touch the area with a heavy hand. You have more access to people's real selves and not their social masks — there's a richness and brutality." An orderly, thrifty people, with few mansions and equally few slums in their town, the residents of Reading were second in the U.S. to elect a socialist government into office.

READING EXCURSION

Many shoppers come here to buy clothes, furniture, luggage and carpeting at factory outlet prices. For information on Reading's shopping bargains, contact the Berks County Pennsylvania Dutch Tourist Association at 538 Court Street.

Unusual dining is available at Stokesay Castle, a copy of a 12th century English castle which is situated on a hill overlooking the town. If you're a mushroom aficionado, Joe's at 450 South 7th Street should be one of your stops. Its owners spend two months a year on the hunt for the succulent fungi, using them in main dishes, soups, and pastries. The tavern in which Joe's is located has stood here for over 150 years.

An annual event, the Cherry Fair, is held in the Oley Valley over Memorial Day weekend. Craft demonstrations, folk music, and lectures on topics as varied as the Conestoga wagon and witchcraft, are traditional.

Your drive from Ephrata will take you north along Route 222.

Reading, Kutztown & Allentown

READING:
(1) Penn's Common (2) The Pagoda
(3) Skew Arch
(4) Historical Society of Berks County
(5) Holy Trinity Church
(6) Reading Public Museum and Art Gallery

KUTZTOWN:
(1) Crystal Cave (2) Roadside America
(3) Hawk Mountain Sanctuary

ALLENTOWN:
(1) Zion Reformed Church and Liberty Bell Shrine
(2) Hess's of Allentown (3) Trout Hall
(4) Trexler Memorial Park

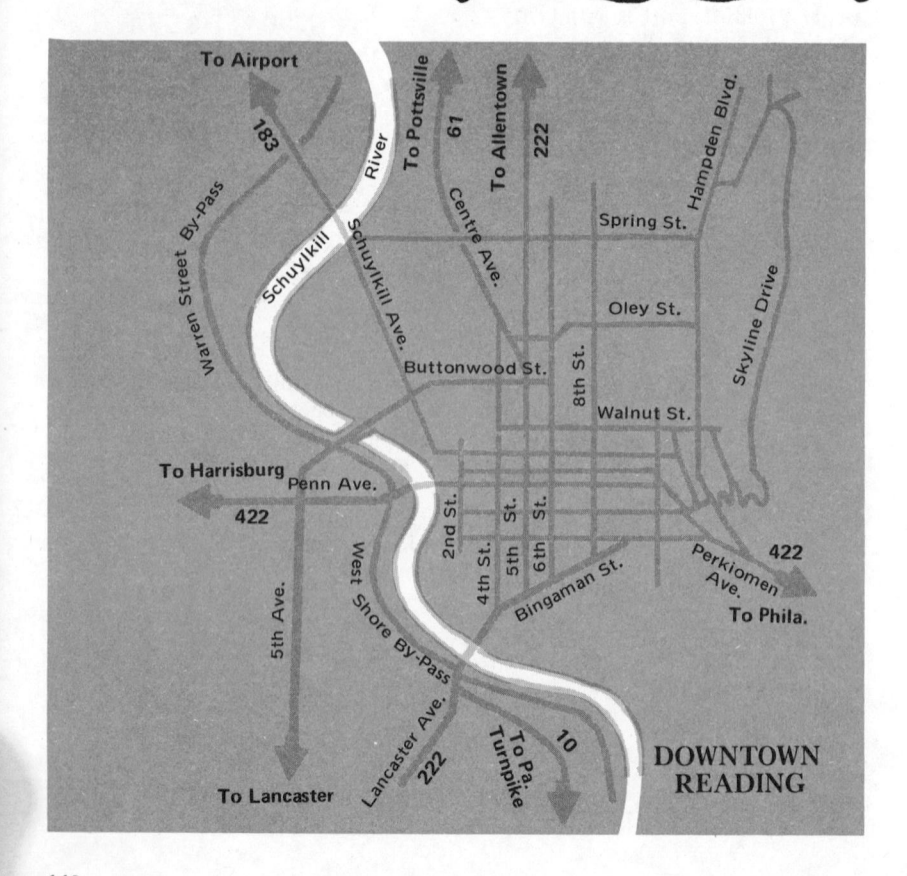

DOWNTOWN READING

DOWNTOWN ALLENTOWN

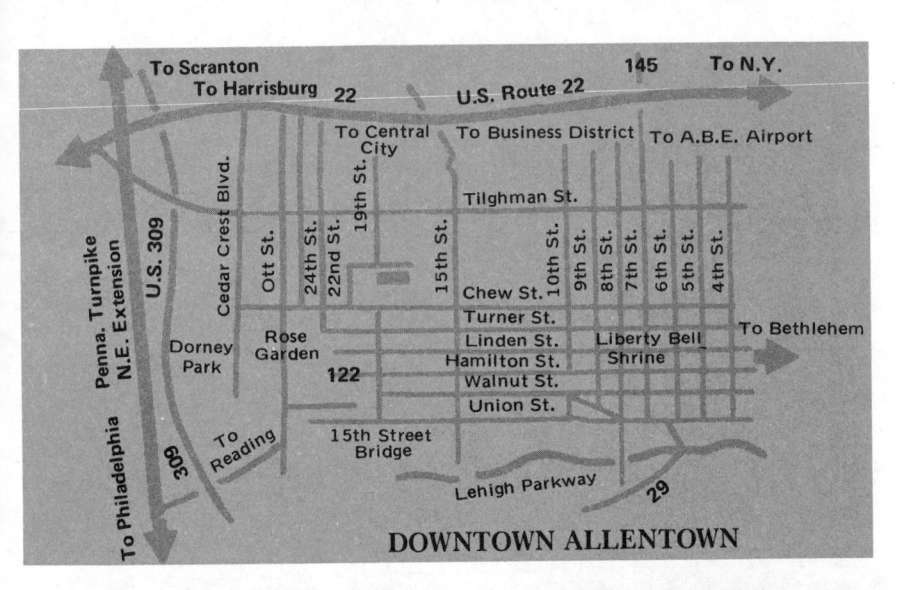

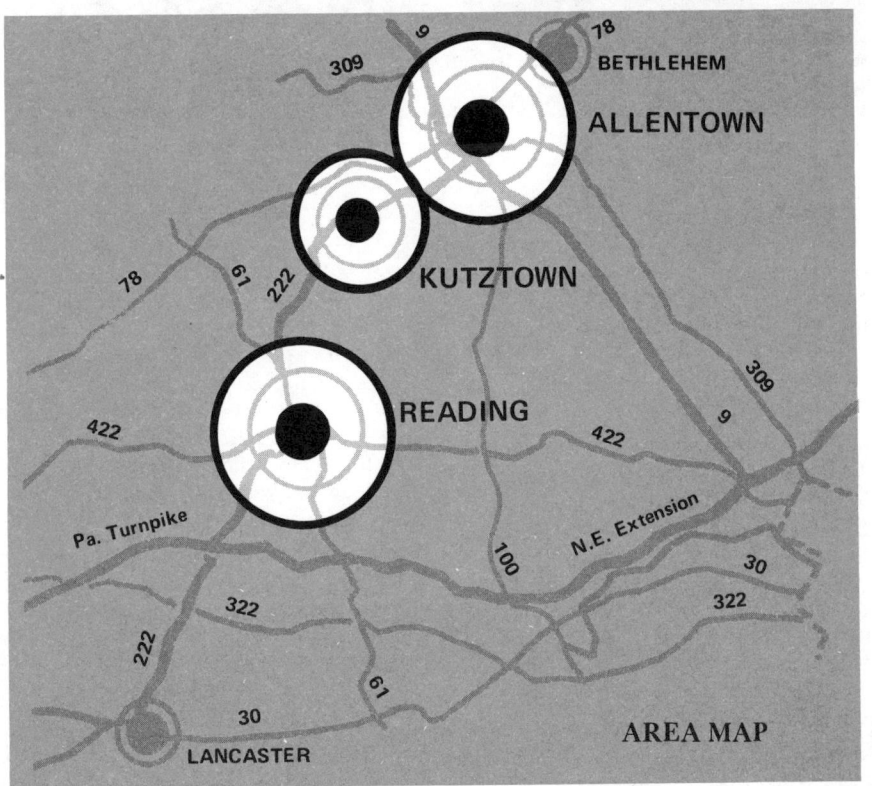

AREA MAP

Industry & Farming Exist Together in the Lebanon Valley of Pennsylvania

1 **Penn's Common,** 11th and Penn Street. This 50-acre park was deeded as a free public commons by the Penns. Formerly the site of public hangings, it now has a more placid existence, with playground, lawns, trees, flower beds and lily ponds.

2 **The Pagoda,** Duryea Drive and Skyline Boulevard. This unusual seven-story Japanese structure, intended but not used as a hotel, was anchored to Mount Penn by ten tons of bolts. Reached from the Common by rough hewn steps, it has an observation tower and picnic area.

Open daily from April through November, 9 a.m. to 11 p.m., rest of year 11 a.m. to 11 p.m., weather permitting; free.

3 **Skew Arch,** Reading Railroad Bridge at 6th and Woodward Street. So named because its courses of brown stone are laid in ellipsoidal curves, the arch was erected in 1857. Since it was constructed from a model made of soap and built by Irish stone masons who were paid partly in whiskey, this is sometimes referred to as "the soap and whiskey" bridge.

4 **Historical Society of Berks County,** 940 Centre Avenue. Local history, decorate arts and antiques are featured in this small red brick structure of Georgian Colonial design, situated on a raised terrace. The Society has the original 1755-56 diary of Conrad Weiser, who helped found Reading and was a leading peacemaker between whites and Indians. There are also several hundred family bibles and an unusual collection of firefighting relics.

Open Tuesdays through Saturdays from 9 a.m. to 4 p.m., also Sundays from October through May from 2 to 5 p.m., closed holidays; free.

5 **Holy Trinity Church**, northwest corner of 6th and Washington. The two-story brick structure was erected in 1972-73 and is of Georgian design. The chief surgeon of the Valley Forge encampment, Dr. Bodo Otto, is buried on its grounds.

6 **Reading Public Museum and Art Gallery**, 500 Museum Road, West Reading. Located in 25 acre Museum Park with botanical garden, streams and pond, this two story structure of Italian Renaissance design contains exhibits of art and science. It has one of the best butterfly collections in the U.S., one of the world's best exhibits of Carboniferous insects, and examples of the local (German folk art) as well as the far away and long ago (Babylonian temple records).

Open July - August Mondays through Fridays 9 a.m. to 4 p.m., September - June Mondays through Fridays 9 a.m. to 5 p.m. and Saturdays to noon; Sundays all year round 2 to 5 p.m.; closed legal holidays except Easter. Free.

KUTZTOWN:
Pennsylvania Dutch Pageantry

Driving north on Route 222 from Reading, you will reach Kutztown which is known for its annual Pennsylvania Dutch Folk Festival. An eight day event held at the end of June and beginning of July, the festival combines folk artistry of bygone times with ample foods and daily demonstrations on how to prepare and preserve everything from pigs to pickles.

Craft demonstrations are given in weaving, soap making, blacksmithing, horseshoeing, quilting and pewtering, and a variety of stage shows include traditional pageants such as the wedding ceremony and barn raising.

$3.00, under 12, 50¢, parking $1. For information on 1976 fair, call 1-717-683-8707.

KUTZTOWN AREA EXCURSION

1 **Crystal Cave**, five miles northwest of Kutztown off U.S. 222. The largest operating cave in Pennsylvania, it was discovered in 1871 by workmen blasting for limestone. Some believe Crystal Cave developed from underground

Baking Fresh Pennsylvania Dutch Rye Bread

streams, others say from seismic action. A guided tour along concrete walks with guard rails reveals a variety of beautiful rock formations, caverns and natural bridges, all enhanced by indirect lighting. Temperature is always 56 degrees. The varied shapes created by nature have inspired such names as "Cathedral Chamber", "Prarie Dogs" and "Rib Roast."

Feb., Mar., Apr., May, June 1-15, Sep., Oct.: 9-5 daily, 9-6 weekends; June 16 through Labor Day: 9-6 daily, 9-7 weekends; Nov., Dec.: Fridays, Saturdays, Sundays only 9-5; closed January. $2.75 adults, $1.35 children 6 to 12, under 6 free.

② Roadside America, west of Kutztown on Route 22 at Shartlesville exit. Two hundred years of American life are depicted here in miniature form. The tiny exhibits include a coal mining scene, a "gay 90's" town, an old style toll gate, and a typical Pennsylvania Dutch farm.

Open weekdays 9 a.m. to 8 p.m. July to September, 10 a.m. to 5 p.m. September to June, Saturdays and Sundays 10 a.m. to 7 p.m. $2 adults, 50¢ those 6 to 11, under 6 free.

③ Hawk Mountain Sanctuary, R.D. 2, Kempton. This unique sanctuary for birds of prey, located north of Kutztown in the the town of Kempton, contains about 2000 acres of rugged terrain on Blue Mountain. Its beautiful forests rise more than 1000 feet to the rocky outcroppings where visitors spend hours and even days waiting for the imposing birds of prey. More than 200 species have been seen here, the chief attraction being the hawk and eagle migration from late August to November. Take along a packed lunch and thermos, wear sturdy shoes, and don't forget the binoculars, cushions for sitting on the rocks, and an adequate supply of patience.

Open every day from 8 a.m. to 5 p.m.; $1 adults, 50¢ for children under 12 and students up to 18.

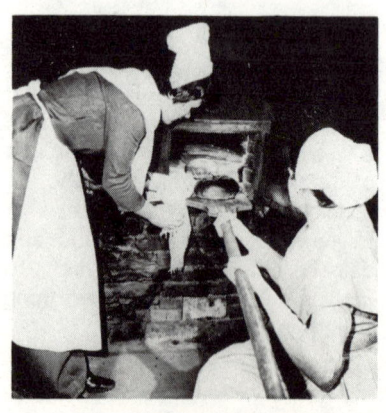

A Typical Pennsylvania Dutch Farmer's Market

ALLENTOWN: Keeper of The Bell

The area that is now Allentown was among the lands acquired — not altogether honestly — from the Lenni Lenape Indians in the "Walking Purchase". Founded in 1762 as "Northampton" by Chief Justice William Allen, it became so widely known as "Allen's Town" that its name finally was changed in 1830 to Allentown.

A munitions-producing center during the Revolution, Allentown gained its enduring fame through a more dramatic role in that war: the secreting of the Liberty Bell. This occurred in September of 1777, one year after the bell had proclaimed "freedom throughout the land". The British occupation of Philadelphia seemed inevitable. It was feared that the enemy, needing ammunition, would take particular delight in melting down the Liberty Bell along with other prize colonial possessions and turning them into cannon. To avoid this fate, the patriots decided to send the Liberty Bell, the chimes and tower bell of Christ Church, and the tower bell of St. Peter's Church — eleven bells in all — to another settlement. Northampton's loyalty to the Continental cause was known and its location safely distant; hence it was chosen as repository for the treasured items. While the transfer was being effected, the British were warned off by an announcement that the Liberty Bell had been buried in the waters of the Delaware.

It was no easy job, moving the huge, cumbersome beacon of freedom from its home at the State House to a place some 50 miles away. But the plan was a clever one. In this era, residents of the rich Pennsylvania Dutch farm region made frequent trips to Philadelphia with wagonloads of produce which they sold there. It was no problem, then, on the return trip home, to place the precious bells in the huge, empty Conestoga wagons, covering them with potato sacks and refuse from the stables. The trip, however, was not without a hitch. According to an entry in the diary of the Moravian Church at Bethlehem dated September 25, 1777, "the bells from Philadelphia brought in wagons. The wagon with the State House bell broke down here, so it had to be unloaded. The other bells went on." Arriving later at Allentown, the Liberty Bell together with the church chimes were hidden under the floor of the old Zion Reformed Church. Here they remained during the Valley Forge encampment and until the British had evacuated Philadelphia in the latter part of 1778.

Rarely has a church been called upon to perform so strange a mission.

ALLENTOWN EXCURSION

Allentown, marketplace for Lehigh County's farm produce, is to the northeast of Kutztown driving along Route 222.

1 Zion Reformed Church and Liberty Bell Shrine, 622 Hamilton at Church Street. The stone church in whose basement the Liberty Bell was secreted no longer exists, but a later church was built on the same site. Extensive excavation revealed the long-buried foundations of the original edifice whose dimensions were exactly copied; a shrine now occupies the space that once held the bell. The focal point of the shrine is an official, full-sized Liberty Bell replica presented to the church by the Commonwealth of Pennsylvania on the 200th anniversary of the original church's construction. In addition, there is a 46-foot painting depicting the journey of the bell and other local events of importance during the War for Independence.

Open Tuesdays - Fridays 1-4 p.m., Saturdays and Sundays 2-4 p.m., closed major holidays; free.

2 Hess's of Allentown, 9th and Hamilton Mall. This department store sells everything from sewing thimbles to $10,000 Dior gowns. It's a favorite visiting spot for fashion-conscious ladies and features an elegant Patio Restaurant.

Open Mondays, Thursdays, Fridays from 10 a.m. to 9 p.m., Tuesdays, Wednesdays, Saturdays from 10 a.m. to 5:30 p.m.

3 Trout Hall, 414 Walnut Street. Built in 1770, this was the summer residence of James Allen, son of Allentown's founder. It later housed Allentown Seminary and Muhlenberg College, then was purchased by the city. Now restored, it is the headquarters of the Lehigh County Historical Society and contains period rooms, a museum and a library.

Open Tuesdays - Fridays, 1-4 p.m., Saturday and Sundays 2-4 p.m., closed major holidays; free.

4 Trexler Memorial Park, Cedar Crest Boulevard. This contains a greenhouse, rose garden (at its peak the second week in June) an old fashioned garden (June - August), trout nursery and fish-for-fun stream, and picnic area.

Open all year; free.

WHILE YOU'RE THERE...

Two of Lehigh County's most historic houses lie north of Allentown. The George Taylor Mansion in Catasauqua was the "Italian Villa" style home of a signer of the Declaration of Independence, and the Troxell-Steckel House erected 1755-6 in the town of Egypt is a fine example of German rural architecture.

When you're in the Allentown area you won't want to miss those intriguing Pennsylvania Dutch attractions you've heard about, or the historic Colonial sites.

For free brochures on all this plus motels, restaurants, and campsites write: Tour Bureau, Box 665, Allentown, PA 18105. In the area, call the Bureau's 24-hour hotline (215) 821-1151.

THE GUIDE RECOMMENDS . . .

Bully Lyon's Saloon Restaurant, in the old Neversink Schoolhouse, Reading, is named for the notorious Reading Sheriff. Delicious steaks, backfin, crab, Grasshopper Pie.

Lunch: 11:30 to 2:00; Dinner: 5:00 to 11:00; Sundays: 5:00 to 9:00.

Interstate 176 to 422 East. Exit at Mount Penn. (215) 779-1086.

Dutch Wonderland . . . an enchanted land of exciting adventure and fun for folks of every age. Drive antique mini cars, ride the giant super slide, see the dolphin show, climb aboard Wonderland railroad, chug down Old Mill Stream in a tugboat, see **Dutch Wonderland** in one of 3 air-conditioned Monorails. Bring your camera. 44 beautifully landscaped acres including the Botanical Gardens to stroll through or glide by in a gondola. Great browsing in **The Castle Gift Shop** (open all year), one of the largest in the country. Appetizing homemade taste treats in **The Kastle Kitchen.** Enjoy dining on the **Castle Terrace** or quick service in the modern cafeteria. Open every day Memorial Day thru Labor Day. Family prices. Route 30 — 4½ miles east of Lancaster, the heart of the Pennsylvania Dutch Country.

To relive Lancaster County's exciting history visit **The National Wax Museum** of Lancaster County Heritage. Inspirational and educational realistic tableaus featuring William Penn, George Washington, Daniel Boone and Abraham Lincoln enhanced by triple-phonic stereo narration. Open all year.

Calling All Campers! Discover the joys of living in the famous Pennsylvania Dutch Country's **Old Mill Stream Camping Manor.** It adjoins the **National Wax Museum** and **Dutch Wonderland.** 15 acres. Complete facilities.

See it like it is. Visit the **Weavertown One-Room Schoolhouse.** Lifelike, costumed pupils and teacher. Animated. Bird-in-Hand. 5 miles east of Lancaster, Route 340 East.

Money-Saving Discovery: You'll probably find it well worth your while to make a small side trip to the "factory outlet capital of the world" in Reading. Fifty percent (and more) off on famous label fashions, in 14 factory outlets in one city block, 110 Moss Street.

Ephrata Cloister, an 18th Century German Protestant monastic settlement (intersection routes 322 & 272 in Ephrata) is a most remarkable American landmark. It's here the **Ephrata Cloister Associates** present **"Vorspiel"**, an outstanding historical pageant with beautiful religious choral music original to

Ephrata. You'll feel part of a bygone world as you walk the shaded paths before viewing this spectacular religious pageant. Tours, crafts demonstrations precede performances.

"VORSPIEL" performed late June to Labor Day, Saturdays; last Sundays in July, August, 9 p.m. Admission $3.00, 12 and over, $1.00, 6 to 11; free, under 6. Group rates on request. (717) 733-4811.

Beautiful crafted items in Cloister Gift Shop.

Cacoosing (Indian for "Land of the Owls") **Farms Store**: R.D. #5, Sinking Spring (Route 422 turn right on Green Valley Road, West of Sinking Spring). Prime beef gift packages shipped anywhere in the United States. Gourmet foods. Also antiques ... period and country pieces displayed in Colonial rooms by Peg Begel. Phone (215) 678-8642.

C.H. Dill Travel Bureau. If the thought of doing **The Whole Thing** on your own wheels staggers you, consult the '76 **Plus Tour** experts. These experienced history oriented people will plan a tailormade tour, right from your home town, in chartered escorted motor coaches. History will come to life, patriotism and friendships bloom, as you ramble through superb scenery in armchair comfort.

Civic organizations, clubs, church groups, schools and individual travelers are cordially invited to write or call: C.H. DILL TRAVEL BUREAU, 623 North Fourth Street, Reading, Pennsylvania. (215) 376-5747.

Kitchen Kettle, Intercourse, Lancaster County, is the heartland of Pennsylvania Dutch Country. You could spend days in this tranquil community of shops and studios, surrounded by lush farmland ... no one will ever hurry you. Local artisans engage in age-old crafts. Handpainted pottery, pewter, handmade leather goods. Glorious aromas rise from Bake House, Smoke House, Fudge Shop, Jam and Jelly Kitchens ... the contents freshly prepared and ready to go. Antiques, paintings, prints.

Open daily, except Sunday, from 9 a.m., Route 772, Newport Road.

Zinn's Country Diner, Lancaster County Landmark, Denver. Pennsylvania Turnpike Exit 21, Route 222 North. Pennsylvania Dutch cooking and baking, family prices. Fast service 24 hours daily. Visit the New Bicentennial Gift Shop, flex travel-weary muscles in the Recreation Park: miniature golf, softball, snack bar, picnics. (215) 267-2210.

Friendly **Dutch Colony Motor Inn**, 4635 Perkiomen Ave., Reading, 10 minutes west on Route 422 from Hopewell Village, Birdsboro. 80 comfortable rooms plus swimming pool. Unique dining in authentic Antique Airplane Restaurant. Specialties: shrimp & scallop casserole, broiled seafood dinners, steaks, chops, garden vegetables. (215) 770-2345.

Jeannette Shops in historic Reading at 5th & Washington and the Berkshire Mall, Wyomissing, for travel coats, dresses, accessories.

Shupp's Grove is the *original* Outdoor Antique and Collectable Market, Adamstown: Pennsylvania Turnpike Exit 21, then Route 222 North two miles to Route 897. Now in its 13th year, this "Collector's Heaven" stands on 30 acres of beautiful shade trees, formerly a family picnic spot since 1911.

Saturdays, Sundays, all day, evenings. (215) 484-9314.

Crystal Restaurants, Reading, Pennsylvania. Marvelous food, warm hospitality ... you'll bask in the true Pennsylvania tradition at the famous restaurants run by the Mantis Family since 1911: **The Crystal Downtown** in the heart of historic Reading on Penn Square; **Crystal West** at the Reading Motor Inn, Park Road and Warren Street, Wyomissing. You'll step into the past when you dine in the **Crystal's** Heritage Room where the color and flavor of Early Reading (founded by William Penn) surrounds you. Great regional dishes, superbly prepared fresh caught fish, seafood delights, gourmet dinners, light luncheons (or fullsome), hearty country breakfasts.

Better phone ahead. Fridays, Saturdays: Downtown (215) 376-2831. West (215) 372-7811.

Stokesay Castle, Hill Road and Spook Lane, Reading's storied replica of a 13th century English Castle, high on a mountainside, magnificent 20 mile view. Superb feasting in spectacular setting. Wine cellar? Positively regal! (215) 375-4588.

Koziar's Christmas Village, just off U.S. Route 183 in Bernville, Pennsylvania, is a dreamworld of Christmas lights and displays.

Founded by William M. Koziar in 1948, the Village features thousands of Christmas lights in a breathtaking panorama across the Pennsylvania Dutch countryside. Here, in glass enclosed buildings, you will see Christmas scenes ... "Twas the Night Before Christmas", "Christmas in Other Lands", "The Manger Scene", and many others.

Fairy tale settings, cartoon settings, snack bar, gift shops, Santa's Workshop ... and real live reindeer.

Saturday and Sunday nights, October through Thanksgiving. Thereafter, every night until January 4th. Night display only. (215) 488-1110.

EXCURSION 10

Bethlehem
The Poconos

This two-day excursion will stop first at the old Moravian town, Bethlehem. Now an industrial center, it still retains its strong religious tradition as "Christmas City U.S.A." and home of the Bach Festival of sacred choral music. Next we will go to Pennsylvania's best known playground, the Poconos — some 2,400 square miles of mountains, lakes, waterfalls and big game country. If you drive to Stroudsburg for your overnight stay, you can devote the next day to sightseeing in this area.

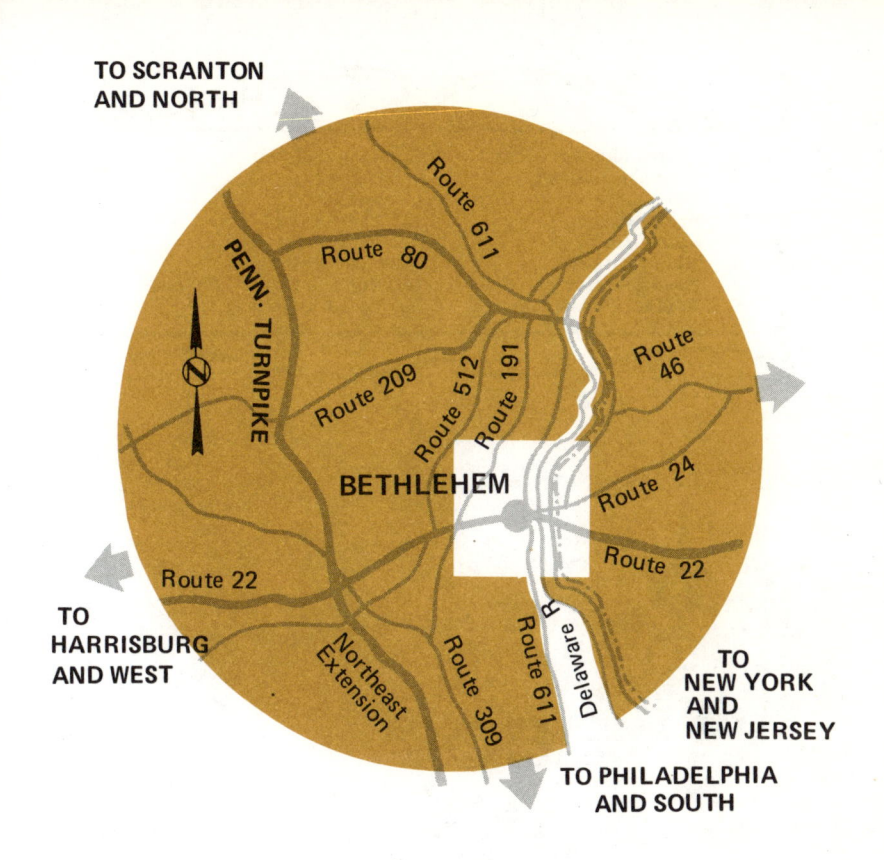

Bethlehem Area

When you are visiting the Bethlehem and Easton areas (Appalachian Trail to Delaware Water Gap) be sure to call (215) 821-1151 for free tourist information service. Or visit the Tourist Information Center at Routes 22 and 512. For brochures and further information write: Northampton County Visitors Council, 11 West Market Street, Bethlehem, PA 18018.

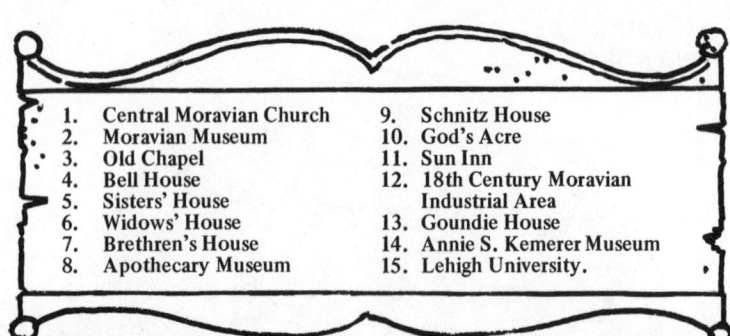

1. Central Moravian Church
2. Moravian Museum
3. Old Chapel
4. Bell House
5. Sisters' House
6. Widows' House
7. Brethren's House
8. Apothecary Museum
9. Schnitz House
10. God's Acre
11. Sun Inn
12. 18th Century Moravian Industrial Area
13. Goundie House
14. Annie S. Kemerer Museum
15. Lehigh University.

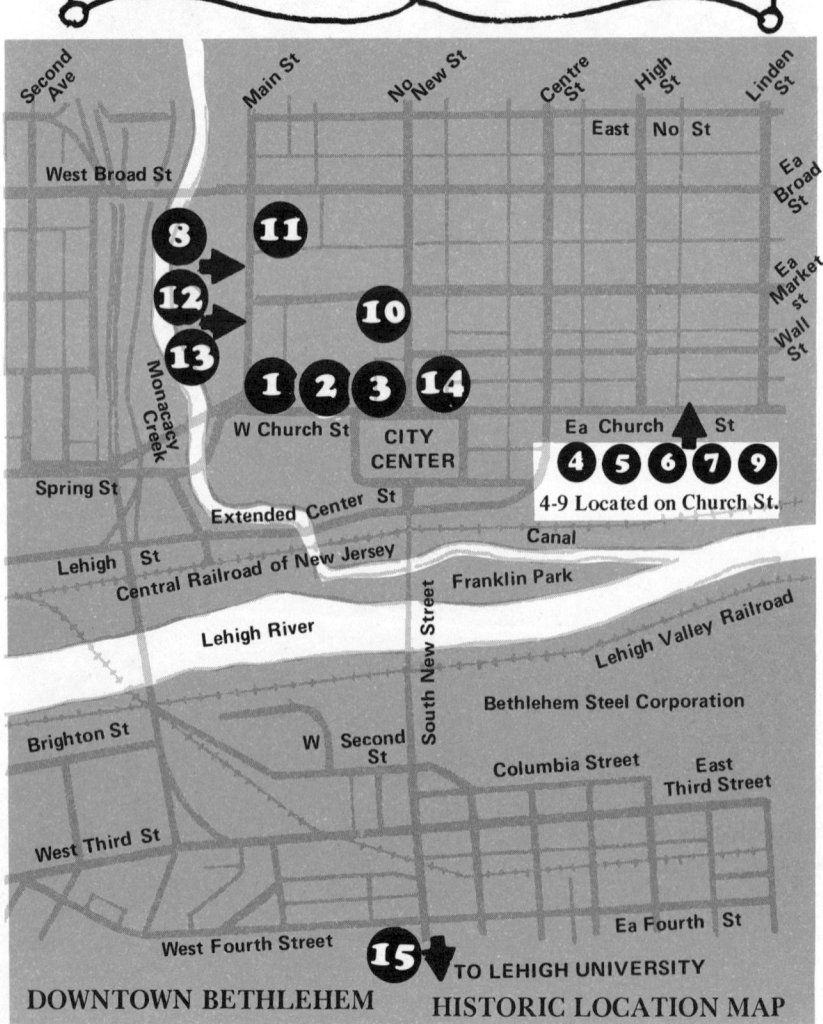

4-9 Located on Church St.

DOWNTOWN BETHLEHEM HISTORIC LOCATION MAP

BETHLEHEM:
Strains of Music, Clanking of Steel

Bethlehem is stamped with the character and personality of its Moravian founders. Indeed, for approximately one hundred years only Moravians were allowed to become residents. Massive limestone buildings arose in which they lived and worked, prayed and sang, the married couples residing separately from the unmarried "sisters" and "brethren". Boys and girls were trained in their schools, an important work of the Church.

Because of their religious beliefs, the Moravians were relieved by the British Parliament from taking oaths or bearing arms, the normal obligation of every resident of Colonial Pennsylvania. They maintained a good relationship with the Indians in the area, succeeding in converting many of them to Christianity. This tranquil life was disrupted by the Revolution, at which time Bethlehem — as befitted its name — became a place of refuge for the ill and wounded. Here soldiers who had fought at Morristown, New Jersey, and the Brandywine in Pennsylvania were treated in temporary hospitals. Lafayette was nursed back to health in a private home, and it is said that Casimir Pulaski, the "father of the American cavalry", protected the young single women from unruly soldiers.

Bethlehem's industrial development began with the opening of the Lehigh Canal and the traffic in coal. Bethlehem Iron Company was founded by a group of Philadelphia industrialists in 1861; this became one of the largest iron works in the world and was reorganized as Bethlehem Steel Corporation in 1899.

BETHLEHEM EXCURSION

This city, the geographical center of the Greater Lehigh Valley, is a one- and one-half hour trip from central Philadelphia. The quickest route is to take the northeast extension of the Pennsylvania Turnpike to the Quakertown Exit and then follow 309 North to 378 into Bethlehem.

Bethlehem is particularly interesting for the strong contrast between the homogeneous old Moravian settlement and the industrial community on the river bank. The Moravian religious heritage is still strong, as is the tie between that first Christmas of 1741 and the present holiday celebration. Bethlehem's historic buildings are especially beautiful at that time, aglow with tiny candles in almost every window. Rising high above the city atop South Mountain is a huge Star of Bethlehem, and a mammoth tree stands near the historic settlement. A favorite tradition is the community *putz* in the Christian Education Building of the Central Moravian Church. Similar to the French *creche,* the *putz* is a representation of the Nativity scene in treasured old miniature figures of carved wood. The high points of the Christmas celebration at the Church are the two Vigils and the "Children's Love Feast", all held on December 24th. The decor is elaborate, centering around a huge painting of the Nativity which hangs behind the pulpit, framed by the great arch. White-clad sacristans carry trays sparkling with fragrant beeswax candles, and choir and orchestra perform chorales, anthems, and traditional hymns, including that one that gave Bethlehem its name.

This fine old church used to be the setting for Bethlehem's annual musical attraction, the 77 year-old Bach Festival, now held in the Packer Memorial Chapel of Lehigh University. In 1748 the Moravians founded the Collegium Musicum which presented secular and sacred concerts. The Bach Festival grew out of this tradition but owes its present form to Dr. J. Fred Wolle, who, after study in Munich, at the turn of this century, devoted the remainder of his life to the interpretation of Bach. It is a remarkable experience, this fusion of a 150-person chorus (members being area residents) with renowned soloists, singing the masterpieces of the sacred musical literature. Visually, too, it is awesome, the darkly clad men in the center flanked by women in white, arranged in tiers in the chancel. During intermission, the Moravian Brass Choir plays chorales from the tower.

In 1976 this annual event will be held May 14 and 15, 21 and 22. Various ceremonial works of Bach and his B Minor Mass will be performed. Seats in the chapel are at a premium, so write for tickets as early as possible to: Bach Choir Office, Main and Church Streets, Bethlehem, PA 18018; the office estimates it will be sold out by mid-March. However, if you miss out on the tickets, you can still listen outside the chapel or in an auditorium which has the performance transmitted by a fine stereo sound system ($1.00 charge).

And if you miss it altogether, don't give up. There is *always* music

Central Moravian Church

in Bethlehem, and many times it's free—as in the late spring and summer when concerts are given in the Rose Garden.

A final word before we begin our sightseeing. As early as 1742, guides were appointed to show interested guests around Bethlehem. The custom continues today.

For full information write or call:

Tourist Information and
 Visitors Center
11 West Market Street
Bethlehem, PA 18018
(215) 867-3788

Historic Bethlehem Inc.
Main and Church Streets
Bethlehem, PA 18018
(215) 868-6311

Moravian Museum and
 Tours of Moravian Buildings
66 West Church Street
Bethlehem, PA 18018
(215) 867-0173

1 **Central Moravian Church,** Main and West Church Streets. This Federal-style building with fine hand-carved detail work is considered the foremost Moravian Church in the U.S. Erected between 1803 and 1806, it was the largest church in Pennsylvania at the time; the entire population of the town could attend services at once. As we have said, it is the location of Bethlehem's special Christmas services. Since 1754 a trombone choir has played here for other special occasions such as Easter and sunrise services.

2 **Moravian Museum (Gemein Haus),** 66 West Church Street. This onetime community house is the oldest building still standing in Bethlehem, erected in 1741. A five story log structure, now covered by protective clapboards, housed the earliest place of worship in the town. Museum exhibits include religious and secular articles such as early furniture, clocks, silver, musical instruments, and seminary art and needlework.

Open Tuesdays through Saturdays, 1 to 4 p.m., closed most holidays and from December 24 to 26; admission $1, students through 12th grade 50¢, and preschoolers free.

3 **Old Chapel, adjoing the Museum.** Erected in 1751, this structure is still used for various small functions but is generally closed to the public. A special service was written in honor of George Washington when he was here. Benjamin Franklin and many members of the Continental Congress also worshipped in this chapel.

4 **Bell House,** Church Street. Built in 1746, it is named for the bell in its tower which called people to services and warned them of peril. The building was once used by the Female Seminary, now a part of Moravian College.

5 **Sisters' House,** Church Street. This German limestone building erected in 1744, was the home of unmarried women. It is now a private residence.

6 **Widows' House**, Church Street. Erected in 1768, it was for widows, who lived separately as did the unmarried women. This, too, is a private residence.

7 **Brethren's House**, Church Street. Erected in 1748, it housed the unmarried men of the community and was later used as a hospital for the Continental Army during the Revolution. Now it contains the offices of Historic Bethlehem Inc.

Open Mondays through Fridays, 8:30 a.m. to 4:30 p.m. The Bach Choir and Music Department of Moravian College are also located in this building.

8 **Apothecary Museum**, set back from Main Street. Exhibited here are items from Bethlehem's 18th century, "Apotheke", including the only complete set of Deflt apothecary jars in the U.S., grinders, mortars and pestles, blown glass bottles, labels, and the original fireplace (1752) where prescriptions were compounded.

Open by appointment through Moravian Museum.

9 **Schnitz House**, Church Street. In this stone structure now covered with stucco, apples were cut and dried into "schnitz" for use during the winter. This is now a private residence.

10 **God's Acre**, on West Market Street, next to the Visitors Center. Here, buried in rows, lie the founders and forefathers of the town, as well as the North American Indians and blacks from Moravian missions in the West Indies. Gravestones were laid flat, indicating that all men are equal in God's eyes.

11 **Sun Inn**, Main Street. Erected in 1758, it was an early Moravian Inn, now planned for restoration.

12 **18th Century Moravian Industrial Area**, along the Monocacy Creek at Ohio Road and Main Street. Industrial development came quickly to early Bethlehem, the first settlers creating some 32 industries. You can see a number of these today, thanks to archaeology and restoration. Predominant is the four-story 1761 Tannery where animal hides were worked into leather. You'll also see the 1762 Waterworks, the reconstructed 1764 Springhouse, the 1869 Grist Mill, and the 1782 and 1830's Gristmiller's House. The high quality of the materials produced in this area made early Bethlehem self-sufficient and supported the missionary effort for many years.

The Industrial Area under the direction of Historic Bethlehem Inc. is open Tuesdays through Fridays, 1 to 4 p.m., Saturdays 10 a.m. to 4 p.m., closed Sundays and the month of January. $1.25 adults, 50¢ students through 12th grade, preschoolers free.

13 **Goundie House**, 501 Main Street. This Federal-style home was built in 1810 for John Sebastian Goundie, a prominent Moravian brewer. The restored home, owned by Historic Bethlehem Inc., now contains the Goundie House Shop and Office.

Open Mondays through Saturdays, 11 a.m. to 3 p.m.

14 Annie S. Kemerer Museum, 427 North New Street. This fine museum, which is housed in a private home, has a great variety of treasures: oriental rugs, Currier & Ives prints, Chippendale chairs, Hepplewhite chests, locally made grandfather clocks. Victorian double parlors with ornate carpeting and red and gold wallpaper display Belter-type rose-carved furniture and a grand piano with a mother-of-pearl inlay. One room is devoted to Bethlehem's German and Moravian heritage; a window-walled hallway is lined with cases of Venetian and American art glass and one of the finest collections known of Bohemian glass. A separate building houses the oldest fire engine in the U.S.; it was built in London in 1698 and was brought to Bethlehem by the Moravians in 1763.

Open 1 p.m. to 4 p.m., Mondays through Saturdays, and 2 to 4 p.m. on the second and fourth Sundays of the month. Closed holidays; contributions.

15 Lehigh University, Brodhead and Packer Avenues. Established in 1865, it has a beautiful 750-acre hillside campus. Located here is Packer Memorial Chapel, one of the campus buildings named after Asa Packer, Lehigh's founder. Packer worked on the canal boats as a boy, later becoming a powerful industrialist. He was responsible for the railroads by which Pennsylvania's anthracite coal was transported to the market.

Campus tours can be arranged, free of charge, through the Office of Admission in the Alumni Memorial Building, and are available weekdays from 1 to 4 p.m. all year, and Saturday 9 to 11:30 a.m. except for the summer months.

WHILE YOU'RE THERE . . .

The town of Easton was developed by Thomas Penn, son of William. It makes for an interesting side trip, being only a 20 minute ride traveling north on Route 22 from Bethlehem. From a tree-studded hill Lafayette College, chartered in 1826 and named after the famous Marquis, looks down on the town which is divided in two by the Lehigh River. Easton's Center Square, featuring a Civil War Monument, is undergoing a facelift for the Bicentennial; there will be a water fountain display with colored lights and a Hall of Flags representative of each of the 13 original colonies.

Easton has many sites of Revolutionary importance. Displayed under glass at the Public Library is the first stars and strips of the states, unfurled July 8, 1776, almost a year before the Continental Congress adopted the Flag Resolution in Philadelphia. The flag is said to have been carried by a local company during the War of 1812 — a present from the women of Easton. The town's First Reform Church, erected in 1776, was used as a hospital during the Revolution and was the site of treaty negotiations with the Indians. You can see the George Taylor House, residence of a signer of the Declaration of Independence. Across the street is the Northampton County Historical and Geneological Society with some fine exhibits of Easton's early history. In the lobby of the Northampton County Court House, erected 1860-61, is the county's own Liberty Bell, rung on the occasion of the official reading of the Declaration of Independence at the old Court House (no longer standing).

Historic Insight...
A Holy Land in The New World

Christmas Eve, 1741: A group of devout Christians of the Moravian Church were gathered in a log cabin, their new home in Pennsylvania being over 3,000 miles distant from the homeland, Herrnhut, Germany. The Moravians had come to these distant parts to serve as missionaries to the Indians. Their faith, which then was almost three centuries old, looked to the Bible as the only source of Christian doctrine. They worshipped according to the Scriptures, were opposed to war, and performed the most beautiful of music.

It had not been an easy task to settle in this strange wilderness, but the cabin sheltered them, and work had begun on the large community house. Now it was the holiest time of the year, a Christmas Eve of snow and howling wind. Inside the shelter, it was warm and comfortable for the missionaries and their sheep and oxen. Adding to the joy of the small band was the presence of their leader, Count von Zinzendorf, who—exiled from Saxony for his religious beliefs—had arrived for the Christmas celebration.

Count von Zinzendorf led this holy service in the first house. With the singing of an old German hymn ("Not Jerusalem—Lowly Bethlehem 'twas that gave us Christ to save us") he was struck by the similarity of this day to the first Christmas. Seizing a candle, he led his followers into the part of the cabin that housed the beasts. Here by the dim light of the candle, the service was completed. According to the diary of one of the Moravians, "Because of the day and in memory of the Birth of our dear Savior, we went into the stable in the tenth hour and sang with feeling, so that our hearts melted."

So it was that the town in America was named for the one in Judea.

Brethren's House Erected in 1748

THE POCONOS: "A Stream Between the Mountains"

The name "pocono" probably derives from an Indian word, "pocohanne", meaning a stream between the mountains. This 2400 square mile, four county area in northeastern Pennsylvania was a favorite hunting and fishing grounds for many tribes—Delaware, Shawnee, Iroquois and Lenape among them.

Industrial development came with the accidental discovery of anthracite coal in Carbon County by an 18th century hunter; this laid the groundwork for the county's later development as a coal-producing region and a railroad center. Honesdale, to the north in Wayne County, is, in fact, the birthplace of the American railroad. Here the first steam locomotive, the British-made "Stourbridge Lion" was set up in 1829 on the tracks of the Delaware and Hudson Canal Company.

Several forts were built in the Poconos during the French and Indian War, and the route of General John Sullivan's famous march of 1778 from Easton to New York State crossed Monroe County. Today the Poconos are filled with remembrances of these early days in the form of old buildings, historic markers, and reconstructed settlements.

Tourism came to these parts in the 1820s, with a boarding house hotel at the Delaware Water Gap. By 1900 thousands were visiting the Poconos each year on their summer vacations. A favorite spot was Mauch Chunk, "the Switzerland of America", now called Jim Thorpe after the great Olympic athlete.

Today tourism is a leading Poconos industry. Indeed, the area is one vast playground, boasting over 20 lakes, 12 ski trails, and more heart-shaped bathtubs per square foot than any other resort area of the world. (This last item derives from its position as the "Honeymoon Capital of the World".) The streams, mountains, waterfalls and woodlands have enough variety to satisfy a multitude of tastes, from the plush to the primitive, and each season of the year has its own visual splendor.

THE POCONOS EXCURSION

The sites listed below will take you roughly in a circle, leaving from and returning to the town of Stroudsburg. Plan a full day of sightseeing, and stay overnight in the area if you can, returning to Philadelphia the next morning.

Coming from Bethlehem, take Route 611 North.

The Poconos

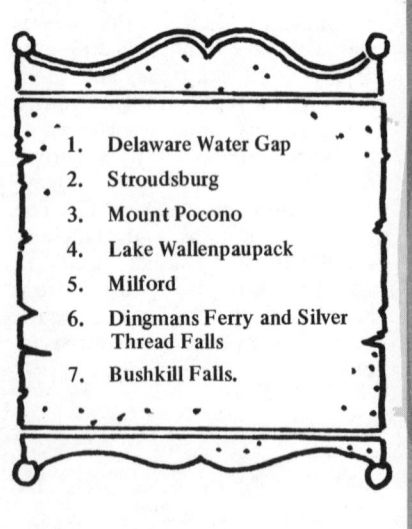

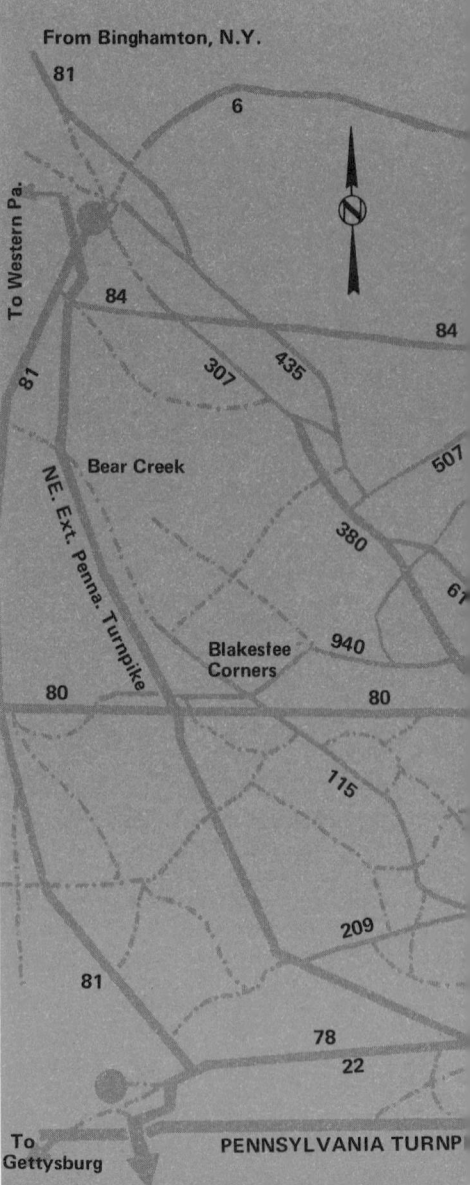

1. Delaware Water Gap
2. Stroudsburg
3. Mount Pocono
4. Lake Wallenpaupack
5. Milford
6. Dingmans Ferry and Silver Thread Falls
7. Bushkill Falls.

HISTORIC LOCATION MAP

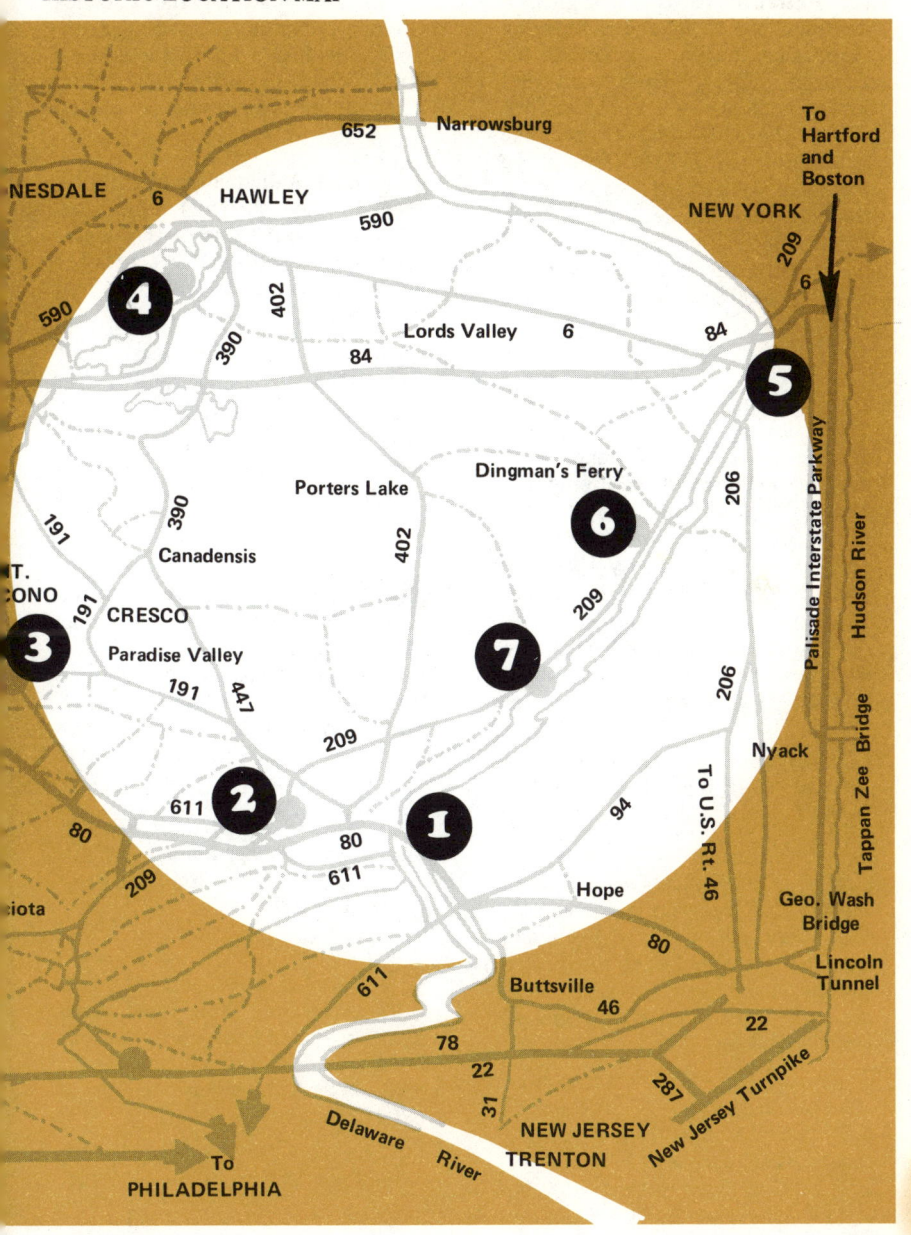

1 **Delaware Water Gap,** on PA. Route 611 and I-80. This is the entrance to the Poconos, a dramatic gorge in the Kittatinny Mountains, located at a bend of the Delaware River. White men first settled here in 1793, and since then visitors have flocked to see the mountains rising 1200 feet above the blue ribbon of water. It is thought that the mountains were formed after the creation of the river, rising up from the earth so slowly that the Delaware was never altered.

2 **Stroudsburg vicinity.** The Monroe County seat was founded in 1776 by Colonel Jacob Stroud, a veteran of the French and Indian Wars. His home at 9th and Main Streets is now headquarters for the Monroe County Historical Society, open Tuesday afternoons. You'll enjoy the Pocono Wild Animal Farm which is on PA 611; here wild animals roam, some of them free, others in cages.

(May to October, weather permitting, daily from 9 a.m. to 5:30 p.m.; $2 adults; $1 for ages 2-12.)

The Quiet Valley Farm Museum on US 209 contains a three-room log house dating from 1765 and nine other original or reconstructed buildings; demonstrations are held of early farm crafts and guided tours are given.

(Late June - Labor Day, Mondays to Saturdays, 9:30 a.m. to 5:30 p.m., Sundays from 1 p.m.; $2 adults, $1.25 ages 3 to 12.)

3 **Mount Pocono,** Route 611. This thriving resort community in the heart of the Poconos offers year-round recreation. Pocono Knob, just a bit to the east on Knob Road, has a fine view of the surrounding countryside.

4 **Lake Wallenpaupack,** PA 390. Formed in 1924, this manmade creation is one of the largest lakes in the state and a center for water sports. There are over 300 campsites at the lake.

5 **Milford,** U.S. 6. This charming town was where noted forester and conservationist Gifford Pinchot lived. His home is now the Pinchot Institute for Conservation Studies.

6 **Dingmans Ferry and Silver Thread Falls,** U.S. 209. These are the two highest waterfalls in the Pocono Mountains; Dingmans tumbles 175 feet over moss covered rocks into a swirling pool. Rhododendrons bloom profusely in July.

Open April 15 to December 15, weather permitting, daily, daylight hours; $1.25 adults, 50¢ ages 6 to 11, under 6 free.

7 **Bushkill Falls,** also off U.S. 209. This "Niagara of Pennsylvania" is the largest series of falls in the Poconos. You can picnic, boat, fish and observe a lot of native animals.

Open April - October, weather permitting, daily, 8 a.m. to dusk; $1.65, 6-12, 50¢.

EXCURSION 11

The Legendary Molly Pitcher

Hershey•Harrisburg Carlisle

From the world of Hershey chocolates to the business of state government and, finally, to a onetime frontier town — these are the ingredients of Excursion 11.

THE GUIDE suggests that you make this a two-day trip, seeing Harrisburg and Carlisle the second day and returning to Philadelphia that evening. An alternate plan is this: Instead of going back to Philadelphia, make your second overnight stop at Gettysburg and visit that historic battlefield as well as York the next day. In this way you would be combining Excursions 11 and 12.

Hershey
Harrisburg
Carlisle

HARRISBURG
(1) Capitol Building
(2) William Penn Memorial Museum
(3) Education Bu...
(4) Home of Joh...
(5) Italian Lake

CARLISLE
(1) Carlisle Barracks
(2) Grave of Molly Pitcher
(3) Carlisle Square
(4) Dickinson Co...
(5) Hamilton Lib...
(6) Western Villa...

HERSHEY MAP NEXT PAGE

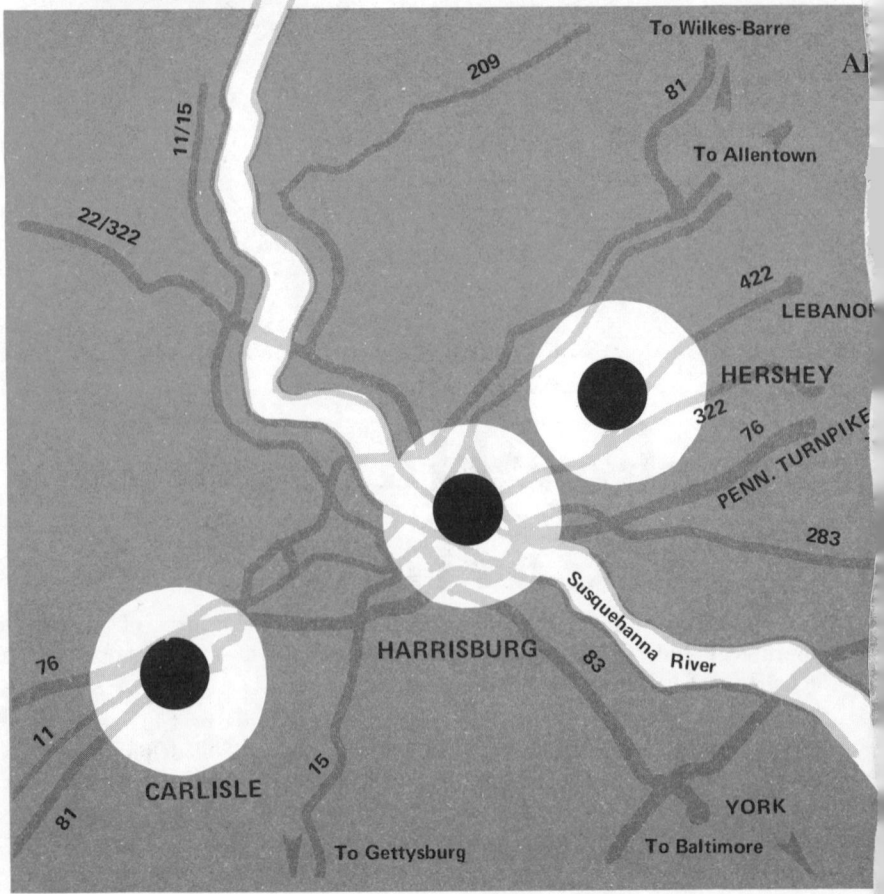

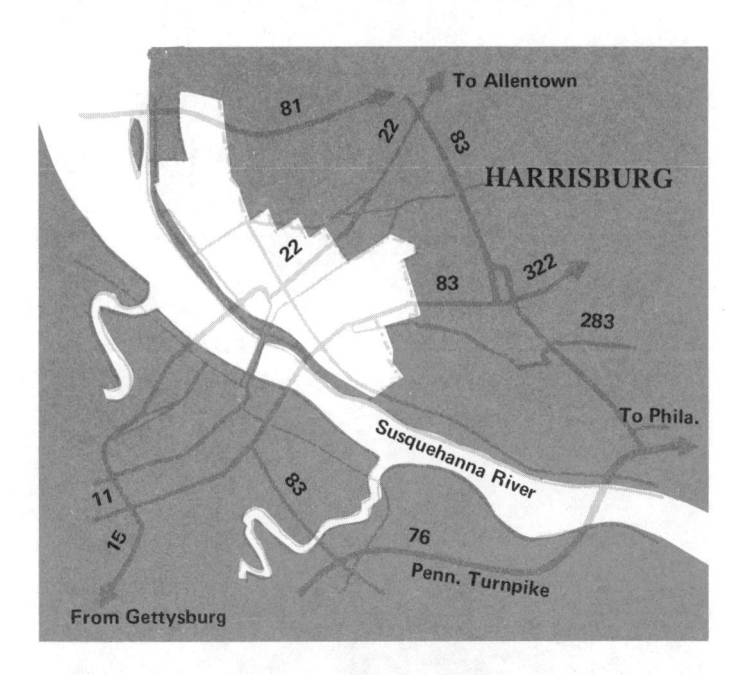

HISTORIC LOCATION MAP

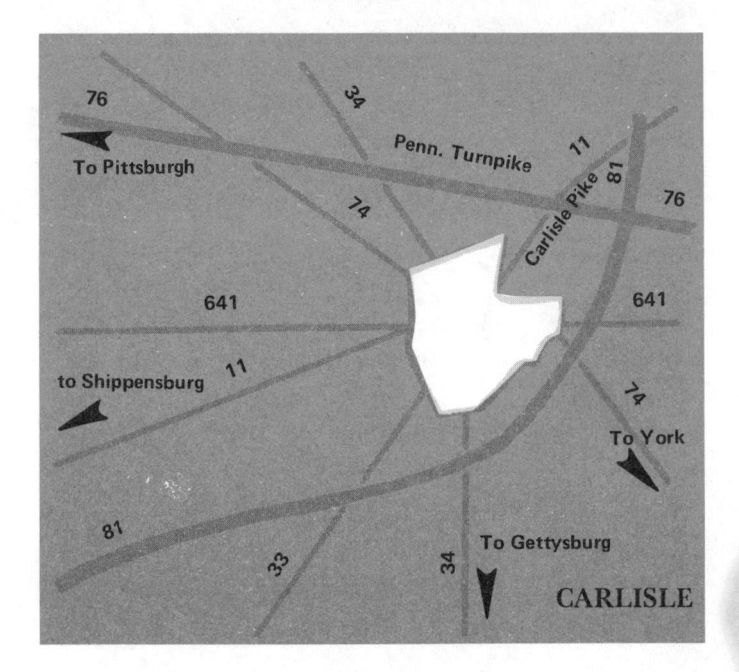

165

HERSHEY'S CHOCOLATE WORLD

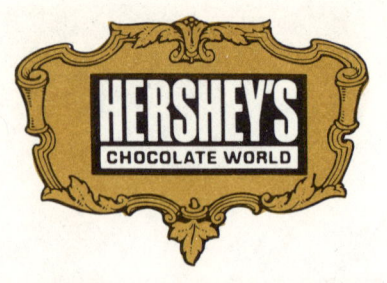

HISTORIC LOCATION MAP

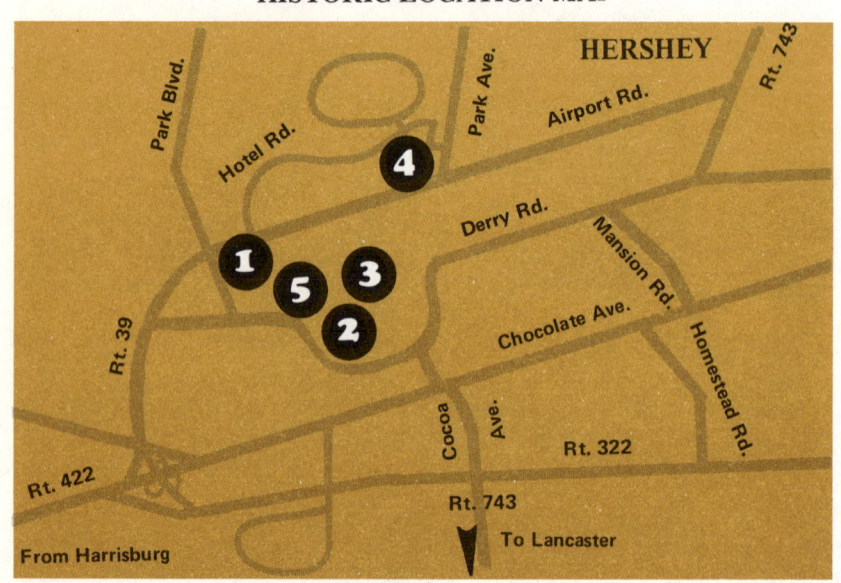

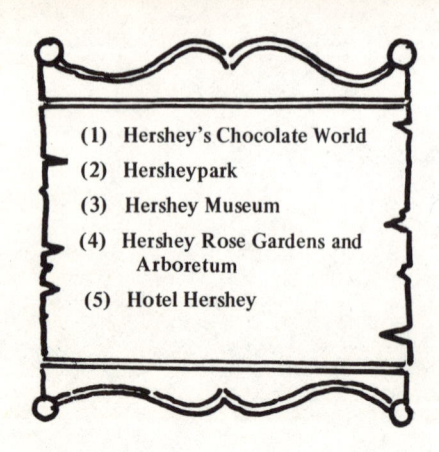

(1) Hershey's Chocolate World
(2) Hersheypark
(3) Hershey Museum
(4) Hershey Rose Gardens and Arboretum
(5) Hotel Hershey

America's Chocolate Town

HERSHEY'S CHOCOLATE WORLD

The saga of Milton S. Hershey and the now extinct five-cent candy bar is one of the most colorful success stories of 20th century America.

Born in 1857 to a Mennonite farming family near Hockersville, Pa., Hershey received schooling only to fourth grade. After a four-year apprenticeship as candymaker in an ice cream parlor, he went to Philadelphia, Denver and New York, seeking his fortune in such sweets as ice cream, salt water taffy and even cough drops. But ambition was not equalled by success until his return to Lancaster where a visiting English candy merchant tasted his milk-based caramels and contracted with him to provide these for export. Before long Hershey had become rich. Caramels, however, were merely a passing fancy for Hershey for by then he had discovered chocolate.

For the sum of one million dollars in cash, Milton Hershey sold out his caramel plant to a rival company and devoted his life to the cocoa bean. With characteristic ability for hard work and endless trial-and-error experimentation, he tried various combinations of ingredients, emerging with the world's first milk chocolate. By this time Lancaster had become too small for him, so Hershey decided to purchase some land and create a town to house his family, factory, employees and the cows that would give milk for the chocolate. This he did in nearby Derry Township. Hershey supervised the building of the entire town from sewers to homes — each of the latter being different from its neighbors. Churches of several faiths were erected; eventually Hershey paid the mortgages on these himself. When the post office was built, a contest was held to name it. The government didn't go for the winning entry of "Hersheykoko", however, and so the town became just plain Hershey.

Its founder lived there in grand style, decorating his mansion with expensive oil paintings, a chandelier bought at the World Exhibition in Paris, and a rooftop duck pond and boardwalk. But he didn't forget the humbler citizens. The most important of his charitable enterprises was a tuition-free school for boys who had only one parent or were orphans. Childless himself, Hershey left most of his money to this school which still exists. It enrolls students from kindergarten age through high school, combining training in academics with various trades. In 1963 $50 million dollars from the Hershey Trust Fund was granted to Penn State University to build a medical center.

World War I affected the chocolate industry as sugar prices mounted, but this was a temporary setback. In the depression years Her-

167

shey began a large number of construction projects such as a sports arena, a hotel, a community center and a high school, in order to assure employment for the people of his town. Later he said that not one man in his employ was dropped by reason of the depression, nor one salary cut. A benevolent autocrat, he was startled when the plant workers first went on strike in 1937, but he adjusted gradually to the principle of collective bargaining.

On Milton Hershey's 80th birthday that same year, his 6,000 employees presented him with a yellow gold octagon-shaped ring with the Hershey trademark (a child emerging from a cacao pod) encircled by 18 blue-white diamonds.

HERSHEY EXCURSION

From Philadelphia by car, take the Pa. Turnpike west to exit 20, go north on Pa. Route 72, west on U.S. Route 322, north on Pa. Route 743. (Gray Line Motor Tours and SEPTA have bus trips to Hershey, too.) This is about a 2 hour trip.

Depending on the degree of interest exhibited by your family in the subject of chocolate, you'll want to spend anywhere from a couple of hours to a full day here. In this Disneyland of the sweet tooth you'll find streetlamps shaped like Hershey kisses and intersections featuring names like Chocolate Avenue and Cocoa Avenue. The clock hands at the plant point not to numerals but to the 12 letters spelling HERSHEY COCOA. Given the shrinking size and soaring cost of candy bars in recent years, chocolate may become a luxury rather than a lunchbox staple, so go

and sniff the chocolate-laden air and see the 15 cent candy bars while they last. If you can avoid the summer months when as many as 15,000 visitors per day appear, you'll have a more relaxed visit.

THE GUIDE lists below the main Hershey attractions. If you wish to spend more time, you might like to visit the elaborate domed Founders Hall of The Milton Hershey School or take in a hockey game at Hershey Park Arena. Hershey Highmeadow Camp has facilities open year round for $5.50 per night per family. Write for reservations to 1 Chocolate Avenue, Hershey, Pa. 17033. An annual event in town is the five day Pennsylvania Dutch festival held during July (call 717-534-3172 for specifics) when early crafts of the country are demonstrated. $2.00 for adults, children under 12 free when accompanied by an adult.

For general information on Hershey, call Hershey Information Center, 717-534-3005.

Milton Hershey's First Automobile

Visitor's to Hershey's Chocolate World
Ride Through a Simulated World of Chocolate

1 **Hershey's Chocolate World.** Visitor used to tour the actual Hershey factory, but the town became such a tourist attraction that in 1973 this was discontinued in favor of a new visitors' center known as Hershey's Chocolate World. Via an automatic conveyance you are whisked on a nine-minute ride past 25 scenes illustrating the story of chocolate, from the growing and harvesting of cocoa beans in the tropics through the basic steps of production at the Hershey plant; the ride accommodates 1,800 people per hour. Afterward you are free to linger in an area depicting Hershey history and browse in a glass-roofed garden with cocoa bean trees and other tropical fruit- and flower-producing trees.

Chocolate World is open Monday through Saturday, 9 a.m. to 5 p.m.; Sunday from noon to 5 p.m. Closed Thanksgiving, Christmas, New Years; free.

2 **Hersheypark.** Truly one of the finest theme parks in America, featuring a 330 foot high Kissing Tower and six theme areas where baby animals roam free, Pennsylvania Dutch crafts, a group of old-fashioned European villages features native dishes, an antique carousel, 36 different rides, and dozens of daily shows. The Monorail trip allows you a bird's eye view of the park, and one-price admission entitles you to take part in all the rides, name acts and cultural attractions:

$7.00 for adults, $5.00 for children 5 to 9; under 4 free. Open every day from mid May through Labor Day, 10:30 a.m.

3 **Hershey Museum.** You'll see exhibits of arts and crafts from North American Indians and the Pennsylvania Dutch, including colonial furniture, Stiegel glass, pewter and ceramics, clocks, musical instruments, firefighting equipment, Conostoga wagons.

Open daily 10 a.m. to 5 p.m.; closed Thanksgiving, Christmas, New Years. Adults $1.50, children 6 to 15, 50¢.

4 **Hershey Rose Gardens and Arboretum:** This 23-acre area of trees, shrubs and flowers is known for its tulip display in April and May, azaleas in May-June, 1200 varieties of roses in June, and chrysanthemums in September-October.

Open April 15 to November 1, daily, 8 a.m. to dusk. Adults $1.00, children 7 to 15, 60¢, under 7 free.

5 **Hotel Hershey.** While you're in town, you should see Hotel Hershey even if you don't plan a stay or a meal here. It was the creation of Milton Hershey himself and gives you an idea of the uniqueness of the man, though its style hardly would be considered admirable by a classically trained architect. Hershey dreamed of a place like this for years, his plan becoming grander with every trip he made to exotic hotels abroad. He paid the architect of the Heliopolis Hotel in Cairo $7,000 for his plans, then made so many changes that the hotel ended up looking more Spanish than Egyptian. It has 150 rooms and luxurious gardens. There are no pillars in the dining room, as Hershey wanted guests to enjoy an unimpeded view of the Blue Mountains on the horizon.

Hershey Rose Gardens & Arboretum

HARRISBURG
From Trading Post to State Capital

The first settler in what is now Harrisburg was John Harris, a pioneer and trader. He came to this Indian village in about 1719 with his wife, opening a trading post and ferry; his stockaded house became a stopping place for travelers. The Harrises raised five children in this wilderness, and their life was not without its dangers. (Mrs. Harris rode several times to Lancaster and Philadelphia to warn the citizens of Indian uprisings.) Tradition tells us that a band of Indians lashed John Harris to a mulberry tree with the intent of burning him alive. The plan was frustrated by the arrival of Harris' black servant Hercules who crossed the river and brought back friendly Indians to rescue his master. By his expressed wish, John Harris was buried next to the mulberry tree alongside his faithful Hercules.

In 1736 the heirs of William Penn acquired a deed for this area, thereby validating a provincial government grant made to Harris a few years before. Harris' son of the same name, said to be the first white child born west of the Conewago, operated the ferry after his father's death and became an Indian agent. With his son-in-law (one of Pennsylvania's first senators) he laid out the town and, believing the capital of the commonwealth might someday be located here, conveyed a certain acreage to be held in trust until the legislature saw fit to use it. When the town became a borough in 1791, officials saw fit to call it Louisbourg in honor of King Louis XVI of France, but Harris would have none of this. "You may Louisbourg all you please," he announced, "but I'll not sell an inch more of land except in Harrisburg."

And Harrisburg it became. It was runner-up as site for the nation's capital but had to settle instead, in 1812, for the secondary role of state capital.

The Capitol Complex at Harrisburg Showing The Capitol Building William Penn Museum and Various Municipal Buildings

HARRISBURG EXCURSION

Harrisburg becomes something of a ghost town during the months when the legislature is not in session, but this quiet can be welcome — especially after the crowds at Hershey. And the city has some lovely areas (particularly the four miles along the River Parkway) which, combined with the rich Capitol complex, make for a most interesting visit. Special events, mostly centered at the State Farm Show Building, offer the visitor an agricultural exhibit in January, antiques in February, dogs in March, roses in June and horses in September.

Try, if you can, to avoid entering or leaving Harrisburg during weekday rush hour traffic. From Hershey the trip is only 12 miles via U.S. #322.

The focal point of our visit will be the Capitol complex at State and 3d Sts. The first three sites in this excursion are part of that complex.

1 **Capitol Building.** This Italian Renaissance building completed in 1906 replaced the old Capitol which had burned down. You can see its fine green dome, modeled on St. Peter's in Rome, from anywhere in the city. The dome is 272 feet high and weighs

26,000 tons; at the top a statue symbolic of the Commonwealth lifts a garlanded mace. The marble staircase in the building was inspired by the Paris Opera House. Many consider this Capitol to be one of the finest in the U.S.

But, alas, the noble edifice has a less exalted story to tell within. It cost $9 million to furnish, of which at least 2/3 was "documentable graft". When the State thought it was getting tile, it got plaster; bronze turned out to be alloy; and the French Baccarat crystal supposedly used under the dome was in actuality Pittsburgh plate glass, overpriced by 1,000%. Chandeliers were leaded to add weight, measurements were grossly exaggerated, the fireplace had no chimney, and even the spittoons, worth $3 apiece at the time, were sold to the State for $16. The rostrum in the House chamber, valued at $4,000, cost $167,438.79.

All this wasn't realized at first and at the Capitol's dedication President Theodore Roosevelt proclaimed it "the handsomest building I ever saw." Thanks largely to Democratic State Treasurer William H. Berry, the scandal was exposed. Berry received little thanks for his efforts and faded from the political scene, shunned by his own party. The administration of honest but incredibly naive Governor Samuel Pennypacker was permanently tainted by the episode. As for the perpetrators of this giant hoax — the crooked interior decorator and the grafters who hired him — they were tried and convicted. Those who didn't die during the lengthy litigation went to jail. The disclosures were believed responsible for at least three suicides.

All this makes the Capitol not less, but more, interesting. Don't miss it, for the beauty of the building itself is unquestionable and a lot of its furnishings and artwork are appropriately grand — the imposing statuary, marbled rotunda, ornate legislative chambers. Note the murals in the Governor's reception room which depict memorable incidents in the life of William Penn. (One of them shows an irate Admiral Penn denouncing his son for having joined the Quaker faith, while a soulful Great Dane offers the young man consolation.) Also, the floor of the Capitol has 400 hand-made mosaic tiles by Dr. Henry Mercer Chapman, considered one of the world's foremost tilemakers.

Guide service is available daily. The Capitol is open every day from 9 a.m. to 4:30 p.m. except New Year's, Election Day and Christmas; free. Phone: (717) 787-2121.

2 William Penn Memorial Museum. This important part of the Capitol complex contains five floors of exhibits and displays depicting Pennsylvania's historic, cultural and natural treasures — from geology to technology, from military history to the fine arts. The Memorial Hall on the first floor, rising three stories, is dominated by an 18-foot stylized bronze statue of William Penn. In an alcove to the rear of the statue are many of the state's most precious documents, including the Charter of 1681 from King Charles II of England which created and named Pennsylvania and designated William Penn as governor and proprietor. Another area contains six period rooms furnished in the major styles of the late 1600s to the 1800s, and a cross-section of early commercial buildings and trade shops is set in a rural village square. In the anthropological hall are artifacts of people who inhabited Pennsylvania 10,000 years before the Europeans arrived. The section on transportation takes the guest from the Indian canoe to the airplane. One of the world's largest framed paintings can be seen in Rothermel's "Pickett's Charge", the climax of the Battle of Gettysburg.

Museum is open Mondays through Saturdays from 9 a.m. to 5 p.m., Sundays 1 to 5 p.m.; closed most holidays. Free. For information call (717) 787-4978.

3 **Education Building.** This grey limestone building is worth seeing especially for the Forum, its lovely semicircular auditorium of neoclassic design. A colonnade of white marble separates the promenade from the tiers of seats. Deep blue is the predominant color of seats, draperies and carpets, and the walls reveal man's progress through time. The ceiling is designed to represent our constellations; stars shine in the proper degree of magnitude by means of a graduated brilliance in lights studding the ceiling.

Open Mondays through Fridays, 8:30 a.m. to 5 p.m.; closed most holidays. Free.

4 **Home of John Harris,** 219 Front Street. This stone house was built in 1766 by Harrisburg's founder near the Susquehanna's best fording place and at the spot where his father had his log trading post. Now the headquarters of the Historical Society of Dauphin County, it is furnished in 18th century style and contains documents of local history.

Open Mondays through Fridays, 1 to 4:30 p.m., Saturdays from September to June, 1 to 4 p.m.; closed holidays and first two weeks in August; free.

5 **Italian Lake,** N. 3d and Division Streets. This artificially created, landscaped lake has ice skating in the winter and in summer is bordered with flowers, shrubs and trees in an Italian garden setting. June is particularly lovely, for there are thousands of rosebushes. From the street you can see the Dance of Spring, a fountain designed by Giuseppe Donato. The fountain depicts three small fawns, each with upturned bowl upon his head, playing flutes for three dancing nymphs. Donato originally was commissioned to do the work by Milton Hershey but the chocolate king considered the uncloaked fawns and nymphs to be obscene and refused to accept the statue. After Donato won a judgment against him, Hershey donated the work to Harrisburg.

WHILE YOU'RE THERE . . .

Near Harrisburg there are several interesting spots to visit if you are not in a rush. Rockville Bridge to the north near Fort Hunter is the longest stone arch bridge in the world; it was constructed with 440 million pounds of stone. Fort Hunter, north of Harrisburg on U.S. 322, was one of a chain of forts erected during the French and Indian War; you can visit the museum and the mansion erected in 1814 which contains exhibits of colonial home life. Automobilorama, one of the largest displays of antique, vintage and classic cars in the country, is located southwest of Harrisburg on U.S. 15. Indian Echo Caverns, east of the city in Hummelstown, has a fairytale display of stalactite and stalagmite formations, with more than 1700 electric lights, walks and handrails.

CARLISLE
Frontier Town
of The Cumberland Valley

The Cumberland Valley played a vital role in Pennsylvania's history as doorway to the west, and Carlisle, founded in 1751, was its heart. This area was settled by the Scotch-Irish, a group that had been harried out of Scotland into Northern Ireland during the 17th century. Almost all Presbyterians, they were an energetic, individualistic people, hungry for land and willing to work hard upon it — their women could wield an axe as well as the men. Progressive in education and religion, jacks-of-all-trades, they often clashed with the Quakers to the east who, they felt, had an unfairly large share of representation in the provincial government. In particular, the Scotch-Irish resented the pacifistic attitudes of the Friends; indeed, the latter could afford to be more generous to potential enemies than could these vulnerable frontier folk. The French and Indian War, during which the French with Indian support battled England to gain domination of Canada and the western lands, was a time of terror and heroic deeds for the inhabitants of the Cumberland Valley. It was a Carlisle man, Col. John Armstrong, who in 1756 marched with 280 men from his town to destroy the Indian village of Kittanning; this was the end of the savage Indian attacks in the state.

Patriotism came naturally to Carlisle's residents. Three of them signed the Declaration of Independence: James Wilson, Thomas Smith, and George Ross. In Carlisle Square, shortly before the Revolution, a mass meeting was held to gauge public opinion. Those in favor of the Revolution were asked to move to the north side, those against it to the south. The entire gathering moved northward. Following the battle of Bunker Hill a contingent of Carlisle and York troops marched from the square to Boston, becoming the First Regiment of the Continental Army; they were led by Colonel William Thompson whose commission was signed by John Hancock.

Barely 20 years later Carlisle Square saw the march of Federal troops against the Whiskey Rebellion. The "whiskey boys" were those western farmers who refused to pay taxes on the Monongahela whiskey that they had been converting from excess grain. (A one gallon jug of "moonshine" passed for 25¢ in every store on the western slopes of the Alleghenies.) Officers endeavoring to collect the excise tax had been tarred and feathered. President Washington called out 15,000 troops and journeyed to Carlisle where he began a march to Bedford. In Carlisle he received an address of welcome and loyalty, and the march was successful. In this episode the Federal government passed the first real test of its ability to enforce law.

Carlisle was later an active station on the underground railroad. In July 1863 a group of Confederate soldiers came here demanding surrender, but finding a Union force instead of the expected Robert E. Lee, shelled the town, burned the U.S. Army barracks and galloped away. This was the northernmost point of penetration by a considerable body of Southern troops during the war.

CARLISLE EXCURSION

Carlisle is now a peaceful college town which has many reminders of gracious 18th century living. Row upon row of authentic colonial homes are surrounded by lovely gardens. The town is located about 17 miles west of Harrisburg via U.S. 11.

If you wish to spend more time than THE GUIDE has allotted for Carlisle, the Cumberland County Tourist Council at 100 Shady Lane has a walking tours brochure listing additional sites.

1 **Carlisle Barracks,** one mile north on U.S. 11. This is the home of the Army War College, senior school in the U.S. Army's educational system. The barracks itself dates from 1757; it is one of the oldest military posts in America and played a notable part in three wars. From this point began the British campaigns that drove the French from the Ohio Valley and the march to capture Fort Duquesne (later Fort Pitt). In Revolutionary days the Hessian Guard House was built here by British prisoners captured at the Battle of Trenton; it was used for the storage of explosive materials. During the Civil War, the barracks was burned during the Gettysburg campaign.

From 1879 to 1918 the Carlisle Indian School was housed here. This was the first non-reservation school for Indians in the United States. An outstanding educational facility, in its heyday it enrolled 1200 redskins from 79 tribes — among them that legendary Oklahoma-born athlete Jim Thorpe, a football and baseball star and Olympic champion.

The post is open from dawn to dusk. Visit the Hessian Guard House, now a museum with historic mementos of the Indian School and Jim Thorpe.

Open May through September, Saturdays and Sundays from 1 to 4 p.m.; closed rest of year and holidays; free. The Omar N. Bradley

Museum has papers and memorabilia of this World War II general. Open May through September, Mondays through Fridays, 11:30 a.m. to 4:30 p.m.; Saturdays and Sundays from 1 to 4:30 p.m.; closed rest of year. Free.

2 Grave of Molly Pitcher, Old Graveyard, South St. Mary Hays served the Revolution as did other women, drawing water for the Continental soldiers during battle. But when her husband, a Carlisle barber, fell mortally wounded in the terrible confrontation of Monmouth, New Jersey in 1778, she went beyond the call of wifely duty, taking his place beside the cannon and firing at the approaching British. Legend has it that after the battle George Washington pensioned the brave soldieress who took to sporting military boots, cropped hair, a tricorn hat, and some unfeminine language.

It is thought that the same Mary Hays was given the nickname of "Molly Pitcher" because she passed back and forth among the troops with her pitcher of water. However, there are strikingly similar accounts of other women who also drew water and took men's places in battle; hence the name might have referred to any of them.

In any case, this particular "Molly Pitcher" is buried here along with other Revolutionary notables; a statue honors her service in battle. *Open at any time; free.*

3 Carlisle Square, intersection of Hanover and High Streets. This square which saw so much history has a few fine buildings that you should not miss. The First Presbyterian Church at the northwest corner is the oldest building in the city. Here, we are told, the "first voice of organized protest against tyranny" was heard on June 12, 1774, and here in May 1776 the local declaration of independence from Great Britain was composed. George Washington worshipped in this building of local grey limestone, erected in 1757. Another corner of the square is occupied by the beautiful St. John's Episcopal Church, erected 1825.

Both houses of worship are open from 9 a.m. to 5 p.m. daily; free.

The old and new courthouses are on the other corners. In its northern drive the Confederate Army bombarded the old courthouse.

You can tour it if you arrange this in advance through the new courthouse whose hours are: 8 p.m. to 4:30 p.m. Mondays through Fridays; free.

4 Dickinson College, High and College Streets. Dickinson College was founded in 1773 by physician Benjamin Rush of Philadelphia. It was the 10th college chartered in the U.S., and among its graduates was the nation's 15th president, James Buchanan.

The institution is named after Maryland-born John Dickinson, an attorney trained in the London courts who became a leading champion of American rights. His eloquent writings — especially "Letters from a Pennsylvania Farmer" — justified the colonies' resistance to British authority and influenced his fellow countrymen more than the words of any other public figure.

The heart of the campus is the U-shaped building known as "Old West" which was constructed in 1803 and designed by Benjamin Latrobe, one of the creators of the Capitol building in Washington, D.C. The imposing, post-colonial edifice is of rough hewn limestone and now houses administrative offices. In the Spahr Library is the Joseph Priestley collection including the burning glass through which oxygen was first liberated.

If you call the admissions office at 243-5121, you will be accorded a full campus tour free of charge.

5 **Hamilton Library (Cumberland County Historical Society),** 21 N. Pitt Street at Dickinson Avenue. In this Victorian structure you'll see relics of colonial days including the oldest American printing press (1787) and the first commission issued for the Continental Army, also mementos of the Carlisle Indian School.

Open Mondays and Tuesdays from 7 to 9 p.m., Wednesdays, Thursdays and Fridays, from 2 to 5 p.m.; closed holidays. Free.

6 **Western Village Park and Museum,** one and one-half miles south of Carlisle on Walnut Bottom Road. If you are traveling with children, they probably have had their fill of serious history by now, so treat them to this reconstructed old western town. It has a blacksmith shop, general store, post office and jail. There are pony rides and picnicking areas as well.

Open late May to early September, daily from 10 a.m. to 8 p.m., closed rest of year. Adults $1.50 weekends and $1 weekdays; ages 6 to 12, 50¢; under 6, free; subject to change.

Hessian Fusilier 1777

ATTRACTIONS IN THE HARRISBURG AREA . . .

For free tourist, group or convention literature, write **The Cumberland County Tourist Council**, 100 Shady Lane, Carlisle, Pennsylvania 17013, or call (717) 249-3293.

Hershey Estates, Hershey, PA, Chocolate Town, U.S.A. — a total travel destination. Hotel Hershey and the spacious Hershey Motor Lodge. Chocolate World, free tour of every step in making the great American Chocolate Bar — open seven days a week. Hersheypark, one of America's top 15 theme parks, open mid-May to Labor Day. Hershey Rose Gardens, Hershey Museum, High-Meadow Camp, Founders Hall and so much more.

Detour for the Economy-Minded. Pennsylvania Outlet Mall, 5103 Carlisle Pike, Mechanicsburg (Harrisburg-Carlisle area). 15 factory outlets under one roof where you can save to 70% on famous label fashions for men, women, and children.

Colonel Johnston House, Route 322 at Boalsburg, is the oldest surviving house in the village. Built in 1811 by Colonel James Johnston, it was a private residence until restoration in 1973. Choose fine Pennsylvania antiques, charming old-fashioned gifts.

10:00 to 5:00, except Sundays.

Dutch Country Antiques, 13 Walnut Street, Bellevue, Pennsylvania, on Route 655. Painstaking hand restoration and fine Pennsylvania Dutch Country Antiques.

Colonial Peddlers is a rustic village of craft and Americana shops in the spirit of 1776. Located just off Route 11 at Pennsylvania Turnpike Interchange 16, Carlisle.

Open every day.

Klinger Farms, Route 26N at State College. The magnificent Pennsylvania barn, built originally in 1814, was remodeled and restored in 1973. It is now the home of Tom Horner, Interior Designer. For sale, in all this authentic rusticity, intriguing furnishings and gifts.

9:00 to 5:30, except Sundays.

Facilities, attractions and history all blend to provide **"Something for Everyone"** in Historic Cumberland County, the vacation hub of Central Pennsylvania. Nestled in the rural center of the state, Cumberland is within one day's drive to Lancaster, Gettysburg or Hershey.

**Historic Locations
at Gettysburg
Battlefield**

EXCURSION 12

2nd U.S. Cavalry

Virginia Cavalry

Gettysburg • York

The first town on this tour, Gettysburg, achieved its fame during the Civil War and the second, York, during the American Revolution. If you are combining this excursion with the preceding one, you might be able to see the highlights of both towns in one — albeit tiring — day. But if you are driving to Gettysburg directly from Philadelphia, plan an overnight stop in the area and see York on your second day. Should you have some spare time, you'll not find a lack of amusement with three state parks containing over 6,000 acres and more golf courses per square mile than anywhere else in the country.

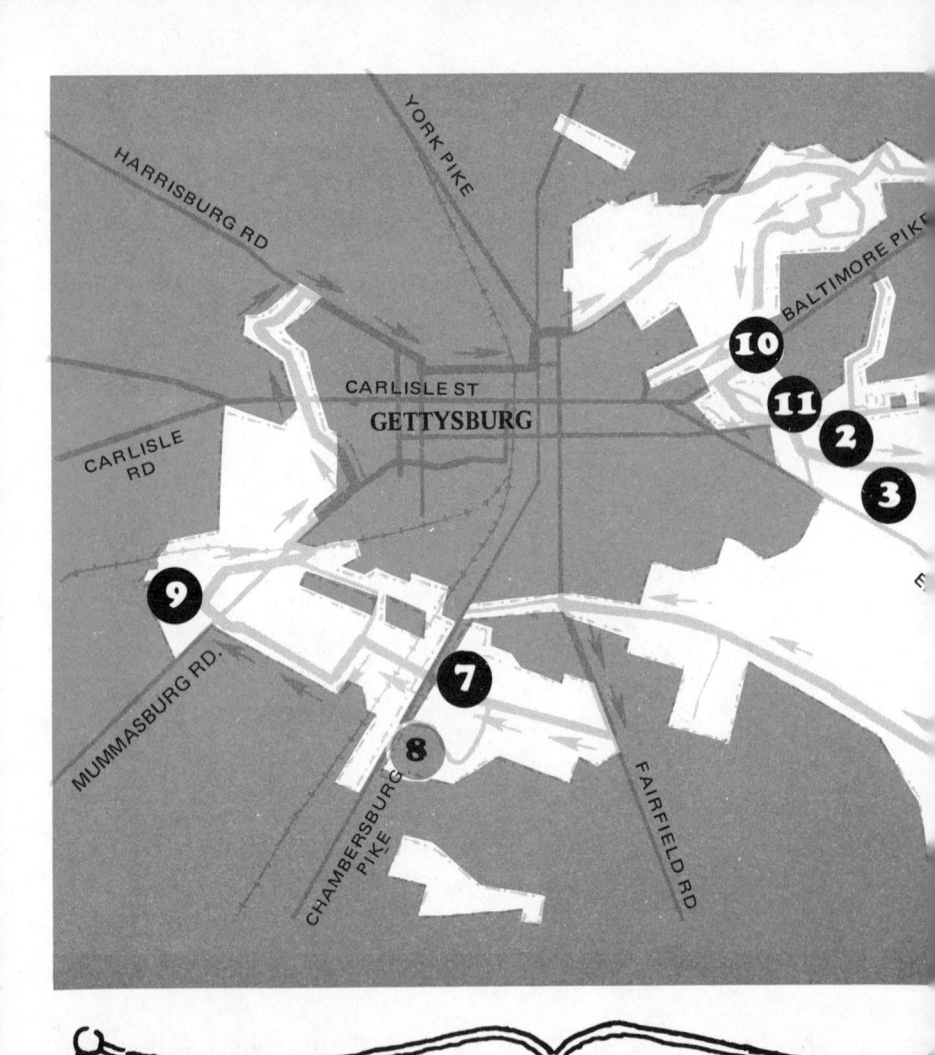

GETTYSBURG

- (1) Gettysburg Travel Council, Inc.
- (2) Visitor's Center
- (3) High Water Mark
- (4) Pennsylvania Memorial
- (5) Little Round Top
- (6) Devil's Den
- (7) McPherson Ridge
- (8) General Lee's Headquarters
- (9) Eternal Light Peace Memorial on Oa
- (10) Cemetery Hill
- (11) National Cemetery
- (12) Eisenhower National Historic Site
- (13) Gettysburg Miniature Horse Farm

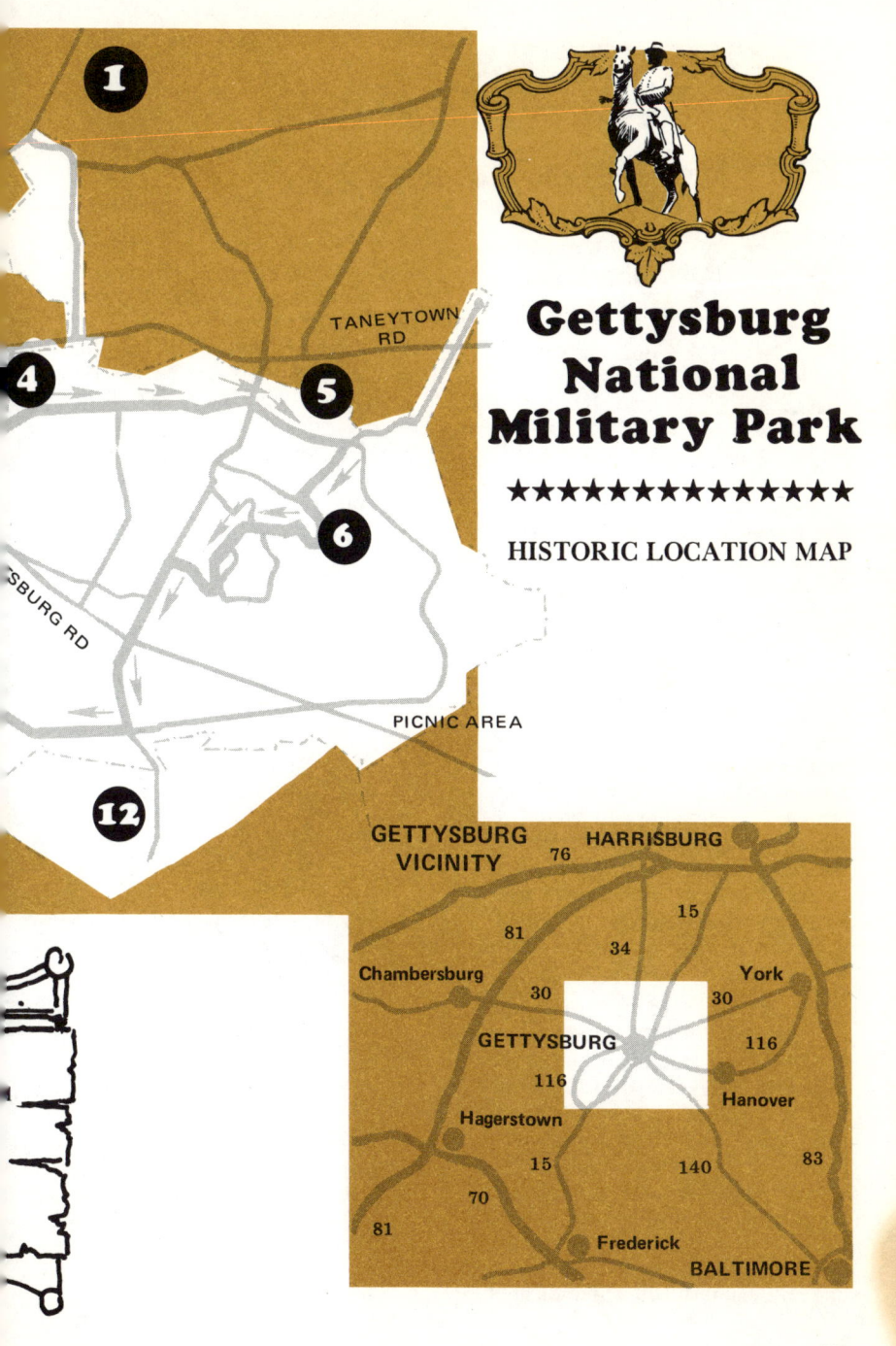

Gettysburg National Military Park

★★★★★★★★★★★★★★★★

HISTORIC LOCATION MAP

TANEYTOWN RD

PICNIC AREA

GETTYSBURG VICINITY

HARRISBURG
76
15
81
34
Chambersburg
30 — 30 — York
GETTYSBURG
116
116
Hanover
Hagerstown
15   140   83
70
81
Frederick
BALTIMORE

183

GETTYSBURG
High Water Mark
of The Confederacy

Gettysburg, the country seat of Adams County, had been a tranquil market and college town before it became the scene of Civil War battle on July 1, 2 and 3 of 1863. The battle occurred by accident — neither the southern Confederates under General Robert E. Lee nor the northern Union Army under Major General George G. Meade planned a confrontation here. Lee had been hoping to take Harrisburg and then Philadelphia on this second — and, as it turned out, last — foray into northern territory. His aim was a negotiated peace on the basis of southern independence. But when his hitherto invincible army detoured to Gettysburg in search of shoes and found the enemy instead, the fight began. When it was over, one-third of the 160,000 men who had participated were killed, wounded or missing, and the victor was now the vanquished.

The first day of battle saw the Confederates pitted against some 18,000 Union troops, including the famed Iron Brigade of 1800 westerns with black slouch hats tilted over their eyes ("those damn black hat fellers," as the rebels called them). These Union troops were hemmed in on all sides and forced to retreat, along with the First Corps. Finally they patched up a line on Cemetery Hill which offered good defense, while the Confederates held the town. On the second day northerners all over the field gave their lives in the valiant and successful effort to win or hold strategic positions at Devil's Den and Little Round Top. Lee's chance for victory came and went that day; the tide had turned. On the third day, the southern general played his desperate last card, hurling 12,000 Confederates across open country right into the Union center.

Confederate Infantryman

Looking across the valley, the northern troops which were protected by a stone wall on the crest of a low ridge, saw a line of battle one and one-half miles long moving inexorably in their direction. A Union staff officer described the scene: "The red flags wave, their horsemen gallop up and down ... barrel and bayonet gleam in the sun, a sloping forest of flashing steel. Right on they move, as with one sound, in perfect order, without impediment of ditch, wall or stream, over ridge and slope, through orchard and meadow and cornfield, magnificent, grim, irresistible."

When they were less than halfway across the wooded ridge, the Union troops opened fire. A little nearer, the batteries on Round Top unleashed a raking fire, tearing great holes in the Confederate ranks. But the southerners didn't stop even with "our guns bellowing in their faces. All along each hostile front, a thousand yards, the narrowest space between, the volleys blaze and roll; as thick the sound as when a summer hail storm pelts the city roofs, as thick the fire as when the incessant lightning fringes a summer cloud." Spearheaded by General George Pickett and his division of 4300 men, southern troops charged up Cemetery Ridge, emerging so near that the expressions on their faces could be seen by the enemy. Every man was on his own and the fate of a nation rode on the outcome. When, in less than an hour, this most terrible battle ever fought on American soil was over, the winner was George G. Meade, a workhorse of a general and a firm disciplinarian who had taken leadership only days before.

The loser: Robert E. Lee, a brilliant man, beloved by his men, who ironically had freed his own slaves because he believed slavery a moral wrong. (Lee had chosen to fight on the side of the Confederates out of loyalty to Virginia and the conviction that a nation divided could function better as two nations.)

The next day scores of grief-stricken women poured onto the battlefield in search of their men. It is said that in their frenzied quest they dug up a thousand bodies before turning away in despair and exhaustion. Shortly afterward it was decided to create a cemetery on 17 acres of the battlefield, bought by the state of Pennsylvania for that purpose. Abraham Lincoln dedicated it that November. In 1895, by an act of Congress, the vast Gettysburg National Military Park was created, memorializing for all America this tragic fight between brothers.

GETTYSBURG EXCURSION

Gettysburg is 140 miles from Philadelphia. It can be reached by driving west on the Pennsylvania Turnpike to the Gettysburg interchange (#17); from here take U.S. Route 15 south. Coming instead from Carlisle (if you are combining this excursion with the previous one), go south on Route 34.

As this is cherry, peach and apple growing country, you'll find an early May visit when the flowering trees are in bloom to be particularly lovely; the second weekend in October is apple harvest festival time.

Gettysburg is a town whose history comes alive to the visitor with almost unbearable realism. But it has another side: the Disneyland aura created by too many picture postcards, dioramas, and generals made of wax. These Civil War-related commercial enterprises vary in quality, and some are quite good. The electric map at Gettysburg National Museum on Route 15 south, for instance, with its accompanying taped description of the battle, can provide an enlightening introduction to the battlefield. Also, the room at Wills House in town where Lincoln revised his Gettysburg Address and stayed overnight has an eerie kind of appeal; it has been refurnished and features a 6'4" Lincoln made of wax sitting in his shirtsleeves while a tape recording simulates the scratching of his pen. If you wish to visit these or other such attractions, be sure to leave enough time to see the battleground. (For an extensive Park tour you will need about three hours.)

1 **Gettysburg Travel Council, Inc.**, Carlisle Street, Business Route 15. The staff here is well equipped to help you choose from among the varied tourist offerings in Gettysburg and to suggest ways for you to see the battlefield (via rented auto tape, by guided bus tour, even by helicopter). The Council also provides an excellent walking tour brochure of the town and a "Scenic Valley Tour" into upper Adams County which includes a number of forts from the French and Indian War. Be sure to take a look at the maroon and grey exterior of this building, for it is of historic importance itself as the one-time Western Maryland Railroad Passenger Depot. Here Lincoln stepped off the train for his sad mission.

Open Mondays through Fridays from 9 a.m. to 5 p.m.; open weekends as well as from March 15 to November 30.

And now, on to the battlefield, which almost completely surrounds the town.

The Park itself is open daily all year from 6 a.m. to 10 p.m., free of charge.

The nine Park sites listed below are only the highlights of the battlefield; as you follow Park routings you will see many more.

③ High Water Mark. Here at the copse of trees and "The Angle", Pickett's Charge was halted on July 3.

Confederate Cavalryman

② Visitor's Center. Should you elect to use one of the highly knowledgeable Park guides to accompany you in your car for a data-packed $8 tour, you would arrange for this here. The Center also shows a free film, "These Honored Dead", provides maps of the Park, and has a 356-foot painting of Pickett's charge accompanied by a sound-and-light story (50¢; free to those 15 and under).

The Center is open every day except Christmas and New Year's Day; hours from 8 a.m. to 9 p.m. July to Labor Day, 8 a.m. to 6 p.m. May – June, 8 a.m. to 5 p.m. rest of year. For information, call (717) 334-1124.

Union Drummer Boy

**Soldiers National Monument
Site of Gettysburg Address**

4 **Pennsylvania Memorial.** On a field noted for its monuments, this one is outstanding. It contains statues of officers and bronze nameplates calling the roll of the nearly 35,000 Pennsylvanians who fought here.

5 **Little Round Top,** the key Union position during the second and third days of battle. Quick action here by General Meade's chief engineer saved Little Round Top from the enemy and a probable victory at Gettysburg. There is a panoramic view of the battlefield from this spot.

6 **Devil's Den,** stronghold of Confederate sharpshooters who fired on Little Round top from this spot.

7 **McPherson Ridge.** Just beyond McPherson's barn the Battle of Gettysburg started early on July 1.

8 **General Lee's Headquarters.** This house contains a collection of historical items from the battlefield. Modern historians do not agree with the claim that it was used as headquarters by the Confederate general.

Open 9 a.m. to 9 p.m. summer and fall; free.

**Robert E. Lee
Commanding General
Army of Northern Virginia**

The Pennsylvania Monument

9 Eternal Light Peace Memorial on Oak Hill. Dedicated by President Franklin D. Roosevelt in 1938, this 40-foot high memorial shaft has a sculpted bas-relief at its base which depicts two figures standing in embrace, holding an olive branch and wreath. In a bronze urn the eternal light traditionally burned at full flame from dusk to dawn until the present energy crisis.

10 Cemetery Hill. Here Union troops rallied late on July 1. The next evening they repelled a Confederate assault that reached the crest of the hill east of this road.

11 National Cemetery. On the spot where Lincoln delivered the Gettysburg Address is the Soldiers' National Monument, commemorating the Union dead who fell here.

12 Eisenhower National Historic Site. Site #12 takes us outside the Park to a favorite tourist attraction: Dwight D. Eisenhower's farm, immediately southwest of the battlefield. It is not open to the public, but you can get a good view from the 75-foot tower at the edge of the Park. The farmhouse was bought by the General in 1951 for his retirement years. After being recalled to active duty as head of the NATO forces in Europe and then on to two terms as President, he visited the 15-room, 230 acre farm often. It was deeded to the government but is now being used as Mamie Eisenhower's residence.

13 **Gettysburg Miniature Horse Farm,** Route 30 west off Knoxlyn Road. The remarkable miniature horses housed here are of a special breed developed within the last hundred years; you'll also find thoroughbreds, appaloosas, palominos and draft horses. Children love riding a wagon or cart down the 1/4 mile tract. Picnic area is available. This is a relaxing and unusual place to visit at the end of your battle-weary day.

Open daily July to Labor Day from 9:30 a.m. to 6:30 p.m.; Good Friday to June and after Labor Day to mid November, 10 a.m. to 5:30 p.m.; closed rest of year. $1.50 adults, 75¢ children 3 to 11, under 3 free.

A Solitary Cannon, one of many used in a withering fire on Pickett's Brigade overlooks the Battlefield

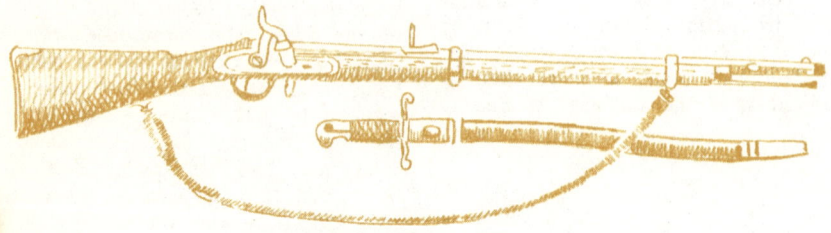

Civil War Enfield Rifle and Bayonet

**Major General
George E. Pickett, C.S.A.**

Pickett's 4300 Man Confederate Division made the famous charge at Cemetery Ridge.

**Brigadier General
John Buford**

Buford's Union Cavalry made initial contact with advance Confederate Forces, in search of shoes.

**Major General
George G. Meade**

Overall Commander of Union Forces at Gettysburg

Historic Insight...
"A Wet Blanket"

November 19, 1863. It was a lovely day of Indian summer, but the crowd was bored and anxious to go home. For two hours the voice of Edward Everett, illustrious orator, had droned on . . . and on.

The setting did not help matters, for it was a graveyard, a field where four months before a terrible battle had raged.

A tall, gaunt man in a black frock coat stood by patiently awaiting his turn. He had arrived at the town's small railway station the day before, having been asked (almost as an afterthought) to deliver "a few appropriate remarks" at the battlefield dedication. In the second floor bedroom of a local house, he had sat in his shirtsleeves redoing the draft of these "appropriate remarks".

Now it was time. Everett finally stopped talking and the crowd of thousands sighed in relief. The tall, gaunt man got up with two sheets of paper in his hand. "Fourscore and seven years ago our fathers brought forth on this continent a new nation, conceived in liberty and dedicated to the proposition that all men are created equal," began President Abraham Lincoln. He spoke of the dedication of the battlefield, the men who died upon it, the great task that remained for his divided nation to assure that "government of the people, by the people, for the people shall not perish from the earth."

In all Abe Lincoln spoke only 272 words in less than three minutes. Then he sat down. The speech was received, said the President himself, "like a wet blanket." Some of the newspapers that covered it were hardly more charitable; among them was a Harrisburg paper that dismissed the address dedicating Soldiers' National Cemetery in Gettysburg as "silly remarks". The Chicago Tribune felt differently — as did posterity — saying it "would live among the annals of men."

Still, the speaker felt he'd done poorly. "I ought to have prepared it with more care," Abe Lincoln said.

YORK America's Unsung Capital

Light Dragoon Pistol 1777

York, founded in 1741, was the first Pennsylvania town west of the Susquehanna. Its Germanic inhabitants developed the area's rich agriculture, while the English settlers gave the town its characteristic Georgian architecture of red brick buildings with white trim.

York's part in America's struggle for independence was a proud one. One of the first military companies to resist the encroachments of Great Britain was organized here in 1774 – its captain, James Smith, who later signed the Declaration of Independence. But the town's real glory occurred from September 20, 1777 to June 27, 1778 when the Continental Congress, having fled from British-occupied Philadelphia to this safer location, met in York's little brick courthouse. During these crucial days of the Revolution, Congress adopted the Articles of Confederation under which the new nation was to be governed. The term "United States of America" was first used in this document, hence York's claim that it was the "first capital of the U.S." News of Burgoyne's surrender at Saratoga, followed by that of France's treaties of alliance with the new nation were received with rejoicing in York, and Von Steuben and Lafayette were commissioned as major generals here. At York Furnace on Codorus Creek iron ore was smelted for cannon balls to be used by General Washington's men. The first National Thanksgiving Proclamation was issued from York's courthouse.

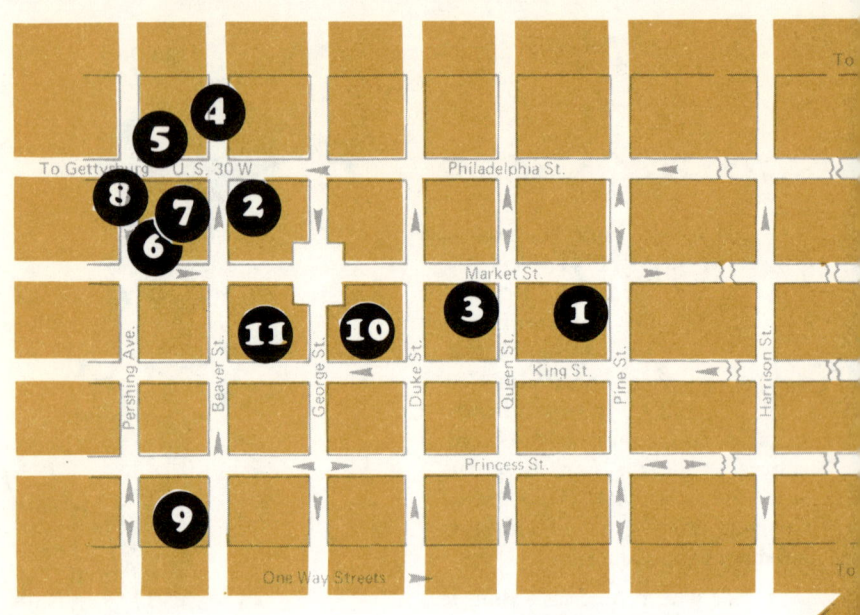

DOWNTOWN YORK

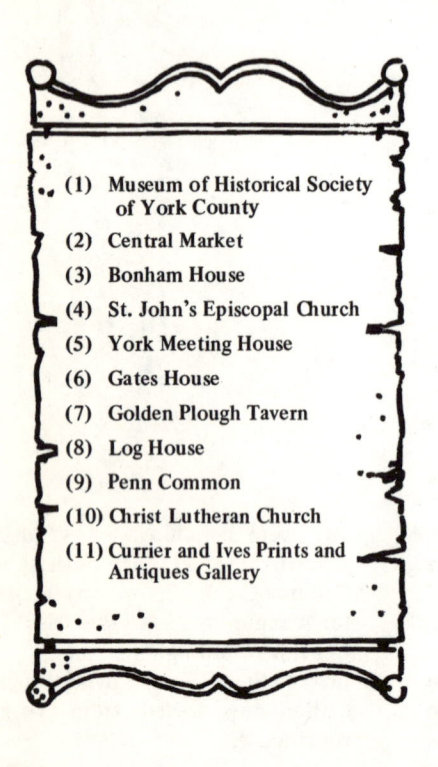

(1) Museum of Historical Society of York County
(2) Central Market
(3) Bonham House
(4) St. John's Episcopal Church
(5) York Meeting House
(6) Gates House
(7) Golden Plough Tavern
(8) Log House
(9) Penn Common
(10) Christ Lutheran Church
(11) Currier and Ives Prints and Antiques Gallery

Historic York County

LOCATION MAP

YORK

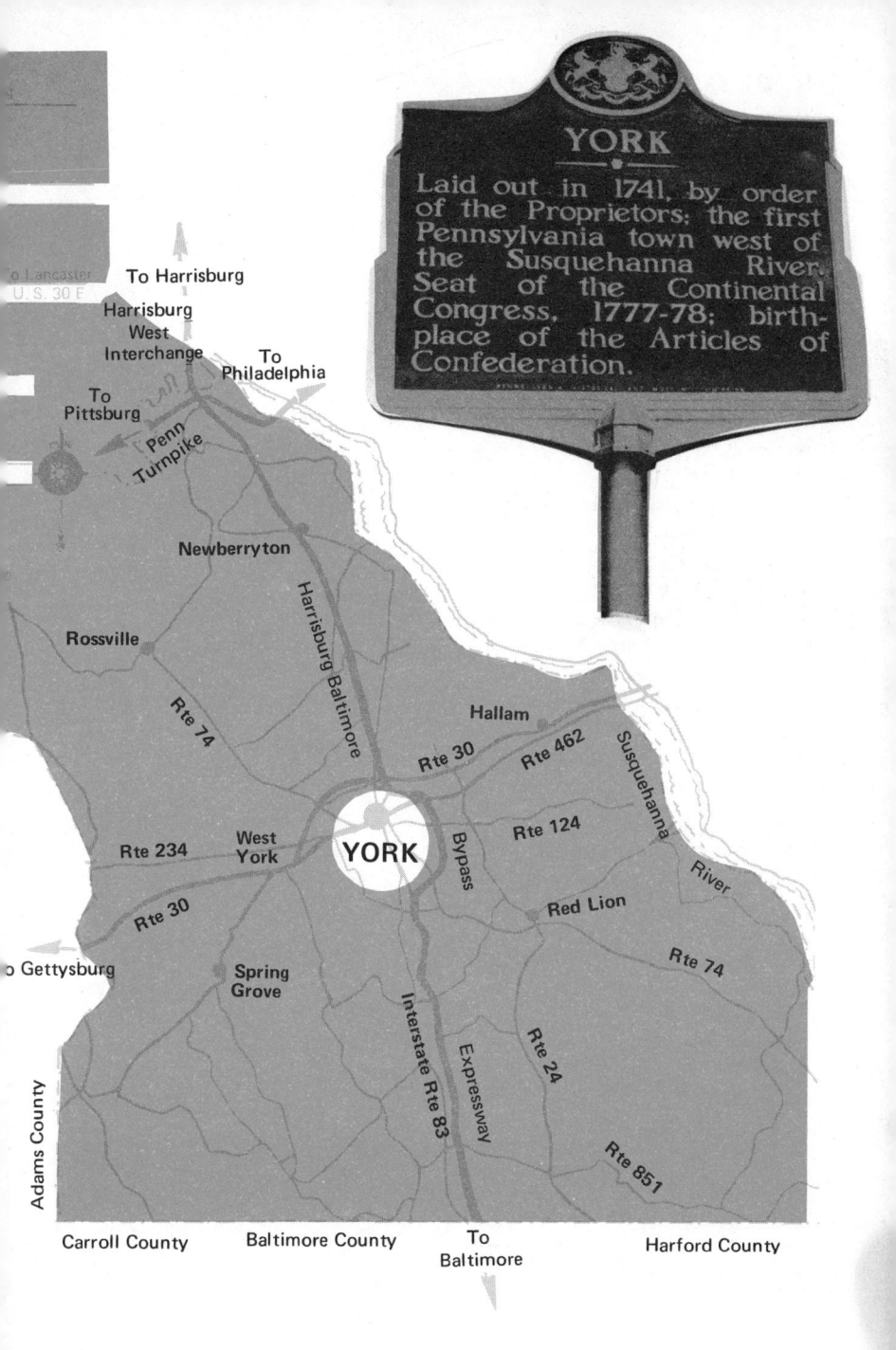

Laid out in 1741, by order of the Proprietors; the first Pennsylvania town west of the Susquehanna River. Seat of the Continental Congress, 1777-78; birthplace of the Articles of Confederation.

YORK EXCURSION

U.S. 30 will take you from Gettysburg to York. Once there, if you wish to tour the town and environs on a guided bus trip, York County Tours, Inc. is set up for that purpose; tickets are available through Colonial York County Visitors and Tourist Bureau, Mount Zion and Route 30. The in-town sites we've chosen, however, lie within easy walking distance of each other. Unfortunately, the most historic site of all, the courthouse, no longer stands, though there are tentative plans to restore it for the Bicentennial.

By the way, if you are visiting during rose-growing season, you'll probably notice an abundance of lovely white blooms at the Visitors Center; this is representative of the friendly competition with neighboring Lancaster County whose roses traditionally are red. The allusion, of course, is to the English royal houses of Lancaster and York whose competition ended in the not-so-friendly War of the Roses.

1 **Museum of Historical Society of York County,** 250 East Market Street. This fine museum has a life-size diorama of Continental Square and a full-scale model of a colonial "Street of Shops", a famed 1804 pipe organ, and a stained glass window display of York County's 41 oldest churches. Housed in the library are geneological records, manuscripts, newspapers, old books, etc. There are also displays relating to the War of 1812.

Open Mondays through Saturdays, 9 a.m. to 5 p.m.; Sundays from 1 to 5 p.m.; closed New Year's, Good Friday, Thanksgiving, Christmas. $1.00 adults, 50¢ for those 12 to 18, under 12 free.

2 **Central Market,** Beaver and Philadelphia Streets. Built in 1888, this is one of York's colorful markets, featuring local delicacies, homemade bread and farm products, all sold by country families.

Open Tuesdays and Thursdays, 8 a.m. to 5 p.m.; Saturdays 7 a.m. to 5 p.m.; if holiday, open previous day.

3 **Bonham House,** 152 East Market Street. Built in 1840, this elegant house is now a museum of mid 19th century furnishings. Note the beautiful green and white jade artifacts and fine works of art. The guide in Bonham House was housekeeper to the last descendent of this wealthy family.

Open June to August, Mondays through Saturdays, 10 a.m. to 5 p.m.; Sundays from 1 to 5 p.m.; rest of year closes at 4 p.m.; 75¢ adults, 35¢ for those 12 to 18, under 12 free.

4 **St. John's Episcopal Church,** 140 North Beaver. The present building incorporates portions of the original brick church built in 1765. York's "Liberty Bell", which used to hang in the old courthouse on the square, can be seen in the vestibule.

Usually open; free.

5 York Meeting House, 135 West Philadelphia Street. Completed in 1766 and expanded in 1783, this Quaker place of worship still has its original virgin pine paneling. It has been in continuous use since its founding but was closed temporarily in 1975; check to see if re-opened.

6 Gates House, West Market Street & Pershing Avenue. General Horatio Gates is not exactly a household name in America, but had history turned out rather differently, it might have been. Gates was president of the nation's Board of War in 1777 and this house was his headquarters while the Continental Congress met in York. It was Gates, an adjutant general, who is believed to have led the plot against General George Washington known as the "Conway Cabal". Its purpose was to unseat him as commander-in-chief and to replace him, probably with Gates himself. Whether the Conway Cabal was really a concerted officers' plot or mere grumbling by malcontents is still a mystery. In any case, the whole idea seemed to have been shelved when the Marquis de Lafayette showed up for a dinner next door at the Golden Plough Tavern (Site #7) and, observing that toasts were being offered to everyone except the nation's leader, quickly stood up and rectified the situation. "Gentlemen," he proclaimed, "there is one you have forgotten. I propose a toast to our Commander-in-Chief: George Washington. May he remain at the head of the army until independence is won." This was fair warning that France was not about to accept anyone in Washington's place. A footnote to the story tells us that one of Gates' staff officers, a man named Wilkinson, revealed the plot. For this disloyalty Gates challenged him to a duel, then thought better of it and arrived at the confrontation unarmed.

Gates House, plus the Golden Plough Tavern and Log House, which are clustered together, can be seen — along with Bonham House — for a combined admission of $1.50, adults; 75¢, 12 to 18; under 12, free with parent. Hours are same as Bonham House, above.

Gates House

7 Golden Plough Tavern. Erected in 1741, the tavern is possibly the last remaining half-timber structure of medieval German design in the U.S.

8 Log House. Built in 1812, this home is typical of those built by early German settlers. With its dirt floors and hard beds it is quite a contrast to the Bonham House.

9 Penn Common, West College Avenue and Beaver. A portion of the original Penn family grant was put to use as a park and later as a military encampment during the Revolution and the War of 1812.

10 Christ Lutheran Church, South George Street and Mason Avenue. This is one of the first Lutheran churches west of the Susquehanna. Many colonial citizens and Revolutionary war dead lie here.

Usually open; free.

11 Currier and Ives Prints and Antiques Gallery, 43 West King Street. This is an unusual collection of 300 prints by famed lithographers Currier and Ives with antiques of the same period, housed in a 19th century mansion. Nathaniel Currier did his first print in 1835 of the ruins of a New York fire. An immediate success, he went on to cover every conceivable event of importance — ship disasters and Civil War battles, deathbed scenes and Indian rampages, Bloomer costumes and woman's suffrage. Currier was joined by James Ives, first as bookkeeper, then as partner; hand-colored prints signed by the two remain favorite collectors' items.

Open Mondays through Fridays, 8:30 a.m. to 5 p.m. June – August; also Saturdays 9 a.m. to 2 p.m.; closed holidays. $1; under 12, free.

WHILE YOU'RE THERE...

Driving by car you'll find a few sites of colonial interest between Gettysburg and York. First, you might like to stop at Conewago Chapel near McSherrystown. The first known worship service west of the Susquehanna was the Catholic mass held about 1721 in the Conewago region; the early mass house was the forerunner of Conewago Chapel built in 1787 and still in use. Further north along Codorus Creek is Colonial Valley at Menges Mills. This village dating back to 1734 has the oldest water-powered grist mill and up-and-down sawmill in the country, as well as the Laucks Museum of Pennsylvania history and a colonial blacksmith shop, bake oven, ice house and hemp mill. Northeast of York, near Starview, you'll find the restored (but not operational) Codorus Furnace built in 1765 which produced shot and cannon for Washington's army at Valley Forge. Nearby is a spot the children will love — Haines Shoe House, a six-room, three-story building shaped like a shoe and built, naturally, by a shoe manufacturer; behind the house is a shoe-shaped doghouse. To the southeast of York is Indian Steps, a very unusual museum of Indian artifacts, some of which have been embedded in the masonry and walls. On the grounds of Indian Steps is the 65-foot high holly tree, now a venerable 300 years of age and believed to be the oldest tree of its kind in the U.S.

For recreation, as we've said, there's no shortage of parks: Codorus, Rocky Ridge and Gifford Pinchot — with lakes and beaches, and camping, boating and fishing facilities. Winter sports buffs will find many different ski runs, and the 2250 acre Pinchot State Park north of Rossville has a 1300 foot toboggan chute as well as ice fishing and ice skating.

The Shoe House

Swetland Homestead, in The Wyoming Valley
Built in the 1790's

Forty Fort Meeting House, Completed in 1808
A Fine Example of Early American Architecture

EXCURSION 13

The Battle of Wyoming - July 3, 1778

The Wyoming Valley

Historic Wyoming Valley, encompassing Wilkes-Barre and nearby communities, is less than a two and one-half hour's drive from Philadelphia. The valley will afford you a full day of sightseeing and enough bloodcurdling tales of history to satisfy the most dramatic of tastes. If you care to combine this with a trip to Pennsylvania's magnificent Endless Mountains, which are replate with canyons, forests and creatures of the wild, you will need a day or two extra. The site of French Azilum lies in this area.

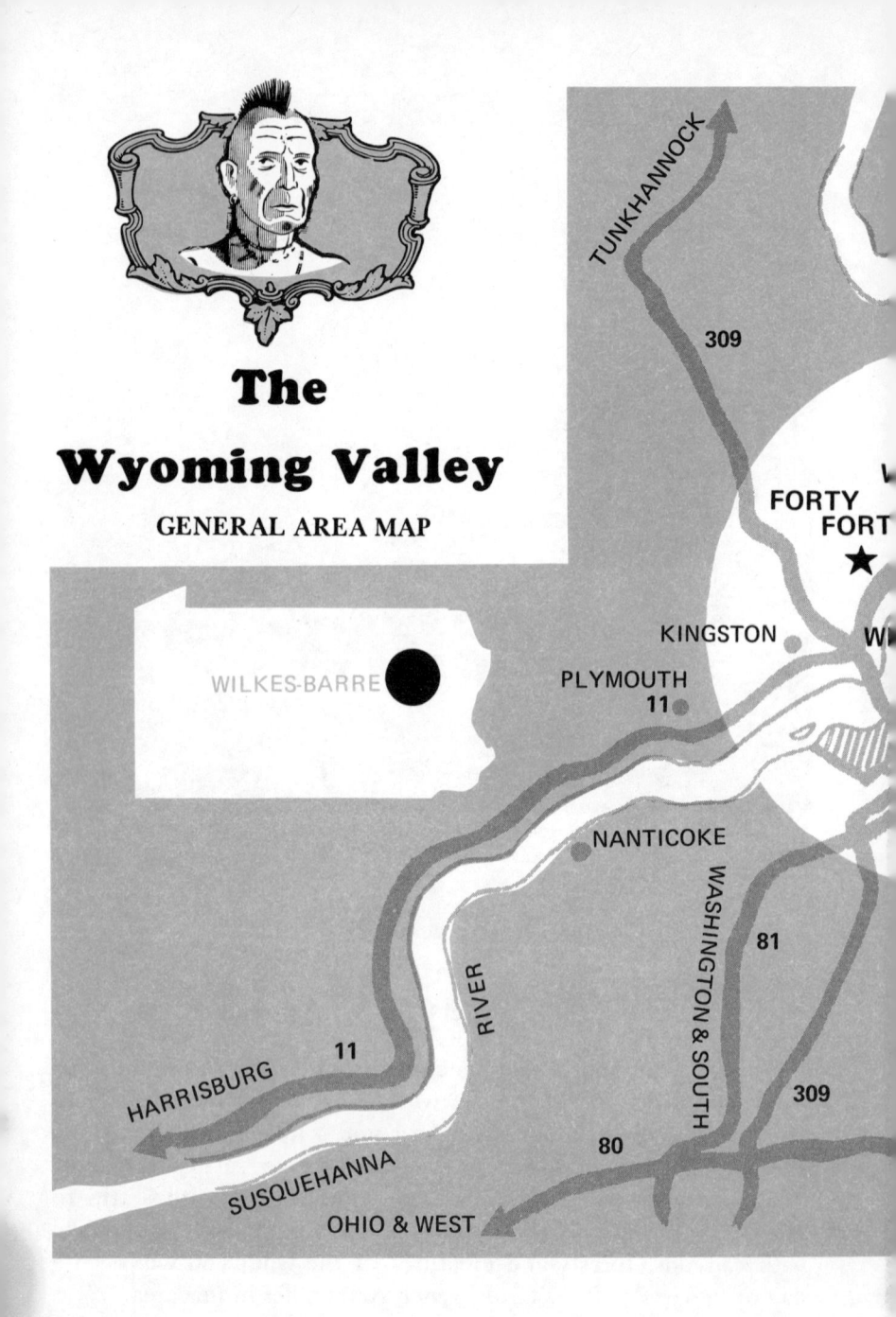

The Wyoming Valley

GENERAL AREA MAP

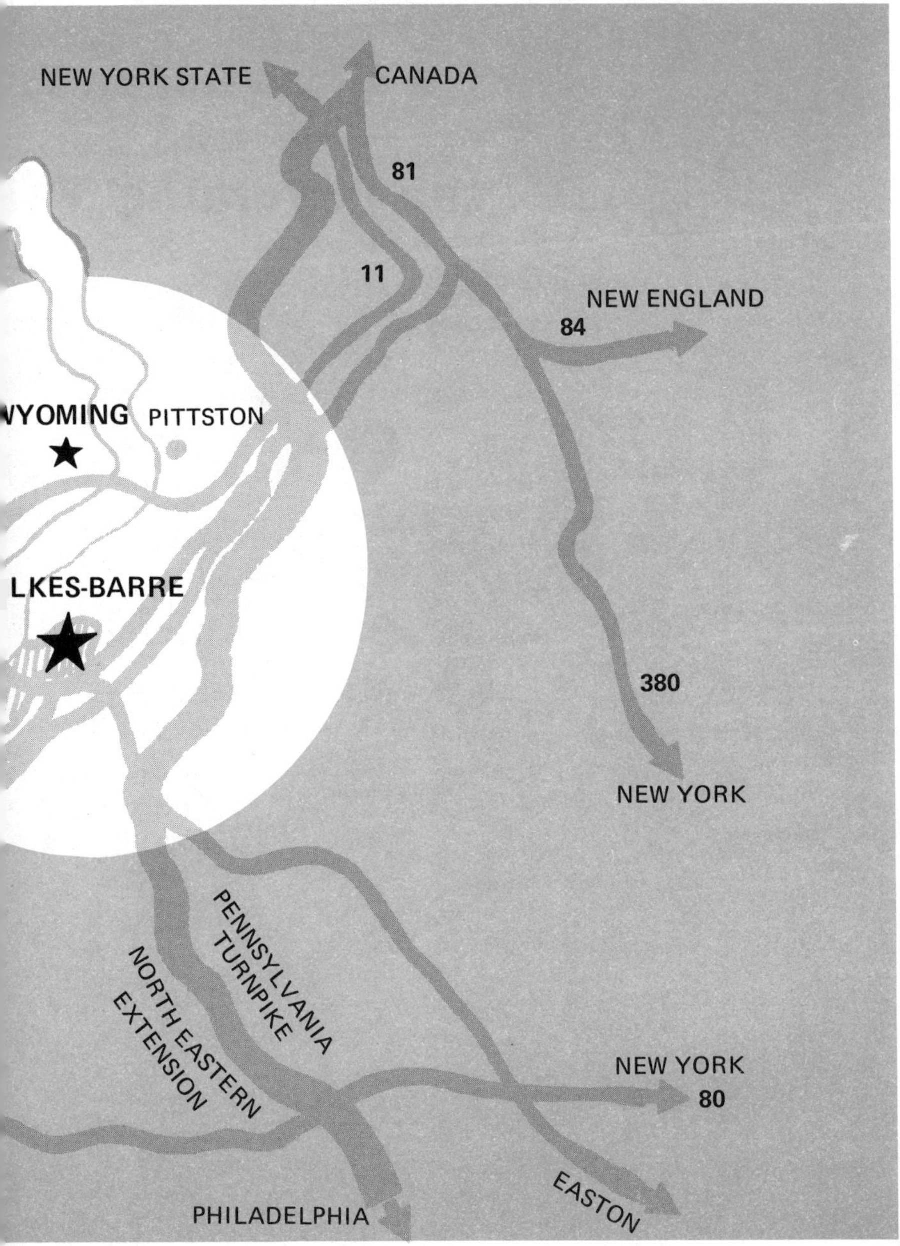
NEW YORK STATE
CANADA
81
11
NEW ENGLAND
84
WYOMING
PITTSTON
LKES-BARRE
380
NEW YORK
PENNSYLVANIA TURNPIKE
NORTH EASTERN EXTENSION
NEW YORK
80
EASTON
PHILADELPHIA

Wilkes-Barre A...
of
the Wyoming Val...

HISTORIC LOCATION MAP

Area Valley

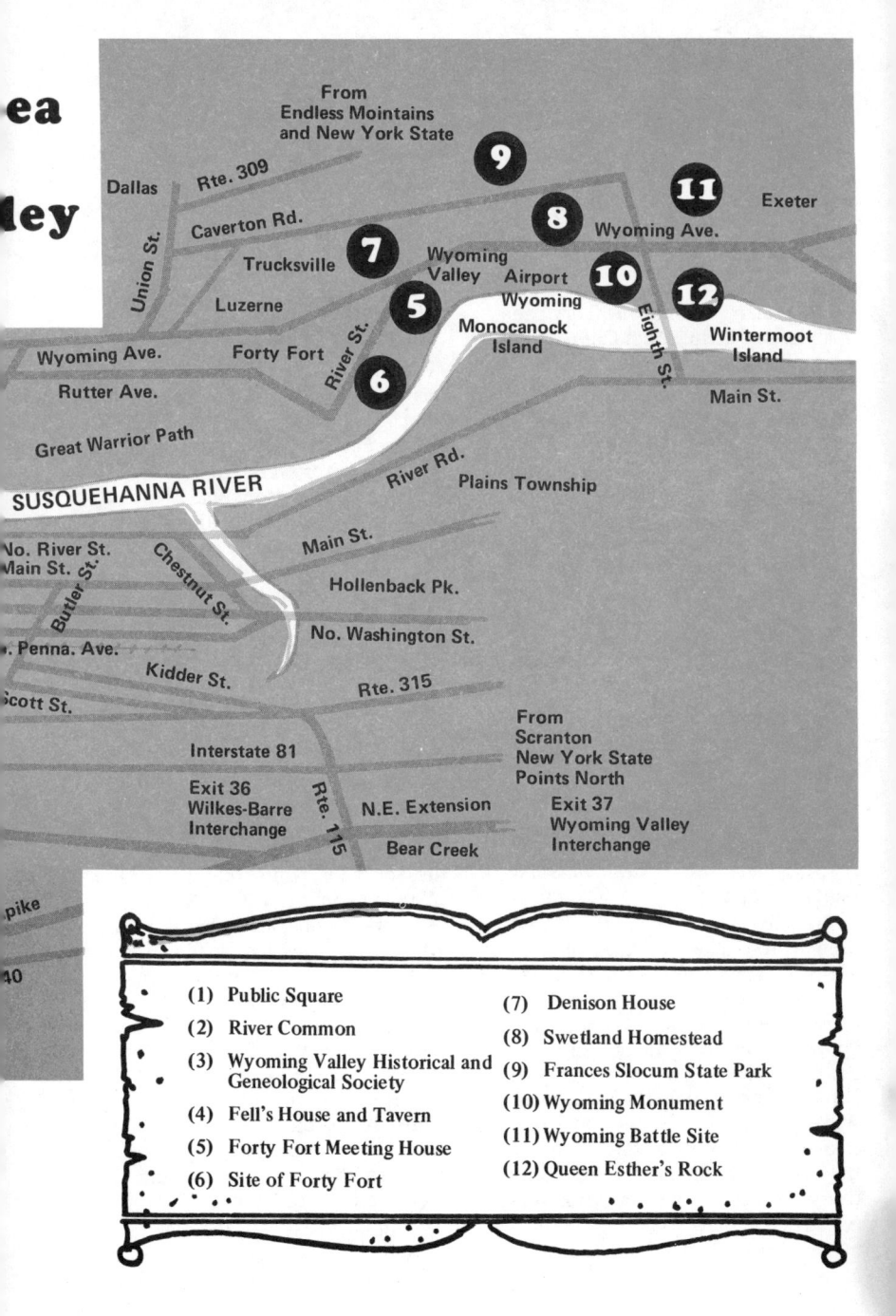

From Endless Mointains and New York State

- Dallas
- Rte. 309
- Caverton Rd.
- Union St.
- Trucksville
- **(7)**
- Wyoming Valley Airport
- **(9)**
- Wyoming Ave.
- **(11)** Exeter
- **(8)**
- **(10)**
- **(12)**
- Luzerne
- **(5)** Wyoming
- Monocanock Island
- Wyoming Ave.
- Forty Fort
- River St.
- Eighth St.
- Wintermoot Island
- Rutter Ave.
- **(6)**
- Main St.
- Great Warrior Path
- River Rd.
- SUSQUEHANNA RIVER
- Plains Township
- No. River St.
- Main St.
- Butler St.
- Chestnut St.
- Main St.
- Hollenback Pk.
- No. Washington St.
- Penna. Ave.
- Kidder St.
- Rte. 315
- Scott St.
- Interstate 81
- Exit 36 Wilkes-Barre Interchange
- Rte. 115
- N.E. Extension
- Bear Creek
- From Scranton New York State Points North
- Exit 37 Wyoming Valley Interchange
- pike
- 40

---

(1) Public Square
(2) River Common
(3) Wyoming Valley Historical and Geneological Society
(4) Fell's House and Tavern
(5) Forty Fort Meeting House
(6) Site of Forty Fort
(7) Denison House
(8) Swetland Homestead
(9) Frances Slocum State Park
(10) Wyoming Monument
(11) Wyoming Battle Site
(12) Queen Esther's Rock

THE WYOMING VALLEY: Scene of Bloodshed...

The beautiful Wyoming Valley has known more than its share of violence — not only battles but massacres, and not just between redskin and white or British and Continental, but between Indian and Indian, American Tory and American Patriot, even Connecticut and Pennsylvania resident. Five long and bitter legacies of hate — and all in one relatively small area of the state of Pennsylvania.

Before it was known to white man, this broad, fertile valley nestled among green mountains was the home of the powerful Iroquois Confederacy which, after long battle with the Susquehannock tribe, took control of the area. Then, early in the 1760s, a group of white settlers from Connecticut entered the valley with the idea that it belonged to their state. Pennsylvania, however, felt differently and responded by jailing some of the Yankees. Actually, the real ownership was unclear, for King Charles II's original land grant had some faulty geography.

In any case, both sides proceeded to stake out their claims, with Connecticut's Major John Durkee supervising the construction of 20 cabins and a palisade and Pennsylvania responding with the erection of its own fort. (It was Durkee who named the settlement Wilkes-Barre in honor of two strongly pro-colonial members of the British Parliament.) The relatively bloodless confrontation between the two states lasted 30 years in the form of the Yankee-Pennamite Wars. Though, in 1782, Congress declared Pennsylvania rightful owner of the disputed territory, it took another 20 years for land claims to be settled. (In the meantime, some Connecticut die-hards actually tried to set up a separate state there.)

With the outbreak of the Revolution, the area took on importance as granary for the colonial forces. Settlers in the valley began to split along Patriot-Tory lines, and several of the latter were shipped off for trial and imprisonment. Not surprisingly, the British under notorious Colonel John Butler saw this provocative area as being a ripe target for Indian raids (they had been able to buy redskin help with such gifts as rum, guns and gold). Faced with the threat of having the entire area pillaged, the Continentals fought back on July 3, 1778, some 300 of their militiamen facing the enemy north of what is now the town of Wyoming.

Led into an ambush, the Americans were cut off from any retreat by Seneca warriors; they lost nearly 250 men in the 30 minute battle. Afterwards the victors began to pay off old grudges by burning farms, driving off livestock, and massacring entire families. A number of the Continentals who had surrendered in hopes of better treatment were led away to a rock on the slopes above the river where they were bludgeoned to death. The term "Wyoming Massacre" refers both to the July 3 battle and the violence that followed.

Seeking to avenge this deed and to wipe out a source of supplies for the British army, the Continental

Congress in 1779 authorized a military expedition to destroy the villages and crops of the Iroquois Confederation, also known as Six Nations. Major John Sullivan was chosen by General Washington to lead this expedition. Announced the Commander-in-Chief: "It is proposed to carry the war into the heart of the country of the Six Nations, to cut off their settlements, destroy their next year's crops, and do to them every other mischief which time and circumstance will permit." In June under Sullivan's command some 3000 hardened Continentals (one-third of Washington's total troops) arrived at their mobilzation point in Wilkes-Barre, camping on the River Common. They spent about six weeks awaiting the arrival of additional troops and supplies and in preparing for the trip; more than 600 boats to carry supplies were constructed during that time. Sullivan's famous march up the Susquehanna began in late July; at Tioga Point he was joined by General Clinton's army. Together, at Newton, they defeated a combined British-Indian-Tory force, then moved north to the Finger Lakes region where they devestated the land as far as the Genesee Valley.

This was one of the most successful campaigns of the Revolution, ending Indian power forever in the Wyoming Valley and destroying the British source of supplies.

It was not until around 1800, with the final settlement of the Connecticut-Pennsylvania claims, that the Wyoming Valley settled down to a period of peace, at which time a new activity took over the scene: coal mining. In 1808 Judge Jesse Fell of Wilkes-Barre successfully burned anthracite or "hard" coal in a common grate without forced draft, thereby proving the value of the substance as a domestic fuel. Immediately he and his brothers began mining and marketing in this coal-rich area. So flourishing an industry did it become that immigrants arrived from many nations of Europe to work in the mines. By around 1920, however, as electricity and heating oil came into prominence, coal mining began to decline; mine disasters and the Great Depression added to the problems of this onetime powerful industry.

WYOMING VALLEY EXCURSION

The Wilkes-Barre area can be reached from Philadelphia by taking I-76 to the Pennsylvania Turnpike and then going east to the Northeast Extension. Follow that all the way to Exit 37 where there are signs to Wilkes-Barre. Our excursion goes to Forty Fort (sites #5 and 6) and Wyoming (sites #7 on) as well.

1 **Public Square,** Main and Market Streets. This landscaped park is the site of Fort Wilkes-Barre, built in 1771 by Pennsylvania, seized by Connecticut, and partially burned by Butler's raiders the day after the battle of Wyoming. Having served as Sullivan's headquarters in 1779, the fort was torn down in 1784. A monument honoring Wilkes and Barre marks the approximate place on which it stood.

Wyoming Monument

house, completed in 1909. The fine structure of Ohio sandstone has four stained glass windows in its large dome, representing the history and industry of the Wyoming Valley.

③ Wyoming Valley Historical and Geological Society, 69 South Franklin Street. Considered to be the oldest historical society in the U.S., this organization has records and relics of the valley's history. Its museum features an electronic relief map of the early valley with an audio-visual description of the Battle of Wyoming. One of the largest collections of Indian relics in the country is located here.

Open Wednesdays, Fridays and Saturdays 10 a.m. to 5 p.m.; free.

② River Common, River Street between North and South Streets. The Common was established in 1770 by Major Durkee near Northampton Street, and here the first two forts in the Wyoming Valley were built – Durkee by the Connecticut settlers and Wyoming by the Pennsylvania claimants. Many skirmishes of the Yankee-Pennamite Wars took place here. Later, General John Sullivan mobilized his army for the march against the Indians at River Common, with 3000 soldiers camping on its ground. The 35-acre plot is dotted with historic markers. It is very pleasant to walk, especially in spring when the Japanese cherry trees are in bloom.

At the north end of River Common is Luzerne County Court-

④ Fell's House and Tavern, Washington and Northampton Streets. Erected in the 1790's, this first tavern in the Wyoming Valley was where Judge Jesse Fell first burned his famous piece of anthracite.

Now a fine restaurant, it is open daily and Sundays from 11 a.m. to 2 a.m.

⑤ Forty Fort Meeting House, River Street. Completed in 1808, this well preserved place of worship is a classic of early American architecture. Timber framed and clapboarded, it is a copy of a Kingston, Rhode Island church.

Non-denominational evening services are held on Sundays in summer.

⑥ Site of Forty Fort, River Street and Wyoming Avenue.

This most important of Connecticut's forts in the valley was named for the early group of settlers who arrived from Connecticut in the 1760s, calling themselves the "First Forty". The fort also served as assembling point for the Americans immediately before the Battle of Wyoming.

7 **Denison House,** Wyoming Avenue above River St. Built in 1790 by John Denison, one of the original Connecticut settlers, this house was modeled on his family's home in Mystic, Conn. Its great central chimney provides a unique New England touch. The house contains relics of the early history of the valley, including the table on which Colonel Denison negotiated the terms of surrender for the survivors of the Battle of Wyoming.

Currently being restored by the Pa. Historical and Museum Commission.

8 **Swetland Homestead,** 885 Wyoming Avenue. This house was built in the 1790's by John Swetland, a Connecticut settler who managed to survive the difficulties of valley life during the Revolution, including a year's imprisonment by the Seneca Indians. Period rooms show the changing ways of life and decor through the late 19th century.

Open Tuesdays through Sundays, from noon to 5 p.m.; 50¢, children with parent, free.

9 **Frances Slocum State Park,** up 8th Street in the mountains immediately above the valley. Kidnapped from her family in 1778 by Delaware Indians, five year old Frances was given up for lost. She was, however, located at age 64 in an Indian village in Indiana. By then she had no desire to return to the culture of her birth, having married a chief of the Miami tribe and borne him four children. Legend has it that Frances spent the first night of her captivity under a gigantic rock. This impressive natural formation is now part of a state park named after her. Picnicking and boating facilities are available.

10 **Wyoming Monument,** 4th Street and Wyoming Avenue. This monument marks the site of a mass grave for the victims of the terrible massacre.

11 **Wyoming Battle Site,** 8th Street along Wyoming Avenue. Here the battle itself took place.

12 **Queen Esther's Rock,** near 8th Street Bridge. This is the site of the murder of about twenty American prisoners after the Battle of Wyoming. Local legend assigns the prime role in the deed to an aged Indian woman known to the whites as Queen Esther. Though this proud and commanding woman who sported showy costumes and glittering ornaments was probably equal to the grisly task, actual evidence indicates that she was not in the area at the time. In any case, many of the Americans captured at the battle were led to this rock and placed around it in a ring, after which an Indian woman passed around the circle chanting like a demon and killing them all with a death-maul. Only two escaped to tell the tale.

WHILE YOU'RE THERE...

If you'd like a break from the fortifications, Harveys Lake only 12 miles north of Wilkes-Barre offers swimming along a nine-mile shoreline. Somewhat further is Ricketts Glen State Park, featuring 33 waterfalls. Young people enjoy Scranton's Nay Aug Park which contains a zoo, swimming pool, model coal mine and the fine Everhart Museum of Natural History, Science and Art.

One can travel on to the beautiful Endless Mountains by going north to New Milford and Montrose by way of I-81 and state 706, or via U.S. 6 which follows the northeast bank of the Susquehanna. On the southeast bank, opposite Rummerfield, is the site of French Azilum. Though the community no longer exists, the admirably preserved LaPorte House, built in 1836 by a son of one of the original settlers, can be seen. Some of the handhewn timbers of La Grande Maison were incorporated into it, and its delicately painted ceilings and interior decoration reflect the French influence. Also, 30 miles up the Susquehanna River, the Tioga Point Museum at Athens has documents and memorabilia which relate to Azilum. Continuing west on U.S. 6, you will travel through Tioga County, the canyon area of Pennsylvania. South of Ansonia, near Wellsboro, is Pine Creek Gorge (the state's "Grand Canyon"); it is located on State route 660. The scenic countryside continues along U.S. 6 to the west of the state.

Driving south from Wilkes-Barre instead, you might like to stop at Eckley, near Hazleton. Discovered a few years ago by the Paramount movie people who were looking for a suitably grim mining town in which to set "The Molly Maguires", Eckley fit the bill to a T. After $500,000 worth of renovations had turned the main paved street into a muddy dirt road and all TV antennas had been removed, Eckley was even bleaker. The object, of course, had been to make it look as it had one hundred years ago in peak mining days. Once the movie was completed, a local banker realized Eckley was now an ideal museum of the period. Hence Paramount left its "improvements", the State took over, and there is now a museum and visitors center. Residents are mostly retired anthracite mine workers.

Refuge in the Wilderness
FRENCH AZILUM, 1793-1803

It was a place of refuge, this crescent-shaped piece of land located on a bend of the Susquehanna River in northern Pennsylvania. The new residents, émigrés from France, could not help but miss the city life of Paris, the theater, fetes and balls that came along with their high station in life. But no longer was France a land hospitable to royalty and nobility. The bloody French Revolution had swept through the streets of Paris, and those sympathetic to King

Louis XVI — indeed, even those of moderate political views — had only prison and the guillotine to look ahead to. Robespierre, the fanatical leader now in power, would not tolerate anything other than Jacobin politics.

So it was that a group of Frenchmen — courtiers, minor nobility, professionals, clergy, merchants, soldiers and a few artisans — being lucky enough to escape with their heads intact, came to the receptive climate of the United States. With them was a group of rich French planters who had fled Santo Domingo when the declaration of equality by the radical French assembly caused a violent uprising by slaves and mulattos in the Gallic portion of that island.

The settlement was thought by Americans both to be a good business deal and a mark of gratitude for French assistance during the War of Independence. Three Philadelphia men of finance were involved: Robert Morris, the "financier of the Revolution", Stephen Girard, banker and philanthropist, and John Nicholson, comptroller general of the state. The Frenchmen who planned the community were no less illustrious. Among them was the Viscount Louis de Noailles, whose wife, mother and grandmother were beheaded without trial during the French Revolution. A brother-in-law of Lafayette, de Noailles had strong ties with America; during the struggle of the colonies for their independence he had fought so bravely that General Washington chose him to receive Cornwallis' surrender at the Battle of Yorktown. General manager of Azilum was the Marquis Antoine Omer Talon, faithful advisor to Louis XVI and head of the royal secret service. To assure his safety, Talon's friends placed him in a wine cask and secreted it in the hold of the ship which took him to America.

The Frenchmen were not laborers, either by training or instinct. Building a home was as foreign to them as attending a king was to their pioneer American neighbors. Hence native labor was utilized, with overcharging and cheating commonplace. Angered, some of the French vowed never to learn the English language. Nor was agricultural development easily achieved. Wrote a British visitor, one Mr. Weld, in 1796: "The French settled here ... seem to have no great ability or inclination to cultivate the earth, and the great part of them have let their lands at a small yearly rental to the Americans, and the Americans in the neighborhood hate and accuse them of being an idle and dissolute set. The manners of the two people are so different that it is impossible they could ever agree."

At its height, the community of French Azilum (its name being a hybrid of the French and English words for "asylum") comprised some 50 or 60 log houses set on one-half acre plots of land; there were over 400 lots in all. Fifteen streets of unusually great width divided the town and a two-acre market square was at the center. Anxious to preserve the niceties of their life, the French added many luxuries to their crude log structures — piazzas, shutters, chimneys, porches, fenced yards and even treasured furniture and musical instruments brought over from the homeland. Gardens, too, were sometimes elaborate. The agreement describing Lot 416 read: "The garden is decorated by a considerable number of fruit trees, young Lombardy poplars and weeping willows, and by a lattice summer house. Next to the garden is a nursery of about 900 apple trees." The Americans shook their heads at the various excesses but, finding that Azilum's shopping and entertainment facilities were far superior to their own, came here frequently to gawk, drink, and stock up on household goods.

In the ten years of its life, Azilum played host to Gallic visitors of renown — Talleyrand, statesman and diplomat, Louis Philippe, Duc d'Orleans, who was later to become king, and the Duc de la Rochefoucauld-Liancourt, first gentleman of Louis XVI's ill-fated court. (It had been the latter's duty to lift the royal bedcurtains and announce the fall of the Bastille.) When such dignitaries arrived, the French settlers put on balls and assemblies, the women attired in sparkling jewels and richly embroidered silks, the men in satin knee breeches and lace-ruffled white suits. Amateur theatricals and picnics, boating and sleighing — there was no end to the entertainment.

The most formal events were held at "La Grande Maison" (The Great House), an 84-foot long, 60-foot wide log structure with eight large fireplaces. Supposedly it was intended for Marie Antoinette herself. But this strawberry-blonde queen with a passion for gambling, jewels, and men other than her husband Louis, was, like him, to die, another victim of revolutionary violence.

Nor was Azilum itself destined for a long life. Tensions between natives and émigrés were heightened by the wartime edicts of the French government that, after 1795, resulted in the seizure and confiscation of American ships and cargoes. After years of financial problems, Azilum's sponsors went into bankruptcy to the tune of $10 million, and French sources of income were cut off. Some of the settlers moved to the south; others, homesick for their native land, returned to France. Talon and de Navailles were among these, the former dying prematurely senile at age 52 after serving a prison sentence for his political offenses, the latter expiring as a brigadier general in the service of France at Havana. (So loved was de Navailles by his men that they enclosed his heart in a silver box and attached it to their flag.) The émigrés' return to France was made easier when Napoleon Bonaparte came to power, for he promised both personal safety and the restoration of estates.

Thus ended the saga of French Azilum. A few of the families remained in the environs, settling in nearby towns as well. But the log houses, the taverns, theater, gardens, the silk-stockinged splendor vanished, giving way to evenly tilled farmlands. Today little remains of the onetime Gallic refuge except for traces of roads, a monument, a millrace, millstones. And the burbling stream that once supplied water for La Grande Maison still flows, knowing much of times long past but telling nothing.

EXCURSION 14

Commander Oliver Hazard Perry

Erie · Waterford Titusville

Today's excursion is a diversified one, taking us first to the scene of a great shipbuilding feat during the War of 1812, then to a fort whose history predates the French and Indian War, when the father of our country was a young British subject. Finally, we visit the place where our oil industry had its beginnings — a fabled era when pioneer tenacity brought riches to some and dashed the dreams of others.

THE GUIDE suggests that you spend one full day in Erie, enjoying not only its historic sites but the fine recreational facilities that derive from its Great Lakes location. On the second day Fort Le Boeuf and Drake Well Park can be seen with ample time for some exploring of nearby lake or forest country. Excursions up to this point have been planned with Philadelphia as the starting and return point. However, Erie — being to the far northwest of the state — makes for an arduous day's drive from Philadelphia. Plan, if you can, to link this excursion with the Pittsburgh one that follows.

ERIE

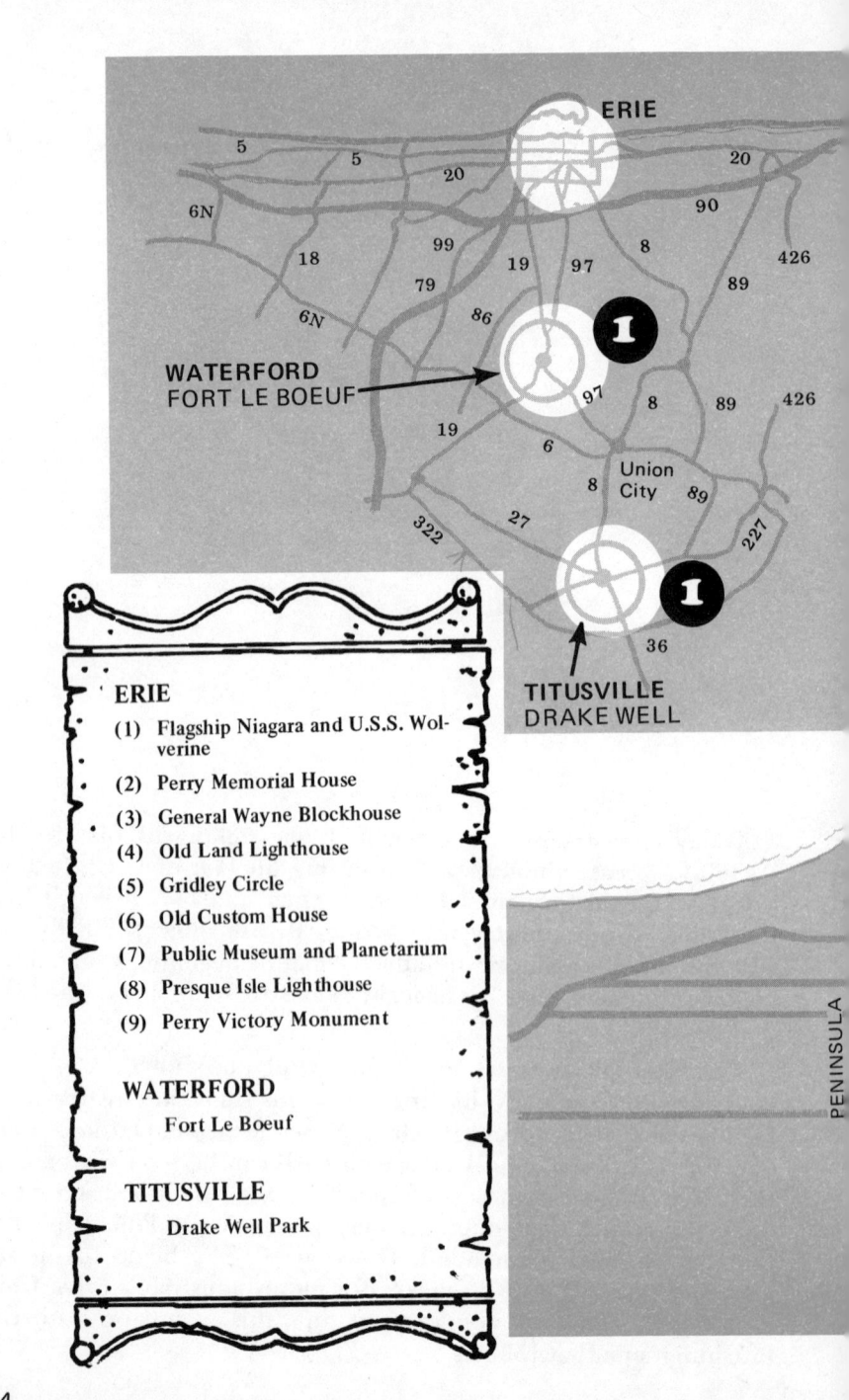

(1) Flagship Niagara and U.S.S. Wolverine
(2) Perry Memorial House
(3) General Wayne Blockhouse
(4) Old Land Lighthouse
(5) Gridley Circle
(6) Old Custom House
(7) Public Museum and Planetarium
(8) Presque Isle Lighthouse
(9) Perry Victory Monument

WATERFORD

Fort Le Boeuf

TITUSVILLE

Drake Well Park

Erie Waterford Titusville

HISTORIC LOCATION MAP

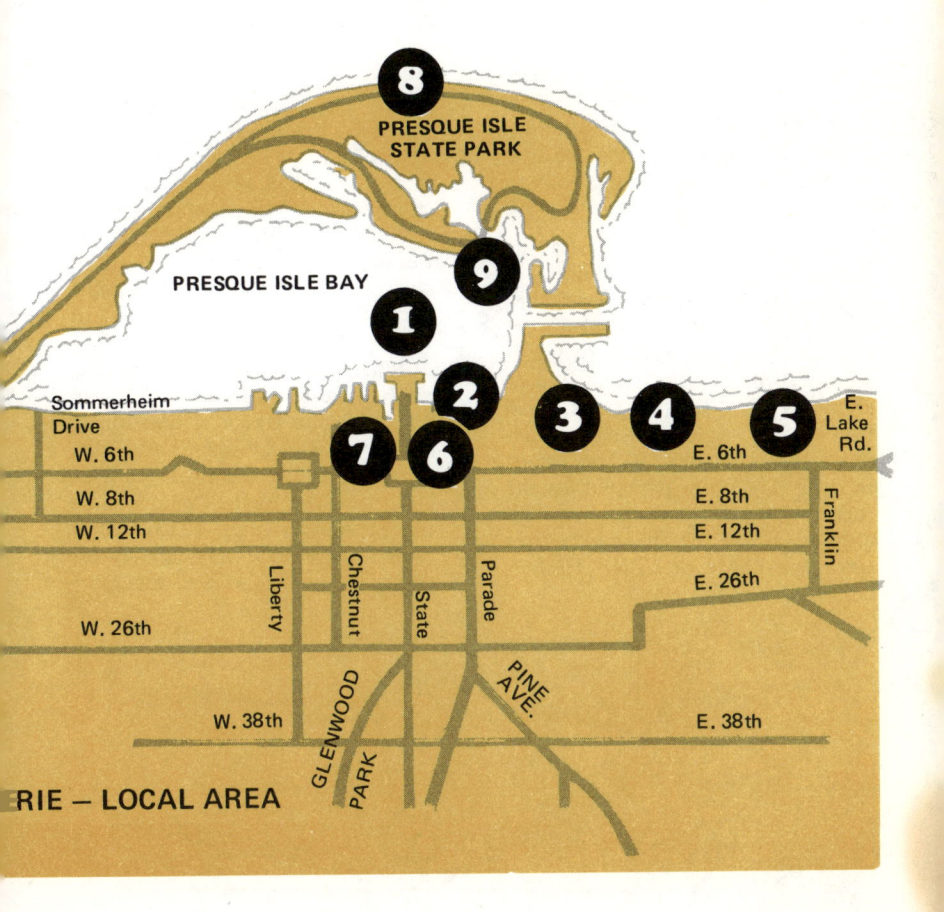

ERIE
"We Have Met The Enemy and They are Ours"

The locale that was to become known as Erie first achieved importance in 1753 when, in the bitter race with England for empire, France built Presque Isle, the first of four forts aimed at control of the Ohio Valley. A few years later the fort was abandoned to the conquering British, and in 1763 it was burned by Indians who were fearful of the white man's encroachment.

In 1792 Pennsylvania paid the U.S. government 75¢ an acre, or $151,640.25 for the so-called "Triangle Lands" which became its northwest border and provided it with a port on the Great Lakes. (New York, Massachusetts, and Connecticut were forced to relinquish their claims to the same territory.) Despite payment to the Indians for this land, violence still erupted between reds and whites until the Battle of Fallen Timbers was waged and won by the great Revolutionary War general, Anthony Wayne. This victory, which broke the spirit of the western Indians, led in 1795 to the Treaty of the Six Nations. That same year the town of Erie was laid out, named after the Eriez Indians who had lived in the region long before its discovery by French explorers.

It was not long before new hostilities broke out: the War of 1812. This was brought on indirectly by American defiance of British supremacy on the seas. It was also believed that Britain was hindering our nation's expansion westward by such means as playing on the anti-American sentiments of the Indians.

When the war began, Great Britain had mastery of the Great Lakes, and soon she was in a position to strike the fatal blow on Lake Erie's south shore. She was thwarted from this, however, in the famous battle of September 10, 1813, when, under incredibly difficult conditions, nine small American ships —

six of them constructed at Erie — challenged the British fleet on Lake Erie. In a bloody duel, the young American navy emerged victorious, removing the British threat to the northwest and opening the supply lines to the military in Ohio.

The construction of the six ships was in itself remarkable. Erie was a small, isolated community, and people and supplies had to be imported: craftsmen from Philadelphia and New York, rigging from Pittsburgh, cannon from Washington, D.C., iron from Meadville. Daniel Dobbins, veteran shipmaster on the Great Lakes was assigned the task of building the fleet, and he worked tirelessly to do so. But the real hero was Commander Oliver Hazard Perry, who arrived at Erie in March from his home in Rhode Island, taking command of the construction, manpower, and ensuing confrontation.

The battle began with the U.S. ship Lawrence challenging the largest of the British ships. After a furious exchange Perry and some of his crew escaped by boat to the Niagara, brought it into the line of fire, and defeated the enemy. In the calm that followed, he wrote his oft repeated report to the Secretary of the Navy: "Dear General — We have met the enemy and they are ours. Two ships, two brigs, one schooner and one sloop. Yours with great esteem. O.H. Perry." Modest, calm, humane, Perry ended his day of glory by showing great kindness to the British prisoners of war.

ERIE EXCURSION

Erie, Pennsylvania's third largest city and its only playground on the Great Lakes, is known for its broad, tree-lined streets and lovely residential areas. It is an important industrial center as well, but retains a feeling of spaciousness that characterized early Washington. (Erie was, in fact, laid out on a modification of the plan for our nation's capital.)

In warm weather, when the lake is open to navigation, Erie's waterfront is full of activity. Presque Isle Peninsula, a curved finger of land seven miles long which stretches into the lake, offers sandy beaches with fine swimming, picnic facili-

Seaman, Colonial Navy

217

ties, lagoons complete with lily pads, and wooded areas of deer and wildflowers. You can enjoy all this recreation and choose among good seafood restaurants at the approach to the pier. These facilities are open all year round and, in summer, late into the evenings. Winter, too, can be most enjoyable in Erie, with skiing, ice skating, and fewer crowds to share it all with.

1 **Flagship Niagara and S.S. Wolverine,** foot of State Street. The sturdy little wooden ship Niagara, black hulled with bands of yellow and a show of brick red, is one of the most renowned of all American naval vessels. After the 1813 battle it decayed and was allowed to sink into Misery Bay (the northeast corner of Presque Isle Bay, so named because of the dreary weather and hardships suffered here after the battle.) To celebrate the centennial of the victory, the Niagara was brought up from its watery grave and reconstructed. Once again it sank, and once more it was brought up and repaired — this time for the Perry Sesqui-centennial in 1963. Still the ship contains a long section of its original keel. With its full rigging and its cannon, the Niagara looks today much as it looked in 1813, according to historians.

The U.S.S. Michigan (later rebuilt and renamed The Wolverine) was the first iron ship in the U.S. Navy and for more than 50 years the only war vessel in the Greak Lakes. Only its bow is left, resting in the shadow of the Niagara.

The Niagara can be toured as follows: daylight savings time — 8:30 a.m. to 5 p.m. Tuesdays - Saturdays, 1 p.m. to 5 p.m. Sundays; in winter — 9 a.m. to 4:30 p.m. Tuesdays - Saturdays, 1 p.m. to 4:30 p.m. Sundays; closed most holidays. Hours are subject to change and a fee may be instituted.

2 **Perry Memorial House,** 201 French Street. Originally Dickson Tavern, this structure, c. 1809, is a splendid and excellently preserved example of that period. Legend has it that Commander Perry made the house his headquarters during the building of the fleet; actually he used Buehler's Tavern, which is no longer standing. Twelve years later, on June 3, 1825, food was prepared here for the Marquis de Lafayette's visit to Erie, a gala occasion for the small frontier village. Later the house was a station on the Underground Railroad; its walls contain hiding places where the slaves stayed until it was safe for them to move on.

Open mid June to mid September, daily from 1 to 4 p.m., rest of year Saturdays and Sundays only; closed New Year's weekend, Easter, Christmas weekend. 25¢, children 10¢.

3 **General Wayne Blockhouse,** 560 East 3d Street. A short distance from the old Fort Presque Isle is a replica of the blockhouse where General Anthony Wayne held a peace treaty with the Indians after his victory at Fallen Timbers and where, two years later, he died.

Wayne's son, hearing that the general's burial place was being neglected, rode on horseback from his home in Radnor at the other end of the state in order to collect his father's remains. The body was boiled to loosen the flesh from the skeleton, the bones were then stored in saddlebags for reburial in

Perry's Brig Niagara

Radnor, and the residue within the kettle was returned to the first resting place.

Open Memorial Day – Labor Day, daily from 10 a.m. to 4 p.m.; closed rest of year except by appointment; free.

4 **Old Land Lighthouse**, foot of Dunn Boulevard. Erected first in 1818, this was the initial lighthouse built on the Great Lakes by the U.S. government. It was replaced in 1858 and again in 1866. The light has not been used since the opening of the present channel in 1885.

5 **Gridley Circle**, Lakeside Cemetery on East 6th Street. Overlooking Lake Erie, this burial place of Charles Vernon Gridley, commander of Admiral Dewey's flagship Olympia in the Battle of Manila Bay, is surrounded by four 18th century Spanish cannons captured by the Americans in that confrontation. It began when Dewey gave his famous order: "You may fire when ready, Captain Gridley." The Spanish-American War of 1898 was declared by the U.S. against Spain to liberate Cuba from Spanish domination and to protect American economic interests in the Caribbean. It resulted in the ceding of the Philippines, Puerto Rico and Guam to the U.S. and the proclaiming of Cuba as an independent territory under U.S. protection.

6 **The Old Custom House**, 407 State Street. This beautiful example of Greek Revival (Doric) architecture was built in 1839 to house a branch of the U.S. Bank of Pennsylvania. The building's front portion of white marble was quarried in the hills of Vermont and

219

hauled by teams of oxen to the Erie Canal and thence to Erie. The mantels are of fine Italian marble. Note the decorated ceiling of the main room. This building and the companion one next door (formerly the Cashier's House) have been renovated.

Hours and fee for Old Custom House not yet available. The Cashier's House is now occupied by the Erie County Historical Society and is open Tuesdays through Fridays 1 to 4:30 p.m., Saturdays 9 a.m. to 12 noon; closed holidays; free.

7 **Public Museum and Planetarium**, 356 W. 6th Street. Regional history, health and natural science are featured in this museum which is located in a lovely old home. Here, if you have a taste for the macabre, you can see the kettle in which General Wayne's body was boiled after disinterment (note site #3).

Open Tuesdays through Saturdays 10 a.m. to 5 p.m., Sundays 2 to 5 p.m., closed holidays. Free. Planetarium shows Sundays at 2:30 p.m.; 50¢ adults, 25¢ children.

8 **Presque Isle Lighthouse**, Peninsula. One of Erie's most charming landmarks, the lighthouse has been in continuous use since 1871. Its light flashes a red and white alternate beam visible for 16 miles out in the lake. No keepers have lived here since 1941 when the Coast Guard took over the light's operation.

9 **Perry Victory Monument**, northeast corner of Presque Isle Bay. This monument was erected by the state of Pennsylvania as a memorial to Commander Perry and his defeat of the British at Put-in-Bay. It overlooks Misery Bay where the fleet wintered after the battle. The tall, beautiful shaft of reinforced concrete faced with royal blue Indiana limestone was built in 1926. It has an eight-foot high tripod of bronze on the top and it rises 101 feet above water level.

Wood Stock Anchor

Famous Erie Landmarks

1) Old Land Lighthouse
2) General Wayne Blockhouse
3) Presque Isle Lighthouse
4) Admiral Penn's Monument

FORT LE BOEUF
France and England Battle for An Empire

Fort Le Boeuf, built the same year as Presque Isle, was one in a chain of four forts intended to link France's domain in Canada with that in Louisiana.

Since this fort was a threat to the expansion of the British colonies, Governor Dinwiddie of Virginia sent George Washington, a 21 year old militia major, to warn the French that they were trespassing on British territory. Starting out October 31, 1753, on this his first public mission, Washington arrived December 11, accompanied by a small party of servants, interpreters and Indians. At the fort he presented to the French commandant Legardeur de St.-Pierre the request of Dinwiddie for "your peaceful departure." St.-Pierre would not heed the suggestion, saying, "As to the summons you sent me to retire, I do not think myself obliged to obey it." Washington returned to Williamsburg by canoe, horseback and on foot, with just one guide for most of the trip. On the way he was fired upon by hostile Indians, nearly drowned crossing the Allegheny, and faced icy winds and snow in "as fatiguing a Journey as it is possible to conceive." He reached Williamsburg January 16, 1754, reporting on what he had seen of the fort and of French preparations for travel down the Ohio.

Fort LeBoeuf Museum

Soon the threat turned into battle, in the form of the French and Indian War. From 1755 to 1758 Fort Le Boeuf served as a way station on the French line of defense to Fort Duquesne (later Pittsburgh). The tide turned with the British capture of Fort Duquesne, and the French, forced to retreat, burned Le Boeuf. The British flag then flew over a new fort, built under Henry Bouquet. During the Indian attack known as "Pontiac's War", in 1763, once again it was destroyed. For 30 years it remained in ruins, but with the end of the Revolution the danger of Indian raids necessitated the establishment by Americans of a defense system, and in 1794 under Major Ebenezer Denny two small blockhouses were erected.

The town of Waterford was laid out here at that time by a group of settlers, and it prospered as a major stopping point on the route from Pittsburgh to the Great Lakes.

FORT LE BOEUF EXCURSION

Located 15 miles south of Erie on U.S. 19, Fort Le Boeuf Museum is administered by the Pennsylvania Historical and Museum Commission. You'll want to visit the museum which explains the role of Indians and Europeans on the Pennsylvania frontier; it features a multi-image theater. Near it is the Judson House, a fine Greek Revival home erected in 1820 by a store owner and early settler of Waterford; it has been partly restored. Across the street in a parklike setting is a statue of George Washington as the brave young emissary from Governor Dinwiddie to the French. Also in this area are the remains of the American fort.

Open Tuesdays through Saturdays 9 a.m. to 4:30 p.m., Sundays 1 to 4:30 p.m.; closed election days and most holidays; admission 50¢.

TITUSVILLE
Birth of A Giant Industry

It was the year 1858. Oil was known to be present in sections of western Pennsylvania, for it floated on the waters as a greasy scum and Indians gathered it up in their blankets to use in mixing war paints and as a medicinal cureall. Scientists realized that if oil could be brought up in quantity, it could be used to make kerosene for the nation's lamps.

At age 40, "Colonel" Edwin L. Drake, a sometime clerk, salesman and train conductor, was an unlikely character to launch a great industry. The one thing he had going for him was free passes on the railroad, for which reason he was hired by a syndicate which had leased a tract near Titusville, Pa. to bring up the oil in that area. How they did not know. Nor did he. Even the townspeople were in doubt, referring to the venture as "Drake's Folly". After his first attempt to dig for the oil proved unsuccessful, Drake had the good idea of hiring one William A. ("Uncle Billy") Smith, a blacksmith who had learned the techniques and tools of drilling from the operation of salt wells. When water began to collapse the sides of their hole, Drake solved the problem by driving sections of cast iron pipe 32 feet to bedrock. Drilling began at that depth in mid-August, 1859.

On Sunday afternoon of August 28, Uncle Billy and his son, Sam, went out to the well, peered down the pipe into the ground and saw a dark brown liquid bubbling near the surface. They used a pitcher pump to fill several barrels. Then Uncle Billy mounted his mule and rode the half mile into town shouting, "Struck oil! Struck oil!"

Soon the countryside was covered by derricks, shacks, tanks, and the people who wanted to "get rich quick". As for Drake, he thought that he had tapped the source of the oil and saw no need to drill all over the countryside. He served as a justice of the peace and oil buyer in Titusville, while others made thousands of dollars from their wells. Crippled by neuralgia and a poor man, Drake left Titusville. Finally the legislature voted him an annual pension of $1500. He died in 1880 and was buried in the town he had made famous. Later on, his bogus title became a real one. Edwin L. Drake was officially appointed a colonel in the Pennsylvania National Guard.

TITUSVILLE EXCURSION

Drake Well Park is located one mile southeast of the town of Titusville off Route 8. It is a short drive from Le Boeuf going east on Route 94 and south on Route 8. The setting is a beautiful one between the hills enclosing Oil Creek. Drake Well Park contains a full-size and operative reproduction of Drake's oil well, derrick and well house. In the $2 million museum you'll learn the story of Pennsylvania's oil country via dioramas, working models and an electric map; there is also a collection of Drake's personal effects and pieces of apparatus from the first well. Picnic areas are available.

Open 9 a.m. to 4:30 p.m. Mondays through Saturdays, Sundays 1 to 4:30 p.m.; closed most holidays; 50¢, under 12 free.

WHILE YOU'RE THERE...

If this introduction to America's early oil days has interested you, a side trip ten miles southeast of Titusville to Pithole City will provide a real conversation piece. The area that became Pithole City was, in the mid 1800s, a series of great bluffs and abrupt hills, covered with tall pines and hemlock. The only signs of human habitation were a few small farm buildings and cleared fields. Then, five years after Drake's venture, they started to drill on Pithole Creek. The first wells came in with thousands of barrels of oil per day; as it gushed adventurers of every description rushed in to make their fortune. Within months some 1,000 homes and businesses dotted the land, and hotels costing from $50,000 to $100,000 sprang up along with dance halls, saloons, restaurants, churches, theaters and a jail. The town population swelled to 15,000. But it was over as suddenly as it began. The oil stopped gushing, terrible fires destroyed houses and hotels, and the "Queen City of Oildom", within a mere two years of her creation had become a ghost town.

The Pennsylvania Historical and Museum Commission is completing a new museum in Pithole City. You'll also see traces of the roads and railroads as well as hundreds of cellar holes, and you can follow the trench of the oil pipeline.

If you'd like to get in some excellent swimming, go west from Titusville on Route 27 toward Lake Conneaut (it's Indian for "Snow Waters") which lies on U.S. 6 and 322. The largest natural lake in the state, this beautiful sheet of water is four miles long and has facilities for boating and fishing, as well as an amusement park.

Wilderness lovers should take advantage of some beautiful forest land to the east. The town of Warren, named after General Joseph Warren (a Revolutionary War patriot who was killed in the Battle of Bunker Hill) lies at the junction of the Allegheny and Conewango Rivers. It is the gateway to the famed Allegheny National Forest whose four million acres of virgin timber are rich in wildlife, streams, dense forest and open meadows. Kane, to the southeast of Warren, has abundant hunting, fishing, and summer and winter sports. The altitude at its golf course is the highest in the state. Kane is sometimes referred to as "the icebox of Pennsylvania" because of its record cold temperatures. Appropriately enough, it was founded by the brother of an Arctic explorer.

Drake Well Museum, Titusville, PA

Limited editions and framing. **Christine Whipple's Gallery,** 2632 West 8th St. Erie (814) 838-4991.

Ye Old Barn Country Store, 23rd & Route 832. Erie.

Replica of Drake's Well House and Derrick

EXCURSION 15

Pittsburgh Old Economy

Pittsburgh, which only 25 years ago was buried under clouds of industrial smoke, has undergone an imaginative program of urban renewal. After the bulldozer did its work, a "new" city emerged with gleaming office buildings, a park setting for the historical treasures, a huge sports arena, and some impressive additions to Pittsburgh's already strong cultural tradition.

Plan two full days here to see most of the sites in our listing, then continue to Old Economy, superb restoration of a 19th century communal society.

Pittsburgh and Old Economy

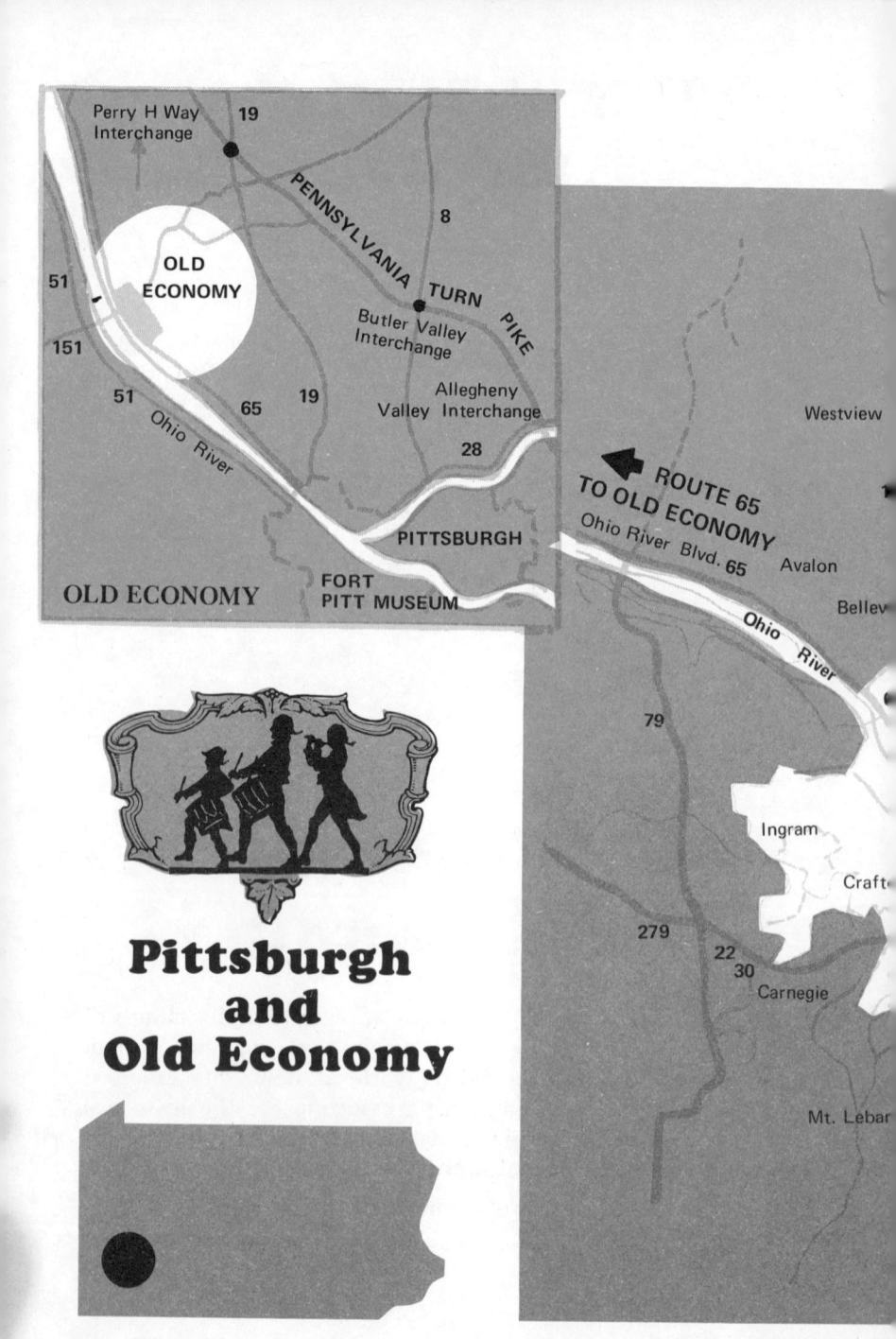

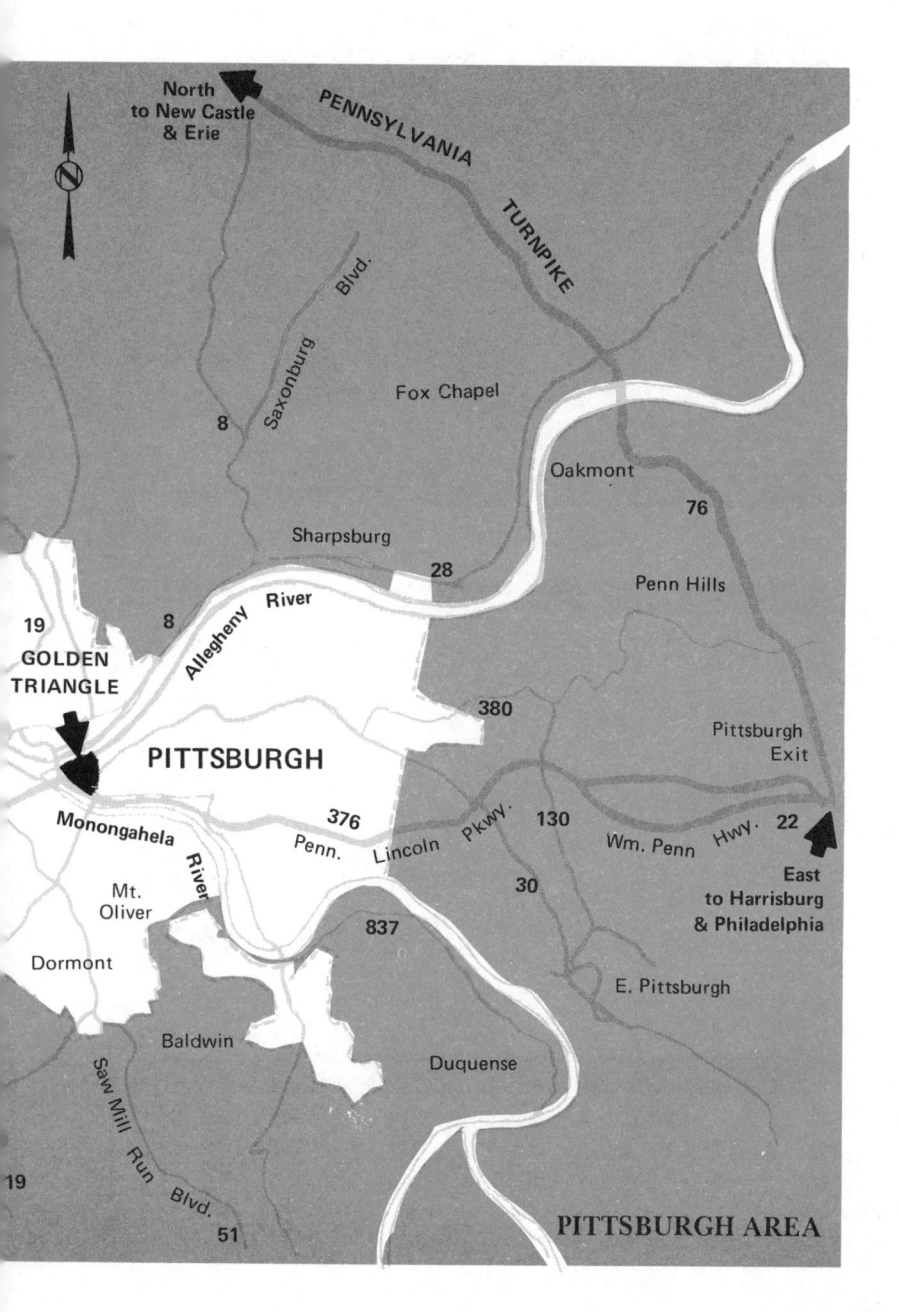

PITTSBURGH AREA

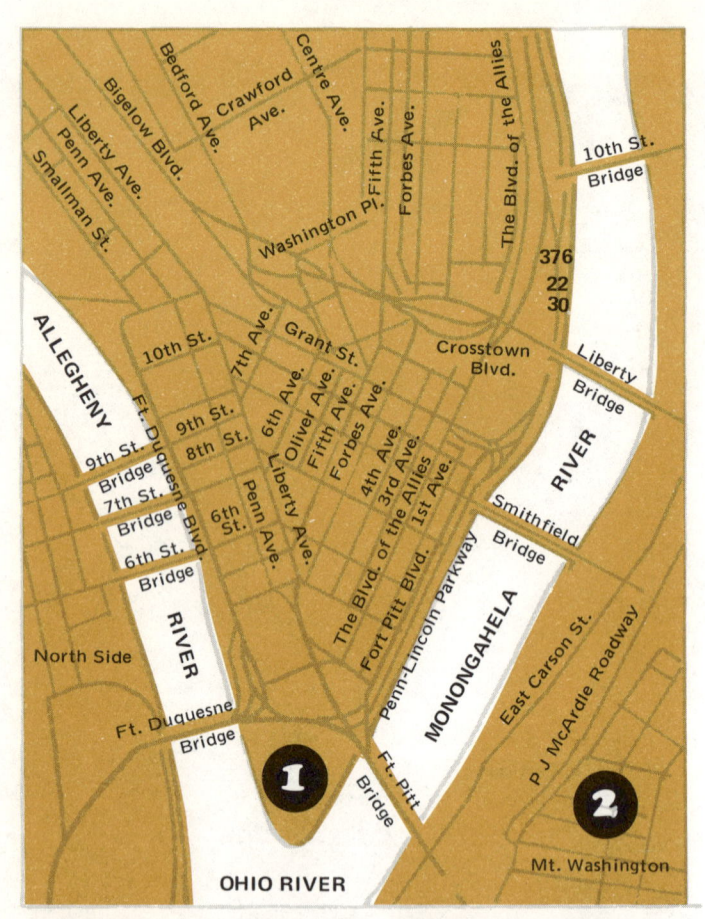

The Golden Triangle

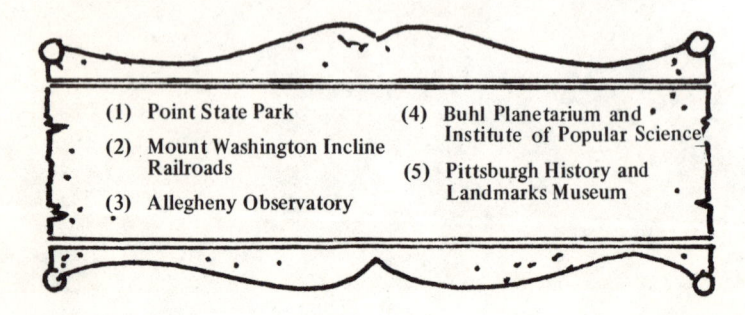

(1) Point State Park
(2) Mount Washington Incline Railroads
(3) Allegheny Observatory
(4) Buhl Planetarium and Institute of Popular Science
(5) Pittsburgh History and Landmarks Museum

230

Pittsburgh North

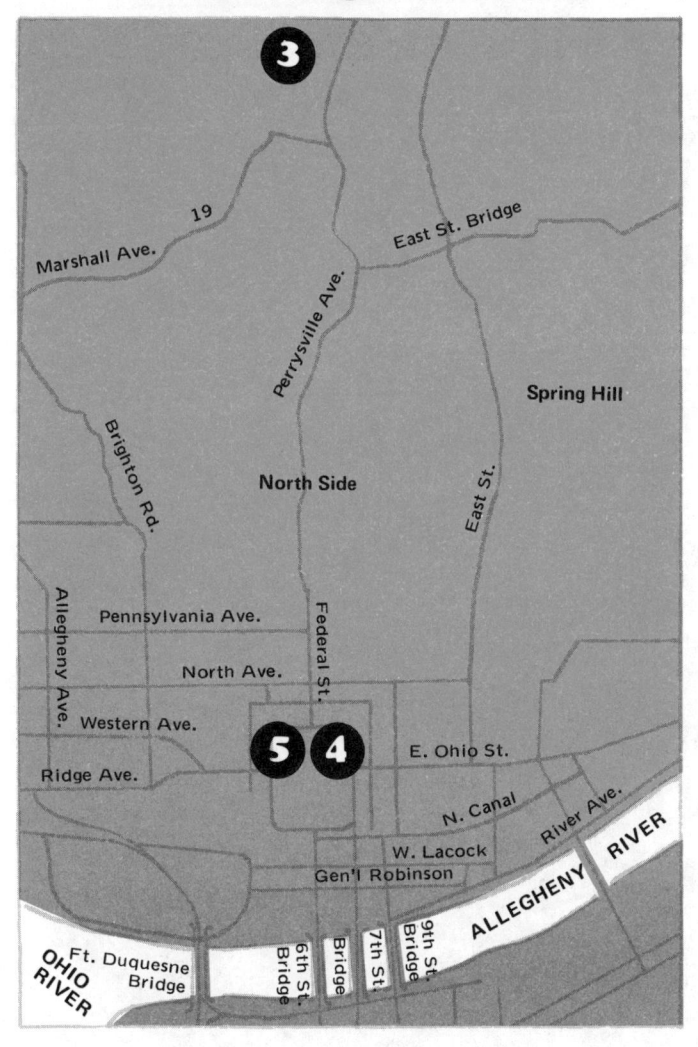

HISTORIC LOCATION MAP

Pittsburgh East

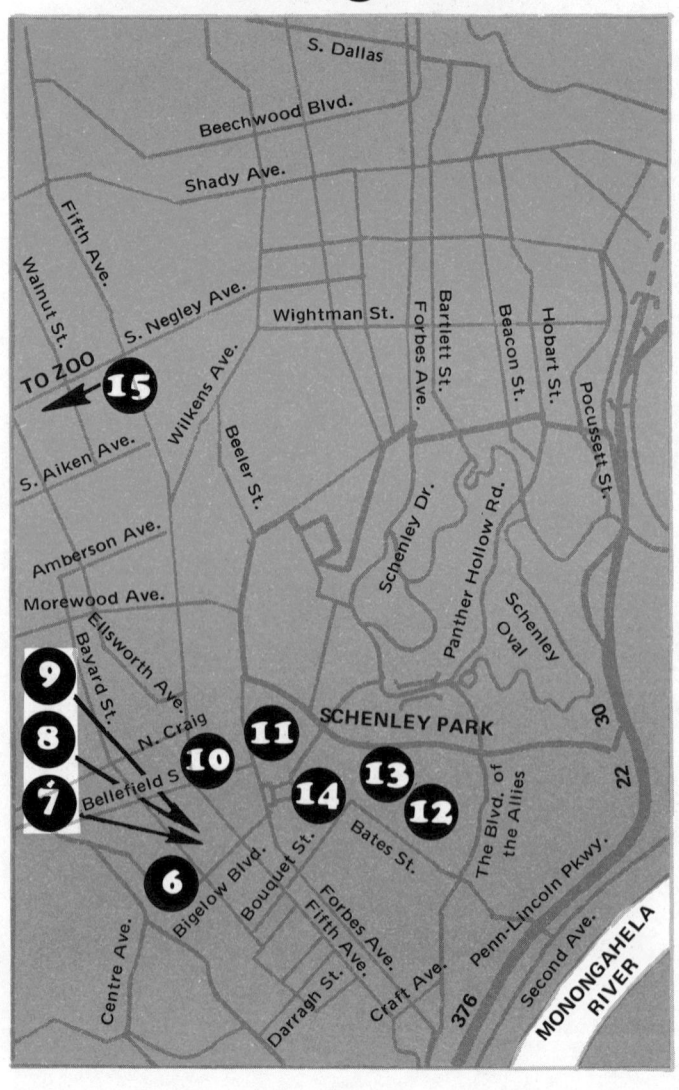

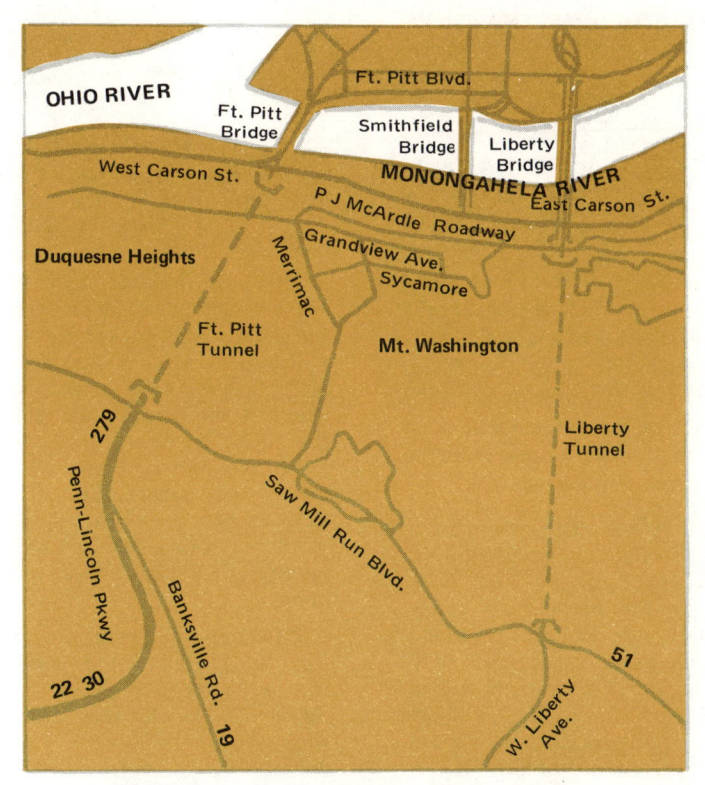

Pittsburgh South & West

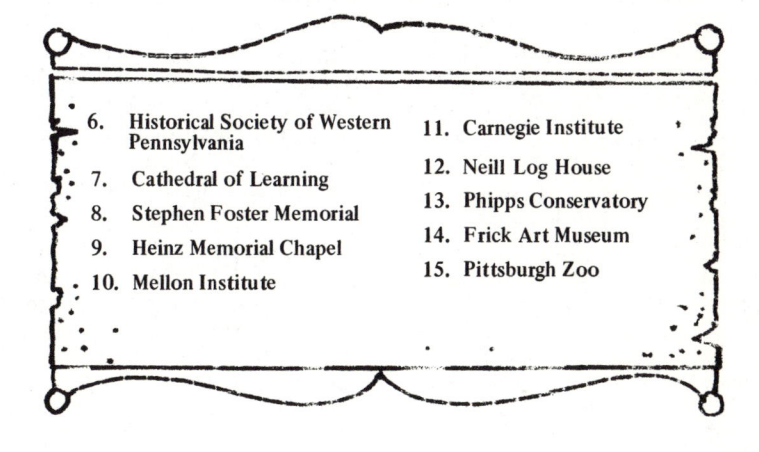

6. Historical Society of Western Pennsylvania
7. Cathedral of Learning
8. Stephen Foster Memorial
9. Heinz Memorial Chapel
10. Mellon Institute
11. Carnegie Institute
12. Neill Log House
13. Phipps Conservatory
14. Frick Art Museum
15. Pittsburgh Zoo

PITTSBURGH: The Golden Triangle

On his way to Fort Le Boeuf in 1753, the young British officer George Washington stopped at the Forks of the Ohio where the Allegheny and Monongahela Rivers meet, noting: "I have spent some time viewing the rivers and the land in the fork, which I think extremely well situated for a fort."

Indeed it was. The next year a group of Virginians attempted to make a settlement there but were ousted by the French who built Fort Duquesne. The area remained in French hands during the early stages of the French and Indian War; then, in 1758, it was abandoned to the advancing British under General John Forbes. On November 25 of that year, Forbes had the English flag raised here, and shortly thereafter Fort Pitt was constructed. Named after the brilliant Prime Minister of Britain, Sir William Pitt, this was the largest and most elaborate inland fort in what was to become the United States.

Finally the brutal war was over and, in 1764, Pittsburgh became a town. But new tensions were not long in coming in the form of British-colonial hostility and, eventually, the American Revolution. Pittsburgh had its own Tea Party when two local men were found selling tea at their store in defiance of the resolves of the Continental Congress. An angry delegation marched there, demanded the surrender of the unsold part of the tea and burned it at the "Liberty Pole". Wrote a visiting Englishman: "The people here are Liberty mad." Neighboring Westmoreland (County) Association raised a flag bearing the figure of a coiled rattlesnake with the motto, "Don't Tread on Me". Settlers were active, too, in guarding the frontier and watching for Tory intrigue. As for the poorly clad, half-starved Pittsburgh regiment, their march through knee-deep snows over the Alleghenies was as heroic a tale as the more celebrated Valley Forge encampment.

Pittsburgh's growth was rather slow during this period, partly due to confusion over titles to real estate. Those who did settle here were a brave and hardy folk, encompassing many trades and professions. A traveler in 1787 noted that there were four attorneys and two doctors in the area; yet, he reported sadly, the inhabitants were "likely to be damned without benefit of clergy." By the turn of the century, Pittsburgh had gained new importance as the "Gateway to the West", with pioneers by the thousands passing through on their way to the Old Northwest and the Mississippi and Missouri River Valleys.

In the early 19th century, industry came to Pittsburgh. Abundant coal deposits in the area led to the metalworking trade and this, in turn, gave birth to the huge steel industry. By the latter part of that century some of the giants of

Mellon Square, Pittsburgh

American industry were located in Pittsburgh: Andrew Carnegie, telegraph boy-turned steel king and railroad magnate; Henry J. Heinz who as a boy sold vegetables from his family's garden and as a man could claim 27 massive buildings of his own which produced the famed "57 varieties"; Henry Clay Frick who pioneered in the manufacture of coke; and Andrew Mellon of banking and aluminum fame.

But with industry had come pollution. British author Charles Dickens was so turned off by Pittsburgh during a visit there that he called it "hell with the lid off." To make matters worse, a devestating fire swept through the city in 1845, causing $9 million worth of damage. (The Mayor, confronting the bleak scene at the meeting of the two rivers, said: "We shall make of this triangle of blackened ruins a golden triangle whose fame will endure as a priceless heritage." Hence the name which still endures.)

Industrial growth continued to take its toll, however, and by the middle of the 20th century Pittsburgh had earned the nickname of "The Smoky City". It was then that a huge renovative effort known as the "Pittsburgh Renaissance" took place, and some of the beauty underneath the mire and soot began to show. The entire Golden Triangle area between the two rivers was cleared, leaving only Fort Pitt blockhouse as the focal point of the new Point State Park. Adjacent to the Park there sprang up a modern business district of tall office buildings known as Gateway Center; here, in shafts of steel, sheaths of glass, thrusts of concrete, are housed some of the world's leading industrial and business enterprises.

Now people tend to give Pittsburgh much more flattering names — like "The City of Bridges" (it has almost 200.) Culture and horticulture stand out, instead of belching fumes. Charles Dickens never would have believed it.

PITTSBURGH EXCURSION

If you are coming from Philadelphia by car, Pittsburgh can be reached via the Schuylkill Expressway to the Valley Forge exit of the Turnpike. Follow this west all the way to exit #6, and then take Interstate 376, into Pittsburgh itself. The journey is three hundred miles long, and one should allow an entire day for travel.

Along with the sites listed below, you will find no shortage of entertainment in Pittsburgh. The city has been a sports center even since it hosted the first World Series back in 1903. At the $22 million Civic Arena, whose retractable dome is three times as large as St. Peter's in Rome, you can see college basketball and professional ice hockey (the Penguins). Three Rivers Stadium is home to Pirate baseball and Steeler football.

Music lovers should take advantage of concerts (including the Pittsburgh Symphony), ballet and opera at Heinz Hall, a magnificent structure of Italian Renaissance design remodeled from an old movie theater.

Hotels are numerous and of good quality, as are restaurants. Best transportation throughout the city is by bus.

Point State Park, The Golden Triangle

1 **Point State Park,** at the point of the Golden Triangle. This is the site of the five 18th century forts that were the beginnings of Pittsburgh. By the 20th century the area had become a slum; happily, it was a major focus of the Renaissance program. After careful excavation, the exact sites and contours of the various forts were identified, lawns planted, and a fountain placed at the tip of the point. The Park contains the following sites of interest:

The Blockhouse, 25 Penn Avenue. Built by British colonel Henry Bouquet as a redoubt outside the walls of Fort Pitt, it is the oldest building still standing in Pittsburgh and the only one that predates the Revolution.

Used as a souvenir stand, it is open Tuesdays through Saturdays, 9 a.m. to 5 p.m., Sundays 2 to 5 p.m., closed Mondays.

Fort Pitt Museum, on the site of one of the bastions of Fort Pitt. The museum contains scale models of the three French and Indian War forts at the Point (Prince George, Duquesne and Pitt). Several dioramas depict the important events in the founding of the city, and artifacts are displayed. On summer Sundays, the Royal American Regiment parades at the Point with fife, musket, drum and cannon, and wearing the red uniforms of General Forbes' British Regulars.

Open Mondays through Saturdays 9:30 a.m. to 4:30 p.m., Sundays from 12 noon to 4:30 p.m.; closed certain holidays; free.

2 **Mount Washington Incline Railroads.** Reminiscent of German alpine railroads, after which they were modeled, these provide an interesting way to view the city, especially the Golden Triangle area. Two separate lines take you up or down the steep Mount Washington inclines, and from the top you will have a magnificent view of the Monongahela and the Triangle beyond it. The Duquesne Incline's lower station is at 1197 W. Carson Street across the river from Point State Park, and its upper station is at Grandview Avenue.

It is operated Mondays through Saturdays, 5:30 a.m. to 1 a.m., Sundays and holidays from 7 p.m. to 1 a.m.; 25¢.

The Monongahela Incline is slightly further up the river, its lower terminus being across from the old Penna. and Erie Railroad Passenger Station and its upper terminus on Grandview Avenue.

This operates Mondays through Saturdays 5:30 a.m. to 12:45 a.m. and Sundays 8:45 a.m. to midnight; 25¢, children 15¢, under 6 free.

3 **Allegheny Observatory,** 159 Riverview Avenue, North Side.

This world-famous observatory for astronomical research is open to the public Mondays through Fridays from 9:30 a.m. to 3:30 p.m.; free.

4 **Buhl Planetarium and Institute of Popular Science,** Allegheny Square, North Side. For additional star-gazing, this is the oldest — and still one of the best — planetariums in the country, featuring "sky dramas" every day at 2:15 and 8:15 p.m.; shows are also given on Saturdays at 11:15 a.m. and Sundays at 4:15 p.m. There are many science exhibits in the Institute, some of them the "do-it-yourself" variety, and a gigantic pendulum measures the motion of the earth.

Open Mondays through Saturdays 1 to 5 p.m. and 7 to 10 p.m., Sundays 1 to 10 p.m. Adults $1.50; children 65¢.

5 **Pittsburgh History and Landmarks Museum,** 322-1204 Allegheny Square, Allegheny Center. Located in the former North Side Post Office, this collection preserves the history of Allegheny County through architectural exhibits, mannequins dressed in 18th and 19th century styles, and artifacts.

Open Tuesdays through Saturdays 10 a.m. to 4:30 p.m., Sundays 1 to 4 p.m.; nominal admission.

6 **Historical Society of Western Pennsylvania,** 4338 Bigelow Boulevard. This is our first stop in the Oakland area, center of the city's cultural and academic life. The Society contains exhibits of weapons such as muskets, guns and swords, paintings, surveying equipment, goblets, decanters and other glass, and additional artifacts of early Pittsburgh. There is a small cherry saddle desk that belonged to George Washington as well as the first piano in Pittsburgh (it was ordered in 1791 by Fort Pitt's commander to make frontier life happier for his homesick daughter). The library contains 12,000 books on the period and many manuscripts.

Open Tuesdays through Fridays 9:30 a.m. to 4:30 p.m., Saturdays 9:30 a.m. to 12:30 p.m.; free.

7 **Cathedral of Learning,** Fifth Avenue and Bigelow Boulevard. This site and the two which follow are part of the University of Pittsburgh campus. The Cathedral of Learning is the only skyscraper college building in the western world. The 42-floor shaft, Gothic in style, has an immense Commons Room which rises four stories and is surrounded by 18 nationality rooms, lavishly furnished in the style of the particular country. Perhaps the most remarkable is the Chinese room whose red lacquer door is guarded by laughing lions; the hall itself is modeled after a room in the Forbidden City at Peiping, its ceiling done in squares of color with the imperial dragon pursuing the sacred pearl.

Tours of the cathedral are held on the hour Mondays through Fridays, 9 a.m. to 4 p.m., Saturdays 11 a.m. to 4 p.m., Sundays noon to 4 p.m. Reservations necessary through visitors center, first floor, or by phone: 624-6000; free.

8 **Stephen Foster Memorial,** adjacent to the Cathedral of Learning. Stephen Foster was an American songwriter of the mid 1800s and a Pittsburgh native. A gentle, sensitive man, he had an innate understanding of the black people as well as their pre-Civil War plantation life — and this although he only traveled south once. Foster's some 200 melodies include "Old Black Joe", "Old Folks at Home", "Beautiful Dreamer" and "O Susanna" which is said to have brought him $100 and his publisher $10,000. Lonely, ill in health, poor, he drank to excess and died penniless in New York City from a fall in a Bowery lodging house at age 37. The Foster Memorial houses thousands of exhibits on American music, in particular Foster's, and there is a concert auditorium.

Open Mondays through Fridays, 9 a.m. to 4:30 p.m., free.

The Blockhouse, Oldest Building Still Standing in Pittsburgh

9 **Heinz Memorial Chapel,** northeast of Cathedral of Learning. This non-denominational place of worship is Gothic in style with a delicate spire and Bedford stone walls. It is the center of the university's religious life.

10 **Mellon Institute,** 4400 Fifth Avenue, Oakland Civic Center. Part of Carnegie-Mellon University and a gift to the city from Andrew Mellon and his brother, the Institute is one of the world's great scientific research centers. The building is designed like a Greek temple with 62 Ionic columns, each hewn from a solid block of limestone. Walk into the lobby to see the four stately figures of Aristotle, Goethe, Huxley and Pasteur; so huge are they (each weighing around 60 tons) that they were brought from the railroad at night so as not to disturb traffic.

Open Mondays through Fridays, 8:30 a.m. to 5 p.m.

11 **Carnegie Institute,** 4400 Forbes Avenue, Oakland Civic Center. This huge and magnificent building of Renaissance design houses myriad wonders. *The Museum of Art* has a large collection of painting, prints and sculpture by old masters and contemporary artists. In cooperation with museums in Brazil and Italy, it holds a major art exhibition every three years that is very highly regarded. There are also special exhibit halls devoted to architecture and the decorative arts. *The Museum of Natural History* has over five million specimens including a gigantic, 150 million year old skeleton of the genre Diplodocus. Birds and mammals, Indian and Egyptian artifacts, even hobbies, are among the subjects of other halls. *Carnegie Music Hall,* not to be confused with the famous Carnegie Hall in New York City, is among the most accoustically perfect concert auditoriums in the world. It boasts one of the largest pipe organs, its pipes ranging in length from 32 feet (and 1000 pounds in weight) to a fraction of an inch. Free organ recitals are given October through March on Sunday afternoons.

The Carnegie Institute is open Tuesdays through Saturdays 10 a.m. to 5 p.m., Sundays 2 to 5 p.m.; free.

12 **Neill Log House,** East Circuit and Serpentine Roads. One of three confirmed 18th century buildings still standing in the city, this one is located in large and beautifully landscaped Schenley Park. The house was built sometime between 1787 and 1795 by a farmer. It gradually fell into disrepair but was restored by the Mellon Foundation after an extensive dig during which some 20,000 artifacts were unearthed. The restoration includes rather primitive and rugged furniture, as suited the original occupant and his era.

Open Tuesdays through Fridays, 10 a.m. to 4:30 p.m.; Saturdays and Sundays 1 to 4:30 p.m.; free.

13 **Phipps Conservatory,** also in Schenley Park. One of the largest botanical conservatories in the U.S., Phipps encompasses 2½ acres under glass with 12 major greenhouses of rare plants and flowers. There is a Charleston-style southern garden and an outstanding collection of orchids.

Open daily 9 a.m. to 4 p.m., free, and evenings during flower shows in March-April and November from 7 to 10 p.m.; evening admission is 50¢ for adults, and 10¢ for children.

14 Frick Art Museum, 7227 Reynolds Street in Point Breeze. The Italian Renaissance style museum provides the setting for an exquisite collection of French, Italian and Flemish Renaissance paintings, 18th century period rooms, French decorative arts and Chinese porcelains of the 18th century. Chamber music concerts are given in an elegant concert hall.

Open Wednesdays through Saturdays, 10 a.m. to 4 p.m., Sundays 1 to 5 p.m.; free.

15 Pittsburgh Zoo, Highland Park, East Liberty. The Zoo contains about 2000 animals in a 75 acre area. Especially interesting is the Twilight Zoo, with a 300 foot tunnel exhibit of rare nocturnal animals. The Aquazoo features Alaskan king crabs, piranhas, and a special exhibit on the voltage produced by electric eels to stun their enemies.

Open daily 10 a.m to 5 p.m., except Sundays and holidays in summer when hours are 10 a.m. to 6 p.m.; admission is $1, children under 2 free; on Saturdays no charge.

Horn of Plenty Buffet Restaurant at Butler, Pa., is an interesting, informal two-level buffet with open selection from 70 items both hot and cold. Local art on display.

5:00 to 9:00 p.m. Tuesday thru Saturday; 12:00 to 9:00 p.m. Sunday.

Route #8, five miles north of Exit 4, Penn. Turnpike.

Henry Bouquet

OLD ECONOMY VILLAGE: Utopian Prosperity

The Great House, home of George Rapp

At the beginning of the 19th century, a group of pious German Lutherans fled the Duchy of Wurtemberg for America because of religious persecution. Led by weaver and vinedresser George Rapp, they set up the communal "Harmony Society" on a piece of land he had purchased in western Pennsylvania. Here they awaited the Second Coming, their lives bound by brotherhood and work. As was common in such communities, members deeded their property to the Society. Father Rapp reigned supreme, accepted by his followers as a prophet — a view he shared. He meditated on a thronelike rock formation (aptly named "Father Rapp's Seat") which stood on a hill overlooking the town. In 1807 the population of Harmony was about 700, at which time the practice of celibacy was introduced as a preparation for Christ's coming.

Industrious and business-minded, the Harmonists moved to Indiana in 1815 to take advantage of better water transportation, then moved back to Pennsylvania ten years later. It was then that the village Economy was founded. Here the group began a profitable industrial operation, particularly in the areas of shoes, cotton and woolen goods, and wines (celibacy may have been the rule but sobriety was not!) Indeed, for a time Economy was the leading industrial community in the west, with surplus funds financing railroads throughout the Upper Ohio Valley.

Except for a split created by a new prophet, Count Leon, in 1832, Economy was relatively placid until the time of the Civil War. Then the death of George Rapp, the advancing Industrial Revolution, unsure investments, and diminishing membership due to celibacy led to a decline. The Harmony Society was dissolved in 1905 by which time it had dwindled to two members.

OLD ECONOMY EXCURSION

The remains of the Harmony Society's Economy settlement were taken over by the State in 1916. Today you can see a two block area containing 17 original and restored buildings at 14th and Ambridge Streets in the town of Ambridge. Thanks to the exhaustive research and renovative effort, Old Economy looks today as it did at the zenith of its career.

Driving from Pittsburgh, go northwest on Route 65.

Among the large number of sites in the community, note particularly the following:

1 **Great House.** George Rapp lived here as did his adopted son and business manager, Frederick. It was the latter who designed the buildings and planned the community.

2 **Feast Hall.** This large building was the cultural center of Economy, housing the museum, printing press and adult school. The love feasts, characteristic of pietist societies, were shared in the great hall on the second floor.

3 **Cabinet shop.** The quality of workmanship was excellent in all of Economy's products.

4 **Feast Kitchen,** where meals for about 800 could be prepared.

5 **Tailor Shop and Wine Cellar;** see the huge wine casks.

6 **Store.** It did as much as $150,000 in business during a single year — no paltry sum back then.

7 **House B.** This is one of the mass-produced houses in which the people lived as brothers and sisters. (It's quite a step down from the Great House.)

8 **Garden Pavilion and Grotto.** The formal garden has vines, arbors and boxwood-lined paths.

9 **Church.** Completed in 1831, it is now St. John's Lutheran.

Old Economy Village is open Mondays through Saturdays from 8:30 a.m. to 5 p.m., Sundays from 1 to 5 p.m.; closed January 1, Easter, Thanksgiving, Christmas and Election Days. 75¢, children and those over 65, free.

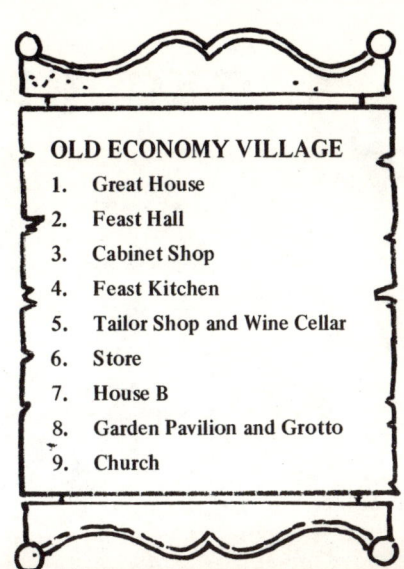

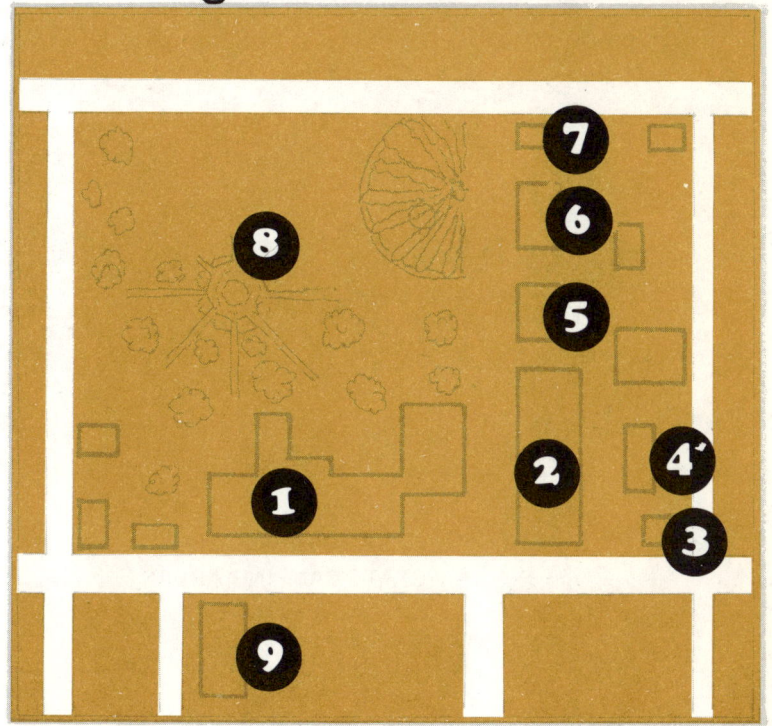

OLD ECONOMY VILLAGE
1. Great House
2. Feast Hall
3. Cabinet Shop
4. Feast Kitchen
5. Tailor Shop and Wine Cellar
6. Store
7. House B
8. Garden Pavilion and Grotto
9. Church

EXCURSION LOCA

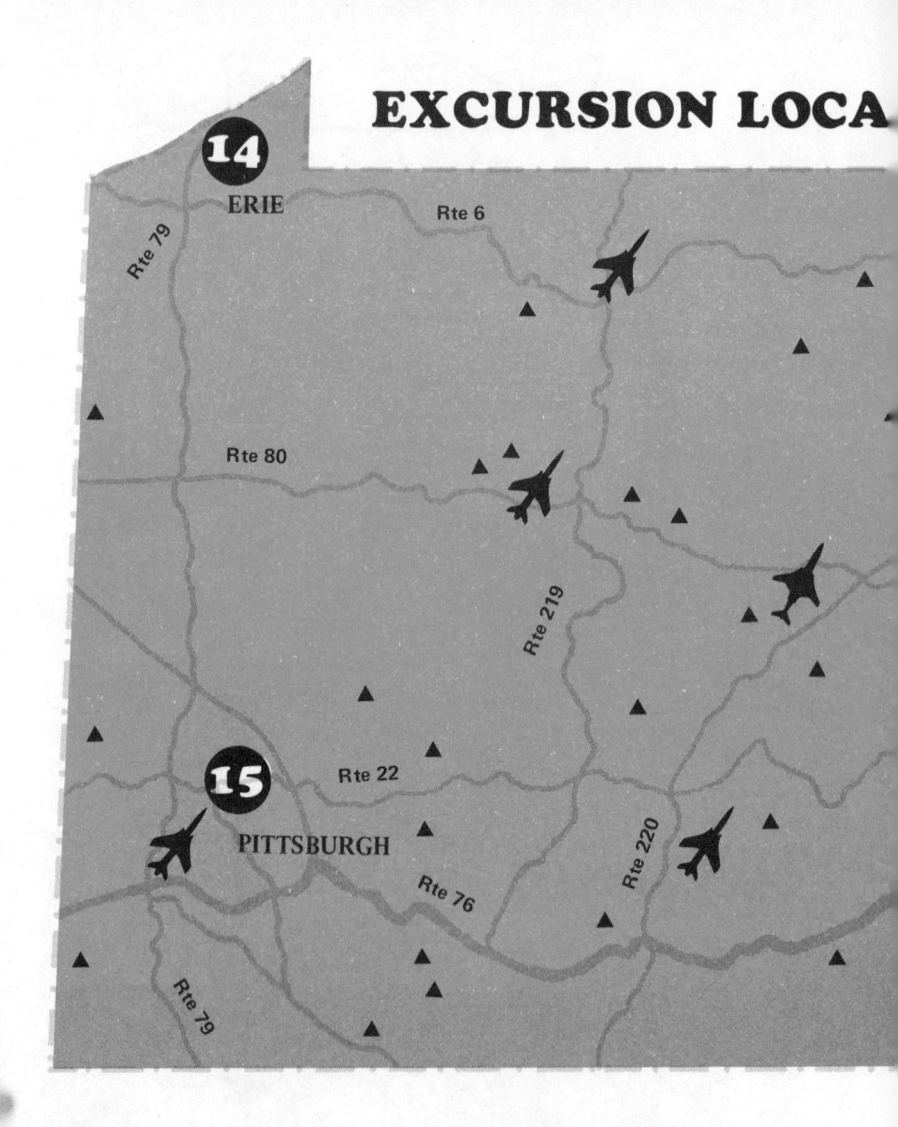

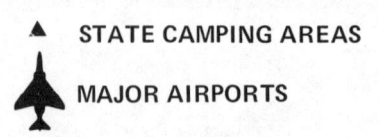

14 ERIE

Rte 79
Rte 6
Rte 80
Rte 219
Rte 22

15 PITTSBURGH

Rte 76
Rte 220
Rte 79

▲ STATE CAMPING AREAS
✈ MAJOR AIRPORTS

ONS & PUBLIC FACILITIES

Tourist Promotion Agencies

If you have questions on the areas covered in the fifteen excursions of this book, the following tourist promotion agencies will be glad to help you:

ALLENTOWN-LEHIGH COUNTY TOURIST-CONVENTION BUREAU
462 Walnut Street • Allentown, Pa. 18105 • Phone: 215-437-9661

BERKS COUNTY PENNSYLVANIA DUTCH TRAVEL ASSOCIATION
538 Court Street • Reading, Pa. 19601 • Phone: 215-376-3931

BUCKS COUNTY HISTORICAL-TOURIST COMMISSION
One Oxford Valley, Suite 410 • Langhorne, Pa. 19054 • Phone: 215-752-2203

CHESTER COUNTY TOURIST PROMOTION BUREAU
Room 108 - Court House • West Chester, Pa. 19380 • Phone: 215-431-6365

COLONIAL YORK COUNTY VISITORS AND TOURIST BUREAU, INC.
1455 Mt. Zion Road • York, Pa. 17402 • Phone: 717-755-9638

CRAWFORD COUNTY TOURIST ASSOCIATION
Court House • Meadville, Pa. 16335 • Phone: 814-336-1151

CUMBERLAND COUNTY TOURIST COUNCIL
100 Shady Lane • Carlisle, Pa. 17013 • Phone: 717-249-3293

DIVISION OF ECONOMIC DEVELOPMENT • STATE OF DELAWARE
45 The Green • Dover, Delaware 19901 • Phone: 302-678-4254

ENDLESS MOUNTAINS ASSOCIATION
Laceyville, Pa. 18632 • Phone: 717-869-1100

GETTYSBURG TRAVEL COUNCIL
35 Carlisle Street • Gettysburg, Pa. 17325 • Phone: 717-334-6274

HARRISBURG-HERSHEY AREA TOURIST PROMOTION AGENCY
114 Walnut Street • Harrisburg, Pa. 17101 • Phone: 717-232-4121

LUZERNE COUNTY TOURIST PROMOTION AGENCY
301 Market Street • Kingston, Pa. 18704 • Phone: 717-288-6784

MONTGOMERY COUNTY TOURIST BUREAU
One Montgomery Plaza • Norristown, Pa. 19404 • Phone: 215-275-5000

NEW JERSEY STATE PROMOTION OFFICE
DIVISION OF ECONOMIC DEVELOPMENT
P.O. Box 400 • Trenton, New Jersey • Phone: 609-292-2448

NORTHAMPTON COUNTY VISITORS COUNCIL
11 West Market Street • Bethlehem, Pa. 18018 • Phone: 215-691-0556

PENNSYLVANIA DUTCH TOURIST BUREAU
1800 Hempstead Road • Lancaster, Pa. 17601 • Phone: 717-393-9705

PHILADELPHIA CONVENTION AND TOURIST BUREAU
1525 John F. Kennedy Boulevard • Philadelphia, Pa. 19102 • Phone: 215-864-1976

PITTSBURGH CONVENTION AND VISITORS BUREAU, INC.
3001 Jenkins Arcade • Pittsburgh, Pa. 15222 • Phone: 412-281-5723

POCONO MOUNTAINS VACATION BUREAU
1004 Main Street • Stroudsburg, Pa. 18360 • Phone: 717-421-5791

TOURIST AND CONVENTION BUREAU OF ERIE COUNTY
1006 State Street • Erie, Pa. 16501 • Phone: 814-454-7191